The Ford Madox Ford Reader

Also published by Carcanet

A Call
The English Novel
The Rash Act

The Ford Madox Ford Reader

Edited by

SONDRA J. STANG

Foreword by

GRAHAM GREENE

CARCANET

First published in Great Britain 1986 by
Carcanet Press Limited
208–212 Corn Exchange
Manchester M4 3BQ

The publisher acknowledges the financial assistance of the Arts Council of Great Britain

Ford, Ford Madox
The Ford Madox Ford Reader.
I. Title II. Stang, Sondra
828′.91209 PR6011.053

ISBN 0-85635-519-4

Typeset by Paragon Photoset, Aylesbury
Printed in England by SRP Ltd, Exeter

CONTENTS

Foreword

There was a small group of novelists at the turn of this century living not far from each other who one believes have a far greater chance of surviving into their second centenary than their successors: Henry James, Joseph Conrad and Ford Madox Ford (although no one seems to have remembered Ford's first centenary twelve years ago). In that period before his death in 1916 James had written his greatest works — *The Wings of the Dove*, *The Ambassadors*, *The Golden Bowl*: Conrad too had published his best — *The Nigger of the Narcissus*, *Heart of Darkness*, *The Secret Agent*, *Under Western Eyes*, *Nostromo* (a whole chapter of which was written by Ford so that his sick friend could fulfil a serial contract): and Ford? Ford had produced four masterpieces, his *Fifth Queen Trilogy* and *The Good Soldier*. It was a golden period for the English novel.

Ford survived after James and Conrad had died and produced in all some eighty books, including another masterpiece of the First World War, the *Tietjens Trilogy* (I insist on calling it a trilogy, for Ford justly disowned the fourth volume which he wrote from financial necessity and under pressure from his publisher), or *Parade's End*.

Sondra Stang has undertaken the enormous task of choosing pages from the whole ground of Ford's work, and no one could have done it better. For reasons of copyright she has not been able to include passages from that finest novel of all, *The Good Soldier*, or from the *Tietjens Trilogy*, but a large number of his other books are represented here. He described himself as an 'old man mad about writing' and the exuberance, the enthusiasm her anthology conveys, a sort of wild delight in the technique of the novel: he was mad about the writing of others as well as his own. No one has ever given so much encouragement to young writers, to Hemingway, Pound, Crane,

Jean Rhys, even to myself at a particularly bad time of failure, and I am happy to have met him once, a year before he died, and as we walked together across a Sussex field to have felt his energy like a shot of vitamin in the veins.

Graham Greene

Introduction

> It is impossible in a short article to do justice to a work which is conceived and executed on such a grand scale. . . . *Parade's End* has never yet been a popular success and few critics, I believe, have paid much attention to it. This neglect passes my comprehension. Of the various demands one can make of a novelist, that he show us the way in which a society works, that he show an understanding of the human heart, that he create characters in whose reality we believe and for whose fate we care, that he describe things and people so that we feel their physical presence, that he illuminate our moral consciousness, that he make us laugh and cry, that he delight us by his craftsmanship, there is not one, it seems to me, that Ford does not completely satisfy. There are not many English novels which deserve to be called great: *Parade's End* is one of them.

AUDEN, writing in 1961, could not state the case for Ford without disbelief that he has been given so little by the literary world to which he gave so much. Critical recognition has been uncommonly slow in coming to Ford: he has had neither a popular success nor a *succès d'estime*. And yet he was one of the most important figures in twentieth-century literature. Every writer, as Gide recognized about himself, has the 'nostalgie du grand public': 'For a writer, talking to a large audience is not at all the same thing as talking to a wall.' Ford made his peace with the small editions of his books and the large piles of remainders. He never stopped writing in the course of a long career, but he never stopped hoping for the collected edition that constantly eluded him and that would have kept his books alive for the reading public. 'Although my kindlier critics assure me', he wrote in 1921, 'that I have written several books of permanent interest, the public finds it very difficult to know where to go to obtain my works.' Only now, with both *The Good Soldier* and *Parade's End* at last firmly in print, with a few titles here and there re-issued from time to time, have the 'other' books begun to be re-issued systematically, by Carcanet Press (UK) and The Ecco Press (USA); and Graham Greene's The Bodley Head Edition, as far as it has been able to proceed, is being kept in print. Perhaps it is all just as well, this temporary disappearance of the larger part of a major writer's life's work. The generation discovering it takes an intense pleasure in its own sense of discovery; an *oeuvre* is unwrapped, still fresh, while some of the approved — and much reprinted — great writers come to seem a little frayed from too much handling.

For whatever reasons, Ford has been, on the whole, a missing person (in spite of his having been 'enormously boomed' for a while) in those historical overviews and anthologies that signal which writers are in favour and which are not. Until the last few years, when Edwardian essayists were cited we could find Chesterton, Belloc, Beerbohm, E. V. Lucas, Alice Meynell, Augustine Birrell, G. S. Street — but no Ford. When Edwardian travel writers were mentioned, there would be Tomlinson, Doughty, Hudson — but again no Ford. In our own day, even *Parade's End*, which many readers believe to be the best English novel about The Great War, receives scant acknowledgement in the literary histories of that war. But our picture of the first few decades of this century is very much in flux; as Irving Howe has said of Kipling, 'It has taken time to sort things out, and the job is by no means finished.'

It was difficult, editing this Reader, to keep up any illusion that I was carving out the right five hundred pages from the great mass of Ford's writing. I could imagine a long shelf of other Ford Readers, each so different from the other as to have in common no more than a dozen or so pages. Ford left — by a rough count — eighty books, over four hundred uncollected essays and articles, and a great pile of unpublished manuscripts. He was a novelist, literary critic, social critic, art critic, biographer, writer of reminiscences, historian, travel writer, poet, journalist, and editor of two remarkable magazines, *The English Review* (1908–09) and *The Transatlantic Review* (1924–25). Prolific even among the Edwardians, Ford has left us an impression of such largeness of personality that comparison with the largest monsters of the deep has been almost inevitable (leviathan, whale, walrus, fabulous monster — as he called Christopher Tietjens), and because he has been so long submerged, perfectly accurate.

My purpose here is to present as many sides of Ford's genius as possible in a single volume and bring to light works that until now, only a handful of readers have been able to enjoy. In a volume of this size, I have had to omit any representation of the fairy tales, half of the books of reminiscence, the biography of Ford Madox Brown, the collaborations with Conrad, in fact most of the novels. Above all, I have had to leave out altogether *The Good Soldier* and the Tietjens books *(Parade's End)*; but I assume that most of Ford's readers already know them because they are readily available. For this reason I have tried to include, among the critical and miscellaneous pieces, material that will be of particular interest to readers of those subtle and demanding novels, who may find in the course of this volume many critical problems illuminated in unexpected places. I have also included a good deal of previously unpublished material that seems to me too important to be left in manuscript.

My premise has been that readers opening this collection would like to see beyond *The Good Soldier* and *Parade's End*: see what surrounds them, where they belong in Ford's *oeuvre* (are they anomalies or part of a continuum?), what other sorts of books Ford wrote, and what they tell us about one another as well as themselves. Not all these questions can be answered by the present selection, but it should begin to reveal something of the variety of Ford's work and the range of his powers.

To suggest his powers — without diminishing them — I have tried to avoid the patchwork approach, aiming rather for an effect of solidity in each of the selections, though a certain amount of respectful cutting and stitching has been inevitable with a writer who left no novellas, as James, Conrad, or Lawrence did — or even novels short enough for inclusion in a volume the size and scope of this one. 'I have written with some violence against the short novel,' Ford reported. Or again, 'The curse that epigram is to literature'. He liked to point out that the word *author* derives from the Latin *auctor*, one who adds.

Ford's characteristic mode is expatiation. Novels rarely lend themselves to excerpting; Ford's are particularly resistant, depending as they do on a complication of pattern that is intrinsic to Ford's idea of writing. Yet Ford thought of himself as primarily the novelist, and as Arthur Mizener has remarked, Ford's novels are the most important things about him. They must be accounted for if readers are to have a true picture of his work. Robert Lowell spoke of Ford's 'ordered, subtly circuitous paragraphs'. Ford's imagination tended toward ordered, subtly circuitous expression pre-eminently in the design of his novels. For this reason alone, excerpting can give no true idea of what the novels are like, and they are therefore under-represented here. All an anthologist can do is refrain from further violence and hope to send readers to the books themselves.

In a short autobiographical sketch dated 1924, Ford set down the salient facts of his early life.

> Born 1873: s.[on] of Francis Hueffer, musical Editor of the *Times*. g.[rand] s.[on] of Ford Madox Brown, painter. Early surroundings Pre-Raffailite [sic]. Rossetti, Swinburne, W. Morris etc. Pub[lishe]d. first book at age of 17.

Ford was proud of those facts — with reason. His father had emigrated from Germany four years before Ford was born and quickly established himself as both the leading English music critic of his day and the strongest advocate of Wagner in England. (Shaw — and Wagner — owed him a good deal.) Dr Hueffer published a number of books of essays on music; he edited four volumes of German lieder and two magazines, *The New Quarterly* (a forum for Schopenhauer) and *The Musical World*. He also edited the correspondence of Wagner and Liszt, which is still in print. In addition, he wrote *The Troubadours: A History of Provençal Life and Literature in the Middle Ages*, a book which greatly influenced Ford's — and Pound's — thinking about culture and art in general and the troubadours in particular.

Ford was fifteen when his father died; he was then raised by his maternal grandfather, Ford Madox Brown, the Pre-Raphaelite painter. Better known in his own day than in ours, Brown was mentor and friend to a large circle of painters and writers, many of whom turn up in the pages of Ford's first book of memoirs, *Ancient Lights* (*Memories and Impressions* in the American edition). Having lost his remarkably gifted son Oliver at nineteen (Dr Hueffer helped to edit his literary remains), the grandfather was, as Ford tells us, intent on training Ford for genius; upon the old man's death, in an act of filial piety, Ford at twenty-three wrote his biography, still the standard work on Ford Madox Brown.

Through his aunt's marriage, Ford came to be related to the Rossettis — William Michael, Christina, and Dante Gabriel. Ford wrote engagingly about those 'early surroundings' among the Pre-Raphaelites in *Ancient Lights*; in the Tietjens books he looked more critically at the movement and its implications. But far more complicated and even less well understood is Ford's relationship to the more significant intellectual currents of the nineteenth century, in which he lived almost half his life. His intellectual life was rooted in the world view of Coleridge and Arnold; he was more indebted to Wordsworth, Ruskin, Carlyle, Browning, and Meredith than he acknowledged. The debts he did pay, fully and explicitly, were to Flaubert, Maupassant, Turgenev, and James. These affinities bound him and Joseph Conrad together during a long and almost daily association from 1898 to 1908. Their collaboration yielded three novels: *Romance*, *The Inheritors*, and *The Nature of a Crime*.

> And it is to be remembered that during all those years the writer wrote every word that he wrote with the idea of reading aloud to Conrad, and that during all those years Conrad wrote what he wrote with the idea of reading it aloud to this writer.

The long vowels in Ford's account of those long sessions with Conrad tell us what they might have sounded like to someone overhearing them. No wonder that both writers came to rely so much on the sound of the human voice narrating. We *hear* Marlow and Dowell tell their stories. Conrad and Ford agreed that the purpose of their art was to make us *see*: it was to make us hear — and listen — as well. On his side Ford left *Joseph Conrad: A Personal Remembrance* as his monument to Conrad; I cannot help reading 'The Secret Sharer' as Conrad's tribute to Ford in rendering so uncannily the psychological experience of close collaboration.

Ford wrote the section of *Nostromo* included in this Reader because Conrad was too ill to meet the deadline for the next installment of the magazine serializing the novel. 'What I actually wrote into Conrad's books was by no means great in bulk and was usually done when he was too ill to write himself and had to catch up with serial publication.' By ill, Ford meant either depressed or down with gout, or sometimes both. Although Ford himself appears to have been suffering from depression at the time, he would, he writes in *Return to Yesterday*, 'manoeuvre him [Conrad] towards writing as the drake manoeuvres the sitting duck back to the nest when she has abandoned her eggs'. When all else failed, Ford would jump in. The question of how much Ford wrote for Conrad is a delicate one (there is no evidence that the arrangement was reciprocal). By Ford's own account, *Under Western Eyes* (which he thought Conrad's greatest novel) was 'almost the only great one in which I had no finger at all'; in the case of *Nostromo*, Ford's claim is fully corroborated.[1] Conrad, unhappy at having to appear in a journal he 'despised', made a good many changes in the text of *Nostromo* when he prepared it for the first English edition. For this reason I have transcribed the manuscript of Ford's original text.

As a man and a novelist, Conrad left an indelible impression on Ford. Among other things, during the years they worked together, the painterly element in Ford's work became intensified, and by the time he wrote *The Fifth Queen* trilogy, he had mastered what V. S. Pritchett calls his 'ingenious system of getting at the inside of things by looking intensely at the surface alone. . . . He may see more than we can in the way people's hands lie in their laps, or how their legs look when they are kneeling, or how much of Henry VIII appeared as he went upstairs.' It should be remembered that Ford was working on his book on Holbein while he was thinking about *The Fifth Queen*, thinking still, in fact, about his original plan to write a history of the reign of Henry VIII. In the British Museum, Ford had read through the letters and papers of Henry VIII published by the Rolls Office, but he abandoned the project, though not before writing a synopsis (and chapter) containing his statement of purpose. 'The author will attempt to make Henry "live" as vividly as do the characters in a work of fiction or as he does in his portrait by Holbein. . . . It will be an attempt at as careful a psychological and picturesque analysis of the King as may be possible. . . . It should contain reproductions of all the Holbeins which are at Windsor Castle, at Hampton Court and in other places at home and abroad.' The subject had run away with him: it had to be done as a novel, and

[1] John Hope Morey, 'Joseph Conrad and Ford Madox Ford', Diss. Cornell University, 1960. The job was made all the more difficult because all correspondence concerning the serialization of the novel was destroyed when the offices of Cassell and Company, publishers of *T. P.'s Weekly*, were bombed in a raid during 1941. My reading of Ford's manuscript differs in certain details from Professor Morey's.

it had to be done as a trilogy. It is impossible to read it without being struck by the quality of its painterliness, its brilliance as tableau. 'It makes most of our historical fiction up to 1914 look like the work of interior decorators' (V. S. Pritchett again). Ford's natural inclination was to understate; the years with Conrad encouraged him not to hold back in describing how things looked. Ford had early absorbed the essential quality of the Pre-Raphaelites — their extreme clarity of local detail; in *The Fifth Queen* he rose to the further challenge that Holbein presented: to suggest living human beings arrested for just a moment and to render them with monumental assurance.

In 1908 Ford founded *The English Review*, and as its editor, he made it one of the most distinguished periodicals ever to be published. But he was unable to put it on a satisfactory financial basis and he lost it. He lost more than the magazine, and by 1915, when he enlisted in the British army at forty-one, his financial and personal problems had come to seem insurmountable. His marriage to Elsie Martindale, with whom he had eloped when he was twenty-one and she was seventeen, had ended not in divorce, as he hoped it would, but in bitterness on her part and a sense of hopeless entanglement and loss on his: after 1916 he never again saw his two daughters, a matter so painful he could not allow it into his novels. His liaison with Violet Hunt was another entanglement: in her refusal to let Ford go she nourished his idea of Sylvia in *Parade's End*. His wife had sued the newspaper that referred to Violet Hunt as Mrs Hueffer; his friends (including Conrad and James), offended by so much scandal, disappeared. The anxiety and humiliation, the depression and physical illness that followed — all this was the raw material that produced the state of mind behind *The Good Soldier*, that most searching of novels about states of mind and the experience of marriage, sexual passion, social taboos, possession and loss.

Ford was easily drawn to women and they to him, particularly women with strong literary or artistic abilities. Elsie Martindale published a volume of translations of Maupassant's stories, with an introduction by Ford. Violet Hunt was a celebrated though minor Edwardian novelist; Ford collaborated with her on two books, *The Desirable Alien* and *Zeppelin Nights*. Stella Bowen, with whom Ford lived after the war and with whom he had a daughter, Julia Madox Loewe, was an Australian painter who, after she and Ford separated, made an independent career as a portrait painter. Janice Biala, with whom Ford lived very happily the last decade of his life, is a well-known painter who illustrated *Provence* and *Great Trade Route* and designed the dust covers for *It Was the Nightingale* and *The Rash Act*. It was for her Ford wrote the poem sequence *Buckshee*. The view — prevailing in his lifetime and after — that he was a sort of feckless Don Juan going from conquest to conquest is at odds with what his books tell us about him: very few male novelists have been able to imagine so completely what being a woman is like. In his affairs with women, he seems to have sought not power over them but imaginative identification with them. To read the novels is to see how far it is possible for a man writing about women to project himself imaginatively into male and female selves.

Readers today warm to Ford as the creator of Valentine — a militant suffragette, invading the golf course (the traditionally male preserve of the Edwardian ruling class) early in *Some Do Not*. Political, athletic, intellectual, she is also sexual, and though we cannot speak of her sexual appetite as we can of Sylvia's, we know Valentine's thoughts, and we know that she lives in a post-Freudian world. But her strong sense of propriety — a shade or two less strong than Christopher's — is not maiming, like his — or like Sylvia's sense of impropriety. And terrible as Sylvia can be, Ford understands her: we see her with her mother (as we do Valentine), and in her own imaginings (as we do Valentine), and her destructiveness is tied to Christopher's: neither character is blamed, neither is absolved. Finally, Tietjens needs Valentine (as he also needed Sylvia), and conversely, Sylvia needs Christopher (as much, in her way, as Valentine does): *Parade's End* explores rather thoroughly a whole complex system of mutual psychological needs. Through them, Ford reveals, as the novelist Mary Gordon has observed, why men need women and women need men.

Valentine is as intelligent and comprehending as Christopher, her wit and capacity for irony are equal to his, but her Latin is better, and she knows more about the English class system than he (having worked as a servant), knows more about how things really are. She is stronger and more resilient; she is his teacher, and she teaches him to find a way of accommodating himself to the world and making a place for himself in it instead of rejecting it outright. In short, she is wiser than he; she is Ford's Mr Knightley. But if Ford pleases today because he creates for us women as they are or might be, rather than as they cannot possibly be or, we feel today, should no longer try to be ('The Woman of the Novelists', Ford calls her in his essay in *The Critical Attitude*, page 149 in this volume), he also creates, for example, Magdalena in *The 'Half Moon'* — passive, domestic, content to polish her furniture with a craftsman's love of the surface; in that novel she is the antithesis of Anne Jeal, who is restless, driven, intent on power. But Ford loves Magdalena as much as he does Valentine, though feminist theoreticians may not. Ford was not tendentious in his novels: while his women (and men) carry forward from book to book qualities that we can recognize (e.g. Sylvia as another version of Florence in *The Good Soldier*), his women are imagined rather than polemically conceived, understood from within, rather than merely visualized.

In *Return to Yesterday* Ford tells of sitting on a terrace in pre-war England and asking the minister with whom he is having tea: 'Why *don't* you give women the vote?' The minister answers: 'My election agent tells me that if women had the vote in my constituency they would vote two to one against me and I should lose my seat. What price my seat?' Ford, picking up the thread of price and valuation, tells us that *This Monstrous Regiment of Women* (see page 304), the pamphlet he wrote for Mrs Pankhurst, is 'the only work of mine that I care to mention by name in these pages . . . and proud of it still!'

> I will give in twenty-three [sic] words the reason for my conviction. In England of those days the only people who were refused citizenship were children, criminals, lunatics — and the mothers of our children.

In the Epistolary Epilogue to *A Call*, written a few years before the pamphlet, Ford alluded to 'something heroic and chivalrous, such as aiding women to obtain the vote'. This is Ford's idea of chivalry, a chivalry so large as to enable women to dispense with the very idea of chivalry. *Women and Men* is the title of one of Ford's books (see the chapter on Meary Walker, page 330); it could have been the subtitle of any of Ford's novels. It is one of his great subjects. 'Do you think one can make a thing interesting without a woman?' Conrad asked. The question would not have occurred to Ford.

I have included in this volume sixty of Ford's letters that have never been published. Richard Ludwig's selection came out in 1965 and is the only volume we have of Ford's letters. But the number still in manuscript is, like everything else about Ford, large, and critical discussion of his books, now that they are being brought back into print, will require that more of the letters be brought to light. Inevitably, they colour the way we read the books. Take, for example, Ford's letter to John Lane dated 28 March 1915 (see page 477). It opens:

> Alas, it does indeed seem a monstrous thing, but after all, what is chaste in Constantinople is frequently regarded as vice. Let us hope that when the Allies have entered the Dardanelles 'The Good Soldier' may come into his own, in several senses. You see, that work is as serious an analysis of the polygamous desires that underlie all men — except perhaps the members of the Publishers' Association — as 'When Blood is Their Argument' is an analysis of Prussian culture.

Ford had an anthropologist's view — as well as a novelist's — of men and women and the way they live in their particular culture. The pages on English conduct in *The Spirit of the People*, the ending of *The 'Half Moon'*, all of *Provence* and *Great Trade Route* surely suggest as much. When Ford speaks of the polygamous desires that underlie all men, he is speaking as inclusively as he can of sexuality released from constraint: at the centre of *The Good Soldier*, as I read it, is Ford's sense of wonder, years before Freud published *Civilization and Its Discontents* and *Beyond the Pleasure Principle*, at the requirements of culture and the cost to the individual personality, the tension that both creates and destroys. Ford's letter to Lane will be seen as extraordinarily suggestive, now that it is available, to readers of *The Good Soldier*, as well as of *Parade's End* ('men' in his letter has to be read as 'men and women'), where Christopher brakes the polygamous impulse with all the force of his character and Sylvia indulges it with all the force of hers.

Ford's phrase resonates. Conrad had written: 'I find I can't live with more than one story at a time. It's a kind of literary monogamism.' In one year (1911), Ford published *The Simple Life Limited* and *Ladies Whose Bright Eyes* (novels) as well as *Ancient Lights* (reminiscences) and *The Critical Attitude* (essays). The following year he published *The Panel* and *The New Humpty-Dumpty* (novels) as well as *High Germany* (poems). In 1924, he was writing *Some Do Not*, editing *The Transatlantic Review*, and upon hearing of Conrad's death, at once wrote *Joseph Conrad: A Personal Remembrance*. Ford sometimes regretted writing so much, but he did describe himself as an old man mad about writing, and I doubt whether he would have been incapable of living with more than one story at a time had he written less. How much more good writing he left than he is commonly thought to have written is becoming clearer as the books are brought back into print. Unlike Conrad and Flaubert, Ford seems to have associated writing with pleasure rather than pain, though there is evidence to suggest that the pleasure was not always unalloyed.

That pleasure derived from a state of mind, one which he connected with the idea of Provence. In his book by that name he explains:

> I am giving you my Provence. It is not the country as made up by modern or German scholarship; it is the Roman Province on the Great Trade Route where I have lived for nearly all my spiritual as for a great part of my physical life.

'Nearly all' his spiritual life: at those times when his powers failed and he would lose the capacity to 'draw strength from the knowledge that that land exists and is unchanging', his language evokes the Romantic poets writing about the sacred breeze of inspiration:

> I sit here in my garret and hammer at phrases; I walk these streets with the dove-coloured paving stones, bemused; if I want to see anything I must make an effort of the will; if I write a sentence it comes out as backboneless as a water-hose; to give it life I must cut it into nine.

But returning to Provence, i.e. living once again in that state of mind, he no longer needs to hammer his phrases and mutilate his sentences (water-hoses 'chopped into nine'!): '. . . When I get back to Provence the world will be astonishingly visible. I shall write little crisp sentences like silver fish jumping out of streams.' Provence represents earthly permanence, an idea of culture in which body and spirit, life and art, past and present, society and the individual are not in conflict but in 'equanimity'. In his long poem 'On Heaven', Ford imagines himself dead for nine years and waiting at his table at a café in a 'shadowy sunlit square' in Provence, where the oddness of being English is thrown into sharp relief:

> But one is English,
> Though one be never so much of a ghost:

And if most of your life has been spent in the craze to relinquish
What you want most,
You will go on relinquishing,
You will go on vanquishing
Human longings, even
In Heaven.

But no harm comes to the lovers because 'all that we desire shall prove as fair as we can paint it': the 'very hardest trick of all' for God is to make a Heaven in which society no longer makes war on the human heart. Provence was for Ford an image of transcendence; 'if not with the eyes of the flesh, then at least with those of the spirit I shall always see it'. The language is Christian, but Ford's Catholicism, not a very clear matter for his readers, is perhaps best thought about in the context of his Provence.

'I give so much of autobiography though these are reminiscences,' Ford writes in *Return to Yesterday*. 'In that form the narrator should be a mirror, not any sort of actor. . . .' Ford makes the distinction because it is important to him. He is not an autobiographer, except insofar as he can supply information about himself that will make the reminiscences more coherent. His affective life belongs to the novels, and he is firm in excluding it from the memoirs. 'I was in those days of an extreme shyness,' he tells us, those days being c.1896 when he was Henry James's admiring young neighbour, 'le jeune homme modeste', as James called him. But Ford's shyness stayed with him, and his refusal to write autobiography rather than reminiscence or memoir is of course related to it. He disliked 'having one's psychology presented to the world'. 'Had I the cap of Fortunatus you should not see even so much of one of my garments.' He had to solve the problem of how to write about himself without, on the one hand, giving too much away, and on the other, unduly thinning out the experience of 'revisiting' the past. All his books in this vein share with one another, as well as with the novels, a power of indirection that requires more skilful reading than their apparent looseness and casualness suggest. Such a power has done his reputation more harm than good with less skilful readers.

If the design is labyrinthine, the thread is always there. Ford never loses it, no matter how slack or thin or tangled it may seem. Over and over it leads to some revelation of himself, ironic and self-deprecating, which he could not make in a more overt way without violating his sense of propriety. In this way, his seriousness is made to seem offhand and his 'constatations' (a favourite word) self-important, but the digressions and elaborations he found necessary all colour the point, when it emerges, so that it is far more saturated and charged than it could be otherwise.

He suffered, perhaps, from the 'habit of anecdote', though many of his readers are grateful for it. He often invented; he could not resist, and his inventions were taken for falsifications. The exaggerations, the tall tales, the 'lies' (how naive those Edwardian charges seem to us now, though they seriously damaged his reputation) were in fact miscalculations on Ford's part. The stories were meant to amuse. More often they only succeeded in outraging readers who did not appreciate his sense of fun or missed the point, camouflaged by so much intricacy of narration. But in fact, his memoirs, which repeatedly laid him open to *ad hominem* attack, are remarkably honest in their refusal to idealize the days before The Great War, marked as they were by widespread urban and rural poverty, the spread of the anarchist movement, the agitation over votes for women, the beginning of mass journalism, and the despoiling of Africa by imperialist policy. In one way or another, when Ford was directly or indirectly connected with these developments they found their way into his pages among, or by means of, his anecdotes. In recalling his times, he was doing what he believed was the real job of the novelist — to write the history of one's own times. In that sense he was a model of honesty, and his books illustrate the degree to which language and style can ultimately be the real test of truth. The only thing that mattered, after all, he believed, was to do good work.

Referring to Ford's criticism, Pound observed: 'He frankly says what he likes — a paradigm for all would-be critics. And for the most part the things he likes are good and the things he dislikes abominable.' Even when the things Ford dislikes are not abominable and he is simply wrong, he is at his best as a reader responding to other literary personalities, one temperament encountering another. 'A writer holds a reader by his temperament,' he wrote. 'That is his true gift.' In his criticism Ford was after something essential, and in one after another of his pieces in this Reader — on Wilde, Wells, Bennett, Hardy, Wyndham Lewis, Flaubert, Pound, James, Conrad, Jean Rhys, Hemingway, Lawrence, and Joyce, he finds it. Never solemn or pretentious, he says what he thinks in prose 'that lay so natural on the page that one didn't notice it' (Pound in his obituary for Ford).

Ford's idea of the function of the critic included looking out for the future of 'humane letters'. His protectiveness toward younger writers in whom he saw promise is by now well-known. He would 'discover' them (Lawrence was a celebrated example), publishing them in his magazines, finding publishers for their books, writing prefatory statements when a publisher was found (often on the strength of the forthcoming preface). In the case of Jean Rhys, he published her in *The Transatlantic Review* and wrote the preface to *The Left Bank and Other Stories* to introduce her to a larger reading public and launch her career at a time when his influence was at its peak. His preface is a model of tact and grace, Ford filling in what the title seems to promise: the details of place, the objective, anchoring visual details that are absent in these stories of a consciousness locked in itself and closed to all but a few external impressions.

In the case of Ernest Hemingway, Ford took him on as assistant editor of *The Transatlantic*; eight years later, Ford wrote an Introduction to *A Farewell to Arms* for the Modern Library edition. That Hemingway had, as acting editor in Ford's absence, dropped the serial installments in the magazine of Ford's *Some Do Not* (the first of the Tietjens books) is perhaps even less admirable than the portrait of Ford he left in *A Moveable Feast*. Ford's Introduction to *A Farewell to Arms* neither rises above matters of a personal nature nor descends to them: they seem not to exist. What matters is good writing, and Ford found Hemingway so good a writer that *A Farewell to Arms* evokes his best writing as a critic.

Ford's last book, his most comprehensive work of criticism, was called *The March of Literature* (1938), a phrase Flaubert might have relished for Bouvard and Pécuchet to add to their Dictionary of Received Ideas. Ford risked the title to put on record his faith in the future and the future of literature a year before the outbreak of World War II. Stock-taking (a word he loved) and at the same time forward-marching, the book was his 'summa litteraria', its subject nothing less than the literature of the world, 'from Confucius' Day to Our Own', in 878 pages. It was the last of his self-portraits. On every page he left the imprint of his strong individuality and the freshness of his literary intelligence. Ford spoke of 'the quality of surprise, which in the end is the supreme quality and necessity of art'. It is the quality that quite overwhelmed me on first looking into his unread books.

Sondra J. Stang

Acknowledgements

I would like to express my gratitude to all who have helped me in preparing this book. Without the generosity and co-operation of Janice Biala, Ford's literary executor, the book could not have been prepared at all; I thank her for making available to me the published and unpublished work of Ford I have selected. I thank Michael Schmidt at Carcanet Press for his enthusiasm and support; I have greatly benefited from both his questions and those of C. H. Sisson, which helped me to clarify my idea of what this book ought to contain. I especially thank my husband, Richard Stang, whose excellent advice I have both sought and taken. Edward Krickel at the University of Georgia and Max Saunders, Selwyn College, Cambridge University, have given me valuable suggestions; Edward Naumburg, Jr. has put me on the track of important material I would not have found without his help. Scott Elledge, George Core, Theodora Zavin, Bruce Hunter, Roger Hecht, and Rita Malenczyk have given me help in their various ways, and I am grateful to them all. I am deeply obliged to Robyn Marsack, my editor, for her patience and decisiveness in solving the many problems this manuscript presented.

I feel very much indebted to William Matheson, Chief of Rare Books at the Library of Congress, who built up the splendid Ford collection at Washington University while he was there and who has, since then, rushed to my rescue whenever I have needed it. Holly Hall, Chief of Rare Books at Washington University, has given me constant aid over the years, and I acknowledge gratefully her superior powers as a literary detective.

I would like to convey my particular thanks to the librarians at the institutions possessing Ford manuscripts. As a group and as individuals, they have been unfailingly helpful and responsible in answering my many requests and seeing me through any difficulties that presented themselves. I thank Donald Eddy, Charles McNamara, and Lucy Burgess at Cornell University; Tim Murray, Ida Holland, Melanie Osborn, Christine Smith, Kay Shehan, Victoria Witte, Alison Verbeck, Kenneth Nabors, B. J. Johnston, and the reference staff at Washington University; Cathy Henderson at the Harry Ransom Humanities Research Center, The University of Texas at Austin; Marjorie Stevens, Olivet College; R. Russell Maylone and Sigrid P. Perry at Northwestern University; Robert J. Berthold, the State University of New York at Buffalo; Sem C. Sutter and Margaret A. Fusco, the University of Chicago; Kenneth A. Lohf, Columbia University; Rodney G. Dennis and Susan Halpert, The Houghton Library, Harvard University; Daniel H. Woodward and Sara S. Hodson, The Huntington; William Hanna, Department of Archives and History, State of Mississippi; Lyman W. Riley and Daniel Traister, University of Pennsylvania; Jean F. Preston and Richard Ludwig, Princeton University; Charles Mann and Robert Secor, Pennsylvania State University; N. Frederick Nash and Annette Schoenberg, University of Illinois at Urbana; Robin W. Smith, University of Virginia; Lola L. Szladits, The Berg Collection, New York Public Library; Jack A. Siggins, Marjorie Wynne, and Patricia M. Howell, Yale University. In addition, I thank James Oliver Brown for permission to use letters on deposit at Columbia University.

The chronology of Ford's life is reprinted by permission of Frederick Ungar Publishing Co., Inc., from Sondra J. Stang, *Ford Madox Ford* (Modern Literature Monographs), 1977. The excerpt from *The Fifth Queen* is reprinted by permission of The Bodley Head Ltd; those from *A Call* and *Great Trade Route* by permission of The Ecco Press; the excerpts from *The March of Literature* by permission of George Allen & Unwin (Publishers) Ltd. Ford's introduction to *A Farewell to Arms* by Ernest Hemingway © 1932 by Random House, Inc., is reprinted by permission of the publisher. The excerpts from *Return to Yesterday* are reprinted by permission of the Liveright Publishing Co. 'Memories of Oscar Wilde' and the letter to the editor on James Joyce's *Finnegans Wake* are reprinted with permission of *Saturday Review*. The excerpt from Conrad's *Nostromo* is published with permission of the Beinecke Rare Book and Manuscript Library, Yale University. The Cornell University Library Rare Book Room has permitted publication of the following manuscripts: Ford's synopsis of *As Thy Day (Henry for Hugh)*, Ford's notes on reading the *Talmud*, and 'A Day of Battle'. 'The Mantle of Elijah' is published here with permission of the Harry Ransom Humanities Research Center, the University of Texas at Austin.

Letters no. 38, 43, 50–52 are cited with the permission of The Poetry/Rare Books Collection of the University Libraries, State University of New York at Buffalo.

The letters to Harriet Monroe (no. 22, 23, 33, 34, and 39) are from the *Poetry* Magazine Papers (1912–1936), Box 32, folder 14; letter no. 54 to Morton D. Zabel is from the Morton D. Zabel papers, Box 1, folder 30. For permission to reproduce these letters I am obliged to Special Collections, The Joseph Regenstein Library, The University of Chicago.

The two letters to George T. Bye (no. 53 and 55) are from the James Oliver Brown Papers, Rare Book and Manuscript Library, Columbia University, and are published here with the permission of Columbia University.

Letters no. 18, 40–42, and 56 are published with the permission of the Department of Rare Books (Ford Collection), Cornell University Library.

Letters no. 25, 35, and 48 are published by permission of the Houghton Library, Harvard University.

Letters no. 7, 9–14, 19–21 and 24 are reproduced by permission of The Huntington Library, San Marino, California: no. 7, FMF 32; no. 9, FMF 163; no. 10, FMF 167; no. 11, FMF 153; no. 12, FMF 201; no. 13, FMF 209; no. 14, FMF 210; no. 19, FMF 242; no. 20, FMF 244; no. 21, FMF 245; no. 24, FMF 4.

Letters no. 57–60 to Eudora Welty are published here with permission of the Department of Archives and History, State of Mississippi.

The letters to Olive Garnett (no. 1–4) and to Richard Garnett (no. 6) are reproduced by permission of the Special Collections Department, Northwestern University Library.

The letter to Theodore Dreiser (no. 45) is from the Theodore Dreiser Collection, Van Pelt Library, University of Pennsylvania, and is published here with the permission of the Library.

Letters no. 5, 8, 15, 26–32, 36, 44, 46, 47, and 49 are published with permission of the Harry Ransom Humanities Research Center, The University of Texas at Austin. I am also grateful to Graham Greene for his permission to publish letters no. 46 and 47.

The letter to J. B. Manson (no. 37) is cited with permission of Special Collections, Washington University Libraries, St. Louis, Missouri, U.S.A.

In addition, I am grateful to Mr James Gilvarry, who sent me for inclusion in this volume photocopies of the two letters to John Lane (no. 16 and 17) in his private collection.

Chronology

1873: Ford Hermann Hueffer is born on 17 December in Merton, Surrey.

1889: Death of father, Dr Francis Hueffer; family moved to house of the grandfather, Ford Madox Brown.

1891: Conversion to Roman Catholicism. His first publication, *The Brown Owl*, a fairy tale for children.

1892: Publication of his first novel, *The Shifting of the Fire*.

1893: Death of grandfather.

1894: Elopement with Elsie Martindale.

1896: Publication of *Ford Madox Brown: A Record of His Life and Work*.

1897: Birth of daughter Christina.

1898: Meeting with Conrad, arranged by Stephen Crane and Edward Garnett; beginning of ten-year collaboration: *The Inheritors* (1901), *Romance* (1903), *The Nature of a Crime* (1909).

1900: Birth of daughter Katharine.

1904: Nervous collapse; trip to Germany.

1906–08: Publication of *The Fifth Queen* trilogy: *The Fifth Queen*, *Privy Seal*, *The Fifth Queen Crowned*.

1908–09: Editorship of the *English Review*.

1908: Meeting with Violet Hunt, with whom he lived until 1915; collaboration with her on *The Desirable Alien* (1913) and *Zeppelin Nights* (1915).

1910: Residence in Germany to obtain a divorce from Elsie under German law.

1910–11: Elsie's refusal to grant divorce and her libel suit of two newspapers referring to Violet Hunt as Mrs Hueffer;

Ford's bankruptcy and sale of all his possessions as a result of legal expenses of attempted divorce and debts of *English Review*.

1915: Publication of *The Good Soldier*. Death of Ford's friend, the sculptor Gaudier-Brzeska, in the war and Ford's enlistment in the British army; active service at the front from July 1916.

1918: Meeting with the painter Stella Bowen, a friend of Ezra Pound.

1919: Change of name to Ford Madox Ford. Move to Sussex with Stella.

1920: Birth of daughter Esther Julia Ford (Julie).

1921: Award by *Poetry* magazine of $100 prize for his poem *A House* (the only literary prize of his career).

1922: Move to France with Stella and Julie.

1924–25: Editorship of the *Transatlantic Review*.

1924: *Some Do Not . . .*; Conrad's death; Ford's *Joseph Conrad: A Personal Remembrance*; affair with Jean Rhys.

1925: *No More Parades*.

1926: *A Man Could Stand Up —*.

1927: Separation from Stella.

1928: *Last Post*.

1930: Meeting with the painter Janice Biala, with whom he lived until his death.

1931–36: Publication of last novels.

1934–36: Travels in the United States.

1936: *Collected Poems* published by Oxford University Press.

1937: Appointment as writer and critic in residence at Olivet College, Michigan.

1939: Death in Deauville, France on 26 June 1939.

I

Novels

from

The Fifth Queen (1906)

Of Ford's thirty-one published novels, nine are historical novels. *The Fifth Queen* was followed by *Privy Seal*, 1907, and *The Fifth Queen Crowned*, 1908, to make up the trilogy that Conrad called 'the swan song of Historical Romance'.

THE Lord Privy Seal was beneath a tall cresset in the stern of his barge, looking across the night and the winter river. They were rowing from Rochester to the palace at Greenwich, where the Court was awaiting Anne of Cleves. The flare of the King's barge a quarter of a mile ahead moved in a glowing patch of lights and their reflections, as though it were some portent creeping in a blaze across the sky. There was nothing else visible in the world but the darkness and a dusky tinge of red where a wave caught the flare of light further out.

He stood invisible behind the lights of his cabin; and the thud of oars, the voluble noises of the water, and the crackling of the cresset overhead had, too, the quality of impersonal and supernatural phenomena. His voice said harshly:

'It is very cold; bring me my greatest cloak.'

Throckmorton, the one of Cromwell's seven hundred spies who at that time was his most constant companion, was hidden in the deep shadow beside the cabin-door. His bearded and heavy form obscured the light for a moment as he hurried to fetch the cloak. But merely to be the Lord Cromwell's gown-bearer was in those days a thing you would run after; and an old man in a flat cap — the Chancellor of the Augmentations, who had been listening intently at the door — was already hurrying out with a heavy cloak of fur. Cromwell let it be hung about his shoulders.

The Chancellor shivered and said, 'We should be within a quarter-hour of Greenwich.'

'Get you in if you be cold,' Cromwell answered. But the Chancellor was quivering with the desire to talk to his master. He had seen the heavy King rush stumbling down the stairs of the

Cleves woman's lodging at Rochester, and the sight had been for him terrible and prodigious. It was Cromwell who had made him Chancellor of the Augmentations — who had even invented the office to deal with the land taken from the Abbeys — and he was so much the creature of this Lord Privy Seal that it seemed as if the earth was shivering all the while for the fall of this minister, and that he himself was within an inch of the ruin, execration, and death that would come for them all once Cromwell were down.

Throckmorton, a giant man with an immense golden beard, issued again from the cabin, and the Privy Seal's voice came leisurely and cold:

'What said Lord Cassilis of this? And the fellow Knighton? I saw them at the stairs.'

Privy Seal had such eyes that it was delicate work lying to him. But Throckmorton brought out heavily:

'Cassilis, that this Lady Anne should never be Queen.'

'Aye, but she must,' the Chancellor bleated. He had been bribed by two of the Cleves lords to get them lands in Kent when the Queen should be in power. Cromwell's silence made Throckmorton continue against his will:

'Knighton, that the Queen's breath should turn the King's stomach against you! Dr Miley, the Lutheran preacher, that by this evening's work the Kingdom of God on earth was set trembling, the King having the nature of a lecher . . .'

He tried to hold back. After all, it came into his mind, this man was nearly down. Any one of the men upon whom he now spied might come to be his master very soon. But Cromwell's voice said, 'And then?' and he made up his mind to implicate none but the Scotch lord, who was at once harmless and unliable to be harmed.

'Lord Cassilis,' he brought out, 'said again that your lordship's head should fall ere January goes out.'

He seemed to feel the great man's sneer through the darkness, and was coldly angry with himself for having invented no better lie. For if this invisible and threatening phantom that hid itself among these shadows outlasted January he might yet outlast some of them. He wondered which of Cromwell's innumerable ill-wishers it might best serve him to serve. But for the Chancellor of the Augmentations the heavy silence of calamity, like the waiting at a bedside for death to come, seemed to fall upon them. He imagined that the Privy Seal hid himself in that shadow in order to conceal a pale face and shaking knees. But Cromwell's voice came harsh and peremptory to Throckmorton:

'What men be abroad at this night season? Ask my helmsmen.'

Two torchlights, far away to the right, wavered shaking trails in the water that, thus revealed, shewed agitated and chopped by small waves. The Chancellor's white beard shook with the cold, with fear of Cromwell, and with curiosity to know how the man looked and felt. He ventured at last in a faint and bleating voice:

What did his lordship think of this matter? Surely the King should espouse this lady and the Lutheran cause.

Cromwell answered with inscrutable arrogance:

'Why, your cause is valuable. But this is a great matter. Get you in if you be cold.'

Throckmorton appeared noiselessly at his elbow, whilst the Chancellor was mumbling: 'God forbid I should be called Lutheran.'

The torches, Throckmorton said, were those of fishers who caught eels off the mud with worms upon needles.

'Such night work favours treason,' Cromwell muttered. 'Write in my notebook, "The Council to prohibit the fishing of eels by night."'

'What a nose he hath for treasons,' the Chancellor whispered to Throckmorton as they rustled together into the cabin. Throckmorton's face was gloomy and pensive. The Privy Seal had chosen none of his informations for noting down. Assuredly the time was near for him to find another master.

The barge swung round a reach, and the lights of the palace of Greenwich were like a flight of dim or bright squares in mid air, far ahead. The King's barge was already illuminating the crenellated arch at the top of the river steps. A burst of torches flared out to meet it and disappeared. The Court was then at Greenwich, nearly all the lords, the bishops and the several councils lying in the Palace to await the coming of Anne of Cleves on the morrow. She had reached Rochester that evening after some days' delay at Calais, for the winter seas. The King had gone that night to inspect her, having been given to believe that she was soberly fair and of bountiful charms. His courteous visit had been in secret and in disguise; therefore there were no torchmen in the gardens, and darkness lay between the river steps and the great central gateway. But a bonfire, erected by the guards to warm themselves in the courtyard, as it leapt up or subsided before the wind, shewed that tall tower pale and high or vanishing into the night with its carved stone garlands, its stone men at arms, its lions, roses, leopards, and naked boys. The living houses ran away from the foot of the tower, till the wings, coming towards the river, vanished continually into shadows. They were low by comparison, gabled with false fronts over each set of rooms and, in the glass of their small-paned windows, the reflection of the fire gleamed capriciously from unexpected shadows. This palace was called Placentia by the King because it was pleasant to live in.

Cromwell mounted the steps with a slow gait and an arrogant figure. Under the river arch eight of his gentlemen waited upon him, and in the garden the torches of his men shewed black yew trees cut like peacocks, clipped hedges like walls with archways above the broad and tiled paths, and fountains that gleamed and trickled as if secretly in the heavy and bitter night.

A corridor ran from under the great tower right round the palace. It was full of hurrying people and of grooms who stood in knots beside doorways. They flattened themselves against the walls before the Lord Privy Seal's procession of gentlemen in black with white staves, and the ceilings seemed to send down moulded and gilded stalactites to touch his head. The beefeater before the door of the Lady Mary's lodgings spat upon the ground when he had passed. His hard glance travelled along the wall like a palpable ray, about the height of a man's head. It passed over faces and slipped back to the gilded wainscoting; tiring-women upon whom it fell shivered, and the serving men felt their bowels turn within them. His round face was hard and alert, and his lips moved ceaselessly one upon another. All those serving people wondered to see his head so high, for already it was known that the King had turned sick at the sight of his bedfellow that should be. And indeed the palace was only awake at that late hour because of that astounding news, dignitaries lingering in each other's quarters to talk of it, whilst in the passages their waiting men supplied gross commentaries.

He entered his door. In the ante-room two men in his livery removed his outer furs deftly so as not to hinder his walk. Before the fire of his large room a fair boy knelt to pull off his jewelled gloves, and Hanson, one of his secretaries, unclasped from his girdle the corded bag that held the Privy Seal. He laid it on a high stand between two tall candles of wax upon the long table.

The boy went with the gloves and Hanson disappeared silently behind the dark tapestry in the further corner. Cromwell was meditating above a fragment of flaming wood that the fire had spat out far into the tiled forehearth. He pressed it with his foot gently towards the blaze of wood in the chimney.

His plump hands were behind his back, his long upper lip ceaselessly caressed its fellow, moving as one line of a snake's coil glides above another. The January wind crept round the shadowy room behind the tapestry, and as it quivered stags seemed to leap over bushes, hounds to spring in pursuit, and a crowned Diana to move her arms, taking an arrow from a quiver behind her shoulder. The tall candles guarded the bag of the Privy Seal, they fluttered and made the gilded heads on the rafters have sudden grins on their faces that represented kings with flowered crowns, queens with their hair combed back on to pillows, and pages with scolloped hats. Cromwell stepped to an aumbry, where there were a glass of wine, a manchet of bread, and a little salt. He began to eat, dipping pieces of bread into the golden salt-cellar. The face of a queen looked down just above his head with her eyes wide open as if she were amazed, thrusting her head from a cloud.

'Why, I have outlived three queens,' he said to himself, and his round face resignedly despised his world and his times. He had forgotten what anxiety felt like because the world was so peopled with blunderers and timid fools full of hatred.

The marriage with Cleves was the deathblow to the power of the Empire. With the Protestant Princes armed behind his back, the imbecile called Charles would never dare to set his troops on board ship in Flanders to aid the continual rebellions, conspiracies and risings in England. He had done it too often, and he had repented as often, at the last moment. It was true that the marriage had thrown Charles into the arms of France: the French King and he were at that very minute supping together in Paris. They would be making treaties that were meant to be broken, and their statesmen were hatching plots that any scullion would reveal. Francis and his men were too mean, too silly, too despicable, and too easily bribed to hold to any union or to carry out any policy. . . .

He sipped his wine slowly. It was a little cold, so he set it down beside the fire. He wanted to go to bed, but the Archbishop was coming to hear how Henry had received his Queen, and to pour out his fears. Fears! Because the King had been sick at sight of the Cleves woman! He had this King very absolutely in his power; the grey, failing but vindictive and obstinate mass known as Henry was afraid of his contempt, afraid really of a shrug of the shoulder or a small sniff.

With the generosity of his wine and the warmth of his fire, his thoughts went many years ahead. He imagined the King either married to or having repudiated the Lady from Cleves, and then dead. Edward, the Seymour child, was his creature, and would be king or dead. Cleves children would be his creations too. Or if he married the Lady Mary he would still be next the throne.

His mind rested luxuriously and tranquilly on that prospect. He would be perpetually beside the throne, there would be no distraction to maintain a foothold. He would be there by right; he would be able to give all his mind to the directing of this world that he despised for its baseness, its jealousies, its insane brawls, its aimless selfishness, and its blind furies. Then there should be no more war, as there should be no more revolts. There should be no more jealousies; for kingcraft, solid, austere, practical and inspired, should keep down all the peoples, all the priests, and all the nobles of the world. 'Ah,' he thought, 'there would be in France no power to shelter traitors like Brancetor.' His eyes became softer in the contemplation of this Utopia, and he moved his upper lip more slowly.

Now the Archbishop was there. Pale, worn with fears and agitation, he came to say that the King had called to him Bishop Gardiner and the more Catholic lords of the Council. Cranmer's own spy Lascelles had made this new report.

His white sleeves made a shivering sound, the fur that fell round his neck was displaced on one shoulder. His large mouth was open with panic, his lips trembled, and his good-natured and narrow eyes seemed about to drop tears.

'Your Grace knoweth well what passed tonight at Rochester,' Cromwell said. He clapped his hands for a man to snuff the candles. 'You have the common report.'

'Ah, is it even true?' The Archbishop felt a last hope die, and he choked in his throat. Cromwell watched the man at the candles and said:

'Your Grace hath a new riding mule. I pray it may cease to affright you.'

'Why?' he said, as the man went. 'The King's Highness went even to Rochester, disguised, since it was his good pleasure, as a French lord. You have seen the lady. So his Highness was seized with a make of palsy. He cursed to his barge. I know no more than that.'

'And now they sit in the council.'

'It seems,' Cromwell said.

'Ah, dear God have mercy.'

The Archbishop's thin hands wavered before the crucifix on his breast, and made the sign of the cross.

The very faces of his enemies seemed visible to him. He saw Gardiner, of Winchester, with his snake's eyes under the flat cap, and the Duke of Norfolk with his eyes malignant in a long, yellow face. He had a vision of the King, a huge red lump beneath the high dais at the head of the Council table, his face suffused with blood, his cheeks quivering.

He wrung his hands and wondered if at Smithfield the Lutherans would pray for him, or curse him for having been lukewarm.

'Why, goodman gossip,' Cromwell said compassionately, 'we have been nearer death ten times.' He uttered his inmost thoughts out of pity: — All this he had awaited. The King's Highness by the report of his painters, his ambassadors, his spies — they were all in the pay of Cromwell — had awaited a lady of modest demeanour, a coy habit, and a great and placid fairness. 'I had warned the Almains at Rochester to attire her against our coming. But she slobbered with ecstasy and slipped side-ways, aiming at a courtesy. Therefore the King was hot with new anger and disgust.'

'You and I are undone.' Cranmer was passive with despair.

'He is very seldom an hour of one mind,' Cromwell answered. 'Unless in that hour those you wot of shall work upon him, it will go well with us.'

'They shall. They shall.'

'I wait to see.'

There seemed to Cranmer something horrible in this impassivity. He wished his leader to go to the King, and he had a frantic moment of imagining himself running to a great distance, hiding his head in darkness.

Cromwell's lips went up in scorn. 'Do you imagine the yellow duke speaking his mind to the King? He is too craven.'

A heavy silence fell between them. The fire rustled, the candles again needed snuffing.

'Best get to bed,' Cromwell said at last.

'Could I sleep?' Cranmer had the irritation of extreme fear. His master seemed to him to have no bowels. But the waiting told at last upon Cromwell himself.

'I could sleep an you would let me,' he said sharply. 'I tell you the King shall be another man in the morning.'

'Ay, but now. But now. . . .' He imagined the pens in that distant room creaking over the paper with their committals, and he wished to upbraid Cromwell. It was his policy of combining with Lutherans that had brought them to this.

Heavy thundering came on the outer door.

'The King comes,' Cromwell cried victoriously. He went swiftly from the room. The Archbishop closed his eyes and suddenly remembered the time when he had been a child.

Privy Seal had an angry and contemptuous frown at his return. 'They have kept him from me.' He threw a little scroll on to the table. Its white silence made Cranmer shudder; it seemed to have something of the heavy threatening of the King's self.

'We may go to bed,' Cromwell said. 'They have devised their shift.'

'You say?'

'They have temporised, they have delayed. I know them.' He quoted contemptuously from the letter: 'We would have you send presently to ask of the Almain Lords with the Lady Anne the papers concerning her pre-contract to the Duke of Lorraine.'

Cranmer was upon the point of going away in the joy of this respite. But his desire to talk delayed him, and he began to talk about the canon law and pre-contracts of marriage. It was a very valid cause of nullity all the doctors held.

'Think you I have not made very certain the pre-contract was nullified? This is no shift,' and Cromwell spoke wearily and angrily. 'Goodman Archbishop, dry your tears. Tonight the King is hot with disgust, but I tell you he will not cast away his kingdom upon whether her teeth be white or yellow. This is no woman's man.'

Cranmer came nearer the fire and stretched out his lean hands.

'He hath dandled of late with the Lady Cassilis.'

'Well, he hath been pleasant with her.'

Cranmer urged: 'A full-blown man towards his failing years is more prone to women than before.'

'Then he may go a-wenching.' He began to speak with a weary passion. To cast away the Lady Anne now were a madness. It would be to stand without a friend before all nations armed to their downfall. This King would do no jot to lose a patch upon his sovereignty.

Cranmer sought to speak.

'His Highness is always hot o'nights,' Cromwell kept on. 'It is in his nature so to be. But by morning the German princes shall make him afraid again and the Lutherans of this goodly realm. Those mad swine our friends!'

'He will burn seven of them on tomorrow sennight,' Cranmer said.

'Nay! I shall enlarge them on Wednesday.'

Cranmer shivered. 'They grow very insolent. I am afraid.'

Cromwell answered with a studied nonchalance:

'My bones tell me it shall be an eastward wind. It shall not rain on the new Queen's bridals.' He drank up his warm wine and brushed the crumbs from the furs round his neck.

'You are a very certain man,' the Archbishop said.

Going along the now dark corridors he was afraid that some ruffling boy might spring upon him from the shadows. Norfolk, as the Earl Marshal, had placed his lodgings in a very distant part of the palace to give him long journeys that, telling upon his asthma, made him arrive breathless and convulsed at the King's rooms when he was sent for.

* * *

The Queen came to the revels given in her honour by the Lord Privy Seal. Cromwell had three hundred servants dressed in new liveries: pikemen with their staves held transversely, like a barrier, kept the road all the way from the Tower Steps to Austin Friars, and in that Lutheran quarter of the town there was a great crowding together. Caps were pitched high and lost for ever, and loud shouts of praise to God went up when the Queen and her Germans passed, with boys casting branches of holm, holly, bay and yew, the only plants that were green in the winter season, before the feet of her mule. But the King did not come. It was reported to the crowd that he was ill at Greenwich.

It was known very well by those that sat at dinner with her that, after three days, he had abandoned his Queen and kept his separate room. She sat eating alone, on high beneath the dais, heavy, silent, placid and so fair that her eyebrows appeared to be white upon her red forehead. She did not speak a word, having no English, and it was considered disgusting that she wiped her fingers upon pieces of bread.

Hostile lords remarked upon all her physical imperfections, which the King, it was known, had reported to his physicians in a writing of many pages. Besides, she had no English, no French, no Italian; she could not even play cards with his Highness. It was true that they had squeezed her into English stays, but she was reported to have wept at having to mount a horse. So she could not go a-hawking, neither could she shoot with the bow, and her attendants — the women, bound about the middle and spreading out above and below like bolsters, and the men, who wore their immense scolloped hats falling over their ears even at meal-times — excited disgust and derision by the noises they made when they ate.

The Master Viridus had Katharine Howard in his keeping. He took her up into a small gallery near the gilded roof of the long hall and pointed out to her, far below, the courtiers that it was safe for her to consort with, because they were friends of Privy Seal. His manner was more sinister and more meaning.

'You would do well to have to do with no others,' he said.

'I am like to have to do with none at all,' Katharine answered, 'for no mother's son cometh anigh me.'

He looked away from her. Down below she made out her cousin Surrey, sitting with his back ostentatiously turned to a Lord Roydon, of Cromwell's following; her uncle, plunged in his silent and malignant gloom; and Cromwell, his face lit up and smiling, talking earnestly with Chapuys, the Ambassador from the Emperor.

'Eleven hundred dishes shall be served this day,' Viridus proclaimed, seeming to warn her. 'There can no other lord find so many plates of parcel gilt.' His level and cold voice penetrated through all the ascending din of voices, of knives, of tuckets of trumpets that announced the courses of meat and of the three men's songs that introduced the sweet jellies which only Privy Seal, it was said, could direct to be prepared.

'Other lordings all,' Viridus continued with his sermon, 'ha' ruined themselves seeking in vain to vie with my lord. Most of those you see are broken men, whose favour would be worth naught to you.'

Tables were ranged down each side of the great hall, the men sitting on the right, each wearing upon his shoulder a red rose made of silk since no flowers were to be had. The women, sitting upon the left, had white favours in their caps. In the wide space between these tables were two bears; chained to tall gilt posts, they rolled on their hams and growled at each other. From time to time the serving men who went up and down in the middle let fall great dishes containing craspisces, cranes, swans or boars. These meats were kicked contemptuously aside for the bears to fight over, and their places supplied immediately with new. Other serving men broke priceless bottles of Venetian glass against the corners of tables, and let the costly Rhenish wines run about their feet.

This, the Master Viridus said, was intended to point out the wealth of their lord and his zealousness to entertain his Sovereigns.

'It would serve the purpose as well to give them twice as much fare,' Katharine said.

'They could never contain it,' Viridus answered gravely, 'so great is the bounty of my lord.'

Throckmorton, the spy, enormous, bearded and with the half-lion badge of the Privy Seal hanging round his neck from a gilt chain, walked up and down behind the guests, bearing the wand of a major-domo, affecting to direct the servers when to fill goblets and listening at tables where much wine had been served. Once he looked up at the gallery, and his scrutinising and defiant brown eyes remained for a long time upon Katharine's face, as if he too were appraising her beauty.

'I would not drink much wine with that man listening at my back. He came from my country, and was such a foul villain that mothers fright their children with his name,' Katharine said.

Viridus moved his lips quickly one upon another, and suddenly directed her to observe the new Queen's headdress, broad and stiffened with a wire of gold, upon which large pearls had been sewn.

'Many ladies will now get themselves such headdresses,' he said.

'That will I never,' she answered. It appeared atrocious and Flemish-clumsy, spreading out and overshadowing the Queen's heavy face. Their English hoods with the tails down made the head sleek and comely; or, with the tails folded up and pinned square like flat caps they could give to the face a gallant or a pensive expression.

'Why, I could never get me in at the door of the confessional with such a spreading cloth.'

Viridus had his chin on the rail of the gallery; he gazed down below with his snaky eyes. She could not tell whether he were old or young.

'You would more prudently abandon the confessing,' he said,

without looking at her. 'My lord is minded that ladies who look to him should wear such.'

'That is to be a bond-slave,' Katharine cried indignantly. He looked round.

'Here is a great magnificence,' he uttered, moving his hand towards the hall. 'My Lord Privy Seal hath a mighty power.'

'Not power enow to make me a laughing-stock for the men.'

'Why, this is a free land,' he answered. 'You may rot in a ditch if you will, or worse if treasonable actions be brought home to you.'

Down below, wild men dressed in the skins of wolves, hares and stags ran round the tethered bears bearing torches of sweet wood, and a heavy and languorous smoke, like incense, mounted up to the gallery. Viridus' unveiled threat made the necessity for submission come once more into her mind. Other wild men were leading in a lion, immense and lean as if it were a fawn-coloured ass. It roared and pulled at the gold chains by which the knot of men held it. Many ladies shrieked out, but the men dragged the lion into the open space before the dais where the Queen sat unmoved and stolid.

'Would your master have me dip my fingers in the dish and wipe them on bread-manchets as the Queen does?' Katharine asked in a serious expostulation.

'It were an excellent action,' Viridus answered.

There was a brazen flare of trumpets so that the smoke swirled among the rafters. Men with brass helmets and shields of brass were below in the hall.

'They are costumed as the ancient Romans,' Katharine said, lost in other thoughts.

Suddenly she saw that whilst all the other eyes were upon the lion, Throckmorton's glare was again upon her face. He appeared to shake his head and to bow his immense and bearded form. It brought into her mind the dangerous visit of Bishop Gardiner. Suddenly he dropped his eyes.

'You see some friends,' Viridus' voice asked beside her.

'Nay, I have no friends here,' Katharine answered.

She could not tell that the bearded spy's eyes were not merely amorous in their intention, for such looks she was used to, and he was a very vile man.

'In short,' Viridus spoke, 'it were an excellent action to act in all things as the Queen does. For fashions are a matter of fashion. It is all one whether you wipe your fingers on bread-manchets or on napkins. But when a fashion becometh general its strangeness departeth and it is esteemed fit for a King's Court. Thus you may earn your bread: this is your duteous work. Observe the king of the beasts. See how it shall do its duty before the Queen, and mark the lesson.' His voice penetrated, low and level, through all the din from below. Yet the men dressed like gladiators advanced towards the dais where the Queen sat eating unmoved. The lion before her growled frightfully, and dragged its keepers towards the men in brass. They drew their short swords and beat upon their shields crying: 'We be Roman traitors that war upon this land.' Then it appeared that among them in their crowd they had a large mannikin, dressed like themselves in brass and running upon wheels.

The ladies pressed the tables with their hands, making as if to rise in terror. But the mannikin toppling forward fell before the lion with a hollow sound of brass. The lean beast, springing at its throat, tore it to reach the highly smelling flesh that was concealed within the tunic, and the Romans fled, casting away their shields and swords. One of them had a red forked beard and wide-open blue eyes. He brought into Katharine's mind the remembrance of her cousin. She wondered where he could be, and imagined him with that short sword, cutting his way to her side.

'That sight is allegorically to show,' Viridus was commenting beside her, 'how the high valour of Britain shall defend from all foes this noble Queen.'

The lion having reached its meat lay down upon it.

Katharine remembered that Bishop Gardiner said that her cousin must be begone. She tried to say to Viridus: 'Sir, I would fain obey you in these things, but I have a cousin that shall much hinder me.'

But the applause of the people below drowned her voice and Viridus continued talking.

Let it be true that the Queen, being alone, showed amongst their English fineries and nicenesses a gross and repulsive strangeness. But if their ladies put on her manners she should no longer be alone, and it would appear to the King and to all men that her example was both commended and emulated. It was a matter of kingcraft, and so the Lord Privy Seal was minded and determined.

'Then I will even get myself such a hat and tear my capons apart with my fingers,' Katharine said.

'You had much the wiser,' he answered.

The hall was now full of wild men, nymphs in white gowns, men bearing aspergers with which to scatter perfumes, and merry andrews, so that the floor could no longer be seen. A party of lords had overset a table in their efforts to get to the nymphs. The Queen was schooled to go out behind the arras, and the ladies, laughing, calling to each other and to the men at the other tables, and pinning up their hoods, filed out after her.

'I shall do my best to please your master and mine,' Katharine said. 'But he must even help me, or I can be no example to emulate, but one at whom the finger of scorn is likely to be pointed.'

Viridus paused before he led his charge from the gallery. His pale-blue eyes were more placable.

'You shall be well seconded. But have a care. Dally with no traitors. Speak fairly of your master's friends.' He touched her above the left breast with a claw-like finger. 'The Italian writes: "Whoso mocketh my love mocketh also mine own self." '

'I mock none,' Katharine said. 'But I have a cousin to be provided for that neither you nor I shall mock with much safety if he be sober enough to stand.'

He listened to her with his hand upon the door of the gallery: his air was attentive and aroused. She related very simply how Culpepper had besieged her door — 'He came to London to help me on my way and to seek fortune in some war. I would that a place might be found for him, for here he is like to ruin both himself and me.'

'We have need of good swordsmen for an errand,' he said, in an absorbed voice.

'There was never a better than Tom,' Katharine said. 'He hath cut a score of throats. Your lord would have sent him to Calais.'

He muttered:

'Why, there are places other than Calais where a man may make a fortune.'

Something sinister in his brooding voice made her say:

'I would not have him killed. He hath made me many presents.'

He looked at her expressionlessly:

'It is very certain that you cannot serve my lord with such a firebrand to your tail,' he said. 'I will find him an errand.'

'But not where he shall be killed,' she said again.

'Why,' he said slowly, 'I will send him where he will make a great fortune.'

'A great fortune would help him little,' she answered. 'I would have him sent where he may fight evenly matched.'

He laid his hand upon her wrist.

'He is in as much danger here as anywhere. This is not Lincolnshire, but an ordered Court.' — A man drew his sword with some peril there, for there were laws against it. If men came brawling in the maids' quarters at nights there were penalties of losing fingers, hands, or even heads. And the maids themselves were liable to be whipped. — He shook his head at her:

'If your cousin hath so violent an inclination to you I were your best friend to send him far away.'

It was in his mind that if they were to breed this girl to be a spy they must keep her protected from madmen. Something of mystery in his manner penetrated to her quick senses.

'God help me, what a dangerous place this is!' she said. 'I would I had never spoken to you of my cousin.'

He eyed her solemnly and said that if she were minded to wed this roaring boy they might both, and soon, earn fortunes to buy them land in a distant shire.

[London: The Bodley Head, 1962: pp. 24–34, 85–92.]

from

The 'Half Moon' (1909)

The title refers to Henry Hudson's ship on his voyage of 1609. In the concluding pages of this little known historical novel, so sympathetic to the American Indian, Ford sees the tragic consequences of colonialism, a theme he took up again in *A History of Our Own Times* (to be published in 1987 by Indiana University Press) as well as in *Provence* and *Great Trade Route*.

IT was on a day in July towards ten o'clock in the morning that first they sighted the shores of the New World, being then well to the north of the island called Newfoundland and farther in, too, to the west. It was a very hot day too, and the wind fell when they came in with the land and found soundings, and there was much of haze in the air. But, from where they let the anchor drop into the steel-like water, they could descry the little mouth of a river or creek, red rocks, many green pine-trees and, farther in, several mountains much more lofty than are to be seen in England or Holland, but more such as they had observed passing Scotland on their northern voyage. So they debated how it would be to call this land New Scotland if it had no other name, and they filled their two boats, called the pinnace and the little-boat, with their water-casks to be filled at the river, and taking their stand-guns and some bows and arrows, all of them but two rowed into the little creek, which, sure enough, they found to be of fresh water.

And as they rowed up this little creek, between rocks and boulders and old grey dead trees, and many trees like pine-trees that were quite still in the unwindy weather, laughing and talking all together, they heard wild cries, resounding and full, like the notes of owls and hawks, and soon they saw great hawks and, soon after, men, leaping along over the fallen trees, all brown, with blankets of brown upon them and with hatchets in their hands and their long hair, all black, floating behind them. In the pinnace where Hudson was he made them sit quietly and observe these indigenes; but the little boat was behind, and they saw old Jan in it stand up and plant his gun on a rest and set his eye along it, and the sound of his shot echoed many times among the deep hills and the white smoke hung in the still air. They could not, in the pinnace, see that he had killed any man, only the Indians, who had been coming close along the right bank, made off into the trees and up the hillsides, calling out mournfully and awakening mournful echoes.

Hudson scowled heavily at this deed, and bade them lay on their oars till the little-boat came up with them. For, he said, and he called it out to the old man, not only are these people a simple and a friendly folk, but here when they came first many vessels would follow them. And if any were shipwrecked how would it fare with the poor crews upon this land if they, the first comers, mishandled thus, without any provocation?

But the old Jan was in no way dismayed or cast down. He answered that these peoples and all peoples with black or brown skins were devils, that was why they had that mark of brownness set upon them by God. And it was his duty and his pleasure to slay some of them that came within reach of pellets or bolts.

'Well,' said Hudson, 'I have in this no command over you. But I hold it for a very wicked thing to do, and I would fain have spoken with these people as to whether near here a strait crosses this land.'

'Why, you cannot speak with them,' old Jan called back, 'for if you have no Dutch asuredly you have not the tongue of devils such as these be. And they would misguide you and lead you astray and murder us all, and they have ways of sending men to hell after having slain them. My grandfather, who was a sailor, heard that of his confessor in the Indies.'

Hudson answered that it was not true, or, if it were, so much the more reason not to slay these poor peoples in their sin, but to bring them to see God.

'I am never for killing,' he said.

But in that mind he had only Edward Colman with him. For the Dutchmen, when they did not incline to believe the teachings of old Jan, said that these brown-skinned peoples were no more than beasts, and you slay a beast when you see it.

'That do I not,' Hudson said, and the boat's crew laughed at him.

For they said that he was a very great man in all else; but in this he was a little simple and foolish. For did he not play with white mice, which, in Holland, was held to be the deed of a natural, since mice were not eatable, neither did they give forth agreeable songs like birds, or make gross antics for men to laugh at like apes?

But, because each man was eager to set forth upon this New World, they gave over this talking and set about to find a convenient landing-place. And, with a few strokes of the oars, they came to a place where a canoe painted with ochre lay upon a pebbly flat. Behind it were three tents of deerskins with the poles crossed above them, and before the openings were fires smouldered down, and the tents were painted with ochre with the figures of monstrous horned beasts where they stood beneath the trunks of great pine-trees in the shadows. So the Dutchmen fired three gun-shots, one into each tent, and a score or so of arrows through the sides to make sure that no savages lurked within. And there came out of them no more than a yellow-furred dog, that howled at them till one shot it with an arrow.

Then they said it was proof of the devilish nature of these brown men that, without message carried to them, they knew that the boats were arrived. So they went ashore and gave thanks to God that had so safely brought them to this land after such many and fearful storms and escapes. For, but four days before, on a dark night they had come very close to an iceberg and had come away only with great peril.

And most of them were filled with a great emotion of wonder and contentment thus, for the first time, to tread upon these shores where each man, after his disposition, imagined that his heart's content was to be found. For some aspired to perfect republics, and some to find places where the True Doctrine, as they took it to be, should flourish in tranquillity, and some desired gold, and some strange sweetmeats and spices and fruits. And each had heard that all these things were to be found in this New World.

So they stretched their legs and rifled the tents, where they found only skins and a few fish, and some hatchets and tools, whose use they did not know, made of stone tied with thongs to sticks, and two carcases of deer hung to a tree, and some baskets of rush-work and a little money, and some strips of leather that had beads of a substance they knew not and sharks' teeth stitched into them, and other strips of leather with coronals of feathers and strips of great eagles' feathers sewn to them. And all these things they carried to their boats, and they filled their casks with water, and four or five of them ran a race along the level ground, and they cut many green boughs of a sort of tree that bore nuts and looked like a hazel. And one man with his bow shot a hawk that was high overhead in the sky. And some stretched themselves on the little pebbles in the hot sunlight and debated of this New World and of all they had heard told of it by other travellers, and they drank wine they had brought with them.

But, to Edward Colman, this did not seem a very good place to found a colony, for the rocks were very dry and had no lichens, and the soil was sand and there was neither grass nor flowers, and the hills were high and precipitous all around that little stream, and there was no level ground, only there was timber enough to build all the navies and fleets of the world.

And Hudson bade him be patient, for farther south he would find him meadows and champaigns and flat places level with river mouths; aye, and timber too, and fruit trees and streams bearing gold in their sands and a great fertility and many sweet flowers.

'This is no good place,' he said, 'or only good in midsummer time, for here we are above the sixtieth parallel, and I know that in winter it is very cold. And you may plainly tell by the poverty of gear in these tents that this is a very poor place.'

Towards sundown there came a great swarm of midges and of flies, and the sun set towards the top of the mountains to a fire and red gold such as they had never seen. And when they had slit the tents to ribands with their swords and set fire to the canoe, that was as thin as paper, they got into their boat, and with their oars tore the satin of the water into foam and made the hills once more echo, this time with psalms in Dutch and some few gunshots.

The next morning they decorated the ship all over the rigging with the boughs of trees that they had cut, and they set a little fir-tree on the high-mast and another on the little mast at the stern, and they declared it a Sabbath day and did nothing but lie at anchor.

Hudson made them also another long speech, telling them what his plans were and how they should sail. They were to search, he said, for a great strait of water that ran right across this continent. Now, north of where they were, the country had been well explored by the French, who, sixty years before, had sent there a great expedition under the Lord of Riverolles. And, since then, every year they had sent there expeditions to the land that they had called Canada; and they brought away furs and skins, and had made friends with and converted the natives to the Papist form of religion, and the French Protestants, called Huguenots, had there attempted to found settlements and colonies, and had set up posts bearing the arms of the Kings of France, and had made excellent good charts. So that, although there was there a very great gulf called the Gulf of St Lawrence, after the day on which it had been found by the Papist French, they were well assured that, to the north of them, there was no strait extending through America.

To the south and west of them the land bowed out to the island called Newfoundland. Here the French fishermen came every year from French Britaigne and fished; and here there were said to be settlements on the shores, and they might have meats and fish and replenish their stores. And from the southern port of America up to the fortieth parallel they were main certain that there was no passage, the French and the Spaniards having searched the coasts so high on the east, and Sir Francis Drake having searched so high on the western or Pacific shore. For this idea of the passage through America was a very old idea that had been pursued by many men.

But the shores in between the southern end of Newfoundland and the fortieth parallel were less well known and charted than any. Only it was known that here were many inlets and sounds such as, if any there were, might well be the western end of such a passage. Therefore he was minded, if they would suffer him, to take them right away from the shore of Newfoundland, not very near to the land, but observing it, down to the fortieth parallel and from there northwards again to nearly Newfoundland, searching all the creeks and inlets till they were well satisfied.

And he made them, at the end, another great speech of the glory and renown to be had in such an enterprise and in setting their names to headlands, saying that their ship and their voyage should live as long in the minds of men as the ship called *Argos* that bore of old Jason and the Argonauts in search of the golden fleece. For were they not in search of a fleece, allegorically, as precious — the gold of a land where men might dwell in peace and unity and concord and affluence and plenty, such as were not in their own lands where too much sorrow was?

But for himself, he confessed to Edward Colman after this speech, whilst he wiped his great forehead with a towel, for it was very hot, he cared much less for the glory of opening new horizons of land. He wished much more to penetrate into new seas. And he was very contented.

For with this voyage he had searched well the northern seas, and was assured that there was no outlet over the Pole, for it was the third time that he had made that essay. And, for himself, he was assured that they would find no strait across this continent; but he was well content to make the essay, since it would set his mind at rest, and being then well assured that there were no other corners of the world to leave unprobed, he could, in subsequent voyages, set to discovering the secrets of the seas and the northward of the Gulf of St Lawrence — more northerly than ever the Frenchmen had sailed.

On this glory he dilated much. And he laid himself upon his couch to sleep through the afternoon. But Edward Colman went with a boat to the shore lower down than where they had landed the day before, for his mind was set upon the land and not upon the inconstant seas, and he dreamed of sending settlements to these shores, and he observed the rocks and the trees and how there was little fresh water there and many flies and little grass and herbage.

* * *

It was only the old Jan who derided without ceasing these New World schemes of theirs. He looked upon the dry and rocky shores that passed slowly before their eyes. And he said, Would there never be an end of this mad sailing? For he was wild to be back in Holland and draw his pay and take his ease and drink much liquor. For he came of an older generation that had held that only in the old world at home was there Christendom. And all the rest was a dark land peopled with beasts with black skins or yellow skins or copper skins. And such of these as had gold it was fitting to slay and take their gold from them, for they were devils; and such as had no gold they should slay at once. And leaning over the bulwarks he spat into the crawling waters, and pointed with gloomy derision at those shores. For, said he, farther south the Spanish conquistadores had had stores of gold from Montezuma's men; and in the East, in the Moluccas and the Philippines and the Islands of Spice they had pepper and gold and nutmegs for the taking. All that had been in the good days of old. But here there was nothing. It was a land accursed of God; for here the Indians that they slew had no wealth but feathers. And that proved the accursed barrenness of the land. For these Indians were devils and sorcerers, and if they could wring from the earth no gold or spices it was a proof that the earth there was poor and useless.

'And aye me!' he said, 'it is in the omens that I shall never go back to Amsterdam. Unlucky me that late in life have set out upon such a voyage that is weary and profitless to me. And we are beset with sorcery and have no rest.'

And he told how he had had it of a Spanish prisoner in Holland before they hanged him, in the centre of this God accursed land there dwelt a sort of Pope, called a Grand Susham, who never died, but lived for ever and instructed all these brown fiends in their devilries. And they danced round fires and howled; and each time they howled the souls in hell had fresh tortures, below in the earth's centre. So that even the Spaniards themselves, who were devils, had not taken this land of fear and horror.

'And never shall there arise out of it any good thing or republic. For it is for ever accursed. Nay,' he said, 'some hold that it hath no corporeal existence, for all you could see it and tread upon it. But it was really only a solidified mist, set there in space to beguile good men into the hands of these brown spirits.'

* * *

So, as they had nothing better to do, Hudson determined that they would ascend and explore this river as high as it was navigable. And to it he gave the name of the Hudson River, to be a token to all time of this, his third great voyage; just as before he had given, on his first voyage, his name to Cape Hudson, and, on his second, to the islands in the Waigatz Sea the name of Hudson's Touches.

He was very contented with himself after he had thus named the river — but there occurred very soon a thing that caused him no little discontent.

It was towards sunset of the 2nd of September that they came into this river, and lay in a great expanse of water like a millpond, with low, dark hills to their left and behind them a little spit of sand, and, a very long way before them, the sun going down beyond level land, as it seemed. And not very high above the sun was a little, silver new moon.

There came out, as if to meet them, from the shores of the bay a large fleet of canoes, with many men to paddle them, each with a coronal of feathers. Three of them, that were so long as to carry thirty rowers, came the first. And in the bows of one sat a man holding a large wooden cross, and in another a man holding up a bough of a tree, and in the third a man with a large flag of white cloth. And from all these canoes, near each other in the sunset light, there went up a sound of singing.

The *Half Moon* had only a few of her sails taken off, yet the wind had fallen so much that they flapped idly in the evening air, and the ship was almost still in the stillness of the water. The canoes came to a stop maybe fifty yards from the ship and lay altogether in a flat group, keeping a little way on them with their paddles. And from the stern Hudson beckoned to them to approach. But from the bows the crew ran out their culverin, and at its sound in the stillness Hudson turned rigid, and said, 'What is that? The anchor?'

And the culverin was fired, whilst the sound of laughter went up, and the stone ball did not even skip over the water, so close they were. But Hudson saw the Indians in one boat throw up their arms, and that canoe turned over, and another, and yet a third, so that there was a clear space of water in the midst of the flotilla. Then those soft songs were changed to horrible cries and calls; the canoes turned and fled, using their paddles furiously, back to the dark shores. The Dutchmen fired arrows and one or two shots from their stand-guns; and the sun went down very suddenly, and the red of the waters changed to grey, and silver, and green.

Then Hudson was very angry. For, said he, this was the first act of white men upon this stream that should bear his name. And it was a very shameful thing. For those men came out with the sign of the Cross — having learned, doubtless, Christianity from the French of Canada — and with green boughs, which were their tokens of peace, and with a flag all white, which was a token of peace to all that were civilized.

And he pointed to the moon and said, full surely, ere that little crescent had waxed and finished its waning, they should rue that day; and he said that the sun hid its face for shame of them. And he wept at last to think that his stream had so, at the offset of its naming, been so baptized with innocent blood.

Whilst he wept the Dutchmen jeered at him; for they said that that sign of the Cross was a Papist emblem, that it was fitting to fire always upon, and that the white flag was an emblem of the treacherous French, for most likely it had *fleur de lis* upon it, and the green boughs were an emblem of the leafage wherewith those devils were wont to hide their guile. And that flotilla, they said, was a very great menace to them; had they come closer the Indians would have shot arrows upon them, and sent their souls to hell. And Dutch, they said, were not come to a far haven to be shot with arrows for an Englishman's whim. And they said that they were weary and needed entertainment; and that, compared with these beasts, they were as gods — and the gods slew whom they would, and there was an end of it.

But Edward Colman did not translate these words to the navigator, who went down to his cabin and covered his head with his cloak. And he did not speak to those Dutchmen any more that night. All through the dark hours they heard, coming from the distant shores, great cries and the groaning of drums. And they saw enormous fires lit in five places on the level beaches, and black figures leaping and roaring before them; and, in the darkness, all that blaze was doubled by the waters, so that it stood out like a fiery portent in the black night. And the Dutchmen said that these were the devils at their horrid antics.

★ ★ ★

The Master Outreweltius and old Jan were very much afraid, for they said that all the wood was alive with devils. And once they saw a man of huge stature, who appeared to be covered with yellow fire and paint and to glide noiselessly over the ground, holding a great bow, and to vanish suddenly.

But, 'Hurry on, my masters,' Edward Colman said, 'for it is very late. Let us come to the water's edge.' And he bade them not to despair; for assuredly these were men, not devils, since the arrow, which he had drawn from the soil, had mortal feathers and a stick of plain wood.

'And,' he said, 'if ye fear them for devils, assuredly they, who are men, fear us for gods, who carry thunder with us and are impregnable to arrows.'

It took them nearly all that afternoon to go over the shoulder of the hill, as if it were ten miles of hard going; and over the tree-tops the sun began to sink.

★ ★ ★

EPILOGUE

Upon the *Half Moon* that had swung a little way up the river with the tide — a matter of six or seven miles or so — Hudson waited with a great impatience after the sun got low. They had dropped the anchor and lay about where the red and rocky wall was in that part at its highest. At one time they had heard a gun-shot from the thick woods on the left-hand side of them when they faced seawards; but they heard no more sounds till towards three of the afternoon, when there were two gun-shots almost abreast of them — but a little far inland. Then there was no more sound — and a great anxiety fell upon Hudson.

He had a little boat out and rowed up and down the rocky shore of the left hand; the trees came almost down to the water's edge; it was a very hot day, and many sea-birds and great eagles sat on the stones of the shore. But the sun went down, and the blood-red light turned the red rocks to a colour so bright that it hurt the eyes to see them. The *Half Moon* lay still on the silent river; fishes sprang up here and there; the night fell and the moon gave a little light. Far up in the hills they thought they saw a glow as of a faint fire, but they could not be certain that it was not a last glimmer of the sunset over the black tree-tops.

At last Hudson swore he heard a faint moaning almost abreast of them, that he saw a faint blackness on the shore or in the water, moving about up and down. He had out a boat and steered through the quiet; and then they knew that it was a faint voice that cried out.

Outreweltius stood there up to his waist in the water. He was quite calm, and still carried his stand gun, but he said that Edward Colman was dead and old Jan either dead or taken. He said that the Indians had ringed them round all that afternoon among the trees as if they were afraid. Once or twice they had fired arrows in showers, but these had always rebounded from their breastplates and helmets, so that he deemed the savages thought them godlike and invulnerable. But at last one arrow had struck the palm of old Jan where it was unprotected, and he had given a great cry of pain. They were in a sort of glade then, with the sunlight upon them — and immediately old Jan cried out the Indians, as if they saw these were no more than men, had burst out twenty or thirty yards above them, bedizened and hideous in the sunlight, all copper-skinned, bedaubed with ochre, waving stone hatchets and leaping in the air, shooting arrows in a cloud as they came, it seemed many hundreds of them among the rocks. An arrow had struck Edward Colman in the soft part of the neck, glancing down off his helm between helmet and cuirass. Both old Jan and himself had fired with their stand-guns, but when he stepped back to reload he had fallen down into a sort of pit that was quite covered with briars and bushes. He had known no more of the fight, for he had lain quite still, only he heard cries and voices and the feet of men going round among the bushes. And he had lain there still, the pit at its top being quite closed out from the sky by the verdure and thorns. But at nightfall he had crept out of the pit and so down to the river, where they had come to take him.

Next morning, whilst they still debated on the *Half Moon*, there came down to the water a great many copper-coloured men with feathers on their backs and painted with ochre. Amongst them they had a white man quite naked. They stayed their howling until the *Half Moon* sent a boat near the shore — and it was to be seen that the white man among them was old Jan with his beard falling upon his naked chest.

One of the Indians, a man of huge stature, made to them in the boat a long speech. He pointed to the sea, to eastward, and to the heavens above; he raised one finger and then six; he affected to draw his bow and shook his head; he made as women do when they cast ashes on their heads and bewail the dead. The warriors around him leaned up in their bows and were silent. From time to time old Jan screamed and jabbered and then the chief paused and looked at him, afterwards resuming his sonorous words. Finally he paused for a long time too, and leaning on his own bow seemed to await speech from the boat. He was a man near seven feet high, and his coronal of feathers made him appear to have a great majesty. Suddenly he uttered one single word, and he and all his companions had vanished into the road as if they had sunk into the ground.

Old Jan remained alone on the shore, naked and gibbering, and when they drove the boat to take him aboard he ran away over the stones of the shore, crying out unintelligible words. But at last he fell down, and they bound him with the rope and took him aboard.

Henry Hudson was like a man mad with grief for a time; he cried out upon the Dutchmen that it was because of their firing on the canoes that the Indians had slain his innocent mate and friend, and he said that the Indians with their clemency were better Christians than they all. But they could not understand one word in ten of what he said, and at last, signing them to up-anchor, he went down into his cabin to be lonely with his grief. So they sailed away up that broad stream.

[London: Eveleigh Nash, 1909: pp. 298–306, 310–11, 316–19, 322–3, 343–6.]

from

A Call (1910)

Thomas Hardy complimented Ford on his 'very clever and modern novel', impressed by both its urbanity and its substance. The title refers to a telephone call as well as the sense of a vocation; the novel deals with repression, marriage, polygamous desire (see Ford's letter on *The Good Soldier*, page 477), the will to silence, psychoanalysis and psychoanalysts.

WITH her eyes on the grey pinnacles of the Scillies, Katya Lascarides rose from her deck-chair, saying to Mrs Van Husum: 'I am going to send a marconigram.'

Mrs Van Husum gave a dismal but a healthy groan. It pleased Katya, since it took the place of the passionately pleading 'Oh, don't leave me — don't leave me!' to which Katya Lascarides had been accustomed for many months. It meant that her patient had arrived at a state of mind so normal that she was perfectly fit to be left to the unaided care of her son and daughter-in-law, Mr and Mrs Clement P. Van Husum, junior, who resided at Wantage. Indeed, Mrs Van Husum's groan was far more the sound of an elderly lady recovering from the troubles of seasickness than that which would be made by a neurotic sufferer from the dread of solitude.

Katya, with her tranquil and decided step, moved along the deck and descended the companion forward to where the Marconi installation sent out its cracklings from a little cabin surrounded by what appeared a schemeless jumble of rusty capstans and brown cables. With the same air of pensive introspection and tranquil resolve she leaned upon the little slab that was devoted to the sender of telegrams, and wrote to her sister Ellida, using the telegraphic address of her husband's office: 'Shall reach London noon tomorrow. Beg you not to meet ship or to come to hotel for three days. Writing conditions.'

And, having handed in this message through the little shutter to the invisible operator, she threaded her way with the same pensiveness between the capstans and the ropes up the companion and on to the upper deck where, having adjusted the rugs around the dozing figure of Mrs Van Husum in her deck-chair, she paused, with her grey eyes looking out across the grey sea, to consider the purplish islands, fringed with white, the swirls of foam in the greeny and slate-coloured waters, the white lighthouse, and a spray-beaten tramp steamer that, rolling, undulating, and battling through the long swell between them and the Scillies, was making its good departure for Mexico.

Tall, rounded, in excellent condition, with slow but decided actions, with that naturally pale complexion and clean-cut run of the cheek-bone from chin to ear which came to her with her Greek parentage, Katya Lascarides was reflecting upon the terms of her letter to her sister.

From the tranquillity of her motions and the determination of her few words, she was to be set down as a person, passionless, practical, and without tides of emotion. But her eyes, as she leant gazing out to landwards, changed colour by imperceptible shades, ranging from grey to the slaty-blue colour of the sea itself, and her brows from minute to minute, following the course of her thoughts, curved slightly upwards above eyes that expressed tender reminiscences, and gradually straightened themselves out until, like a delicate bar below her forehead, they denoted, stretched and tensile, the fact that she had arrived at an inflexible determination.

In the small and dusky reading-room, that never contained any readers, she set herself slowly to write.

> My dear Ellida (her letter ran), I have again carefully read through your report of what Dr Tressider says of Kitty's case, and I see no reason why the dear child should not find it in her to speak within a few weeks — within a month even. Dr Tressider is certain that there is no functional trouble of the brain or the vocal organs. Then there is just the word for it — obstinacy. The case is not so very uncommon: the position must be regarded psychologically rather than by a pathologist. On the facts given me I should say that your little Kitty is indulging in a sort of dramatic display. You say that she is of an affectionate, even of a jealously affectionate, disposition. Very well, then; I take it that she desires to be fussed over. Children are very inscrutable. Who can tell, then, whether she has not found out (I do not mean to say that she is aware of a motive, as you or I might be) — found out that the way to be fussed over is just not to speak. For you, I should say, it would be

> almost impossible to cure her, simply because you are the person most worried by her silence. And similarly with the nurses, who say to her: 'Do say so-and-so, there's a little pet!' The desire to be made a fuss of, to occupy the *whole* mind of some person or of many persons, to cause one's power to be felt — are these not motives very human? Is there any necessity to go to the length of putting them down to mental aberration?

Katya Lascarides had finished her sheet of paper. She blotted it with deliberate motions; and, leaving it face downwards, she placed her arms upon the table, and, her eyelashes drooping over her distant eyes, she looked reflectively at her long and pointed hands. At last she took up her pen and wrote upon a fresh sheet in her large, firm hand: 'I am diagnosing my own case!'

Serious and unsmiling she looked at the words; then, as if she were scrawling idly, she wrote: Robert.

Beneath that: Robert Hurstlett Grimshaw.

And then: σας ἀγαπω!

She heaved a sigh of voluptuous pleasure, and began to write, 'I love you! I love you! I love you . . .' letting the words be accompanied by deep breaths of solace, as a very thirsty child may drink. And, having written the page full all but a tiny corner at the bottom, she inscribed very swiftly and in minute letters: 'Oh, Robert Grimshaw, why don't you bring me to my knees?'

She heaved one great sigh of desire, and, leaning back in her chair, she looked at her words, smiling, and her lips moving. Then, as it were, she straightened herself out; she took up the paper to tear it into minute and regular fragments, and, rising, precise and tranquil, she walked out of the doorway to the rail of the ship. She opened her hand, and a little flock of white squares whirled, with the swiftness of swallows, into the discoloured wake. One piece that stuck for a moment to her forefinger showed the words: 'My own case!'

She turned, appearing engrossed and full of reserve, again to her writing.

> No, (she commenced) do not put down this form of obstinacy to mental aberration. It is rather to be considered as a manifestation of passion. You say that Kitty is not of a passionate disposition. I imagine it may prove that she is actually of a disposition passionate

in the extreme. *But all her passion is centred in that one desire* — the desire to excite concern. The cure for this is not medical; it is merely practical. Nerve treatment will not cure it, nor solicitude, but feigned indifference. You will not touch the spot with dieting; perhaps by . . . But there, I will not explain my methods to you, old Ellida. I discussed Kitty's case, as you set it forth, very fully with the chief in Philadelphia, and between us we arrived at certain conclusions. I won't tell you what they were, not because I want to observe a professional reticence, but simply so that, in case one treatment fails, you may not be in agonies of disappointment and fear. I haven't myself much fear of non-success if things are as you and Dr Tressider say. After all, weren't we both of us as kiddies celebrated for fits of irrational obstinacy? Don't you remember how one day you refused to eat if Calton, the cat, was in the dining-room? And didn't you keep that up for days and days and days? Yet you were awfully fond of Calton. . . . Yes; I think I can change Kitty for you, but upon one condition — that you never plead for Robert Grimshaw, that you never mention his name to me. Quite apart from any other motive of mine — and you know that I consider mother's example before anything else in the world — if he will not make this sacrifice for me he does not love me. I do not mean to say that you are to forbid him your house, for I understand he dines with you every other day. His pleadings I am prepared to deal with, but not yours, for in you they savour of disrespect for mother. Indeed, disrespect or no disrespect, I will not have it. If you agree to this, come to our hotel as soon as you have read it. If you disagree — if you won't, dear, make me a solemn promise — leave me three days in which to make a choice out of the five patients who wish to have me in London, and then come and see me, bringing Kitty.

Not a word, you understand — not one single word!

On that dreadful day when Robert told us that father had died intestate and that other — I was going to add 'horror', but, since it was mother's doing, she did it, and so it must have been right — when he told us that we were penniless and illegitimate, I saw in a flash my duty to mother's memory. I have stuck to it, and I will stick to it. Robert must give in, or I will never play the part of wife to him.

She folded her letter into the stamped envelope, and, having dropped it deliberately into the ship's letter-box, she rejoined Mrs Van Husum, who was reading *The Mill on the Floss*, on the main deck.

§

In the shadow of a huge mulberry-tree, upon whose fingerlike branches already the very light green leaves were begining to form a veil, Katya Lascarides was sitting in a deck-chair. The expression upon her face was one of serenity and of resigned contentment. She was looking at the farmhouse; she was knitting a silk necktie, a strip of vivid green that fell across her light grey skirt. With a little quizzical and jolly expression, her hands thrust deep into the pockets of cream-coloured overalls, Kitty Langham looked sideways for approval at her aunt. She had just succeeded in driving a black cat out of the garden.

They lived down there in a deep silence, Katya never speaking and eliciting no word from the child. But already the child had made concessions to the extent of clearing her throat or emitting a little 'Hem!' when she desired to attract her aunt's attention; but her constant occupation was found in the obstinate gambols of a pet lamb — a 'sock', as the farm people called it — which inhabited the farmhouse, bleated before the door, or was accustomed by butting to send the garden gate flying back upon its hinges.

This creature, about one-third the size of a mature ram, was filled with obstinacies apparently incomprehensible; it was endowed with great strength and a considerable weight. With one push of its head it would send the child rolling several feet along the grass; it would upset chairs in the dining-room; it bleated clamorously for milk at all meals when Kitty had her milk and water.

Against its obstinacies Kitty's was valiant but absolutely useless. With her arms round its neck — a little struggling thing with dark eyes and black hair, in her little white woollen sweater — she would attempt to impede the lamb's progress across a garden bed. But the clinching of her white teeth availed nothing at all. She would be dragged across the moist earth, and left upon her back like a little St Lawrence amongst the flames of the yellow crocuses. And at these struggles Katya Lascarides presided with absolute deafness and with inflexible indifference; indeed, after their first meeting, when Ellida Langham had brought the child with her nurse to the gloomy, if tranquil, London hotel, where Katya had taken from Mrs Van Husum a parting which lasted three days, and ended in Mrs Van

Husum dissolving into a flood of tears — at the end of that meeting Ellida had softly reproached Katya for the little notice she had taken of what was, after all, the nicest child in London.

But cool, calm, tall, and dressed in a grey that exactly matched her eyes, Katya 'took charge'. And, during the process, whilst she said, 'I shall want this and that,' or 'The place must be on a hill; it must face south-west; it must be seven miles from the sea; it must be a farm, with plenty of livestock but no children,' Ellida watched her, silent, bewildered, and admiring. It seemed so improbable that she should have a sister so professional, so practical, so determined. Yet there it was.

And then they descended, Katya and Kitty alone, into the intense silence of the farm that was found. It was on a hill; it faced south-west; it was seven miles from the sea, and the farmer's wife, because she was childless, surrounded herself with little animals whose mothers had died. And there the child played, never hearing a word, in deep silence with the wordless beasts. This had lasted three weeks.

The gate was behind Katya's back as she smiled at the rolling hills below the garden. She smiled because the night before she believed she had overheard Kitty talking to the lamb; she smiled because she was exhausted and quivering and lonely. She knitted the green necktie, her eyes upon the April landscape, where bursts of sunlight travelled across these veil-like films of new leaves that covered tenderly the innumerable hedgerows.

And suddenly she leaned forward; the long fingers holding the knitting-needles ceased all motion. She had heard a footstep — and she knew every footstep of the farm. . . .

He was leaning over the back of her chair; she saw, against the blue when she opened her eyes, his clear, dark skin, his clear, dark contemplative eyes. Her arms slowly raised themselves; her lips muttered unintelligible words which were broken into by the cool of his cheek as she drew him down to her. She rose to her feet and recoiled, and again, with her arms stretched straight before her, as if she were blind and felt her way, her head thrown back and her eyes closed, an Oriental with a face of chiselled alabaster. And with her eyes still closed, her lips against his ear as if she were asleep, she whispered: 'Oh, take me! Take me! Now! For good. . . .'

But these words that came from her without will or control ceased, and she had none to say of her own volition. There fell upon them the silent nirvana of passion.

And suddenly, vibrant, shrill, and interrupted by sobs and the grinding of minute teeth, there rose up in the child's voice the words: 'Nobody must be loved but me. Nobody must be loved but me.'

They felt minute hands near their knees; they were parted by a little child, who panted and breathed through her nostrils. They looked at each other with eyes into which, very slowly, there came comprehension. And then, over the little thing's head, Katya repeated:

'Nobody must be loved but me. Nobody must be loved but me.' And with a quick colour upon her cheeks and the wetness of tears in her eyes, 'Oh, poor child!' she said.

For in the words the child had given to her she recognized the torture of her own passion.

That night quite late Katya descended the stairs upon tiptoe. She spoke in a very low voice: 'The little thing's been talking, talking,' she said, 'the quaintest little thoughts. I've seen it coming for days now. Sometimes I've seen her lips moving. She's the most precise enunciation in the world.'

'I wired Ellida this afternoon,' Robert Grimshaw said.

'Then Ellida will be down here by the last train?' Katya answered, and he commented: 'We've only got an hour.'

'But little Kitty,' she was beginning.

'No, no,' he interrupted. 'Nobody must be talked about but us. Nobody must be talked about but us. I'm as glad as you or Ellida or Paul could possibly be about Kitty, but now that I have got you alone at last you're bound to face the music.'

'But little Kitty?' Katya said. She said it, however, only for form's sake, for Robert Grimshaw's gentle face was set in a soft inflexibility, and his low tones she knew would hold her to the mark. She had to face the music. In the half-darkness his large eyes perused her face, dark, mournful and tender. The low, long farmhouse room with its cheap varnished furniture was softened by the obscure light from the fire over which he had been standing for a very long hour.

'Is it the same terms, then?' he asked slowly, and she answered: 'Exactly the same.'

He looked down at the fire, resting his hand on the chimney-piece. At last she said: 'We might modify it a little;' and he moved his face, his eyes searching the obscurity in which she stood, only one of her hands catching the glow from the fire.

'I cannot modify anything,' he said. 'There must be a marriage, by what recognized rite you like, but — that.'

Her voice remained as level as his, expressing none of the longing, the wistfulness. that were in her whole being.

'Nobody knew about mother,' she said. 'Nobody seems to have got to know now.'

'And you mean,' he said, 'that now you consent to letting nobody know it about you?'

'You did succeed,' she evaded him, 'in concealing it about mother. It was splendid of you! At the time I thought it wasn't possible. I don't know how you managed it. I suppose nobody knows about it but you and me and Ellida and Pauline.'

'You mean,' he pursued relentlessly, 'you mean that now you consent to letting nobody know it about you? Of course, besides us, my solicitor knows — of your mother.'

'At the first shock,' she said, 'I thought that the whole world must know, and so I was determined that the whole world should know that I hadn't deserted her memory. . . .' She paused for a wistful moment, whilst inflexibly he reflected over the coals.

'Have you,' she said, 'the slightest inkling of why she did it?'

He shook his head slowly; he sighed.

'Of course I couldn't take you even on those terms — that nobody knew,' he said, with his eyes still averted. Then he turned upon her, swarthy, his face illumined with a red glow. The slow mournfulness of their speeches, the warmth, the shadow, kept him silent for a long time. 'No,' he said at last, 'there isn't a trace of a fact to be found. I'm as much in the dark as I was on that day when we parted. I'm not as stunned, but I'm just as mystified.'

'Ah!' she said, 'but what did you feel — then?'

'Did you ever realize,' he asked, 'how the shock came to me? You remember old Partington, with the grey beard? He asked me to call on them. He sat on the opposite side of his table. He handed me the copy of some notes your father had made for their instructions as to his will. It was quite short. It ran: "You are to consider that my wife and I were never married. I desire you to frame a will so phrased that my entire estate, real and personal, should devolve upon my two daughters, Ellida and Katharine, without revealing the fact that they are illegitimate. This should not be difficult, since their mother's name, which they are legally entitled to bear, was the same as my own, she having been my cousin." ' Grimshaw broke off his low monologue to gaze again at her, when he once more returned his eyes to the coals. 'You understand,' he said, 'what that meant to me. It was handed to me without a word; and after a long time Partington said: "You understand that you are your uncle's heir-at-law — nothing more." '

Katya whispered: 'Poor old Toto!'

'You know how I honoured your father and mother,' he said. 'They were all the parents I ever knew. Well, you know all about that. . . . And then I had to break the news to you. . . . Good God!'

He drew his hands down his face.

'Poor old Toto!' Katya said slowly again. 'I remember.'

'And you won't make any amends?' he asked.

'I'll give you myself,' she said softly.

He answered: 'No! no!' and then, wearily, 'It's no good.'

'Well, I did speak like a beast to you,' she said. 'But think what a shock it was to me — mother not dead a month, and father not four days, and so suddenly — all that. I'll tell you how I felt. I felt a loathing for all men. I felt a recoiling from you — a recoiling, a shudder.'

'Oh, I know,' he said, and suddenly he began to plead: 'Haven't you injured me enough? Haven't I suffered enough? And why? why? For a mad whim. Isn't it a mad whim? Or what? I can understand you felt a recoil. But . . .'

'Oh, I don't feel it now,' she said; 'you know.'

'Ah yes,' he answered; 'but I didn't know till today, till just now when you raised your arms. And all these years you haven't let me know.'

'How did you know?' she asked. 'How did you know that I felt it? But, of course, you understand me even when I don't speak.'

'It's heaven,' he said, 'to know that you've grown out of it. It has been hell to bear the thought. . . .'

'Oh, my dear! . . .' she said.

'Such loneliness,' he said. 'Do you know,' he continued suddenly, 'I came back from Athens? I'm supposed to be a strong-minded man — I suppose I am a strong-minded man — but I turned back the moment I reached Greece because I couldn't bear — I could not bear the thought that you might still shudder at my touch. Now I know you don't and . . .'

'Ellida will be here soon,' Katya said. 'Can't you hear her train coming down the valley . . . there . . . ? And I want to tell you what I've found out about mother. I've found it out, remembering what she said from day to day. I'll tell you what it was — it was trustfulness. I remember it now. It was the mainspring of her life. I think I know how the very idea came into her mind. I've got it down to little details. I've been inquiring even about the Orthodox priests there were in England at the time. There wasn't a single one! One had just died suddenly, and there did not come a successor for six months. And mother was there. And when she was a young thing, mother, I know, had a supreme contempt — a bitter contempt — for all English ideas. She got over it. When we children were born she became the gentlest being. You know, that was what she always was to me — she was a being, not a woman. When she came into the room she spread soothing around her. I might be in paroxysms of temper, but it died out when she opened the door. It's so strong upon me that I hardly remember what she looked like. I can't remember her any more than I can conceive of the looks of a saint. A saint! well, she was that. She had been hot-tempered, she had been contemptuous. She became what you remember after we were born. You may say she got religion.'

Katya, her eyes full of light, paused; she began again with less of exultation.

'I dare say,' she said, 'she began to live with father without the rites of the Church because there was no Church she acknowledged to administer them; but later, she didn't want them. I remember how she always told us, "Trust each other, trust each other; then you will become perfectly to be trusted." And again, she would never let us make promises one to another. Don't you remember? She always said to us: "Say that you will do a thing. Never promise — never. Your word must be your bond." You remember?'

Grimshaw slowly nodded his head. 'I remember.'

'So that I am certain,' she said, 'that that was why she never married father. I think she regarded marriage — the formality, the vows — as a desecration. Don't you see, she wanted to be my father's chattel, and to trust him absolutely — to trust, to trust! Isn't that the perfect relationship?'

Grimshaw said: 'Yes, I dare say that is the explanation. But . . .'

'But it makes no difference to you?' she pleaded.

In the distance she heard the faint grind of wheels.

'No,' he said, 'not even if no one else knew it. I'm very tired; I'm very lonely. I want you so; I want you with all my heart. But not that — not that.'

'Not ever?' she said.

'No,' he answered; 'I'll play with my cards on the table. If I grow very tired — very, very tired — if I cannot hold out any longer, well, I may consent — to your living with me as your mother lived with your father. But' — and he stood up briskly — 'I'll tell you this: you've strengthened me — you've strengthened me in my motive. If you had shuddered at me as you did on that day years ago, I think I should have given in by now. But you didn't any longer. You've come to me; you raised your arms to me. Don't you see how it has strengthened me? I'm not alone any more; I'm not the motherless boy that I was . . . Yes, it's heaven.'

Her hands fell by her side. The sound of wheels filled the room, and ceased.

'If I'd repulsed you, you'd have given in?' she said.

The door fell violently back, and from the black and radiant figure of Ellida came the triumphant cry: 'Kitty's spoken! Kitty's spoken! You've not deceived me!'

[Manchester: Carcanet Press, 1984: pp. 59-72.]

from

The Simple Life Limited (1911)

The Simple Lifers are a self-enclosed community animated by a mixture of Fabianism, vegetarianism, and Edwardian medievalism — as well as a dubious business sense. Ford's *roman à clef* needed the camouflage of a pseudonym (Daniel Chaucer) behind which he could satirize the circle around the Garnetts and include Wells, Conrad, Marwood, and even himself in the fun. See also the story 'The Mantle of Elijah', page 430.

MR LUSCOMBE was standing with his hands deep in his pockets, his chin resting upon the dishevelled crown of the head of his little boy called Bill, who stood upon the window-seat before him and, like him, gazed at the pouring rain. It came down in such sheets that a small river flowed on each side of the carriage-drive. Because the County did not call upon Mr Luscombe and his wife, Mr Luscombe was solitary in his habits. He was friendly with the Vicar and he had some acquaintances whom he met at the Golf Club on the neighbouring common. But his most constant companion was his little boy Bill who was then aged seven, had dark, uncombed hair, a brownish, freckled face, wore a rumpled blue jersey and short blue knickerbockers.

'By Jove, we'd better ask them to come in,' Mr Luscombe exclaimed. 'That tree's no kind of a shelter. The rain comes through it like a sieve.'

The boy continued to gaze out of the window. 'Don't ask them, father,' he said: 'they are ugly people.'

'They're jolly wet people,' Mr Luscombe said. 'You couldn't even ask Sitting Bull to look beautiful with all the paint washed off him.'

'But,' the little boy retorted, 'they don't look like pirates, and they don't look like Indians, and they don't look like highwaymen or anything nice.'

'But they look wet, Bill,' his father urged.

'They look like wet tramps,' the little boy said. 'They'll come in and they'll spoil our game, and Filson says that tramps are poison.'

'But they don't look like tramps, Bill,' his father pleaded. 'I should say they were foreigners if they weren't so fair.'

'Then they're German spies,' the boy said. 'Filson says the country is full of German spies.'

'Then,' Mr Luscombe said triumphantly, 'our duty is to lure them into the house and then to have them arrested.'

'That,' the little boy answered, 'would be against the laws of hospitality.'

'Isn't it,' his father said, 'still more against the laws of hospitality to let them get wet? They're the strangers within the gates, you know. For they are inside the carriage gates. If they'd stayed outside it would be different.'

'Then if you give them anything to eat,' Bill uttered firmly, 'I shall drop some salt into it as Morgiana did to the captain of the Forty Thieves.'

'I don't think you've got the hang of that, old man,' his father said. 'It was that she got suspicious when the captain said he wanted his food cooked without salt.'

Mr Luscombe went from the large and rather gloomy dining-room into the large and rather gloomy hall. He opened the door and stood in the pillared porch. The rain poured down and in the long drive the cypresses and holly trees drooped dejectedly beneath the weight of water. Above the gate that gave on to the road there towered two enormous chestnut trees, against whose trunks were pressed the backs of two slight figures. Mr Luscombe stood as far out in the porch as the driving rain would permit: a blonde, rather heavy man of perhaps thirty-five or a little more, he was dressed in a shooting-jacket, had a heavy jaw, a thick moustache and sagacious, rather dog-like eyes. He was a little slow in his actions and he had a pleasant smile which uncovered white and level teeth. He stood just six feet high, his shoulders were more than usually broad and his chest more than usually full. When he had beckoned three times with his hand he succeeded in attracting the attention of the cyclists but, in answer to his gestures, both the young creatures — who in spite of their costumes, which he found so extraordinary, appeared to him of a dazzling fairness — vigorously shook their heads.

'Damn them,' Mr Luscombe exclaimed good humouredly, 'I believe they think I am telling them to go away.'

He repeated his gestures, bowing his body forward and shovelling with his hand towards the doorway as if he were inviting pigs to enter a sty. But his efforts were rewarded only by a similar indifference. He breathed little sounds of vexation between his teeth, and returning into the flagged hall he came out with a large umbrella which was used by his coachman upon wet days. Having opened this he walked gingerly — for he still wore his slippers — down the carriage-drive, picking his way over little runlets of water in the sandy track. The heavy drops fell with loud sounds from the boughs on to the surface of his umbrella and the rain itself made a loud and continuous crepitation.

'Why the deuce,' Mr Luscombe exclaimed, 'did you not come in when I beckoned you? You've made me get my feet wet.'

Both the young people gazed at him with expressions of singular solemnity and portentousness.

The girl, who was of singular fairness, wore upon her head an ungracious cap. It appeared to have been crumpled haphazard together out of a piece of the grey cloth of which her dress was made. She wore also a coat of grey so ill fitting that one of her shoulders appeared to be higher than the other. Her short skirt only just reached to her knees, her stockings were of grey worsted and her cycling shoes were laced with pieces of string. Her male companion, who was as fair, as young and even more slender, had the greater part of his form concealed by a grey horse-blanket, through a hole in whose centre his head stuck out. Upon his head, itself, there was crushed a grey wide-awake so sodden by the rain that it flapped down on each side, concealing the greater portion of each cheek. From between it his pink and white cultured features looked out like an old woman's from a deep poke-bonnet. The girl was about to speak when the young man spoke in tones that combined at once a quality of gentlemanliness and aggression:

'We ought,' he said, 'to inform you that we object to the abominable institution of marriage. We were married yesterday morning, but we desire to enter the strongest possible protest.'

Mr Luscombe raised his eyebrows, whistled between his teeth, and smiled in a slightly puzzled manner.

'Well, well,' he said. 'I've heard of repenting at leisure, but I never heard of a couple who found out their mistake so soon. Consider the protest made and carried and come in out of the rain.'

The young man after a pause was about to speak when the young girl spoke. Her voice was lady-like and she, too, appeared to force into it a certain note of aggression.

'Do you own this property?' she asked.

'Oh,' Mr Luscombe said, 'I own this house and grounds and the cottages round the Common and a certain portion of the Common itself. You can hardly call it a property.'

'But it is a property,' the young girl said. 'You ought not to own it.'

A slight shade of vexation came into Mr Luscombe's face.

'How do you know?' he said. 'Is this an impertinence? Are you connections of mine?'

The young man spoke again in his high tones:

'Except in so far as all men are brothers,' he said, 'we cannot claim connectionship with you. But we object . . .'

The young girl raised her hand as if she were addressing a meeting.

'We object,' she began, 'to all such things as individual property, marriage, revealed religion, the unequal distribution of wealth . . .'

'Oh, well,' Mr Luscombe said, 'you don't seem to object to rain. Come in and we will have a fire lit.'

The young man said:

'We think we ought to tell you all the things we object to, for we have been told that we have a corrupting influence, whereas our consciences make us see that we must never cease to proselytize. So we warn you . . .'

'Oh,' the young girl suddenly exclaimed, 'if you own all the cottages round the Common you own the one with the yellow jasmine on it and the seat in the porch just beyond the duck-pond. Will you let it to us?'

Mr Luscombe regarded them reflectively. 'To do that,' he said, 'I should have to turn out the people who are there now.'

'You could find them another cottage,' the boy said. 'We have decided that that one would exactly suit us.'

'We desire,' the girl exclaimed, 'to lead the Simple Life.'

* * *

'Our name,' the boy said, 'is "Bransdon", and we both have the Celtic temperament. That is what you might expect, for Ophelia's father is the great Mr Bransdon and mine is his chief disciple, Mr Gubb. We have neither of us tasted flesh meat or alcohol in our lives and we are compiling a book called "Health Resides in Sandals."'

Mr Luscombe said: 'Well, now!'

Mr Gubb's son fetched the bicycles from outside the wall. From the handle-bar of each of them depended a net bag containing a very sodden loaf of bread and a paper bag so melted that raisins dripped from them here and there as the bicycles shook. But the showers of talk continued undamped, as if they were veritable bursts of sunshine beneath the liquid downfall. Nevertheless, when they were about half-way up the carriage drive the great Mr Bransdon's daughter exclaimed: 'Ugh!' and wriggled her shoulders inside her ill-fitting clothes. 'The rain has gone through! It's trickling down my spine!'

She had interrupted a dissertation of her husband who was explaining that though both Mr Bransdon and Mr Gubb objected to bicycling it was never their way to employ a blind subservience towards their distinguished parents. Indeed, their parents had not exacted it. They had never commanded either of their children to do anything. They had simply appealed to their reason. Thus, though the fathers strongly objected to bicycles because they were vulgar, were not employed in mediaeval times, were machines manufactured by other machines and had never been ridden by either Mr Bransdon or Mr Gubb — in spite of these very weighty reasons the children had decided to inaugurate their common life by a bicycle tour. They did it for the sake of the experience and they did it because, also, they were upon a crusade.

'We want to spread our ideas,' the boy explained. 'We want to preach here and there in the hedgerows and by-ways. And so the more quickly we can get from audience to audience the better. Our desire is to do something fine. That, for instance, is why for the first time in our lives we have put on stockings.'

Mr Luscombe said that he did not follow their course of reasoning.

'You see, it's like this,' the boy continued, 'we desire to talk to all sorts of people and we have observed that even round Court Street, where we are comparatively well-known figures, we are sometimes laughed at as we go along the road. Now it cannot be a good opening for a lecture if the lecturer is laughed at. It takes away considerably from your chance of a hearing. Usually I wear a smock frock and Ophelia a single garment of a clinging and flowing design and we have always walked about bare-foot, carrying our sandals in our hands for rough places. But we have decided that if we are to see people as they actually are and if we are to be listened to with attention at a first hearing we must appear as nearly like ordinary people as possible. With the results that you see. We feel that we are hideous but it is in a good cause. And we can put it to our account that all of our garments have been manufactured by our own hands from fabrics actually woven by our fathers and their disciples.'

He stopped for a moment to look himself down and to survey the figure of his wife. Underneath their misshapen and sodden clothes their figures appeared, as if they were something foreign and disconnected from their attire, to be lithe, rounded and glowing. It was as if antelopes had put on coats and trousers.

'Hideous, but certainly to be excused,' the boy was beginning with complacency but at this point the girl interrupted him with the little scream to the effect that the water was trickling down her back. There was just the slightest suspicion of annoyance in the boy's voice as he said:

'Well, you won't take cold: we never take cold. We have been brought up on rational, hygienic principles.'

'But it's horribly uncomfortable,' the girl said. 'Horribly! I've never felt anything so cold.'

This gave Mr Luscombe the chance for a word and he suggested that he would lend the young man some of his own clothes and the girl some of his wife's.

'I shall wear nothing of the sort,' the young man said. 'I have always been of the opinion that we should allow our clothes to dry upon us. If animals can do it why should not we?'

The girl hesitated for a moment and then as a fresh little runlet of water reached her skin, she excalimed:

'I shall go off my head if I don't get these things off. It's like being tickled to death with icicles.'

She started forward into the porch and Mr Luscombe followed her. The young man remained to stack the bicycles against one of the large stone pilasters. He took the loaves of bread from the string bags and set them on a carved oak chair in the hall, and the raisins he laid out to dry on the hall table. Then, having shaken the wet out of his wide-awake with a circular sweep of his arm, he was about to follow Mr Luscombe into the drawing-room when the crash of falling bicycles warned him that his work was to do all over again.

* * *

On its rubber tyres the brougham ran up the drive almost noiselessly and stopped before the pilasters of the porch. Mrs Luscombe descended in a cloud of very light pink. She was wearing in addition a great black hat shaped like a mushroom across the front of which there ran a single white ostrich feather. She had a very light step, and she passed almost soundlessly through the hall with the intention of not being heard by her little boy. With the Londoner's bewilderment before all phases of weather and forgetful of the green marks that damp lawns will leave on the bottom of skirts, Mrs Luscombe had dressed herself for the Vicar's wife's garden party as if she had been going to Goodwood during a period of profoundest drought, and she knew herself that she looked so well that no warnings would prevent her little boy from rushing upon her, springing up and transferring the greater part of the dirt from his blue jersey to her delicate blouse, and from perforating with his heavy boots her skirt which was still more delicate in texture. She wished to get up to her room and to change before she met the little boy. Her son, however, was actually in the stables with Filson, the under-gardener, listening with awe to that gloomy and Conservative politician's version of the relative strengths of the British and German navies.

A large female form in very tight white was standing before the pier-glass in her bedroom and adjusting by its aid one of those turn-down collars that were then not quite beginning to be worn. Only the day before Mrs Luscombe had received from her dress-maker a costume that she imagined to be just such another. And she had already pictured to herself the thrill of pleasure that it would give her when she appeared white and shining upon Lady Crested Joins' tennis lawn next Saturday wearing assuredly the first lace frock and the first Peter Pan collar to be seen in that district. On the other hand, the girl appeared so large, so sunny and so voluptuous! Mrs Luscombe couldn't in the least fix her amongst the number of her friends, but it gave her a distinct feeling of pleasure to see so pagan a figure in her rather grim bedroom, the furniture of which was all of shiny red mahogany and all whose cut looking-glasses had a slightly bluish tinge as if smoke had passed across them. Ophelia Bransdon, indeed, had about her at the moment a touch almost of the sinister. The immoral, Mrs Luscombe would have called it, had not a slight suspicion of immorality of appearance been considered to be in the fashion of that date. The dress which fitted Mrs Luscombe exactly, was slightly tight for Ophelia, so that her ample proportions seemed accentuated in almost more ample curves and the then indispensable corsets thrust her figure forward in an attitude that remotely suggested the predatory.

Ophelia, however, was gazing into the blue-grey glass with a rapt expression. She had such a little catch in her throat at the sight of her white reflection that she could not even speak. The garments she had taken off lay behind her in untidy coils upon the floor, wet, brown, sandy with the sand of the Surrey heaths so that they resembled sea-weed and sacking. Ophelia had seen the Duchess of Portarlington once get out, all in white, from her carriage just beside the large gates at New Hatch. But except for that she had never seen anything like herself, and not even the Duchess, she thought, quite came up to it.

Mrs Melville, a small woman with her black lace cap like a d'oyley, stood just to the right of the mirror holding forward her thin, delicately wrinkled hands in that position that one woman always adopts when she has just 'turned out' another woman — mute, contemplative, attentive, but at the same time very much as if she expected her hairpins to fall out. It was as if she were an allegorical figure who had just shoved off a nymph upon a voyage into another world.

'As I was saying,' Ophelia suddenly continued addressing Mrs Melville, 'you people who have never done anything and have led sheltered and orderly lives all your days can have very little idea of what it means to be absolutely free. I mean to be free not only now but for ever. You think because I was married yesterday I'm going to acknowledge ties. But nothing of the sort. The marriage was entered into with "reservations" as the Catholics say, in deference to the vulgar opinions of the majority of the State. Outwardly in deference, this is to say, but inwardly in defiance.'

Mrs Melville remained motionless; only her eyelids blinked, and a certain measure of panic appeared in the lines of her face as she regarded Ophelia and her daughter-in-law by turns.

'Oh, she's taken your new frock!' she gasped, and her hands, from which there descended a small shower of at least a dozen pins, fell helplessly to her sides.

'That!' Mrs Luscombe exclaimed. 'Mine!' And though her eyes fell upon the distasteful mass of Ophelia's damp garments upon the ground, she couldn't exactly for the moment figure that the white lace gown was her own. She had always considered it as destined to present at a garden party her own thinnish lines that were so long from the breast to the hips — something tight and trim. Ophelia seemed to swell it out, to round it off, as it were, into large bubbles of a decidedly substantial white froth.

Ophelia swayed round with an awkward and toppling, but still imperious motion. She had never before been so confined at the knees, so that she had the appearance of being about to topple over and of extending her hands to preserve her balance.

'You are,' she addressed Mrs Luscombe, 'another of these purely conventional beings. You probably married under the influence of a passion and swore to remain faithful for the rest of your life. And no doubt you will. Your sort of person is quite capable of it.'

Mrs Luscombe ejaculated clearly and emphatically: 'Good God!'

She had certainly never in her life used that ejaculation before, and it was only part of her extraordinary bewilderment that she found it in her vocabulary at all. She had had no preparation for Ophelia, she had never had any experience of anything of the sort, she could not begin to classify it. She could not say whether it was — this column in white — of the abandoned aristocracy, or of the licentious stage or of the incalculable societies for procuring the franchise for women.

'Who is the girl?' she exclaimed to Mrs Melville, 'Where does she come from?'

She had one brief moment of imagining that Ophelia must be from Idaho or from Montana, or at any rate from the State of New York. Then Ophelia overwhelmed her with another torrent of words.

'But as for us,' the young lady continued, 'ours is a union of reason. We enter upon it without any passion; it is purely utilitarian.'

'My dear,' Mrs Melville said admiringly, 'you do speak like a book. I wish I could.'

'It's practice,' Ophelia said. 'We have been being trained to be public speakers — apostles, that is, of the Simple Life ever since we were twelve and thriteen respectively.'

Mrs Melville suddenly went down on her knees to gather up the pins that she had dropped, and Mrs Luscombe, who couldn't see her mother-in-law do anything of the sort alone and who was herself too speechless to say any words to prevent it — Mrs Luscombe also knelt down and aided her. So that it was as if she were triumphing over captives when Ophelia Bransdon continued her oration.

'You,' she said, addressing the back and the back of the head of Mrs Luscombe — 'you would never leave your husband if you desired to do it, or if you were overcome by another passion. Or perhaps *you* might, for you are upstanding and when you have listened to reason you may be fitted to become a banner-bearer in the cause of Freedom. But *you*,' and she addressed Mrs Melville, '*you* would never do anything of the sort. Of that I am convinced, for you are not of the stuff of which heroines are made.'

Mrs Melville slowly raised her head and a deep flush as slowly covered her face.

'You are talking nonsense,' she said sharply, 'and moreover you are exceedingly cruel. What can you know of these things?'

'In the cause of spreading the light,' Ophelia Bransdon exclaimed, 'cruelty is a merit. We shall have to take many hard blows. We shall have to be stoned perhaps, but we mean to hit back. For that reason we have determined to get our blows in first. That is why I am sometimes called a little aggressive.'

Mrs Melville had risen to her feet and stood with her hands clasped before her.

'You are more than aggressive,' she said with a sharpness that appeared extraordinary. 'You are even odious. And if being put into people's best gowns is what you call being stoned. . . .' Mrs Melville, faced with the cruelty of youth, had a gentle little passion of extreme anger. She remembered how obstinately and how helplessly in her obstinacy she had done exactly what this ignorant child had said she would never be capable of doing. And at the same time she felt oddly bitter to think that all the obloquy which she had had to endure had not been enough to insure her immunity on such a subject from this child's tongue. For she was certain that Ophelia had never heard of it: if she had she would never have spoken. But Mrs Luscombe, looking up from her knees, interrupted her suddenly with:

'How in the world does she come to have on my dress and who in the world is she?'

'You know,' Ophelia said with a bland reasonableness as if she were about to concede a point, 'there is really no such thing in the world as property. This dress is very much more mine than yours by reason of my necessity. Just as it's very much more poor Betty Higden's than mine. For poor Betty hasn't sufficient clothes at all, whereas mine only need drying.'

'I don't know who she is,' Mrs Melville said, relapsing into a sort of helplessness when she had to face her daughter-in-law. 'Gerald invited the two of them to come out of the rain.'

'I went through the rest of your wardrobe that was offered to me,' Ophelia explained, 'and it appeared to me to be frivolous and unsuitable, with the exception of this garment. This in some ways fulfils the canons of our requirements, since it is made all in one piece and of a fabric which, if it is slightly ornate, does not appear to be exceedingly costly.'

'My real lace dress!' Mrs Luscombe exclaimed. 'You'll have stretched it till it hangs round me like a blanket. And oh, it's the first of this model to reach England!'

'I might buy it of you,' Ophelia said hesitatingly. It was the first hesitation she had shown since she was a child.

'It cost eleven hundred and twenty-five francs!' Mrs Luscombe rejoined. 'And even if you could buy it, it wouldn't help me — for I should have *nothing* new to wear at Lady Joins' on Saturday.'

'Oh!' Ophelia said with the air of a child who is startled at a tremendous falsehood. 'There are eleven dresses on that bed — I've been through them and counted them. And you can't have worn the oldest of them five times.'

'The child, my dear,' Mrs Melville, said, 'is just a savage. It was *Gerald* who told me to bring her up here and lend her a dress of yours, not I.'

'I didn't suppose you would have,' Mrs Luscombe answered.

'And she seized on that,' Mrs Melville continued to excuse herself. 'I believe her parents are quite respectable — friends of Miss Stobhall's — but odd!'

'I don't care how respectable or how odd they are,' Mrs Luscombe said rising from her knees. 'If it's merely a question of a change while her things are drying, a blouse and skirt are good enough for her.'

'I told her so: oh, I told her so!' Mrs Melville exclaimed.

Mrs Luscombe approached Ophelia who was saying:

'One thousand, one hundred and twenty-five francs are forty-five pounds — enough to keep Hamnet and me for a year, for our habits are very simple!'

'I don't,' Mrs Luscombe said with a good humoured determination, 'in the least want to keep anybody for a year.'

She had walked round Ophelia and suddenly put her hands to the hooks and eyes that fastened the dress on the shoulder.

'And I want you out of my frock,' she added with determination. 'Keep deadly still if you don't want to die.'

'Oh,' Ophelia pleaded, 'couldn't I keep it on just a little longer?'

Her fair brow clouded over: her blonde hair seemed to droop: a corner of her bare shoulder appeared through the opening.

'Keep still,' Mrs Luscombe said grimly.

'Oh, I *should* have liked,' Ophelia said, 'to discuss it with Hamnet. We *never* could sanction a blouse and skirt. I'm certain of that. But this is all in one piece and if it's foolishly luxurious there is possibly something to be said. . . .'

Mrs Luscombe had moved round to the front of her motionless and columnar figure. She was sedulously and delicately drawing the sleeve off Ophelia's white arm.

'You can have a tea-wrap if you don't like a blouse and skirt,' she added. 'You and the gentleman called Hamnet will have plenty of opportunity to discuss this frock. But it will have to be . . .' she paused for a moment of anxiety as the lace slipped down Ophelia's other arm . . .'on me!' she added with relief as the dress dropped free on to the girl's hips.

[London: John Lane, The Bodley Head, 1911: pp. 3-8, 17-20, 40-47.]

Ladies Whose Bright Eyes (1911)

The title is taken from Milton's 'L'Allegro'; the ostensible subject, from Mark Twain. 'The Idea of this book was suggested to me by Mark Twain's Yankee at the Court of King Arthur. It occurred to me to wonder what would really happen to a modern man thrown back into the Middle Ages . . .' (Inscription in a copy of the novel owned by Mr Edward Naumburg.) *Ladies* was revised in 1935 with a much changed ending.

MR SORRELL was accustomed to regarding himself as a typical representative of the Homo-Sapiens-Europaeus. He was rising forty; he was rather fair with fresh, brown hair; he had a drooping brown moustache and a pink, clear skin. His eyes were blue and slightly threatening, as if his condition in the world was that of militant assertion of his rights and rectitude. He had been nearly married several times, and he had had one or two affairs of the heart that he did not particularly care to think about, and in one case he had burned his fingers rather severely. His rival in the affections of an erratic married lady having persuaded her to give up to him Mr Sorrell's letters, which the rival afterwards, to save his own skin, handed over to a remarkably injured husband, it was only by the most extraordinary exertions that Mr Sorrell had kept out of the Divorce Courts, and this had proved to him such a warning that, as he stood there reflecting, nothing in the world would have persuaded him, except on shipboard, to have had anything whatever to do with Mrs Lee-Egerton. It was not that anybody knew anything against her: it was that there was always enveloping her such a perpetual and cloudy feeling of insecurity. Her husband was the sort of man who was always shooting in the Rockies. He was, indeed, shooting in the Rockies at that moment, which made it all the more remarkable that Mrs Lee-Egerton should have appeared anywhere as near him as New York. Lee-Egerton was the son of a peer of so many descents that Mr Sorrell would have been glad to know him. To know Mrs Egerton was not, however, nearly so remarkable, since it was so extraordinarily easy to come across her, attended as it seemed always by a band of laughing cavaliers. On the other hand Lee-Egerton, whom few people ever saw, was said to be a happy, dangerous person, who might descend upon you at any time with a magazine rifle or worse. Nevertheless, with the idea of this rather thunderous personality at the back of his head, Mr Sorrell had felt himself quite remarkably soothed by her frequent companionship. He had not, indeed, ever been soothed by anything or anybody quite so much for quite a long time. It was not that she was in her first youth, for she had a son, as Mr Sorrell had remarkable reason at that moment to know, actually at Cambridge, where he had got himself into scrapes, all the more damnably complicated in that he was the heir-presumptive to the title, though his uncle could not be got to speak to any of his relatives. But Mrs Egerton had a sort of haggard, pale, passionate repose. She was very dark and very tall and very aquiline, and her eyes appeared perpetually to be searching into mysteries. She was, moreover, exceedingly thin, and Mr Sorrell imagined that he found her so infinitely restful because she was so exactly the opposite of himself. In the last five years, that is to say, he had been putting on flesh. As a mining engineer he had been rather thin and hard-bitten, but five years of publishing, though he kept himself fit with Turkish baths and mechanical exercises, had contrived considerably to obscure the former outlines of his figure, and the face that looked out at him from the glass was much more heavy-jowled and deep and threatening-eyed than he at all cared to see. That middle age was descending upon him did not distress him so much, but he strongly objected to being fat.

And whereas Mr Sorrell was distinctly bulky, Mrs Lee-Egerton was exceedingly thin and graceful; whereas upon the whole he was exceedingly prosperous, she was oppressed by a very great grief. The great grief was her confounded son. And to him, feeling, as he did, large, fatherly, and protective, Mrs Egerton had confided her almost unbearable sorrow. She had started for the United States, intending a campaign of social pleasures and triumphs that was to begin in New York, end in Washington, and culminate in a scandalous book of which, with immense success, she had already written two or three. But in New York itself, before she had had time to get her foot really planted, she had received a most lamentable letter from her son at Cambridge. This she had shown to Mr Sorrell on the second night out, whilst after dinner they had reclined side by side in armchairs in a pleasant nook on the upper deck. Mr Sorrell had taken it to a porthole to read, and he had gathered from it that young Egerton would be in the most damnable scrape in the world if he could not have two hundred and fifty pounds on the very moment that Mrs Egerton landed at Southampton. Mr Sorrell had returned to Mrs Egerton in a frame of mind as grave as it was consolatory. He said that she might be quite sure it would be all right, though it was quite certain that the young Jack must be in as disgusting a hole as it was by any means possible for a young man to be in. And Mrs Egerton, the enormous tears in her enormous eyes, plainly visible in the Atlantic moonlight, had declared to him that he could not by any possible means imagine what a mother's feelings were like, or what a good boy her Jack really was. And at the thought that he might have to go to prison she shuddered all over her long and snake-like body. Mr Sorrell said that of course it could not possibly come to that. Next evening, whilst they sat side by side at dinner in the *à la carte* restaurant of the upper deck, she suddenly thrust over his plate of *hors-d'oeuvre*, whilst the select band played, and the waiters appeared to skim through the air, a marconigram form bearing the words:

'Bulmer pressing. All up if necessary not here by eight tomorrow. God's sake help. —Jack.'

'Oh well,' Mr Sorrell had said cheerfully, 'you must send your husband's solicitors a message to wire the money to him.'

Mrs Egerton stared at him with huge eyes. She swallowed an enormous something in her throat, and since she ate nothing else during that meal, Mr Sorrell's dinner was completely spoilt. She disappeared, indeed, before he had finished it, and Mr Sorrell went to pace in solitude upon the comparatively deserted deck where, although they were only two days out and were not yet past the Banks, he had acquired the habit of expecting to find this charming lady. It was not, however, for at least an hour and a half, which in his impatience seemed an interminable agony, that, through the moonlight, she came to him and, exclaiming 'I can't do it!' burst into tears.

'You can't do what?' Mr Sorrell asked. And then there came out the whole lamentable story. Mr Sorrell imagined that he must be the only man in London, or in the space between London and New York, who really understood what Mrs Egerton was, just as he was the only one who would be really absolutely able from henceforth to champion her. But the immediately active part of her sad history was the fact that her husband allowed her the merest pittance — not twenty pounds a week — for her private needs; that his solicitors were instructed in the most peremptory manner never to advance her a penny of this pittance; that having come out expecting to exist upon the hospitality of the United States, she had upon her hardly more than her return ticket; that the real stones of her jewellery were all in pawn and replaced by imitations; and that she could not anyhow in the rest of the world, although she was surrounded by seeming friends, raise anything like the sum of a quarter of a thousand pounds. Her husband was fourteen days' journey beyond the nearest telegraph station in the middle of a savage region.

'And oh,' she said, with a glance at the heaving bosom of the sea, 'I couldn't *live* if anything happened to Jack. I understand that they'd shave off the little ringlets that I used to twine round my fingers when he was an innocent boy saying his prayers at my knee.'

'Oh, of course, they wouldn't do it at first,' Mr Sorrell said. 'Not while he was under remand. But it's quite beastly enough that he should have committed — er — er — done the thing, without his being punished for it. In fact . . . ' And after a good deal of hesitation and stammering Mr Sorrell got out the offer to lend the lady the required sum.

She said, of course, she could not think of it; as her son had made his bed so he must lie; comparative strangers, however intimate their souls might feel, could not bring financial matters into their relationships; her husband would murder her if he came to hear of it, for Mr Sorrell could have no conception of that gentleman's ferocity. But the more she protested the more Mr Sorrell thrust it upon her, and at last, in the midst of a burst of tears, Mrs Lee-Egerton came to a pause. 'There's the Tamworth-Egerton crucifix,' she said.

Mr Sorrell had never heard of the Tamworth-Egerton crucifix, and she explained to him that it was a gold beaten cross of unknown antiquity that had been in the hands of the family ever since the thirteenth century. It was considered to be of almost inestimable value and indeed the Jewellery Insurance Company had granted upon it a policy of £1,000. She had it actually upon the boat with her, for she had desired to impress certain choice members of American society by the sight of it now and then. If Mr Sorrell would lend her the money, or still better, would wire it to her son, she would at once give the cross into his keeping until she could repay him.

Mr Sorrell without more bargaining — for at the moment he did not want a cross or anything but this woman's gratitude, had routed out the Marconi operator from his supper, and had telegraphed by private code to his bankers instructing them to pay £250 to Mr Jack Lee-Egerton before noon on the morrow. And shortly afterwards in the public boudoir of the ship, Mrs Egerton had handed over to him the Egerton cross in its leather case, in return for an acknowledgement from him, that he held it against the sum of £250 that day advanced.

In the corridor of the train Mr Sorrell opened the leather case and looked at the battered, tarnished, light gold object. It was about the size of a dog biscuit and the thickness of a silver teaspoon, the cross being marked upon the flat surface with punched holes much indeed like those on the surface of a dog biscuit itself. And the feeling that had been lurking in the mind of Mr Sorrell ever since, quitting the glamour of the ship, he had stepped upon the gangway at Southampton, put itself into the paralysing words: 'Supposing I have been done!'

After all, he did not know anything about Mrs Lee-Egerton, except that she was a Mrs Lee-Egerton, and the other things that she had told him might or might not be true. This thing might just as well be a gilt fragment of a tin canister for all he knew. And upon the moment he snapped the case to and determined to return it to the lady. After all, if she were honest, she would pay him back the money in any case. If she was not the thing would not be worth keeping. And he swayed back into their compartment and sat down opposite her.

'I don't at all like this speed,' she said. The train was shooting through round level stretches of heather. It seemed to sway now upon one set of wheels, now upon the other.

'That's all right,' Mr Sorrell said. 'Nothing ever happens in these days. I've travelled I don't know how many thousand miles in my life without coming across the shadow of an accident.' And he extended the jewel-case towards her. 'Look here,' he said, 'this thing's too valuable for me to have in my possession. You take it. After all, you're the best person to keep it.'

In the unromantic atmosphere of the railway carriage Mrs Egerton appeared much older. She was dressed all in black and her face was very white and seamed, with dark patches of shadow like fingerprints beneath her eyes.

'No, you must keep it,' she said earnestly. 'After all, it's a thing to have had in one's possession. Why, it was brought back from Palestine by Sir Stanley Egerton of Tamworth. Tamworth is quite close to here, and Sir Stanley, they say — that's the touching old legend — died on landing on English soil, and the cross was carried to Tamworth by a converted Greek slave, who was dressed only in a linen shift and knew only two words of English — Egerton and Tamworth. Of course, Tamworth has been out of the family many centuries now, but the cross never has, never till this moment.'

And if Mrs Egerton appeared to have grown older she appeared also to have grown more earnest. She leaned forward, and taking the cross out of the case she put it into Mr Sorrell's hands.

'Look at the funny, queer old thing,' she said. 'And think of all it means, of loyalty and truth.'

'Well, I suppose it does if you say so,' Mr Sorrell said. 'You mean about the chap who carried it about in his nightshirt? I wonder how *he* travelled? I suppose they had stage coaches then, didn't they?'

'Oh, good gracious no!' Mrs Egerton answered. 'He walked bare foot, and the country was beset with robbers all the way from Sandwich to here.'

'I don't know that I should like to do that,' Mr Sorrell said. 'Though I suppose it would take off some flesh! But you don't mean to say that they didn't have any kind of public conveyance?'

'Dear me, no!' the lady answered. 'It was in the year of the battle of Bannockburn. Sir Stanley set out with twenty knights and more than a hundred men-at-arms, and when he came back they were all dead and his only companion was this slave.'

'Well, that was a pretty heavy bill of mortality,' Mr Sorrell said cheerfully. 'The army doctors can't have been worth very much in those days!'

'No, but don't you see?' Mrs Egerton said. 'That's why I should like you to keep the cross, if only for a little time. Since it was in the hands of that slave it hasn't been out of the hands of an Egerton until now. But my son is the last of the family, and you've saved him from a dishonour worse than death quite as certainly as it is said that slave many times saved his master.'

'I guess,' Mr Sorrell said, 'that chap must have been a handy sort of fellow to have about one. You don't get them like that now for thirty shillings a week. I'd just like to see one of my clerks walking from London to Brighton in his nightshirt carrying my gold stylo!'

'They say,' Mrs Egerton went on, 'he lived for some time at Tamworth and then he died. He's said to have had weird gifts of prophecy and things. He prophesied steam-engines and people being able to speak to each other hundreds of miles apart and their flying about in the air like birds. That's recorded in the chronicle.'

'You don't say!' Mr Sorrell said. And he took the cross out of the case by the heavy gold ring at its top. 'I should think he must have scared them some. I rather like those faithful characters of the Dark Ages. They didn't produce much else that was worth speaking of, but they did invent the trusty servant. Did you ever see the picture at Winchester? It was called the trusty servant, and it had a head like a deer and half a dozen other assorted kind of limbs. I've forgotten about it now.'

'Oh, that doesn't matter,' Mrs Egerton said. 'I don't think people have very much changed even nowadays.' And leaning forward she spoke with a deep and rather sonorous earnestness. 'They say that in all the ages the blessing of a mother upon the preserver of her child—'

'Oh come!' Mr Sorrell said. And he felt himself grow pink even down into his socks.

'No it hasn't,' Mrs Egerton continued. 'It hasn't ever lost its power to console the unhappy. So that if ever you find yourself in a tight place—'

'Oh well, that's never likely to happen,' Mr Sorrell said. 'You'd have to bring down the country before you could bring our house down. Why, we're—'

Mrs Egerton suddenly clutched at her heart. Her eyes became filled with an agony of panic, her mouth opened to scream. The smooth running of the train had changed into a fantastic hard jabbing. The glass of the inner windows cracked with a sound like a shriek and fell splintering over her knees. There was a rattle like the volley of machine-guns. He was thrown forward on to Mrs Egerton and she thrown back upon him. Then with a frightful jerk all motion ceased. Mr Sorrell perceived that the glazed photographs of beauty spots served by that line, together with all the wall of the carriage, were descending upon his upturned forehead. The two opposite seats of the carriage were crushed one in upon the other so that he screamed with the pain it caused his legs. The carriage turned right over; he was hanging head downwards in a rush of steam. For a moment he was conscious of a great pain in his temples.

[London: Constable, 1911: pp. 12-21.]

from

The Young Lovell (1913)

Ford's most mysterious romance, *The Young Lovell*, takes place in the Border country in the fifteenth century under Henry VII. Ford thought of the novel as 'a pretty big and serious historical work': 'it is really literature and I have spread myself enormously over it.' Two years later, he published *The Good Soldier*, his 'great auk's egg': the two books are more closely related than they seem.

IN the darkness Young Lovell of the Castle rose from his knees, and so he broke his vow. Since he had knelt from midnight, and it was now the sixth hour of the day, he staggered; innumerable echoes brushed through the blackness of the chapel; the blood made flames in his eyes and roared in his ears. It should have been the dawn, or at least the false dawn, he thought, long since. But he knew that, in that stone place, like a coffer, with the ancient arched windows set in walls a man's length deep, it would be infinitely long before the light came to his eyes. Yet he had vowed to keep his vigil, kneeling till the dawn . . .

When the night had been younger it had been easier but more terrible. Visions had come to him; a perpetual flutter of wings, shuddering through the cold silence. He had seen through the thick walls, Behemoth riding amidst crystal seas, Leviathan who threw up the smoke and flames of volcanoes. Mahound had passed that way with his cortège of pagans and diamonded apes; Helen of Troy had beckoned to him, standing in the sunlight, and the Witch of Endor, an exceedingly fair woman, and a naked one, riding on a shell over a sea with waves like dove's feathers. The Soldan's daughter had stretched out her arms to him, and a courtesan he had seen in Venice long ago, but her smile had turned to a skull's grinning beneath a wimple. He had known all these for demons. The hermit of Liddeside with his long beard and foul garments, such as they had seen him when they went raiding up Dunbar way, had swept into that place and had imperiously bidden him up from his knees to drive the Scots from Barnside, but he had known that the anchorite had been dead this three years and, seeing that the Warden of the Eastern Marches and the Bishop of Durham, with all his own father's forces and all theirs, lay in the castle and its sheilings, it was not likely that the false Scots would be so near. Young gallants with staghounds, brachets and Hamboro dogs had bidden him to the chase; magicians with crucibles had bidden him come view their alembics where the philosopher's stone stood revealed; spirits holding flames in their hands had sought to teach him the sin against the Holy Ghost, and Syrians in robes of gold, strange sins. There had come cooks with strange and alluring messes whose odours make you faint with desires, and the buttling friars from friaries with great wine-skins of sack. But all of them, too, he had known for demons, though at each apparition desire had shaken him.

All these he had taken to be in the nature of the very old chapel, since it had stood there over the tiresome and northern sea ever since Christendom had come to the land, and it was proper to think that, just as those walls had seen the murdering of blessed saint Oddry by heathens and Scots whilst he sang mass, and even as pagans and sorcerers had in the old times contended for that ground, now, having done it in the body, in their souls they should still haunt that spot and contend for the soul of a young lording that should be made a knight upon the morrow. But when the tower-warden had churned out four o'clock the bird of dawn had crowed twice. . . .

Three times would have been of better omen. At that moment Satan himself, the master fiend, with legs of scarlet, a bull's hide sweeping behind and horns all gold and aquamarine, had been dancing with mighty leaps above a coal fire, up through which, livid and in flaming shrouds, there had risen the poor souls of folk in purgatory. And with a charter from which there dangled a seal dripping blood to hiss in the coals and become each drop a viper — with this charter held out towards Young Lovell, Satan had offered him any of these souls to be redeemed from purgatory at the price of selling his own to Satan.

He had been about to say that he knew too much of these temptations and that the damnation of one soul would be infinitely more grievous to Our Lady than the temporary sojourn in purgatory of an infinite number. But at the crowing of the cock Satan and his firelit leer had vanished as if a candle had been blown out in a cavern. . . .

There had begun an intolerable period of waiting. He tried to say his sixty Aves, but the perpetual whirling of wings that brushed his brow took away his thoughts. He knew them now for the wings of anxious bats that his presence disturbed. When he began upon his Paters, a rat that had crept into his harness of proof overset his helmet and the prayer went out of his head. When he would have crossed himself, suddenly his foster-brother and cousin, Decies of the South, that should have watched in the chapel porchway, began to snore and cried out in his sleep the name 'Margaret'. Three times Decies of the South cried 'Margaret'.

Then Young Lovell knew that the spirits having power between cockcrow and dawn, in the period when men die and life ebbs down the sands — that these spirits were casting their spells upon him.

These were the old, ancient gods of a time unknown — the gods to whom the baal fires were lit; gods of the giants and heroes of whom even his confessor spoke with bated breath. Angels, some said they were, not fallen, but indifferent. And some of the poor would have them to be little people that dwelt in bogs and raths, and others held them for great and fair. He could not pray; he could not cross himself; his tongue clove to his jaws; his limbs were leaden. His mind was filled with curiosity, with desire, with hope. He had a great thirst and the cramp in his limbs. He could see a form and he could not see a form. He could see a light and no light at all.

Yet it was a light. It was a light of a rosy, stealing nature. It fell through one of the little, rounded windows, the shadows of the crab-apple branches outside the wall, moving slowly across the floor. When he looked again it was gone and not gone. Without a doubt some eyes were peering into the chapel; eyes that could see in the dark were watching him. Kind eyes; eyes unmoved. His heart beat enormously. . . .

And then he was upon his feet, reeling and stretching out his arms, with prayers that he had never prayed before upon his lips. Then prudence came into his heart and he argued with himself. It was to himself and to no other man or priest that he had vowed to watch above his harness from midnight to dawning. That was a newish fashion and neither the Border Warden nor the Prince Bishop would ask him had he done it or no. They would knight him without this new French manner of it. Then he might well go to see if the dawn were painting the heavens. He fumbled at the bar and cast the door open, stepping out.

It was grey; the sea grey and all the rushes of the sands. The foam was grey where it beat on the islands at sea and in the no-light the great cliff of his father's castle wall was like grey clouts hung from the mists. He perceived an old witch toiling up the dunes to come to him. She had a red cloak and a faggot over her shoulder. She waved her crutch to make him await her, and suddenly he thought she sailed, high in the air from the heavy sand to the stone at his feet. He thought this, but he could not be sure, for at that moment he was rubbing the heavy sleep from his eyes.

'That ye could do this, well I knew,' he said, 'but I had not thought to see ye do it over my ground.'

Often he had seen the old witch. Sometimes she was in the form of a russet hare, slinking into her bed when he had been in harness without bow or light gun or hounds to chase her with. At other times he had seen her in her red cloak creeping about her affairs in the grey woods byBarnside.

Her filthy locks fell across her red eyes and she laughed so that he repented having spared her life in the woods.

'Gowd ye sall putten across my hand,' she said, and her voice was like the wither of dried leaves and the weary creak of bough on bough in a great gale when the woods are perilous because of falling oaks. He answered that he had no gold because he had left his poke in his chest in the castle.

And with great boldness she bade him give her one of the pearls from the cap that hung at his belt. He reached to his left side for his sword, but it lay in the chapel across his armour of damascened steel and bright gold.

'Ye shall drown in my castle well when I have this business redded up,' he said, but he wished he had slain her with his sword, for she was a very evil creature and it was not well in him to let her corrupt the souls of his poor. He lifted from his girdle his tablets to write down that the witch must drown, but the tablets the pen and the knife were tangled with their red silken tassels and skeins. A heavy snore came from within the chapel porch where Decies of the South was sleeping against the wall.

'If my bride had not begged your life of me . . .' the Young Lovell began.

Decies of the South muttered: 'Margaret,' just at his left hand.

'Bride,' the old witch tittered. 'Ye shall never plight your troth. But that sleeper shall be plighted to my lording's bride and take his gear. And another shall have his lands.'

'Get you back to Hell!' the Young Lovell said.

'Look,' the witch cried out.

She pointed down the wind, across the miles of dim dunes underneath where the Cheviots were like ghosts for the snow. The dunes rose in little hummocks amongst grey fields. A high crag was to the left. It was all grey over Holy Island; smoke rose from its courtyard. Dunstanburgh was lost in clouds of white sea spray, and in great clouds the sea-birds were drifting inland in strings of thousands each. Still no sun came over the sea.

The witch pointed with her crutch. . . .

A little thing like a rabbit was digging laboriously at the foot of the crag; it ran here and there, moving a heavy stone.

'That man shall be your master,' the witch cried.

A white horse moved slowly across the dunes. It had about it a swirling cloud of brown and a swirling cloud of the colour of pearly shells.

'And that shall be your bane,' the witch said, in a little voice. 'Ah me, for the fine young lording.'

Young Lovell coursed to the shed beyond the chapel yew where his horse whinnied at the sound of his voice. He haled out the goodly roan that was called Hamewarts because they had bought him in Marseilles to ride homewards through France; his father and he had been to Rome after his father did the great and nameless sin and expiated it in that journey. He had ridden Hamewarts up from the Castle of Lovell so that, standing in the shed whilst his master kept his vigil, the horse might share his benediction.

The roan stallion lifted his head to gaze down the wind. He drew in the air through his nostrils that were as broad as your palm; he sprang on high and neighed as he had done at the battle of Kenchie's Burn.

The horse had no need of spurs, and young Lovell had none. It ran like the wind in the direction of the white steed at a distance. Nevertheless, the rider heard through the muffled sound of hoofs on the heavy sand the old witch who cried out, 'Eya,' to show that she had more to say, and he drew the reins of his charger. The sand flew all over him from beneath the horse's feet, and he heard the witch's voice cry out:

'Today your dad shall die, but you's get none of his lands nor gear. From the now you shall be a houseless man.'

But when he turned in his saddle he could see no old beldam in a scarlet cloak. Only a russet hare ran beneath the belly of Hamewarts and squealed like a new-born baby.

Whilst he rode furiously as if he were in chase of the grey wolf Young Lovell had leisure to reflect, he had ample time in which to inspect the early digger and the beclouded horse. At eight o'clock he was to be knighted by the double accolade of the Warden of the Eastern Marches and of the Prince Bishop, following a custom that was observed in cases of great eminence or merit in the parties. And not only was Young Lovell son to Lord Lovell of the Castle, but he had fought very well against the Scots, in the French wars and in Border tulzies. So at eight, that he might not fast the longer, he was to be knighted. It was barely six, for still no sun showed above the long horizon of the northern sea.

It was bitter cold and the little digger, with his back to the rider, was blowing on his fingers and muttering over a squared stone that had half of it muddied from burial. At first Young Lovell took the little man for a brownie, then for an ape. Then he knew him for Master Stone, the man of law.

He cried out:

'Body of God, Master Furred Cat, where be's thy gown?'

And the little man span round, spitting and screaming, with his spade raised on high. But his tone changed to fawning and then to a complacence that would have done well between two rogues over a booty.

'Worshipful Knight,' he brought out, and his voice was between the creak of a door and the snarl of a dog fox, though his thin knees knocked together for fear. 'A man must live, I in my garret as thou in thy castle bower with the pretty, fair dames!'

'Ay, a man mun live,' the Young Lovell answered. 'But what sort of living is this to be seeking treasure trove on my land before the sun be up?'

'Treasure trove?' the lawyer mumbled. 'Well, it is a treasure.'

'It is very like black Magic,' Young Lovell said harshly. 'A mis-likeable thing to me. I must have thee burnt. What things a man sees upon his lands before the sun is up!'

'Magic,' the lawyer screamed in a high and comic panic. 'God help me, I have nothing of Mishego and Mishago. This is plain lawyer's work and if your honour will share, one half my fees you shall have from the improvident peasants.'

At the high sound of his voice Hamewarts, who all the while was straining after the white horse, bounded three strides; when Young Lovell took him strongly back, he had the square stone at another angle. Upon its mossed side he saw a large 'S' carved that had two crosses in its loops, upon the side that was bare was one 'S' with the upper loop struck through.

'Body of God, a boundary stone,' he cried out. 'And you, Furred Cat, are removing it.' He had got the epithet of Furred Cat from talking to the Sire de Montloisir whilst they played at the dice.

'Indeed it is more profitable than treasure-troving and seeking the philosopher's stone,' the lawyer tittered, and he rubbed, from habit, his hands together, so that little, triturated grains of mud fell from them into the peasant's poor, boggy grass. 'This is Hal o' the Mill's land, and I have moved the stone a furlong into the feu of Timothy Wynvate. There shall arise from this a lawsuit that shall last the King's reign out. Aye, belike, one of the twain shall slay the other. His land your honour may take back as forfeit, and the other's as deodand. I will so contrive it, for I will foment these suits and have the handling of them. By these means, in time, your lordingship may have back all the lands ye ever feu'd. In time. Only give me time. . . .'

The Young Lovell lifted up his fist to the sky. The most violent rage was in his heart.

'Now by the paps of Venus and the thunder of Jove, I have forgotten the penalty of him that removeth his neighbour's landmark! But if I do not die before night, and I think I shall not, that death you shall die. Say your foul prayers, filth, your doom is said. . . .'

Master Stone lifted up both his hands, clasped together, to beg his life of this hot but charitable youth. But Young Lovell had leaped his horse across a dune faster than the words could follow him.

He came upon a narrow strip of nibbled turf running down a valley of rushy sand-hills. Hamewarts guided him. They went over one ridge and had sight of the white horse; they sank into another dale and lost it.

On the summit of the next ridge Hamewarts became suddenly like a horse of bronze and the Young Lovell had a great dizziness. He had a sense of brown, of pearly blue, of white, of many colours, of many great flowers as large as millstones. With a heavy sense of reluctance he looked behind him. The mists were rising like curtains from over Bamborough; since the tide was falling the pall of spray was not so white on Dunstanburgh. Upon his own castle, covering its promontory near at hand, they were hoisting a flag, so that from there the tower warden must have already perceived the sun. From over the castle on Holy Island the pall of smoke was drifting slowly to sea. No doubt in the courtyard they had been roasting sheep and kine whole against the visit of the Warden and the Prince Bishop who would ride on there with all their men by nine of the clock.

In every bay and reedy promontory the cruel surf gnawed the sand; the ravens were flying down to the detritus of the night, on the wet margins of the tide. The lawyer was climbing over the shoulder of a dune, a sack upon his back; a shepherd, for the first time that spring, was driving a flock of sheep past the chapel yew. There was much surf on Lindisfarne.

Suddenly, from the middle of bow of the grey horizon there shot up a single, broadening beam. Young Lovell waved his arm to the golden disk that hastened over the grey line.

'If you had come sooner,' he said to the sun, 'you might have saved me from this spell. Now these fairies have me.'

Slowly, with mincing and as if shy footsteps, Hamewarts went down through the rushes from that very real world. Young Lovell perceived that the brown was a carpeting that fluttered, all of sparrows. It had a pearly and restless border of blue doves, and in this carpet the white horse stepped ankle-deep without crushing one little fowl. He perceived the great-petalled flowers, scarlet and white and all golden. On a green hill there stood a pink temple, and the woman on the back of the white horse held a white falcon. She smiled at him with the mocking eyes of the naked woman that stood upon the shell in the picture he had seen in Italy.

'But for you,' he heard himself think, 'I might have been the prosperest knight of all this Northland and the world, for I have never met my match in the courteous arts, the chase or the practice and exercises of arms.'

And he heard her answering thoughts:

'Save for that I had not called thee from the twilight.'

[London: Constable, 1913: pp. 1-12.]

from

The Rash Act (1933)

See pages 266–9 for Ford's comments on *The Rash Act* and its sequel, *Henry for Hugh*, 1934.

HE could not be certain whether the motor was running quite smoothly. Usually its sound was an agreeable murmur. But perhaps, just as colours will not have full brightness if you are financially worried so the sound of engines will not be altogether soothing if you have been up all night.

Dawn had come very suddenly. It is the misfortune of certain landscapes of great beauty that human arts have banalized their most wonderful or unusual effects. On the stage when an actor lights a candle the whole large stage will be flooded as if with sunlight. It was so with this dawn of the fifteenth of August, nineteen hundred and thirty-one.

You cannot spoil dark night and immense, wheeling stars by any parody. In such a place when the air is just flesh-heat you are conscious only of being at one with immensity. You are no separate being and even to you your weightiest preoccupations are without importance. You say: 'If I had acted then in another way my situation would now be less unfortunate . . .' But your regrets have little poignancy.

But that dawn flickered suddenly into existence. The islands were illuminated. A white sail showed on the horizon. Sea birds called. The sea itself, as if awakening, threw a single, long-resounding wave along the miles of shingle. The stage was suddenly set. You could no longer commune with infinity. These were the great boards on which to enact tragedy.

A grotesque — an almost abhorrent — message from Destiny opened the ball. An immense, skeleton-grey bird was flying slumberously along the edge of the sea. At little more than the height of a man. With dawn its labours were no doubt ended and it was going to rest on some solitary crag. With the slow beating of its vast spread of wings it had all by itself the air of a portent.

It was sleepily almost upon him . . . six feet away. It screamed with rage and fear. Its immense wings beat the air in untidy panic: it towered. Straight up. Towering and screaming it let fall a small fish. The fish struck smartly on Henry Martin's left shoulder. . . . An omen!

If a raven in those regions dropped excrement on the left shoulder of a Roman it was the best omen of all. He did not know what that bird was. . . . A stork, possibly. A pelican? A flamingo? . . . A fish dropped by a stork might be of better omen than excrement from a raven. The fish was silver . . . a fortune must be coming to him. . . . It was a grim and atrocious pleasantry on the part of Destiny. It struck him as something indecent. Destiny had driven him to death. His end was tragedy, not mere death. A hundred slowly converging things were forcing him over the edge of the boat. Not mere despair because you had lost a woman. Or a million dollars.

He had been doomed in his mother's womb. It had been decreed that the seed of a wild boar of the Ardennes meeting the lymphatic stock of over-old New England should beget one who danced without giving pleasure.[1] That was reasonable. . . . As it were within the rights of Destiny. Destiny had the prerogative of dooming you within the womb.

But to conduct you within a foot or two of death and then, grinningly to throw a fish at you. That was execrable. In execrable taste. . . .

He ran suddenly into the gloomy cavern of the inn-door. He clumped up the dark, carpetless stairs. . . . On the staircase at least he had recovered the night. Shadows.

It had struck him when the dawn had fallen suddenly on him that he had taken his call too soon.

He ought to have descended two hours later into a brilliantly illuminated stage. He would have received the plaudits of the islands, the innumerable smiling wavelets, the pine trees, the pebbles. Of the sirens too, perhaps! He would then have been the hero of tragedy, stepping gallantly to his doom. Then he would have danced. And all that applause would have shown that he had given pleasure.

As it was, the curtain — the dawn — had gone up too soon. He had been without make-up — cothurnus, parsley fillet, pine cone sceptre. And Destiny, in the audience had chucked fish at him! . . .

[1] See *Provence*, p. 343, where Ford speaks of the memorial tablet for the boy of Antibes who 'danced and gave pleasure'. — Ed.

He had actually been prepared enough and might then have taken his call. . . .

In his bare room his papers were all burnt, his grips packed. His drawers all stood open as witness of the fact that, the night before, he had taken the proper precautions to leave nothing.

There hung nevertheless on the wall a little card calendar. It had been given to him last year in return for his *étrennes* to the postman . . . his five-franc tip. It had a pink and grey picture representing children feeding pigeons beside the Medici fountain. In the Luxembourg Gardens. . . .

The incredible thing! . . . It was incredible! . . .

He had mistaken the date!

It was today, Sunday, August 16th. . . . He had taken it to be the 15th . . . the feast of the Assumption. . . . It stood there on the Calendar.

15 S. ASSOMP

16 D. St. Roch

The Assumption in good fat capitals. St. Roch in tiny type.

It was disillusionment. He had imagined himself going up to heaven in a festival of glory. The Assumption was regarded as the most important feast of the French year. Gipsies from all over the world came to celebrate it to the Stes. Maries, a few miles away. . . . Gipsies, cardinals, *vaqueros*. . . . The tenders of the wild bulls of the Carmargue. They swam their wild bulls across the Rhone and back and were blessed by the Cardinals. . . . The bulls for the bull fights. . . . For the *Salta della Muerta*. . . . The dance of death. . . .They placed, those bull fighters, their feet on the horns of the charging bulls and sprang right over them. . . . *Salta* . . . the spring . . . *Saltaverunt*. . . . They sprang amidst wild applause. If they didn't die they were lucky. If they did they got more applause.

He had taken pleasure at the thought that, whilst he drifted over the waving fronds at the bottom of the Mediterranean, those excitements would be taking place over the blazing pebble of the Carmargue. Almost within sight.

But S. Roch . . . who was Saint Roch! . . . He was represented as fainting, with a dog licking his hand, a great loaf and a bamboo cross. There was a statue of him in the church of his name in the rue St. Honoré at Paris. As far as Henry Martin could remember he was a local saint . . . . Local to Marseilles and these parts. He must have been born in Montpellier. . . . Yes, there had been a pestilence and

M. Roch had gone about curing the sufferers and probably feeding them from the great loaf. He had been himself succumbing to the plague. But the dog had rescued him.

How could a dog rescue you from the plague? . . .

Was that the sort of story you wanted to have attending on your extinction? . . . It was another grin of Destiny.

On the other hand . . . perhaps if a local saint had been appointed for the day of his death his soul might expect to receive more immediate attention. . . . *Anima* . . . *vagula* . . . *blandula*. . . . Little, pale, wandering, new wet soul. It might be glad of a dog and a big loaf. . . . A more homelike reception than to have all the Archangels and the morning stars singing in glory.

He pulled down the sheets and laid himself full-dressed on his bed. He didn't know why he wanted to stage his end in that way. But he certainly desired to leave the impression that he had spent his last night in bed.

Why should he desire to leave impressions? It was nevertheless a strong urge and no doubt there is something vital in all strong urges. Something going to the root of life. An intimation perhaps of immortality.

If hell consisted of floating between the tides of the winds and worrying, one might as well worry about what happened to one's reputation as about anything else. It might be agreeable to hear them say: 'He was hard boiled. He slept in his bed before the rash act — as if nothing had happened.' . . . Or rather it might be extremely disagreeable if they said he had been in such a stew that he *hadn't* slept.

That was no doubt it. He had examined the bill-fold twice already and he felt that he was about to do it again. That was because he extremely disliked the idea of having his body searched by whoever found him. That wallet contained — A: his passport and identity card. B: a letter to Alice. C: a cable to his father. D: a hundred franc note. E: a letter to whoever found him. He begged them to send the cable to father — a night letter costing thirty-five francs; to mail the letter to Alice; to believe that there was nothing else in any of his other pockets and to retain the remaining sixty-five francs for any incidental expenses they might be put to. He said, too, that his heir and next male representative was his father and that he had nothing against anybody. The Crisis alone was responsible for his taking his own life.

He could think of nothing else to add to that collection of exhibits. He had done everything he could invent to keep his body from being handled. He had even tried to invent some way of leaving his wallet attached to his hand so that they might not even need to visit his pockets. If he had been going to shoot himself that would have been simple. If you died by a shot in the brain your hand closed irrevocably on whatever it held. He imagined himself lying on the ground — on the pine needles under an umbrella pine. Then the first thing that met the eye would be the oiled silk wrapping of the wallet. . . . Or no, it would be the wallet itself. If he had not been going to die in the water there would have been no need for the wrapper.

Some people had all the luck — the people who shot themselves. They could lie with their proof of identity in their hand. . . .

He lay with a nearly vacant mind till a ray of sun-light touched the extended fingers of a branch of the stone pine that grew at the house-end. He had long since hocked his watch. And it was odd how little he needed it. He had, of course, gone native: he had pretty well acquired the ability to tell the time by the sun. A year ago he would have laughed at you if you had told him he would one day live watchless. The watch was the badge of American manhood. . . . Free, male and twenty-one: complete with timepiece. . . . Incomplete without. How could you make dates? You could not be American and not make them.

Four days ago he had verified by the *salle à manger* clock that the sun just touched the branch at five-fifty-two. Giving the sun two minutes a day of delay, this morning it would touch it at six.

When the dark needles grew suddenly golden he started. He could not remember what he had been thinking of. He must have dozed off. That gave him pleasure. He had actually slept. Then he would not be obtaining applause by false pretences. He was indeed hard-boiled. Before the rash act he had really slept in his bed!

He took his call from the end of the little pier at six-fifteen. It had taken him a quarter of an hour, accompanied by old Marius Vial, to walk there from the bed in which he had slept. He had a sense that the mountains and islands 'Ho-ho'd,' the innumerable wavelets clapped, the umbrella and stone pines waved commendations.

Somewhere the sirens smiled. Heartlessly! He remembered a picture he had once seen, of a smiling siren plunging down, beneath the sea. A classical-featured youth was tight bound in her arms. As if there had been a hundred ropes twining round his limbs. Iridescent bubbles shot up through the air. Her smile was gleeful but aloof. As if she were thinking of something else. . . . If you were carrying down to your grotto a stalwart youth whose blood you were going to suck it would be more polite to think of him. . . .

So there he stood amongst all that applause!

On the terrace of the inn the silver fish that the bird had dropped had still lain on the gravel. . . . Destiny could hardly have been pelting him off the stage with it. He had acted as became a hero of tragedy. He had slept with refreshment and come there for all to see. Spectators, mad with enthusiasm, throw to a great torero in the arena fans, cigarettes, hats, jewels . . . whatever they have to hand. So Destiny had thrown the silver fish. Silver you observe!

The sheaf of thousand pound notes that Hugh Monckton had thrown to him the night before had for some reason or another seemed to represent great quantities of silver. Perhaps because they were silvery white. So Destiny might have been trying, with silver, to persuade him not to commit . . . the rash act. Destiny might very well think him the hell of a fine fellow.

Well, wasn't he? There he stood on high amongst the applause of a world. Nothing Destiny might have done had been able to deter him. He had marched there to his end, Nordic hero. Taking his call.

He was not wrong in calling it that. An author took his call when the curtain came down at the end of his play. And the curtain had come down on the end of his tragedy. Of that he was both hero and author.

He bowed to the right; to his left; before him. As if he had been an Oriental saluting the sun. His mind was full of sardonic gaiety. He remembered to have read somewhere that trapeze performers felt hatred for a public that applauded their living in mortal danger. So he hated that heartless, smiling landscape. When he had finished bowing he ran down the steps to his boat.

His left foot was poised above it, his right was still on the granite of the quay when he thought: 'This is my last contact with dry land.'

He imagined that his soul had shrunk within him to the dimensions of a shrivelled walnut. A walnut in a cavern. That was his soul. It was already dissociated from his body.

Marius Vial appeared to be speaking. Henry Martin did not hear what he said. The boat floated free. He went forward and pulled back the starting lever. Marius Vial had already set the engine running. Henry Martin turned the wheel on its joy-stick. He considered that a minute ago he had been mad. You do not bow to mountains, islands and waves. It is not done.

He had secretly wondered for a long time how fear would take him.

It had made his throat horribly dry. At this moment, too, he noticed that the engine was not running smoothly.

It annoyed his head. It was as if a mourner had behaved indecorously at his funeral. He had been used to take pleasure in the deep tones of his motor.

It was perhaps no more than the hangover after a sleepless night. . . . But it had not been sleepless.

He had had five very small drinks of that amazing *fine* the night before. Minute drinks because it had been so precious. It would be treason to that sanctified liquor to think that it had given him a hangover.

Then this was fear!

The boat had rounded the rocky bluff and opened out the great bay. The 'port exterior' as they called it. He thought that in English they called it 'roads'. 'The English fleet lay in Toulon Roads.' The level sea spread before him, between the headland and the mainland. The headland was a peninsula parallel with the mainland. Those words brought back to him moods of his young boyhood. 'Mainland.' 'Headland.' 'Roads.' 'Bluff.'

Well, his bluff had been called all right.

'Oh, little did my mother think the day she cradled me
Of the lands that I should travel in and the death that I should dee!'

His mother had been proud of the fact that he had never been rocked in a cradle. His first crib had stood in the sun-parlour. It gave on to the garden that was behind the drug-store. It had the model of a caravel, time of Columbus, that mother had brought from Fall River after Grandfather Smith's death. But before his — Henry Martin's birth. He supposed Grandfather Smith had had some movable property in Fall River at his death. Mother must have gone over there to collect it.

She had had the proud idea that rocking babies injured their brains. He could still hear the inflection of her voice as she told other mothers that Henry Martin had *never* been rocked. . . . That was the baby-raising craze those years. . . .

Perhaps that was why he and the boys born about then were now the Lost Generation. They probably needed rocking to form their characters. Well, Providence was about to make up for it. He was going to be. . . . What was the old song?

'Rocked in the cradle of the deep!'

His throat was deplorably dry, the missing beat of the engine exasperated his brain. He might go ashore in the little cove called St. Mejean where there was an *estaminet:* he might stop the engine and try sailing. There was a bright little breeze from behind.

If he went ashore it would look as if he were faltering in his purpose: if he took to sailing he would appear to be playing for delay. Besides he had not a penny in the world beside the hundred franc note in his bill-fold. . . . Hugh Monckton had not in the end returned the three hundred and ninety-four francs . . . was it three hundred and ninety-four? He could not remember. The momentary recollection of last night gave him pleasure. It reminded him of the dark girl. He wondered if she was wearing his ring or had hocked it. He would never know.

There were five bright sails in the bay before him. Pleasure craft. It was Sunday. There would be hundreds of them before the day was done. There was a very full-membered sailing boat club at a little placed called Mourillon that had a seventeenth-century castle and a tiny harbour behind a mole. The little space of water was as thick with them as if they had been sardines in a tin. Before noon they would be all out and the bay would be as gay as Miami in a record season.

He was glad of it. It pleased him to think of going out of the world in a sort of watery Coney Island. Besides he might be seen to go overboard. . . . Then they would be fairly certain to look out for his body. It was his body he was anxious about.

Dreadful fear beset him at the thought of his last minute. He imagined that you struggled, suffocated. At last you breathed. What happened then? When the water entered your lungs? Apparently you died then. You became for the rest of the world no longer 'he' but 'it'. But what exactly happened to you? A desperate running together of thoughts. Panic? Regret? Your lungs no longer supplied your heart with air and the want of aeration of your blood stupefied your brain. . . . So you died poisoned. . . . He had wanted to avoid dying poisoned. Poison distorted your face and caused pain like flame. Similarly he disliked the idea of cutting his throat. It would make you repulsive. So would death by shooting. Besides he had hocked his gun long ago.

He would not have been averse to putting his head inside a gas oven and turning on the gas. But he disliked the idea of dying in a room. He wanted to see a bright sky with his dying eyes. . . . And he had heard that the drowned had serene faces. He had never actually seen a dead man. Mother's coffin had been screwed down before he reached Springfield from Dartmouth. He had imagined that that had been an act of spite on the part of father. But, of course, it had not been. He heard afterwards that mother had had a look of terrible agony and father wanted to spare his children.

He had misjudged father. Father had told the cook to cook Luxemburg-fashion and had taken his gold-headed cane out of the drawer immediately after he had come back from the funeral. That had looked like callousness. It hadn't been. Long after, father had told Sister Carrie that he had done it as a tribute to mother. He had been so certain of her saintliness that he knew she had gone straight to Heaven. If he had had any doubt or considered that she had earned a period in Purgatory he would have waited till he thought that period had ended. But, in Heaven, she would see all things in the right light. She would see that Luxemburg-fashion cooking was the best for him, and that gold-knobbed canes became men of his generation. She would be glad when from the battlements in the sky she saw him eating his first *plat de côte* and Kramyk.

A queer old fellow, father — in some ways his mind worked singularly like his son's.

Of course Henry Martin had thought that death by drowning would be the most painless.

He stopped the engine and throwing up one of the deck boards took out two heavy pigs of iron ballast. He dropped one into either pocket. That was to show that though he might be delaying his death he was still determined on it. After all there was no hurry. If he had set six o'clock for the hour of his rising he had set none for his death. And he had all eternity before him. And a lovely day. He had always luxuriated in that sort of brightness. He imagined that Heaven would be all sunlight and little bright objects.

As soon as the boat had lost way the scarlet, triangular sail bellied out nicely. Henry Martin had never ascertained what such sails were called in English. 'Lateen' he imagined. But he had a vague idea that lateen sails were made of rush. Probably that was wrong. He was pretty sure that the rig when there were several masts was called 'felucca'. A brave word, felucca. It made you think of Salee rovers, corsairs. He was familiar with the look of the rig from a set of nacred tea-trays that his mother had had. They showed Mediterranean scenes with the curved felucca yards bending romantically this way and that.

It was a nice rig. So extraordinarily easy to handle that he had often wondered why it was not used all the world over. This particular boat had the disadvantage that, when the sail was furled, if you had forgotten, or if you had not had time, to secure the yard it would swing round and round on the mast and might catch you a tidy crack if you were in the way — say in the rounded seat behind the joy-stick. Then it swung round again and caught you on the other side. Precisely like a vindictive boxer delivering a left and right.

That had happened to him three days ago, the nose of the yard catching him such a crack on each shoulder that he had two immense bruises on his upper arms.

He retreated to the stern where there was a tiller that he used instead of the motorwheel when the engine was not running. The stern seat was the more comfortable. You could stretch your legs to the full with one arm over the bar. It was one of his favourite positions. From there he could handle the sheet of the mainsail without getting up.

He lay for a long time with a completely vacant mind. The very high bow of the boat towered up to a sharp point and hid the greater part of the roads before him. It was complete luxury. This was how he had imagined it.

After a time the wind fell completely. The sail flapped now and then against the mast. Why not be delayed when you could suffer it in complete luxury? The sails of the approaching flotilla of pleasure-seekers grew brighter and brighter. He could see them beyond the side of the port bow if he leaned his head over to one side. It pleased him to see them. They were like a gay fleet coming to lead him to a feast of garlands.

The sunlight grew whiter and more white. The day hung breathless. The sea was like a looking-glass: infinitely blue and getting bluer and ever more blue against the bright green of the promontory. He was by now well into the roads.

But, by Jove, the water was not blue between him and the mainland. It was a reddish chocolate. And opaque! There must have been an immense rainstorm somewhere in the mountains during the night. Old Marius Vial's *trombio*. Henry Martin had seen the water looking like that once already after an immense storm, taking up exactly half the inlet so that, from above, it had seemed to be two streaks . . . of red-brown and blue. The storm had gone pounding along the foothills of the Alps and then out to sea beyond Hyères. Cyclonic! These storms with a circular itinerary were not unusual in that neighbourhood during early August. The amount of water that fell during one of them was incredible. You could tell that because though the actual number of days on which rain fell in that neighbourhood was the lowest in all Western Europe the rainfall itself was the highest in all France. It was of course practically the tropics.

A feeling of unease was coming over him. He felt as if someone was watching him from behind his back. That was absurd. But the feeling grew until it was as if the something was an immense feline creature. That was more absurd. You should not yield to these feelings. There was no knowing how your character might not deteriorate if you did! . . .

With his face looking backwards, his right hand, mechanically, but with frantic speed, released the sheet of the sail from its cleat. He had seen three boats against a grey curtain — slate grey triangles of supernatural leaden-whiteness! They had stood out against the leaden curtain. One: two: three! They had gone over, flat. One: two: three! It was incredible that they could have capsized. But the air was moaning for them.

The immense grey-black curtain towered up to the peak of the heavens. It advanced with unbelievable rapidity. Before it the white villas half hidden in the tropical trees, the fort on the top of Cap Brun, the white semaphore over the highest part of St. Mandrier — all these things sparkled and were distinct in the sunlight. When it reached them they disappeared. There was nothing but the leaden grey pall with the fringe of sea beaten into an agony of whiteness.

It threatened unimaginable horrors. It advanced with the speed of a racehorse. God knew what went on within it. Lightning tore it and glowed from within. The screams of the drowning were thin but incessant. Those three sails had gone over, flat, with the precision of flaps on the edge of a machine. . . . It was Hell that was advancing — the Hell of primitive imagination.

If he could get the boat round! He had sprung to the engine. There was no time to let down the yard. The sail, let free, might not exercise much leverage. Not enough to turn that large boat over. The noise was now so great that he could not hear if the engine responded. . . . It had sounded out of order! . . .

It had sounded out of order. But, if he could not get her head round they were lost. Her stern was so low that those white seas would poop her, without a chance of escape. He jammed and jammed at the starting lever. He cursed but could not hear his oaths. The sounds advancing were like the screams of demoniac birds. . . . Like the scream of that bird. He did not dare to look behind him. He had been contemplating a sin — Hell was advancing on him.

She could never run before it. She had a trick of speed: she was a good filly. They must not be lost: they must not be lost. Time moved so slowly that when, in the now steaming heat he moved his hand from the wheel to wipe his wet forehead with the back it seemed to take whole minutes to get it up to his head. . . . One day is as a thousand years in Hell. Then perhaps the engine was not refusing. It was time that had broken down.

There was a faint vibration on the wheel in his hands. . . . He felt his body sway back in his seat. If he could get her round. She must know she could never stand those seas on her broadside. She had way on. She was starting engrossedly over the still placid sea in the sunlight that was already livid.

He said:

'Now for it, old girl.'

He pressed on the wheel a little but steadily. A big boat like that could not be turned very sharply. It was at any rate not one of her virtues. Besides, if that sea caught her heeling for the turn it would swamp her in a minute.

To his breathlessness her high bow moved slowly to the right. Along the flank of the mountain that is over Les Sablettes. Behind the inner harbour. A heavy, squarish mass of cloud was attached to the peak, going away to the right like a shock of hair. The bow moved round, obscuring in its deliberate motion, grey-white ravines and little trees each of which had its separate shadow. He was then in the shadow and chill of what was advancing. But out there the sunlight still fell. Objects were amazingly distinct: seven miles away. But the shadows were ink-black.

On the beach at Les Sablettes there would already be a thick, gay, unsuspecting crowd of Sunday holiday seekers. As they said there:

You would not be able to smell the sea for the babies. . . . And unsuspecting!

She had come half round. The bows were obscuring the flowered gardens and the palms and pines of the mainland. He had made the inland turn. He would have preferred to make for the open, left-handed. But there might be some shelter near the land. He was about a mile out. People in white clothes were running in crowds along the smugglers' path. Along the face of the rock.

Suddenly he looked at the approaching *trombio*. She was now broadside on to it and turning slowly. As if unconcernedly. Like a woman occupied with her cooking during a bombardment. He still lay back. Luxuriously! Leaning slackly on the tiller. He considered for a moment and then sprang for the wheel. The tiller might be jerked out of his hand in the approaching torrent.

That Thing of God appeared to go perfectly straight across the inlet. Like a great wall with a whitewashed foot. It towered completely up into invisibility. But, as she moved slowly round, he saw that the face of the wall was in vaporous motion. It was as if cloudy beings rushed violently to right or left or upwards. Or as if. . . .

He said:

'By God!'

It was now that he was taking his call before the mocking beings of the Universe. It was now . . . now . . . now that he was going behind the curtain.

As soon as she was round he had unthrottled the engine. The sea was now agitated. She had come alive. Under the new force she seemed to spring towards her doom. He discovered that he was panting.

Darkness descended on him. It came like a whip. With a roaring rush. The air was full of missiles. It was as if a hundred pails of wheat had been hurled at him. Just before the darkness he had looked at the compass. Whilst he could still see the land. By steering due east with a little south to allow for drift if the wind beat inshore he ought just to shave the headland behind which lay Carqueiranne. But he was blinded. Heavy veils of water were in his eyelashes as he shivered. They seemed glutinous, one succeeding another as he brushed them away with the back of his hand. The rain drove straight through his shirt. It was icy and impelled him to rage. He would best this damned imbecility of the elements. And save the boat. It was as if she trusted him to save her. He exclaimed:

'By God, she is the only friend I have.'

Damn all women! A woman by now would have been shrieking or fainting. Not Alice perhaps. But she had gone Lesbian.

The noise was as if a thousand lunatics were rubbing sheets of corundum paper one on the other. The rain was solid on his skin. It was as if he were at the bottom of the sea.

He remembered the little flask in his pocket: the one he had not offered to Hugh Monckton the night before. *That* was fiery, cheap stuff. Having drunk half of it he seemed to be on fire within and frozen outside. What pastry-cooks call a *chaud-froid*. It seemed to fill him with savage gaiety.

She was labouring slowly into the teeth of the wind. She took the short seas as if she were a hunter at a horse-show taking in and out fences. It was impossible to see what progress she made if she made any. He steered to the left, towards the land. Very gradually. She shipped a little water. He imagined himself to be about level with Cap Brun.

He knew all the beaches along there. But he was not enough of a sailor to know how she would take landing on the shingle in this sea. He was, however, certain that she would be all right if she struck a patch of sand. Or, if he got under the lea of Carqueiranne mole he might risk landing on the hard stones.

Suddenly land loomed up before him. Reddish perpendicular rocks with the spindrift shooting before it. She was going at it, nose on. And travelling rather fast.

That would not do. Even in smooth water she would stave her bows in if she charged red granite rocks. He wanted her to come off without a scratch, and he felt full of confidence that he could do it. He headed her seawards. It was no doubt the brandy that had given him confidence. But that did not matter. He caught, near his left hand in large white letters the word RESERVE. He must be within ten yards of the land but the water was deep there. He knew the place but not its name. He was more than half way back to Carqueiranne and he knew approximately the pace at which they were travelling.

Out of the shelter of the land the storm blew again more furiously. She began once more her gait of the jumping hunter. It made his teeth chatter. He reckoned it would cut her travelling down to about half. They would have to stand it for a full hour more.

The wind howled: the rain beat upon him: the engine ran well now. He could feel its pulsations on the wheel. The monotony grew insupportable. Once there was a moment of calm in the air. He put her at it, cramming in the gasoline. He imagined himself to have made three hundred yards at racing speed. Then she washed into it again. As if she had gone at. . . . What was it called? A bullfinch. The sort of hedge Hugh Monckton had said he was going to put his car at.

There must be a pocket of calm travelling in the middle of the storm. He thought they called it the cyclonic centre. That must mean they were in the middle of the disastrous affair. They would have to go through as much again as they had already gone through. He doubted if he could do it. He was insufferably weary and cold. His hands on the wheel ached with cramp. His eyes were painful with gazing into the wind. He would have given anything to lie down on dry land. On pine-needles. . . . What a hope! as Hugh Monckton had said.

The fumes of the brandy were surging up within him. . . . You had to remember that his stomach must be quite empty. He had eaten nothing since dinner-time last night. He remembered to have read that, taken on an empty stomach brandy reached its maximum effect in a quarter of an hour. After that it acted as a soporific. Weakening you.

It was perhaps half an hour since he had taken that gulp. Then he must be feeling the weakening effect. That was damnable.

Suddenly he put her about. It was perhaps the recklessness of brandy. He must have underestimated her seaworthiness. The la Seyne boatbuilders probably knew their job and those waters. She was like a cork. Even when she was broadside on to the direction of the wind she shipped next to no water. Before the wind she fairly raced the wave crests.

He felt wild elation. Like a drunken motorist racing through traffic. Or like Hugh Monckton charging his bullfinch. Well, he was probably the better man of the two. It was unlikely that he had done what he said. Whereas he, Henry Martin, was actually charging an unknown obstacle at breathless speed. . . .

He would have to borrow some money of Hugh Monckton. So as to be able to sleep for two days on end. He would have to have two days' sleep before he would have the nerve to commit suicide again.

Well, why not borrow of Hugh Monckton? They had been in the same regiment! Besides, Hugh Monckton had offered to lend him twenty thousand pounds to have a gamble with. Surely he would let him have five hundred francs for a sleep. . . . One five-thousandth of the sum!

He exclaimed suddenly:

'Good God!'

They had leapt into perfectly still water. They were doing very likely thirty! With a furious kick at the pedal and pushing the lever completely over he reversed the engine. He did not dare to go about in the effort to reduce speed. They must have struck the mouth of the little cove beneath the stone pines. He was thrown against the wheel as the reversing engine began to take effect. All the breath left his body. The cove was perhaps two hundred yards across and a quarter of a mile deep. The sides were lined with red granite but at the bottom was the stretch of silver sand. The very thing to land on if they were not going at express speed.

But there was no knowing how far they were down the cove. The cove it must be because there was no other. But the rain falling direct into the windless space hid everything. He might well be going to crash her on to that sand with a force that might stave her bottom. What a thing to do to your only friend!

But perhaps Hugh Monckton was also a friend. He seemed to hear his voice say: 'Old Bean!' . . . Male and female created He them. . . . The boat was a female. . . .

There appeared dim and wet through the glassy rods of the rain a red brick blockhouse, a hillside and a white path that divided it at a slant. It was indeed the cove.

These things came toward him rapidly. But the reversed screw had taken hold. Every half second the speed decreased. He stood up to see exactly at what moment to stop the engine. Some men were running out of the red blockhouse. If the engines ran after she was stopped they might strain their bearings. He thought so.

She checked glutinously as she were on the bottom ooze. He half fell forward. She proceeded: then checked more determinedly. He felt a violent, an incredible blow on his cheek. Incredible pain.

The yard that had been completely divested of its canvas had swung round on the mast at the checking of the keel. The end of the yard was bound in iron.

The blow knocked him sideways. Immediately a fearful sear of pain existed in his right temple. That flail had swung completely round on the mast. He screamed. He fell desperately forward on to the hood that covered the engines. . . .

The only thing that existed was pain. Men stopped him on the sand and told him he was bleeding.

'Vous saignez!' . . . 'Mais vous saignez!' . . . 'Saignez.'

He struck at them and ran. He thought that if he ran fast enough he could escape from the pain. And they were barring his way. . . . What sort of life was this?

They shuffled back stupidly. He ran for the foot of the path. He must obtain insensibility. He desired to bite at the tufts of rosemary that on the pathside brushed his cheek. He was past them before he could bite.

He came to the top and sat down on a ledge. The rain had stopped. The sunshine fell on the island of Porquerolles — the high blue island over the ruffled sea. He could do no more.

He held his hand to his right temple. It came down glutinous and scarlet. He held his other hand to his other cheek. He desired to vomit. To have escaped war, tempest and self-given death and to come to this! The impulse to vomit made him remember his brandy flask. It was still half full.

The men on the sand below had given up looking at him and had gone back to the blockhouse. With the impulse of the brandy within him he stood up. The day was growing brighter and brighter. He must be going on!

[Manchester: Carcanet Press, 1982: pp. 181-203.]

II

Reminiscences

from

Ancient Lights (1911)

This was published in America as *Memories and Impressions*. 'I give so much of autobiography though these are reminiscences. In that form the narrator should be a mirror, not any sort of actor. . .' (*Return to Yesterday*, p.139). *Ancient Lights*, the first of Ford's volumes in which he looked back over the events of his lifetime, recalls his childhood in Pre-Raphaelite London and is as much an autobiography as a series of reminiscences. Ford's other books in this mixed genre were *Thus to Revisit*, 1921; *Return to Yesterday*, 1931; and *It Was the Nightingale*, 1933. See also *Henry James*, 1913; *Joseph Conrad*, 1924; and *Portraits from Life*, 1937. *No Enemy* is in a class by itself: see page 110 in this volume.

DEDICATION: TO CHRISTINA AND KATHARINE

MY Dear Kids — Accept this book, the best Christmas present that I can give you. You will have received before this comes to be printed, or at any rate before — bound, numbered, and presumably indexed — it will have come in book form into your hands — you will have received the amber necklaces and the other things that are the outward and visible sign of the presence of Christmas. But certain other things underlie all the presents that a father makes to his children. Thus there is the spiritual gift of heredity.

It is with some such idea in my head — with the idea, that is to say, of analysing for your benefit what my heredity had to bestow upon you — that I began this book. That, of course, would be no reason for making it a 'book', which is a thing that appeals to many thousands of people, if the appeal can only reach them. But to tell you the strict truth, I made for myself the somewhat singular discovery that I can only be said to have grown up a very short time ago — perhaps three months, perhaps six. I discovered that I had grown up only when I discovered quite suddenly that I was forgetting my own childhood. My own childhood was a thing so vivid that it certainly influenced me, that it certainly rendered me timid, incapable of self-assertion, and, as it were, perpetually conscious of original sin, until only just the other day. For you ought to consider that upon the one hand as a child I was very severely disciplined, and, when I was not being severely disciplined, I moved among somewhat distinguished people who all appeared to me to be morally and physically twenty-five feet high. The earliest thing that I can remember is this, and the odd thing is that, as I remember it, I seem to be looking at myself from outside. I see myself a very tiny child in a long, blue pinafore, looking into the breeding-box of some Barbary ring-doves that my grandmother kept in the window of the huge studio in Fitzroy Square. The window itself appears to me to be as high as a house, and I myself to be as small as a doorstep, so that I stand on tiptoe and just manage to get my eyes and nose over the edge of the box, while my long curls fall forward and tickle my nose. And then I perceive greyish and almost shapeless objects with, upon them, little speckles like the very short spines of hedgehogs, and I stand with the first surprise of my life and with the first wonder of my life. I ask myself, can these be doves — these unrecognizable, panting morsels of flesh? And then, very soon, my grandmother comes in and is angry. She tells me that if the mother dove is disturbed she will eat her young. This, I believe, is quite incorrect. Nevertheless, I know quite well that for many days afterward I thought I had destroyed life, and that I was exceedingly sinful. I never knew my grandmother to be angry again except once when she thought I had broken a comb which I had certainly not broken. I never knew her raise her voice, I hardly know how she can have expressed anger; she was by so far the most equable and gentle person I have ever known that she seemed to me to be almost not a personality but just a natural thing. Yet it was my misfortune to have from this gentle personality my first conviction — and this, my first conscious conviction, was one of great sin, of a deep criminality. Similarly with my father, who was a man of great rectitude and with strong ideas of discipline. Yet for a man of his date he must have been quite mild in his treatment of his children. In his bringing up, such was the attitude of parents toward children that it was the duty of himself and his brothers and sisters at the end of each meal to kneel down and kiss the hands of their father and mother as a token of thanks for the nourishment received. So that he was, after his lights, a mild and reasonable man to his children. Nevertheless, what I remember of him most was that he called me 'the patient but extremely stupid donkey'. And so I went through life until only just the other day with the conviction of extreme sinfulness and of extreme stupidity.

God knows that the lesson we learn from life is that our very existence in the nature of things is a perpetual harming of somebody — if only because every mouthful of food that we eat is a mouthful taken from somebody else. This lesson you will have to learn in time. But if I write this book, and if I give it to the world, it is very much that you may be spared a great many of the quite unnecessary tortures that were mine until I 'grew up'. Knowing you as I do, I imagine that you very much resemble myself in temperament, and so you may resemble myself in moral tortures. And since I cannot flatter myself that either you or I are very exceptional, it is possible that this book may be useful not only to you for whom I have written it, but to many other children in a world that is sometimes unnecessarily sad. It sums up the impressions that I have received in a quarter of a century. For the reason that I have given you — for the reason that I have now discovered myself to have 'grown up' — it seems to me that it marks the end of an epoch, the closing of a door.

As I have said, I find that my impressions of the early and rather noteworthy persons among whom my childhood was passed — that these impressions are beginning to grow a little dim. So I have tried to rescue them now, before they go out of my mind altogether. And, while trying to rescue them, I have tried to compare them with my impressions of the world as it is at the present day. As you will see when you get to the last chapter of the book, I am perfectly contented with the world of today. It is not the world of twenty-five years ago, but it is a very good world. It is not so full of the lights of individualities, but it is not so full of shadow for the obscure. For you must remember that I always considered myself to be the most obscure of obscure persons — a very small, a very sinful, a very stupid child. And for such persons the world of twenty-five years ago was rather a dismal place. You see there were in those days a number of those terrible and forbidding things — the Victorian great figures. To me life was simply not worth living because of the existence of Carlyle, of Mr Ruskin, of Mr Holman Hunt, of Mr Browning, or of the gentleman who built the Crystal Palace. These people were perpetually held up to me as standing upon unattainable heights, and at the same time I was perpetually being told that if I could not attain these heights I might just as well not cumber the earth. What then was left for me? Nothing. Simply nothing.

Now, my dear children — and I speak not only to you, but to all who have never grown up — never let yourselves be disheartened or saddened by such thoughts. Do not, that is to say, desire to be Ruskins or Carlyles. Do not desire to be great figures. It will crush in you all ambition; it will render you timid, it will foil nearly all your efforts. Nowadays we have no great figures, and I thank Heaven for it, because you and I can breathe freely. With the passing the other day of Tolstoy, with the death just a few weeks before of Mr Holman Hunt, they all went away to Olympus, where very fittingly they may dwell. And so you are freed from these burdens which so heavily and for so long hung upon the shoulders of one — and of how many others? For the heart of another is a dark forest, and I do not know how many thousands other of my fellow men and women have been so oppressed. Perhaps I was exceptionally morbid, perhaps my ideals were exceptionally high. For high ideals were always being held before me. My grandfather, as you will read, was not only perpetually giving; he was perpetually enjoining upon all others the necessity of giving never-endingly. We were to give not only all our goods, but all our thoughts, all our endeavours; we were to stand aside always to give openings for others. I do not know that I would ask you to look upon life otherwise or to adopt another standard of conduct; but still it is as well to know beforehand that such a rule of life will expose you to innumerable miseries, to efforts almost superhuman, and to innumerable betrayals — or to transactions in which you will consider yourself to have been betrayed. I do not know that I would wish you to be spared any of these unhappinesses. For the past generosities of one's life are the only milestones on that road that one can regret leaving behind. Nothing else matters very much, since they alone are one's achievement. And remember this, that when you are in any doubt, standing between what may appear right and what may appear wrong, though you cannot tell which is wrong and which is right, and may well dread the issue — act then upon the lines of your generous emotions, even though your generous emotions may at the time appear likely to lead you to disaster. So you may have a life full of regrets, which are fitting things for a man to have behind him, but so you will have with you no causes for remorse. So at least lived your ancestors and their friends, and, as I knew them, as they impressed themselves upon me, I do not think that one needed, or that one needs today, better men. They had their passions, their extravagances, their imprudences, their follies. They were sometimes unjust, violent, unthinking. But they were never cold, they were never mean. They went to shipwreck with high spirits. I could ask nothing better for you if I were inclined to trouble Providence with petitions.

F.M.H.

P.S. — Just a word to make plain the actual nature of this book: it consists of impressions. When some parts of it appeared in serial form, a distinguished critic fell foul of one of the stories that I told. My impression was and remains that I heard Thomas Carlyle tell how at Weimar he borrowed an apron from a waiter and served tea to Goethe and Schiller, who were sitting in eighteenth-century court dress beneath a tree. The distinguished critic of a distinguished paper commented upon this story, saying that Carlyle never was in Weimar, and that Schiller died when Carlyle was aged five. I did not write to this distinguished critic, because I do not like writing to the papers, but I did write to a third party. I said that a few days before that date I had been talking to a Hessian peasant, a veteran of the war of 1870. He had fought at Sedan, at Gravelotte, before Paris, and had been one of the troops that marched under the Arc de Triomphe. In 1910 I asked this veteran of 1870 what the war had been all about. He said that the Emperor of Germany, having heard that the Emperor Napoleon had invaded England and taken his mother-in-law, Queen Victoria, prisoner — that the Emperor of Germany had marched into France to rescue his distinguished connection. In my letter to my critic's friend I said that if I had related this anecdote I should not have considered it as a contribution to history, but as material illustrating the state of mind of a Hessian peasant. So with my anecdote about Carlyle. It was intended to show the state of mind of a child of seven brought into contact with a Victorian great figure. When I wrote the anecdote I was perfectly aware that Carlyle never was in Weimar while Schiller was alive, or that Schiller and Goethe would not be likely to drink tea, and that they would not have worn eighteenth-century court dress at any time when Carlyle was alive. But as a boy I had that pretty and romantic impression, and so I presented it to the world — for what it was worth. So much I communicated to the distinguished critic in question. He was kind enough to reply to my friend, the third party, that, whatever I might say, he was right and I was wrong. Carlyle was only five when Schiller died, and so on. He proceeded to comment upon my anecdote of the Hessian peasant to this effect: at the time of the Franco-Prussian War there was no emperor of Germany; the Emperor Napoleon never invaded England; he never took Victoria prisoner, and so on. He omitted to mention that there never was and never will be a modern emperor of Germany.

I suppose that this gentleman was doing what is called 'pulling my leg', for it is impossible to imagine that any one, even an English literary critic or a German professor or a mixture of the two, could be so wanting in a sense of humour — or in any sense at all. But there the matter is, and this book is a book of impressions. My impression is that there have been six thousand four hundred and seventy-two books written to give the facts about the Pre-Raphaelite movement. My impression is that I myself have written more than seventeen million wearisome and dull words as to the facts about the Pre-Raphaelite movement. These, you understand, are my impressions; probably there are not more than ninety books dealing with the subject, and I have not myself really written more than three hundred and sixty thousand words on these matters. But what I am trying to get at is that, though there have been many things written about these facts, no one has whole-heartedly and thoroughly attempted to get the atmosphere of these twenty-five years. This book, in short, is full of inaccuracies as to facts, but its accuracy as to impressions is absolute. For the facts, when you have a little time to waste, I should suggest that you go through this book, carefully noting the errors. To the one of you who succeeds in finding the largest number I will cheerfully present a copy of the ninth edition of the Encyclopaedia Britannica, so that you may still further perfect yourself in the hunting out of errors. But if one of you can discover in it any single impression that can be demonstrably proved not sincere on my part I will draw you a cheque for whatever happens to be my balance at the bank for the next ten succeeding years. This is a handsome offer, but I can afford to make it, for you will not gain a single penny in the transaction. My business in life, in short, is to attempt to discover and to try to let you see where we stand. I don't really deal in facts; I have for facts a most profound contempt. I try to give you what I see to be the spirit of an age, of a town, of a movement. This cannot be done with facts. Supposing that I am walking beside a cornfield and I hear a great rustling, and a hare jumps out. Supposing now that I am the owner of that field and I go to my farm bailiff and should say: 'There are about a million hares in that field. I wish you would keep the damned beasts down.' There would not have been a million hares in the field, and hares being soulless beasts cannot be damned, but I should have produced upon that bailiff the impression that I desired. So in this book. It is not always foggy in Bloomsbury; indeed, I happen to be writing in Bloomsbury at this moment and, though it is just before Christmas, the light of day is quite tolerable. Nevertheless, with an effrontery that will, I am sure, appal the critic of my Hessian peasant story, I say that the Pre-Raphaelite poets carried on their work amid the glooms of Bloomsbury, and this I think is a true impression. To say that on an average in the last twenty-five years there have been in Bloomsbury per three hundred and sixty-five days, ten of bright sunshine, two hundred and ninety-nine of rain, forty-two of fog, and the remainder compounded of all three, would not seriously help the impression. This fact I think you will understand, though I doubt whether my friend the critic will. F.M.H.

P.P.S. — I find that I have written these words not in Bloomsbury, but in the electoral district of East St Pancras. Perhaps it is gloomier in Bloomsbury. I will go and see.
P.P.P.S. — It is.

MUSIC AND MASTERS

When I was a very small boy indeed I was taken to a concert. In those days, as a token of my Pre-Raphaelite origin, I wore very long golden hair, a suit of greenish-yellow corduroy velveteen with gold buttons, and two stockings, of which the one was red and the other green. These garments were the curse of my young existence and the joy of every street-boy who saw me. I was taken to this concert by my father's assistant on the *Times* newspaper. Mr Rudall was the most kindly, the most charming, the most gifted, the most unfortunate — and also the most absent-minded of men. Thus, when we had arrived in our stalls — and in those days the representative of the *Times* always had the two middle front seats — when we had arrived in our stalls Mr Rudall discovered that he had omitted to put on his necktie that day. He at once went out to purchase one and, having become engrossed in the selection, he forgot all about the concert, went away to the Thatched House Club, and passed there the remainder of the evening. I was left, in the middle of the front row, all alone and feeling very tiny and deserted — the sole representative of the august organ that in those days was known as 'The Thunderer'.

Immediately in front of me, standing in the vacant space before the platform, which was all draped in red, there were three gilt arm-chairs and a gilt table. In the hall there was a great and continuing rustle of excitement. Then suddenly this became an enormous sound of applause. It volleyed and rolled round and round the immense space; I had never heard such sound, and I have never again heard such another. Then I perceived that from beneath the shadow of the passage that led into the artists' room — in the deep shadow — there had appeared a silver head, a dark-brown face, hook-nosed, smiling the enigmatic Jesuit's smile, the long locks falling backward so that the whole shape of the apparition was that of the Sphinx head. Behind this figure came two others that excited no proportionate attention, but, small as I then was, I recognized in them the late King and the present Queen Mother.

They came closer and closer to me; they stood in front of the three gilt arm-chairs; the deafening applause continued. The old man with the terrible enigmatic face made gestures of modesty. He refused, smiling all the time, to sit in one of the gilt arm-chairs. And suddenly he bowed down upon me. He stretched out his hands; he lifted me out of my seat, he sat down in it himself and left me standing, the very small, lonely child with the long golden curls, underneath all those eyes and stupefied by the immense sounds of applause.

The King sent an equerry to entreat the Master to come to his seat; the Master sat firmly planted there, smiling obstinately. Then the Queen came and took him by the hand. She pulled him — I don't know how much strength she needed — right out of his seat and — to prevent his returning to it she sat down there. After all it was *my* seat. And then, as if she realized my littleness and my loneliness, she drew me to her and sat me on her knee. It was a gracious act.

There is a passage in Pepys's *Diary* in which he records that he was present at some excavations in Westminster Abbey when they came upon the skull of Jane Seymour, and he kissed the skull on the place where once the lips had been. And in his *Diary* he records: 'It was on such and such a day of such and such a year that I did kiss a Queen,' and then, his feelings overcoming him, he repeats: 'It was on such and such a day of such and such a year that I did kiss a Queen.' I have forgotten what was the date when I sat in a Queen's lap. But I remember very well that when I came out into Piccadilly the cabmen, with their three-tiered coats, were climbing up the lamp-posts and shouting out: 'Three cheers for the Habby Liszt!' And, indeed, the magnetic personality of the Abbé Liszt was incredible in its powers of awakening enthusiasm. A few days later my father took me to call at the house where Liszt was staying — it was at the Lytteltons', I suppose. There were a number of people in the drawing-room and they were all asking Liszt to play. Liszt steadfastly refused. A few days before he had had a slight accident that had hurt one of his hands. He refused. Suddenly he turned his eyes upon me, and then, bending down, he said in my ear:

'Little boy, I will play for you, so that you will be able to tell your children's children that you have heard Liszt play.'

And he played the first movement of the 'Moonlight Sonata'. I do not remember much of his playing but I remember very well that I was looking, while Liszt played, at a stalwart, florid Englishman who is now an earl. And suddenly I perceived that tears were rolling down his cheeks. And soon all the room was in tears. It struck me as odd that people should cry because Liszt was playing the 'Moonlight Sonata'.

Ah! that wonderful personality; there was no end to the enthusiasms it aroused. I had a distant connection — oddly enough an English one — who became by marriage a lady-in-waiting at the court of Saxe-Weimar. I met her a few years ago, and she struck me as a typically English and unemotional personage. But she had always about her a disagreeable odour that persisted to the day of her death. When they came to lay her out they discovered that round her neck she wore a sachet, and in that sachet there was the half of a cigar that had been smoked by Liszt. Liszt had lunched with her and her husband thirty years before.

And ah! the records of musical enthusiasms! How dead they are and how mournful is the reading of them! How splendid it is to read how the students of Trinity College, Dublin, took the horses out of Malibran's carriage and, having amid torchlight drawn her round and round the city, they upset the carriage in the quadrangle and burnt it to show their joy. They also broke six hundred and eighty windows. The passage in the life of Malibran always reminds me of a touching sentence in Carlyle's Diary:

'Today on going out I observed that the men at the corner were more than usually drunk. And then I remembered that it was the birthday of their Redeemer.'

But what has become of all the once-glorious ones? When I was a boy at Malvern my grandfather went about in a Bath-chair because he was suffering from a bad attack of gout. Sometimes beside his chair another would be pulled along. It contained a little old lady with a faint and piping voice. That was Jenny Lind.

I wonder how many young persons of twenty-five today have ever heard the name of Jenny Lind? And this oblivion has always seemed to me unjust. But perhaps Providence is not so unjust after all. Sometimes, when I am thinking of this subject, I have a vision. I see, golden and far away, an island of the Hesperides — somewhere that side of heaven. And in this island there is such an opera-house as never was. And in this opera-house music is forever sounding forth, and all these singers are all singing together — Malibran and Jenny Lind and Schlehi, and even Carolina Bauer. And Mario stands in the wings smoking his immense cigar and waiting for his time to go on. And beside him stands Campanini. And every two minutes the conductor stops the orchestra, so that twenty bouquets, each as large as a mountain, may be handed over the footlights to each of the performers.

The manifestation of the most virtuous triumph that was ever vouchsafed me to witness occurred when I was quite a child. A *prima donna* was calling upon my father. She had been lately touring round America as one of the trainloads of *prime donne* that Colonel Mapleson was accustomed to take about with him. Mme B. was a dark and fiery lady, and she related her triumphant story somewhat as follows:

'My best part it is Dinorah — my equal in the "Shadow Song" there is not. Now what does Colonel Mapleson do but give this part of Dinorah to Mme C. Is it not a shame? Is it not a disgrace? She cannot sing, she cannot sing for nuts, and she was announced to appear in "Dinorah" for the whole of the tour. The first time she was to sing it was in Chicago, and I say to myself: "Ah! only wait, you viper, that has stolen the part for which the good God created me!" Mme C., she is a viper! I tell you so, I, Eularia B.! But I say she shall not sing in "Dinorah". You know the parrots of Mme C. Ugly beasts, they are the whole world for her. If one of them is indisposed she cannot sing — not one note. Now the grace of God comes in. On the very night when she was to sing in "Dinorah" in Chicago I passed the open door of her room in the hotel; and God sent at the same moment a waiter who was carrying a platter of ham upon which were many sprigs of parsley. So by the intercession of the blessed saints it comes into my head that parsley is death to parrots. I seize the platter from the waiter' — and Mme B.'s voice and manner became those of an august and avenging deity — 'I seize the platter, I tear from it the parsley, I rush into the room of Mme C. By the grace of God Mme C. is absent, and I throw the parsley to the ugly green fowls. They devour it with voracity, and they die; they all die. Mme C. has fits for a fortnight, and I — I sing Dinorah. I sing it like a miracle; I sing it like an angel, and Mme C. has never the face to put her nose on the stage in that part again. Never!'

This was perhaps the mildest of the stories of the epic jealousies of musicians with which my father's house re-echoed, but it is the one which remains most vividly in my mind, I suppose because of the poor parrots.

* * *

PRE-RAPHAELITES AND PRISONS

When I was a little boy there still attached something of the priestly to all the functionaries of the Fine Arts or the humaner Letters. To be a poet like Mr Swinburne or like Mr Rossetti, or even like Mr Arthur O'Shaughnessy, had about it something tremendous, something rather awful. If Mr Swinburne was in the house we children knew of it up in the nursery. A hush communicated itself to the entire establishment. The scullery maid, whose name I remember was Nelly; the cook, whose name was Sophy; the housemaid, who was probably Louie, or it may have been Lizzie, and the nurse, who was certainly Mrs Atterbury — she had seen more murders and more gory occurrences than any person I have ever since met — even the tremendous governess, who was known as Miss Hall, though that was not her name, and who had attached to her some strange romance such as that she was wooed too persistently by a foreign count with a name like Pozzo di Borgo — though that was not the name — we all of us, all the inhabitants of the back nooks and crannies of a large stucco house, fell to talking in whispers. I used to be perfectly convinced that the ceiling would fall in if I raised my voice in the very slightest. This excitement, this agitation, these tremulous undertones would become exaggerated if the visitor was the editor of the *Times*, Richard Wagner, or Robert Franz, a composer whom we were all taught especially to honour, even Richard Wagner considering him the greatest song-writer in the world. And, indeed, he was the mildest and sweetest of creatures, with a face like that of an etherealized German pastor and smelling more than any other man I ever knew of cigars. Certain other poets — though it was more marked in the case of poetesses — made their arrival known to the kitchen, the back, and the upper parts of the house by the most tremendous thunders. The thunders would reverberate, die away, roll out once more and once more die away for periods that seemed very long to the childish mind. And these reverberations would be caused, not by Apollo, the god of song, nor by any of the Nine Muses, nor yet by the clouds that surrounded, as I was then convinced, the poetic brow. They were caused by dissatisfied cabmen.

And this was very symptomatic of the day. The poet — and still more the poetess — of the seventies and eighties, though an awful, was a frail creature, who had to be carried about from place to place, and generally in a four-wheeled cab. Indeed, if my recollection of these poetesses in my very earliest days was accompanied always by thunders and expostulations, my images of them in slightly later years, when I was not so strictly confined to the nursery — my images of them were always those of somewhat elderly ladies, forbidding in aspect, with grey hair, hooked noses, flashing eyes, and continued trances of indignation against reviewers. They emerged ungracefully — for no one ever yet managed to emerge gracefully from the door of a four-wheeler — sometimes backward, from one of those creaking and dismal tabernacles and pulling behind them odd-shaped parcels. Holding the door open, with his whip in one hand, would stand the cabman. He wore an infinite number of little capes on his overcoat; a grey worsted muffler would be coiled many times round his throat, and the lower part of his face and his top hat would be of some unglossy material that I have never been able to identify. After a short interval, his hand would become extended, the flat palm displaying such coins as the poetess had laid in it. And, when the poetess with her odd bundles was three-quarters of the way up the doorsteps, the cabman, a man of the slowest and most deliberate, would be pulling the muffler down from about his mouth and exclaiming: 'Wot's this?'

The poetess, without answering, but with looks of enormous disdain, would scuffle into the house and the front door would close. Then upon the knocker the cabman would commence his thunderous symphony.

Somewhat later more four-wheelers would arrive with more poetesses. Then still more four-wheelers with elderly poets; untidy-looking young gentlemen with long hair and wide-awake hats, in attitudes of dejection and fatigue, would ascend the steps; a hansom or two would drive up containing rather smarter, stout, elderly gentlemen wearing as a rule black coats with velvet collars and most usually black gloves. These were reviewers, editors of the *Athenaeum* and of other journals. Then there would come quite smart gentlemen with an air of prosperity in their clothes and with deference somewhat resembling that of undertakers in their manners. These would be publishers.

You are to understand that what was about to proceed was the reading to this select gathering of the latest volume of poems by Mrs Clara Fletcher — that is not the name — the authoress of what was said to be a finer sequence of sonnets than those of Shakespeare. And before a large semicircle of chairs occupied by the audience that I have described, and with Mr Clara Fletcher standing obsequiously behind her to hand to her from the odd-shaped bundles of manuscripts the pages that she required, Mrs Clara Fletcher, with her regal head regally poised, having quelled the assembly with a single glance, would commence to read.

Mournfully then, up and down the stone staircases, there would flow two hollow sounds. For, in those days, it was the habit of all poets and poetesses to read aloud upon every possible occasion, and whenever they read aloud to employ an imitation of the voice invented by the late Lord Tennyson and known, in those days, as the *ore rotundo* — 'with the round mouth mouthing out their hollow o's and a's.'

The effect of this voice heard from outside a door was to a young child particularly awful. It went on and on, suggesting the muffled baying of a large hound that is permanently dissatisfied with the world. And this awful rhythm would be broken in upon from time to time by the thunders of the cabman. How the housemaid — the housemaid was certainly Charlotte Kirby — dealt with this man of wrath I never could rightly discover. Apparently the cabman would thunder upon the door. Charlotte, keeping it on the chain, would open it for about a foot. The cabman would exclaim, 'Wot's this?' and Charlotte would shut the door in his face. The cabman would remain inactive for four minutes in order to recover his breath. Then once more his stiff arm would approach the knocker and again the thunders would resound. The cabman would exclaim: 'A bob and a tanner from the Elephant and Castle to Tottenham Court Road!' and Charlotte would again close the door in his face. This would continue for perhaps half an hour. Then the cabman would drive away to meditate. Later he would return and the same scenes would be gone through. He would retire once more for more meditation and return in the company of a policeman. Then Charlotte would open the front door wide and by doing no more than ejaculating, 'My good man!' she would appear to sweep out of existence policeman, cab, cab-horse, cabman and whip, and a settled peace would descend upon the house, lulled into silence by the reverberation of the hollow o's and a's. In about five minutes' time the policeman would return and converse amiably with Charlotte for three-quarters of an hour through the area railings. I suppose that was really why the cabmen were always worsted and poetesses protected from these importunities in the dwelling over whose destinies Charlotte presided for forty years.

The function that was proceeding behind the closed doors would now seem incredible; for the poetess would read on from two to three and a half hours. At the end of this time — such was the fortitude of the artistic when Victoria was still the Widow at Windsor — an enormous high babble of applause would go up. The forty or fifty poetesses, young poets, old poets, painter-poets, reviewers, editors of *Athenaeums* and the like would divide themselves into solid bodies, each body of ten or twelve surrounding one of the three or four publishers and forcing this unfortunate man to bid against his unfortunate rivals for the privilege of publishing this immortal masterpiece. My grandfather would run from body to body, ejaculating: 'Marvellous genius!' 'First woman poet of the age!' 'Lord Tennyson himself said he was damned if he wasn't envious of the sonnet to Mehemet Ali!'

Mr Clara Fletcher would be trotting about on tiptoe fetching for the lady from whom he took his name — now exhausted and recumbent in a deep armchair — smelling bottles, sponges full of aromatic vinegar to press upon her brow, glasses of sherry, thin biscuits, and raw eggs in tumblers. As a boy I used to think vaguely that these comestibles were really nectar and ambrosia.

In the early days I was only once permitted to be present at these august ceremonies. I say I was permitted to be present, but actually I was caught and forced very much against my will to attend the rendition by my aunt, Lucy Rossetti, who, with persistence, that to me at the time appeared fiendish, insisted upon attempting to turn me into a genius too. Alas! hearing Mr Arthur O'Shaughnessy read 'Music and Moonlight' did not turn poor little me into a genius. It sent me to sleep, and I was carried from the room by Charlotte, disgraced, and destined from that time forward only to hear those hollow sounds from the other side of the door. Afterward I should see the publishers, one proudly descending the stairs, putting his cheque-book back into his overcoat pocket, and the others trying vainly to keep their heads erect under the glances of scorn that the rest of the departing company poured upon them. And Mr Clara Fletcher would be carefully folding the cheque into his waistcoat pocket, while his wife, from a large reticule, produced one more eighteenpence wrapped up in tissue-paper.

This would today seem funny — the figure of Mrs Clara Fletcher would be grotesque if it were not for the fact that, to a writer, the change that has taken place is so exceedingly tragic. For who nowadays would think of reading poetry aloud, or what publisher would come to listen? As for a cheque . . . ! Yet this glorious scene that I have described these eyes of mine once beheld.

And then there was that terrible word 'genius'. I think my grandfather, with his romantic mind, first obtruded it on my infant notice. But I am quite certain that it was my aunt, Mrs William Rossetti, who filled me with a horror of its sound that persists to this day. In school-time the children of my family were separated from their cousins, but in the holidays, which we spent as a rule during our young years in lodging-houses side by side, in places like Bournemouth or Hythe, we were delivered over to the full educational fury of our aunt. For this, no doubt, my benevolent but misguided father was responsible. He had no respect for schoolmasters, but he had the greatest possible respect for his sister-in-law. In consequence, our mornings would be taken up in listening to readings from the poets or in improving our knowledge of foreign tongues. My cousins, the Rossettis, were horrible monsters of precocity. Let me set down here with what malignity I viewed their proficiency in Latin and Greek at ages incredibly small. Thus, I believe, my cousin Olive wrote a

Greek play at the age of something like five. And they were perpetually being held up to us — or perhaps to myself alone, for my brother was always very much the sharper of the two — as marvels of genius whom I ought to thank God for merely having the opportunity to emulate. For my cousin Olive's infernal Greek play, which had to do with Theseus and the Minotaur, draped in robes of the most flimsy butter-muslin, I was drilled, a lanky boy of twelve or so, to wander round and round the back drawing-room of Endsleigh Gardens, imbecilely flapping my naked arms before an audience singularly distinguished who were seated in the front room. The scenery, which had been designed and painted by my aunt, was, I believe, extremely beautiful, and the *chinoiseries*, the fine furniture, and the fine pictures were such that, had I been allowed to sit peaceably among the audience, I might really have enjoyed the piece. But it was my unhappy fate to wander round in the garb of a captive before an audience that consisted of Pre-Raphaelite poets, ambassadors of foreign powers, editors, poets-laureate, and Heaven knows what. Such formidable beings at least did they appear to my childish imagination. From time to time the rather high voice of my father would exclaim from the gloomy depths of the auditorium, 'Speak up, Fordie!' Alas! my aptitude for that sort of sport being limited, the only words that were allotted to me were the Greek lamentation 'Theu! Theu! Theu!' and in the mean while my cousin, Arthur Rossetti, who appeared only to come up to my knee, was the hero Theseus, strode about with a large sword, slew dragons, and addressed perorations in the Tennysonian 'o' and 'a' style to the candle-lit heavens, with their distant view of Athens. Thank God, having been an adventurous youth, whose sole idea of true joy was to emulate the doings of the hero of a work called *Peck's Bad Boy and His Pa*, or at least to attain to the lesser glories of Dick Harkaway, who had a repeating rifle and a tame black jaguar, and who bathed in gore almost nightly — thank God, I say, that we succeeded in leading our unsuspecting cousins into dangerous situations from which they only emerged by breaking limbs. I seem to remember the young Rossettis as perpetually going about with fractured bones. I distinctly remember the fact that I bagged my cousin Arthur with one collar-bone, broken on a boat slide in my company, while my younger sister brought down her cousin Mary with a broken elbow, fractured in a stone hall. Olive Rossetti, I also remember with gratification, cut her head open at a party given by Miss Mary

Robinson, because she wanted to follow me down some dangerous steps and fell on to a flower-pot. Thus, if we were immolated in butter-muslin fetters and in Greek plays, we kept our own end up a little and we never got hurt. Why, I remember pushing my brother out of a second-floor window so that he fell into the area, and he didn't have even a bruise to show, while my cousins in the full glory of their genius were never really all of them together quite out of the bonesetter's hands.

My aunt gave us our bad hours with her excellent lessons, but I think we gave her hers; so let the score be called balanced. Why, I remember pouring a pot of ink from the first-story banisters on to the head of Ariadne Petrici when she was arrayed in the robes of her namesake, whose part she supported. For let it not be imagined that my aunt Rossetti foisted my cousin Arthur into the position of hero of the play through any kind of maternal jealousy. Not at all. She was just as anxious to turn me into a genius, or to turn *anybody* into a genius. It was only that she had such much better material in her own children.

Ah, that searching for genius, that reading aloud of poems, that splendid keeping alive of the tradition that a poet was a seer and a priest by the sheer virtue of his craft and mystery! Nowadays, alas! for a writer to meet with any consideration at all in the world he or she must be at least a social reformer. That began, for the aesthetic set at least, with William Morris, who first turned all poets and poetesses into long-necked creatures with red ties, or into round-shouldered maidens dressed in blue curtain serge. For, indeed, when aestheticism merged itself in social propaganda the last poor little fortress of the arts in England was divested of its gallant garrison. It might be comic that my Aunt Lucy should turn her residence into a sort of hothouse and forcing-school for geniuses; it might be comic that my grandfather should proclaim that Mrs Clara Fletcher's sonnets were finer than those of Shakespeare. It might be comic even that all the Pre-Raphaelite poets should back each other up, and all the Pre-Raphaelite painters spend hours every day in jobbing each other's masterpieces into municipal galleries. But behind it there was a feeling that the profession of the arts or the humaner letters was a priestcraft and of itself consecrated its earnest votary. Nowadays . . .

⋆ ⋆ ⋆

CHANGES

I was walking the other day down one of the stretches of main road of the west of London. Rather low houses of brownish brick recede a little way from the road behind gardens of their own, or behind little crescents common to each group of houses. Omnibuses pass numerously before them, and there is a heavy traffic of motor-vehicles, because the road leads out into the country toward the west. But since this particular day happened to be a Sunday, the stretch of road, perhaps half a mile in length, was rather empty. I could see only two horse 'buses, a brougham, and a number of cyclists. And at that moment it occurred to me to think that there were no changes here at all. There was nothing at that moment to tell me that I was not the small boy that thirty years ago used, with great regularity, to walk along that stretch of road in order to go into Kensington Gardens. It was a remarkably odd sensation. For the moment I seemed to be back there, I seemed to be a child again, rather timid and wonderingly setting out upon tremendous adventures that the exploring of London streets then seemed to entail.

And having thus dipped for a moment into a past as unattainable as is the age of Homer, I came back very sharply before the first of the horse 'buses and the fourth small band of cyclists had passed me — I came back to wondering about what changes the third of a century that I can remember had wrought in London and in us. It is sometimes pleasant, it is nearly always salutary, thus to take stock. Considering myself, it was astonishing how little I seemed to myself to have changed since I was a very little boy in a velveteen coat with gold buttons and long golden ringlets. I venture to obtrude this small piece of personality because it is a subject that has always interested me — the subject, not so much of myself, as in how far the rest of humanity seem to *themselves* to resemble me. I mean that to myself I never seemed to have grown up. This circumstance strikes me most forcibly when I go into my kitchen. I perceive saucepans, kitchen spoons, tin canisters, chopping-boards, egg-beaters, and objects whose very names I do not even know. I perceive these objects, and suddenly it comes into my mind — though I can hardly believe it — that these things actually belong to me. I can really do what I like with them if I want to. I might positively use the largest of the saucepans for making butterscotch, or I might fill the egg-beater with ink and churn it up. For such were the adventurous aspirations of my childhood when I peeped into the kitchen, which was a forbidden and glamourous place inhabited by a forbidding moral force known as *Cook*. And that glamour still persists, that feeling still remains. I do not really very often go into my kitchen, although it, and all it contains, are my property. I do not go into it because, lurking at the back of my head, I have always the feeling that I am a little boy who will be either 'spoken to' or spanked by a mysterious *They*. In my childhood *They* represented a host of clearly perceived persons: my parents, my nurse, the housemaid, the hardly ever visible cook, a dayschool master, several awful entities in blue who hung about in the streets and diminished seriously the enjoyment of life, and a large host of unnamed adults who possessed apparently remarkable and terrorizing powers. All these people were restraints. Nowadays, as far as I know, I have no restraints. No one has a right, no one has any authority, to restrain me. I can go where I like; I can do what I like; I can think, say, eat, drink, touch, break, whatever I like that is within the range of my own small empire. And yet till the other day I had constantly at the back of my mind the fear of a mysterious *They* — a feeling that has not changed in the least since the day when last I could not possibly resist it, and I threw from an upper window a large piece of whiting at the helmet of a policeman who was standing in the road below. Yesterday I felt quite a strong desire to do the same thing when a bag of flour was brought to me for my inspection because it was said to be mouldy. There was the traffic going up and down underneath my windows, there was the sun-light, and there, his buckles and his buttons shining, there positively, on the other side of the road, stalked the policeman. But I resisted the temptation. My mind travelled rapidly over the possibilities. I wondered whether I could hit the policeman at the distance, and presumed I could. I wondered whether the policeman would be able to identify the house from which the missile came, and presumed he would not. I wondered whether the servant could be trusted not to peach, and presumed she could. I considered what it would cost me, and imagined that, at the worst, the price would be something less than that of a stall at a theatre, while I desired to throw the bag of flour very much more than I have ever desired to go to a theatre. And yet, as I have said, I resisted the temptation. I was afraid of a mysterious *They*. Or, again, I could remember very distinctly as a small boy staring in at the window of a sweet-shop near Gower Street Station and perceiving that there brandy balls might be had for the price of only fourpence a pound. And I remember thinking that I had discovered the secret of perpetual happiness. With a pound of brandy balls I could be happy from one end of the day to the other. I was aware that grown-up people were sometimes unhappy, but no grown-up person I ever thought was possessed of less than fourpence a day. My doubts as to the distant future vanished altogether. I knew that whatever happened to others, I was safe. Alas! I do not think that I have tasted a brandy ball for twenty years. When I have finished my day's work I shall send out for a pound of them, though I am informed that the price has risen to sixpence. But though I cannot imagine that their possession will make me happy even for the remaining hours of this one day, yet I have not in the least changed, really. I know what will make me happy and perfectly contented when I get it — symbolically I still desire only my little pound of sweets. I have a vague, but very strong, feeling that every one else in the world around me, if the garments of formality and fashion that surround them could only be pierced through — that every one else who surrounds me equally has not grown up. They have not in essentials changed since they were small children. And the murderer who tomorrow will have the hangman's noose round his neck — I am informed at this moment that criminals are nowadays always executed on Tuesdays at eleven o'clock — so let us say that a criminal who will be executed next Tuesday at that hour will feel, when the rope is put round his throat, an odd, pained feeling that some mistake is being made, because you do not really hang a child of six in civilized countries. So that perhaps we have not any of us changed. Perhaps we are all of us children, and the very children that we were when Victoria celebrated her first jubilee at about the date when Plancus was the consul. And yet we are conscious, all of us, that we have tremendously changed since the date when Du Maurier gave us the adventures of Mr Cimabue Brown.

We have changed certainly to the extent that we cannot, by any possibility, imagine ourselves putting up for two minutes with Mr Brown at a friend's At Home. We could not possibly put up with any of these people. They had long, drooping beards; they drawled; they come back to one as being extremely gentle, and their trousers were enormous. Moreover, the women wore bustles and skin-tight jerseys. (I have a friend the top cushions of whose ottomans are entirely filled with her discarded bustles. I cannot imagine what she could have been doing with so many of these articles. After all, the fashion of wearing them did not last for ten years; and the bustle was itself a thing which, not being on view, could hardly have needed to change its shape month by month. So that, although the friend in question already possesses nine Chantecler hats and may, in consequence, be said to pay some attention to her personal appearance, I cannot imagine what she did with this considerable mass of unobtrusive adornments.)

In those days people seem to have been extraordinarily slow. It was not only that they dined at seven and went about in four-wheelers; it was not only that they still asked each other to take pot luck (I am just informed that no really modern young person any longer understands what this phrase means). It is not only that nowadays if we chance to have to remain in town in August we do not any longer pull down the front blinds, live in our kitchen, and acquire by hook or by crook a visitor's guide to Homburg, with which we could delude our friends and acquaintances on their return from Brighton into the idea that in the German spa we had rubbed shoulders with the great and noble. It is not only that our menus now soar beyond the lofty ideal of hot roast beef for Sunday, cold for Monday, hash for Tuesday, leg of mutton for Wednesday, cold on Thursday, and so on; it is that we seem altogether to have changed. It is true that we have not grown up, but we are different animals. If we should open a file of the *Times* for 1875 and find that the leader writer agreed with some of our sentiments today, we should be as much astonished as we are when we find on Egyptian monuments that the lady who set snares for the virtue of Joseph was dissatisfied with the state of her linen when it came home from the wash.

Now where exactly do these changes, as the phrase is, come in? Why should one feel such a shock of surprise at discovering that a small slice of High Street, Kensington, from the Addison Road railway bridge to the Earl's Court Road has not 'changed'? Change has crept right up to the public-house at the corner. Why, only yesterday I noticed that the pastry cook's next door to the public-house was 'to let'. This is a great and historic change. As a boy I used to gaze into its windows and perceive a model of Windsor Castle in icing-sugar. And that castle certainly appeared to me larger and more like what a real castle ought to be than did Windsor Castle, which I saw for the first time last month. I am told that at that now vanished confectioner's you could get an excellent plate of ox-tail soup and a cut off the joint for lunch. Let me then give it the alms for oblivion of this tear. Across the front of another confectioner's near here is painted the inscription, 'Routs catered for'. What was a rout? I suppose it was some sort of party, but what did you do when you got there? I remember reading a description by Albert Smith of a *conversazione* at somebody's private house, and a *conversazione* in those days was the most modern form of entertainment. Apparently it consisted in taking a lady's arm and wandering round among showcases. The host and hostess had borrowed wax models of anatomical dissections of a most realistic kind from the nearest hospital, and this formed the amusement provided for the guests, weak negus and seed biscuits being the only refreshment. This entertainment was spoken of in terms of reprobation by Mr Albert Smith — in the same terms as we might imagine would be adopted by a popular moralist in talking of the doings of the smart set today. Mr Smith considered that it constituted a lamentably wild form of dissipation and one which no lady who was really a lady ought to desire to attend.

Yes, very decidedly, we have changed all that. Though we have not grown up, though we are still children, we want something more exciting than anatomical dissections in glass cases when we are asked out of an evening. We have grown harder, we have grown more rapid in our movements, we have grown more avid of sensation, we have grown more contemptuous of public opinion, we have become the last word.

But if we are more avid of sensations, if we are restless more to witness or to possess, to go through or to throw away always a greater and greater number of feelings or events or objects, we are, I should say, less careful in our selections. The word 'exquisite' has gone almost as completely out of our vocabulary as the words 'pot luck'. And for the same reason. We are no longer expected to take pot luck, because our hostess, by means of the telephone, can always get from round the corner some sort of ready-made confection that has only to be stood for ten minutes in a *bain-marie* to form a course of an indifferent dinner. She would do that if she were mildly old-fashioned. If she were at all up to date she would just say, 'Oh, don't bother to come all this way out. Let's meet at the Dash and dine there.' In either case pot luck has gone, as has 'dropping in of an evening'. Social events in all classes are now so frequent; a pleasant, leisurely impromptu foregathering is so seldom practicable that we seldom essay it.

Dining in restaurants is in many ways gay, pleasant, and desirable. It renders us on the one hand more polite, it renders us on the other less sincere, less intimate with our friends, and less exacting. We have to be tidier and more urbane, but on the other hand we cannot so tyrannically exact of the cook that the dishes shall be impeccable. We are democratized. If in a restaurant we make a horrible noise because the fish is not absolutely all that it should be, we shall have it borne in upon us that we are only two or three out of several hundred customers, that we may go elsewhere, and that we shall not get anything better anywhere else. If the tipping system were abolished it would be impossible to get a decent meal anywhere in London.

At present it is difficult. It is difficult, that is to say, to get a good meal anywhere with certainty. You may patronize a place for a month and live well, or very well. Then suddenly something goes wrong, everything goes wrong, a whole menu is uneatable. The cook may have gone; the management, set on economizing, will have substituted margarine for real butter in cooking; the business may have become a limited company with nothing left to it but the old name and redecorated premises. And five hundred customers will not know any difference. Provided that a book has a binding with a sufficiency of gilt; provided that a dinner has its menu; provided that a picture has its frame, a book's a book, a dinner's a dinner, a picture will cover so much wall-space, and being cheapened, will find buyers enough.

[New York: Chapman and Hall, 1911: pp. vii-xvi, 70-76, 95-105, 252-61.]

from

No Enemy (1929)

Although it was published in 1929, the book was written much earlier. '*No Enemy* is in effect my reminiscences of active service under a thinly disguised veil of fiction. . . . It has, such as it is, a certain additional value because it was written during the war and the armistice by an actual ordinary combatant, part of it having been actually written in the line. So it seems to me to be of a certain documentary weight. . . . It is, I believe, regarded as the best prose I have written. . . .' (Letter to Victor Gollancz, 1 March 1932). Elsewhere Ford described the book as 'the war-reminiscences of the only British novelist of anything like, say, my age who actually took part in hostilities as an infantry officer.' (Letter to Hugh Walpole, 28 May 1930). See also letter no. 19 in this volume.

BEFORE the war Gringoire was an ordinary poet, such as you might see in Soho or in various foreign underground haunts by the baker's dozen, eating nasty meats, drinking nasty wines, usually in nasty company. How the war changed his heart is here recorded.

This is therefore a Reconstructionary Tale.

* * *

'I wonder,' then, he asked on one of these evenings, 'if my experience of landscape during the war has been that of many people.' And without waiting he continued much as follows: 'For I may say that before August, 1914, I lived more through my eyes than through any other sense, and in consequence certain corners of the earth had, singularly, the power to stir me.' But from the moment when, on the 4th of August, 1914, the Germans crossed the Belgian frontier 'near a place called Gemmenich,' aspects of the earth no longer existed for him.

The earth existed, of course. Extending to immense distances of field-grey; dimly coloured in singularly shaped masses, as if the colours on Mercator's projection had been nearly washed out by a wet brush. Stretching away, very flat, silenced, in suspense, the earth — *orbis terrarum veteribus notus* — seemed to await the oncoming legions, grey too, but with the shimmer of gold standards that should pour out from that little gap, 'near a place called Gemmenich,' and should obscure and put to shame all the green champaign lands of the world, as the green grass of meadows is put to shame and obscured by clay, water pouring through a gap in a dike. That was the earth.

There were no nooks, no little, sweet corners; there were no assured homes, countries, provinces, kingdoms, or races. All the earth held its breath and waited.

'And it is only today,' my friend went on, 'that I see again a little nook of the earth; it forms the tiniest of hidden valleys, with a little red stream that buries itself in the red earth beneath the tall green of the grass and the pink and purple haze of campions, the occasional gold of buttercups, the cream of meadowsweet. The plants in the garden wave in stiffness like a battalion on parade — the platoons of lettuce, the headquarters' staff, all sweet peas, and the colour company, which is of scarlet runners. The little old cottage is under a cliff of rock, like a gingerbread house from a Grimm's fairy tale; the silver birches and the tall pines confront it; the sunlight lies warmer than you could imagine in the hollow, and a nightingale is running in and out of the bean-stalks. Yes, a nightingale of midsummer that has abandoned the deep woodland and runs through the garden, a princess turned housekeeper, because it has young to feed. Think of noticing that!'

During the four years that the consciousness of the war lasted, he had noticed only four landscapes and birds only once — to know that he was noticing them — for themselves. Of course, one has memories of aspects of the world — but of a world that was only a background for emotions.

Even, for instance, when one saw poor Albert, by some trick of mnemonics, from the lettering of the huge word 'Estaminet' across the front of a battered house in the Place where, in the blinding sunlight, some Australian transport men were watering their mules, and one recognized it for a place one had visited twenty years before and had forgotten — even when one saw the remains of the garden where, twenty years before, we had waited whilst our lunch of omelette, cutlets, and salad was prepared, or even when one saw the immense placard with 'Caution' erected in the centre of the white rubbish and white rubble of the Place, or the desecrated statue of the Madonna, leaning in an abandoned attitude from the church tower

— even then one was so preoccupied, so shut in on one's self that these things were not objects that one looked at for themselves. They were merely landmarks. Divisional Headquarters, one had been told, was behind the N.E. corner of the Place, the notice-board was to the N.E. of one's self, therefore one must pass it to reach Divisional Headquarters. It was Headquarters one wanted, not the storing of the mind with observed aspects.

So Gringoire had four landscapes, which represent four moments in four years when, for very short intervals, the strain of the war lifted itself from the mind. They were, those intermissions of the spirit, exactly like gazing through rifts in a mist. Do you know what it is to be on a Welsh mountain side when a heavy mist comes on? Nothing remains. You are there by yourself. . . . And the only preoccupation you have with the solid, invisible world is the boulders over which you stumble and the tufts of herbage that you try to recognize as your path. Then suddenly the mist is riven perpendicularly, and for a moment you see a pallid, flat plain stretching to infinity beneath your feet and running palely to a sea horizon on a level with your eyes. There will be pale churches, pale fields, and on a ghostly channel the wraiths of scattered islands. Then it will be all gone.

* * *

'I wonder,' Gringoire asked again that evening, 'if other people had, like myself, that feeling that what one feared for was the land — not the people but the menaced earth with its familiar aspect. And I wonder why one had the feeling. I dare say it was just want of imagination: one couldn't perhaps figure the feelings of ruined, fleeing and martyred populations. And yet, when I had seen enough of those, the feeling did not alter. I remember that what struck me most in ruined Pont de Nieppe, by Armentières, was still the feeling of abashment that seemed to attach to furniture and wall-paper exposed to the sky — not the sufferings of the civilian population, who seemed to be jolly enough — or at any rate sufficiently nonchalant — with booths erected under ruined walls or in still whole cottages, selling fried fish to the tanneries. No! what struck me as infinitely pathetic was lace curtains: for there were innumerable lace curtains, that had shaded vanished windows, fluttering from all the unroofed walls in the glassless window-frames. They seemed to me to be more forlornly ashamed than any human beings I have ever seen. Only brute beasts ever approach that: old and weary horses, in nettle-grown fields; or dogs when they go away into bushes to die.'

* * *

I do not know why it is that now, when I think of Gaudier [-Brzeska], the cadence that I hear in my mind should be one of sadness. For there was never any one further from sadness than Henri Gaudier, whether in his being or in his fate. He had youth; he had grace of person and of physique; he had a sense of the comic. He had friendships, associates in his work, loves, the hardships that help youth. He had genius, and he died a hero.

He comes back to me best as he was at a function of which I remember most, except for Gaudier, disagreeable sensations — embarrassments. It was an 'affair' — one of two — financed by a disagreeably obese Neutral whom I much disliked. That would be in late July, 1914. The Neutral was much concerned to get out of a country and a city which appeared to be in danger. Some one else — several some ones — were intensely anxious, each of them, to get money out of the very fat, very monied, disagreeably intelligent being. And I was ordered, by *Les Jeunes*, to be there. It was a parade, in fact. I suppose that even then I was regarded as a, I hope benevolent, grandfather, by a number of members of an advanced school.[1] Anyhow, that comes back to me as a disagreeable occasion of evil passions, evil people, of bad, flashy cooking in an underground haunt of pre-war smartness.

I daresay it was not really as bad as all that — but when I am forced to receive the hospitality of persons whom I dislike, the food seems to go bad, and there is a bad taste in the mouth, symbol of a disturbed liver. So the band played in that cave and the head ached and there were nasty foreign waiters and bad, very expensive, champagne.

There were also speeches — and one could not help knowing that the speeches were directed at the Neutral's breeches pockets. The Neutral leaned heavily sideways at table, devouring the bad food at once with gluttony and nonchalance. It talked about its motor car, which apparently was at Liverpool or Southampton — somewhere

[1] For the benefit of the uninstructed reader, I may say that new Schools of Art, like new commercial enterprises, need both backers with purses and backers of a certain solid personal appearance or weight in the world. And it is sometimes disagreeable, though it is always a duty, to be such an individual.

where there were liners, quays, cordage, cranes; all ready to abandon a city which would be doomed should Armageddon become Armageddon. The speeches went on. . . .

Then Gaudier rose. It was suddenly like a silence that intervened during a distressing and ceaseless noise. I don't know that I had ever noticed him before except as one amongst a crowd of dirtyish, bearded, slouch-hatted individuals, like conspirators; but, there, he seemed as if he stood amidst sunlight; as if indeed he floated in a ray of sunlight, like the dove in Early Italian pictures. In a life during which I have known thousands of people; thousands and thousands of people; during which I have grown sick and tired of 'people' so that I prefer the society of cabbages, goats and the flowers of the marrow plant; I have never otherwise known what it was to witness an appearance which symbolized so completely — aloofness. It was like the appearance of Apollo at a creditors' meeting. It was supernatural.

It was just that. One didn't rub one's eyes: one was too astounded. Only, something within one wondered what the devil he was doing there. If he hadn't seemed so extraordinarily efficient, one would have thought he had strayed, from another age, from another world, from some Hesperides. One keeps wanting to say that he was Greek, but he wasn't. He wasn't of a type that strayed: and indeed I seem to feel his poor bones moving in the August dust of Neuville St Vaast when I — though even only nearly! — apply to him a name that he would have hated. At any rate, it was amazing to see him there; since he seemed so entirely inspired by inward visions that one wondered what he could be after — certainly not the bad dinner, the attentions of the foreign waiters, a try at the Neutral's money-bag strings. No, he spoke as if his eyes were fixed on a point within himself; and yet, with such humour and such good-humour — as if he found the whole thing so comic!

One is glad of the comic in his career; it would otherwise have been too much an incident of the Elgin marble type. But even the heroism of his first, abortive 'joining up' was heroico-comic. As I heard him tell the story, or at least as I remember it, it was like this:

He had gone to France in the early days of the war — and one accepted his having gone as one accepted the closing of a door — of a tomb, if you like. Then, suddenly, he was once more there. It produced a queer effect; it was a little bewildering in a bewildering world. But it became comic. He had gone to Boulogne and presented himself to the Recruiting Officer — an N.C.O., or captain, of the old school, white moustachios, *cheveux en brosse*. Gaudier stated that he had left France without having performed his military duties, but, since *la patrie* was in danger, he had returned like any other good little *piou-piou*. But the sergeant, martinet-wise, as became a veteran of 1870, struck the table with his fist and exclaimed:

'*Non, mon ami*, it is not *la patrie*, but you who are in danger. You are a deserter; you will be shot.' So Gaudier was conducted to a motor, in which, under the military escort of two files of men, a sergeant, a corporal, and a lieutenant, he was whirled off to Calais. In Calais Town he was placed in an empty room. Outside the door were stationed two men with large guns, and Gaudier was told that, if he opened the door, the guns would go off. That was his phrase. He did not open the door. He spent several hours reflecting that though they manage these things better in France, they don't manage them so damn well. At the end of that time he pushed aside the window blind and looked out. The room was on the ground floor; there were no bars. Gaudier opened the window; stepped into the street, just like that — and walked back to Boulogne.

He returned to London.

He was drawn back again to France by the opening of the bombardment of Rheims Cathedral. This time he had a safe conduct from the Embassy. I do not know the date of his second joining up or the number of his regiment. At any rate, he took part in an attack on a Prussian outpost on Michaelmas Eve, so he had not much delayed, and his regiment was rendered illustrious, though it cannot have given him a deuce of a lot of training. He did not need it. He was as hard as nails and as intelligent as the devil. He was used to forging and grinding his own chisels. He was inured to the hardships of poverty in great cities; he was accustomed to hammer and chisel at his marble for hours and hours of day after day. He was a 'fit' townsman — and it was 'fit' townsmen who conducted the fighting of 1914 when the war was won: it was *les parigots*.

Of his biography I have always had only the haziest of notions. I know that he was the son of a Meridional craftsman, a carpenter and joiner, who was a good workman and no man could have a better. His father was called Joseph Gaudier — so why he called himself B'jesker, I do not know. I prefer really to be hazy; because Gaudier will always remain for me something supernatural. He was for me a 'message' at a difficult time of life. His death and the death at the same time of another boy — but quite a commonplace, nice boy — made a rather doubtful way quite plain to me.

All my life I have been very much influenced by a Chinese proverb — to the effect that it would be hypocrisy to seek for the person of the Sacred Emperor in a low teahouse. It is a bad proverb, because it is so wise and so enervating. It has 'ruined my career'.

When, for instance, I founded a certain Review, losing, for me, immense sums of money on it, or when the contributors unanimously proclaimed that I had not paid them for their contributions — which was not true because they certainly had among them a quantity of my money in their pockets — or when a suffrage bill failed to pass in the Commons; or when some one's really good book has not been well reviewed; or when I have been robbed, slandered, or abortively blackmailed — in all the vicissitudes of life, misquoted on it, I have always first shrugged my shoulders and murmured that it would be hypocrisy to seek for the person of the Sacred Emperor in a low tea-shop. It meant that it would be hypocrisy to expect a taste for the finer letters in a large public's discernment in critics; honesty in aesthetes or literati; public spirit in lawgivers; accuracy in pundits; gratitude in those one has saved from beggary, and so on.

So, when I first noticed Henri Gaudier — which was in an underground restaurant, the worst type of thieves' kitchen — these words rose to my lips. I did not, you understand, believe that he would exist and be so wise, so old, so gentle, so humorous, such a genius. I did not really believe that he had shaved, washed, assumed garments that fitted his great personal beauty.

For he had great personal beauty. If you looked at him casually, you imagined that you were looking at one of those dock-rats of the Marseilles quays, who will carry your baggage for you, pimp for you; garotte you and throw your body overboard — but who will do it all with an air, and ease, an exquisiteness of manners! They have, you see, the traditions and inherited knowledge of such ancient nations in Marseilles — of Etruscans, Phoenicians, Colonial Greeks, Late Romans, Troubadours, Late French — and that of those who first sang the Marseillaise! And many of them, whilst they are young, have the amazing beauty that Gaudier had. Later, absinthe spoils it — but for the time, they are like Arlésiennes.

All those wisdoms, then, looked out of the eyes of Gaudier — and God only knows to what he threw back — to Etruscans or

Phoenicians, no doubt, certainly not to the Greeks who colonized Marseilles, or the Late Romans who succeeded to them. He seemed, then, to have those wisdoms behind his eyes somewhere. And he had, certainly, an astounding erudition.

I don't know where he picked it up — but his conversation was overwhelming — and his little history of sculpture by itself will give you more flashes of inspiration than you will ever, otherwise, gather from the whole of your life. His sculpture itself affected me just as he did.

In odd places — the sitting-rooms of untidy and eccentric poets with no particular merits, in appalling exhibitions, in nasty night clubs, in dirty restaurants one would be stopped for a moment in the course of a sentence by the glimpse of a brutal chunk of rock that seemed to have lately fallen unwanted from a slate quarry, or, in the alternative, by a little piece of marble that seemed to have the tightened softness of the haunches of a fawn — of some young creature of the underwoods, an ancient, shyly-peopled, thicket.

The brutalities would be the work of Mr Epstein — the other, Gaudier. For Gaudier's work had just his own, personal, impossible quality. And one did not pay much attention to it simply because one did not believe in it. It was too good to be true. Remembering the extraordinary rush that the season of 1914 was, it appears a miserable tragedy, but it is not astonishing, that one's subliminal mind should whisper to me, every time we caught that glimpse of a line: 'It is hypocrisy to search for the person of the Sacred Emperor in a low tea-house.' It was of course the devil who whispered that. So I never got the sensation I might have got from that line. Because one did not believe in that line. One thought: 'It is just the angle at which one's chair in the restaurant presents to one an accidental surface of one of these young men's backs.'

And then a day came when there was no doubt about it. Gaudier was a Lance Corporal in the 4th Section, 7th Company, 129th Regt. of Infantry of the Line.[1] Gaudier was given his three stripes for 'gallantry in face of the enemy'. One read in a letter: 'I am at rest for

[1] The knowledgeable reader will observe that here Gringoire has consulted the monograph on Gaudier by Mr Pound — the best piece of craftsmanship that Mr Pound has put together; or at least the best this writer has read of that author's.

three weeks in a village, that is, I am undergoing a course of study to be promoted officer when necessary during an offensive.'

Or in another letter:

'I imagine a dull dawn, two lines of trenches, and in between explosion on explosion with clouds of black and yellow smoke, a ceaseless noise from the rifles, a few legs and heads flying, and me standing up among all this like to Mephisto —commanding: "*Feu par salves à 250 mètres — joue — feu!*"

Today is magnificent, a fresh wind, clear sun, and larks singing cheerfully. . . .'

That was it!

But just because it was so commonplace; so sordid, so within the scope of all our experiences, powers of observation, and recording, it all seemed impossible to believe that in *that* particular low tea-house there were really Youth, Beauty, Erudition, Fortune, Genius — to believe in the existence of a Gaudier! The devil still whispered to me: 'That would be hypocrisy!' For if you would not believe that genius could show itself during the season of 1914, how *could* you believe that, of itself, inscrutable, noiseless, it would go out of our discreditable world where the literati and the aesthetes were sweating, harder than they ever, ever did after *le mot juste* or the Line of Beauty, to find excuses that should keep them from the trenches — that, so quietly, the greatest genius of them all would go into that world of misery.

And then I read:

'*Mort pour la patrie*.

After ten months of fighting and two promotions for gallantry, on the field, Henri Gaudier-Brzeska, in a charge at Neuville St Vaast. June 5, 1915.'

Alas, when it was too late, I had learned that, to this low tea-shop that the world is, from time to time the Sacred Emperor may pay visits. So I began to want to kill certain people. I still do — for the sake of Gaudier and those few who are like him.

For the effect of reading that announcement was to make me remember with extraordinary vividness a whole crowd of the outlines of pieces of marble, of drawings, of tense and delicate lines at which, in the low tea-house of the year before's season, I had only nonchalantly glanced. The Sacred Emperor, then, had been there. He seemed, at last, to be an extraordinarily real figure — as real as one of the other sculptor's brutal chunks of granite. Only, because of the crowd one hadn't seen him — the crowd of blackmailers,[1] sneak-thieves, suborners, pimps, reviewers, and the commonplace and the indifferent — the Huns of London. Well, it became — and it still more remains one's duty to try to kill them. There are probably several Sacred Emperors still at large — though the best of them will have been killed, as Gaudier was.

★ ★ ★

I don't know how it is: but from the moment when I first saw that highlight — and it had been certainly three hours before — I had been perfectly sure that that was what it was — the forehead of a quiet woman bending her head forward to have more light from the high window whilst she sewed in the dusk. In a way it was not what one expected: the town had been evacuated of its civilian population the Sunday before, when the Huns — as it seemed, for the love of God — started shelling the church just as it had emptied after benediction. And they had shelled from six o'clock till midnight; and every night since then, from six o'clock till midnight they had shelled the church. And they were shelling it now — eighty yards away. It was a desolate, and it seemed a stupid business. But no doubt they had their purpose, though it was difficult to see what it was.

That was how Rosalie Prudent put it, as she sat sewing my wristbands by the stove, in the wash-house. I sat nearer the stove, naked to the waist, the red glow and the warmth that came from the red-hot iron of the circular furnace being, I can tell you, very agreeable to my shivering skin. Opposite me sat the orderly drinking a bottle of Burgundy — which he had richly deserved. The steam went up from his wet clothes and was tinged red by the light of the coke. . . .

In the extremely clean *salle-à-manger*, with a high faïence stove of

[1] Gringoire is too fond of this word — which he uses in a special sense to indicate persons — mostly reviewers — who do not appreciate the work of himself and his school. In his conversation he introduced at this point a long denunciation of the — Literary Supplement, principally because, whilst purporting to be a literary paper, it devotes, according to him, 112/113ths of its space to books about facts, at the expense of works of the imagination. So he calls that respectable journal a blackmailing organ. Since, however, this is a topic that can hardly interest the non-literary, and since the literary are hardly likely to read these pages, the compiler has taken the liberty of not reporting these sallies. It may be true that Pontius Pilate is more criminal than the crucified thieves — but it is *never* politic to say so.

blue and white tiles, a colza lamp with a white globe, a buffet in the Nouvel Art style, of yellow Austrian oak with brass insertions; at a yellow oak table covered with a green velvet table-cover fringed with lace, sat my friend the Sinn Feiner learning the French that is spoken in Plugstreet from the niece, Beatrice Prudent. She was teaching him French by selling him handkerchiefs edged with lace in whose corners she had embroidered multicoloured initials. In two very clean, lavender-papered bedrooms, upstairs, with white bedsteads, strips of carpet beside them on the waxed floors, with valises opened and showing works of devotion, altar vases, empty biscuit tins containing unconsecrated wafers of the sacrament, trench boots, gas helmets, tin hats — sat two padres composing their sermons for the next day. The Roman Catholic — for I heard him preach on it next day — was meditating on the doctrine of the Immaculate Conception. I don't know what the Presbyterian was writing about.

But there the house was, large, quiet but for the shells, kept spotless by the labours of Rosalie and her niece Beatrice, and, as yet untouched — just as it had been evacuated by the factory manager and his family, who had fled on the Sunday after benediction. In one of the roomy, very tall parlours there was, over the fireplace, a gigantic figure of the Saviour, standing in robes of blue, white, and scarlet plaster of paris, holding on his left arm a great sheaf of white lilies and resting one hand on the head of a very thin plaster sheep of, I should think, a Rhineland breed. That was perhaps why the owner of the house had not trusted to its miraculous intervention in favour of his dwelling. He might have — for I heard the other day that the house remained intact until the 11/11/18.

Rosalie profited — for, when the French inhabitants fled, the British authorities allowed Belgian refugees to take their places on condition that they billeted the troops. So perhaps it had been to protect her that the immense Bon Dieu waited! She deserved it.

She came from Plugstreet, of which town she had been one of the richest bourgeoises, her husband being the miller. She had had a large, roomy house, a great yard with stables and carts; she had had a wealthy, goodish, but possibly too jovial husband, two affectionate, dutiful, and industrious sons, and two obedient daughters. On Sundays she had gone to mass wearing a black satin gown, and, on her breast, a gold-framed cameo as large as a saucer. It represented a very classical Paris, seated, I don't know why, apparently between the horns of a lyre and stretching out one hand — which no doubt contained an apple — toward three grouped Goddesses in rather respectable Flemish *déshabillé*. Mme Prudent retained this work of art, but her wardrobe was reduced to two blue cotton dresses.

I gathered all this, whilst I dozed by the black iron stove, from her conversation with the orderly. She spoke Flemish, and he, Wiltshire, but they understood each other. Of course, they used signs and facial expressions. The flames through the interstices of the stove poured upward to the dim rafters of the washhouse roof, and, by its light, Mme Rosalie sewed as if she had no other pride and no other purpose in the world. For she told of the fate of her men and her womenfolk abstactedly and passionlessly; pride only showed itself when she talked of the state of the house in which she had found a refuge. From time to time she would say that if Mm. the Proprietors returned, they would find the floors waxed; the stair-rods shining, the windows polished; woodruff and sweet herbs amongst the bed linen in the presses, and not a speck of dust on the plaster-robes of the great Bon Dieu in the *salon de réception*. That was her pride. . . .

As for the rest . . . On the 18th of August, 1914, her man had been killed in the Belgian Reserve somewhere near Liège; on the 20th of the same month her eldest son had been killed in the Belgian regiment of the Guides. He had expected to have an excellent career in the office of an *avocat* — in Bruges, I think. On the 8th of November, 1914, her remaining son had been killed in the 76th French Regiment of Infantry of the Line. He had been chief clerk to an architect of Paris. Her daughters had been, one apprentice and the other chief saleswoman of a celebrated *couturière* of Liège. She had heard of them once since the Germans had entered the city. A Belgian priest had written to her from the Isle of Wight in December, 1914, to say that some nuns had taken in Aimée and Félicité. Those were the names of her two daughters. . . .

And at the moment she started up. She remembered that she had forgotten the potatoes for Monsieur — Monsieur being myself. So out she went into the black garden and returned with a tin platter of potatoes.

On it were ten tubers of which she weighed each in her hand inscribing what they came to on a slate — so that she might account to Messieurs the owners, on their return, for the potatoes that she had dug from the garden. Then she called her niece from the dining room to wash and slice the potatoes. She was going to give me an omelette with bacon and fried potatoes for my supper. She sat down again and went on, sewing and talking to the orderly.

She began talking of the interior of her house in Plugstreet; she described minutely all the furniture in all the apartments. In each of the bedrooms there was a night commode in mahogany and a statue of the Virgin, also one of the Blessed Saints, and a *prie-dieu*, also in mahogany. . . . And now there was nothing. Every fortnight she was permitted by the British military police to visit her house — and she stayed there, in Nieppe, so that every fortnight she might revisit her house — which now, she said, contained nothing. The shells were shaking it to pieces. The tiles were all gone; the rain was soaking into the upper floors. The furniture was all gone — the great presses with her linen, the wardrobes — *en acajou* — which had contained her black satin dress and her husband's Sunday clothes. . . .

But she continued to catalogue to the orderly the contents of her residence. I don't know why it should interest him, but it did; for he nodded sagely when she talked of the *bahûts en bois de chêne*, and the immortels in vases on the piano. . . .

Suddenly she turned her head to me and said to me, where I sat writing with my tablet on my knee:

'And I ask you, *M. l'officier*, for what purpose is it that one brings men children into the world if this is to be the end? They cause great pain in their entry, greater than at the entry of little girl children. It is difficult to keep them alive so that they reach men's estate. And then it is difficult to keep them in the paths of virtue. And then they are gone.'

[New York: Macaulay, 1929: pp. 18, 21–4, 26–7, 204–17, 250–57.]

from

Return to Yesterday (1931)

Written ten years after *Ancient Lights*, *Return to Yesterday* takes up where the earlier book leaves off and covers the period from 1894 to the outbreak of World War 1. In the chapter represented here, 'Farthest Left', Ford writes from his first-hand acquaintance with many of the anarchists in London he had met through David Soskice, a Russian émigré who had married his sister, Juliet.

To Dr Michael & Mrs Eileen Hall Lake

MY DEARS, —

It was whilst looking up at the criss-cross of beams in the roof of your tall studio that the form of this book was thought out. Micky had admirably bandaged up my unfortunate foot and you had given up that room to me and there I lay looking up and thinking of Henry James who had been born only a few yards away. So, as I go through these pages I seem to see that criss-cross in your gracious old house and the literary form of the work is inextricably mingled with those Cubist intricacies.

You will say that volumes of memories have no forms and that this collection of them is only a rag-bag. It isn't really. The true artfulness of art is to appear as if in disordered habiliments. Life meanders, jumps back and forwards, draws netted patterns like those on the musk melon. It seems the most formless of things. One may know that one has lived a life of sturt and strife and will probably die by treachery in the approved Border fashion. But if one is to set down one's life — for which there is only one excuse — one should so present the pattern of it that, insensibly, it in turn, presents itself to your awareness.

The excuse for setting down one's life on paper — the only excuse — is that one should give a picture of one's time. I believe that hardly anyone — and certainly not I — so lives that his personal adventures whether on the high seas or in criticism can be well worth relating. But certain restless spirits roll, as the saying is, their humps into noteworthy cities or into the presence of human notables. So, if one can keep oneself out of it, one may present a picture of a sort of world and time.

I have tried to keep myself out of this work as much as I could — but try as hard as one may after self-effacement the great 'I', like cheerfulness will come creeping in. Renan says that as soon as one writes about oneself one poetises a little. I don't think I do. On the other hand, being a novelist, it is possible that I romance. For about as long as the lives of the two of you young and gallant things together I have gone about the world looking for the person of the Sacred Emperor in low tea-shops — or in such lofty places as your studio. I have seen some Emperors — and not a few pretenders. These and the tea-shops of the Chinese proverb I have tried to make you see. If you sometimes see my coat-tails whisking round the corners you must pardon it. My true intent is only for your delight. Had I the cap of Fortunatus you should not see even so much of me or my garments. The Chinese proverb I have mentioned says that it is hypocrisy to seek for the person of the Sacred Emperor in a low tea-shop; they are cynics those fellows — or pessimists. There is really no other pursuit in life. Our geese *must* be swans.

So this is a novel: a story mirroring such pursuits. If that pursuit is indeed hypocrisy that is the only hypocrisy in this book — but this book is all that homage paid to virtue by one who errs. Where it has seemed expedient to me I have altered episodes that I have witnessed but I have been careful never to distort the character of the episode. The accuracies I deal in are the accuracies of my impressions. If you want factual accuracies you must go to. . . . But no, no, don't go to anyone, stay with me!

I don't know how much of my writing you have read. It is probably little enough; you have better things to do and be. But it is certainly more than I shall ever read of my own. I am one with the struggling millions who cannot read me. So, if you have read me at all, you may here find things I have written before. Please don't mind that. Often enough it is unconscious: at my age one does repeat oneself and, since I possess practically none of my own books I cannot refer to them to see what I have written before and I should not have the patience to read them if I had them. But in a number of cases I have done it advisedly to keep the thread of the novel together. Thus one chapter is reprinted from a long forgotten book of mine that was never published in America and part of another is reprinted from a book that was never published in either England or the United States.[1] If I could have rewritten these chapters better I would have done so. As I did not think I could I have let them stand as they were. In certain cases I have here modified details of stories that I know I have told before. That is because in their original form I had to deviate from factual exactitude because I was afraid of hurting feelings. The versions here printed are nearer what actually happened.

So, humbly, gratefully and affectionately, I subscribe myself your mirror to my times. This was begun to the tune of the agreeable noises of West 12th Street and to the taste of the admirable Caribbean confections of your Antiguan *cordon brun*. It finishes to the rhythm of the sirocco in the ears of sweet corn that I can see agitated in front of the Mediterranean azure. When I have written my name hereunder I shall grill myself an ear or two for my supper. That is pleasure enough. But if the South Wind would change to the West it might over the Atlantic bring you two sailing. That surely would be the proudest sight this poor old mirror has now to reflect and — whatever may be the case with tea-shops — I should surely against the sea of Ulysses see on my terraces sacred and Imperial Personages.

F.M.F.

Cap Brun
14th July, 1931.

The world in turning towards universal industrialism was undergoing immense growing pains. The distress which goes with developments, as with stagnations of trade is accompanied by widespread and atrocious suffering. The hideousness of the poverty in the early nineties the world over would now be incredible were it not that some of them are only too visible today. And it is not merely that hunger, cold and squalour beset the actually destitute. It was the terrible anxiety that for ever harassed the minds of those who were just above the starvation line. You were in work one day; you were out the next. Thus even whilst you were in work you had no rest at the thought of the morrow. Worklessness meant the gradual disintegration of your home, the wearing out of the shoes of your children, if your children had shoes; it meant thus slow starvation,

[1] Ford is referring here to *Women and Men* (see p. 330) and to the unpublished *A History of Our Own Times*. — Ed.

your moral decay, your slowly sinking away from all the light. I remember Charles Booth saying fiercely in 1892: 'Do you realize that there are now in London 250,000 people — and in Lancashire God knows how many — who in this December weather have no fire in the grate, no meal on the table, no stick of furniture on the floor, no door in the doorway, no handrails to the stairs and no candle to go to bed by?' Mr Booth was a great shipowner but he was also a statistician. His statistics affected him at that time almost to madness.

If that could happen to a very rich man with great powers of alleviating suffering, what would take place in the minds of those who, just not starving themselves, lived as if buried beneath the foodless, the unclothed, the unwarmed, who dwelt in darkness? And it is to be remembered that if things were that bad in London they were infinitely worse in every other country in the world. It was a day of nightmares universal and showing no signs of coming to an end. Nothing could happen but what did — a world-wide flood of disorder ending in Anarchism. That was inevitable.

The state of affairs in some of the Continental cities was incredible. I remember Paris in 1892 as being absolutely paralysed. I was stopping with American relatives who belonged to the rich Anglo-American Catholic circle that solidly ornamented in those days the French capital. That colony and the rich and solid French families with whom they mingled and intermarried lived again as if in the days of the siege. They dared not go to theatres, to restaurants, to the fashionable shops in the rue de la Paix, to ride in the Bois where there were Anarchists behind every tree. The most terrible rumours ran round every morning: the Anarchists had undermined the churches of Paris; they had been caught pouring prussic acid into the city reservoirs; the New York *Herald* came out one day with a terrifying story of Anarchists having been hidden beneath the seats of the tiny black and yellow fiacres and coming out and robbing and murdering rich American ladies in the Champs Elysées.

The Anarchists did not of course hide beneath the seats of fiacres because those little vehicles had no spaces beneath their seats. The axles of the wheels were there. Nevertheless today the catalogue of their outrages reads like an improbable nightmare. They bombed the cafés where the rich took their *apéritifs* and the more costly restaurants; then they bombed poor restaurants where their comrades had been arrested; they bombed theatres, railway stations, the

Chamber of Deputies, the President of the Republic himself. Merely to consider how they could have done it in the face of the most skilful and remorseless police force in the world is an amazing speculation.

'Paris,' says a contemporary journalist, Fernand Evrard, writing in 1892, 'offers the spectacle of a besieged city: the streets are deserted, the shops closed, the omnibuses without passengers, the museums and the theatres barricaded. The police are invisible but ubiquitous; the troops assembled in the suburbs are ready to march at the first command. The rich foreign families take flight, the hotels are empty, the takings of shops dwindle. After some weeks of relative quiet the populace takes hope again and the red sequence seems at an end. Then the terrible bomb in the police station of the rue des Bons Enfants, followed immediately by the discovery of the dynamite cartridge in the Prefecture of Police causes new panic and despair. . . . There is cholera in the outskirts of the city, the Panama scandal within the walls . . . one hundred and four deputies are suspected of complicity. The year 1892 may well bear on its brow the words "Death to Society", and "Corruption to Politics".'

The passion that inspired these paralysers of a whole society was probably nothing else but pity. Ravachol, who committed the outrage in the rue de Clichy, was arrested because he could not restrain himself from saying to a waiter in a *bistrôt*: 'How can you call that an outrage when there is so much suffering in the world?' The queerly paradoxical and reckless speech might well stand for the philosophical basis of the whole movement, more especially when you consider that neither Ravachol nor Vaillant nor yet the assassin of President Carnot had suffered much themselves from poverty. And indeed the relative prosperity of England and possibly the more considerable voice that the poorer classes had in the government of the country may have been as much accountable for the absence of Anarchist activities in London as the fact that, the police letting them alone, the Anarchists were determined not to close to themselves their only safe refuge.

Kropotkin's was the only name of the movement that is likely to remain in the annals of those times. A prince and officer of the Imperial body-guard he was in addition a very distinguished scientist. His investigations led him irresistibly towards the frame of mind that is called non-resistance and he was one of the most determined opponents of the theory of evolution as one upholding conquests. Eventually, like Tolstoy and so many of the Russian aristocracy, he abandoned his career and his vast properties and lived the life of a poor man among the poor.

From that to the bombing of the commissariat in the rue des Bons Enfants may well seem a far cry but the workings of the human mind are always mysterious and when they take place under conditions of great stress there is no saying whither they may not tend. Kropotkin's great sympathy for the very poor and the very oppressed made him seek their company and they his. That he never counselled violence or excused it when it had taken place is certain enough, but the essence of his philosophy being that laws by their very existence incite to crime, it was not a great progression for a hunger-weakened brain to imagine that the destruction of those who benefit by or enforce laws will bring about a reign of peace upon earth.

I will not undertake to say that I ever heard him deprecating violence to Ravachol or Vaillant, though I certainly was in the same room with Vaillant if not with Ravachol on more than one occasion at a Socialist club, but I do remember Kropotkin speaking with great emphasis against physical force and even against revolution brought about by violence, the occasion coming back to me very vividly.

It was during the great coal strike of 1893 and Charles Rowley had invited me to dine with some other labour leaders with the idea of converting me to advanced opinions, such as they were in those days. The meal took place in the Holborn Restaurant, a haunt of everything that was middle-class and Free Masonic. There were present Mr Ben Tillet, Mr Tom Mann, Charles Rowley, the Manchester Socialist, and Prince Kropotkin, and since the restaurant was so very middle-class the presence of those notorious promoters of disorder created a sufficient agitation so that the management tucked us away in a quiet alcove where the waiters hovered about us with scared faces.

As long as the discussion remained on general lines of the relief of suffering or even of strikes these leaders of advanced thought got on very well together, and that stage lasted for the greater part of the meal. But the moment it came to the discussion of remedies Kropotkin's quietism acted like a bomb at the table, the Labour representatives being all for strong measures against authority. Kropotkin was all for non-resistance, meditation and propaganda so that eventually we broke up in disorder after a deadlock in which Mr Mann, who was dark and of Celtic animation with an immense harsh voice, had gone on for a long time striking the palms of his left hand with the clenched fist of his right and exclaiming over and over again, 'We must destroy! We must pull down! We must be rid of tyrants!'

Mr Tillet, little, blond and virulent, echoing in a soft but even more destructive voice:

'Yes, we must tear down! We must make a clear space!' And Charles Rowley with his red beard and Lancashire brogue, trying uselessly to quiet the noises. But always in the pauses came the quiet, foreign accent of the Prince, who, with the eyes of a German scientist behind his gleaming spectacles fixed intently on his interlocutors, exclaimed gently and unceasingly:

'No, there must be no destruction. We must build. We must build the hearts of men. We must establish a kingdom of God.'

That seemed to drive the others mad.

When the party broke up, I stood for a long time with the Prince under the portico of the restaurant whilst the rain poured down. He asked me what I was doing and I told him that I was just publishing a fairy tale. He said that that was an admirable sort of thing to do. Then he said that he hoped the fairy tale was not about Princes and Princesses — or at least that I would write one that would be about simple and ordinary people. I have been trying to do so ever since. Indeed I tried to do so at once with the singular result that although my first invention had a great — indeed a prodigious — sale I could not even find a publisher for the second. My subsequent difficulties have been technical. I always want to write about ordinary people. But it seems to be almost impossible to decide who are ordinary people — and then to meet them. All men's lives and characteristics are so singular.

I do not think I saw much of Kropotkin after that in political gatherings though I must have seen him once at the office of *The Torch* in Goodge Street. But I did not much frequent that establishment. Until my aunt's death, the Rossettis' house being her property, my juvenile relatives carried on their activities at home. Why my aunt permitted them to run in her basement a printing press that produced militant Anarchist propaganda I never quite knew. She no doubt would have approved of any activities of her children, so long as they were active in a spirited and precocious way. But I imagine she would have preferred their energies to continue to be devoted to the productions of the Greek plays which caused me so much suffering. In any case the world was presented with the extraordinary spectacle of the abode of Her Majesty's Secretary to the Inland Revenue, so beset with English detectives, French police spies and Russian *agents provocateurs* that to go along the sidewalk of that respectable terrace was to feel that one ran the gauntlet of innumerable gimlets. That came to an end.

My uncle William was a man of the strongest — if slightly eccentric — ethical rectitude and, as soon as my aunt was dead and the house become his property, he descended into its basement and ordered the press and all its belongings to be removed from his house. He said that although his views of the duties of parenthood did not allow of his coercing his children, his sense of the fitness of things would not permit him to sanction the printing of subversive literature in the basement of a prominent servant of the Crown. *The Torch* then had to go.

It removed itself to Goodge Street, Tottenham Court Road — a locality as grim as its name. There it became a sort of club where hangers-on of the extreme Left idled away an immense amount of time whilst their infant hosts and hostesses were extremely active over their forms. I did not myself like it much and only went there I think twice — to see about the printing of my first poem. This was not very Anarchist in coloration. It ran:

'Oh, where shall I find rest?'
Wailed the wind from the West,
'I've sought in vain on dale and down,
In tangled woodland, tarn and town
But found no rest.'

'Rest thou ne'er shalt find,'
Answered Love to the wind.
'For thou and I and the great, grey sea
May never rest till Eternity
Its end shall find.'

It seems to be a fairly orthodox piece of verse to find publication in a Red journal.

The other piece of imaginative literature to which *The Torch* committed itself was Mr George Bernard Shaw's pamphlet entitled *Why I am an Anarchist*. That had an amusing sequel.

When Mr Shaw first came to London he was a true-red Anarchist. A little later he changed his coat and became a Socialist, at first of the

William Morris and then of the Marxian school. In the early days of the nineties the quarrels between Socialist and Anarchist were far more bitter than those between either and constituted Society. These quarrels as often as not ended in free fights. I have said that I remember seeing several meetings in Hyde Park break up in disorder, the Socialists being always the aggressors and usually the victors. One meeting at Kelmscott House was brought to an end by someone — I presume an Anarchist — putting red pepper on the stove. Poor William Morris, with his enormous mop of white hair, luxuriant white beard and nautical pea-jacket, used to preside at these meetings of his group. I never heard him speak. But he walked up and down in the aisle between the rows of chairs, his hands in his jacket-pockets, with the air of a rather melancholy sea-captain on the quarter-deck. He disliked the violence that was creeping into his beloved meetings. He had founded them solely with the idea of promoting human kindness and peopling the earth with large-bosomed women dressed in Walter Crane gowns and bearing great sheaves of full-eared corn. On this occasion his air was most extraordinary as he fled uttering passionate sneezes that jerked his white hairs backwards and forwards like the waves of the sea.

Mr Shaw imprudently addressed a meeting of Socialists in Hyde Park. It was perhaps his one mistake in tactics. As soon as he announced the title of his address which was *The Foolishness of Anarchism* childish voices arose on the silence. They repeated and repeated: 'Buy *Why I Am an Anarchist* by the lecturer. *Why I Am an Anarchist* by the lecturer. One penny.' The high skies towered above the trees of the Park; in the branches birds sang. Those fresh young voices mounted to heaven. Mr Shaw's did not. Every time he opened his mouth that anthem: '*Why I Am an Anarchist* by the lecturer. One penny,' began again. Every now and then they added: 'And worth it!' I suppose it would be worth ten thousand pence today. And then some!

Those young people shortly afterwards arrived at the conclusion that they were being victimised, and *The Torch* was discontinued.

It had one other curious literary offshoot. That was *The Secret Agent* by Joseph Conrad. In one of my visits to *The Torch* office I heard the inner story of the Greenwich Observatory outrage. It was subsequently confirmed and supplemented to me by Inspector French of Scotland Yard after first my mother's and then my own house had been burgled by a professional cracksman employed by the Russian

Embassy. I happened to tell the story to Conrad shortly after my burglary and, since he detested all Russians, and the Russian Secret Police in particular, he made his novel out of it. In his attribution to me of the plot which will be found in the Preface to the book he says he is sure that the highly superior person who told him the tale could never have come into contact with Anarchists. I have recounted above how I did.

A short time after that dinner at the Holborn Restaurant, I forsook London and took to agriculture.

* * *

But in great part, the prominence taken by the intelligentsia and Nihilists in English intellectual — and certainly in my own — life was due to Mrs Constance Garnett. That lady's family had long been engaged in Russian trade and she herself gave to the world one of its noblest literary monuments — her translation of the works of Turgenev. For me Turgenev is the greatest of all writers and Mrs Garnett's rendering of his Russian into English is the most flawless and limpid of carryings across from one country to another of a literary masterpiece.

Her circle of friends and admirers was enormous and international — the foreign element being mostly Russian and thus a constant transfusion of Russian ideas into English life went on around the *Cearne*. In the meantime Mr Edward Garnett was achieving one of his meteoric publishing successes. That was the *Pseudonym Library* — a collection of little yellow covered books which spread all over England and the continent of Europe with a most astonishing rapidity. Its contents were largely Slav in tone — with stories of Russia or translations from the Russian.

What exact part the activities that went on round the *Cearne* played in Russian history I don't propose to estimate. Certainly it must have been considerable. English Left opinion heartily espoused the cause of Nihilism, supported it with funds, found houses and even wives for its more destitute exiles. My brother-in-law, Dr Soskice, had been imprisoned without trial or charge in St Petersburg. He was sent to Siberia, escaped and found himself in Paris with badly damaged nerves. He was recommended to work in the open air. He came to Limpsfield to work in the garden of the *Cearne* and indeed worked in the garden of my cottage which was next door. Eventually he married my sister. My sister helped Mrs Garnett with her later translations of Dostoevsky, Mrs Garnett's eyes troubling her. Soskice played a considerable part in the political events in Russia up to the ending of the Kerensky Republic.

A curious detail of life at Limpsfield comes back to me. The Garnetts had an odd-looking yellow dog. The dog met a fox in the deep woods of the Chart. The fox bit out one of the dog's eyes. Mr Garnett dispatched the dog with an axe on the porch of the *Cearne*. This immensely impressed Bunny — afterwards David — Garnett, then aged perhaps four. His childish stutterings largely concerned themselves with the wickedness of foxes. Later he wrote *Lady into Fox*.

My own most glamorous connections with the Russian branch of the Slav family dated from earlier. They centred round Sergius Stepniak and Felix Volkhovsky, who were Nihilists, and as I have said, round Kropotkin.

Stepniak was huge, flat-featured, with small, fiery black eyes and an enormous dark beard. He was always serious. He once came to sit for my grandfather but could not sit still long enough. He carried always an enormous despatch case of great weight. I imagined it to contain the secret service money of the Russian Revolution.

Volkhovsky edited *Free Russia*. It was a rather lugubrious sheet. But he himself was small, lean, grey and always humorous. He told almost as many stories as poor Borschitzky[1] and in much the same accent. Here is one of them:

'Zair vas once Gipsy and a Ukrainian. Ze Gipsies are very clever people and the Ukrainians very stchupid. Zay vas going along a road and zay saw a porg tchop lying on it. "Zat is my porg tchop," said ze Gipsy. "No, zat is my porg tchop," said ze Ukrainian. "You poor Ukrainian," said ze Gipsy, "you are too stchupid to have ze porg tchop. Zay are for fine Gipsy fellows."

So zay agreed to go to sleep and zer one zat should have ze pudifullest dream should have ze porg tchop. In a little while: "Wake up, wake up, you stchupid Ukrainian," said ze Gipsy. "I have had ze pudifullest dream. O it was a lofly dream: I dream I come into a mos' lofly prairie; zer vas lofly green, green grass and flowers bright, bright like enamel. And zer came running to me like ze wind a mos'

[1] 'I used to have violin lessons from the queer, tragic Borchitzky whose dismal adventure caused Euston Square to be re-christened . . . and it became Endsleigh Gardens.' *Return to Yesterday*, p. 84.

wonderful charger. And his saddle vas of silver and his reins of gold and fire flashed from his eyes and smoke from his nostrils. And he say: 'Get up on my back, you fine Gipsy man, and I will carry you to ze Lord God,' and I get up on his back and 'e run swift, like ze wind till he come to a mos' lofly golden ladder. An' ze angels of God was flying up and down it and they help me climb up it like it was no labour at all.

And when I get up into Heaven zere I see ze Lord God sit at dinner. And He say: 'Come an' 'ave dinner wiz me, you fine Gipsy man. It will be honour to 'ave you at my table.' . . . Vos zat not a mos' lofly dream, you stchupid Ukrainian?"

"Zat is very sdtrange," said ze Ukrainian. "I also have a dream — but it vas a mos' wretched dream. I dream I come into a prairie but it was not a lofly prairie. It vas a wretched desert of dust an' dirt an' ol' rags. An' zer came toward me vairy, vairy slowly a miserable ol' 'oss. And 'is lungs wheezed an' ze tears dripped from 'is eyes an' 'e 'ad a rope of straw for 'is reins an' 'e 'adn't got no saddle at all. An' I git on 'is back an' 'e go vairy, vairy slowly till 'e come to a miserable old broken ladder and zer vas no angels going up nor coming down. An' I clumb panting up ze ladder till I come to ze back door of Evan. An' I see a fine Gipsy fellow sitting at ze table of ze Lord God. . . ." "Zat was me," said ze Gipsy. "Yes, zat vos you," said ze Ukrainian. "An' ze Gipsy he say to me: 'You poor stchupid Ukrainian, I am 'avin' a fine dinner wiz ze Lord God, you can go down an' eat ze porg tchop.' An' so I did! . . ." "You fool," said the Gipsy, "it vos only a dream." "Ow could I tell zat," said ze Ukrainian. "E vos too stchupid." '

Mr Volkovsky was a Ukrainian.

An examination of the amount of harm that the Russian Imperial Secret Police must have done to Russian international relations would be a very profitable and instructive proceeding. Every nation had, and still of course has, its secret police, *agents provocateurs* and bands of active semi-criminals, but these activities are as a rule limited to the territories and crimes of the nation itself and international preventive measures are carried on by officials of the respective police services. The secret police of Russia spread themselves in armies of spies and *agents provocateurs* over pretty nearly the surface of the habitable globe. They were most active in England which had then a name for being the land of freedom. I can remember about 1897 seeing shiploads of Russian and Polish Jews escaped from pogroms in their native lands and, as they came off the gangways of their ships in London Docks, falling on their knees and kissing the sacred soil of freedom — a thing that may be put to the credit of England who gets very little in matters international.

I knew, vaguely hanging about the skirts of the Russian exiles group in London, a vague, quite not political Russian then calling himself Grumeisen. He was the cause of Russia's early failure to effect an alliance with France — a dim, stoutish person with a grievance. There had been in the early eighties some sort of attempt to de-rail an Imperial train in Russia. Grumeisen was at that time a fur merchant in Paris. For some obscure reason — Grumeisen said it was because he had refused to pay money to a blackmailer who was also a Russian *agent provocateur* — the Russian secret police insisted that he was a perpetrator of the outrage. To please the Imperial Government the French police detained Grumeisen. M. De Freycinet and Prince Orloff were then engaged in the lively and picturesque conversation that would certainly have led to a Franco-Russian alliance. But there was not a shadow of proof that poor Grumeisen had had anything to do with the attempted outrage. The photographs supplied by the secret police in no way resembled him; he was able to prove that he had been in Paris at the time of the outrage. The French police were forced to release him. The Russian secret service was so strong in the entourage of the Tzar that the negotiations for the alliance were summarily broken off. The bitterness of the matter from poor Mr Grumeisen's point of view was that the French police released him only on condition that he went to England. He did not want to go to England; he was doing pretty well in the French fur trade and all his friends were Parisians.

But the fact that England was the international refuge for all exiles was not agreeable to the Russian police who filled the country with an incredible number of spies. There must have been at least one for every political exile and the annoyance that they caused in the country was extreme. I remember between 1893 and 1894 going home for longish periods almost every night from London University to a western suburb with Stepniak, Volkhovsky or Prince Kropotkin who were then the most prominent members of the Russian extreme Left and who were lecturing at the university on political economy, Russian literature and, I think, biology respectively. And behind us always lurked or dodged the Russian spies allotted to each of those distinguished lecturers. Stepniak or Volkhovsky dismissed them at

Hammersmith station, as often as not with the price of a pint, for the poor devils were miserably paid, and also because, the spies and their purpose being perfectly well known in the district where the Russians lived, they were apt to receive very rough handling from the residents who resented their presences as an insult to the country. One or two quite considerable riots were thus caused in the neighbourhoods of Hammersmith proper and Ealing.

Those matters caused at one time a very considerable friction between the British and the Russian courts. The redoubtable Azev, who was the Russian chief spy-master and *agent provocateur*, conceived the fantastic idea that an outrage in England might induce the British Government and British public opinion to decree the expulsion of all political exiles from their shores, the exiles themselves being remarkably law-abiding., He accordingly persuaded a half-witted youth to throw a bomb into Greenwich Observatory. The boy, however, stumbling over a tree-stump in the Observatory Park was blown to pieces and the whole matter came to light. For diplomatic reasons, the newspapers made very little of it. But the Home Secretary, Sir William Vernon Harcourt, made such caustic remarks over it to the Russian First Secretary of Embassy that Russian activities on the Afghan border became very marked for a considerable period.

I happen accidentally to know a good deal of these episodes. My own house was once — and my mother's twice — burgled by emissaries of the Russian Embassy in search of documents. In my case, I being the owner of *The English Review*, the above-mentioned scoundrel Azev sent me by one of his emissaries a volume of the diary of the late Tzar; he imagining that I might like to publish it — which I didn't. I didn't want to have it in my house for more than a minute and took it round to my bank for internment whilst I informed the police. In the interval between then and my return, a little after midnight, my house had been carefully gone through and all my papers, which were very many, had been thrown all over the floor. In my mother's case, the same thing happened twice, during the time that Father Gapon, the heroic leader of the peasants to the Tzar's palace on Bloody Sunday, was being housed by her, my mother being very charitable but by no means interested in politics. Eventually Gapon was sandbagged outside the house and the burglar — a Russian — given a long term of imprisonment. The Embassy naturally denied all knowledge of or responsibility for him. I came in that way a good deal in contact with the Scotland Yard Inspector who had charge of that sort of case and he told me a great deal about not only the activities of the Russian spies but gave me an — I daresay highly coloured — account of what the Home Secretary had said to the Secretary of the Embassy. I may add as a note that the reputed Tzar's journal turned out to be nothing more than a list of trials and executions of Nihilists, with comments of an extreme naïveté in that sovereign's hand. Words like 'Horrible', 'Unimaginable', or 'How can he speak thus of his Little Father?' being scrawled beside reports of Nihilists' professions of faith.

[London: Gollancz, 1931: pp. vii-ix, 102-11, 129-35.]

'Memories of Oscar Wilde'

IN December of the year before the trial of Oscar Wilde the writer's uncle called the male children of his family together and solemnly informed them that if any older man made to us 'proposals or advances of a certain nature', we were morally and legally at liberty to kill him 'with any weapon that offered itself'. The person speaking thus was not merely the brother of Dante Gabriel Rossetti, the Pre-Raphaelite poet, but also her Majesty's Secretary of the Inland Revenue; one of the most weighty and responsible of Great Britain's permanent officials, and the most reasonable human being ever sent on this earth.

From that you may understand that London parents of adolescent male children of the end of '94 saw 'perverters' lurking in all the shadows; and Wilde and Oscarisms, in their several kinds, were the preoccupation of that metropolis almost to the exclusion of all other intellectual pabula. And, beneath the comfortable strata of Society, growled the immense, frightening quicksand of the Lower Classes and the underworld, with ears all pricked up to hear details of the encounters of their own Fighting Marquis, a toff called Wilde, and the riff-raff of the Mews. Every two or three days, inspired by the generous port of his lunch, the Home Secretary issued a warrant against Mr Wilde; but in the mists of before-dinner indigestion ordered it withdrawn. The Queen and Mr Gladstone, then retired, were mercifully shielded from these whisperings — or Heaven knows what they would not have done!

The writer, however, was conscious of none of these things . . . until the first night of *The Importance of Being Earnest*. Instances — or indeed knowledge — of what was called 'perversion' had never come his way; even Mr Rossetti's exhortation had seemed nearly unmeaning. And that any blame could attach to Mr Wilde would have seemed fantastic. Mr Wilde was a quiet individual who came every Saturday, for years, to tea with the writer's grandfather — Ford Madox Brown. Wilde would sit in a high-backed armchair, stretching out one hand a little towards the blaze of the wood fire on the hearth and talking of the dullest possible things to Ford Madox Brown, who, with his healthy coloured cheeks and white hair cut like the King of Hearts, sat on the other side of the fire in another high-backed chair and, stretching out towards the flames his other hand, disagreed usually with Mr Wilde on subjects like that of the Home Rule for Ireland Bill or the Conversion of the Consolidated Debt.

Mr Wilde was, in fact, for the writer and, as far as he knows, for his cousins, the younger Rossettis, what we should have called one of the common objects of the countryside. Like Ford Madox Brown's other old friends or protégés and poor relations he had his weekly day on which to pay his respects to the Father of the Pre-Raphaelites. He had begun the practice during a long period of very serious illness on the part of the older man and he continued it, as he said later, out of liking for the only house in London where he did not have to stand on his head.

Certainly, there, he could be as quiet as he liked, for, as often as not, he and Madox Brown would sit silent for minutes on end in the twilight. So that the painter was accustomed to deny that the young poet who sat at his feet possessed any wit at all and, since Madox Brown died the year before the Wilde-Queensberry trial, he went to his death without any knowledge at all of the singular nature of the bird of paradise who had nestled on Saturday afternoons in the high-backed *bergère* beside the fire. Thus the only utterance of that date that comes back to the writer as at all weighty on the part of Mr Wilde, the private gentleman, was an admission that he had been mistaken in a political prophecy. The Tory Government of that day had decided to reduce the rate of interest on Consols. Mr Wilde had prophesied that that 'conversion' would be disastrous to the finances of the country. The rate was, however, reduced from 3 to 2¾% without any panic on the Stock Exchange. The Government had triumphed, and the writer still remembers very vividly the, by then extremely bulky, figure of Wilde as he entered the studio in a Saturday dusk, came to a standstill, loosened his great overcoat, removed his gloves and in the fashion of the day, smacked them against his left hand palm, and exclaimed in a voice of unusual sonority: 'I see I was wrong, Brown, about Consols!'

And the writer might add that the last poem of Christina Rossetti — the manuscript of which he happens to possess — is written on the back of a used envelope on the front of which the poetess had made a number of jottings — as to fluctuations in the price of Consols. So much did that resemble our own!

Thus, the first intimation of what, whether it were irresponsible or sinister, Wilde meant to London and later to the world, came with Lord Queensberry's presentation of his bouquet to Wilde on the first night of *The Importance of Being Earnest*. That was an occasion! The writer may have been obtuse or may have been merely inexperienced. But it was impossible during the performance of the play not to feel that both the audience and the quality of that audience's emotions were something different from those of any other first night he had attended. That audience was almost infinitely 'smart'. It consisted, presumably, one-half of 'decadents' more or less reckless and irresponsible, and of rich, more or less cultured and titled people who were, at least, in the know and presumably did not disapprove of what Wilde represented. What exactly Wilde represented at that moment it would be too complicated here to analyse.

On the fall of the curtain, Wilde appeared, rather pallid, blinking against the glare of the footlights and singularly prophetic of what Mr Morley looked like in 'Oscar Wilde' at the Fulton Theatre the other day. He said some words, in the voice of Mr Morley, that singular mixture of Balliol and brogue. Then unrest in the audience made him hesitate. His eyes, always uneasy, roved more uneasily than usual over the whole audience from gallery to pit. An immense pink and white bouquet was being carried down the gangway between the stalls.

That alone was sufficient to cause tittering emotion — because bouquets were only handed to women. But when the bouquet reached that solitary black figure with the pallid face and the audience could realize of what it consisted, then an extraordinarily black undertone of panic surged right through that semi-oval bowl. You saw men starting to their feet and women pulling their ermine cloaks hastily up over their shoulders — as if they felt they must incontinently flee from a scene on which violence was about to burst out.

For that bouquet consisted, plain to the view, of carrots and turnips framed in a foam of coarse lace paper. The panic in the face of Wilde exceeded the final panic that came over him under the cross-examination of Sir Edward Carson in *Wilde vs. Queensberry*. He shook and his lips bubbled. During the trial his breakdown was very gradual; there behind the footlights he was struck by a thunderbolt. For he and all the hundreds in the theatre realized within a second that this was Queensberry's final insult to the author of that play. The whole matter *could* no longer keep under ground. And the hurried exit of all that audience from the theatre was like a public desertion of that unfortunate idol of the unthinking. You saw people running to get out and the cries of encouragement of the few decadents who had the courage to take it were completely drowned in the voices of those departing who were explaining to each other what it all meant. And next day all whispering London heard that the Marquis had left in the hall of Wilde's club a card of his own bearing an unmistakable insult.

Thus, the libel action of Wilde against the Marquis was a really horrible occasion. It was not so much Wilde as the spirit of irresponsibility that was on its trial and so many of us all — all London that in the remotest degree counted — had been guilty of sympathizing with the spirit of irresponsibility.

And there was another feature. It should be remembered that for the first and last time in the whole history of London the Arts, at least of painting and poetry, had really for a year or so counted as one of the important attributes of the metropolis. We, the poets and painters of London, had for the first time in the history of the world, become front-page news. Our hearths, our bookshelves, our favourite dogs, our back-yards, were photographed for publication with all the honours of flashlights. Yes, the very pen of this writer here writing was reproduced in the shiny papers of the capital's weeklies and his inkpot, too.

This accounted for the hesitation of the Home Secretary in issuing and withdrawing his warrant. People who then used the pen in London were a clan with whom one must very seriously take account. And the same fact accounted for the final downfall of Wilde. He could not believe that the Victorian state would dare to measure itself against the chief pre-Raphaelite poet and the foremost playwright of the day.

His breakdown at the Queensberry trial came very slowly and was, therefore, the more agonizing. The cross-examination at the hands of Carson lasted at least as long as the whole play of 'Oscar Wilde' at the Fulton. And it was obviously impossible that our sympathies should not go out to that doomed rat in that rat-pit without issue. Every time that he got back on Carson — as when he said: 'No, it is not poetry when you read it,' one breathed with relief as if a sorry hero had achieved the impossible. For in the arid panoply of English law procedure the dice are so weighted in favour of the cross-examiner that one would doubt if the archangel Michael or in the alternative Machiavelli could ever finally get back on learned counsel. Wilde, however, came very near it once or twice.

No, your sympathies were bound to be with Wilde in that place and on that occasion. It is a detail that is by no means a criticism of the art displayed on the Fulton stage that the cross-examination there shown in no way duplicated the process of the London law-courts. There was none of the shouting and parading about the court by counsel that the Fulton stage showed. Sir Edward Carson spoke from a sort of a box, at some distance from the plaintiff and in a quite low if very clear voice. It made it the more horrible when suddenly you saw that pallid man's left hand begin to quiver along the lower edge of his waistcoat. And then a long time afterwards his right hand, holding his gloves, quivering on the lapel of his coat. You just waited and waited for the next sign of discomfiture until finally it came with his throwing his gloves hysterically into the well of the court, his lips bubbling with undistinguishable words until they ended in silence. The whole three stages of breakdown took perhaps an hour and a half to accomplish.

Yes, Wilde overestimated the position in the Victorian hierarchy of a poet-playwright who was the cynosure of two continents. He felt behind him all the reckless and unthinking of London, Paris, New York, and why not the boundless prairies of the Middle West? Chicago had given him a king's reception.

Thus, immediately after the end of the Queensberry trial, the Home Secretary let it be signified to Robert Humphreys who was Wilde's lawyer — and happened also to be the writer's — that a warrant would be issued for the arrest of Wilde at 6:51 that evening. That was a word to the wise, its significance being that the boat-train for Paris left Victoria station at 6:50. There was a sufficient crowd of the smart that left by that train but Wilde unfortunately was not one of them. He came into Humphrey's office about two o'clock that afternoon and before Humphreys could get words spoken, he had sunk into a chair, covered his face with his hands, and sobbingly deplored the excesses of his youth, his wasted talent, and his abhorred manhood. He spread himself in Biblical lamentation. But when Humphreys, coming round his table, was intent on patting him on the shoulder and telling him to cheer up and be a man and cut his stick for Paris, Wilde suddenly took his hands down from his face, winked jovially at Bob, and exclaimed: 'Got you there, old fellow.'

And no persuasions of Humphreys could make him leave for Paris. No. He drew himself up: assumed his air of an autocrat and exclaimed : 'Do you think they dare touch me! The author of *Lady Windermere's Fan*! I tell you the Government must fall if they did it. Why, the French would declare war. Even America!' He really believed it.

He was, by the bye, much more erect in figure than Mr Morley made him. The writer remembers seeing him in the sunlight at the Bishop of London's garden party at Fulham in a white top-hat and a grey frock coat with black buttons and braiding, much too tight across him. And he seemed, as we have said, very erect, a rather virile figure, if much too stout. The writer has very strongly the vision of Mr Wilde, who was a common object of the countryside, who sat in a high-backed chair, consuming tea and muffins with the luxury of a great Persian cat coiled up before the fire. And wasn't that in all probability the real Wilde? The man who sighed with relief to to find himself in the one house in London where he did not have to stand on his head?

Even today, the writer or painter who is to secure even a modicum of thin oatmeal that will keep the skin over his bones, has to perform a sufficiency of antics in the securing of publicity for himself. But in Victorian days those antics must be still more fantastic because press agents did not yet exist and the public was even more indifferent to the Arts. Almost no Victorian great poet or painter did not owe at least half of the impress that he made on the public to one singularity or another of costume or one or another eccentricity of behaviour in public. The process was called alternately *épater les bourgeois*, or 'touching the philistine on the raw'. And since Wilde was determined and was successful in keeping himself monstrously in the centre of the picture, it would seem to have been inevitable that he should have landed where he did whether on account of his personal taste or the remorseless logic of publicity.

The writer is hardened in his half-conviction that Wilde *péchait par snobisme* by the nature of his few contacts with Wilde in Paris during the later days. Certainly Wilde, weeping and slobbering and surrounded by teasing students, was a sufficiently lamentable spectacle of indigence, solitude, and alcoholism. The students carried on with him an almost nightly comedy. Those were the days of the great Apache scares. Wilde possessed only one thing of value and that he treasured excessively. It was a heavy black ebony cane with a crook for a handle, inlaid with numerous little pin-points of ivory. The students would come up to his table and say:

'You see Bibi la Touche, the King of the Apaches, there? He has taken a fancy to your fine stick. You must give it to him or your life will not be worth a moment's purchase.'

And after they had kept this up for a long time, Wilde, weeping still more copiously, would surrender his stick. The students would take the trouble to take it home to his hotel in the rue Jacob and next morning, Wilde, who was presumed to have forgotten the overnight incident, would find his stick, sally forth to Montmartre, and the whole thing would begin all over again.

And one may be quite uncertain as to whether the whole thing was not one last, or nearly last, attempt to *épater les bourgeois*. Wilde was so obviously — so almost melodramatically — degenerated, deserted, and soaked in alcohol that one was apt to suspect that that lamentable *mise en scène* was put up for the benefit of the bystander. The writer's contacts with him at that date limited themselves solely to buying him rather rare drinks, or, if the hour were very late and Wilde quite alone, to taking him to the rue Jacob in a *fiacre*.

One doesn't, of course, know to what extent Wilde was really deserted by his friends. He did, perhaps, tire out the patience of people. But it pleases the writer to consider that, perhaps, Wilde in all this was really scoring a world at which he had consistently mocked.

At any rate, one night very late, the writer found Wilde, hopelessly drunk, sprawled over a table outside of one Montmartre bistro or another. The writer was in the embarrassing position of having at the moment only exactly two francs. Wilde might be presumed to be completely penniless. It was, therefore, necessary to walk him quite a long way before arriving at a place that would be a reasonable two franc cab-fare from his hotel. It was at first very difficult to rouse the poet; but when he realized who was talking to him, he came to himself rather suddenly exclaiming: 'Hey, oh yes, I'll come without resistance.' He staggered for some yards, true to character, and then threw back his shoulders and we walked quite a distance side by side down the dark rue Pigalle, he talking with quite sensible regret of the writer's grandfather and the great old house in Fitzroy Square. He seemed to retain even then quite an affection for the memory of Madox Brown who was by that time dead. The walk comes back to this writer as having been excruciatingly painful. He was very young at the time and that the quiet gentleman of Madox Brown's Saturdays should have fallen so low seemed to him terribly a part of the tears of things. Suddenly Wilde exclaimed:

'Hello, what is all this? Why are we walking? Man was not made to walk when there are wheels on the streets.'

I said: 'I'm very sorry, Mr Wilde; I haven't got the money to pay for a cab.'

He said: 'Oh, is that all.' And thrusting his right hand deep into his trouser pocket produced quite a respectable roll of small notes. He waved to a cab, got into it and drove off, like any other English gentleman, leaving the writer planted there on the curb.

So one may take it as one likes. And as far as this writer is concerned he likes to take it that Wilde did in the end get a little of his own back — out of this writer and all us other imbeciles — and that he died as he lived, not beyond his means, but keeping, as the phrase is, his eyes quite consummately in his own boat. It is at least pleasant to think of him winking at St Peter as before he winked at Bob Humphreys and exclaimed: 'Had you there, old fellow.'

[Reprinted from *The Saturday Review of Literature*, XX, 27 May 1939, pp. 22-31.]

III

Literary Criticism

from

The Critical Attitude (1911)

The Critical Attitude was a collection of essays, most of which Ford had written for the *English Review* when he was its editor (December 1908–December 1909). The essay published here, which is Chapter VII of the book, had appeared in four consecutive issues of *Vote*, 1910.

THE WOMAN OF THE NOVELISTS

An open Letter, To . . .

MY DEAR Mesdames, X, Y, and Z.

We should like you to observe that we are writing to you not on the women, but on the Woman of the novelists. The distinction is very deep, very serious. If we were writing on female characters — on the women of the novelists — we should expect to provide a series of notes on the female characters of our predecessors or our rivals. We should say that Amelia (Fielding's Amelia) was too yielding, and we should look up Amelia and read passages going to prove our contention. Or we should say we envied Tom Jones — and again give our reasons for that envy. We should say that Amelia Osborne (Thackeray's Amelia) was a bore. And we should bore you with passages about Amelia. We should flash upon you Clarissa and Pamela; Portia and the patient Grisel; Di Vernon and Lady Humphrey's Daughter (perhaps that is not the right title); Rose (from *Evan Harrington*) — we adore Rose and very nearly believe in her — and Mr Haggard's *She*. We should in fact try to present you with a series of Plutarch's *Lives* in tabloid form, contrasting Amelia Osborne with Fielding's Amelia; Rose Harrington with Lady Rose's Daughter (we have got the title right this time) or Portia with the heroine of *What Maisie Knew*. It would be fun and it would be quite easy: we should just have to write out a string of quotations, and there would be an end of it.

But the 'Woman of the Novelists' is quite other guess work. It is analysis that is called for — analysis that is hard to write and harder to read. To put it as clearly as we can, all the women of the novelists that you have read make up for you the Woman of the Novelists. She is, in fact, the creature that you average out as woman.

For you who are women, this creature is not of vast importance as an object lesson. For us men she is of the utmost. We fancy that, for most of us she is the only woman that we really know. This may seem to some of you an extravagant statement. Let us examine it a little more closely.

Has it occurred to you to consider how few people you really know? — How few people, that is to say, there are whose biographies, whose hearts, whose hopes, whose desires and whose fears you have really known and sounded! As you are women and a good many of you are probably domestic women, this will not appear to you as clear as it will to most men. Yet it will be clear enough. Let us put a case — the case we know best — our own, in fact.

We have a way of putting ourselves to sleep at night by indulging in rather abstruse mental calculations. Lately we figured out for ourselves how many people we know, however slightly. The limits we set were that we should know their names, be able to sit next them at table. We could reckon up rather over a thousand — to be exact, one thousand and forty.

But of all of these how many do we really *know*? The figure that we have arrived at may seem a little preposterous, but we have considered them rather carefully. We know intimately the circumstances and the aspirations of eight men and two women and we are bound to say that both women say we do not understand them. Still for the purposes of our argument we will say that we do.

In the present-day conditions of life, as we have said, men are more prone to these acquaintanceships that are not knowledge. They go to business and negotiate with great numbers of simulacra in the shape of men. Some have eyes, beards, voices, humours and tempers; some are merely neckties, waistcoats or penholders. But as to how these simulacra live, what they really desire — apart from their functional desires to outwit us in the immediate business in hand — as to what they are as members of society, we have, as a rule, no knowledge at all.

We meet at our club every day from twenty to thirty men of whose circumstances we have not the least idea. One of them is, for instance, quite good company, distinguished and eminently conversational. We know what his public function is: we know his politics: we know his vices. But as for knowing *him*: why, we have never even looked him up in *Who's Who* to see if he is married!

And, if we are so walled off from men, how much more are we walled off from women? I should say that, out of that odd thousand acquaintances, about six hundred are women. Yet the conventions of modern life prevent us from really knowing more than two — and those two, we are told, we do not understand.

We daresay we don't. But who is to blame? Why, the Woman of the Novelists.

We trust that, by now, you know what we are driving at.

For the conditions of modern life are such that for experience of our fellow men we have to go almost entirely to books. And the books that we go to for this knowledge are those of the imaginative writers.

(Thus among novelists — or the greatest of English novelists — we should include Shakespeare. We should also include Chaucer and perhaps the English dramatists up to Sheridan — the dramatists like Congreve, that is, who are read and not performed. We have reasons for making these inclusions that we will not dwell upon.)

We may take ourself to be the average man: the man in the street. And you will find that the man in the street — or rather the men on your hearthstones — your husbands and brothers — are in much the same case as ourself. You will find that they know up to a score or so of men. You will — if you are the average wife — take care that they don't know more than a couple of women, one of them being yourself. And you will all agree with us when we say that your husbands and your brothers do not understand you. They think they do; but they do not. Poor simple, gross creatures, for them two and two will be four. For you — I wonder how much two and two are?

Yet your man of the hearthstone will talk about woman. He will talk about her with a simple dogmatism, with a childish arrogance. He will tread on all your corns. He will say that women are incapable of humour. (Of course, in his mind he will exclude you and his sister and mother — but he will never make you believe that.) He will say that women are changeable. (He will probably include you in that.) He will say that every woman is at heart a rake. (We do not know where you come in there.) He will say that a certain lane is called Dumb Woman's Lane because it is so steep that no woman's feet ever carried her up it. Well, you know all about what he will say as well as we do.

But you observe: he is talking about Woman; he talks with the confidence of an intimate. But what woman is it that he talks of? Why is it that you are not torn with pangs of jealousy when he thus speaks? Who is this creature; incapable of humour, steadfastness, virtue or reticence? You are not alarmed: you do not suddenly say to yourself: 'Are these the women he spends his time with when he pretends to be at his office, his club, his golf-links or his tailor's?' You are quite tranquil on that account; you hate him for his conceit, but you know you have him safe. This is no woman of prey that he is analysing. Women of prey are more attractive: they bewilder, they ensnare, they do not leave room for dogmatism. No, This is the Woman of the Novelist!

We do not mean to say that there have never been men whose views of women were founded upon actual experience, who took lines of their own and adhered to them. There have even been imaginative writers who have done this: there have been, that is to say, misogynists, as there have been women worshippers, and there have been a few men to whom the eternal feminine presents eternal problems for curiosity.

We do not recall, at this moment, any great novelist who has actually been a misogynist: it would indeed be a little difficult to write a novel from a misogynistic point of view — though there are several novelists who come as nearly as is possible to a pitch of altogether ignoring the Fair Sex.

The Fair Sex! Do not these two words bring to mind the greatest of all misogynists — Arthur Schopenhauer? For, says he, that we should call the narrow-chested, broad-hipped, short-legged, small waisted, low-browed, light-brained tribe, the Fair Sex, is that not a proof of the Christo-Germanic stupidity from which all we Teutons suffer?

We wonder how many of you have read Schopenhauer's 'Über die Weiber'? If you have not you should certainly do so. It is an indictment of what — owing to various causes — women may sink to. It is, of course, exaggerated; but it is savagely witty in the extreme. (And, if it enrage you, go on to read the other monograph in *Parerga and Paralipomena* in which Schopenhauer attacks carters who crack whips. 'Über Lärm und Geräusch' it is called. There you will see that what Schopenhauer attacks — along with one type of woman — is the middling sorts of men.)

The one type of woman that he attacks — the garrulous, light-headed, feather-brained type that he says includes all woman-kind

— this one type was drawn from the one woman from whom Schopenhauer really suffered. Schopenhauer was — his pasquinades apart — a mystic and dogged thinker, and the thinker is apt to consider that his existence is the all important thing in this world — and that the disturber of his existence is the greatest of criminals.

The one woman from whom he suffered was his mother. All other women he stalled off; his mother he could not. And Johanna Schopenhauer was what you might call a terror.

To begin with, for a considerable portion of Schopenhauer's life, she held the purse strings. She was an indomitable, garrulous creature. (Need we say that she was one of the most successful women novelists of her day?) She had the power to approach Schopenhauer at all times: to talk to him incessantly: to reproach this needy and lofty thinker with his want of success as a writer: to recommend him to follow her example and become a successful novelist.

So that, actually, it was his mother's type that he was attacking when he thought — or pretended to think — that he was attacking all womenkind. And that, upon the whole, is what has happened to most of the few writers who have systematically attacked women. We do not think, as we have said, that there are many of these, but some writers have had rather narrow escapes. There was, for instance, Gustave Flaubert.

Flaubert was several times pressed to marry, but he always refused and he gave his reason that: 'Elle pourrait entrer dans mon cabinet' — 'She might come into my study.' From this you will observe that he found just such another woman as was Johanna Schopenhauer. And indeed it *was* just such another — the lady he called La Muse — that he found. The Muse was the only woman with whom he came really into contact — and she was a popular novelist, a writer of feuilletons and of fashion pages, an incessant chatterer. She was no doubt a sufficiently attractive woman to tempt Flaubert towards a close union. But his own wisdom and the fact that she plagued him incessantly to read her manuscripts let him save himself with a whole skin. He was not minded to give her the right — or at any rate the power — to come into his study.

If he had done so — who knows? — under the incessant stimulus of her presence he might have joined the small band of writers who have been women haters.

As it is he was – not so much a misanthropist — a hater of his kind as a lover of what is shipshape. He had in fact the Critical Attitude. And seeing how badly — how stupidly — the affairs of this world are governed — this loving the Shipshape rendered him perpetually on the look-out for the imbecilities of poor humanity.

If he was hard upon women, he was harder, without doubt, upon men. Madame Bovary is idle, silly, hyper-romantic, unprincipled, mendacious — but she is upon the whole more true to her poor little lights than most of the male characters of the book — than Homais the quack, than her two lovers — and she is less imbecile than her husband. And indeed, the most attractive and upon the whole the wisest in the conduct of life and in human contacts — the most attractive and wisest character that Flaubert ever drew is Madame Arnoux in *L'Education sentimentale*. She is nearly a perfect being, recognizing her limitations and fulfilling her functions. I do not think that Flaubert drew more than one other such — the inimitable Félicité, the patient household drudge, in the *Coeur Simple*. Bouvard and Pécuchet are lovable buffoons or optimists, brave and impracticable adventurers into the realms of all knowledge: these two dear men are one or the other as you look at them. Flaubert drew them lovingly but we are not certain that he loved them; it is impossible to doubt that he loved Madame Arnoux, the lady, and Félicité of the Simple Soul. He drew each of them as being efficient — and since he drew two efficient women, and no efficient man at all — we may consider him to have given us the moral that, in an imbecile world, as he saw it, woman had a better chance than man.

We are not quite certain whether we regard Flaubert or Turgenev as having been the greatest novelist the world ever produced. If we introduce a third name — that of Shakespeare — we grow a little more certain. For we should hesitate to say that Flaubert was greater than Shakespeare — in fact we are sure we should not say it — but we are pretty certain that Turgenev was.

His personality was more attractive that Flaubert's — and his characters are more human than Shakespeare's were. So we should give the palm of the supreme writer to Turgenev — and so, we fancy, would every woman if she were wise. For Turgenev was a great lover — a great champion — of women. He was a great lover — a great champion, too, we may say — of humanity. Where Flaubert saw only that humanity was imbecile, Turgenev, kindlier and more sympathic, saw generally that men were gullible and ineffectual angels. And it is significant that all the active characters —

all the persons of action — in Turgenev's novels are women. There is just one man of action — of mental and political action — in all Turgenev's works, — and that man, Solomin, the workman agitator, is the one great failure of all Turgenev's projections. He is wooden and unconvincing, an abstractly invented and conventional figure.

And this preponderance of the Fair Sex in Turgenev's action does not come about because Turgenev was a champion of women: it arises simply because of the facts of Russian life as Turgenev saw them. (And let us offer you as an argument, when you are most confounded with the dogma that women never *did* anything political, the cases of Russia and Poland. For, when the history of the Russian Revolution comes to be written it will be seen that an enormous proportion of the practical organizing work of the revolution was done by women, the comparatively ineffectual theorizing has been in the main the work of men. As for Poland — the Polish national spirit has been kept alive almost solely by the women.)

So with Turgenev: if you take such a novel as *The House of Gentlefolk* you will find that it is Lisa who is the active character, taking a certain course which she considers as the course of duty and persevering in it. Her lover, Lavretsky, on the other hand, is an ineffectual being, resigned if you will, but resigned to the action of destiny. And, roughly speaking, this is the case with all Turgenev's characters. It is Bazaroff the Nihilist who is in the hands of the woman he loves: it is only in the physical activities of the peasants that the man takes the upper hand.

But Turgenev, if he was a great lover of women, did not idealize them. We love Lisa with a great affection: she might be our patient but inflexible sister: we love her and believe in her because she is the creation of a patient and scrupulous hand.

Let us now consider the woman of the English novelist — because, alas, we are a nation of readers so insular that only a few thousands of us have heard of Madame Bovary and a very few hundreds of Lisa. Consequently, these figures hardly bulk at all as colouring the figure of the Woman of the Novelist as she affects us English.

Let us consider the best known woman of action in English imaginative writing; let us consider Portia. Here we have a woman witty a little beyond woman's wit: graceful a little beyond woman's grace: gracious a little beyond the graciousness of women: with a knowledge of the male heart a little beyond the knowledge that woman ever had. She is, in fact, the super-woman.

If we love Lisa, we adore Portia: but if we believe in Turgenev's heroine do we ever quite believe in Shakespeare's? Do we ever quite — to the very back of our minds — believe in Cordelia? Or in Beatrice? Or in Desdemona? Or in Juliet? Do we believe that we shall ever meet with a woman like these? And — what is more important still — do we ever believe that these women will 'wear', that their qualities will not pall, their brilliances create in us no impatience, or cause in them no reactions that in their effects would try us beyond bearing? Portia might get us out of a scrape: Juliet might answer passion with passion: Desdemona might bear with our ill-humours: Beatrice would pique us delightfully whilst we were courting. We might, in fact — we *do* certainly — believe in these super-women during certain stages of our lives. But . . . what a very big 'But' that is!

And yet, with the women of Shakespeare the tradition of the Woman of the Novelist is already in full swing. This particular good woman — the heroine of an episode — is a peculiarly English product — a product of what Schopenhauer called, as we have said, Christo Germanisch Dummheit (Christo-Germanic stupidity.) It is hardly, in fact, stupidity: it is rather idealism. (But then in the practical affairs of the world idealism is very nearly the same thing as stupidity.) The man, in fact, who would marry Beatrice would be a stupid man, or one obsessed by erotic idealism. (For certainly — quite certainly — she would 'entrer dans son cabinet'.)

Do not please imagine that these are mere cheapnesses. Or, if they are, consider how life itself is a matter of infinite cheapnesses. And then consider again how this tradition of the super-woman heroine — the woman who is the central figure of an episode — has come right down to our own time on the wings of the English novel. She is always, this super-woman, gliding along some few inches above the earth, as we glide when we dream we are flying. She is a sort of Diana with triumphant mien before whose touch all knotted problems dissolve themselves. So she has traversed, this woman of the novelist, down and across the ages until we find her, triumphant and buoyant still, in the novels of Mr Meredith. Do not we all adore Rose and Diana and Letty — and all these other wonderful creatures? And do not we all, at the back of our minds, disbelieve in them?

You will say that Mr Meredith is the great painter of your sex. But you will not believe that: the statement is a product of emotion. You mean that he is the great pleader for your sex.

Ah! the Woman of the Novelist — the Woman of the Novelist: what great harm she has done to the cause of women in these days and for centuries back!

For consider what she has done: when Elizabethan England put Portia on the stage the Elizabethan Englishman considered that he had in public treated Woman so handsomely that she had got as much as she could reasonably expect. He proceeded in private, to cheat her out of nine-tenths of what she deserved.

You have only to read any of the innumerable 'Advices to a Son', written by various Tudor gentlemen to realize to what an extent this was really the case. The son was advised to regard his wife as a very possibly — a very probably — dangerous adjunct to a house. She was esteemed likely to waste a man's substance, to cheat his heirs in the interests of an almost inevitable second marriage. She was not to be chosen for her talkativeness as that would distract a man: (elle pourrait, in fact, entrer dans son cabinet). She was not to be of a silent disposition because she could not entertain him when he needed entertainment.

And so — hardly and coldly — with that peculiar hardness and coldness that distinguished all the real manifestations of Tudor prudence — were the lines of women's life laid down in these Tudor testaments. Woman was a necessary animal, a breeder of children; but she was a very dangerous one, or at least a very uncertain beast — a chestnut horse exhibited most of her characteristics. Desdemona and the patient Grisel were acknowledged to be dreams: Beatrice of the ready tongue was to be eschewed, and as for Portia — the Elizabethan was pretty sure, even *his* lawyers with their settlements could not bind her!

So that, in Elizabethan days, as today, you had a Woman of the Novelists, a Super-Woman — set on high and worshipped. But you had a very different woman whom you contemplated — if you were a man — from behind the locked doors of your *cabinet*.

Today we have still the Woman of the Novelists — the woman of Mr Meredith. Like Portia she is inimitable in episodes: she will get a man out of a scrape: she will be inimitable too during a season of courtship. We do not, being English, go in for the novel of life: we do not want to: we do not want to face life. When we marry, it is a woman something like Portia, or Di Vernon or Sophia Western, or Rose Harrington that we marry. We have given up as impracticable the Elizabethan habit of attempting, by selection or settlements, to choose and to tie down a partner for life. We have given it up; we say: 'The Woman of the Novelists is one thing; but as for the woman we shall marry, she is an incomprehensible creature, bewildering and unknowable. We must take our chance.'

But we should like to point out to you that we might say almost the same thing if we were going to make an indissoluble life-partnership with any man. We have, as it were, a romantic — a novelist's — idea that men, as distinguished from women, are upright, logical, hardworking, courageous, businesslike. We do not really believe this. But, if we go into partnership with a man, we do it because we like him or believe in him; because, in fact, he appeals to us. We cannot tell how he will wear, any more than we can tell how the woman we marry, or want to marry, will wear. He may go off with the till: it may prove intolerable to sit day after day in the same office with such a bounder; the fact that he comes in at night full of energy and loquacity may be intolerable, too, if he is sharing our rooms.

This will not much surprise us in a man. It is apt to disconcert us very much in our Portia — and we say: 'What a strange beast woman is! She was so clever with Shylock. Has not she got the tact to see that we need our studies to ourselves?'

Of course, the woman that we know, the woman, that is to say, that eventually each of us gets to know, is fused at last into the Woman of the Novelists. This invariably happens, for we woo a Portia who has neither a past nor a future, and life welds for us this Portia into an ordinary woman. This combination of the Woman of the Novelists who is always in one note with a creature of much the same patiences, impatiences, buoyant moments, reactions, morning headaches and amiabilities, as our own — this hybrid of a conventional deity and a quite real human being is a very queer beast indeed. We wonder if you ever quite realize what you are to the man on your hearthstone? We do not know if any woman ever really thinks — really — truly — and to the depths of her whole being — thinks that she has a bad husband. We do not know about this, but we are perfectly certain that no husband ever thinks that he has a bad wife. You see — poor, honest, muddled man with the glamour of the novelist's woman on him — he is always looking about somewhere in the odd and bewildering fragments of this woman who has the power to bedevil, to irritate, to plague and to madden him. He looks about in this mist of personal contacts for the Cordelia that he still believes must be there. He believes that his Sophia Western is still the wise, tolerant, unjealous Sophia, who once made him with the blessing of some Parson Adams, the happiest of men. God forbid that we should say she is not there. We are certain that the man believes she is, only he cannot find her. He is so close to her, and you know that if you hold your nose very close to a carpet, it is useless to hope to see its pattern. But no — believe us when we say that no man in the silence of his study believes that he has a bad wife. She may drink, but he will think that some action, some attribute, or the circumstances of the life that she has led with him, gives excuse. She may nag, but he will believe that it is because he has never really taken the trouble to explain the excellencies of his motives and his actions. She may be unfaithful, but in his heart he will believe that it is because he has been unable to maintain the strain of playing Benedick to her Beatrice. And this poor, honest, simple man may declaim against his wife to his friends, may seek in new Amelias new disillusionments, may seek amid the glamour of *causes célèbres* his liberty — but he will listen to the words of his K.C. — of his special pleading conscience — with a certain contrition, for before his eyes, dimly radiant, there will stand the figure of the Woman of the Novelists.

Now, if this man never believes that his wife is a bad wife he will yet pick up certain little salient peculiarities. He will not believe that any given manifestation of unreasonableness is a part of the real character of his Di Vernon; he will regard it as an accidental, as what Myers called a supra-liminal, exhibition, just as when he himself, having travelled first class with a third-class ticket, neglects to pay the excess fare. It is not the sort of thing he would do, it is only what by accident he has done. He remains honest and upright in spite of it. So when his wife calls him a beast he does not believe that the word 'beast' is really a part of the vocabulary of, let us say, Dolly of the 'Dolly Dialogues'. It is all one with his excess fare that he carelessly — and it was so unlike him! — neglected to pay.

At the same time a constant aggregation of these little nothings becomes impressed upon his mind. They are the reaction from the Woman of the Novelists. He does not believe that they are part of his individual woman's nature, he cannot quite make them out — so he attributes them to her sex. (If he lived with a man he would not attribute them to this man's sex but he would say it was because poor so-and-so went to Eton instead of Winchester, or because he smokes too much, or because he takes after his parents.)

The woman of the music-hall, in fact — 'My wife who won't let me' and 'My wife's mother who has come to stay' — this creature is the direct product *à rebours* of the Woman of the Novelists. For, if no man really believes that his wife is a woman of the music-hall, he is not so loyal to the wife of his friend Hunter. His own wife was *Diana of the Crossways*. She still, if she would only be serious for a minute — is Diana of the Crossways. Mrs Hunter, however, is only Mrs Hunter. To Hunter she was once St Catherine of Siena and still is saintly. But our friend catches certain phases of the intercourse of the Hunters; he hears an eloquent discourse of Hunter about the action of the tariff on the iron industry in Canada, he hears this eloquent and learned discourse interrupted by Mrs Hunter's description, let us say of the baby linen of the Prince of the Asturias. He does not know that Mrs Hunter was once St Catherine — is still St Catherine — and, as such, has a right to be more interested in infants than in iron trades. And, just as in the newspapers, crimes are recorded and the normal happenings of life let alone, so a number of irrational, unreasonable, illogical actions of real women become stored in our poor friend's mind. Thus he arrives at his grand question with which he will attempt to stump you, when you ask for a certain little something:

'Why can't you,' he asks, 'learn to be logical, patient, businesslike, self-restrained? You cannot because of your sex? Then give up talking and try to be the womanly woman.'

And by the womanly woman he means the Woman of the Novelists. And if you achieved this impossibility, if you became this quite impossible she, he would still squash you with the unanswerable question:

'What does St Catherine, what on earth does St Catherine of Siena, want with a vote?'

You see this terrible creation, this Woman of the Novelists has you both ways. Man has set her up to do her honour, and you, how foolishly and how easily you have fallen in the trap! — you, women, too, have aided and applauded this setting up of an empty convention. Women are not more illogical than men, but you are quite content as a rule to allow yourselves to be called illogical if only you may be called more subtle. Women are not less honourable than men, but you are quite content to be called less honourable than men if only you may be called long-suffering. In the interests of inflated virtues you have sacrificed the practical efficiencies of life, you are content to be called hysterical, emotional and utterly unworthy of a place in any decently ordered society, in order that you may let men bamboozle themselves into thinking that in other ways you are semi-divine. Well, this has recoiled upon your own heads and now the average man, whilst believing that in certain attributes you are semi-divine, believes that in the practical things of this life you are more incapable — the highest and most nearly divine of you is more incapable of exercising the simplest functions of citizenship than the lazy and incompetent brute who carries home your laundryman's washing. I do not know which of you, woman or novelist, is the more culpable. The novelist, being a lazy brute, has evolved this convenient labour-saving contrivance. You, thinking it would aid you in maintaining an ascendancy over a gross and stupid creature called man, have aided and abetted this crime against the Arts, and the Arts have avenged themselves, the gross and stupid creature has found his account and you are left as the Americans say 'in the cart'.

Whether there will ever come a reaction, the God Who watches over all tomorrows alone can tell. But you have the matter a great deal in your own hands, for to such an extent is the writer of imaginative literature dependent on your suffrages, that if women only refused to read the works of any writer who unreasonably idealizes their sex, such writers must starve to death. For it should be a self-evident proposition that it would be much better for you to be, as a sex, reviled in books. Then men coming to you in real life would find how delightful you actually are, how logical, how sensible, how unemotional, how capable of conducting the affairs of the world. For we are quite sure that you are, at least we are quite sure that you are as capable of conducting them as are men in the bulk. That is all we can conscientiously say and all, we feel confident, that you will demand of us.

[London: Constable, 1911: pp. 147–69.]

Literary Portraits

The following six literary portraits are taken from a series Ford wrote weekly for *The Outlook* between 1913 and 1915, about the time he was writing *The Good Soldier*. He had written two other series of portraits, one for the *Daily Mail* in 1907, the other for the *Tribune* (London) in 1907–08; in December of 1908, Ford began his brilliant editorship of the *English Review*.

MR H. G. WELLS AND THE 'PASSIONATE FRIENDS'

I

MR WELLS's is an exceedingly difficult figure at all to define. When you are irritated or exasperated with him — and that happens upon occasion; when for instance, he writes to the papers or wastes his time with a shillelagh at the Fabian Society — you exclaim, 'This man is a damned journalist!' When however you come across one of his books you find yourself reading it and all unconsciously, from time to time, saying to yourself: 'This fellow is a simple genius!' And that is about all there is to it.

Our author, indeed, though I believe a Kentish man — which is by no means the same as a man of Kent, who is a stolid being — is the most Irish of the Irish, to the extent that whenever any head pops up anywhere, bang, Mr Wells's club must come down upon it! He will 'go for' myself, Mr Shaw, the Liberal Government, the *Daily Mail*'s scheme for giving country cats a day in town, distraint of princes, the acts of God or the King's enemies — he will go for anything, all of a sudden and without rhyme or reason, And he is, I suppose, the greatest influence in England today! These two things are at once his greatest good fortune and his greatest bane. For the tendency to go for things, if it is apt to lead a writer into dragging matters neck and crop into his books, so that he will bring in a wholly superfluous character in order to hold up some harmless poor devil to opprobrium, or will carry off the whole of his story to South Africa in order to have a shot at some man in Park Lane who once omitted to send the author home from a party in his motor — if it is apt to cause certain defects, this tendency to go for things is at least a symptom of the greatest blessing that God can confer on an author. For it means that that author is able to take a keen interest in the things of this odd, this exasperating, this infinitely diverting world of ours.

God knows, myself, the Fabian Society, or the present Government are sufficiently harmless and unobtrusive things, creeping about in the hollows of this large ant-hill and hoping that God will look sideways on us. You would think that an author of position, a really great influence on his nation, would be altogether too high above the clouds to notice such minute inhabitants of what is merely his footstool. When you can write *Tono Bungay* you ought to be able to take even the present Government with complacency. The book will so long outlast that poor old link in the chain of Administrations. But that is not so. (I do not mean the last statement, but the penultimate dogmatising!) The true diagnosis of the case is that if Mr Wells had been able to take the present Government — or anything else in the world — with complacency he could not possibly have written *Tono Bungay*. For that is the book of a man to whom everything — everything in the world — is vividly interesting: the book of a man who can throw himself into — and get a lark, oh, the hugest of larks! out of just any situation, institution, law, custom, or children's game. And of course if, behind you, you have the whole force of a nation, if you are a tremendous influence, your interest — which is the same thing as sympathetic imagination — will lead you into taking sides, into setting the poor dear world straight. Personally, I sometimes wish that some way could be devised for making our author keep his hands off the poor old world and his fingers out of the works of the clock. I sometimes wish that the grateful nation would present him with £190,000 a year, a dukedom, precedence before the Archbishop of Canterbury and the Roman Cardinals, and Buckingham Palace, crammed from roof to cellars with costly and interesting toys, for a home. Mr Wells would like all these things; he could get more out of them than ever could you or I or any created being. And they might keep him quiet. (Perhaps one ought to add in addition power of life and death over certain men.). . . He would then go on writing his so beautiful, his so tenuous, his so moving and so convincing fairy-tales. But I don't know . . . A world without 'H.G.' to bang it about would be a dull place. At any rate I wish this tricksy genius could have whatever in the wide world he desired. For it is his fairy-tales that we want; it is the reading of the *Passionate Friends* that has brought me to this. . .

II

For years I have thought that the *Invisible Man* and the short story called *The Man Who Could Work Miracles* were the two most perfect expressions of Mr Wells's genius. I have been browbeaten by the world, by my friends, by Mr Wells and Mr Wells's friends, from time to time into thinking that the synchronising series of works by our author — that *The Wheels of Chance, Love and Mr Lewisham, Kipps, Ann Veronica* (I except *Tono Bungay* for the moment), and *Marriage* — that these more portentous and less imaginative works had a greater significance. But I have always come back, at other intervals, to the feeling that pure — or, as musicians would call it, 'absolute' — poetry is the true occupation of Mr Wells's genius. . . I don't mean to say that *The War of the Worlds* is more significant than *Love and Mr Lewisham* or *The Food of the Gods* than *Kipps*. They are not; they are really only just pieces of 'prentice work, of preparation for the phase of non-realistic, but very real, imaginative work upon which our author seems to be very happily entering. For the *Passionate Friends* has a great charm — a greater quality of pure charm than any one of Mr Wells's books of whichever class. And the quality of that charm again is a certain quality of serenity that hangs over the book like haze over a landscape on a still clear day. I fancy that serenity has come just because *Passionate Friends* is a piece of imagination — is, if you like, a piece of dreaming. Most of Mr Wells's other 'realistic' novels have been renderings of or inversions of Mr Wells's biography — they have been realism tinged with acrimony, as if our author had felt personal irritations against persons or institutions that had surrounded him in his passage through life. So that, all admirable as they were, they have never rung quite real; one had always the sneaking subconscious feeling that each of these books was a little more Mr Wells scoring off his destiny rather than Mr Wells passionlessly recording the results of his observations — which is your only realism. With *Tono Bungay* alone this was not so.

I have followed Mr Wells's literary career for years; and with each successive masterpiece of one kind or other I have said to myself —

after the publication of *The Invisible Man* I said it, as after the publication of *Love and Mr Lewisham* and *Tono Bungay* — I have always said to myself: 'Well, here's an end of "H. G." He will never do better than this; there's no other place for him to come out at. He will just now go along in this vein to the end.' With *Tono Bungay* this seemed to me to be extraordinarily the case. I could not for the life of me see where Mr Wells was going to come out, after that. I ought to have known better; I ought to have seen the writing on the wall. For *Tono Bungay* is so much bigger, is so much finer, than anything else that Mr Wells had ever written that I ought to have seen that the difference was due to a new impulse welling up in our author, not to any remaking of old moods, however ingenious. *Ann Veronica*, the *New Machiavelli*, and *Marriage* simply confirmed me in my error. Frankly speaking, they seemed monotonous. (I can afford to say it now.) I said to myself — (and with very sincere regret, for I cannot sufficiently express how much for how many years I have wished that 'H. G.' should make good artistically. [I don't care a bit about his sales.] This has really been in me a desire far more occult than any desire I have ever had for my own 'coming off' as a writer; because this man is so vivid, so striving, so keen, that he ought to be happy) — I said to myself: 'Oh, well, here's an end of "H. G." at last.' For these books seemed to be — as indeed they were — the merest tiltings at points of the universe in the vein, with the trick but without the spirit, of Tono. Well, thank heaven, it isn't so. With the *Passionate Friends* our friend breaks ground in a territory that is as boundless as the plains of the south; a territory of fine country in which he may now travel for ever and be ever so 'happy'. For the difference between Mr Wells imagining and Mr Wells remembering past bitterness is the difference between the poet and the man with a grievance; the difference precisely between a pure genius and a damned journalist. (I mean a journalist with Satanic sounds in his voice.)

No, *Passionate Friends* is a daydream; it is rather the career that Mr Wells would have liked to have had than that — wonderful enough in all conscience — that he has had. Into all sorts of imagined places Mr Wells takes you — into the life of a parson's son; into love with a Lady Mary; into relations with a kind scholarly father; into the South African War; into the East. . . And how beautifully, how happily, it is done! I don't mean to say that there aren't any portentous passages; the whole book pretends to be a father's advice to a son and so on;

and there are pages about the ideal city of the future. But they don't much count; you can skip them easily enough, and then you get to the real right thing — to Mr Wells dreaming daydreams. For Mr Wells is just a poet — and he has found it out.

[*The Outlook*, 27 September 1913.]

MR ARNOLD BENNETT AND 'THE REGENT'

I

I PRIDE myself on having been the first person to take Mr Arnold Bennett really seriously. I am aware that, as soon as some twenty-five to thirty persons read these words those same twenty-five to thirty persons will at once take pen in hand and write to the editor of this Journal protesting that they, and not I 'discovered' this considerable writer. There must have been the publisher's reader who first recommended the printing of Mr Bennett's first book; there must have been the publisher who presumably first ventured real money upon that writer (and heaven knows real money is the only important thing in the literary career!). There must have been from ten to twenty ladies and gentlemen who wrote the First Review that Counted of the First Book. There must have been the one hundred and twenty editors who, at about that time, began to publish the one hundred and twenty different kinds of advice that Mr Arnold Bennett, equally about that time, began to give to a world wholly ignorant, across which Mr Bennett stalked in the guise of one infinitely all-wissend. That, at least, is the impression that one has of the matter.

One seemed to be being advised in those days by that amazing professor of what's what, as to how to write novels, short stories, dramas, epics, and snappy paragraphs for the halfpenny papers. As to the choice of socks one was advised and as to the selection of dishes in cheap restaurants, as to voyages in the Ardennes, as to the proper sort of card-index and paper-clips, as to one's demeanour before waiters, as to one's selection of a wife, of a club, of a daily paper, of a brand of cigarettes, of an imitation gold tooth-pick, and a mowing-machine for suburban gardens. I am not sure that every one of these matters was treated of by Mr Bennett in what he was pleased to call his Savoir Faire series; indeed I am not absolutely certain that our Author actually contributed one hundred and twenty series of articles to the daily, weekly, fortnightly, monthly, quarterly, annual, and biennial Press. But that was the sort of impression that one had. It may, for the matter of that, have been short of the mark! There is no knowing the prodigious record! Even to this day Mr Bennett, I am told, is still advising the world. He tells us how to write plays; that Flaubert is not much of a writer; or, again (by presumption in his latest work), how to behave at Clxxxdge's Hotel. And since, as I believe, Mr Bennett has written wildly successful plays; since he receives, so I have been assured (indeed I am not certain that Mr Bennett himself has not assured me that he receives), one shilling for every word he writes or utters, so that Midas himself may be put to shame, — may we not well take his advice, dramatic or literary, eschew the reading of Flaubert (who made but one centime a word!), and so comport ourselves, when our avocations take us to Clxxxdge's, that we may do credit to our mentor?

Nevertheless it was not — as it still is not — this kind of Mr Bennett that one was looking for. But years ago — years and years ago it seems! — I happened to pick up in Mr Joseph Conrad's study a book that Mr H. G. Wells had dropped in that room. (I think that Mr Wells had before them mildly, and as if uneasily, suggested that I should read this book. And I like to exaggerate in my memory Mr Wells's mildness and uneasiness, because it gives me my chance of nursing my pride at having been the first person to take Mr Bennett seriously, for heaven knows, in this world one needs something to be proud of! At any rate I like to think that Mr Wells was not *quite* certain about the book — not quite absolutely cocksure.) Mr Conrad said something like: 'Cela existe — et c'est déjà quelque chose.' But as for me, beneath my modest obscurity in the presence of those two shining celebrities, on reading the first page of this book I felt an absolute conviction that its writer had about him the correct, austere, authentic touch of the real writer. The book was *The Man from the North*.

Mr Bennett, in short, like all the rest of us is homo duplex: he has a talent that kicks up a devil of a row in the world, and he has a real genius, which is a much quieter affair. Savoir Faire Papers, Advices to Authors, Grand Babylon Hotels, Cards, Milestones, et patati et patata, — these one accepts with patience and resignation. They are a nuisance; but one is given to understand that they represent Mr

Bennett patiently and advisedly collecting the quarter of a million pounds upon which he will retire from the business of Cook's Tours and Conductor-in-Chief to the world. One says, 'Oh, well! . . .'; one waits. Then there appears an *Anna of the Five Towns*, there appears an *Old Wives' Tale*, or a *Matador of the Five Towns*, and one is happy as one is at the feeling of contact with the Real Right Thing. I think indeed I have seldom experienced a greater sensation of pleasure than came to me at reading the *Matador of the Five Towns* in MS. It was the sensation of travel, of lights, of streets, of being introduced to real people. It was the rare sensation at once of living and being conscious of life. I don't know a better piece of work in the English language, or a job better executed. I had the honour of publishing it in the *English Review*.

Naturally Mr Bennett quarrelled with me about the price I paid his agent for this piece of work. He would. And in the midst of a rather grotesque correspondence I made this distinguished author's acquaintance. (He persisted in saying that his work was worth many, many hundreds of pounds, and I retorted that he had chosen to send it me through an agent, and that the price was agreed. And, as I am not really a business man, it seemed to me that I was in the right!) Anyhow, in making our Author's acquaintance beneath this cloud of grotesquerie, I had the sensation (as I had had in reading *The Man from the North*) of coming into contact with a being of extraordinary wisdom — with the wisest personality I had ever imagined. I use the words 'wisdom' and 'wise' after weighing them carefully enough. I don't mean to say that the Mr Bennett who advises us as to safety-razors and the vintage-years of petits gris wines is wise any more than a person very skilful at declarations in Auction. That is a sort of stamp-collecting. No! Mr Bennett's wisdom is that deep, stable, tranquil knowledge of the values of life (hominibus bonae voluntatis!). It doesn't matter that his values are purely materialistic. That is a better outlook than any idealism compounded of platitudes, banalities, confusions of values, and accepted ideas. It is a sane, a national, and, above all, a workmanlike affair, and one which is of infinite use to a writer. For if any writer can render, as Mr Bennett can, the materialistic value of the external world (and that he probably learned of poor dear old Flaubert), then the supernatural, the subliminal, the inner values will suggest themselves, as inevitably as night follows day, to any reader of good will. More no writer can hope for.

II

The Regent is another nuisance. I don't know why Mr Bennett wrote it — to fulfil a contract? to complete his quarter-million guinea fund? to add, in short, another stamp to his collection? One is *so* tired of these self-made men posing before the head-waiters of Clxxxdge's. Dickens, one would have thought, did it once for all . . . One is *so* tired of gentlemen setting sail for New York à propos des bottes . . . One is *so* tired . . .

The Town Council of K——am-Rhein are marching with red and white ribbons round their stomachs beneath the window of my hotel. They have several bands, and each of them from seven to twenty orders in his buttonhole. They wear opera-hats, black frock-coats, and lavender trousers, and each — oh, each of them is a self-made man, a regular card! They manage perhaps these things better on the Rhine.

[*The Outlook*, 4 October 1913.]

MR THOMAS HARDY AND 'A CHANGED MAN'

I

I WAS once in the same company as Mr Hardy in a house by the sea, the guest of a hospitable but militant atheist of the 1880 type. After dinner they all began talking about religion. It was an occasion that I cannot forget — that, I suppose, I never shall be able to forget!

The room was darkish and low; the open windows gave upon the sea and the night that was traversed, here and there across the casements, by lanthorns of ships, like moving pin-points of light. So there was a certain solemnity about the occasion — not too much, but enough to render it vivid, or, if not vivid, then touching; for the night, the sea, and the discussion of religion are queer human futilities in the face of ships'-lanthorns, in a low room. There were present a Cambridge professor of classics, who was an avowed Spiritualist; two lady novelists — one, like our host, an atheist of the eighties; one a Roman Catholic; there was a Servian representative of the Press, like one of the lady novelists — and, like myself, for the matter of that — a Papist; there were our host and Mr Thomas

Hardy. It is not my business to record the discussion; its only salient point was the odd bringing out of the fact that the rationalism of the eighties appeared to be as dead as a door-nail, and, minute by minute, to be disappearing — rusting away — before the oncoming tide of Spiritualism, Catholicism, and everything that atheists call superstition.

And then, suddenly, Mr Hardy, with his kindly, modest manner, that has the odd quality of making you feel like a good or a bad child, as the case may be, announced from the shadows that he believed in ghosts. In good old-fashioned ghosts!

Our host threw up his hands; I am not certain that he did not tear his hair. Was it for this, he asked, that he and his doughty peers had fought and suffered in the eighties? — to see this tide creeping up again as, in the dark ages, bogeys had crept upon the world!

And then, at the urging of the lady novelist who was not a Papist, Mr Hardy told us the story of Wild Darrell! I don't know how many of us believed in ghosts till that moment, but I will bet that every one of us, whilst that tale was telling — the tale of the midwife carried off through the darkness to Littlecote, of the throwing of the newborn child into the fire, of the woman's cutting the little piece from the bed-curtains, by means of which she afterwards identified the place — I will bet anything you like that every one of us — including our host — for the time being believed in the ghost of Wild Darrell!

It wasn't, I think, that Mr Hardy employed any particular artifice of description or verbiage — and it wasn't only that, in the nature of things, one listens to Mr Hardy with the deepest of attentiveness, of respect, and, if I may so, of affection; though these things tell. It is, I think, that in certain natures there is a particular gift for telling a certain type of tale. Perhaps it is that they love that type, and that, as it were, the love shows through.

I suppose that, if I may be permitted to stand for anything, if I have been permitted to preach anything in these columns, it would, on the face of it, be something to which the art of Mr Hardy would be anathema. In cold blood the critic of my type would have to say that Mr Hardy's art was no art at all, except when it was hopelessly wrong. But I can't myself get cold-blooded enough to say these things in face of the charm, the sweetness, the entire *goodness* that is caused to come up within me by the remembrance of certain novels by our author and of certain verses by this great poet. Perhaps that is the cult that I owe to Aesculapius . . .

Or perhaps it is something more. Some time ago, during a period of long illness — a period lasting years, characterized by great depression — I read firstly the whole works of Samuel Johnson, including Boswell; then the whole works of Turgenev, and then all the novels and poems of the author of the *Return of the Native*, one after the other. Johnson meant for me a return to interest in the facts of life; the Russian author gave me again the rest, the happiness, and (if I may be pardoned for using a word that I should not use save in connection with the feelings of convalescence after long weakness) all the bliss of connection with, of the observation of, a supreme Art at work. But Mr Hardy's books gave me a sensation as strong as either — a sensation of dark charm . . .

The Mayor of Casterbridge, The Trumpet Major, The Woodlanders: God knows, according to my own critical standards, and if I had the books beneath my hands, I could point out whole bushelsful of faults of diction; in the handlings of conversations; in the management of plots. But, thank goodness, I have not the books beneath my hands, so that there remain only the sensations — the sensations of the dark charm, the gloomy sweetness as of a great façade of ancient tree-trunks, and the goodness, the personal fascination.

For the personal fascination of the face that looks up at you out of the pages, of the human being that lives between the covers of Mr Hardy's books — as if each volume were a dark crystal with the flame of a kind soul moving within it — gets beyond the vicissitudes of conscious Art into a realm altogether differing.

To get hold of a formula I am inclined to say that there are only two schools of Art of any authenticity: that of the conscious artist who is ground as fine as a needle by the necessities of conscious self-expression, and that of the peasant who is ground down into a knowledge of how life works by the hard necessities of the wind, the soil, and by hunger and death that accompany all weathers. You have to formularize yet more closely, the French school, the product of the only real city life of the world; you have the Russian peasant tale-tellers — the Tolstoys, the Dostoevskys, the Chekhovs — who sit, as it were, by the stoves and are driven by the necessities of their lives to express themselves in such a way as to engross the attentions of their hearers. For, let me again repeat, Art is nothing more nor less than the faculty, conscious or unconscious, of engrossing the attention of passers-by.

II

And here I have Mr Hardy's latest volume to support me in this theory. *The Changed Man* (Macmillan, 6s.) shows us, authentically enough, I think, our author sitting beside stoves and penning peasants' stories, and then getting up and going out along the road to other firesides, where he relates such stories as have appealed to him to persons to whom they may appeal — telling them with such modifications as, upon the one hand, he needs to make to satisfy himself, or, on the other hand, with such as he feels will make the tale more engrossing to his readers. Thus, in the truest sense, these are tales — things told rather than stories — histories — which are written things. That, I think, is one of the secrets of this author's charm — that he is always attentive to an audience. He writes sagas — things said to a present hearer. Here is an opening for you:

> I lately had a melancholy experience . . . that of going over a doomed house . . . Some of the thatch, brown and rotten as the gills of old mushrooms, had, indeed, been removed before I walked over the building. Seeing that it was only a very small house . . . situated in a remote hamlet, and that it was not more than a hundred years old, if so much, I was led to think, in my progress through the hollow rooms, with their cracked walls and sloping floors, what an exceptional number of abrupt family incidents had taken place therein . . .

Isn't that jolly! Isn't that a picture! Isn't it a good device for making you want to hear what had happened in the house! And isn't it Thomas Hardy!

Isn't it again unlike Maupassant? — and, once more, isn't it a little like the opening of one of the *Sportsman's Sketches* of Turgenev — those peasant's tales that caused a revolution in Holy Russia?

And, reading again a book by this author, don't I get again exactly the feeling — from *The Grave by the Hand-post, Enter a Dragoon, What the Shepherd Saw,* or *A Committee Man of the 'Terror'* — exactly the feeling of dark charm, of engrossment, of sincerity, that I had when, years ago, I read through all Mr Hardy's work. And, because the feeling is so exactly the same, I am pretty certain that the quality of charm of this great poet is authentic, founded in the hearts of men, and enduring.

[*The Outlook*, 8 November 1913.]

MR WYNDHAM LEWIS AND 'BLAST'

I

IT was on a hot noontide of the month of——, A.D. 19——, when three persons might have been observed sitting at lunch in an upper room of a western district of this great Metropolis. He whom by his stature you might have known to be part proprietor of the *E——h Re——w* addressed thus, in tones of despair, him whom by his demeanour you could discern to be the editor of that periodical. 'It's a perfectly rotten number! We haven't got a single article that an intelligent cow would want to read.' Said the editor to her who, you must by now recognize from her competent yet respectful bearing and from her attire, was the secretary of that charitable institution: 'Go down, Miss ——, and say a prayer before the image of St Anthony to the end that he may find us an article suited for our needs.' The fair secretary descended, and very soon her lips might have been heard moving as she stood before the saint who is invaluable for his aid in discovering lost or not easily findable articles — the saint who still confronts us as we search our minds for the words that so difficultly come. There he stands, tranquil upon the mantelpiece between an Egyptian image and a Welsh wooden dog, obscuring, modest saint that he is, the greater part of an invitation from Mr Lane — an invitation to celebrate the birth of his new periodical. But to our tale. . . . Suddenly from below there sounded a minute but unmistakable feminine shriek. It was followed by the quick patter of footsteps upon the stair. The secretary reappeared. 'There is,' she exclaimed, 'an awfully funny-looking man coming into the office.'

With that courage which we hope will always distinguish him, and at the same time with the caution which should also be a characteristic of the truly brave, the editor crept slowly down the narrow stair, availing himself of the protection that was afforded him by the nooks and angles of that means of communication. In the luxuriously appointed office stood an individual whom with his unerring eye the editor at once took to be a Russian moujik. The long overcoat descending to the feet, the black wrappings to the throat, the black hair, the pallid face, the dark and defiant eyes — all, all indicated the Slav. With swiftness and vehemence natural to the situation the editor remarked: 'We don't want any accounts of the methods of the secret police. We don't want to print any secrets of the Imperial Court. We don't want to buy any diary of the Tsar. We don't want . . .'

Slowly and with an air of doom the stranger began to draw out manuscripts — from his coat-pockets, from his trouser-pockets, from his breast-pockets, from the lining of his conspirator's hat. The dark stranger uttered no words; his eyes remained fixed on the editor's face so that that official quailed. He quailed so much that, in spite of himself, his unwilling hands accepted the piles of manuscripts that were thrust into them. His unwilling eye descended upon the pages. With one shout he turned and, rushing from the room with the manuscripts waving above his head, he ascended the stairs three at a time, his dressing-gown waving too in the wind of his passage. 'Eureka!' he exclaimed, 'The good saint has answered our prayer.' The dark stranger — the man of destiny — meanwhile stood alone and silent in the luxuriously appointed office.

This is a true story, written in a Pastist manner.

Well, that is how Mr Wyndham Lewis rose over my horizon. Today Mr Lewis is decorating everybody's house — or at any rate he is decorating the houses of most people who count, and who do not go in for 'Chippendale'; his name is on most people's lips; we sit with folded hands listening to his rare but incisive words, and I permit myself these indiscretions. (I hope I shall one day become more phlegmatic — more English in the best sense. But I am reminded of the Greek woman's prayer, 'The dear gods make me chaste — but not soon!')

At any rate I do take a very serious view of the movement that contains Mr Lewis and his followers, or his associates, or whatever is the right word. Putting aside for the moment the intrinsic value of Futurism, Cubism, Imagism, or Vorticism, it must from bitter experience be manifest to the most academic of mortals that you cannot afford to despise a movement conducted by young men who are loud-voiced, tapageux, vigorous, and determined to arrive. You can afford to throw bricks at any one young man; you may successfully down him — which is the natural desire of the middle-aged, the aged, the sluggish, the official, of those who have arrived, and more particularly of those who have nearly arrived. But not even if you be the president of the British Academy can you prudently afford to despise a body of young men kicking up a more or less unanimous row, all in a phalanx. That is no go.

It is no go, simply because those young men will survive you. They will be the judges when you are dead. So the young are always in the right; the old always in the wrong. The young always have the right of it, simply because with their inexperience they can get hold of a point of view and stick to it and shout about it. The middle-aged are always in the wrong because they have learned caution, desire rest, and have no point of view. Caution is no good; if a king desires rest he abdicates. These young men will survive us for the simple reason that there is no such thing as the abstractly beautiful or the abstractly virtuous. If a number of young men, shouting together, insist that an old ruin is beautiful, insist on it loud enough and for a sufficiently extended period — they will in the end find thousands of people to admire old ruins, to erect false old ruins, to muse over artificial skulls. In that way you had the Romantic movement, with its profound effect on the art, the international politics, the morality of Europe. (My motives you will observe to be entirely cowardly. You will perceive that I support these young men simply because I hope that in fifteen years' time Sir Wyndham Lewis, Bart., P.R.A., may support my claim to a pension on the Civil List, and that in twenty years the weighty voice of Baron Lewis of Burlington House, Poet Laureate and Historiographer Royal, may advocate my burial in Westminster Abbey.) One is only mortal.

II

And indeed Vorticism, Cubism, Imagism — and Blastism — may well sweep away anything for which I have stood or fought. That is the luck of the game; that is how we are laid to rest by inscrutable but august destiny. Let us however consider what chance Blastism has of becoming permanent. It has this chance . . .

All great art has been produced by people interested in their own ages and their own climes. I do not mean to say that it was produced by men solely interested in their own day; but if they looked at the past they saw it in terms and represented it in the idiom of their own climes and nations. Homer was a Presentist writing in terms of his own epoch and seeing the figures of the past with blind eyes that yet saw as his hearers saw. Horace was a Presentist, writing of his present. Dante was a Presentist, so interested in his day that he made hell the vehicle for abusing all the men that he disliked. So did the

Provençal poets; so did the Meistersingers; so did the Elizabethan English, since whom nothing of any particular value has been produced in these islands.

Well, in *Blast* you have Messrs Aldington, Brzeska, Pound, Wadsworth, Lewis, and others corporately blasting what in our time they dislike and blessing what appeals to them. And the blasting makes very amusing reading. You can laugh for an hour over their manifestoes. It is no good saying that *Blast* is vulgar and contains many misprints. That was said of Shakespeare and the Folios bristle with misprints too. It was said of Shakespeare with such effect that he went and hid himself inStratford — as if Mr Lewis should retire to Surbiton and pretend that he had made his fortune in the pork-trade. The parallels are quite exact — the British academic school of today hating to see their own times in terms of their own times just as did the upholders of the unities, and Gorboduc and Ferrex and Porrex, in the day when they frightened poor Shakespeare out of town. Of course Mr Lewis is not yet Shakespeare; neither is Mr Pound; I am only talking of the chances of permanence in the new movement.

And its chance of permanence consists in the fact that its method in attack is the obviously right one of being amusing and taking an interest in its own day. It is no good being not amusing, however earnest you may be. It is no good being serious if you cannot find hearers; it is no good avoiding sensationalism in an affair, like that of the arts, whose whole purpose is sensationalism and appeals to the emotions. It is no good being so careful to avoid misprints that you get nothing done. *Blast* is very amusing, very actual, very impressive now and then; it contains less dullness than any periodical now offered to this sad world. Mr Pound goes on uttering what a late Academician called 'barbaric yawps', Mr Lewis presents you with a story that is to other stories what a piece of abstract music by Bach is to a piece of programme-music. I don't just figure out what it means, but I get from it ferociously odd sensations — but then I do not understand what Bach meant by the Fourth Fugue, and I don't want to. I get sensations enough from it. Mr Brzeska's vortex about sculpture is another singularly fine piece of abstract incomprehensibility. I am not sure that Mr Brzeska's is not the most pleasurable piece of writing of the lot. Mr Pound's vortex does not so much appeal to me — it is too moral; but I like the little poem by H. D. with which he concludes his apostrophe. That is perhaps because I have a soft spot for H. D.; perhaps it is because H. D. is the best poet that we have. Of work in the past method there is a magnificent nightmare by Rebecca West, and a portion of a novel by myself which appears unexciting when I see it in print.

Anyhow I fancy that these young men are going to steamroller out this poor old world of ours. And I am very glad of it; it has been a dull place enough. Of course I do not expect that Mr G. will install its purple in his library; that Mr H. will retire with it to his mediaeval moat; that Mr X. will really mean the three lines of praise that he writes about it in the *Daily* _____, or that Mr Y. will really really like it. It remains a hypocrisy to seek for the person of the sacred emperor in a low tea-house. But I who am, relatively speaking, about to die, prophesy that these young men will smash up several elderly persons — and amuse a great many others.

[*The Outlook*, 4 July 1914.]

UN COEUR SIMPLE

I

'PENDANT un demi-siècle, les bourgeoises de Pont-l'Evêque envièrent à Mme Aubain sa servante Félicité.'

This simple sentence is the beginning of the story which, at this moment, is of most significance to the world. It means that for fifty years the middle-class housewives of Pont-l'Evêque envied Mme Aubain her servant Félicité. Nevertheless, exactly and rightly to translate that simple sentence is a task of almost unheard-of difficulty. Let us consider for a moment these verbal exactitudes. Let us take the words 'Pendant un demi-siècle.' If we say 'During half a century,' the words have not a quite English sound. If we say 'For fifty years,' the period is too exact in appearance. It would give the suggestion that Mme Aubain was about to celebrate a golden jubilee. And the opening words of a story are of immense importance because they strike a note in the reader's mind, so that if we start the reader anticipating the celebration of a golden jubilee, and if no such celebration takes place, the reader's mind will be a little confused. In the French the sentence suggests no event of any kind, not so much as the shadow of an event. The clear, cold sentence, with its cadence just sufficiently long to leave the reader wishing for the next syllables, dictatorially limits the mind to the consideration, firstly, of

Mme Aubain, and then, by the careful reservation of the servant's name to the last words, indicates with absolute precision that the main interest of the story will be the servant Félicité. The use of the word 'bourgeoises' indicates that Pont-l'Evêque is a town, or a large village, of sufficient importance to contain several families in fairly comfortable circumstances. The note thus exactly struck in the reader's mind amounts to this: that the story will concern itself with an affair lasting fifty years, that the affair will not contain any memorable events, and that it will centre round the life of a faithful servant — for Félicité was for fifty years in the service of her mistress, and the other housewives of the place envied Mme Aubain.

We must therefore not commence our rendering by saying 'For fifty years'. On the other hand 'During half a century' is not quite right. I do not know why it is not quite right — I fancy that the word 'during' rather implies sequences of similar or dissimilar but not continuous actions spread over a given period. I think we should be using correct English — correct idiomatic English — if we said 'During the next two centuries the Danes made repeated attempts to break the power of the Heptarchy;' but I think we should have to say 'For the last twenty-five years' — or, if we wanted to be more literary, 'For the last quarter of a century Admiral von Tirpitz was, or has been, unceasingly engaged in the long effort to raise a High Seas Fleet for the German Empire.'

Thus, in the case of Félicité we might say that for half a century the housewives, etc. On the other hand, 'For half a century' is too literary a phrase to satisfy an absolutely delicate ear. Personally, if I were writing the story on these lines I should begin with an exact statement of the number of years, softening off the exactness with the qualificative 'more than'. 'For more than thirty-seven years', I should say, and I think I should arrive at about the sense of Flaubert's phrase. I am not, of course, suggesting that Flaubert is at fault in the matter. 'Pendant un demi-siècle' is a phrase in general use amongst simple people in France to imply a long period — anything between thirty-seven and fifty years. Similarly with the word 'envièrent'.

In English we should probably have to translate this: 'Envied her her servant,' and the phrase might possibly serve the turn. Nevertheless some trace of the original meaning of the word 'envy', which was a cardinal sin, still attaches to the dissyllable in certain cases. Of course in such a phrase as 'I envy So-and-So his good teeth' or 'his sound digestion', the original sense of the word 'envy' has completely disappeared. Nevertheless the necessity to use the phrase 'envied her her servant' is regrettable, though I cannot think of any more advantageous synonym. In England, I fancy, we are accustomed to associate the word 'housewives' to some extent with malicious gossip, so that the collocation of the words 'housewife' and 'envy' has a faint flavour of the disagreeable. In France when a 'bourgeoise' of Pont-l'Evêque met Mme Aubain in the market-place or came once a week to the 'salle' of Mme Aubain to play floral loto she would felicitate Mme Aubain upon Félicité and would really mean what she said. This is the precise meaning of the word 'envièrent'.

So that, if I had to translate *Un Coeur Simple* for publication, which God forbid that I should have to do, I should work out from the story as nearly as possible how many years Félicité was in the service of Mme Aubain, and I should begin: 'For more than forty years the housekeepers of Pont-l'Evêque envied Mme Aubain because of her servant Félicité'. I am aware of the objections to this rendering. In the first place many reviewers might — and with some justice — object to the rendering 'For more than forty years', and I do not know whether they would be right or whether they would be wrong. Still, I have the rather strong feeling that the business of a translator is to take over rather the atmosphere than the exact wording of the original. For 'housewife' it will be observed that I have substituted 'housekeeper', and the word 'housekeeper' generally implies a paid upper servant. That I should have to chance. I have got to imply that the persons who envied Mme Aubain were in a position to keep servants; 'housewife' is a dangerous word because, in its proper pronunciation of 'hussif', it sounds too like 'hussy' to go near the word 'envied'. After the word 'envied' I have inserted the words 'because of' so as still further to get away from the implication of mortal sin. For it seems to me that if I say: 'I envy the editor of this journal his position', that might mean that I was attempting to get him out of his job and to obtain it for myself; whereas, if I say that I envy him because of his position, it would at the most imply that I should like to have a similar one — as indeed I should.

II

The reader will say: 'What is the use of all this fuss about the exact incidence of a few commonplace words?' I can only answer that that is my job and that the exact use of words seems to me to be the most important thing in the world. We are, in the end, governed so much more by words than by deeds that I would rather have said to me by one person, 'Well done, thou good and faithful servant,' than receive, from the hand of another, the Order of the Garter and half the wealth of the Indies.

And I do stoutly maintain that this very exact examination and weighing of French words is of the most enormous importance to the inhabitants of these islands. It is of enormous importance to us to realize that they have in France these faithful servants, these market-towns where the housekeepers really go to market, these quiet, simple people contented with their humble and useful careers. If you will read with great care and assimilate with a humble intelligence — for humility is necessary in approaching the study of words and your mind must be utterly cleared of any trace of preconception — if, then, with humility and attention you will read the following sentences you will know more of France than if you spend months and months and months in one of the large hotels near the Tuileries Gardens:

> Un vestibule étroit séparait la cuisine de la *salle* où Mme Aubain se tenait tout le long du jour, assise près de la croisée dans un fauteuil de paille. Contre le lambris, peint en blanc, s'alignaient huit chaises d'acajou. Un vieux piano supportait, sous un baromètre, un tas pyramidal de boîtes et de cartons. Deux bergères de tapisserie flanquaient la cheminée en marbre jaune et de style Louis XV. La pendule, au milieu, représentait un temple de Vesta — et tout l'appartement sentait un peu le moisi, car le plancher était plus bas que le jardin.

You will know, then, something of France, for France is 'la salle de Mme Aubain', where she sits day after day against the white wainscoting; there will be the eight mahogany chairs, an old piano under a barometer; an armchair with a tapestry back will be on each side of the yellow marble mantelpiece, Louis Quinze in style. The clock in the centre of the mantelpiece will represent a temple of Vesta, and all the room will smell a little of mould because the floor is a little lower than the garden. And when you have this picture well before you you will find that there will rise in your mind the reasonably correlated idea that there must be thousands and thousands of such houses all over France from Alsace to the Rhone

— thousands and thousands of tranquil, useful households where there is a touch of style in the tapestried armchairs, the yellow marble mantelpiece, Louis Quinze in tradition, the clock and barometer — where, in fact, life is quite decorous, sober, and more tenacious than the life of any other country in the world. Out of such small material indeed, and managing life with such frugality, these people achieve an existence of dignity and commonsense. And that should be a great lesson to us.

It is a lesson that we immensely need, and that only France can give us.

Modern life, the modern life of our great cities, has got hideously too far from the quiet rooms where sit the mothers of the race — the quiet rooms that smell faintly of mould because they are a little below the level of the garden. And, if these are hideous days, with hideous occurrences devastating appalling nights, that is very much because the world has got too far away from Mme Aubain and her servant Félicité. It is directly because of this. The Germans have devastated Belgium because every German has been taught to desire to be a pig of a millionaire in a vast, gilded, modern hotel, with central heating and vast basements, far underground, filled with an army of sweated parasites.

The salvation of the world, if it be to be saved, will come from Mme Aubain and her servant Félicité — the moral as much as, or even more than, the bellicose salvation. And, for my part, if I could have my way, I would introduce a conscription of the French language into this country and a conscription of the English language into France, so that every soul from County Galway to the Alpes Maritimes was transfused with the double civilization. For it is only through language that comprehension and union can arise, and it is only by the careful and strained attention to the fine shades of language in common use that comprehension of language can be reached. And it is perhaps only Flaubert who ever paid sufficient attention even to the French language to reach its thorough understanding, and thus to appreciate the value to the world of the mind of Félicité, who for more than forty years was the servant of Mme Aubain of Pont-l'Evêque.

[*The Outlook*, 5 June 1915.]

FROM CHINA TO PERU [Ezra Pound]

I

THE interdict of the Editor of this Journal upon my writing about things as to which I know or care anything being still unremoved, I find myself reduced to writing about the Far East and the Far West; though it is true that this happens by hazard of book post. I have received, that is to say, during the last week two publications, the one entitled *Yerba Maté*, by Mrs Cloudesley Brereton, Officier d'Académie, Member of the Royal Sanitary Institute, Fellow of the Institute of Hygiene; and the other *Cathay*, by Ezra Pound. The first volume sings the praises of a beverage; the second contains renderings of Chinese poems that are a thousand years old — at least I suppose that they are renderings and not part of a mystification by the bard of Idaho — or is it Montana? For, if these are original verses, then Mr Pound is the greatest poet of this day.

The magic word 'maté' has been with me all my life, and, by writing about the beverage, by telling me where it may be procured, and by thus introducing it vicariously to my mouth, Mrs Cloudesley Brereton has done me a service almost equal to that which has been done to this country and to me by her distinguished husband.

Maté, then, is an Indian weed. It grows presumably in South American forests along with lianas and orchids and caymans and other exotics; just as, beneath the underwood of many years it has bloomed in my mind. I think I first became acquainted with maté when I first read Waterton's *Wanderings*, and I first read Waterton's *Wanderings* when I was eight. I wonder if you are acquainted with the narrative of that good squire of Elmete who wandered all through South America and returned to die in Yorkshire, a very St Francis of the birds in a blue Windsor uniform with golden buttons. He rode upon a cayman, it is true, but the feat of his which most endeared him to me was the fact that he used to stick wooden birds in his shaws and coppices so that the night-wandering poachers would discharge hails of rattling shot upon these inanimate objects, and the good Squire could sleep soundly while the guns roared in his coverts. He himself never had a bird shot on all his estates — game or garden.

It was, then, in Waterton's *Wanderings*, that delight of my earliest years, that I first made the acquaintance of maté; it is in the works of

Mr W. H. Hudson, the constant solace of my declining years as of my maturity, that that acquaintance has been matured. And surely if Mr Waterton was a St Francis of the Birds, Mr Hudson is their St Jerome and *Green Mansions* their Vulgate.

Birds, green mansions, vicarious wanderings on the Amazon, these have been great delights of my life, and they are united by the magic word 'maté'. Now, by the kindly graces of Mrs Cloudesley Brereton, the circle is complete and my acquaintance with the green, herb-odorous liquid is consummated. Happy Mrs Cloudesley Brereton! For what fate can be more enviable than that of singing the praises of a beverage? Omar Khayyam hymned wine, so did Horace, so did Rabelais; Mr Belloc, I think it was, who sang of the pleasures of drinking ale in the village of one's name; someone else has whispered, rather than sung, of the cup that cheers and not inebriates. Nothing but doubly decasyllabic Homerics will do for chanting praises of maté, since maté is the beverage of super-heroes. Do we not read that the Brazilian Army lived for twenty-two days upon maté alone without any food or drink? But Mrs Cloudesley Brereton does not write in verse; she uses solid prose — good, solid, sober prose such as our ancestors devoted to serious matters.

> Now, maté [writes Mrs Brereton] is no new-fangled drink, nor is it a manufactured article. It is a green herb, in appearance and flavour not unlike the green tea esteemed by our grandparents, with the bitter and aromatic flavour already mentioned, and somewhat resembling China tea if the latter be served without milk or sugar. For generations it has been the staple drink of millions of people, while from the earliest times those great huntsmen and warriors, the South American Indians, have known and appreciated its worth. So great is the sustaining power of the infusion that horsemen in South America constantly ride for a hundred miles or so and go all day without any other food and drink.

What a jolly sentence is this last! And how I wish it had fallen to my lot to write 'so great is the sustaining power of the infusion'! I have all my life been certain that the drinking of the infusion of this herb conferred upon the imbiber heroism, sobriety, chastity, hardihood, and endurance. Now that I daily drink it I know that I have all these virtues.

II

And, gazing into the depths of the mysterious green liquid in my fragrant cup, I realize that this lady has dealt a final blow to poor old China. Never again, after a few more years, will chests of Souchong, Orange Pekoe, and Gunpowder come to us from the Yang-tse-Kiang; never again will Borrovian old gentlemen pick up the Chinaman's language from hieroglyphics on the porcelain that comes embedded in the chests. We shall all be drinking maté. But here comes Mr Ezra Pound with *Cathay*. Mrs Brereton has called the New World in to redress the balance of the unchanging East; but Mr Pound brings us the poetry of the unchanging East to redress the equilibrium of beverages.

The poems in *Cathay* are things of a supreme beauty. What poetry should be, that they are. And, if a new breath of imagery and of handling can do anything for our poetry, that new breath these poems bring.

In a sense they only back up a theory and practice of poetry that is already old — the theory that poetry consists in so rendering concrete objects that the emotions produced by the objects shall arise in the reader — and not in writing about the emotions themselves. What could be better poetry that the first verse of 'The Beautiful Toilet'?

Blue, blue is the grass about the river
And the willows have overfilled the close garden.
And within, the mistress, in the midmost of her youth,
White, white of face, hesitates, passing the door.
Slender, she puts forth a slender hand;

Or what could better render the feelings of protracted war than 'The Son of the Bowman of Shu'?

Here we are, picking the first fern-shoots
And saying: When shall we get back to our country? . . .
Our defence is not yet made sure, no one can let his
  friend return.
We grub the old fern-stalks.
We say: Will we be let to go back in October?
  . . . Whose chariot? The General's.
Horses, his horses even, are tired. They were strong.
We have no rest, three battles a month.

By heaven, his horses are tired.
The generals are on them, the soldiers are by them.
The horses are well trained, the generals have ivory arrows
  and quivers ornamented with fish skin.
The enemy is swift, we must be careful.
When we set out, the willows were drooping with spring,
We come back in the snow,
We go slowly, we are hungry and thirsty,
Our mind is full of sorrow, who will know of our grief?

Or where have you had better rendered, or more permanently beautiful a rendering of, the feelings of one of those lonely watchers, in the outposts of progress, whether it be Ovid in Hyrcania, a Roman sentinel upon the Great Wall of this country, or merely ourselves in the lonely recesses of our minds, than the 'Lament of the Frontier Guard'?

By the North Gate, the wind blows full of sand,
Lonely from the beginning of time until now!
Trees fall, the grass goes yellow with autumn.
I climb the towers and towers to watch out the barbarous land:
Desolate castle, the sky, the wide desert.
There is no wall left to this village.
Bones white with a thousand frosts,
High heaps, covered with trees and grass;
Who brought this to pass?
Who has brought the flaming imperial anger?
Who has brought the army with drums and with kettledrums?
Barbarous kings.
A gracious spring, turned to blood-ravenous autumn,
A turmoil of warsmen, spread over the middle kingdom.
Three hundred and sixty thousand,
And sorrow, sorrow like rain.
Sorrow to go, and sorrow, sorrow returning.
Desolate, desolate fields,
And no children of warfare upon them,
    No longer the men for offence and defence.
Ah, how shall you know the dreary sorrow at the North Gate,
With Rihaku's name forgotten,
And we guardsmen fed to the tigers.

Rihaku.

Yet the first two of these poems are over two thousand years old and the last more than a thousand.

And Mr Pound's little volume is like a door in a wall, opening suddenly upon fields of an extreme beauty, and upon a landscape made real by the intensity of human emotions. We are accustomed to think of the Chinese as arbitrary or uniform in sentiment, but these poems reveal as being just ourselves. I do not know that that matters much; but what does matter to us immediately is the lesson in the handling of words and in the framing of emotions. Man is to mankind a wolf — homo homini lupus — largely because the means of communication between man and man are very limited. I daresay that if words direct enough could have been found, the fiend who sanctioned the use of poisonous gases in the present war could have been so touched to the heart that he would never have signed that order, calamitous, since it marks a definite retrogression in civilization such as had not yet happened in the Christian era. Beauty is a very valuable thing; perhaps it is the most valuable thing in life; but the power to express emotion so that it shall communicate itself intact and exactly is almost more valuable. Of both of these qualities Mr Pound's book is very full. Therefore I think we may say that this is much the best work he has yet done, for, however closely he may have followed his originals — and of that most of us have no means whatever of judging — there is certainly a good deal of Mr Pound in this little volume.

[*The Outlook*, 19 June 1915.]

from

Henry James, A Critical Study (1914)

I HAVE said elsewhere that, considering that our contacts with humanity are nowadays so much a matter of acquaintanceship and so little a matter of friendship, considering that for ourselves, moving about as men do today, we may know so many men and so little of the lives of any one man, the greatest service that any novelist can render to the Republic, the greatest service that any one man can render to the State, is to draw an unbiased picture of the world we live in. To beguile by pretty fancies, to lead armies, to invent new means of transport, to devise systems of irrigation — all these things are mere steps in the dark; and it is very much to be doubted whether any lawgiver can, in the present state of things, be anything but a curse to society. It seems at least to be the property of almost every law that today we frame to be infinitely more of a flail to a large number of people than of a service to any living soul. Regarding the matter historically, we may safely say that the feudal system in its perfection has died out of the world except in the islands of Jersey, Guernsey, Alderney, and Sark. The Middle Ages with their empirical and tricky enactments against regrating and the like; the constitutional theories, such as they were, of the Commonwealth and the Stuart age, have disappeared; the Whigism of Cobden and Bright, the bourgeois democracy of the first and third Republics and the oppressive, cruel, ignorant and blind theorizing of later Fabianism have all died away. We stand today, in the matter of political theories, naked to the wind and blind to the sunlight. We have a sort of vague uneasy feeling that the old feudalism and the old union of Christendom beneath a spiritual headship may in the end be infinitely better than anything that was ever devised by the Mother of Parliaments in England, the Constituent Assemblies in France, or all the Rules of the Constitution of the United States. And, just at this moment when by the nature of things we know so many men and so little of the lives of men, we are faced also by a sort of beggardom of political theories. It remains therefore for the novelist — and particularly for the realist among novelists — to give us the very matter upon which we shall build the theories of the new body politic. And, assuredly, the man who can do this for us, is conferring upon us a greater benefit than the man who can make two blades of grass grow where one grew before; since what is the good of substituting two blades for one — what is the benefit to society at large if the only individual to benefit by it is some company promoter?

That is the reason for my saying that I consider Mr James to be the greatest man now living. He, more than anybody, has observed human society as it now is, and more than anybody has faithfully rendered his observations for us. It is perfectly true that his hunting grounds have been almost exclusively 'up town' ones — that he has frequented the West End and the country house, practically never going once in his literary life east of Temple Bar or lower than Fourteenth Street. But a scientist has a perfect right — nay more, it is the absolute duty of the scientist — to limit his observations to the habits of lepidoptera, or to the bacilli of cancer if he does not feel himself adapted for enquiry into the habits of bulls, bears, elephants or foxes. Mr James, to put the matter shortly, has preferred to enquire into the habits of the comfortable classes and of their dependants, and no other human being has made the serious attempt to enquire with an unbiased mind into the habits and necessities of any other class or race of the habitable globe as it is. That is why Mr James deserves so well of the Republic.

I am aware that my penultimate statement is what is called a large proposition, but I think I am justified in making it. The English novel has hitherto occupied a very lowly position, whether in the world of art or in the world where sermons are preached, political speeches listened to, railway trains run, or ships plough the sea; and, in both these worlds, its lowly position has upon the whole been justified. The critic has been forced to say that the English novelist has hardly ever regarded his art as an art; the man of affairs has said that to read English novels was waste of time. And both the critic and man of affairs have hitherto been right. The worlds of art and affairs are widely different spheres, but that is not to say that they are spheres that should not interact one upon the other. Indeed, my grand-aunt Eliza amply summed the matter up, busy woman as she was, when she exclaimed that sooner than be idle she would take a book and read. But this attitude is only justifiable in a world of affairs that can't get hold of books worth reading. For, when books are worth reading the world of affairs that omits to read them is lost both commercially and spiritually. You cannot have a business community of any honesty unless you have a literature to set a high standard.

★ ★ ★

If Mr James, then, has given us a truthful picture of the leisured life that is founded upon the labours of all this stuff that fills graveyards, then he, more than any other person now living, has afforded matter upon which the sociologist of the future may build — or may commence his destructions.

For, given that he has achieved this, the problem which will then present itself to the sociologist is no more and no less than this — are the prizes of life, is the leisured life which our author has depicted for us, worth the striving for? If, in short, this life is not worth having — this life of the West End, of the country house, of the drawing-room, possibly of the studio, and of the garden party — if this life, which is the best that our civilization has to show, is not worth the living; if it is not pleasant, cultivated, civilized, cleanly and instinct with reasonably high ideals, then, indeed, Western civilization is not worth going on with, and we had better scrap the whole of it so as to begin again. For, you may by legislation increase the earnings of the labourer; you may by organizing or by inventing increase the wealth of our particular Western communities, but what is the use of this wealth if the only things that it can buy are no better than are to be had in any city store — unless, along with material objects that it does buy, it gets 'thrown in', as the phrase is, some of the things that were never yet bought by mortal's money. For it is no use saying anything else than that the manual labourer, if you give him four hundred a year and an excellent education, will have no ambition to live any otherwise, things being as they are, than as the dwellers in any suburb. And, supposing that you gave him a thousand a year he would, as things at present stand, have no other ambition than to live like one of the less wealthy characters of any one of Mr James' books. There is no getting away from these facts in any Anglo-Saxon community, and even in France and Germany the tendency is much the same; though, of course, in both of those countries you happen upon such phenomena as farmers of very large income who continue to live the life and to wear the dress of farmers, without any thought of snobbishly imitating the lives and habits of suburban clerks or of hunting gentry.

So that the problem remaining to the sociologist, the politico-economist or the mere voter, after reading Mr James' work is simply this: is the game worth the candle; is the prize worth the life? If they are not, then political economists must entirely change their views of what is meant by supply and demand, introducing a new factor which I will call the 'worth whileness' of having one's demands supplied; the sociologist must shut up all the books that he has ever read until he, too, has evolved some theory of what is worth while; and the voter must insist upon the closing of all the legislatures known to this universe — until some reasonable plan of what they are all striving for shall have been arrived at. For the fact is that our present systems of polity and laws, being entirely based upon theories of economics, we have paid — none of us who are interested in public questions — any heed at all to the purchasing power of that money which by our activities we produce and which by our legislation we seek as equally as possible to distribute.

It is because Mr James has so wonderfully paid attention to this question that I have advanced for him — and heaven knows he won't thank me for it — the claim to be the greatest servant of the State now living. Heaven knows too, that, things being as they are, it isn't much of a claim.

* * *

But it has been necessary for Mr James' immense process of refining himself, that he should keep away from the manifestations of the uncontrollable, and so very high-voiced, West. I have said earlier in this little study, that Mr James has had no public mission in life. But that is only a half truth, if it is not an absolute lie. For, during the whole seventy years of his life which began in New England in 1843, Mr James has had just one immense mission — the civilizing of America. New England presented our subject with glimpses of what a civilization might be. But you have only got to go to New England today to realize all that New England hadn't got, in those days, in the way of civilization. You have only got to go to Concord, Massachusetts with its dust, its heat, its hard climate, its squalid frame houses, its mosquitoes, to realize how little, on the luxurious and leisured side of existence, New England had to offer to a searcher after a refined, a sybaritic civilization.

I am not saying that there wasn't, between Salem and Boston, enough intellectual development to provide a non-materialistic state with fifty civilizations. It is obvious that you could not have produced an Emerson, a Holmes, a Thoreau or a Hawthorne — or for the matter of that a Washington Irving — without having a morally, an intellectually and even a socially refined atmosphere. Hampstead itself could not more carefully weigh its words or analyse its actions. But it would be fairly safe to say that, except for some few specimens of 'Colonial' ware and architecture you wouldn't in the '60s have found in the whole of New England a single article of what is called *vertu*. If you will look at the photograph which forms the frontispiece of *The Spoils of Poynton*, in Mr James' collected edition, you will see the sort of civilization for which Mr James must obviously have craved and which New England certainly couldn't have produced.

I must confess that I myself should be appalled at having to live before such a mantelpiece and such a *décor* — all this French gilding of the Louis Quinze period; all these cupids surmounting florid clocks; these vases with intaglios; these huge and floridly patterned walls; these tapestried fire-screens; these gilt chairs with backs and seats of Gobelins, of Aubusson, or of *petit point*. But there is no denying the value, the rarity and the suggestion of these articles which are described as 'some of the spoils' — the suggestion of tranquillity, of an aged civilization, of wealth, of leisure, of opulent refinement. And there is no denying that not by any conceivable imagination could such a mantelpiece with such furnishings have been found at Brook Farm.

It was in search of these things that Mr James travelled, as he so frequently did, to Florence where palazzi, and all that palazzi may hold, were so ready of access, so easy of conquest for the refined Transatlantic. In various flashes, in various obscurities, hints, concealments, reservations and reported speeches, Mr James has set us the task of piecing together a history of his temperament. The materials for this history are contained in various volumes. There is, for instance, his very last production, *A Small Boy*; there are the prefaces to the volumes of his collected editions; there are his comparatively scanty collections of criticisms, the most important of which are contained in the volume called *French Poets and Novelists*; there is the life of Hawthorne; there are the books about places such as *A Little Tour in France, English Hours,* and *The American Scene*. It is therefore to these works that I shall devote my consideration for the space of this section.

A Small Boy, which is a touching tribute to the memory of our subject's brother, adumbrates the existence, mostly in the state of New York, of a young male child — of two young male children in a household of the most eminent and of the most cultivated. As far as one can make the matter out — as far, that is to say, as it is necessary to make it out for a work which is in no sense biographical — Mr James' father, Henry James senior, was a person of great cultural position in what is now called the Empire State. He was not so much a representative citizen as a public adornment. He was occupied in the something like the reconciling of revealed religion with science, which was then beginning to adopt the semblance of a destroyer of Christianity. His published works were numerous; his eloquence renowned; his refinement undoubted. For the matter of that it was demonstrable, so that we have the image of two small boys, whether in the clean, white-porticoed streets of Buffalo or of Albany, or in the comparative rough-and-tumble and noise of a yellow-painted New York that contained nevertheless at that date gardens and pleasaunces. We have the impression of these two small boys of the '50s, pursuing a perhaps not very strenuous, but certainly a very selected, educational path towards that stage in which William James displayed all the faculty of analysis of a novelist, and Mr Henry James all the faculties of analysis of a pragmatic philosopher.

And there is no doubt that there were afforded to the quite young James — the small boy — a quite unusual number of contacts with quite the best people. Figuratively speaking, not only did this particular small boy live amongst the placid eccentrics of New England but, in his father's house, he was exposed to the full tide that, running counter to the Gulf stream, from quite early days of the Victorian age, bathed the shores of the Western World — the tide, I mean, of European celebrities. I am not, of course, writing a history of American culture — though indeed a history of Mr James' mind might well be nothing more nor less than that; but a very interesting subject lies open for some analyst in recording the impressions and adventures of the early tourists who entered on the formidable task of visiting, lecturing in, or, in whatever other intellectual way, exploiting the States of before the War. You will find traces of them in The Mississippi Pilot of Mark Twain where the formidable author tomahawks Mrs Trollope, and several French and English writers who, having visited that gigantic but uninteresting and desolate stream, failed of seeing its snags and bluffs and steamer saloons eye to eye with Mr Clemens. You will read the actual impressions of such a visit in Martin Chuzzlewit and in American Notes; or, in later American Memoirs you will read of the disappointment caused to distinguished hearers by Matthew Arnold's faulty delivery of his lectures — his mumbling voice, his frigid, English mannerisms. (How, alas, one sympathizes with the unfortunate author of The Forsaken Merman!)

At any rate, lecturing and acclaimed, or lecturing and appalled, and in either case overwhelmed by that immense and blinding thing, the world-famed American Hospitality — they came, those pilgrims, in a steady trickle. And it passed, that trickle, through the house of Mr Henry James, Senr, under the no doubt observant eyes of Henry James, Junr. It is not my business to particularize who they exactly were — those great figures. In order to catalogue them, I should have to fall back on the record of conversations with our subject; and although I should unscrupulously resort to this, if it suited my turn, it simply does not. It suffices to say that, whatever may have been our subject's personal contacts with Dickens, Thackeray, Arnold or any other English celebrity to whom Henry James, Senr, offered his fine hospitality, nothing of their personalities, 'rubbed off', as you might say, on to the by then adolescent James — or, if anything came at all it was only from the restrained muse of Matthew Arnold, whose temperament, in its rarefied way, was as 'New England' as was ever that of Emerson of James Russell Lowell.

* * *

Balzac we may take to have been our subject's first serious literary model — or at any rate his first conscious one; and it is interesting to consider how, at any rate on the surface, in their late flowering and in their determination to produce contemporary history, the voluminous author of the series of fairy tales called the Comédie Humaine and the author of the series of stories about worries and perturbations resembled each other.

* * *

As regards the second of the golden spoons that Mr James had in his mouth — I mean when he was born an American. . . .

There can be no doubt that this in itself is very largely responsible for his knowledge — apart from his mere surmises as to the human heart and as to human manners. The position of the American of some resources and of leisure was, in European society of the nineteenth century, one of a singular felicity. Without, or almost without, letters of introduction or social passports of any kind, the American 'went anywhere'. Anywhere in the world — into the courts of the Emperors of Austria as into the bosom of English county families! To know, or to admit an American into your family circle, appeared to commit you to nothing. There was the whole immense Herring Pond between yourself and their homes and you just accepted the strange and generally quiet creatures on their face values, without any question as to their origins, and taking their comfortable wealths for granted. Thus Mr James could really get to 'know' people in a way that would be absolutely sealed to any European young writer whether he were Honoré de Balzac or Charles Dickens. You can figure him (I am not in any way attempting to do more than draw a fancy portrait) — a quiet, extremely well-mannered and unassuming young gentleman, reputed to be very wealthy and in command of an entire leisure, without indeed even so much tax on his time as an occasional professional call in at the Legation or ministry of his country. Still he would be — he was — taken on the footing of a young diplomat and, if he proved, on nearer acquaintance, to be a thought more 'intellectual' than one is accustomed to find in the young men that one meets in good houses, that was only part of a transatlantic oddness. Some oddnesses the amiable creatures must be allowed to possess, considering their distant and hazy origins; you could be thankful if they did not sleep with derringers under their pillows — which they sometimes did — or pick their teeth with bowie knives.

Thus we may consider that Mr James, starting upon his European career, came in, at once, upon the very top. If he had been an English writer he would have been at it twenty years before he knew an English countess; he would die without having exchanged ten words with the wife of a duke, just as Balzac died without having had a glimpse of an interior of the Faubourg St Germain. But that street of high walls had no terrors for Mr James, and if his Madame de Bellegarde in some ways resembles a Balzac Marchioness, that is much more owing to the hold that Balzac and his methods had over our subject's imagination than to any want of social knowledge.

* * *

A critic may like a class of subject or may dislike them — for myself I like books about fox-hunting better than any other book to have a good read in. I would rather read Tilbury Nogo than *Daniel Deronda*, and any book of Surtees than any book of George Meredith — excepting perhaps *Evan Harrington*, which is a jolly thing with a good description of country house cricket. But that is merely a statement of preferences, like any other English writing about books. This latter leads the reader, as a rule, no further than to tell him that Messrs Lang, Collins, or who you will, like reading about golf, Charlotte Corday, the Murder in the Red Barn and, what you will — facts which may be interesting in themselves but which have nothing to do with how a book should be, or is not, written.

Similarly with disquisitions upon the temperament of a writer — since temperament is a thing like sunshine or the growing of grass, a gift of the good God. One may write about it if one likes, if one has nothing better to do; it is a sort of gossip like any other sort of gossip and, if it does no good in particular, it breaks no bones. Twenty of us, confined in a country house by a south-westerly gale, may well set to work to discuss the temperaments of our friends. 'I like so and so,' one of us will say, 'he is so considerate'; 'I prefer Mrs Dash,' another replies, 'she is so forceful.' But all the talk will not make the friend of So-and-so, with a taste for the milder virtues, like Mrs Dash whose attractions are of a more vigorous type. That is as much as to say that any penny-a-liner might call your attention to the temperament of Mr W. H. Hudson, which is the most beautiful thing that God ever made, though twenty thousand first-class critics thundering together could not make Mr James like Flaubert. Still, disquisitions upon temperament may do this amount of good: Supposing that the only work of Mr James that you had happened to glance at had been *The Great Good Place*, and supposing that you had no taste for mysticism, preferring the eerily horrible or the suavely social! You would have put Mr James' volume down and would have sworn never to take another up. Then — coming in some newspaper quotation upon some passage about *The Turn of the Screw*, which is the most eerie and harrowing story that was ever written — you might discover that here was a temperament, after all, infinitely to your taste. So that some profit might come from that form of writing.

But criticism concerns itself with methods and with methods and again with methods — and with nothing else. So that, having waded wearily through a considerable amount of writing that I can only compare to duty-calls, I was rejoicing at the thought of letting myself go. I felt as a horse does when, after a tiring day between the shafts, it is let loose into a goodly grass field. There seemed to be such reams that one might, all joyfully, write about the methods of this supremely great master of method. I had promised myself the real treat of my life. . . .

But alas, there is nothing to write! I do not mean to say that nothing could have been written — but it has all been done. Mr James has done it himself. In the matchless — and certainly bewildering series of Prefaces to the collected edition, there is no single story that has not been annotated, critically written about and (again critically) sucked as dry as an orange. There is nothing left for the poor critic but the merest of quotations.

I desired to say that the supreme discovery in the literary art of our day is that of Impressionism, that the supreme function of Impressionism is selection, and that Mr James has carried the power of selection so far that he can create an impression with nothing at all. And, indeed, that had been what for many years I have been desiring to say about our master! He can convey an impression, an atmosphere of what you will with literally nothing. Embarrassment, chastened happiness — for his happiness is always tinged with regret — greed, horror, social vacuity — he can give you it all with a purely blank page. His characters will talk about rain, about the opera, about the moral aspects of the selling of Old Masters to the New Republic, and those conversations will convey to your mind that the quiet talkers are living in an atmosphere of horror, of bankruptcy, of passion hopeless as the Dies Irae! That is the supreme trick of art today, since that is how we really talk about the musical glasses whilst our lives crumble to pieces around us. Shakespeare did that once or twice — as when Desdemona gossips about her mother's maid called Barbara whilst she is under the very shadow of death; but there is hardly any other novelist that has done it. Our subject does it, however, all the time, and that is one reason for the impression that his books give us of vibrating reality. I think the word 'vibrating' exactly expresses it; the sensation is due to the fact that the mind passes, as it does in real life, perpetually backwards and forwards between the apparent aspect of things and the essentials of life. If you have ever, I mean, been ruined, it will have been a succession of pictures like the following. Things have been going to the devil with you for some time; you have been worried and worn and badgered and beaten. The thing will be at its climax tomorrow. You cannot stand the strain in town and you ask your best friend — who won't be a friend any more tomorrow, human nature being what it is! — to take a day off at golf with you. In the afternoon, whilst the Courts or the Stock Exchange or some woman up in town are sending you to the devil, you play a foursome, with two other friends. The sky is blue; you joke about the hardness of the greens; your partner makes an extraordinary stroke at the ninth hole; you put in some gossip about a woman in a green jersey who is playing at the fourteenth. From what one of the other men replies you become aware that all those three men know that tomorrow there will be an end of you; the sense of that immense catastrophe broods all over the green and sunlit landscape. You take your mashie and make the approach shot of your life whilst you are joking about the other fellow's necktie, and he says that if you play like that on the second of next month you will certainly take the club medal, though he knows, and you know, and they all know you know, that by the second of next month not a soul there will talk to you or play with you. So you finish the match three up and you walk into the club house and pick up an illustrated paper. . . .

That, you know, is what life really is — a series of such meaningless episodes beneath the shadow of doom — or of impending bliss, if you prefer it. And that is what Henry James gives you — an immense body of work all dominated with that vibration — with that balancing of the mind between the great outlines and the petty details. And, at times, as I have said, he does this so consummately that all mention of the major motive is left out altogether. But it is superfluous for me to say this because it is already said — in a Preface. Consider this:—

> Only make the reader's general vision of evil intense enough, I said to myself —

Mr James is considering how to make *The Turn of the Screw* sufficiently horrible —

> — and that already is a charming job — and his own experience, his own imagination, his own sympathy (with the children) and horror (of their false friends) will supply him quite sufficiently with all the particulars. Make him *think* the evil, make him think it

> for himself, and you are released from weak specifications. This ingenuity I took pains — as indeed great pains were required — to apply; and with a success apparently beyond my liveliest hope. . . . How can I feel my calculation to have failed . . . on my being assailed, as has befallen me, with the charge of a monstrous emphasis, the charge of indecently expatiating [upon the corruption of soul of two haunted children]? There is . . . not an inch of expatiation . . . my values are positively all blanks save so far as an excited horror . . . proceeds to read into them more or less fantastic figures. . . .

Here again is one passage which exactly gives you the measure of how the horror is suggested. You are dealing with a little boy who has been expelled from school on a vague charge. This little boy and his sister have been corrupted — in ways that are never shown — by a governess and a groom in whose society they had been once left and who now, being dead, haunt, as *revenants*, the doomed children. The new governess is asking him why he was expelled from school, and the little boy answers that he did not open letters, did not steal.

> 'What then did you do?'
>
> He looked in vague pain all round the top of the room and drew his breath two or three times as if with difficulty. He might have been standing at the bottom of the sea and raising his eyes to some green twilight. 'Well — I said things.'
>
> 'Only that?'
>
> 'They thought it enough!'. . .
>
> 'But to whom did you say them? . . . Was it to every one?' I asked.
>
> 'No, it was only to ——' But he gave a sick little headshake. 'I don't remember their names.'
>
> 'Were they then so many?'
>
> 'No — only a few. Those I liked.'
>
> '. . . And did they repeat what you said,' I went on after a pause. . . .
>
> 'Oh, yes,' he nevertheless replied — 'they must have repeated them. To those *they* liked.'
>
> 'And those things came round ——?'
>
> 'To the masters? Oh yes!' he answered very simply.

I have stripped this episode of all its descriptive passages save one in order to reduce it to the barest and most crude of bones, in order to show just exactly what the hard skeleton is. And it will be observed that the whole matter — the whole skeleton or the only bone of it — is the one word 'things' — 'I said things'.

[London: Martin Secker, 1913: pp. 46-50, 62-5, 94-101, 107, 124-6, 150-57.].

from

The Transatlantic Review, vol. I, no. 1, January 1924

The first issue of the magazine Ford edited in Paris in 1924, with Hemingway as his associate editor, contained *The Nature of a Crime* by Conrad and Ford, the first instalment of *Some Do Not* (the first of the Tietjens books), two cantos by Pound, four poems by Cummings, and editorial matter by Ford in the form of 'Communications' and 'Stock Taking' (the latter signed with the pseudonym Daniel Chaucer he had used for two early novels). Subsequent issues included Gertrude Stein, William Carlos Williams, Joyce, Valéry, Juan Gris, Cocteau, Selma Lagerlof, Djuna Barnes, Jean Rhys, and Hemingway.

COMMUNICATIONS

PERIODICALS starting on careers have as a rule some difficulty in obtaining from an unmoved world those personal utterances of the interested that seem to give piquancy to the ends of what otherwise are seriousness. That difficulty has not beset the birth of the *Transatlantic Review* — because perhaps the birth is in truth a re-birth. It is held that Anglo-Saxondom cannot support a periodical purely literary in its aims; nevertheless the attempt to organize such a periodical is forever being made. One man has a try and fails; then another, and fails again. Then man number one takes it up again and one attempt is but the re-birth of the older failure. The older failure as like as not has begotten kindly memories and so, good wishes. Some of those attendant on the birth of the *Transatlantic Review* follow here.

The old *English Review* was started many years ago in order to print a poem called a 'Sunday Morning Tragedy' by Mr Thomas Hardy. The strong and generous impulse came from the late Mr Arthur Marwood. The writer remembers better than most episodes in his life the quiet morning — it was a Sunday too — on which Marwood burst into his garden that overlooked the Romney Marsh and exclaimed: 'The *Dash* has refused to print some of Hardy's poems for fear of shocking its readers. We must start a Review to print them'. — Marwood was of the Tory, North Country Squire type, full of lofty scepticisms and full too of generous enthusiasms and contempts. He had the most powerful intelligence that distinguished any man it has been the writer's fortune to meet: but by a grim stroke of destiny a tormenting disease made it impossible for him to be anything more than a looker on at that life of careers and movement in which he took so keen an interest and for which he was so marvellously equipped. It would be difficult to overestimate the number of predictions, all since borne out by the course of public events, to which before his untimely death he gave utterance.

We opened the *English Review*, then, blessed by George Meredith and with, as it were, on our foreheads the poem of Mr Hardy that had spread terror in the hearts of the Conductors of the *Dash*. We had hoped to open the *Transatlantic Review* with a poem from the same pen. Alas: our first COMMUNICATION runs:

Max Gate, Dorchester

Dear Mr Madox Ford,

As Mr Hardy continues rather unwell — which he has been the last fortnight, though not seriously except on account of his age — I reply to your last letter that you may not be inconvenienced by further delay.

In the circumstances he fears he can do nothing now beyond sending the general message that, believing International understandings should become thorough for the good of mankind, he wishes every success to the *Transatlantic Review*, since it may help such understandings.

Yours truly

F. E. Hardy

Our next COMMUNICATION is more difficult to handle and we handle it early to solve a problem as soon as we may. It runs:

Eastern Glebe, Dunmow

My Dear. . .

Good luck to the *Transatlantic Review*. I have always considered you to be one of the greatest poets and one of the greatest Editors alive and it gladdens my heart to think that you are creating a successor to the wonderful *English Review*.

Yours ever H.G.

this being addressed to a member of our editorial staff. It being a principle of all sound businesses that its employees must not receive valuable presents — and indeed the Reader who carefully studies our Advertisement Pages will see the condign punishment reserved for members of the *Transatlantic* staff who *do* receive presents — we shall take care that no poems by Mr Wells' protégé appear in these columns. As for the Editing — we can't help that. What — in the end — is an Editor more or less?

Mr T.S. Eliot, the editor of the only other purely literary periodical that reaches us shall answer with his definition of what is the task of the Perfect Editor: He writes:

THE CRITERION
A QUARTERLY REVIEW
17 Thavies Inn, London E.C.1

Dear Ford,

I welcome with extreme curiosity the appearance of the *Transatlantic Review*. If it is similar to the *Criterion* I shall take it as the best possible testimony of the blessings of the gods on our enterprises; in so far as it be different I hope that the differences will be complementary or at least antagonistic.

But from the prospectus which you have sent me I take no prescience of antagonism. Personally, I have always maintained what appears to be one of your capital tenets: that the standards of literature should be international. And personally, I am, as you know, an old-fashioned Tory. We are so far in accord.

The present age, a singularly stupid one, is the age of a mistaken nationalism and of an equally mistaken and artificial internationalism. I am all for empires, especially the Austro-Hungarian Empire, and I deplore the outburst of artificial nationalities, constituted like artificial genealogies for millionaires, all over the world. The number of languages worth writing in is very small, and it seems to me a waste of time to attempt to enlarge it. On the other hand, if anyone has a genuine nationality — and a genuine nationality depends upon the existence of a genuine literature, and you cannot have a nationality worth speaking of unless you have a national literature — if anyone has a genuine nationality, let him assert it, let the Frenchman be as French, the Englishman as English, the German as German, as he can be; but let him be French or English or German in such a way that his national character will complement, not contradict, the other nationalities. Let us not have an indiscriminate mongrel mixture of socialist internationals, or of capitalist cosmopolitans, but a harmony of different functions. But the more contact, the more free exchange there can be between the small number of intelligent people of every race or nation, the more likelihood of general contribution to what we call Literature.

I agree also that there can only be one English literature; that there cannot be British literature, or American literature.

You say that you wish to provide another vehicle for the younger writers. I object that this is an unnecessary discrimination in favour of youth. In America there seem to be a considerable number of periodicals, appearing more or less periodically, for this same purpose and in England there do not seem to be any younger writers anyway. That is one advantage in living in England: one remains perpetually a very young writer. I have enquired after younger writers; but those who are young in years seem anxious to pretend that they are round about forty, and try as hard as possible to assimilate themselves to the generation which has just gone out of date. They have no politics, or liberal politics (which is much the same thing); and if they had any politics, they would mix them up with their literature instead of keeping their literature clean. They have nothing. It is your business to help create the younger generation, as much as to encourage it. It does not need much encouragement.

But a review is not measured by the number of stars and scoops that it gets. Good literature is produced by a few queer people in odd corners; the use of a review is not to force talent, but to create a favourable atmosphere. And you will serve this purpose if you publish, as I hope you will find and publish, work of writers of whatever age who are too good and too independent to have found other publishers. I know that there are good writers, young and old, who belong in this category. In the *Criterion* we have endeavoured not to discriminate in favour of either youth or age, but to find good work which either could not appear elsewhere at all, or would not appear elsewhere to such advantage.

But I have only one request to make: give us either what we can support, or what is worth our trouble to attack. There is little of either in existence.

Sincerely yours,
T.S. Eliot

It is usual for periodicals nowadays to add notes as to the past histories of their contributors. Of our poets Messrs Cummings, Pound and Coppard are too well known in the United States to need our introduction there. For the benefit of the British reader — who however will manifest no curiosity — and of the French who in these days are almost too generously avid of information concerning those who write in English we may just call attention to the fact that Mr Pound has fathered a whole generation of younger writers; to the fact that, if American magazines did not print with eagerness all that Mr Coppard vouchsafed them we should have started the *Transatlantic Review* to print him — and we may as well say a word as to the typographical felicities of Mr Cummings. The man of letters is continually troubled by the problem that, — in cold print, the inflections and the tempi of the human voice are as impossible of rendering as are scents and the tones of musical instruments. It is to be doubted if there is any one who ever used a pen who has not from time to time tried by underlinings, capitals and queerly spacing his words to get something more on the paper than normal paper can bear. Mr Cummings with the bravery and logic of relative youth attempts cadences and surprises that we who are old, old and not brave long since abandoned and in so far as he succeeds he deserves well of all humanity who use the pen for even so little a matter as a note to go by the post.

For ourselves we limit ourselves to the use of. . . . to indicate the pauses by which the Briton — and the American now and then — recovers himself in order to continue a sentence. The typographical device is inadequate but how in the world. . . . how in the whole world else? — is one to render the normal English conversation? The last one at which we attended on English soil ran as follows: (We were in our club waiting for the waiter to bring change for a cheque)

First Club Member. What sort of a feller is. . . er. . . ? *(He points with his chin at an individual by the further fireplace)*

Second Ditto. Oh. . . . He's. . . . He's a;;. . . . Er;;;;;; Er. . . . .

First Ditto (Briskly) Ah!;;;. . . . Ialwaysthoughtso.

Of our other contributors Mr Luke Ionides is a member of one of those old Greek families who for a century or so by their encouragements of the Arts have added to the amenities and dignity of London life; Mr Chaucer, a veteran long hidden in Paris emerges in the hope of adding somewhat to the irritations caused by his books which, a decade ago, amused parts of the British metropolis and annoyed other parts. Miss Mary Butts is a writer of a younger school upon whom, if we may use the phrase, we have had our eye longer than most people; Mr Robert McAlmon represents — though geography is not our strongest point — that West-Middle-West-by-West of which we have been taught to and *do* expect so much. MM. Jean Cassou and Phillippe Soupault being French exact a greater privacy as to their personalities. The charm of their prose may be left for itself to work on the Reader; so may the vivacities of Mrs Jeanne Foster of New York.

The story by Mr Conrad and his collaborator who then signed himself Mr F. M. Hueffer was published firstly under a German pseudonym. As Mr Conrad himself says in his letter authorizing the re-publication 'Why on earth did we do it? Is it because the stuff is introspective and redolent of weltschmerz?' We continue to quote this last COMMUNICATION since we have no answer to give:

The early E.R. is the only literary business that in Bacon's phraseology ever came home to my bosom. The mere fact that it was the occasion of you putting on me that gentle but persistent pressure which extracted from the depths of my then despondency the *Personal Record* would be enough to make its memory dear. Do you care to be reminded that the editing of the first number was finished in the farm-house we occupied near Luton? You arrived one evening with your amiable myrmidons and parcels of copy. I shall never forget the cold of that night, the black grates, the guttering candles, the dimmed lamps and the desperate stillness of that house where women and children were innocently sleeping, when you sought me out in my dismal study to make me concentrate suddenly on a two-page notice of the *Île des Pingouins*; A marvellously successful instance of editorial tyranny. I suppose you were justified. The Number One of the E.R. could not have come out with two blank pages on it. It would have been too sensational. I have forgiven you long ago.

My only grievance against the early E.R. is that it didn't last long enough. If I say that I am curious to see what you will make of this venture it isn't because I have the slightest doubts of your consistency. You have a perfect right to say that you are 'rather unchangeable'. Unlike the Serpent (which is Wise) you will die in your original skin. But for one of your early men it will be interesting to see what men you will find now and what you will get out of them in these changed times . . .

Lastly. The paragraphs about *Romance* which you plan to include in your chronique. . . I suppose our recollections agree. Mine, in their simplest form, are:

First Part, yours; Second Part, mainly yours, with a little by me on points of seamanship and suchlike small matters; Third Part, about 60% mine with important touches by you; Fourth Part, mine, with here and there an important sentence by you; Fifth Part practically all yours, including the famous sentence at which we both exclaimed: 'This is Genius', (Do you remember what it is?) with perhaps half a dozen lines by me . . .

Mr Conrad's recollections — except for the generosity of his two 'importants' — tally well enough with those of the writer if conception alone is concerned. When it comes however to the writing the truth is that Parts One, Two, Three and Five are a singular mosaic of passages written alternately by one or other of the collaborators. The matchless Fourth Part is both in conception and writing entirely the work of Mr Conrad. It had been the intention of the editor of the Review to include in the present number some specimen pages from *Romance* with phrases allotted to one or the other of the collaborators. The process of collation of mss. and proofs has however proved so much more laborious than was anticipated that this must be deferred to a later number. Literary interest in the question of collaboration as such and the interest of the public in this particular collaboration may be taken to warrant the labour.

from

Joseph Conrad: a Personal Remembrance (1924)

Ford wrote this tribute to Conrad within two months of hearing of his death. 'I wrote this book at fever heat — in an extraordinarily short time for I had, as it were, to get it out of my system. Nevertheless I see very little that I want to change in it and I think it remains a very accurate account of our relationship — Conrad's and mine.' (Inscription in a copy of the book, December 1926, cited by David Dow Harvey, *Ford Madox Ford: A Bibliography*.)

PREFACE

NINE years ago the writer had occasion to make a hasty will. Since one of the provisions of his document appointed Conrad the writer's literary executor, we fell to discussing the question of literary biographies in general and our own in particular. We hit, as we generally did, very quickly upon a formula, both having a very great aversion to the usual official biography for men of letters whose lives are generally uneventful. But we agreed that should a writer's life have interests beyond the mere writing upon which he had employed himself, this life might well be the subject of a monograph. It should then be written by an artist and be a work of art. To write: *Joseph Conrad Korzeniowski was born on such a day of such a year in the town of 'So and So' in the Government of Kieff*, and so to continue would not conduce to such a rendering as this great man desired. So, here, to the measure of the ability vouchsafed, you have a projection of Joseph Conrad as, little by little, he reveal'ed himself to a human being during many years of close intimacy. It is so that, by degrees, Lord Jim appeared to Marlow [sic], or that every human soul by degrees appears to every other human soul. For, according to our view of the thing, a novel should be the biography of a man or of an affair, and a biography, whether of a man or an affair, should be a novel, both being, if they are efficiently performed, renderings of such affairs as are our human lives.

This then is a novel, not a monograph; a portrait, not a narration: for what it shall prove to be worth, a work of art, not a compilation.

It is conducted exactly along the lines laid down by us, both for the novel which is biography and for the biography which is a novel. It is the rendering of an affair intended first of all to make you see the subject in his scenery. It contains no documentation at all; for it no dates have been looked up; even all the quotations but two have been left unverified, coming from the writer's memory. It is the writer's impression of a writer who avowed himself impressionist. Where the writer's memory has proved to be at fault over a detail afterwards out of curiosity looked up, the writer has allowed the fault to remain on the page; but as to the truth of the impression as a whole, the writer believes that no man would care — or dare — to impugn it. It was that that Joseph Conrad asked for: the task has been accomplished with the most pious scrupulosity. *For something human was to him dearer than the wealth of the Indies.*

Guermantes, Seine et Marne, August
Bruges, October, 1924

from PART II, 'EXCELLENCY, A FEW GOATS. . . .'

The difference between our methods in those days was this: We both desired to get into situations, at any rate when any one was speaking, the sort of indefiniteness that is characteristic of all human conversations, and particularly of all English conversations that are almost always conducted entirely by means of allusions and unfinished sentences. If you listen to two Englishmen communicating by means of words, for you can hardly call it conversing, you will find that their speeches are little more than this: A. says 'What sort of a fellow is . . . *you* know!' B. replies, 'Oh, he's a sort of a . . .' and A. exclaims, 'Ah, I always thought so. . . .' This is caused partly by sheer lack of vocabulary, partly by dislike for uttering any definite statement at all. For anything that you say you may be called to account. The writer really had a connection who said to one of her nieces, 'My dear, never keep a diary. It may one day be used against you', and that thought has a profound influence on English life and speech.

The writer used to try to get that effect by almost directly rendering speeches that, practically, never ended, so that the original draft of *The Inheritors* consisted of a series of vague scenes in which nothing definite was ever said. These scenes melted one into the other until the whole book, in the end, came to be nothing but a series of the very vaguest hints. The writer hoped by this means to get an effect of a sort of silverpoint: a delicacy. No doubt he succeeded. But the strain of reading him must have been intolerable.

Conrad's function in *The Inheritors* as it today stands was to give to each scene a final tap; these, in a great many cases, brought the whole meaning of the scene to the reader's mind. Looking through the book the writer comes upon instance after instance of these completions of scenes by a speech of Conrad's. Here you have the — quite unbearably vague — hero talking to the royal financier about the supernatural-adventuress-heroine. Originally the speeches ran:

'You don't understand. . . . She. . . . She will. . . .'

He said: 'Ah! Ah!' in an intolerable tone of royal badinage.

I said again: 'You don't understand. . . . Even for your own sake. . . .'

He swayed a little on his feet and said: 'Bravo. . . . Bravissimo. . . . You propose to frighten. . . .'

I looked at his great bulk of a body. . . . People began to pass, muffled up, on their way out of the place.

The scene died away in that tone. In the book as it stands it runs, with Conrad's addition italicised:

'*If you do not* (cease persecuting her had been implied several speeches before), *I said*, '*I shall forbid you to see her.* And I shall. . . .'

'*Oh, Oh!' he interjected* with the intonation of a reveller at a farce. 'We are at that — we are the excellent brother —' *He paused and then added:* '*Well, go to the devil, you and your forbidding.*' *He spoke with the greatest good humour.*

'I am in earnest,' I said, 'very much in earnest. *The thing has gone too far*. And even for your own sake you had better. . . .'

He said: 'Ah, ah!' in the tone of his 'Oh, oh!'

'*She is no friend to you*,' I struggled on, '*she is playing with you for her own purposes*; you will. . . .'

He swayed a little on his feet and said: '*Bravo . . . bravissimo. If we can't forbid him we will frighten him. Go on, my good fellow. . . .*' and then, '*Come, go on.*'

I looked at his great bulk of a body. . . .

'*You absolutely refuse to pay any attention?*' I said.

'*Oh, absolutely*,' he answered.

At that point Conrad cut out a page or two of writing which was transferred to later in the book and came straight on to:

'Baron Halderschrodt has *committed suicide*,' which the writer for greater delicacy had rendered, 'Baron Halderschrodt has . . .' Conrad, however, added still further to the effect by adding: 'Half sentences came to our ears from groups that passed us: *A very old man with a nose that almost touched his thick lips was saying*:

"*Shot himself. . . . Through the left temple. . . . Mon Dieu!*" '

If the reader asks how the writer identifies which was his writing and which Conrad's in a book nearly twenty-five years old, the answer is very simple. Partly the writer remembers. This was the only scene in the book at which we really hammered away for any time and the way we did it is fresh still in his mind. Partly it is knowledge; Conrad would never have written 'a very old man' or 'almost'. He would have supplied an image for the old man's nose and would have given him an exact age, just as he had to precise the fact that Halderschrodt had shot himself, and through the left temple at that.

⋆ ⋆ ⋆

It has to be remembered that he had to wrestle, not with one language only, but with three. Or, say with two and the ghost of one, for it happened to him occasionally to say, 'There's a word *so and so* in Polish to express what I want.' But that happened only very seldom. All the rest of the time he got an effect to satisfy himself in French. This was of course the case preponderantly in passages of some nicety of thought and expression. He could naturally write 'Will you have a cup of tea?' or 'He is dead,' without first expressing himself to himself in French. But when he wrote a set of phrases like 'the gift of expression', 'the bewildering', 'the illuminating', 'the most exalted', 'the most contemptible', 'the pulsating stream of light', or 'the deceitful flow from the heart of an impenetrable darkness', he was translating directly from the French in his mind. Or when he wrote, 'Their glance was guileless, profound, confident and trusting', or, 'The offing was barred by a black bank of clouds, and the tranquil waterway leading to the uttermost ends of the earth flowed sombre under an overcast sky — seemed to lead into the heart of an immense darkness.' Naturally, as a British master mariner, he did not *have* to think of the offing as *le large*, but when he was trying the sound of that sentence for his final cadence he *did* first say *le large* and then said, 'The open sea; the *way* to the open sea. No, *the offing*.' That the writer very well remembers. . . . Conrad moreover had for long intended to end the story with the words, 'The horror! The horror!' '*L'horreur!*' having been the last words of Kurtz; but he gave that up. The accentuation of the English word was different from the French; the shade of meaning, too. And the device of such an ending, which would have been quite normal in a French story, would have been what we used to call *chargé* — a word meaning something between harrowing, melodramatic, and rhetorical, for which there is no English equivalent. Perhaps 'overloaded with sentiment' would come as near it as you can get: but that is clumsy. . . .

But the mere direct translation from imagined French into English was just child's play. It was when you came to the transposing precisely, of such a word as *chargé* from French into English, that difficulties began. The writer remembers Conrad spending nearly a whole day over one word in two or three sentences of proofs for the Blackwood volume called *Youth*. It was two words, perhaps — serene and azure. Certainly it was azure. 'And she crawled on, do or die, in the serene weather. The sky was a miracle of purity, a miracle of azure.' Conrad said, *azure*, the writer *ay*sure — or more exactly *ays*yeh. This worried Conrad a good deal since he wanted *azure* for his cadence. He read the sentence over and over again to see how it sounded.

The point was that he was perfectly aware that azure was a French word, or in English almost exclusively a term of heraldry, and his whole endeavour was given to using only such words as are found in the normal English vernacular — or thereabouts, for he never could be got really to believe how poverty-stricken a thing the normal English vernacular is. The vocabulary that he used in speaking English was enormous and he regarded it as a want of patriotism to think that the average Englishman knew his language less well than himself.

Mr Henry James used to call Marlowe, the usual narrator for many years of Conrad's stories, 'that preposterous master mariner'. He meant precisely that Marlowe was more of a philosopher and had a vocabulary vastly larger and more varied than you could possibly credit to the master mariner as a class. Conrad, however, persisted that Marlowe was little above the average of the ship's officer in either particular, and presumably he knew his former service mates better than did Mr James — or the rest of us. . . . Still he *did* think that the word azure would be outside the ordinary conversational vocabulary of a ship's captain. . . .

We talked about it then for a whole day. . . . Why not say simply 'blue'? Because really, it is not blue. Blue is something coarser in the grain; you imagine it the product of the French Impressionist painter — or of a house painter — with the brush strokes showing. Or you think so of blue after you have thought of azure. Azure is more transparent. . . .

Or again the word 'serene'. . . . Why not calm? Why not quiet? . . . Well, quiet as applied to weather is — or perhaps it is only was — part of the 'little language' that was being used by the last Pre-Raphaelite poets. That ruled quiet out. Calm on the other hand is, to a master mariner, almost too normal and too technically inclusive. Calm is in a log-book almost any weather that would not be agitating to a landsman — or thereabouts. Dead calm is — again to a seaman — too technical. Dead calmness precludes even the faintest ruffle of wind, even the faintest cat's-paw on the unbroken surface of the sea.

The writer has heard it objected that Conrad was pernicketty; why should he not use technical sea terms and let the reader make what he could of it? But Conrad's sea is more real than the sea of any other sea writer; and it is more real, because he avoided the technical word.

The whole passage of *Youth* under consideration is as follows — the writer is quoting from memory, but as far as this passage is concerned he is fairly ready to back his memory against the printed page:

'And she crawled on, do or die, in the serene weather. The sky was a miracle of purity, a miracle of azure. The sea was polished, was blue, was pellucid, was sparkling like a precious stone, extending on all sides, all round to the horizon. As if the whole terrestrial globe had been one jewel, one colossal sapphire. And on the lustre of the great calm waters the *Judea* moved imperceptibly, enveloped in languid and unclean vapours. . . .'

That is as far as the writer's memory will carry him, though the paragraph ends with the words, 'The splendour of sea and sky'.

This then is almost the perfection of sea writing of its type. (Stephen Crane could achieve another perfection by writing of the waves as barbarous and abrupt: but that in the end is no less anthropomorphic.) And the words serene and azure remained after an infinite amount of talking so that the whole passage might retain its note of the personality of Destiny that watched inscrutably behind the sky. It was Destiny that was serene, that had purity, that was azure . . . and that ironically set that smudge of oily vapour from the burning vessel across the serenity of the miraculous sapphire — so that youth might be enlightened as to the nature of the cosmos, even whilst in process of being impressed with its splendours.

'Serene' as applied to weather; 'azure' as applied to the sky are over-writing a shade, are a shade *chargés* if they apply merely to the sea and merely to the sky. . . . But Conrad was obsessed by the idea of a Destiny omnipresent behind things; of a Destiny that was august, blind, inscrutable, just, and above all passionless, that has decreed that the outside things — the sea, the sky, the earth, love, merchandising, the winds — shall make youth seem tenderly ridiculous and all the other ages of men gloomy, imbecile, thwarted — and possibly heroic. . . . Had the central character of this story been a fortyish man you would have had, added to the burning ship with its fumes, dirty weather, dripping clothes, the squalid attributes of the bitter sea. As it was an affair of *youth* you have serene weather and a miracle of purity, to enhance the irony of Destiny.

from PART III, 'IT IS ABOVE ALL TO MAKE YOU SEE. . . .'

The time has come, then, for some sort of critical estimate of this author. Critical, not philosophical. For the philosophy of Joseph Conrad was a very simple one; you might sum it all up in the maxim of Herrick's: To live merrily and trust to good letters. Himself he summed it up in the great word 'Fidelity', and his last great novel turned upon a breach of trust by his typical hero, his King Tom. It is the misfortune of morality that the greatest thrills that men can get from life come from the contemplation of its breaches!

About Conrad there was, however, as little of the moralist as there was of the philosopher. When he had said that every work of art has — must have — a profound moral purpose, and he said that every day and all day long, he had done with the subject. So that the writer has always wished that Conrad had never written his famous message on Fidelity. Truly, those who read him knew his conviction that the world, the temporal world, rests on a very few simple ideas — and it might have been left at that. For it was the very basis of all Conrad's work that the fable must not have the moral tacked on to its end. If the fable has not driven its message home the fable has failed, must be scrapped and must give place to another one.

But the impulse to moralize, to pontify, is a very strong one, and comes in many treacherous guises. One may so easily do it unawares: and instances of Conrad's pontifications are far enough to seek, considering the temporal eminence to which he attained. He let, otherwise, his light so shine before men that few would be inclined to claim him amongst the preachers.

He was before all things the artist and his chief message to mankind is set at the head of this chapter. . . . 'It is above all things to make you *see*. . . .' Seeing is believing for all the doubters of this planet, from Thomas to the end: if you can make humanity see the few very simple things upon which this temporal world rests you will make mankind believe such eternal truths as are universal. . . .

That message, that the province of written art is above all things to make you see, was given before we met; it was because that same belief was previously and so profoundly held by the writer that we could work for so long together. We had the same aims and we had all the time the same aims. Our attributes were no doubt different. The writer probably knew more about words, but Conrad had certainly an infinitely greater hold over the architectonics of the novel, over the way a story should be built up so that its interest progresses and grows up to the last word. Whether in the case of our officially collaborated work or in the work officially independent in which we each modified the other with almost as much enthusiasm and devotion as we gave to work done together, the only instance that comes to the writer's mind in which he of his own volition altered the structure of any work occurred in the opening chapters of *The Rescue*.

★ ★ ★

Openings for us, as for most writers, were matters of great importance, but probably we more than most writers realized of what primary importance they were. A real short story must open with a breathless sentence; a long-short story may begin with an 'as' or a 'since' and some leisurely phrases. At any rate the opening paragraph of book or story should be of the tempo of the whole performance. That is the *règle generale*. Moreover, the reader's attention must be gripped by that first paragraph. So our ideal novel must begin either with a dramatic scene or with a note that should suggest the whole book. *The Nigger of the Narcissus* begins:

Mr Baker, chief mate of the *Narcissus*, stepped in one stride out of his lighted cabin into the darkness of the quarter deck. . . .

The Secret Agent:

Mr Verloc, going out in the morning, left his shop nominally in charge of his brother-in-law. . . .

The End of the Tether:

For a long time after the course of the steamer *Sophala* had been altered. . . .

this last being the most fitting beginning for the long-short story that *The End of the Tether* is.

Romance, on the other hand begins:

To yesterday and to today I say my polite *vaya usted con dios*. What are those days to me? But that far-off day of my romance, when from between the blue and white bales in Don Ramon's darkened store room in Kingston. . . .

an opening for a long novel in which the dominant interest lies far back in the story and the note must be struck at once.

The Inheritors' first lines are:

'Ideas,' she said. 'Oh, as for ideas . . .'

an opening for a short novel.

Conrad's tendency and desire made for the dramatic opening; the writer's as a rule for the more pensive approach; but we each, as a book would go on, were apt to find that we must modify our openings. This was more often the case with Conrad than with the writer, since Conrad's books depended much more on the working out of an intrigue which he would develop as the book was in writing: the writer has seldom begun on a book without having, at least, the intrigue, the 'affair', completely settled in his mind.

The disadvantage of the dramatic opening is that after the dramatic passage is done you have to go back to getting your characters in, a proceeding that the reader is apt to dislike. The danger with the reflective opening is that the reader is apt to miss being gripped at once by the story. Openings are therefore of necessity always affairs of compromise.

The note should here be struck that in all the conspiracies that went on at the Pent or round the shores of the Channel there was absolutely no mystery. We thought just simply of the reader. Would this passage grip him? If not it must go. Will this word make him pause and so slow down the story? If there is any danger of that, away with it. That is all that is meant by the dangerous word *technique*.

★ ★ ★

It might be as well here to put down under separate headings, such as 'Construction', 'Development', and the like, what were the formulae for the writing of the novel at which Conrad the writer had arrived, say in 1902 or so, before we finally took up and finished *Romance*. The reader will say that that is to depart from the form of the novel in which form this book pretends to be written. But that is not the case. The novel more or less gradually, more or less deviously, lets you into the secrets of the characters of the men with whom it deals. Then, having got them in, it sets them finally to work. Some novels, and still more short stories, will get a character in with a stroke or two as does Maupassant in the celebrated sentence in the 'Reine Hortense' which Conrad and the writer were never tired of — quite intentionally — misquoting: '*C'était un monsieur à favoris rouges qui entrait toujours le premier*. . . .' He was a gentleman with red whiskers who always went first through a doorway. . . . *That* gentleman is so sufficiently got in that you need know no more of him to understand how he will act. He has been 'got in' and can get to work at once. That is called by the official British critics the static method and is, for some reason or other, condemned in England.

Other novels, however, will take much, much longer to develop their characters. Some — and this one is an example — will take almost a whole book to really get their characters in and will then dispose of the 'action' with a chapter, a line, or even a word — or two. The most wonderful instance of all of that is the ending of the most wonderful of all Maupassant's stories, 'Champs d'Oliviers', which, if the reader has not read, he should read at once. Let us now take a heading. (This method has the advantage that the lay reader who cannot interest himself in literary methods and the Critic-Annalist whose one passion is to cut the cackle and come to the horses can skip the whole chapter, certain that he will miss none of the spicy titbits.)

GENERAL EFFECT

We agreed that the general effect of a novel must be the general effect that life makes on mankind. A novel must therefore not be a narration, a report. Life does not say to you: In 1914 my next-door neighbour, Mr Slack, erected a greenhouse and painted it with Cox's green aluminium paint. . . . If you think about the matter you will remember, in various unordered pictures, how one day Mr Slack appeared in his garden and contemplated the wall of his house. You will then try to remember the year of that occurrence and you will fix it as August, 1914, because having had the foresight to bear the municipal stock of the City of Liège you were able to afford a first-class season ticket for the first time in your life. You will remember Mr Slack — then much thinner because it was before he found out where to buy that cheap Burgundy of which he has since drunk an inordinate quantity, though whisky you think would be much better for him! Mr Slack again came into his garden, this time with a pale, weaselly-faced fellow, who touched his cap from time to time. Mr Slack will point to his house wall several times at different points, the weaselly fellow touching his cap at each pointing. Some days after, coming back from business, you will have observed against Mr Slack's wall. . . . At this point you will remember that you were then the manager of the fresh-fish branch of Messrs Catlin and Clovis in Fenchurch Street. . . . What a change since then! Millicent had not yet put her hair up. . . . You will remember how Millicent's hair looked, rather pale and burnished in plaits. You will remember how it now looks, henna'd; and you will see in one corner of your mind's eye a little picture of Mr Mills the vicar talking — oh, very kindly — to Millicent after she has come back from Brighton. . . . But perhaps you had better not risk that. You remember some of the things said by means of which Millicent has made you cringe — and her expression! . . . Cox's Aluminium Paint! . . . You remember the half-empty tin that Mr Slack showed you — he had a most undignified cold — with the name in a horseshoe over a blue circle that contained a red lion asleep in front of a real-gold sun. . . .

And, if that is how the building of your neighbour's greenhouse comes back to you, just imagine how it will be with your love affairs that are so much more complicated. . . .

IMPRESSIONISM

We accepted without much protest the stigma 'Impressionists' that was thrown at us. In those days Impressionists were still considered to be bad people: Atheists, Reds, wearing red ties with which to frighten householders. But we accepted the name because Life appearing to us much as the building of Mr Slack's greenhouse comes back to you, we saw that Life did not narrate, but made impressions on our brains. We in turn, if we wished to produce on you an effect of life, must not narrate but render impressions.

SELECTION

We agreed that the whole of Art consists in selection. To render your remembrance of your career as a fish salesman might enhance the story of Mr Slack's greenhouse, or it might *not*. A little image of iridescent, blue-striped, black-striped, white fish on a white marble slab with water trickling down to them round a huge mass of orange salmon roe; a vivid description of a horrible smell caused by a cat having stolen and hidden in the thick of your pelargoniums a cod's head that you had brought back as a perquisite, you having subsequently killed the cat with a hammer, but long, long before you had rediscovered her fishy booty. . . . Such little impressions might be useful as contributing to illustrate your character — one should not kill a cat with a hammer! They might illustrate your sense of the beautiful — or your fortitude under affliction — or the disagreeableness of Mr Slack, who had a delicate sense of smell — or the point of view of your only daughter, Millicent.

We should then have to consider whether your sense of the beautiful or your fortitude could in our rendering carry the story forward or interest the reader. If it did we should include it; if in our opinion it was not likely to, we should leave it out. Or the story of the cat might in itself seem sufficiently amusing to be inserted as a purposed *longueur*, so as to give the idea of the passage of time. . . . It may be more amusing to read the story of a cat with your missing dinner than to read, 'A fortnight elapsed. . . .' Or it might be better after all to write boldly, 'Mr Slack, after a fortnight had elapsed, remarked one day very querulously, "That smell seems to get worse instead of better." '

SELECTION (SPEECHES)

That last would be compromise, for it would be narration instead of rendering: it would be far *better* to give an idea of the passage of time by picturing a cat with a cod's head, but the length of the story must be considered. Sometimes to render anything at all in a given space will take up too much room — even to render the effect and delivery of a speech. Then just boldly and remorselessly you must relate and *risk* the introduction of yourself as author, with the danger that you may destroy all the illusion of the story.

Conrad and the writer would have agreed that the ideal rendering of Mr Slack's emotions would be as follows:

> A scrawny, dark-brown neck, with an immense Adam's apple quivering over the blue stripes of a collar, erected itself between the sunflower stems above the thin oaken flats of the dividing fence. An unbelievably long, thin gap of a mouth opened itself beneath a black-spotted handkerchief, to say that the unspeakable odour was sufficient to slay all the porters in Covent Garden. Last week it was only bad enough to drive a regiment of dragoons into a faint. The night before the people whom he had had to supper — I wondered who could eat any supper with any appetite under the gaze of those yellow eyes — people, mind you, to whom he had hoped to sell a little bit of property in the neighbourhood. Good people. With more than a little bit in the bank. People whose residence would give the whole neighbourhood a lift. They had asked if he liked going out alone at night with so many undiscovered murders about. . . . 'Undiscovered murders!' he went on repeating, as if the words gave him an intimate sense of relief. He concluded with the phrase, 'I *don't* think!'

That would be a very fair *rendering* of part of an episode: it would have the use of getting quite a lot of Mr Slack in; but you might want to get on towards recounting how you had the lucky idea of purchasing shares in a newspaper against which Mr Slack had counselled you. . . . And you might have got Mr Slack in already!

The rendering in fact of speeches gave Conrad and the writer more trouble than any other department of the novel whatever. It introduced at once the whole immense subject of under what convention the novel is to be written. For whether you tell it direct and as author — which is the more difficult way — or whether you put it into the mouth of a character — which is easier by far but much more cumbersome — the question of reporting or rendering speeches has to be faced. To pretend that any character or any author writing directly can remember whole speeches with all their words for a matter of twenty-four hours, let alone twenty-four years, is absurd. The most that the normal person carries away of a conversation after even a couple of hours is just a salient or characteristic phrase or two, and a mannerism of the speaker. Yet, if the reader stops to think at all, or has any acuteness whatever, to render Mr Slack's speech directly, 'Thet there odour is enough to do all the porters in Common Gorden in. Lorst week it wouldn' no more 'n 'v sent a ole squad of tinwiskets barmy on the crumpet . . .' and so on through an entire monologue of a page and a half, must set the reader at some point or other wondering how the author or the narrator can possibly, even if they were present, have remembered every word of Mr Slack's long speech. Yet the object of the novelist is to keep the reader entirely oblivious of the fact that the author exists — even of the fact that he is reading a book. This is of course not possible to the bitter end, but a reader *can* be rendered very engrossed, and the nearer you can come to making him entirely insensitive to his surroundings, the more you will have succeeded.

Then again, directly reported speeches in a book do move very slowly; by the use of indirect locutions, together with the rendering of the effects of other portions of speech, you can get a great deal more into a given space. There is a type of reader that likes what is called conversations — but that type is rather the reader in an undeveloped state than the reader who has read much. So, wherever practicable, we used to arrange speeches much as in the paragraph devoted to Mr Slack above. But quite often we compromised and gave passages of direct enough speech.

This was one of the matters as to which the writer was more uncompromising than was Conrad. In the novel which he did at last begin on his forty-first birthday there will be found to be hardly any direct speech at all, and probably none that is more than a couple of lines in length. Conrad indeed later arrived at the conclusion that, a novel being in the end a matter of convention — and in the beginning too, for the matter of that, since what are type, paper, bindings and all the rest, but matters of agreement and convenience — you might as well stretch convention a little farther, and postulate that your author or your narrator is a person of a prodigious memory for the spoken. He had one minute passion with regard to conversations: he could not bear the repetition of 'he said's' and 'she said's', and would spend agitated hours in chasing those locutions out of his or our pages and substituting 'he replied', 'she ejaculated', 'answered Mr Verloc' and the like. The writer was less moved by this consideration; it seemed to him that you could employ the words 'he said' as often as you like, accepting them as being unnoticeable, like 'a', 'the', 'his', 'her', or 'very'.

CONVERSATIONS

One unalterable rule that we had for the rendering of conversations — for genuine conversations that are an exchange of thought, not interrogatories or statements of fact — was that no speech of one character should ever answer the speech that goes before it. This is almost invariably the case in real life where few people listen, because they are always preparing their own next speeches. When, of a Saturday evening, you are conversing over the fence with your friend Mr Slack, you hardly notice that he tells you he has seen an incredibly coloured petunia at a market gardener's, because you are dying to tell him that you have determined to turn author to the extent of writing a letter on local politics to the newspaper of which, against his advice, you have become a large shareholder.

He says, 'Right down extraordinary that petunia was . . . .'

You say, 'What would you think now of my . . . .'

He says, 'Diamond-shaped stripes it had, blue-black and salmon. . . .'

You say, 'I've always thought I had a bit of a gift. . . .'

Your daughter Millicent interrupts, 'Julia Gower has got a pair of snake-skin shoes. She bought them at Wiston and Willocks's.'

You miss Mr Slack's next two speeches in wondering where Millicent got that bangle on her wrist. You will have to tell her more carefully than ever that she must *not* accept presents from Tom, Dick and Harry. By the time you have come out of that reverie Mr Slack is remarking:

'I said to him use turpentine and sweet oil, three parts to two. What do you think?'

* * *

But, on the whole, the indirect, interrupted method of handling interviews is invaluable for giving a sense of the complexity, the tantalization, the shimmering, the haze, that life is. In the pre-War period the English novel began at the beginning of a hero's life and went straight on to his marriage without pausing to look aside. This was all very well in its way, but the very great objection could be offered against it that such a story was too confined to its characters and, too self-centredly, went on, *in vacuo*. If you are so set on the affair of your daughter Millicent with the young actor that you forget that there *are* flower shows and town halls with nude statuary your intellect will appear a thing much more circumscribed than it should be. Or, to take a larger matter. A great many novelists have treated of the late War in terms solely of the War: in terms of pip squeaks, trench coats, wire aprons, shells, mud, dust, and sending the bayonet home with a grunt. For that reason interest in the late War is said to have died. But, had you taken part actually in those hostilities, you would know how infinitely little part the actual fighting itself took in your mentality. You would be lying on your stomach, in a beast of a funk, with an immense, horrid German barrage going on all over and round you and with hell and all let loose. But, apart from the occasional, petulant question, 'When the deuce will our fellows get going and shut 'em up?' your thoughts were really concentrated on something quite distant: on your daughter Millicent's hair, on the fall of the Asquith Ministry, on your financial predicament, on why your regimental ferrets kept on dying, on whether Latin is really necessary to an education. . . . You were there, but great shafts of thought from the outside, distant and unattainable world infinitely for the greater part occupied your mind.

It was that effect, then, that Conrad and the writer sought to get into their work, that being Impressionism.

But these two writers were not unaware that there are other methods; they were not rigid in their own methods; they were sensible to the fact that compromise is at all times necessary in the execution of every work of art.

Let us come, then, to the eternally vexed seas of the Literary Ocean.

* * *

We used to say that a passage of good style began with a fresh, usual word, and continued with fresh, usual words to the end; there was nothing more to it. When we felt that we had really got hold of the reader, with a great deal of caution we would introduce a word not common to a very limited vernacular, but that only very occasionally. Very occasionally indeed; practically never. Yet it is in that way that a language grows and keeps alive. People get tired of hearing the same words over and over again. . . . It is again a matter for compromise.

Our chief masters in style were Flaubert and Maupassant: Flaubert in the greater degree, Maupassant in the less. In about the proportion of a sensible man's whisky and soda. We stood as it were on those hills and thence regarded the world. We remembered long passages of Flaubert; elaborated long passages in his spirit and with his cadences and then translated them into passages of English as simple as the subject under treatment would bear. We remembered short, staccato passages of Maupassant; invented short, staccato passages in his spirit and then translated them into English as simple as the subject would bear. Differing subjects bear differing degrees of simplicity. To apply exactly the same timbre of language to a dreadful interview between a father and a daughter as to the description of a child's bedroom at night is impracticable because it is unnatural. In thinking of the frightful scene with your daughter Millicent which ruined your life, town councillor and parliamentary candidate though you had become, you will find that your mind employs a verbiage quite different from that which occurs when you remember Millicent asleep, her little mouth just slightly opened, her toys beside the shaded night-light.

Our vocabulary, then, was as simple as was practicable. But there are degrees of simplicity. We employed as a rule in writing the language that we employed in talking the one to the other. When we used French in speaking we tried mentally to render in English the least literary equivalent of the phrase. We were, however, apt to employ in our conversation words and periphrases that are not in use by, say, financiers. This was involuntary, we imagining that we talked simply enough. But later a body of younger men with whom the writer spent some years would say, after dinner, 'Talk like a book, H. . . . Do talk like a book!' The writer would utter some speeches in the language that he employed when talking with Conrad; but he never could utter more than a sentence or two at a time. The whole mess would roar with laughter and, for some minutes, would render his voice inaudible.

If you will reflect on the language you then employed — and the writer — you will find that it was something like, 'Cheerio, old bean. The beastly Adjutant's Parade is at five ack emma. Will you take my Johnnie's and let me get a real good fug in my downy bug-walk? I'm fair blind to the wide tonight.' That was the current language then and, in the earlier days of our conversations, some equivalent with which we were unacquainted must normally have prevailed. That we could hardly have used in our books, since within a very short time such languages become incomprehensible. Even today the locution 'ack emma' is no longer used and the expression 'blind to the wide' is incomprehensible — the very state is unfamiliar

— to more than half the English-speaking populations of the globe.

So we talked and wrote a Middle-High English of as unaffected a sort as would express our thoughts. And that was all that there really was to our 'style'. Our greatest admiration for a stylist in any language was given to W. H. Hudson of whom Conrad said that his writing was like the grass that the good God made to grow and when it was there you could not tell how it came.

Carefully examined, a good — an interesting — style will be found to consist in a constant succession of tiny, unobservable surprises. If you write — 'His range of subject was very wide and his conversation very varied and unusual; he could rouse you with his perorations or lull you with his periods; therefore his conversation met with great appreciation and he made several fast friends' — you will not find the world very apt to be engrossed by what you have set down. The results will be different if you put it, 'He had the power to charm or frighten rudimentary souls into an aggravated witch-dance; he could also fill the small souls of the pilgrims with bitter misgivings; he had one devoted friend at least, and he had conquered one soul in the world that was neither rudimentary nor tainted with self-seeking.'

Or, let us put the matter in another way. The catalogue of an ironmonger's store is uninteresting as literature because things in it are all classified and thus obvious; the catalogue of a farm sale is more interesting because things in it are contrasted. No one would for long read: Nails, drawn wire, ½ inch, per lb. . . . ; nails, do., ¾ inch, per lb. . . . ; nails, do., inch, per lb. . . . But it is often not disagreeable to read desultorily: '*Lot 267*, Pair rabbit gins. *Lot 268*, Antique powder flask. *Lot 269*, Malay Kris. *Lot 270*, Set of six sporting prints by Herring. *Lot 271*, Silver caudle cup . . .' for that, as far as it goes, has the quality of surprise.

That is, perhaps, enough about Style. This is not a technical manual, and at about this point we arrive at a region in which the writer's memory is not absolutely clear as to the points on which he and Conrad were agreed. We made in addition an infinite number of experiments, together and separately, in points of style and cadence. The writer, as has been said, wrote one immense book entirely in sentences of not more than ten syllables. He read the book over. He found it read immensely long. He went through it all again. He joined short sentences; he introduced relative clauses; he wrote in long sentences that had a gentle sonority and ended with a dying fall.

The book read less long. Much less long.

Conrad also made experiments, but not on such a great scale since he could always have the benefit of the writer's performances of that sort. The writer only remembers specifically one instance of an exercise on Conrad's part. He was interested in blank verse at the moment — though he took no interest in English verse as a rule — and the writer happening to observe that whole passages of *Heart of Darkness* were not very far off blank verse, Conrad tried for a short time to run a paragraph into decasyllabic lines. The writer remembers the paragraph quite well. It is the one which begins: 'She walked with measured steps, draped in striped and fringed cloths, treading the earth proudly with a slight jingle and flash of barbarous ornaments. . . .'

But he cannot remember what Conrad added or took away. There come back vaguely to him a line or two like:

> She carried high her head, her hair was done
> In the shape of a helmet; she had greaves of brass
> To the knee; gauntlets of brass to th' elbow.
> A crimson spot. . . .

That, however, may just as well be the writer's contrivance as Conrad's: it happened too long ago for the memory to be sure. A little later, the writer occupying himself with writing French rhymed *vers libre*, Conrad tried his hand at that too. He produced:

> Riez toujours! La vie n'est pas si gaie,
> Ces tristes jours quand à travers la haie
> Tombe le long rayon
> Dernier
> De mon soleil qui gagne
> Les sommets, la montagne,
> De l'horizon. . . .

There was a line or two more that the writer has forgotten.

That was Conrad's solitary attempt to write verse.

* * *

Probably the mere thought of reading aloud subconsciously aroused memories of once-heard orations of Mr Gladstone or John Bright; so, in writing, even to himself he would accentuate and pronounce his words as had done those now long defunct orators. . . . And it is to be remembered that during all those years the writer wrote every word that he wrote with the idea of reading aloud to Conrad, and that during all those years Conrad wrote what he wrote with the idea of reading it aloud to this writer.

STRUCTURE

That gets rid, as far as is necessary in order to give a pretty fair idea of Conrad's methods, of the questions that concern the texture of a book. More official or more learned writers who shall not be novelists shall treat of this author's prose with less lightness — but assuredly too with less love. . . . Questions then of vocabulary, selection of incident, style, cadence and the rest concern themselves with the colour and texture of prose and, since this writer, again, will leave to more suitable pens the profounder appraisements of Conrad's morality, philosophy and the rest, there remains only to say a word or two on the subject of form.

Conrad, then, never wrote a true short story, a matter of two or three pages of minutely considered words, ending with a smack . . . with what the French call a *coup de canon*. His stories were always what for lack of a better phrase one has to call 'long-short' stories. For these the form is practically the same as that of the novel. Or, to avoid the implication of saying that there is only one form for the novel, it would be better to put it that the form of long-short stories may vary as much as may the form for novels. The short story of Maupassant, of Chekhov or even of the late O. Henry is practically stereotyped — the introduction of a character in a word or two, a word or two for atmosphere, a few paragraphs for story, and then click! a sharp sentence that flashes the illumination of the idea over the whole.

This Conrad — and for the matter of that, the writer — never so much as attempted, either apart or in collaboration. The reason for this lies in all that is behind the mystic word 'justification'. Before everything a story must convey a sense of inevitability: that which happens in it must seem to be the only thing that could have happened. Of course a character may cry, 'If I had then acted differently how different everything would now be.' The problem of the author is to make his then action the only action that character could have taken. It must be inevitable, because of his character, because of his ancestry, because of past illness or on account of the gradual coming together of the thousand small circumstances by which Destiny, who is inscrutable and august, will push us into one certain predicament. Let us illustrate:

In rendering your long friendship with, and ultimate bitter hostility towards, your neighbour Mr Slack, who had a greenhouse painted with Cox's aluminium paint, you will, if you wish to get yourself in with the scrupulousness of a Conrad, have to provide yourself, in the first place, with an ancestry at least as far back as your grandparents. To account for your own stability of character and physical robustness you will have to give yourself two dear old grandparents in a lodge at the gates of a great nobleman: if necessary you will have to give them a brightly polished copper kettle simmering on a spotless hob, with silhouettes on each side of the mantel: in order to account for the lamentable procedure of your daughter Millicent you must provide yourself with an actress or gipsy-grandmother. Or at least with a French one. This grandmother will have lived, unfortunately unmarried, with some one of eloquence — possibly with the great Earl-Prime Minister at whose gates is situated the humble abode of your other grandparents — at any rate she will have lived with some one from whom you will have inherited your eloquence. From her will have descended the artistic gifts to which the reader will owe your admirable autobiographic novel.

If you have any physical weakness, to counter-balance the robustness of your other grandparents, you will provide your mother, shortly before your birth, with an attack of typhoid fever, due to a visit to Venice in company with your father, who was a gentleman's courier in the family in which your mother was a lady's maid. Your father, in order to be a courier, will have had, owing to his illegitimacy, to live abroad in very poor circumstances. The very poor circumstances will illustrate the avarice of his statesman father — an avarice which will have descended to you in the shape of that carefulness in money matters that, reacting on the detrimental tendencies inherited by Millicent from her actress-grandmother, so lamentably influences your daughter's destiny.

And of course there will have to be a great deal more than that, always supposing you to be as scrupulous as was Conrad in this matter of justification. For Conrad — and for the matter of that the writer — was never satisfied that he had really and sufficiently got his characters in; he was never convinced that he had convinced the reader; this accounting for the great lengths of some of his books. He never introduced a character, however subsidiary, without providing that character with ancestry and hereditary characteristics, or at least with home surroundings — always supposing that character had any influence on the inevitability of the story. Any policeman who arrested any character must be 'justified', because the manner in which he effected the arrest, his mannerisms, his vocabulary and his voice, might have a permanent effect on the psychology of the prisoner. The writer remembers Conrad using almost those very words during the discussion of the plot of *The Secret Agent*.

This method, unless it is very carefully handled, is apt to have the grave defect of holding a story back very considerably. You must as a rule bring the biography of a character in only after you have introduced the character; yet, if you introduce a policeman to make an arrest the rendering of his biography might well retard the action of an exciting point in the story. . . . It becomes then your job to arrange that the very arresting of the action is an incitement of interest in the reader, just as, if you serialize a novel, you take care to let the words *to be continued in our next* come in at as harrowing a moment as you can contrive.

And of course the introducing of the biography of a character may have the great use of giving contrast to the tone of the rest of the book. . . . Supposing that in your history of your affair with Mr Slack you think that the note of your orderly middle-class home is growing a little monotonous, it would be very handy if you could discover that Mr Slack had a secret, dipsomaniacal wife, confined in a country cottage under the care of a rather criminal old couple; with a few pages of biography of that old couple you could give a very pleasant relief to the sameness of your narrative. In that way the sense of reality is procured.

PHILOSOPHY, ETC

We agreed that the novel is absolutely the only vehicle for the thought of our day. With the novel you can do anything: you can inquire into every department of life, you can explore every department of the world of thought. The one thing that you cannot do is to propagandize, as author, for any cause. You must not, as author, utter any views; above all, you must not fake any events. You must not, however humanitarian you may be, over-elaborate the fear felt by a coursed rabbit.

It is obviously best if you can contrive to be without views at all; your business with the world is rendering, not alteration. You have to render life with such exactitude that more specialized beings than you, learning from you what are the secret needs of humanity, may judge how many white-tiled bathrooms are, or to what extent parliamentary representation is, necessary for the happiness of men and women. If, however, your yearning to amend the human race is so great that you cannot possibly keep your fingers out of the watch-springs there is a device that you can adopt.

Let us suppose that you feel tremendously strong views as to sexual immorality or temperance. You feel that you must express these, yet you know that like, say, M. Anatole France, who is also a propagandist, you are a supreme novelist. You must then invent, justify and set going in your novel a character who can convincingly express your views. If you are a gentleman you will also invent, justify and set going characters to express views opposite to those you hold. . . .

You have reached the climax of your long relationship with Mr Slack; you are just going to address a deputation that has come to invite you to represent your native city in the legislature of your country. The deputation is just due. Five minutes before it arrives to present you with the proudest emotion of your life, you learn that your daughter Millicent is going to have a child by Mr Slack. (Him, of course, you will have already 'justified' as the likely seducer of a young lady whose cupidity in the matter of bangles and shoes you, by your pecuniary carefulness, have kept perpetually on the stretch.) Mr Slack has a dipsomaniac wife so there is no chance of his making the matter good. . . .

You thus have an admirable opportunity of expressing with emphasis quite a number of views through the mouth of the character whom you have so carefully 'justified' as yourself. Quite a number of views!

That then was, cursorily stated, the technique that we evolved at the Pent. It will be found to be nowadays pretty generally accepted as the normal way of handling the novel. It is founded on common sense and some of its maxims may therefore stand permanently. Or they may not.

PROGRESSION D'EFFET

There is just one other point. In writing a novel we agreed that every word set on paper — *every* word set on paper — must carry the story forward and that, as the story progressed, the story must be carried forward faster and faster and with more and more intensity. That is called *progression d'effet*, words for which there is no English equivalent.

One might go on to further technicalities, such as how to squeeze the last drop out of a subject. The writer has, however, given an instance of this in describing how we piled perils of the hangman's rope on the unfortunate John Kemp. To go deeper into the matter would be to be too technical. Besides enough has been said in this chapter to show you what was the character, the scrupulousness and the common sense of our hero.

There remains to add once more:

But these two writers were not unaware — were not unaware — *that there are other methods of writing novels. They were not rigid even in their own methods. They were sensible to the fact that compromise is at all times necessary to the execution of a work of art.*

The lay reader will be astonished at this repetition and at these italics. They are inserted for the benefit of gentlemen and ladies who comment on books in the Press.

LANGUAGE

It would be disingenuous to avoid the subject of language. This is the only matter on which the writer ever differed fundamentally from Conrad. It was one upon which the writer felt so deeply that, for several years, he avoided his friend's society. The pain of approaching the question is thus very great.

Conrad's dislike for the English language, then, was, during all the years of our association, extreme, his contempt for his medium unrivalled. Again and again during the writing of, say, *Nostromo* he expressed passionate regret that it was then too late to hope to make a living by writing in French, and as late as 1916 he expressed to the writer an almost equally passionate envy of the writer who was in a position to write in French, propaganda for the government of the French Republic. . . . And Conrad's contempt for English as a prose language was not, as in the writer's case, mitigated by love for English as the language for verse poetry. For, to the writer, English is as much superior to French in the one particular as French to English in the other.

Conrad, however, knew nothing of, and cared less for, English verse — and his hatred for English as a prose medium reached such terrible heights that during the writing of *Nostromo* the continual weight of Conrad's depression broke the writer down. We had then published *Romance* and Conrad, breaking, in the interests of that work, his eremitic habits, decided that we ought to show ourselves in Town. The writer therefore took a very large, absurd house on Campden Hill and proceeded to 'entertain'. Conrad had lodgings also on Campden Hill. At this time *Nostromo* had begun to run as a serial in a very popular journal, and on the placards of the journal Conrad's name appeared on every hoarding in London. This publicity caused Conrad an unbelievable agony, he conceiving himself for ever dishonoured by such vicarious pandering to popularity.

It was the most terrible period of Conrad's life and of the writer's. Conrad at that time considered himself completely unsuccessful; ignored by the public; ill-treated by the critics (he was certainly at that date being treated with unusual stupidity by the critics); he was convinced that he would never make a decent living. And he was convinced that he would never master English. He used to declare that English was a language in which it was impossible to write a direct statement. That was true enough. He used to declare that to make a direct statement in English is like trying to kill a mosquito with a forty-foot stock whip when you have never before handled a stock whip. One evening he made, in French, to the writer, the impassioned declaration which will be found in French at the end of this volume. On the following afternoon he made a terrible scene at the writer's house. . . .

The writer was at the time very much harassed. The expense of keeping up a rather portentous establishment made it absolutely necessary that he should add considerably to his income with his pen — a predicament with which he had not yet been faced. There was nothing in that except that it was almost impossible to find time to write. An epidemic of influenza running through the house crippled its domestic staff so that all sorts of household tasks had of necessity to be performed by the writer: there were, in addition, social duties — and the absolute necessity of carrying Conrad every afternoon through a certain quantum of work without which he must miss his weekly instalments in the popular journal. . . .

At an At Home there, amongst eminently decorous people, a well-meaning but unfortunate gentleman congratulated Conrad on the fact that his name appeared on all the hoardings and Conrad considered that these congratulations were ironical gibes at him because his desperate circumstances had forced him to agree to the dishonour of serialization in a popular journal. . . .

Conrad's indictment of the English language was this, that no English word is a word; that all English words are instruments for exciting blurred emotions. 'Oaken' in French means 'made of oak wood' — nothing more. 'Oaken' in English connotes innumerable moral attributes: it will connote stolidity, resolution, honesty, blond features, relative unbreakableness, absolute unbendableness — also, made of oak. . . . The consequence is that no English word has clean edges: a reader is always, for a fraction of a second, uncertain as to which meaning of the word the writer intends. Thus, all English prose is blurred. Conrad desired to write prose of extreme limpidity. . . .

We may let it go at that. In later years Conrad achieved a certain fluency and a great limpidity of language. He then regretted that for him all the romance of writing was gone — the result being *The Rover*, which strikes the writer as being a very serene and beautiful work. . . . In between the two he made tributes to the glory of the English language, by implication contemning the tongue that Flaubert used. This struck the writer, at that time in a state of exhausted depression, as unforgivable — as the very betrayal of Dain by Tom Lingard. . . . Perhaps it was. If it were Conrad faced the fact in that book. There are predicaments that beset great Adventurers, in dark hours, in the shallows: the overtired nerve will fail. . . . We may well let it go at that. . . .

'For it would be delightful to catch the echo of the desperate and funny quarrels that enlivened these old days. The pity of it is that there comes a time when all *the fun of one's life must be looked for in the past. . . .'*

Those were Conrad's last words on all the matters of our collaborations here treated of. They were, too, almost his last words. . . . For those who can catch them here, then, are the echoes. . . .

from PART IV, 'THAT, TOO, IS ROMANCE. . . .'

He [Conrad] may have had affection for the writer or he may not; he may have had admiration for his gifts or he may not. The one thing certain is that he really regarded him as omniscient. Otherwise he would never have put him at the jobs that he did put him at. For of our establishment the writer was Bill the Lizard. It was, 'Here Bill. . . . Where's Bill? . . . Bill, the master says that you've got to go up the chimney!' all day long. . . . And proud, too! The writer would have to supply authentic information about Anarchists as about Cabinet Ministers, about Courts of Justice as about the emotions of women, about leases, mining shares, brands of cigarettes, the verse of Christina Rossetti. . . . He did, too, and was mostly treated with an exaggerated politeness. As to the accusation of omniscience and the politeness there is documentary evidence: you may read in the preface of *The Secret Agent* of 'the omniscient friend who first gave me the first suggestion of the book'. Or again — this is Conrad giving you the writer:

> The subject of *The Secret Agent* — I mean the tale — came to me in the shape of a few words uttered by a friend, in a casual conversation about anarchists or rather anarchists' activities; how brought about I do not remember now. . . .
>
> I remember, however, remarking on the criminal futility of the whole thing, doctrine, action, mentality. . . . Presently . . . we recalled the already old story of the attempt to blow up Greenwich Observatory. . . . That outrage could not be laid hold of mentally in any sort of a way. . . .
>
> I pointed all this out to my friend who remained silent for a while, and then remarked in his characteristically casual and omniscient manner: 'Oh, that fellow was half an idiot. His sister comitted suicide afterwards.'. . . It never occurred to me later to ask how he arrived at his knowledge. I am sure that if he had once in his life seen the back of an anarchist, that must have been the whole of his connection with the underworld. . . .

That passage is curiously characteristic Conrad. . . . For what the writer really did say to Conrad was, 'Oh, that fellow was half an idiot! His sister murdered her husband afterwards and was allowed to escape by the police. I remember the funeral. . . .' The suicide was invented by Conrad. And the writer knew — and Conrad knew that the writer knew — a great many anarchists of the Goodge Street group, as well as a great many of the police who watched them. The writer had provided Conrad with anarchist literature, with memoirs, with introductions to at least one anarchist young lady who figures in *The Secret Agent*. Indeed, the writer's first poems were set up by that very young lady on an anarchist printing press.

Acquiring such knowledge is the diversion of most youths, the writer having once been young. There are few English boys of spirit who have not at one time or other dressed up in sweaters and, with handkerchiefs round their necks, gone after experience amongst the cut-throats at Wapping Old Stairs. . . . But Conrad, when he met the writer after the publication of *The Secret Agent* with preface in 1920, remarked almost at once and solicitously: 'You know. . . . The preface to *The Secret Agent*. . . . I did not give you away too much. . . . I was very cautious.'. . . He had wished politely to throw a veil of eternal respectability over the writer. And he had been afraid that the suggestion that the writer had once known some anarchists, thirty-five years before, might ruin the writer's career! . . . And of course few men in self-revelations and prefaces have ever so contrived under an aspect of lucidity to throw over themselves veils of confusion.

L'ENVOI

In the days here mostly treated of, Conrad had a very dreadful, a very agonizing life. Few men can so much have suffered; there was about all his depressed moments a note of pain — of agony indeed — that coloured our whole relationship; that caused one to have an almost constant quality of solicitude. It is all very well to say that he had his marvellous resilience. He had, and that was his greatness. But the note of a sailor's life cannot be called preponderantly cheerful whose whole existence is passed in a series of ninety-day passages, in labouring ships, beneath appalling weathers, amongst duties and work too heavy, in continual discomfort and acute physical pain — with, in between each voyage, a few days spent as Jack-ashore. And that, in effect, was the life of Conrad.

His resilience was his own; his oppressions were the work of humanity or of destiny. That is why his personality struck so strong a note of humour. The personality of Conrad as it remains uppermost in the reader's mind was threefold, with very marked divisions. There was the Conrad with the sharp, agonizing intake of the breath who feared your approach because you might jar his gout-martyrised wrist, or the approach of fate with the sharp pain of new disaster. There was the gloomy aristocrat — as man and as intellect — who mused unceasingly upon the treacheries, the muddles, the lack of imagination, the imbecilities which make up the conduct of human affairs; who said after the relation of each new story of incapacity and cruelness: '*Cela vous donne une fière idée de l'homme*.'. . . But most marked in the writer's mind was the alert, dark, extremely polished and tyrannous personality, tremendously awake, tremendously interested in small things, peering through his monocle at something close to the ground, taking in a characteristic and laughing consumedly — at a laborious child progressing engrossedly over a sloping lawn, at a bell-push that functioned of itself in the door-post of a gentleman who had written about an invisible man — or at the phrase: 'Excellency, a few goats. . . .'

[Boston: Little, Brown, and Co., 1924: pp. 143-7, 168-74, 177-9, 181-4, 191-202, 204-6, 208-14, 217-30, 244-7, 255-6.]

Preface to Jean Rhys, *The Left Bank and Other Stories* (1927)

Ford, having published Jean Rhys in the *Transatlantic*, wrote this preface to her first book, launching her career at a time when his influence as a literary personality was at its height. This and the next piece are only two of the more than twenty prefaces or introductions he wrote for the work of writers and painters.

RIVE GAUCHE

THE Left Bank, for as long as I can remember, has always seemed to me to be one of the vastest regions in the world. Always. When I was a boy and lived mostly, as far as Paris was concerned, in the Quartier de l'Étoile, there were five Quarters of the world. They were Europe, Asia, Africa, the Romney Marsh — and the Left Bank. Today, for me, the world consists of the Left Bank, Asia and Africa. The Romney Marsh is no doubt still in its place too.

In my hot youth I disliked Paris. She was stony and infested with winds; I suppose because it was mostly in the winters that I was in Paris. Stony, windy, expensive, solitary — and contemptuous; that was Paris. And I hated her.

I know next to nothing about architecture, but it has always seemed to me that it was the job of the architect, if he worked in stone, not to leave his building looking stony. A building, not a gaol or a workhouse, should look as if it were soft and warm to the touch — and that dictum wipes out all Haussmannized Paris. She is never soft, she is never warm; she is in fact obviously the creation of a gentleman with a name like Haussmann working under the patronage of an Imperial *rasta* like Napoleon III: she is incapable of mellowing like the wines they serve you in all the *Hotels Splendides et des États-Unis* of the sleeping-car world; as incapable of supporting life as the refrigerated meat that in those establishements you must eat, and, like them, she is inhabited solely by — financiers!

I am talking, of course, of the Quartier de l'Étoile of my youth. Today I never go there, or not more than a dozen times in a year, and then only in a vehicle of sorts, going for an evening drive in the Bois de Boulogne. But the straight, hateful, stony streets still run out, the Avenue Victor Hugo, the Avenue Wagram, and all the rest of them, like the spokes of a wheel from the Rond Point de l'Étoile. (I except from my general malediction the Avenues of the Champs-Élysées and du Bois de Boulogne, where I lived as a boy. They have some of the qualities and dignities of mainroads; you go along them to get to somewhere, even if it is only to the Lacs of a summer evening: they are so broad that from a horse-cab in the roadway you hardly note the unweathering stoninesses of the house-fronts. Certainly you have not the feeling that you are sunk deep in hideous canyons peopled by — Financiers — the feeling that broods over all the rest of that Quarter.)

One may say what one likes about Napoleon III: better men than myself have seen in him a better man than most — an idealist, a dreamer of frail dreams. But certainly when, with Haussmann he set to at the transmogrification of North-Western Paris his frail dream was a lasting prophecy. Not only did he find it brick and leave it machine-sawed stone, but he built a home for the worst ruling classes the world has ever seen — a home for today — or, perhaps, leave out the adjective. The world has seen a good many bad men, if never so many built to one pattern.

Anyhow, driving through those Avenues one does not seem to notice that they have much changed, either as to surfaces or as to populations: the financiers on the sidewalks seem leaner and less exotic, less Levantine , more American. And indeed the Levantine bucketshop keeper has been largely replaced by the Confidence Trick man of one type or the other. The world progresses . . . but the change has come in the view that, from one's one-horse fiacre, one finds that one has of the Rive Gauche. It remains geographically the same, but the mental image has how much altered!

When I was a boy The Left Bank was a yellow-purplish haze: today it is a vast, sandy desert, like the Sahara . . . but immense. More immense than the world of Europe, more immense than even Australia, which, Australians tell me is the largest continent in the world. Why I should have these two images I hardly know — perhaps because in my boyhood The Left Bank was a distant city, and of distant cities one sees, at night, in the sky, a yellow-purplish glow — and perhaps again because now that I know The Left Bank better than any other portion of the surface of the globe I have realized how minutely little one can know even of one street thickly inhabited by human beings. Or perhaps, still more because I should find it less fatiguing to take the train from Paris to Constantinople than, at half-past six in the evening, when it is impossible to get a place in a bus, or any other type of conveyance, to have to walk from the Seine, up the rue du Bac and the Boulevard Raspail to anywhere on the Boulevard du Montparnasse. . . . I am talking of course only of half-past six when the spirits are low and vehicles unprocurable. I have as a matter of fact frequently walked quite buoyantly from the Île St Louis to the Observatoire at a time of day when taxicabs were plenty. . . . But the impression of infinitely long walks with the legs feeling as if you dragged each step out of sands . . . remains.

And the place is upon the whole, perfection.

There is here no stoniness: heaven knows what the houses are made of, but never having been cleaned or re-painted since 1792, all the houses have so rich a patina that you may well think they were originally constructed of patina alone — of the very Dust of Ages. And the streets are all so narrow and crooked that no winds have ever entered them. Not even into the rue de Quatre Vents does the breath of heaven ever enter . . . or into the rue du Cherche Midi! Austere, frugal, still, greyish: here indeed is the region of Pure Thought and of the Arts.

It is of course a region of a great many other things — of the incomprehensible noisinesses of the Palais Bourbon as of the more massed movements of the Senate in the Palace of the Luxembourg: of the constantly growing fringe of internationalisms and of cafés more alcoholic than were the cafés of my hotter youth when one ordered a *café au lait* and mused over it for a whole evening for four sous and a sou to the waiter. Alas, today, in the most austere cafés of the real Latin Quarter a *café au lait* is called a *café crême* — and the crême, quite often, late of an evening, is condensed milk. It costs fifteen sous!

But the real Latin Quarter does maintain its austerities: they still, for instance, there serve you orange-flower water with your infusion of tilleul, though few students today know what to do with it, and still, the students of the Sorbonne in conclave and riotous are strong enough to make a government fall if they dislike a professor, or suspect infringements of their privileges. Yes, they will mob a Minister of Education sitting in the Café du Pantheon, and he will only get away under the protection of gendarmes and firemen — with the loss of his hat. . . .

Let me please dwell a little on the real Latin Quarter, though the subject is off my line of the moment: but, in the end, the region that surrounds the Sorbonne is the living heart of the South Side — perhaps of France, perhaps still more of the world. For France has many and famous Universities, but the world has only one Latin Quarter.

It is not merely that this Quarter contains the Sorbonne, or even the Sorbonne plus the Beaux Arts: it is that these two institutions attract an infinite number of youths seriously intent on absorbing pure thought on authorized and academic lines, and, much more important still, an infinite number of youths who re-act instinctively against thought and the arts as enjoined by authorized or academic teachers. The Sorbonne and the Beaux Arts are minatory institutions in that without their warrant you cannot make any sort of official career in France or in countries where French Academic diplomas carry weight. So that, if you come into opposition with either body your chance of an official livelihood is gone: you think twice about it; your opposition is the more bitter . . . and Thought is promoted. In that way the Quartier Latin lives in a sense that can be advanced for none of our, say, Anglo-Saxon Universities which have the gift of surrounding even the most advanced of opposed thought with suavity — as you pack nitroglycerine in cocoa-butter to keep it from exploding. . . .

Around, then, this intensely living Quarter stretch infinite vastnesses of arrondissements, known and unknown. For The Left Bank is a great city in itself. Where the Boulevard du Montparnasse, running east and west, turns into the Boulevard du Pont Royal, you have a huge Quarter of hospitals, clinics, dispensaries, slums — if there can be said to be slums in Paris — the Observatory, and the great gaol. This is the XIIIth Arrondissement of which it is said that it is the largest of all in extent and the most sparsely populated, since the hospitals, clinics, Protestant Training Colleges and Institutions in general have all spacious grounds and are slowly pushing out the more densely populated slum-lands. . . .

In my hot youth — which was a pretty cool affair — all this quarter was reputed to be glamorous and filled with dangers — for it was the quarter of the Apache. Unsafe at dusk and later . . . I remember going, in the nineties, several times to visit an old artist, a friend of my grandfather's in his Paris days. He lived in the small village of studios that is next door to the Santé prison. It was enjoined on me by my careful guardians that I must never, never, find myself south of the end of the Boulevard St Michel after dusk because of the thugs and garotters: never indeed even in the Boulevard St Michel itself after nightfall — because of the allurements. But the old artist painted sedulously till dusk or almost, and would not much talk till afterwards, and since I came to hear him talk of my grandfather and himself in a Latin Quarter of before even the days of Murger and Schaunard and Mimi and the others — which he did very fascinatingly! — the shades were usually much more than crepuscular when, unobtrusively, I would slip out of the gates of that enclosed village. . . . A long boulevard, lined all the way with blank, high, very grim walls, darkened by plane trees then newly planted with very dim gas lamps. Then one evening, forty yards behind my back, footsteps began to run. Until they were very close I did not even quicken my pace: when they *were* very close I ran. I ran like hell. But they gained and gained. And they gained on me. I stood at bay under a gas lamp, beneath the walls of the prison. They emerged from the gloom — two men. They ran. . . .

They were Apaches all right: they wore the casquettes with the visor right down over the eyes, the red woollen muffler floating out, the skin-tight jacket, the trousers ballooning out over the hips: and one of them had an open jack-knife. . . . I suppose they had been in an affray lower down the boulevard. The spot was just where they guillotine such inmates of the Santé as are not there for their healths. . . . For that too is one of the professions of this technical quarter. But the Apache is now extinct. He is extinct in the Avenue d'Orleans into which the Boulevard Arago prolongs itself, as in the Quarter of the Gobelins, further to the east where Industrialism which has ruined the modern world fights with the applied sciences for ground-space. For even into the otherwise nearly Utopian community of the Left Bank Industrialism must creep — and you have tanneries, producers of chemicals, of cheap footwear, of packing cases, of cheap printing — and of course of tapestry.

Along the Avenue d'Orleans, behind the cheap emporia, run the poor quarters, as far as, and no doubt further than, Montrouge. Here you have a population of *marchands des quatre saisons* — costermongers — market porters, odours of cabbage leaves, an Anglo-Saxon lady artist or so, a sculptor or so, window-cleaners, those who occupy themselves with graveyards because of the vicinity of the great cemetery, small — nay tiny! — shopkeepers, whose whole wares will be a peck or so of onions, five or six fish or three second-hand chairs and an ormolu mantel-clock. All in among these native dwellers push, where they can find a garret or half a garret, or a quarter, a few law students or medical students — though the student quarters are as a rule in the grim, tall eighteenth-century buildings on the high ground that supports, to the greater glory of Ste Genevieve, the Panthéon. But nowadays the students and the Anglo-Saxon lady artist or so must push in where they can and with their tiny purses and their heroically frugal lives get some shelter from the skies. So must the sculptors from every nation under the sun. And so emphatically and much more, must the midinettes, the seamstresses, the lesser mannequins of the greater or lesser couturieres of the Other Side, and the lesser figurantes of the theatres and all the cheerful, sensible, careless, efficient populations of Paris that, in so far as Paris is France, make France what she is.

For one is accustomed loosely to say that Paris is not France: and indeed for the Paris of the Other Side, of the Quartier de l'Étoile, of the newspapers, of the *Hotels Splendides et des États-Unis* or *de l'Univers et de Portugal*, of the Financiers and the rest, the saying is true enough, or would appear to be. You get the sort of thing on the Côte d'Azur, at Cairo, at Brighton, at Colombo, no doubt at Palm Beach and very probably in Buenos Aires. But, regarded from the Rive Gauche, Paris is infinitely more French than much of France. You get here, concentrated, the efficiency, the industry, the regard for the métier, the seriousness, the frugality, and the *terre à terre*, cheerful philosophy that account for the fact that only in France can a Paris of the Other Side be a very extended affair. As I have pointed out elsewhere, women from all over the world buy their hats in Paris of the Other Side not merely for the chic of the design but because the extreme care of the seamstresses of the Rive Gauche gets an exactness of line and ensures that that exactness of line will be commensurate with the life of the hat, or at any rate of the fashion. If, that is to say, you buy a hat in London or in Frankfurt or New York, or anywhere else, except possibly Vienna, you may possibly get something that you can wear, but it will lose its exactness of line after you have worn it twice. . . .

And, as with women's hats, so with thought. The thought of France pervades the world — because the Rive Gauche is French.

In the centre of this realm lie the Luxembourg Gardens and the difference between the Luxembourg Gardens and Hyde Park or

Central Park New York is the difference between French and Anglo-Saxon thought. We Anglo-Saxons believe in letting Nature alone in dreary stretches of damp turf and the depressed trees of cities whose air is full of coal smoke. The French are more bold, and, facing problems more, more exact. There is in fact no day on which a child may not be abroad on the ordered gravel of the Luxembourg; the days are very few in which a child can play on the grass in Regent's Park. The French — or the Cosmopolitan — child on the 31st of December, between showers, can go into the walks round the fountain in front of the palace and a kindly attendant will deposit for it, a little off the middle of the walk, a little mound of sand and pebbles in which you, the child, squatting and intent, will incontinently grub with your spade and pail. There will approach you, be-caped and mournful, a Gardien — a sort of policeman. Slowly and distinctly he will pronounce to you the words Ça c'est défendu! Dé . . . fen . . . *du*! You will go on grubbing. He will repeat the words to your parent or guardian and your parent or guardian will completely ignore him. (I have done this scores of times.) The agent of the law will continue to regard you mournfully for a long interval, will then shrug his shoulders and, with sad dignity, approach another child squatting over another gravel heap. . . . Thus you will learn the lesson that Laws are made only for those who choose to keep them.

Returning to your lunch you will perceive the statues of Margaret of Anjou in plaster, of the Comic Muse, in copper, nude and on one foot, of Georges Sand, of Flaubert. You will perceive the pleached trees that run from the foot of the Medicis basin to the Odéon entrance, the very tall trimmed elms that in an admirable perspective run towards the Observatory with its austere metal domes. About these things you will ask, as successively at ten minutes to twelve each day you are conducted back home. So your earliest impression will be of serenities, austerenesses, placidities, of order, of perspective, of History, of Classic Lore, of Pure Literature; and already before you are six you will be in miniature a little man or a little woman of the French Haute Bourgeoisie, your eyes looking meditatively up the steps towards the dome of the Panthéon with its inscription in gold: AUX GRANDS HOMMES LA PATRIE RECONNAISSANTE. . . . And you, considering whether you shall go there in the end as Pasteur, as Renan, as Puvis de Chavannes, as Hugo — a little belated — or as, let us say, Marshal Pétain! The impressions that the children living round Kensington Gardens or Central Park are other ones, so they grow up . . . well, different. And round the Luxembourg Gardens, in eighteenth-centuryish, tall grey houses, live the French Haute Bourgeoisie, austerely, frugally, coldly, with minds exact and exactingly poised, in large rooms, on Aubusson carpets, with tapestried, old, pale oak, begarlanded bergères, all set ranged for eternal Saturday afternoon conversations on serious subjects. . . . The professors, the surgeons, the doctors of law, the senators, the administrators of museums . . . the French, in fact. . . .

But, with here and there in a nook in the great courtyards behind the houses, an Anglo-Saxon lady artist or so, or a transatlantic sculptor . . . or the atelier of a professor of painting admired by Scandinavians: these, however, in the background. . . .

That then is the Rive Gauche as far as I am here concerned. It will be observed that it contains no Financiers. And indeed, what above all marks it is a certain exiguity in matters financial, and indeed the step from the houses of the Haute Bourgeoisie round the Luxembourg Gardens, to the hand to mouth of the more distinctively Montparnassian-international regions, and to the absolute starvation of the outer fringes of those regions is but a step. The margin is the merest pie crust, for even the professors, the surgeons, the doctors of law and the rest of the proud façade of France work for honoraria, as often as not, that an Anglo-Saxon coal-miner would despise: so do great sculptors here and painters of international fame. And if that be the lot of the accepted what — what in heaven's name? — is the lot of the opposition who must wait till their Thought is the accepted Thought of tomorrow? . . .

To some extent the answer will be found in Miss Rhys' book for which I have not so much been asked, as I have asked to be allowed the privilege of supplying this Preface. Setting aside for a moment the matter of her very remarkable technical gifts, I should like to call attention to her profound knowledge of the life of the Left Bank — of many of the Left Banks of the world. For something mournful — and certainly hard-up! — attaches to almost all uses of the word *left*. The left hand has not the cunning of the right: and every great city has its left bank. London has, round Bloomsbury, New York has, about Greenwich Village, so has Vienna — but Vienna is a little ruined everywhere since the glory of Austria, to the discredit of European civilization, has departed! Miss Rhys does not, I believe, know Greenwich Village, but so many of its products are to be found on the Left Bank of Paris that she may be said to know its products. And coming from the Antilles, with a terrifying insight and a terrific — an almost lurid! — passion for stating the case of the underdog, she has let her pen loose on the Left Banks of the old World — on its gaols, its studios, its salons, its cafés, its criminals, its midinettes — with a bias of admiration for its midinettes and of sympathy for its law-breakers. It is a note, a sympathy of which we do not have too much in Occidental literature with its perennial bias towards satisfaction with things as they are. But it is a note that needs sounding — that badly needs sounding, since the real activities of the world are seldom carried much forward by the accepted, or even by the Hautes Bourgeoisies!

When I, lately, edited a periodical, Miss Rhys sent in several communications with which I was immensely struck, and of which I published as many as I could. What struck me on the technical side — which does not much interest the Anglo-Saxon reader, but which is almost the only thing that interests me — was the singular instinct for form possessed by this young lady, an instinct for form being possessed by singularly few writers of English and by almost no English women writers. I say 'instinct', for that is what it appears to me to be: these sketches begin exactly where they should and end exactly when their job is done. No doubt the almost exclusive reading of French writers of a recent, but not the most recent, date has helped. For French youth of today, rejecting with violence and in a mystified state of soul, all that was French of yesterday, has rejected neatness of form as it eschews the austere or the benignant agnosticisms of Anatole France, of Renan and of all the High Bourgeoisie that eleven years ago today stood exclusively for France. The youth of France today is constructive, uncertain, rule of thumb, believing, passionate, and, aware that it works in a mist, it is determined violently not to be coldly critical, or critical at all.

Amongst the things that French youth rejects more violently than others is the descriptive passage, the getting of what, in my hot youth, used to be called an atmosphere. I tried — for I am for ever meddling with the young! — very hard to induce the author of the *Left Bank* to introduce some sort of topography of that region, bit by bit, into her sketches — in the cunning way in which it would have been done by Flaubert or Maupassant, or by Mr Conrad 'getting in' the East in innumerable short stories from *Almayer* to the *Rescue*. . . . But would she do it? No! With cold deliberation, once her attention was called to the matter, she eliminated even such two or three words of descriptive matter as had crept into her work. Her business was with passion, hardship, emotions: the locality in which these things are endured is immaterial. So she hands you the Antilles with its sea and sky — 'the loveliest, deepest sea in the world — the Caribbean!' — the effect of landscape on the emotions and passions of a child being so penetrative, but lets Montparnasse, or London, or Vienna go. She is probably right. Something human should, indeed, be dearer to one than all the topographies of the world. . . .

But I, knowing for my sins, the book market, imagined the reader saying: 'Where did all this take place? What sort of places are these?' So I have butted in.

One likes, in short, to be connected with something good, and Miss Rhys' work seems to me to be so very good, so vivid, so extraordinarily distinguished by the rendering of passion, and so true, that I wish to be connected with it. I hope I shall bring her a few readers and so when — hundreds of years hence! — her ashes are translated to the Panthéon, in the voluminous pall, the cords of which are held by the most prominent of the Haute Bourgeoisie of France, a grain or so of my scattered and forgotten dust may go in too, in the folds.

Introduction to Ernest Hemingway, *A Farewell to Arms* (1932)

I EXPERIENCED a singular sensation on reading the first sentence of *A Farewell to Arms*. There are sensations you cannot describe. You may know what causes them but you cannot tell what portions of your mind they affect nor yet, possibly, what parts of your physical entity. I can only say that it was as if I had found at last again something shining after a long delving amongst dust. I daresay prospectors after gold or diamonds feel something like that. But theirs can hardly be so coldly clear an emotion, or one so impersonal. The three impeccable writers of English prose that I have come across in fifty years or so of reading in search of English prose have been Joseph Conrad, W. H. Hudson . . . and Ernest Hemingway. . . . Impeccable each after his kind! I remember with equal clarity and equal indefinableness my sensation on first reading a sentence of each. With the Conrad it was like being overhwelmed by a great, unhastening wave. With the Hudson it was like lying on one's back and looking up into a clear, still sky. With the Hemingway it was just excitement. Like waiting at the side of a coppice, when foxhunting, for the hounds to break cover. One was going on a long chase in dry clear weather, one did not know in what direction or over what country.

The first sentence of Hemingway that I ever came across was not of course: 'In the late summer of that year we lived in a house in a village that looked across the river and the plain towards the mountains.' That is the opening of *Farewell to Arms*. No, my first sentence of Hemingway was:

'Everybody was drunk.' *Tout court!* Like that!

Exactly how much my emotion gained from immediately afterwards reading the rest of the paragraph I can't say.

It runs for the next few sentences as follows:

Everybody was drunk. The whole battery was drunk going along the road in the dark. We were going to the Champagne. The lieutenant kept riding his horse out into the fields and saying to him, 'I'm drunk, I tell you, mon vieux. Oh, I am so soused.' We went along the road in the dark and the adjutant kept riding up alongside my kitchen and saying, 'You must put it out. It is dangerous. It will be observed.'

I am reading from '*N° 3 of 170 hand-made copies printed on* rives *hand-made paper.*' which is inscribed: 'to robert mcalmon and william bird *publishers of the city of paris* and to captain edward dorman-smith m.c., of *his majesty's fifth fusiliers* this book is respectfully dedicated.' The title page, curiously enough bears the date 1924 but the copy is inscribed to me by Ernest Hemingway 'march 1923' and must, as far as I can remember have been given to me then. There is a nice problem for bibliophiles.

This book is the first version of *In Our Time* and is described as published at 'paris, *printed at* the three mountains press *and for sale at* shakespeare & company *in the rue de l'odéon; london:* william jackson, *took's court, cursitor street, chancery lane.*'

Those were the brave times in Paris when William Bird and I, and I daresay Hemingway too believed, I don't know why, that salvation could be found in leaving out capitals. We printed and published in a domed wine-vault, exceedingly old and cramped, on the Ile St Louis with a grey view on the Seine below the Quais. It must have been salvation we aspired to for thoughts of fortune seldom came near us and Fortune herself, never. Publisher Bird printed his books beautifully at a great old seventeenth-century press and we all took hands at pulling its immense levers about. I 'edited' in a gallery like a bird-cage at the top of the vault. It was so low that I could never stand up. Ezra also 'edited' somewhere, I daresay, in the rue Notre Dame des Champs. At any rate the last page but one of *In Our Time* — or perhaps it is the *feuille de garde*, carries the announcement:

Here ends *The Inquest* into the state of
contemporary English prose, as
edited by EZRA POUND and printed at
the THREE MOUNTAINS PRESS. The six
works constituting the series are:
Indiscretions *of* Ezra Pound
Women and Men *by* Ford Madox Ford

Elimus *by* B. C. Windeler
with Designs *by* D. Shakespear
The Great American Novel
by William Carlos Williams
England *by* B. M. G. Adams
In Our Time *by* Ernest Hemingway
with portrait *by* Henry Strater.

Mr Pound you perceive did believe in CAPITALS and so obviously did one half of Hemingway for his other book of the same date — a blue-grey pamphlet — announces itself all in capitals of great baldness. (They are I believe of the style called *sans-sérif*):

THREE STORIES
& TEN POEMS
ERNEST HEMINGWAY

it calls itself without even a *by* in italics. There is no date or publisher's or distributor's name or address on the title page but the back of the half-title bears the small notices

Copyright 1923 by the author
Published by
Contact Publishing Co.

and the last page but one has the announcement

PRINTED AT DIJON
BY
MAURICE DARANTIERE
M. CX. XXIII

This copy bears an inscription in the handwriting of Mr Hemingway to the effect that it was given to me in Paris by himself in 924. That seems almost an exaggeration in antedating.

Anyhow, I read first *In Our Time* and then *My Old Man* in *Ten Stories* both in 1923. . . .

Those were exciting times in Paris. The Young-American literature that today forms the most important phase of the literary world anywhere was getting itself born there. And those were birth-throes!

Young America from the limitless prairies leapt, released, on Paris. They stampeded with the madness of colts when you let down the slip-rails between dried pasture and green. The noise of their advancing drowned all sounds. Their innumerable forms hid the very trees on the boulevards. Their perpetual motion made you dizzy. The falling plane-leaves that are the distinguishing mark of grey, quiet Paris, were crushed under foot and vanished like flakes of snow in tormented seas.

I might have been described as — by comparison — a nice, quiet gentleman for an elderly tea-party. And there I was between, as it were, the too quiet aestheticisms of William Bird, publisher supported by Ezra Pound, poet-editor, and, at the other extreme, Robert McAlmon damn-your-damn-highbrow-eyes author-publisher, backed by a whole Horde of Montparnasse from anywhere between North Dakota and Missouri. . . . You should have seen those Thursday tea-parties at the uncapitalled *transatlantic review* offices! The French speak of 'la semaine à deux jeudis' . . . the week with two Thursdays in it. Mine seemed to contain sixty, judging by the noise, lung-power, crashing in, and denunciation. They sat on forms — school benches — cramped round Bird's great hand press. On the top of it was an iron eagle. A seventeenth-century eagle!

Where exactly between William Bird, hand-printer and publisher and Robert McAlmon, nine-hundred horse power linotype-publisher Hemingway came in I never quite found out. He was presented to me by Ezra and Bill Bird and had rather the aspect of an Eton-Oxford, husky-ish young captain of a midland regiment of His Britannic Majesty. In that capacity he entered the phalanxes of the *transatlantic review*. I forget what his official title was. He was perhaps joint-editor — or an advisory or consulting or vetoing editor. Of those there was a considerable company. I, I have omitted to say, was supposed to be Editor in Chief. They all shouted at me: I did not know how to write, or knew too much to be able to write, or did not know how to edit, or keep accounts, or sing *Franky & Johnny*, or order a dinner. The ceiling was vaulted, the plane-leaves drifted down on the quays outside; the grey Seine flowed softly.

Into the animated din would drift Hemingway, balancing on the point of his toes, feinting at my head with hands as large as hams and relating sinister stories of Paris landlords. He told them with singularly choice words in a slow voice. He still struck me as disciplined. Even captains of his majesty's fifth fusiliers are sometimes amateur pugilists and now and then dance on their toe-points in private. I noticed less however of Eton and Oxford. He seemed more a creature of wild adventures amongst steers in infinitudes.

All the same, when I went to New York, I confided that review to him. I gave him strict injunctions as to whom not to print and above all whom not to cut.

The last mortal enemy he made for me died yesterday. Hemingway had cut *his* article and all those of my most cherished and awful contributors down to a line or two apiece. In return he had printed all *his* wildest friends *in extenso*. So that uncapitalised review died. I don't say that it died of Hemingway. I still knew he must somehow be disciplined.

But, a day or two after my return, we were all lunching in the little bistro that was next to the office. There were a great many people and each of them was accusing me of some different incapacity. At last Hemingway extended an enormous seeming ham under my nose. He shouted. What he shouted I could not hear but I realized I had a pencil. Under the shadow of that vast and menacing object I wrote verses on the tablecloth.

Heaven over-arches earth and sea
Earth sadness and sea-hurricanes.
Heaven over-arches you and me.
A little while and we shall be
Please God, where there is no more sea
   And no . . .

The reader may supply the rhyme.

That was the birth of a nation.

At any rate if America counts in the comity of civilized nations it is by her new writers that she has achieved that immense feat. So it seems to me. The reader trained in other schools of thought must bear with it. A nation exists by its laws, inventions, mass-products. It lives for other nations by its arts.

I do not propose here to mention other names than those of Ernest Hemingway. It is not my business to appraise. Appraisements imply censures and it is not one writer's business to censure others. A writer should expound other writers or let them alone.

When I thought that Hemingway had discipline I was not mistaken. He had then and still has the discipline that makes you avoid temptation in the selection of words and the discipline that lets you be remorselessly economical in the number that you employ. If, as writer you have those disciplined knowledges or instincts, you may prize fight or do what you like with the rest of your time.

The curse of English prose is that English words have double effects. They have their literal meanings and then associations they attain from other writers that have used them. These associations as often as not come from the Authorised Version or the Book of Common Prayer. You use a combination of words once used by Archbishop Cranmer or Archbishop Warham or the Translators in the XVI & XVII centuries. You expect to get from them an overtone of awfulness, or erudition or romance or pomposity. So your prose dies.

Hemingway's words strike you, each one, as if they were pebbles fetched fresh from a brook. They live and shine, each in its place. So one of his pages has the effect of a brook-bottom into which you look down through the flowing water. The words form a tessellation, each in order beside the other.

It is a very great quality. It is indeed the supreme quality of the written art of the moment. It is a great part of what makes literature come into its own at such rare times as it achieves that feat. Books lose their hold on you as soon as the words in which they are written are demoded or too usual the one following the other. The aim — the achievement — of the great prose writer is to use words so that they shall seem new and alive because of their juxtaposition with other words. This gift Hemingway has supremely. Any sentence of his taken at random will hold your attention. And irresistibly. It does not matter where you take it.

> I was in under the canvas with guns. They smelled cleanly of oil and grease. I lay and listened to the rain on the canvas and the clicking of the car over the rails. There was a little light came through and I lay and looked at the guns.

You could not begin that first sentence and not finish the passage.

That is a great part of this author's gift. Yet it is not only 'gift'. You cannot throw yourself into a frame of mind and just write and get that effect. Your mind has to choose each word and your ear has to test it until by long disciplining of mind and ear you can no longer go wrong.

That disciplining through which you must put yourself is all the more difficult in that it must be gone through in solitude. You cannot watch the man next to you in the ranks smartly manipulating his side-arms nor do you hear any word of command by which to time yourself.

On the other hand a writer holds a reader by his temperament. That is his true 'gift' — what he receives from whoever sends him into the world. It arises from how you look at things. If you look at and render things so that they appear new to the reader you will hold his attention. If what you give him appears familiar or half familiar his attention will wander. Hemingway's use of the word 'cleanly' is an instance of what I have just been saying. The guns smelled cleanly of oil and grease. Oil and grease are not usually associated in the mind with a clean smell. Yet at the minutest reflection you realize that the oil and grease on the clean metal of big guns are not dirt. So the adverb is just. You have had a moment of surprise and then your knowledge is added to. The word 'author' means 'someone who adds to your consciousness'.

When, in those old days, Hemingway used to tell stories of his Paris landlords he used to be hesitant, to pause between words and then to speak gently but with great decision. His temperament was selecting the instances he should narrate, his mind selecting the words to employ. The impression was one of a person using restraint at the biddings of discipline. It was the right impression to have had.

He maintains his hold on himself up to the last word of every unit of his prose. The last words of *My Old Man* are: 'But I don't know. Seems like when they get started they don't leave a guy nothing.'

The last words of *In Our Time*: 'It was very jolly. We talked for a long time. Like all Greeks he wanted to go to America.'

A Farewell to Arms ends incomparably: 'But after I had got them out and shut the door and turned out the light it wasn't any good. It was like saying good-by to a statue. After a while I went out and left the hospital and walked back to the hotel in the rain.'

Incomparably, because that muted passage after great emotion still holds the mind after the book is finished. The interest prolongs itself and the reader is left wishing to read more of that writer's.

After the first triumphant success of a writer a certain tremulousness besets his supporters in the public. It is the second book that is going to have a rough crossing. . . . Or the third and the fourth. So after the great artistic triumph of William Bird's edition of *In Our Times* Hemingway seemed to me to falter. He produced a couple of books that I did not much like. I was probably expected not much to like them. Let us say that they were essays towards a longer form than that of the episodic *In Our Time*. Then with *Men Without Women* he proved that he retained the essential gift. In that volume there is an episodic-narrative that moves you as you will — if you are to be moved at all — be moved by episodes of the Greek Anthology. It has the same quality of serene flawlessness.

In the last paragraph I have explained the nature of my emotion when I read a year or so ago that first sentence of *Farewell to Arms*. It was more than excitement. It was excitement plus reassurance. The sentence was exactly the right opening for a long piece of work. To read it was like looking at an athlete setting out on a difficult and prolonged effort. You say, at the first movement of the limbs: 'It's all right. He's in form. . . . He'll do today what he has never quite done before.' And you settle luxuriantly into your seat.

So I read on after the first sentence:

> In the bed of the river there were pebbles and boulders dry and white in the sun, and the water was clear and swiftly moving and blue in the channels. Troops went by the house and down the road and the dust they raised powdered the leaves of the trees. The trunks of the trees were dusty and the leaves fell early that year and we saw the troops marching along the road and the dust rising and the leaves, stirred by the breeze, falling and the soldiers marching and afterwards the road bare and white except for the leaves.

I wish I could quote more, it is such a pleasure to see words like that come from one's pen. But you can read it for yourself.

A Farewell to Arms is a book important in the annals of the art of writing because it proves that Hemingway, the writer of short, perfect episodes, can keep up the pace through a volume. There have been other writers of impeccable — of matchless — prose but as a rule their sustained efforts have palled because precisely of the remarkableness of the prose itself. You can hardly read *Marius the Epicurean*. You may applaud its author, Walter Pater. But *A Farewell to Arms* is without purple patches or even verbal 'felicities'. Whilst you are reading it you forget to applaud its author. You do not know that you are having to do with an author. You are living.

A Farewell to Arms is a book that unites the critic to the simple. You could read it and be thrilled if you had never read a book — or if you had read and measured all the good books in the world. That is the real province of the art of writing.

Hemingway has other fields to conquer. That is no censure on *A Farewell to Arms*. It is not blaming the United States to say that she has not yet annexed Nicaragua. But whatever he does can never take away from the fresh radiance of his work. It may close with tears but it is like a spring morning.

Paris,
January 1932

from

Portraits from Life (1937) [published in England as *Mightier than the Sword*, 1938]

D.H. LAWRENCE

IN THE year when my eyes first fell on words written by Norman Douglas, H. M. Tomlinson, Wyndham Lewis, Ezra Pound, and others, amongst whom was Stephen Reynolds, who died too young and is much too forgotten — upon a day I received a letter from a young schoolteacher in Nottingham. I can still see the handwriting — as if drawn with sepia rather than written in ink, on grey-blue notepaper. It said that the writer knew a young man who wrote, as she thought, admirably but was too shy to send his work to editors. Would I care to see some of his writing?

In that way I came to read the first words of a new author:

> The small locomotive engine, Number 4, came clanking, stumbling down from Selston with seven full waggons. It appeared round the corner with loud threats of speed but the colt that it startled from among the gorse which still flickered indistinctly in the raw afternoon, outdistanced it in a canter. A woman walking up the railway line to Underwood, held her basket aside and watched the footplate of the engine advancing.

I was reading in the twilight in the long eighteenth-century room that was at once the office of the *English Review* and my drawing-room. My eyes were tired; I had been reading all day so I did not go any further with the story. It was called 'Odour of Chrysanthemums'. I laid it in the basket for accepted manuscripts. My secretary looked up and said:

'You've got another genius?'

I answered: 'It's a big one this time,' and went upstairs to dress. . . .

It was a Trench dinner at the Pall Mall Restaurant — a Dutch Treat presided over by Herbert Trench, the poet, and Dutch Treats being then new in London, Trench dinners were real social events. You sat in groups of five at little tables and the big hall of the restaurant was quite full.

I was with Mr H. G. Wells, Mr Hilaire Belloc, Mr Maurice Baring, and Mr G. K. Chesterton. At other tables were other celebrities. In the middle of an astounding story about the Russian court, told by Mr Baring, who had lately returned from being first secretary or something at our embassy in St Petersburg, Mr Belloc's magnificent organ remarked to an innocent novelist called Kinross, who at the next table was discussing the New Testament with Ladies Londonderry and Randolph Churchill, the reigning beauties of that end of a reign:

'Our Lord?' Mr Belloc's voice pealed among the marble columns and palms. 'What do *you* know about Our Lord? Our Lord was a Gentleman.'

To turn the discussion I remarked to Mr Wells that I had discovered another genius, D. H. Lawrence by name; and, to carry on the good work, Mr Wells exclaimed — to some one at Lady Londonderry's table:

'Hurray, Fordie's discovered another genius! Called D. H. Lawrence!'

Before the evening was finished I had had two publishers asking me for the first refusal of D. H. Lawrence's first novel and, by that accident, Lawrence's name was already known in London before he even knew that any of his work had been submitted to an editor. . . . The lady who had sent this story to me chooses to be known as 'E.T.' and she had not even told Lawrence that she was sending the mss.

So next morning I sent Miss E.T. a letter, a little cautious in tenor, saying that I certainly liked the work she had sent me and asking her to ask her friend to call on me when he had the opportunity. I appear to have said that I thought Lawrence had great gifts, but that a literary career depended enormously on chance, and that if Lawrence had a good job in a school he had better stick to it for the present. It was probably a stupid thing to do and I have regretted it since for I was certain that that writer had great gifts and the sooner a writer who has great gifts takes his chance at writing, the better.

Miss E. T. in her lately published little book on the youth of Lawrence — and a very charming and serviceable little book it is — seems to be under the impression that she sent me as a first instalment only poems by Lawrence. Actually she first asked me if I would care to see anything — and then should it be poetry or prose. And I had replied asking her to send both, so that she had sent me three poems about a schoolmaster's life . . . and 'Odour of Chrysanthemums'. I only mention this because I found the poems, afterwards, to be nice enough but not immensely striking. If I had read them first I should certainly have printed them — as indeed I did; but I think the impact of Lawrence's personality would have been much less vivid. . . . Let us examine, then, the first paragraph of 'Odour of Chrysanthemums'.

The very title makes an impact on the mind. You get at once the knowledge that this is not, whatever else it may turn out, either a frivolous or even a gay, springtime story. Chrysanthemums are not only flowers of the autumn: they are the autumn itself. And the presumption is that the author is observant. The majority of people do not even know that chrysanthemums have an odour. I have had it flatly denied to me that they have, just as, as a boy, I used to be mortified by being told that I was affected when I said that my favourite scent was that of primroses, for most people cannot discern that primroses have a delicate and, as if muted, scent.

Titles as a rule do not matter much. Very good authors break down when it comes to the effort of choosing a title. But one like 'Odour of Chrysanthemums' is at once a challenge and an indication. The author seems to say: Take it or leave it. You know at once that you are not going to read a comic story about someone's butler's omniscience. The man who sent you this has, then, character, the courage of his convictions, a power of observation. All these presumptions flit through your mind. At once you read:

'The small locomotive engine, Number 4, came clanking, stumbling down from Selston,' and at once you know that this fellow with the power of observation is going to write of whatever he writes about from the inside. The 'Number 4' shows that. He will be the sort of fellow who knows that for the sort of people who work about engines, engines have a sort of individuality. He had to give the engine the personality of a number. . . . 'With seven full waggons.'. . . The 'seven' is good. The ordinary careless writer would say 'some small waggons.' This man knows what he wants. He sees the scene of his story exactly. He has an authoritative mind.

'It appeared round the corner with loud threats of speed.'. . . Good writing; slightly, but not *too* arresting . . . 'But the colt that it startled from among the gorse . . . outdistanced it at a canter.' Good again. This fellow does not 'state'. He doesn't say: 'It was coming slowly,' or — what would have been a little better — 'at seven miles an hour'. Because even 'seven miles an hour' means nothing definite for the untrained mind. It might mean something for a trainer of pedestrian racers. The imaginative writer writes for all humanity; he does not limit his desired readers to specialists. . . . But anyone knows that an engine that makes a great deal of noise and yet cannot overtake a colt at a canter must be a ludicrously ineffective machine. We know then that this fellow knows his job.

'The gorse still flickered indistinctly in the raw afternoon.'. . . Good too, distinctly good. This is the just-sufficient observation of Nature that gives you, in a single phrase, landscape, time of day, weather, season. It is a raw afternoon in autumn in a rather accented countryside. The engine would not come round a bend if there were not some obstacle to a straight course — a watercourse, a chain of hills. Hills, probably, because gorse grows on dry, broken-up waste country. They won't also be mountains or anything spectacular or the writer would have mentioned them. It is, then, just 'country'.

Your mind does all this for you without any ratiocination on your part. You are not, I mean, purposedly sleuthing. The engine and the trucks are there, with the white smoke blowing away over hummocks of gorse. Yet there has been practically none of the tiresome thing called descriptive nature, of which the English writer is as a rule so lugubriously lavish. . . . And then the woman comes in, carrying her basket. That indicates her status in life. She does not belong to the comfortable classes. Nor, since the engine is small, with trucks on a dud line, will the story be one of the Kipling-engineering type, with gleaming rails, and gadgets, and the smell of oil warmed by the bearings, and all the other tiresomenesses.

You are, then, for as long as the story lasts, to be in one of those untidy, unfinished landscapes where locomotives wander innocuously amongst women with baskets. That is to say, you are going to learn how what we used to call 'the other half' — though we might as well have said the other ninety-nine hundredths — lives. And if you are an editor and that is what you are after, you know that you have got what you want and you can pitch the story straight away into your wicker tray with the few accepted manuscripts and go on to some other occupation. . . . Because this man knows. He knows how to open a story with a sentence of the right cadence for holding the attention. He knows how to construct a paragraph. He knows the life he is writing about in a landscape just sufficiently constructed with a casual word here and there. You can trust him for the rest.

And it is to be remembered that, in the early decades of this century, we enormously wanted authentic projections of that type of life which hitherto had gone quite unvoiced. We had had Gissing, and to a certain degree Messrs H. G. Wells and Arnold Bennett, and still more a writer called Mark Rutherford who by now, I should imagine, is quite forgotten. But they all wrote — with more or less seriousness — of the 'lower middle' classes. The completely different race of the artisan — and it was a race as sharply divided from the ruling or even the mere white-collar classes as was the Negro from the gentry of Virginia — the completely different class of the artisan, the industrialist, and the unskilled labourer was completely unvoiced and unknown. Central Africa and its tribes were better known and the tombs of the Pharaohs more explored than our own Potteries and Black Country.

It was therefore with a certain trepidation that I awaited the visit of Lawrence. If he was really the son of a working coal-miner, how exactly was I to approach him in conversation? Might he not, for instance, call me 'Sir' — and wouldn't it cause pain and confusion to stop him doing so? For myself I have always automaticallyregarded every human being as my equal — and myself, by corollary, as the equal of every other human being — except of course the King and my colonel on — not off — parade. But a working man was so unfamiliar as a proposition that I really did not know how to bring it off.

Indeed, E. T. in her account of the first lunch that I ever gave Lawrence and herself, relates that Ezra Pound — who has a genius for inappropriate interpolations — asked me how I should talk to a 'working man'. And she relates how she held her breath until, after a moment's hesitation, I answered that I should speak to him exactly as I spoke to anybody else.

Before that I had had some little time to wait for Lawrence's visit. I found him disturbing enough. It happened in this way:

It would appear that he was on his holidays and, as one can well believe, holidays on the seashore from a Croydon board-school were moments too precious to be interrupted even for a visit to a first editor. Indeed, as I heard afterwards, he had talked himself into such a conviction of immediate literary success that he could not believe in the existence of a literary career at all. He had, I mean, said so often that he was going to make immediately two thousand — pounds, not dollars — a year and had so often in schemes expended that two thousand a year in palaces with footmen that, when he came to himself and found that he had not so far printed a word, a literary career seemed part of a fairy tale such as no man had ever enjoyed. And there were no doubt shynesses. Obviously you cannot approach the utterly unknown without them. Yes, certainly there were shynesses.

It must have been on a Saturday because otherwise Lawrence would not have been free to leave his school and come up from Croydon, which was a suburb but not part — as poor Lawrence was to find to his cost — of London, and it cannot have been a Sunday because we were working. And I certainly must have been in the relaxed frame of mind that comes just before the end of the week. I was, I suppose, reading a manuscript or some proofs in a chair that looked towards the room door. My secretary, Miss Thomas, who afterwards won renown as the war secretary of Mr Lloyd George, presumably heard someone knocking at the outer door, for I was dimly aware that she got up from her desk, went out, and returned, passing me and saying, Mr Someone or other.

I was engrossed in my manuscript or proofs. Miss Thomas, imagining that she had been followed by the individual she had found at the outer door, sat down at her desk and became engrossed in her work. And deep peace reigned. The room was L-shaped, the upright of the L being long and low, the rest forming an alcove in which was the door. . . . And suddenly, leaning against the wall beside the doorway, there was, bewilderingly . . . a fox. A fox going to make a raid on the hen-roost before him. . . .

The impression that I had at my first sight of Lawrence is so strong with me at this minute that the mere remembrance fills me with a queer embarrassment. And indeed, only yesterday, reading again — or possibly reading for the first time, for I did not remember it — Lawrence's story called 'The Fox', I really jumped when I came to his description of the fox looking over its shoulder at the farm girl. Because it was evident that Lawrence identified himself with the russet-haired human fox who was to carry off the as-it-were hen-girl of the story.

And that emotion of my slightly tired, relaxed eyes and senses was not so bad as a piece of sensitized imagination. The house itself was old and reputed full of ghosts, lending itself to confusions of tired eyes. . . . My partner Marwood, sitting one evening near the front windows of the room whilst I was looking for something in the drawer of the desk, said suddenly:

'There's a woman in lavender-coloured eighteenth-century dress looking over your shoulder into that drawer.' And Marwood was the most matter-of-fact, as it were himself eighteenth-century, Yorkshire Squire that England of those days could have produced.

And I experienced then exactly the feeling of embarrassment that I was afterwards to feel when I looked up from my deep thoughts and saw Lawrence, leaning, as if panting, beside the doorpost. . . . It was not so bad an impression, founded as it was on the peculiar, as if sunshot tawny hair and moustache of the fellow and his deep-set and luminous eyes. He had not, in those days, the beard that afterwards obscured his chin — or I think he had not. I think that on his holiday he had let his beard grow and, it having been lately shaved off, the lower part of his face was rather pallid and as if invisible, whereas his forehead and cheeks were rather high-coloured. So that I had had only the impression of the fox-coloured hair and moustache and the deep, wary, sardonic glance . . . as if he might be going to devour me — or something that I possessed.

And that was really his attitude of mind. He had come, like the fox, with his overflood of energy — his abounding vitality of passionate determination that seemed always too big for his frail body — to get something — the hypnotic two thousand a year; from somewhere. And he stood looking down on the 'fairish, fat, about forty' man — so he described me in his letter home to E. T. — sprawling at his mercy, reading a manuscript before him. And he remarked in a curiously deep, rather musical chest-voice:

'This isn't my idea, Sir, of an editor's office.'

That only added to my confusion. I had not the least idea of who this fellow was — and at the same time I had the idea from his relatively familiar address that it was someone I ought to recognize. But I was at least spared — since I did not know it was Lawrence — the real pain that his 'Sir' would have caused me had I known. For I should have hated to be given what I will call a caste Sir by anybody who could write as Lawrence could. But I was able to take it as the sort of 'Sir' that one addresses to one's hierarchically superior social equals . . . as the junior master addresses the Head, or the Major the

Colonel. And that was it, for when a little later I reproached him for using that form of address, he said:

'But you are, aren't you, everybody's blessed Uncle and Headmaster?'

For the moment, not knowing how to keep up the conversation with an unknown, I launched out into a defence of my room. I pointed out the beauty of its long, low, harmonious proportions; the agreeable light that fell from windows at both ends with trees beyond one half of them; the pleasant nature of the Chippendale chairs and bureaux that had been in my family for several generations; the portrait of myself as a child by my grandfather, and his long drawings for stained glass. And I ended up by saying:

'Young man, I never enter this room, coming from out of doors, without a feeling of thankfulness and satisfaction such as I don't feel over many things in this world.'. . . All the while asking myself when I was going to pluck up my courage to say to this super-vitalized creature from a world outside my own that I could not for the life of me remember who he was.

He continued to stand there, leaning still slightly against the doorpost with his head hanging a little as if he were looking for his exact thoughts. Then he raised his sardonic eyes to mine and said:

'That's all very well. But it doesn't look like a place in which one would make money.'

I said with the sort of pained gladness that one had to put on for that sort of speech:

'Oh, we don't make money here. We spend it.'

And he answered with deep seriousness:

'That's just it. The room may be all right for your private tastes . . . which aren't mine, though that does not matter. But it isn't one to inspire confidence in creditors. Or contributors.'

That fellow was really disturbing. It wasn't that his words were either jaunty or offensive. He uttered them as if they had been not so much assertions as gropings for truth. And a little, too, as if upon reflection I might agree with his idea and perhaps change my room or neighbourhood. And he added:

'So that, as a contributor, the first impression . . .'

And he answered my immediate question with:

'You are proposing to publish a story of mine. Called "Odour of Chrysanthemums." So I might look at the matter from the point of view of a contributor.'

That cleared the matter up, but I don't know that it made Lawrence himself seem any less disturbing. . . .

I have had indeed the same experience lately whilst I have been re-reading him for the purpose of this article. Each time that I have opened one of his books, or merely resumed reading one of his novels, I have had a feeling of disturbance — not so much as if something odd was going to happen to me but as if I myself might be going to do something eccentric. Then when I have read for a couple of minutes I go on reading with interest — in a little the spirit of a boy beginning a new adventure story. . . . I will return to that side of the matter later.

Enthusiastic supporters of the more esoteric Lawrence will say that my perturbation is caused by my coming in contact with his as-it-were dryad nature. As if it were the sort of disturbing emotion caused in manufacturers or bankers by seeing, in a deep woodland, the God Pan — or Priapus — peeping round beside the trunk of an ancient oak. I daresay that may be something like it. At any rate if the God Pan did look at one round a trunk one might well feel as one felt when the something that was not merely eyesight peeped out at you from behind Lawrence's eyes.

For that was really what the sensation was like — as if something that was inside — inhabiting — Lawrence had the job of looking after him. It popped up, took a look at you through his pupils and, if it were satisfied, sank down and let you go on talking. . . . Yes, it was really like that: as if, perhaps, a mother beast was looking after its young. For all I know it may have been that.

[Boston: Houghton Mifflin, 1937: pp. 70–9.]

Prefatory Note to the English Edition of *When the Wicked Man* (1932)

THE following note is for the English reader:

I publish this novel in England only with reluctance and under the action of a *force majeure* as to whose incidence I cannot here be explicit. I must, therefore, in conscience insist upon the fact that this book is in no sense a picture of American, and still less of New York, manners. It is nothing more than a lucubration on an individual problem such as besets most men at one period or another, of their lives. The scene might just as well have been set in Berlin except that I do not know Berlin. The background, in short, happens to be New York, because Gotham is the only city with which the writer has today any intimate acquaintance — in which, that is to say, he feels completely at home.

In addition the reader will observe that no single character in this book is a born New Yorker. Eighty per cent of the principal characters are of British, and ninety of European birth. That is the disaster of that, for me, much loved, ancient and staid city. For, if I pass any quiet hours in great towns, it is there that I pass them.

So that if the gentle reader wishes to draw from these pages any deductions as to deterioration of manners on the Western Atlantic seaboard it is on the deterioration of those there alien that he should draw them. That old bottle is too strong for their new vintages.

I do not apologize for a pompous introduction to a silly novel. It is the unfortunate character of our day with its monstrous facilities of inter-communication that enormous harm between peoples may be done by any ill-considered phrase. Yet our poor civilization is at stake because of the refusal of aid between nations. Immense, weighty, admirably documented tomes are daily written to prove that without mutual comprehension, co-operation and tolerance our ship is lost. Yet any phrase of any Tom Fool may wither the fruits of all those labours. So I have permitted myself the above remarks although knowing well that, even as a woman, according to St Paul, should hold her tongue in church, a novelist should be silent in the Roman Numerals of his concoctions.

Paris, 6 March MCMXXXII

Autocriticism

THE RASH ACT

THE more modern novelists — or, at any rate, those of the school to which Mr Ford Madox Ford belongs — write with two purposes. They try to produce work according to the canons that they have derived from the light vouchsafed them. Within those limits they try to render — not to write about — their times without *parti pris*. For them the conception and preliminary working out of a novel become an investigation. They say: Given such and such characters, public events of the day being so and so and the set of circumstances being so and so, what will eventuate? The main point is that public events play a principal part in the scheme as they do in our lives.

It would be hypocrisy to expect the lay reader to be interested in a novelist's method of writing — in his technique. Still more would it lack humour to imagine that novelists of other persuasions or the academically entrenched critic will be any more thrilled. But one remark as to the more modern world methods may be hazarded. It is a matter of what in America is called the 'time-shift'. It consists in not telling a story chronologically. No person in telling a story in real life, if the story is at all long, begins at the beginning of his subject's life. Nor do you do so in telling or remembering your own life, for it will come back to you in patches, an incident here, another of ten years earlier, a prevision of the future prepared for you by memories of twenty years of earlier happenings. . . . The 'technique' of the modern novelist is merely an attempt to tell his story as stories are really told. There is nothing more highbrow than that about it. It is the desire to be interesting. Everyone knows — even the most hardened academicist — that you would not be inclined to pursue a story of any person as to whom the first thing you heard was that at the age of three he was put into shorts.

No one rebukes or suspects the writer of detective stories for attending to his technique; yet his sole essential device is, precisely, the 'time-shift'. He knows that if he began one of his romances with the earlier years of his characters no one would read him. So he begins with a murder, harks back, returns to the present, harks back again, exactly like a hound quartering a field, until, pop, you have the *coup de canon* of the French short story writers of the nineties. The gallows or the electric chair — and not unusually Hymen — can then do their work. These works when they are good are often miracles of conscientious and conscious workmanship. They are read by the million — and very properly — simply because the device of the poor old time-shift gives to their pages an illusion of reality that no other device can convey. The breathless reader thus obtains vicarious experience. He has lived those scenes. The more modern novelist has no other ambition. He wants you, without being conscious that you are reading, to have the illusion that you are actually living in a real affair. You are in a real place in our own real times, with all their vicissitudes and reactions going strong.

The Rash Act is the elaborately time-shifted story of a man driven to the very edge of suicide and almost over. The world-crisis has ruined him. The writer's main impulse was what may be called historic. He desired to tell that story in an atmosphere of our own world with the effects and echoes of the Crisis and its machinery creeping in as nowadays it does for all of us. It would be too much to say that the writer also had the purpose of familiarizing Europe with the real America of quiet homes, old memories, entrenched traditions and cultivated, almost hypersensitized people — as opposed to the gangster, high-jacker, big business visage that America usually presents to these shores. *The Rash Act* might or might not serve that public purpose. At any rate, for the last twenty years the writer, always a wanderer, has had the idea of familiarizing widely separated peoples the one with the other somewhere at the back of his mind.

The crux of the plot was suggested by an incident of the great storm of three Augusts ago in Toulon Roads. An unknown foreigner was actually wounded by his boat in the manner described in the book. Maddened by pain, he dashed, when he had succeeded in landing, through a small crowd that had waited on the shore to help him. He disappeared into the woods of the island of St Mandrier. The body of a suicide was afterwards found in those woods, and local opinion had it that that was the man who had rushed out of the boat. The local police, however, came to the conclusion that the man was a down-and-outer, whom, for unexplained reasons, they presumed to be an American.

An apology is due to such readers as this book may find for the fact that its central figure is an American and not even of Anglo-Saxon origin. That is because two years ago America was the cyclonic centre of the disturbance and the immense majority of American citizens are non-Anglo-Saxon in origin. So that to get a real sense of how that cataclysm affected the individual a non-Anglo-Saxon American had to be selected to bear the brunt of the book. Future volumes will become increasingly European as the storm-centre shifts to these shores. And even as to the present instalment consolation may be found. For the second central figure of the book is English enough, and, as is not unusual in Anglo-American contacts, it is he who gets the most of the heroic meat.

FORD MADOX FORD

[The *Week-End Review*, 9 September 1933.]

AS THY DAY

Ford wrote this synopsis as a blurb for *Henry for Hugh*, 1934, originally called *As Thy Day*, the sequel to *The Rash Act*. Published here with permission of the Rare Book Room, Cornell University, from the typescript in the Ford Madox Ford Collection.

WITH *As Thy Day* Mr Ford Madox Ford adds another to the lengthening chain of novels, beginning with the pre-war *Good Soldier* and going on through the 'Tietjens' novels which dealt with the war years to his present group, in which he deals with the Crisis. The whole series thus forms an extended chronicle of our own times. These books thus differ from the more usual novel of the day in that world circumstances impinge on his characters as much as or almost more than their private vicissitudes. *As Thy Day* has a certain universality of theme, the private life of Henry Martin illustrating a phase of universal desire whilst all around him civilization quakes. There can be few men who have not wished at one time or another to change identities with some more fortunate being and this Henry

Martin has contrived to do, aided by tempest, suicide, the exigencies of the stock-markets and the enthusiasms of Southern natures. But, having achieved the exchange, he finds himself wishing wholeheartedly that he could once again be the normal American citizen that he once was. *As Thy Day* shows the workings out of his destinies in what is in effect an inverted detective story, the almost innocent misdemeanant, watching the sleuths getting on to his tracks, rather than the functionings of the ministrants of justice being what occupies the reader's attention. The main story passes on the Côte d'Azur, with reminiscential excursions to New York, the Middle West, Cardiff, London and other regions and the book is the most wound-up example of the use of the time-shift that Mr Ford has yet given us, the greater part of it passing, as is the case with our lives, in memories superimposed on the present and intimately affected by anticipations of the more or less distant future. The subject was suggested by an incident of the great storm of Toulon in August 1930. A man, badly injured by the yard of his boat landed on the shores of the island of St Mandrier and, maddened by the pain of his wounds, dashed through the group of spectators who were waiting to help him and disappeared into the woods on the top of the rocky island. Later in the day a man was found dead in the woods, his face having been rendered unrecognizable by a bullet wound. The police decided, on grounds they did not give the public, that the dead man was the man who landed from the boat and also that he was an American down and outer who had been ruined by the Crisis. The affair was never further cleared up.

from

The March of Literature (1938)

Ford's last book, written for the most part while he was teaching at Olivet. To write the *March*, he set himself a monumental course of re-reading so that he could report freshly to a new generation of readers what the world's literature looked like to him. One of his secretaries who typed the manuscript was Robert Lowell.

A DEDICATION WHICH IS ALSO AN AUTHOR'S INTRODUCTION

To
Joseph Hillyer Brewer and Robert Greenlees Ramsay
President and Dean of Men, Olivet College, Michigan

My dear Mr President and Mr Dean,

It is usual for a dedicator to assure his dedicatees that without their help he could not successfully have concluded his labours. That is true in a literal and physical sense, in this case, because, had you not provided me with a room in your admirable library, I should never have been able to finish this book — or not in ten years. But my spiritual obligation to you is no less deep. We have been working together for some time now, I under your presidency and deanship, in the attempt to restore to the youth of this state a lost art — that of reading . . . and in the hope that that art may spread from this state in ever widening practice to the ends of the earth.

Its present condition must be humiliating to every thinking man. The population of your nation is 150,000,000, that of mine over 450,000,000, every soul of whom is at least taught to read English in the schools. Yet of those six hundred million how many do, after their school days, read any books at all, much less any book that a reasonably cultivated man would not be ashamed to be seen reading? Well, a good — a very good — sale for a book of any literary merit whatsoever would be in my country, 14,000 copies; in yours 40,000. There are also, I have seen it estimated, in our joint vast realms, over 50,000 professors of literature. That means that one professor in a life of conscientious labour induces about 1.08 pupils to become, after tuition, reasonably civilized human beings. . . . And, in addition, there must be in existence hundreds and hundreds of thousands of learned works dealing with literature.

So it occurred to us three that there must be something wrong with the way in which the attractions of literature and the other arts are presented to our teeming populations. The solution of the problem seemed to us to be that that presentation must be in the wrong hands — that, in fact, such tuition, whether by word of mouth or in books, should be, not in the hands of the learned, but in those of artist-practitioners of the several arts — in the hands, that is to say, of men and women who love each their arts as they practise them. For it is your hot love for your art, not your dry delvings in the dry bones of ana and philologies that will enable you to convey to others your strong passion.

So you set up your educational institution in which the professoriate consists solely of practising artists — amongst whom it was my pride to enroll myself and my pleasure to serve. And having, thus, your corporate assurance that I was an artist, I thought I might undertake this book.

It is the book of an old man mad about writing — in the sense that Hokusai called himself an old man mad about painting. So it is an attempt to induce a larger and always larger number of my fellows to taste the pleasure that comes from always more and more reading. But that imposes on me certain limitations — the first being that, contrary to the habits of the learned, I must write only about the books that I have found attractive: because if I lead my reader up to unreadable books I risk giving him a distaste for all literature. Too many of the classics that the learned still mechanically ram down the throats of their pupils or their readers have lost the extra-literary attractions that once they had and so have become but dry bones, the swallowing of which can only inculcate into the coerced ingurgitators a distaste for all books. At the same time, I have such a distaste myself for writing injuriously about my fellows of the pen, though they may have been dead a thousand years, that I have, as you would say, panned hardly any writer, except for one or two stout fellows whose reputations may be considered as able to take care of themselves. So there may well be here certain omissions that may astonish you until you reflect upon the matter.

I have, in fact, tried to do here, making allowance for the differing nature of the medium, what you do with your students. You turn them loose in your library. You say: 'Choose a book. Try it out thoroughly. If, after a sincere trial, you find it distasteful, reject it and try something else. If you like it, study it carefully and study the other books of its author and his circle, observing what you can of his methods as to which we shall afterwards speak to you. Then try other books until you find more to which you are attuned. . . .'

I, of course, have had to dilate upon the methods of authors when recommending readers to read various books, otherwise my method has been the same as yours. I have taken book after book that I liked — and that in so many cases I have liked since my adolescence — and have suggested that if the reader likes the idea of the writer that I present to him, he should try steeping himself in that author's books, and so I have attempted to trace for that reader the evolution from the past of the literature of our own day and our own climes.

In any case, I beg you to accept the assurance of my affectionate thanks, of my hopes for the continued success of your admirable labours, and of the fact that I am

Your humble and, as I hope you have always found me,
Obedient servant,

F.M.F., D.Litt

Olivet College, Michigan
14 July mcmxxxviii

HERODOTUS

But Herodotus is something finer than either the genialities of Xenophon or the relatively pompous philosophic analyses of Thucydides. Herodotus is so interested in the world that surrounded him that he hardly had time to leave any impress of himself on his writings. You don't ever see him. He is a being with a voice saying continually, 'Look, look, how thrilling that is!' Like the prophet Amos he would seem to have been a man of a middling station of wealth — of a wealth sufficient to let him, with his insatiable curiosity, travel incessantly about the whole of the world that was known (or that was at least important) to the metropolitan and colonial Greeks of his day. He visited Asia Minor, Babylon, Phoenicia, Egypt, Thrace, the Ionian Islands, nearly the whole of Greece and very much of the greater Greece of the colonial system. And during all his travels he conversed unceasingly — with priests, with peasants, with satraps, with women carting wool, with packmen leading their mules down the rocky ways beneath the great pine trees of the Mediterranean basin. So that when, towards the age of forty, he was tired of travel or his funds gave out, he settled for a time in Athens with a head stuffed with the most delightful ana of the world. He knew what really happened to Helen after she was supposed to have eloped with Paris. He was acquainted with the most remarkable of all detective stories — how Rhampsinitus found out and rewarded with his sister's hand the thief who had stolen innumerable pieces of gold from the Imperial Treasury. He was at once credulous and cynical. He would recall marvels as if he believed every word that he was told, and in the end would slip in: 'This is hardly to be believed.' Or as in the case of the miraculous extinction of the fire that was to have burned Croesus, he would add: 'Others tell this story differently.' You see before your eyes the whole stretch of those singular climes from which have come all that is most bright and beautiful in our modern temperaments. You see spread out beneath you whilst you read him, the mountains between Thebes and Babylon, the seas from Asia Minor to Sicily, the Aegean Islands and the palms on the Nile bank. But, above all, you commune with a beautiful and humane spirit. For, after having spent some time in idleness or in the observation of the manners and customs of the citizens of Athens, Herodotus removed himself to one of the colonies that the Greeks were establishing in Italy. His removal is said to have taken place in the year 453 — in which case he would have been forty-one years of age — and the colony was that of Thurium, otherwise Thurii in Lucania. Here he would seem to have been settled on a farm such as the Greeks provided for their colonists, the gift including a small income. The colony, as we know, suffered from inroads of the Italian barbarians and it never prospered very much. Nevertheless, in his office or in his home, Herodotus found time to write his matchless projection of the world of his day. His book purports to be the history of the struggle between the Greeks and the Persians which ended successfully for Greece when he was aged about four. But between the beginning and the end of that war he contrives to insert so many digressions as to the habits and customs of any of the tribes mentioned that, though the actual main subject of the war never goes completely by the board, his work presents the aspect of extreme and engrossing complexity. It is sufficient for any new character to be introduced into his pages to let

Herodotus go off at once upon a new journey. Supposing a new character came, say, from Hyrcania: he would set forth either in person or imagination for that distant spot and would bring into his narrative descriptions of the religious rites, the agricultural customs and the vicissitudes of the inhabitants for generations back. That done, he would return to Babylon or Thebes or wherever he last left the seat of the war and after some digressions as to the habits and lore of the priests of Thebes with its hundred gates, he would record, as we have already seen, the Theban account of the wanderings of Helen of Troy and so carry Cyrus and his wars forward for a month or two until once more the opportunity for a digression permitted him to escape from his main stream.

The instructed reader will perceive that in thus handling his matter, Herodotus, 2,500 years ago, anticipated the technique most usual to the novelist and historian of the present day. His history of his own time, had it been written by, say, either the late Joseph Conrad or the living Aldous Huxley, could scarcely have differed in form, though obviously the recording temperament would be different. On the face of it, it might have seemed better to begin the story of the war at the beginning and to carry it straightforwardly onwards until it arrived at the Grecian victory. Actually, as Herodotus knew, if you wish to present, say, Cyrus, as he lived, it is a good thing to get him in with some vividness and then to abandon him for a time in favour of Rhampsinitus. Because, when you return to Cyrus, you will seem to be taking up an acquaintance again with an already known figure, and you will seem to deepen your knowledge of his habits or vicissitudes quite disproportionately. But whether you approve or disapprove of the literary methods of the great historian, you could never deny that the main astonishing note of this chronicle is that of humaneness. Croesus, the great and externally fortunate — but last — King of Lydia, drew from Solon, the Athenian lawgiver, as we have seen, the apophthegm 'Deem no man fortunate till his death.' And with his great and always increasing fortune in gold, with his splendid fleets and his noble alliances, Croesus received the saying at once with distaste and incredulity. But Nemesis attended on him, though what sin he had committed other than that of being too fortunate is not recorded. At any rate, it was his one misfortune that saved his life. He had, to his mortification, a deaf and dumb son. He conquered Asia Minor and the fame of his exploits and wealth became so great that they must needs attract the attention of Cyrus, the humane rebuilder of the Temple of Solomon. Cyrus, looking about for new worlds to conquer, led his legions against Croesus, and after a number of coincidental failures of his troops or the troops of his allies to arrive in time on the fields of battle, Croesus found himself shut up in the citadel of Sardis and surrounded by the troops of Cyrus. The citadel was supposed to be impregnable but, as happened in the Siege of Quebec by Wolfe, a certain number of Persian soldiers scaled its heights and, entering the chamber in which Croesus found himself, prepared to slaughter him. But at the sight, his deaf and dumb son suddenly recovered his voice and exclaimed, 'Soldier, do not dare to slay Croesus, the King.' So Croesus was temporarily spared and carried before Cyrus. Cyrus prepared to put him to death by burning. And just as Joan of Arc upon her pyre exclaimed three times 'Jesus!', so on his, Croesus, remembering the Athenian lawgiver's dictum, cried out three times the name of Solon. And having not Anglo-Saxons but Persians to listen to him, and crying out not the name of his and their Redeemer but merely that of a revered lawgiver, Croesus was spared. For Cyrus, the humane and the pensive, remembered that of Cyrus, too, it might be said that he could not be deemed fortunate until he was dead, and decided to extinguish the brands beneath the body of the man who had brought that saying back to his memory. Nay, more, he made Croesus his counsellor in the conduct of his wars, and this proved admirably helpful not only to Cyrus, but to the subjects of Croesus himself. For Croesus, observing that the Persian soldiery were setting fire to the city of Sardis, disgorging its citizens and carrying off their wealth, exclaimed drily to his conqueror that it would be more profitable if he prevented his men from doing anything of the sort. For, said he, if Cyrus permitted his men to turn that opulent city into a desert and to slay its citizens, thus putting an end to their earning power, not only would Cyrus himself be impoverished to the extent that he would not be able to tax those citizens and otherwise enrich himself at their expense, but his troops being rendered fabulously wealthy would at least desire to desert his army, even if they were not rendered so proud-stomached as to attempt to mutiny against their owner with a view to assuming his royal dignities. So the inhabitants of Sardis were saved, and Cyrus, observing the humane rule of Croesus, not only prospered to the day of his death, but established one of the mightiest and most civilized empires that the world has ever known. For instead of attempting to establish, after the habit of most other conquerors to the present day, a homogeneous empire with all its subject citizens ruined and enslaved and bound down to the worship of the conqueror's god and the observance of his moral code, he permitted those he conquered to retain not only their creeds, habits and moral standards, but the greater part of their wealth, contenting himself by exacting in the form of normal taxes the tribute that enabled him to maintain his empire in peace or to go upon further wars. So that, although he perished gloriously in battle with the Masagetes, his son Cambyses succeeded to his wealth and power, and Cyrus himself, as we have seen, was blessed by Jehovah.

> Thus saith Cyrus king of Persia, All the kingdoms of the earth hath the Lord God of heaven given me; and he hath charged me to build him an house in Jerusalem, which *is* in Judah. Who *is there* among you of all his people, the Lord his God *be* with him, and let him go up.

So that there in one story you perceive what must be so far the moral of this work, the doctrines of humaneness going, coiling as it were, from Sardis and Lydia to Babylon and again to Jerusalem and coming thus to us who sit here in times so infinitely more ferocious, to be to us at once a cause of shame and enlightenment.

LANGLAND and CHAUCER

By the middle of the fourteenth century — say about 1350 — the whole of the literary field was beginning to change its aspect. In a little more than a hundred years the change was to be completed.

In 1350 Chaucer was either ten or twenty, the date of his birth being disputed by the learned. Boccaccio was thirty-seven and had certainly begun the *Decameron* which was given to the world in 1353; Petrarch was forty-six and Froissart twelve. Langland, author or part author of the *Vision of Piers Plowman* was eighteen, Wycliffe was already contemplating the translation of the Scriptures. Let us then make the initial note that in England Chaucer was to be called the father of English poetry; in Italy Boccaccio, the father of Italian prose, and in France Froissart may certainly be regarded as the father of French prose. In Germany, as we have just seen, the three great preaching friars were writing and delivering their sermons that later were considered the beginnings of aesthetic prose in the Northlands.

Another note which it is important to make is that of the eminence of authors. Roughly speaking, from the death of Virgil until the birth of Dante the author was relatively of little national or social distinction. We may make an exception for the cases of the troubadours and the *minnesingers*; but in both cases it is the literature rather than the isolated figure that would appear to be of importance. This is a literary factor that will vary according to social conditions and the spirit of the age. But, as a general rule, when you have great literary figures, literature will be in abeyance, whereas where you have a very high level of literature a great figure will be absent. Bertran de Born the troubadour, was great in his day, but rather as a political and martial figure who fought with all the kings of the earth than as the author of *sirventes*, even though one of them should be as famous as the *Lament for the Son of Henry II*. And the other troubadours are merely part of a great literary movement. Or, to carry the idea one stage further forward, you had in Germany the very remarkable literature of the folksong and there, although we know that the regional poets must have achieved a certain output and local celebrity, we are unable to recapture the name of any one of them. Or, if we take the case of England, you will find a great work like the *Vision of Piers Plowman* which is popular in its inspiration and yet with a quite indefinite authorship. The poem is usually given to William Langland or Langley who was an almost exact contemporary of Chaucer. But we know next to nothing of this author. And his poem has curiously the air of having been written in a place of public assembly. As if, while he wrote, individuals came up and whispered into his hooded ear: 'Don't forget the poor cooks', or: 'Remember the hostlers', or: 'Whatever you do, don't forget to expose the scandalous living of the lousy friars'.

* * *

In England, on the other hand, at least a proportion of the popular mind was given to social matters. The *Vision of Piers Plowman*, whilst being in parts a poem of extreme beauty, is, in other parts — and those the majority — an attempt to assert human rights. Or, at any rate, an assertion that in heaven, which this earth should — if it didn't — resemble, the poor would have equal rights with their lords. The keynote of the poem is, as we have already said, sounded in the words: 'There the poor dare plead.'

It was thus — and the poem with its infinite number of readers is evidence of the fact if any evidence were needed — that the attention of the populace was not merely fixed on public affairs alone. And public affairs were disastrous enough. In 1349 came the first great pestilence, called the Black Death; in 1362 the second; in the same year an immense tempest wrought such great damage in England that it was said that half of the wealth of the country was destroyed in seven hours. (It was in this year also that the first draft of *Piers Plowman* was written.) In 1369 came the third invasion by the Black Death; in 1375-6 the last. In 1377 the second version of *Piers Plowman* was published. From 1361 onwards, England had had peace from foreign wars. Popular unrest grew. Promoted by the preachings of John Ball, it was occasioned by the loss of population and of wealth caused by the successive Deaths and by great frosts and tempests and the miserable condition and serfdom of the common people. Thus, while the author of the *Vision* and Chaucer wrote, you had the revolt of the peasants under Wat Tyler and John Ball, the preacher, their capture of London, and the burning of the Savoy Palace of John of Gaunt. You had also in the same year — 1381 — the denial of transubstantiation by Wycliffe and his followers. So Chaucer wrote his *Canterbury Tales* between 1386 and 1387; the *Confessio Amantis* of Gower, a relatively humdrum achievement, was completed in 1390, and the final text of *Piers Plowman* was written about 1392. And it is interesting to consider that in 1388 was fought the Battle of Otterburne or Chevy Chase, when the Scots under the Douglas defeated Lord Henry Percy. And presumably the first draft of the most famous of all Border ballads was written.

The House of Lancaster, under King Henry IV, who had murdered Richard II, came into power in 1399, and both Langland and Chaucer died in the following year.

So that the poetry produced in this age goes little towards deciding whether or no the best literature is produced by those who are what is called socially minded or no. The lives of Chaucer and Langland coincided almost to a day, and, although it would be bold to compare the genius of Langland with that of Chaucer, the *Vision of Piers Plowman* is a poem sufficiently inspired by genius not to give away the whole case of propagandist literature. It is true that when it becomes propagandist it becomes also tiresomely allegorical, but, nevertheless, in its passages of realism — and they are frequent enough — the genuis of the poet shines without shadow. And the frame and detail of the *Vision* have a marked resemblance to those of the *Tales*:

I saw in that assembly, as ye shall hear hereafter,
  Bakers, butchers, and brewers many,
Woollen weavers, and weavers of linen,
Tailors, tanners, and fullers also,
Masons, miners, and many other crafts,
Ditchers and delvers, that do their work ill,
And drive forth the long day with '*Dieu vous sauve*, dame Emma.'
  Cooks and their boys cry 'Hot pies, hot!
Good geese and pigs, go dine, go dine!'
Taverners to them told the same tale
With good wine of Gascony and wine of Alsace,
Of Rhine and of Rochelle, the roast to digest.
All this I saw sleeping, and seven times more.

So runs a sort of programme of the poem given in the prologue, and it has about it the real Chaucerian — or, perhaps, it would be more just to say the real late fourteenth century — touch. It has, moreover, nearly all Chaucer's genius of language.

That overtone of the written or printed page which conveys the genius of the great writer is one of those standing miracles which has its most striking exponents in such poets as Chaucer — if, indeed, there is any other poet like the author of *Palamon and Arcite*.

Why is it that when for the many hundredth time you read:

Whanne that April with his shoures sote
The droughte of March hath perced to the rote,
And bathed every veine in swiche licour,

you feel a sort of quickening of the veins, a sort of re-oxygenation of the blood, as if from your usual dimnesses you had come out into a keener and purer air? Or, perhaps, to make the image more precise still, one should say: as if one were setting out on a journey to where the air should be pure and alive. . . . At any rate, it is an excitement.

Yet the content of the words is merely meteorological, and not strikingly exact at that. Nevertheless, the words live and, as it were, bubble in a little cauldron and, as if the friction evolved electricity, they exhale it. . . . And still the explanation is insufficient. You may add, say, that the contrast of the three 'ou' sounds in 'shoures' and 'droughte' and 'licour' contrasted with the 'o's' of 'sote' and 'rote' give the effect — the 'ou' being properly pronounced 'oo' — of cuckoos calling in a spring shower. They probably do. And that gives pleasure.

Nevertheless, all that is insufficient to account for the standing-aloneness of Chaucer. Because, like Dante and, in his different degree, like Heine, he is completely solitary, deriving solely from the world that surrounded him and in which he delighted, without predecessor or school. It is, in short, probably the quality of having lived, and remaining self-contained. Dante took for his motto the proud words: '*Fidandomi di me piu che di un altro*' ('Trusting to myself better than to any other man'), and one may imagine that the great — perhaps the greatest — English poet was upheld by a similar self-trust. He was probably, however, insufficiently self-analytical to put that characteristic into the form of the Dantean boast. His work is in the highest sense as impersonal as that of most modern writers. Nay, as impersonal as that of Flaubert. When you read *Palamon and Arcite* you are so carried away by the story that you have no time to bother your head about what manner of man the author was. You are enveloped in an affair. That is the quality of great art. He was obviously a moralist — everyone in his day was — but his moralizings are so exactly those of everyone else of his day that they in no way distinguish him from anyone else. He was a moralist, as proper men today are clean. Then, you washed yourself in a certain quality of moralizing, as today you use soap. The celebrated characterization of Chaucer to be found in the *Canterbury Tales* is generally disputed by the learned for one of those reasons known only to the learned themselves. The host of the Tabard, catching sight of Chaucer amongst the other pilgrims, shouts at him thus:

> What man are thou? quod he.
> Thou lookest as thou wouldst find an hare,
> For ever upon the ground I see thee stare.
> Approache near, and looke merrily.
> Now ware you, sire, and let this man have space.
> He in the waist is shapen as well as I;
> This were a puppet in an arm, to embrace
> For any woman, small, and fair of face.
> He seemeth elvish by his countenance,
> For unto no wight doth he dalliance.

This would seem, as a portrait, to be convincing enough. But since

Chaucer in various places, but notably in the *House of Fame*, is accustomed to make fun of his own person and everywhere to depreciate his own talent, the too ingenious learned enjoin upon you that you must take him to have been the exact opposite of what he herein describes himself as being. But his portrait is so exactly brought in and so convincing that the artist, knowing better than a professor how a brother artist would get his effects, will almost certainly accept this portrait as the just one. In any case we have no real means of knowing since there exist no memoirs of Chaucer or of other people that, by the way, tell us how Chaucer looked or how he lived and talked. The host's portrait does at least tally with the little miniature in the margin of one of the Chaucerian manuscripts.

One perceives a specifically little, hooded man, with a small beard, and eyes obviously accustomed to gaze to the side — with eyes, that is to say, that will see what, to his right or left, you are doing, whilst, his face being not towards you, you are unaware that he is observing you. . . . But within that definite frame everyone must make his own portrait of the great, little poet.

One imagines him, then, with the quality of the unobserved observer that distinguishes the naturalist like the late W. H. Hudson, that incomparable writer of English prose. He was so unobtrusive that neither man nor bird took alarm at his presence, and so observant that without taking a note he could give you the exact fold of a hood, detail of an ornament, facial wrinkle or trick of speech. You get, indeed, from the host's address to him that he was considered as somewhat of a snooper; nevertheless, the characteristic was unresented. Some men have that attribute; when they write they become great writers.

And he had lived before he wrote. The son of a vintner of the city of London, he began life in a situation full of interests for a note-taker. How he became in boyhood a 'valettour' of princes at the King's court, one has no means of knowing — but the relations of wine merchant and client are frequently intimate. Between one wrinkling of the nose over a titillating cup and another, Chaucer *père* may well have slipped in a plea to have his son given a gentleman's place about the court. Once there, he behaved with modest efficiency and captured the heart of Philippa, a lady of honour whose family name has not come down to us, but one of whom everyone in those treacherous circles spoke more than well — and who was beloved by her Lady Princess. You do not, then, need more explanation of

Chaucer's honourable career at court. It is all the battle won to have behind you a lady universally beloved.

CASANOVA

The journal of Giovanni Giacomo Casanova de Seingalt (1725–98), if we regard it as the most monstrous and egregious of picaresque novels, may well pass for a piece of writing of international importance, though not of international literary importance. The writer cannot call to mind any large crops of works that can be alleged to imitate the *Journals*. During our own middle years it was generally taken for fact that the *Journals* were in great part a forgery of that singular figure, the bibliophile Jacob. But today the balance of belief would seem to tend towards agreeing that they are almost altogether the writing of Casanova himself, the published form of the book being the result of a compilation of manuscripts left by Casanova in the library of Dax in Bohemia. Casanova passed the last years of his life as librarian in that castle. The vast majority of his readers today probably read him for the records of his innumerable seductions, which give to the book a certain monotony so that if an *édition du Dauphin* could be prepared leaving out the majority of passages of that kidney we should probably have something much more readable and inspiring, whilst the man of the world and the adolescent seeking useful knowledge would be advantaged by having all the salacious episodes grouped together at the end of the book. The *Memoirs* were actually published in French, so it is perhaps a solecism to call them an Italian masterpiece, though masterpiece they are. As an extended picture of the conditions of an era and a portion of the world's surface in a state of cultural decay and political horrors they have no equal and certainly no parallel save the diary of Pepys. And, as a work of art, the book probably merely gains in attractiveness because a large proportion of the work — as is conceded even by the staunchest believers in the Casanovian authorship — was magnificent lying, particularly in its non-amorous aspects. Casanova was by his own showing rogue, thief, pimp, spy, secret agent, suspect diplomat, gambler, sham magician, purveyor of obscenities, gaolbird, rake and optimist throughout half a Latin world that was staggering through political grafts, felonies, betrayals, candle-lit festivals, debauches lit by burning towns, delicate music, elegances, wantonnesses — towards bankruptcies, revolutions and heroic struggles for national freedom from international oppressions. You might, indeed, read it as a book of prophecies whose results are not exhausted even in our own day. But, however you read it, you will become acquainted with a personality extraordinarily marked and defined, so that according to our late definition, it may well pass as a work of art. . . . Casanova was perhaps surpassed as a liar by Benvenuto Cellini, but he would certainly have made a more agreeable housemate for anyone of a disposition at all leaning towards the contemplative.

CHATEAUBRIAND

It is necessary, then, to read Chateaubriand because he was the last of the great writers. He survived Goethe by sixteen years, and with him he had great resemblances — a sort of marmoreal calm intershot by a singularly tender sensibility. That was something that they added to the characters presented by Plutarch. You can not imagine Cicero with his eyes near to tears as he reads Calderón, nor Brutus writing: 'How sad it is to think that eyes that are too old to see are yet not too old to shed tears. . . .'

That is what Chateaubriand wrote one day when he had been talking to an aged, blind Indian sachem who had passed without wincing a life of infinite hardship and courage and yet was finally moved to emotion by the news of a domestic disaster — the wiping out by enemies of a whole branch of his young family.

And it is that sentence of Chateaubriand's, read long ago, that this writer most has taken away from reading his works. It is an incentive to carry one's fortitude into the extremes of age, so it is, like all great tragic writing, a stimulant. And it is, if that were needed, evidence that Chateaubriand as traveller was more than just a coverer of waste spaces. For it is a touching little vignette from the past to think of that young French noble in tie wig, plumed hat and satin knee breeches standing in the virgin forest looking down on the ancient chief and condensing that human contact into that admirable thought. It justifies him as being the last of a line — a line of writers who were not hacks.

STENDHAL

The fact is that Stendhal was almost ignored by writers and public together until the seventies of the last century. By that decade the literati began to develop an enthusiasm for him; by the nineties his name was continually on the lips of all the intelligentsia of France, Russia, Italy and Germany and even of a portion of the more advanced literary coteries of London. Thus, of the powerful clique known as Henley's Gang in the London nineties, W. E. Henley and Messrs Whibley, Wedmore and Anderson Graham were all in varying degrees interested in *Le Rouge et le Noir* and perhaps even more in *De l'Amour*. And, according to Mr James, Robert Louis Stevenson was almost morbidly affected by both Stendhal's romances and the book on love. He immensely admired Stendhal's dry, direct style and also the manner in which he handled incident. He, nevertheless — again according to Mr James — deliberately avoided reading or thinking of Stendhal for fear the influence should 'spoil his market'.[1]

It is the complete equanimity with which Stendhal regards his characters that gives to his pages their extraordinary effect of reality. He will record, with the passionlessness of a Chancery lawyer commenting on an act of Parliament concerning the doctrine of redemption, how his hero, by then become an archbishop, wishing to enjoy some undisturbed days with his mistress, casually asks the prime minister of the principality that they all inhabit, to remove the extremely noble and wealthy husband of the lady for a week or ten days. The prime minister, *'qui fut attendri de cette histoire d'amour,'* says: 'Certainly. When would the archbishop like the marquis removed?'

In a day or two the archbishop says: 'Now is the time.' And on the same day, the marquis, returning from a ride on horseback from one of his more distant estates, is politely seized by some brigands, near Mantua, confined on a barque which descends the River Po for three days, and is then set free on an island from which, all his money and

[1] Those are Mr James's exact words. In the writer's almost daily colloquies with Mr James, which extended over a number of years, the literary figure of Henri Beyle, known as Stendhal, must have been the most frequent subject of their conversation as far as it concerned itself with literature. And this writer must at one time or another have heard Conrad read with enthusiasm, commenting as he went on the technique there employed, at least half of *Le Rouge et le Noir*.

valuables having been removed from him, he finds some difficulty in returning home.

The marquis, taking the kidnapping as an 'affair of private vengeance', seems to regard it as the most natural thing in the world, and we are not even told that the lovers particularly enjoyed themselves during his absence. Indeed, we know that owing to excruciations of psychological and moral scruples on the part of the lady — who had made a vow to the Blessed Virgin never to see her lover again and who in consequence would only receive him in pitch darkness — they probably did not have a very good time. The highest ecclesiastical authorities of the See of Rome being consulted as to the lady's rash vow, give the verdict that, in certain circumstances, the lady would be justified in seeing her lover by at least candlelight. But when the child of their union dies, the lady is convinced that that is the punishment for breaking her vow to the Virgin and so dies in the archbishop's arms.

Treated by Mrs Radcliffe or Monk Lewis, or even by Victor Hugo or Dumas, these incidents would seem to be of the height of improbability or grotesqueness. But knowing what we do — if only from Manzoni's *Promessi Sposi* — of the nature of Italian higher officials of that day, and drily recounted as they are in the admirably dispassionate style of Stendhal, they seem the most natural and, indeed, logical of occurrences. And we are prepared by the *Princesse de Clèves* of Mme de Lafayette — who is another writer to whom Stendhal must have been electively related — for the moral scruples of the archbishop's Clélia. Or, indeed, we are provided by Manzoni with another instance of a girl's vowing to the Virgin that she will never see her lover again — and of her obtaining a dispensation from the vow by higher ecclesiastical authority.

But, indeed, the literary personality of Stendhal was so magisterial that, had he, instead of Swift, related the conditions of the kingdom of Laputa, we should take them to be a literal constatation of an existing, if distant, state of things.

[THE DETECTIVE NOVEL]

Today's craving for the romance of crime is perfectly healthy, proper and aesthetically justifiable. If you will take up a good — and that means a popular — detective story you will see that its construction is admirable; its style fluid; it will of necessity employ the modern aesthetic device called the 'time shift', which the established critics of the more pompous journals still find esoteric. And it gives information as to the workings of life that is certainly of value — much as the historic romance in its heyday supplied the public with all the information as to history that ninety per cent of us ever had.

On the intellectual side, it is perhaps to seek, and its values of life are apt to be very conventionally estimated. That is because the superior intelligences of the day do not usually — and they are quite wrong — apply themselves to the mystery story. Yet the great novels of the world, whether of the romantic, the classical or the realistic modern schools, have all — and this is no paradox — been mystery stories. *Vanity Fair* is a mystery story, worked from the inside instead of from the out. So is *Madame Bovary*; so is Conrad's *The Secret Agent*; so, for the matter of that, is *Tom Jones* with its working up to the triumphant exposure of young Mr Blifil; so is *The Vicar of Wakefield*; so, substituting psychological for material values, is almost every novel of Henry James.

It is true that the writer of the greater fiction works as a rule from the inside — with the criminal — instead of exteriorly with the detector of crime. That is because, keeping company with the criminal, you have a better opportunity for following the psychological involutions of that character, and to the reflecting writer the psychological developments of his characters, or his affairs, is his reason for writing. Just imagine *Madame Bovary* worked from the outside, a psychologically acute investigator of crime being called to Emma Bovary's bedside the moment after her death and having to unroll, from all the data given by the author, the history of poor Emma's gradual deterioration from her gentle but indomitable romanticism, through sordid intrigues and peculations to her inevitable suicide. What a *roman policier* that would be!

And let that Gallicism serve to remind us that in France the considerable psychological romancers have already turned their attention to the esoteric psychology of crime. The most distinguished of the younger Gallic *romanciers* is M. Georges Bernanos — a writer most admirable in his construction, his writing, his progression of effect and the poetry of his outline. And his *Sous le Soleil de Satan* is an immense theological argument around a perfectly bloodthirsty murder. It passes, nevertheless, for a great product of fictional imagination. Or consider the *Pendu de St. Phollien* or the *Ombres Chinoises* of M. Georges Simenon, the one, precisely, a solution of a perfectly psychological murder mystery in which the whole story turns on the effects of a hyper-romantic economo-political crowd brainstorm on an impoverished group of intellectuals attached to a provincial university; the other being an analysis of an impulsion towards crime of a French bureaucratic household under the impulsion of the insupportable poverty that is the lot of so many French minor officials. It is Dostoevsky . . . and Dostoevsky, *corsé*, constructed, economized and filled with the poetry of pity. . . .

[New York: Dial Press, 1938: pp. v–vii, 98–102, 403–04, 406–11, 527–8, 700–01, 782–4, 832–3.]

Finnegans Wake

Joyce referred to this letter of Ford's as 'possibly the last public act of his life'.

SIR: — I trust you will be good enough to spare space for a protest against the tepidity of the review of James Joyce's *Finnegans Wake* in your issue of May 6. Mr Rosendfeld has borne the burden of several frays on several intellectual and agnostic forefronts but, having been reared in an atmosphere of pure reason, he is unfitted to appreciate to the full the peculiar, hieratic qualities of Mr Joyce's mind. If you are not attuned to the instrument you can hardly do justice to its sound. Hence, Mr Rosenfeld's lack of sensuous appreciation of the 'wit and mysterious poetry' that, intellectually, he perceives in the book. To get a full joy out of Mr Joyce's polychromaticfugal effects of language, one must have been brought up in either Jesuit or high Anglican neighbourhoods, or in any of the vast territories that lie between those two extremes. Your ears must have been at an early age so impregnated with the verbiage of the mass, the Book of Common Prayer, the Vulgate, and the Authorized Version that the mere vowel sequences of certain passages will be sufficient to call back to you all the associations of your youth. If, say, in the three most impressionable years of your life, you have heard the burden of Collects, Prayers, and Novenas 10,950 times (3 times 10 times 365) in school or seminary chapels, the mere sequence of the vowel colouring of that phrase will give you acute pleasure if you hear it in quite other verbiage. Imagine a paragraph of Mr Joyce recounting how a Bloom or a Finnegan refuses an invitation to sit at the groaning board of him who had great possessions whilst accepting one to share the unleavened hoe-cake of Lazarus. Imagine the Cranmerian rhythm of the whole paragraph and then the ending: 'Rather the bun of the lowly host'. To Mr Rosenfeld that might not be very great fun. But we who recognize the triple fugue implicit in those words, feel the joy that cannot be known to those without the Pale. You have, as first subject, the content paraphrasing the Beatitude, 'Blessed are the humble and meek'. You have as second subject, the vowel colouring. And as third subject, the suggestion of the continual burden of the church's unceasing dedication of herself to the persons of the Trinity. As a free fantasia accompanying the counterpoint, you will have your own emotions in remembrance of shivering winter mornings in the frosty school chapel.

Or again, rightly to get joy out of Mr Joyce, you must appreciate his chief note, which is a kind of tender picking on God and his Mother such as the pupils of Jesuits will get a tittering joy at bringing out whilst chancing that their innocuous blasphemies shall bring down upon their heads the stern voice of their teacher, saying, 'Boy, let down your small clothes'.

The comprehension of these primary characteristics must be yours if you desire to taste all the joy that can be got out of Bloom or Finnegan; but Mr Joyce's universality is founded on what Mr Rosenfeld perspicaciously styles 'Mr Joyce's half tender and half savagely blasphemous picture of human life' . . . and on his unparalleled investigation into the uses to which words and their associations can be put.

English is a language ill-suited to good prose because of the associations that, like burrs, cling undetachable to every English word, and the simplest English sentence is forever blurred because it can always have several meanings. Even 'the Cat is on the Mat' can mean so much more than meets the eye. If, for instance, you met the statement on top of a newspaper column you would at once guess that Parliament was discussing the abolition of flogging in the Services. Or Mr Norman Douglas was right in considering that 'They Went' as a title for one of his books would arouse curiosity, since so bold a statement must seem to convey implications such as They Went, flying from fear of disgrace, of threats, of physical violences, of inundations, of earthquakes — with the corollary that you couldn't see their going for dust.

Most of us weaker brothers of the pen try to get round this characteristic of our language by using simpler and always more simple words and constructions. But, wiser and more brave, Mr Joyce seizes the polysignificance of English as the philosophic basis of his labours, and attracts always more associations to his words until the literal meaning of almost every word is lost in a burr-mantle of local or colloquial colourings. And the world owes gratitude to his huge prodigality, since not only does his prose prove how magnificently hued our language may be but it affords us lesser navigators in the sea of words a chart to show us how far we may go. It maps the verges of the word user's habitable universe.

Thus, *Finnegans Wake* stands up across the flat lands of our literatures as does the first Pyramid across the sands of Egypt, and its appearance at this moment is almost the one event of amazing importance sufficient to withdraw our attention from public events. And thus, Mr Rosenfeld's attempt to turn readers from this masterpiece is one contrary to the interests of the Republic, for, if we are deterred from removing our attention from public circumstances today, there can be no end for us but a blithering lunacy of imbecile phraseologists.

I have the honour to be, Sir,

Your obedient servant,

FAUGH AN-BALLAGH FAUGH.

New York City.

[Letter to the Editor, *Saturday Review of Literature*, 3 June 1939.]

IV

Cultural Criticism

from

The Spirit of the People (1907)

This excerpt from chapter V, 'Conduct', is taken from the American edition of *England and the English* (1907), which combined three volumes published separately in England: *The Soul of London* (1905), *The Heart of the Country* (1906) and *The Spirit of the People*.

THE defects of the Englishman's qualities are strange in practice, but obvious enough when we consider the root fact from which they spring. And that root fact is simply that the Englishman feels very deeply and reasons very little. It might be argued, superficially, that because he has done little to remedy the state of things on the Congo, that he is lacking in feeling. But, as a matter of fact, it is really because he is aware — subconsciously if you will — of the depth of his capacity to feel, that the Englishman takes refuge in his particular official optimism. He hides from himself the fact that there are in the world greed, poverty, hunger, lust or evil passions, simply because he knows that if he comes to think of them at all they will move him beyond bearing. He prefers, therefore, to say — and to hypnotize himself into believing — that the world is a very good — an all-good — place. He would prefer to believe that such people as the officials of the Congo Free State do not really exist in the modern world. People, he will say, do not do such things.

As quite a boy I was very intimate with a family that I should say was very typically English of the middle class. I spent a great part of my summer holidays with them and most of my week-ends from school. Lady C —, a practical, comfortable, spectacled lady, was accustomed to call herself my second mother, and, indeed, at odd moments, she mothered me very kindly, so that I owe to her the recollection of many pleasant, slumberous and long summer days, such as now the world no longer seems to contain. One day I rowed one of the daughters up a little stream from the sea, and halting under the shade of a bridge where the waters lapped deliciously, and swallows flitted so low as to brush our heads, I began to talk to the fair, large, somnolent girl of some problem or other — I think of poor umbrella-tassel menders and sweated industries that at that time interested me a great deal. Miss C — was interested or not interested in my discourse; I don't know. In white frock she lay back among the cushions and dabbled her hands in the water, looking fair and cool, and saying very little. But next morning Lady C — took me into the rose garden, and, having qualified her remarks with: 'Look here. You're a very good boy, and I like you very much,' forbade me peremptorily to talk to Beatrice about 'things'.

It bewildered me a little at the time because, I suppose, not being to the English manner born, I did not know just what 'things' were. And it harassed me a little for the future, because I did not know at the time, so it appeared to me, what else to talk about but 'things'. Nowadays I know very well what 'things' are; they include, in fact, religious topics, questions of the relations of the sexes; the conditions of poverty-stricken districts — every subject from which one can digress into anything moving. That, in fact, is the crux, the Rubicon that one must never cross. And that is what makes English conversation so profoundly, so portentously, troublesome to maintain. It is a question of a very fine game, the rules of which you must observe. It is as if one were set on making oneself interesting with the left hand tied behind one's back. And, if one protests against the inconveniences attendant upon the performance of this prime conjuring trick, one is met by the universal: 'Oh, well; it's the law!'

The ramifications of this characteristic are so infinite that it would be hopeless to attempt to exhaust them. And the looking out for them leads one into situations of the most bizarre. Thus, I was talking about a certain book that was hardly more than mildly 'shocking' to a man whose conversation among men is singularly salacious, and whose life was notoriously not clean. Yet of this particular book he said, in a manner that was genuinely shocked:

'It's a thing that the law ought to have powers to suppress.' There was no doubt that he meant what he said. Yet he could recount with approval and with gusto incidents that rendered pale and ineffectual the naïve passions depicted in the work in question. But Mr N — 's position was plainly enough defined and sufficiently comprehensible; it said in effect: 'These things are natural processes which must exist. But it is indelicate to mention them.' And you may set it down that 'delicacy' is the note of the English character — a delicacy that is almost the only really ferocious note that remains in the gamut. It is retained at the risk of honour, self-sacrifice, at the cost of sufferings that may be life-long; so that we are presented with the spectacle of a whole nation that permits the appearance of being extraordinarily tongue-tied, and extraordinarily unable to repress its emotions.

I have assisted at two scenes that in my life have most profoundly impressed me with those characteristics of my countrymen. In the one case I was at a railway station awaiting the arrival of a train of troops from the front. I happened to see upon the platform an old man, a member of my club, a retired major. He, too, was awaiting the train; it was to bring back to him his son, a young man who had gone out to the war as of extraordinary promise. He had, the son, fulfilled this promise in an extraordinary degree; he was the only son, and, as it were, the sole hope for the perpetuation of an ancient family — a family of whose traditions old Major H — was singularly aware and singularly fond. But, at the attack upon a kopje of ill-fated memory, the young man, by the explosion of some shell, had had an arm, one leg, and one side of his face completely blown away. Yet, upon that railway platform I and the old man chatted away very pleasantly. We talked of the weather, of the crops, of the lateness of the train, and kept, as it were, both our minds studiously averted from the subject that continuously was present in both our minds. And, when at last, the crippled form of the son let itself down from the train, all that happened was the odd, unembarrassing clutch of left hand to extended right — a hurried, shuffling shake, and Major H — said:

'Hullo, Bob!' his son: 'Hullo, Governor!' — And nothing more. It was a thing that must have happened, day in day out, all over these wonderful islands; but that a race should have trained itself to such a Spartan repression is none the less worthy of wonder.

I stayed, too, at the house of a married couple one summer. Husband and wife were both extremely nice people — 'good people', as the English phrase is. There was also living in the house a young girl, the ward of the husband, and between him and her — in another of those singularly expressive phrases — an attachment had grown up. P — had not merely never 'spoken to' his ward; but his ward, I fancy, had spoken to Mrs P — At any rate, the situation had grown impossible, and it was arranged that Miss W — should take a trip round the world in company with some friends who were making the excursion. It was all done with the nicest tranquillity. Miss W —'s luggage had been sent on in advance; P — was to drive her to the station himself in the dog-cart. The only betrayal of any kind of suspicion that things were not of their ordinary train was that the night before the parting P — had said to me: 'I wish you'd drive to the station with us tomorrow morning.' He was, in short, afraid of a 'scene'.

Nevertheless, I think he need have feared nothing. We drove the seven miles in the clear weather, I sitting in the little, uncomfortable, hind seat of the dog-cart. They talked in ordinary voices — of the places she would see, of how long the posts took, of where were the foreign banks at which she had credits. He flicked his whip with the finest show of unconcern — pointed at the church steeple on the horizon, said that it would be a long time before she would see that again — and then gulped hastily and said that Fanny ought to have gone to be shod that day, only she always ran a little lame in new shoes, so he had kept her back because Miss W — liked to ride behind Fanny.

I won't say that I felt very emotional myself, for what of the spectacle I could see from my back seat was too interesting. But the parting at the station was too surprising, too really superhuman not to give one, as the saying is, the jumps. For P — never even shook her by the hand; touching the flap of his cloth cap sufficed for leave-taking. Probably he was choking too badly to say even 'Good-bye' — and she did not seem to ask it. And, indeed, as the train drew out of the station P — turned suddenly on his heels, went through the booking-office to pick up a parcel of fish that was needed for lunch, got into his trap and drove off. He had forgotten me — but he had kept his end up.

Now, in its particular way, this was a very fine achievement; it was playing the game to the bitter end. It was, indeed, very much the bitter end, since Miss W — died at Brindisi on the voyage out, and P — spent the next three years at various places on the Continent where nerve cures are attempted. That I think proved that they 'cared' — but what was most impressive in the otherwise commonplace affair, was the silence of the parting. I am not concerned to discuss the essential ethics of such positions, but it seems to me that at that moment of separation a word or two might have saved the girl's life and the man's misery without infringing eternal verities. It may have been desirable, in the face of the eternal verities — the verities that bind and gather all nations and all creeds — that the parting should have been complete and decently arranged. But a silence so utter: a so demonstrative lack of tenderness, seems to me to be a manifestation of a national characteristic that is almost appalling.

Nevertheless, to quote another of the English sayings, hard cases make bad law, and the especial province of the English nation is the evolution of a standard of manners. For that is what it comes to when one says that the province of the Englishman is to solve the problem of how men may live together. And that, upon the whole, they are on the road to the solution of that problem few people would care to deny. I was talking in Germany last year to a much travelled American, and he said to me that it might be taken for granted that English manners were the best in the world. In Turks, in Greeks, in Americans, in Germans, in French, or in Redskins certain differing points were considered to distinguish the respective aristocracies — morals, quiet cordiality, softness of voice, independence of opinion and readiness of quiet apprehension — each of these things were found in one or the other nations separately and were regarded as the height of manners. And all these things were to be found united in the Englishman.

Personally, I think that the American was right; but I do not wish to elevate the theory into a dogma. And against it, if it be acknowledged, we must set the fact that to the attaining of this standard the Englishman has sacrificed the arts — which are concerned with expression of emotions — and his knowledge of life; which cannot be attained to by a man who sees the world as all good — and much of his motive-power as a world force which can only be attained to by a people ready to employ to its uttermost the human-divine quality of discontent.

It is true that in repressing its emotions this people, so adventurous and so restless, has discovered the secret of living. For not the railway stations alone, these scenes of so many tragedies of meeting and parting, but every street and every office would be uninhabitable to a people could they see the tragedies that underlie life and voice the full of their emotions. Therefore, this people which has so high a mission in the world has invented a saving phrase which, upon all occasions, unuttered and perhaps unthought, dominates the situation. For, if in England we seldom think it and still more seldom say it, we nevertheless feel very intimately as a set rule of conduct, whenever we meet a man, whenever we talk with a woman: 'You will play the game.' That an observer, ready and even eager to set down the worst defects of the qualities in a people, should have this to say of them is a singular and precious thing — for that observer at least. It means that he is able to go about the world in the confidence that he can return to a restful place where, if the best is still to be attained to, the worst is nevertheless known — where, if you cannot expect the next man in the street to possess that dispassionate, that critical, that steady view of life that in other peoples is at times so salutary, so exhilarating and so absolutely necessary, he may be sure that his neighbour, temperamentally and, to all human instincts, will respect the law that is written and try very conscientiously to behave in accordance with that more vital law which is called Good Conduct. It means that there is in the world a place to which to return.

[New York: McClure, Phillips & Co., 1907: pp. 334–41.]

from

'The Future in London' (1909)

IT IS this tyranny of the Past that is one of the main obscurers of our view of the Future. In the ceaseless and inscrutable battle that is being waged between the forces of these two tyrants, who can tell what petty and imbecile habit of today will not hinder some beneficent change of the Future? For the Future has only the idealism of a dim and unbefriended reason to wage war with. The Past uses this idealism of the picturesque, the Ancient, the Faith of our Fathers. It arms itself with the weapons of pathos, of habit, of want of imagination, and of an irrational reason.

★ ★ ★

A friend of mine of German extraction has told me of the amazement he felt when visiting his ancestral city — which he had thought he knew very well — after an absence of ten or a dozen years. This city was in its circumstances very like a miniature London. It is the administrative capital of an ancient Kingdom; it is at one end of the Kingdom, the immense, hideous, and wealthy manufacturing tract of country is at some distance — at much such a distance as are the Midlands — Lancashire-cum-Yorkshire — from London. And, just as London began to grow in the twenties of last century, with the growth of the industrial movement after the Napoleonic war, so after the seventies, when manufactories began to be established at the other end of the Kingdom, this German city began to grow.

It contained a core of very ancient buildings, high gabled, arcaded, round an ancient parliament hall, an ancient cathedral, an ancient Mansion House. For a while — until the eighties and nineties — builders did very much what they pleased with additional houses. Then they threatened to invade this ancient and venerable centre. They proposed to pull down some of the arcaded houses, and to erect what we call shops and offices. And at this the city consciousness awoke! It awoke not merely to the extent of protecting the old buildings, it began to consider the future, for a huge outer ring was threatening to develop.

It was the effects of this city awakening that amazed my friend. He had been visiting an estate, perhaps seven or eight miles from the city, and, finding no convenient train by which to return, he had walked home. He met the city at an inordinate distance from what he had been used to consider its limits. But it was not the ten-year growth that so much impressed him as the evidences of a control of that growth — the feeling of spaciousness, the wideness of the streets, the attractive character of the houses, the elbow room, the spacious meeting places of roads, the greens, the parks, and pleasure grounds.

This was because the city itself had taken hold of its fore towns. The roads, it had said, were to be straight enough to act, as it were, the part of air shafts into the inner city: the houses were to be far enough apart, one from another, to allow for the entry of the sunbeams. There were little white houses for the employed, and large white houses for the employers; but they were houses, not suburban villas. They spread out over the ground and did not stand as if with their shoulders hunched together like men in a crowd. There was space in each of the large roads for a tramway; there were trees for shadow in rows, right from the city gates to beyond the further outskirts. Wide stretches of land had been acquired all around the green battlements, a great bit of forest was preserved round the Governor's Schloss. And here there were Zoological Gardens, playgrounds for the children, a great avenue of ancient trees encircling the whole inner city; there were birds, squirrels, rabbits, even a few fallow deer. Think of what London Wall is!

Within the city they had cleared down patches of unsightly slums that had obscured the high and ancient buildings, giving the owners patches of land in the outskirts in compensation. In one case, where the owner had refused a reasonable amount, they had simply walled him round with the view of starving him out. It cannot be alleged, as regards the outer ring, that every one of the houses was artistically delightful. The Nouvel Art, and the parodies of the Nouvel Art, to which Germany has fallen so severely a victim, had scattered here and there odd dwellings of toadstool greens and yellows, with lines suggested by cigarette smoke, and windows whose outlines suggested those of an English county. Our own aesthetic movement, which raged severely in Germany till lately, was responsible for some sadly mediaeval eccentricities, and there were some old German buildings that filled my friend with dismay, side by side with Swiss chalets and Italian palazzi. But, upon the whole, the buildings were simple, businesslike, and spaciously proportioned. So that, if city life can be ideal, this city in its material aspects very nearly appeared to offer ideal conditions. And similar city evolutions are taking place all over Germany.

The word that expresses these things is 'attractiveness'. For a city to have a future, it must grow; in cities, as in Love, there is no standing still, you go either forward or backward. And, if the Future of London is to be one of growth, sanity, and health, some such revolution in the Londoner's consciousness of his city must take place as has taken place all over Germany.

It is not to be said that London is at the present day actually behind in the race for open spaces: we have the parks; we have benevolent societies that acquire tracts of ground in Hampsteads and Highgates. But the speculative builder is a stealthy figure — no one knows quite what he will be up to next — and just because we none of us know how many treasures we have in London, so we cannot tell what, in the night, we may not lose. The person who cares about these things trembles sometimes.

There stands, for instance, in the heart of one of the inner suburbs a Tudor manorhouse with Italian terraces and gardens, with acres and acres of grounds, paddock, and coppices, where the pheasants still breed and creep about the lawns in the early mornings. Bits of this property have been built into. What is to prevent its all going? Why should its owner sacrifice so much wealth for much longer?

There is nothing to prevent such capital catastrophes as this: nothing but an awakening of a city consciousness. For it is certain that the semi-private bounties of societies and subscriptions cannot save more than a small proportion of these oases.

As for the likelihood of such an awakening of city ideals in the Londoner it is hardly possible for one to speak. That any large percentage of the citizens should suddenly be seized upon by this holy fire is not likely. But that the more enlightened — enlightened, I mean, in this direction — that the more enlightened leaders of opinion and guides of the destinies of cities may come before very long to take some such views is just possible, and just possible it is that they may prevail against the heavy mass of the general indifference.

* * *

Already there are many men who live at Brighton, on the Kentish heights, or as far into the shires as Aylesbury — men who come daily into town to perform their functions and return nightly to the same distances to restore their energies. The clearings, the little chippings out of fragments of the inner fabric of the city, are daily taking place. It is only a question of how swiftly these changes shall take place: of whether they shall be conscious or unconscious, enlightened or enforced by the slow grinding of the mills of time.

⋆ ⋆ ⋆

Upon the whole the signs are favourable. We are certainly more careful of open spaces than ever we were before; indeed, it would be strange if we were not, since it is to seek these that we travel so far afield, or seek illusory and unreal rusticity in week-end cottages or garden cities. The garden cities are, on principle, satisfactory enough; but just because they seek to withdraw the population into small knots they tend to produce a spirit that is narrow and provincial. And it is just the narrow and the provincial that we should avoid. Our problem is to make of the whole of Outer London one garden city. But even the speculative builder finds his account in offering, along with his indifferent erections, public lawns, common spaces and fragments of parks that he might have built upon but for his desire to attract patrons. An awakened corporate spirit — the spirit of which I have spoken as existing in almost every German city — how much more beneficent that would be. Upon the whole, the conditions of modern life make inevitably for improvement in these material factors. A little reflection will make that manifest. We travel more easily, we have better artificial light, we widen our roads, we pull down rookeries and let in the air. But I doubt if even today there are many Londoners who are proud of their home, if there are many to echo the excellent boast that they are citizens of no mean city. I should like to meet a few men who would utter those words upon convenient occasions. I should like to meet them; I never do — at any rate, amongst the articulate classes. I have heard dock labourers and charwomen say, 'Ah, London's the place!' but upon the whole, the literate, the educated classes, if they have an affection for this great and lovable place, cherish that affection in secret, and profess that their real home would be — if they had the chance — the boundless pampas, the limitless seas, or the moors of Devonshire. That has always appeared to me to be a mean and a detrimental spirit in men who seek their bread in a place. Where we go for gain, there, too, we should leave something of ourselves; are we lesser men in conscience than Socrates, who acknowledged his and our debt to Aesculapius? I suppose we are; but I wish we were not; and it is with the desire to preach this lesson, to spread this spirit, to embolden those of us who are afraid to speak their minds, and to aid in awakening that corporate spirit of which I have spoken that, as much as for any other reason, I have written these pages. For, after all, the Future of London is very much in our hands. We are the tyrants of the men to come; where we build roads, their feet must tread; the traditions we set up, if they are evil, our children will find it hard to fight against; if for want of vigilance we let beautiful places be defiled, it is they who will find it a hopeless task to restore them.

[Essay in W. W. Hutchings, *London Town Past and Present*, 1909: pp. 1100-01, 1103-05, 1109-10.]

This Monstrous Regiment of Women (1912)

The year before, in *Ancient Lights*, Ford had written: 'Personally, I am an ardent, I am an enraged, suffragette.' He contributed this pamphlet to the Women's Freedom League, which published it.

THERE are certain facts so plain — as plain as the nose on your face — that you never seem to see them, just as you never see that useful organ unless you happen to look in the looking-glass. In these days and years we are filled with Imperial and political consciousness. Today we crown a King; tomorrow we revise a Constitution. Last year we mourned; this year we rejoice — and always there are crowds in the street, so that it is difficult — indeed, it is inappropriate — to think in the very moment of celebration. But perhaps when you go home tired you won't object to reflecting for a moment — you won't object to reflecting for a moment upon the Empire, upon its greatness and upon some of the things that we celebrate.

One of the things that is remarkable about the Empire is that in certain ages it has immensely increased its boundaries, and in certain other ages it has immensely increased the prestige of the throne or of one or other of the constituents going to make up the body politic of Great Britain and of Great Britain beyond the seas.

Let us consider then these two things: When did Great Britain begin to go abroad upon the great waters, and when did the throne appear to become settled and unassailable?

In the year 1558 there was an immense Empire — the Empire of Spain. Spain had all the power in the world, simply because Spain possessed, roughly speaking, all the gold in the world. In 1558 England was just nothing, and if one had said that in less than fifty years Spain would have fallen before the power of England a sane and proper man would have laughed, as today you might laugh if someone suggested that Great and Greater Britain would fall before the Federal Republic of Switzerland. Spain had all the gold in the world; Spain occupied all the trade routes in the world; there were no seas upon which the banner of Spain was not dreaded; there was no realm of Incas from which Spain was not drawing a tide of gold. And England was just a little half-island. That was in 1558.

In 1837 there was no institution that seemed more decrepit than the British throne. The last of the four Georges had hopelessly discredited the personal side of Kings. The last of the Williams viewed his position as a Sovereign with a sort of dreary disdain. Revolutions were brewing everywhere. Industries were rising up that were changing the face of the whole world. And, amongst the spectators of the Coronation that took place that year, there was no one who would not have laughed loudly if you had said that in seventy years time or so the power of the Throne, adapting itself to the great material, industrial and political changes, would be more firmly based upon the popular will than was ever the case, let us say, since Elizabeth sat on the throne of England.

Yet it is impossible to doubt that in the forty-five years that came after 1558 the ships of England occupied all the sea that before then had seen the banners of Spain float unchallenged. And it is impossible to doubt that, in the seventy and odd years that succeeded the year 1837 the one thing, astonishingly, that proved stable amidst innumerable changes, was the British crown.

And it is impossible to doubt that from the year 1558 to the year 1603, and from the year 1837 for seventy years or so, women sat upon the throne of England.

It is almost impossible to doubt it, that is to say. The other day, however, I was talking to a distinguished personage, who was loudly contending against the claims of women to have any administrative faculties. And I mentioned that during these two great periods of British expansion and British prosperity, women sat upon the throne of England. My argumentative friend said:

'Oh! as for Victoria, she was a nasty old woman, and Queen Elizabeth ought to have been a man.'

This is the sort of argument that has to be met by those of us who support the claims of women to political equality with boot-blacks and uncertified imbeciles.

There is no word in the English language so suggestive of great adventures, of romantic literature, of fine hazards and of the Golden Age, as the word 'Elizabethan'. There is no word in the English language so suggestive of the spread of the arts of peace, and of the peaceful penetration throughout the world of British ideals — so suggestive of progress in science, and in all the things with which by material means the State can render happy the lives of its constituents — there is no word in the English language so suggestive as the word 'Victorian'. What, for instance, does the word 'Tudor' suggest? Or what, again, does 'Jacobean'? Or what, once more, 'Georgian'? These words suggest just Domestic Architecture. They imply nothing more than a certain type of house. And, if this in itself be a great achievement, cannot a Queen of England be an equal in that field, too, for don't we speak of a Queen Anne mansion?

It may be said that these matters of nomenclature are pure accidents. It might be said that had a King sat on the throne during these two ages the results for England would have been the same. But would they? Are these things just an accident? Let us consider for a moment.

For it is at least remarkable that, if we consider the Tudor Age until the ascent to the throne of Elizabeth, we find nothing very definite to distinguish the history of the country. From the usurpation of Henry VII to the death of Henry VIII, England was distinguished more than anything else by its endless wranglings. It wrangled at home, it wrangled abroad; it ejected the Church; it hung several hundred thousand tramps; it beheaded almost every one of its heads of great families. And it had done none of these things effectually. Its wranglings abroad had left it powerless in the councils of Europe; its ejection of the Church had left it a perfectly open question whether the Church would not come back again. Its hanging of innumerable tramps did not seem in the least to have solved any social problem, but had simply plunged the whole question of dealing with the poor in this country into a state of hopeless confusion which persists to this day. So that, of the Tudor Sovereigns up to 1558 no traces now remain to us except this confusion of the Poor Laws, and some fine palaces as well as some country houses distinguished by square windows with mullions.

If we consider the Jacobean Age we see again nothing but a period of wrangling. James I rendered his dreaded England contemptible abroad; Charles I plunged the country into an unending feud; Cromwell made us, it is true, dreaded abroad, but for how short a period, and how little lasting effect his sway had upon the country at home! Charles II turned England into nothing more than the pimp of France; James II was nothing. That was all that remained of the Jacobean Age except a few lyrics like those of Herrick and Donne, and except a few plays like those of Wycherly. It hardly left us even any houses.

Under the Georges, it is true, the State was consolidated, for Walpole invented the National Debt. And the National Debt meant that the British State must be continued, with whatever modifications, simply because the British State was such a huge creditor. We have, in fact, even today, to keep the State going whether we like it or not, because it owes us so much money that if it failed financially we should all be ruined. But this is all that the Georgian Age left us with the exception of some few houses, of several literary works by writers like Pope and Addison, whom we pretend to esteem but don't much read. It gave us certainly the British School of Painting, which was a fine thing in its way, but with the assistance of Mynheer Handel, it killed British music for ever. Owing to the personal union of Hanover, it kept us perpetually in a state of concern with the quarrels and broils of the Continent. Who knows what the Battle of Blenheim was about? Why did we fight Malplaquet, Dettingen, Fontenoy, or Minden? Who knows? But it had something to do with the personal affairs of William III or with Hanover, and the Georges were Kings of Hanover — those extraordinary masculine, obstinate Kings who were always embroiling us in matters that did not concern us. George I and George II kept us worried about their Continental possessions. George III was English enough, but he lost us our Colonies which we had begun to settle under Elizabeth, so that it remained for the Age of Victoria to begin rebuilding the Empire. George IV brought the Crown into absolute disrepute. The only creditable thing that I ever remember having come across concerning him as a King was that out of some gambling winnings he founded a Home for the orphan daughters of State Officials in the City of Hildesheim, in Hanover, so that the only real benevolence of this monarch was given to the land of the personal union. William IV was a dismally stupid person with what on the Continent is called the 'Englishman's spleen'; he objected to being crowned, he didn't care about reigning; he made himself as disagreeable as he could to a number of persons, including his successor and her family, and then he died in 1837.

Now it is a somewhat remarkable fact, it is surely something more than coincidence, that if we take the three and a half centuries from the accession of Henry VII to the death of Queen Victoria, the two periods that have been times of peace on the whole, of internal tranquillity and foreign respect that was at all lasting — it is a little remarkable that these periods should have occurred when women sat upon the throne, just as it is a little remarkable that what distinguished the early 'Tudor', the 'Jacobean' and the 'Georgian' periods was endless wrangling.

Of course, it does not do to run a theory too hard, or rather it does not do to shut one's eyes to what may tell against one's theory. During this period of time there reigned two other Queens — Mary, who is generally known as 'bloody', and Anne, who is principally known because she is dead. The reign of Mary was certainly not a happy reign, but she was a woman very much warped, and she had to deal with problems that had been left her by her predecessors. We don't want particularly to excuse Mary because she was warped, except that it might reasonably be said that her mind was affected by her father, who was one sort of King, and by her husband, who was another. And if she lost Calais she had at least the grace to say that its name would be found graven on her heart. We have not any of the reflections of George III upon the loss of our North American Colonies. And if we have really to consider the case of Mary we have to see that, after her lights, she dealt conscientiously and effectively with the problems that her predecessors had left her. She burnt a number of Protestants and, without doubt, if she had reigned another fifty years, she would have re-established Catholicism in these kingdoms, for her predecessors had done no more than leave it an open question that Elizabeth had eventually to decide.

Indeed, had Elizabeth died in 1568 or Victoria in 1848, they would have left the country in a condition parlous enough, for Elizabeth was trying to deal with Spain by the lies and false pretences that she found so effectual, and in 1848, the year of revolutions all over Europe, there would not have appeared to be one chance in ten of the throne remaining had Victoria died.

And if we balance Mary against Charles II or even against his brother James, we shall see that her record is a comparatively creditable one. It is much the same with the late Queen Anne, though at any rate at home her reign was one of comparative peace. Abroad, of course, there were the wars of Marlborough, but these she had as a succession, a legacy from William III. William III, that is to say, was much more interested in Continental questions and in the upholding of Protestantism by armed force, than he was in anything connected with these islands. And it was only towards the end of the

Reign of Anne that this comparatively peaceful lady succeeded in attaining to peace and the leisure to devote herself to the quarrels of Sarah, Duchess of Marlborough, and of Mrs Masham. And as I have said, at home it was a period, if not of peace, then at least of a sort of truce. During Anne's reign the Jacobites without doubt intrigued, but there were not any sanguinary attainders; there was not the forty-five, with George by the Grace of God letting loose Butcher Cumberland and the Campbells upon his devoted islands. No, the reign of Anne was characterized upon the whole by political suavity, the politics of the day being carried on in the coffee houses where gentlemen of the race of Addison and Steele met in satin coats and ruffles, or by gentlemen like Swift, who intrigued for places and for bishoprics that no one nowadays would much think worth the trouble of intriguing for. It might be said that by the reign of Anne, civilization in the mass was becoming more gentle and less fond of the axe, the firebrand, and the rope. Unfortunately for this contention, thirty years after the death of Anne, we had the forty-five, and the rope was unsparingly used — the gallows were the common coin of the day — right up to about the year 1842. There were, for instance, the 'Peterloo Massacre' or the 'Gordon Riots'.

And the reign of Victoria saw comparatively few wars. There was the Crimea, which was a foolishness, and there was the Boer War, which was a sheer imbecility. Apart from these there was only the Indian Mutiny, which was not, in the strict sense, a war at all. In the reign of Elizabeth there was only the one war — the long struggle with Spain, and this was not so much a war as a long series of piratical expeditions — a really remarkably good commercial undertaking.

Let us, then, consider the personal characteristics of these two Sovereigns. My friend who objected to the right of women to have any administrative functions said:

'Victoria was a nasty old woman, and Elizabeth ought to have been a man.' I wonder what would have been the fate of England if Elizabeth had been a man? I think it is fairly certain that for many centuries these countries would have been like the Netherlands, a province of Spain. For the war which Elizabeth carried on with Philip was, at least for the first thirty years of her reign, a war purely 'feminine'. In the first place she flirted; later she lied, and only in the last resort, and then with extreme economy, did she resort to cannon-balls. Elizabeth was a remarkable woman, the product of a remarkable house, and of a remarkable age. No one, I think, will ever be able really to sum up the character of her father, Henry VIII. He was a person too complicated. And no one, I think, will ever be able to sum up the character of her mother, Anne Boleyn, for all the accounts of Anne Boleyn are too coloured by partisanship. But when it comes to the age in which, amidst hardship and contempt, Elizabeth was a child, there is much less difficulty in summing it up; it was an age in statecraft of certain ideals. Thus on the one hand there was the ideal of the Papacy, and, on the other hand, there was Thomas Cromwell's ideal of Kingcraft, and there was Thomas More's ideal of an Utopia, which was the ideal of a large band of reformers who in those days were known as the 'Humanists'. So for ideals the world of Elizabeth's youth was not a poor one. But when it came to the practice of statecraft, as opposed to the ideals for which the statesman strove, then the picture entirely changed. For, in statesmanship all the world over, the early 'Tudor' practice was one simply of remorseless cunning, of unscrupulous lying, of murder, of despoiling and of mutilations. And when you come to consider Elizabeth, you have to remember that it was in this atmosphere that she was brought up. It may appear to us rather scandalous today that, after Drake had gone plundering round the world, Elizabeth could write on the one hand to Philip of Spain that she would satisfy his desire for justice at her hands against her mutinous subject, Francis Drake. At the same time she wrote to Drake two letters. One was public, and in that she said that none of his spoils from Spain were to be put out of the way. On the contrary, she directed that they were to be kept by strict watchers under the custody of public servants until an account of them could be rendered to the King of Spain, from whose subjects they had been stolen. At the same time she wrote in private that the greater part of this booty was to be conveyed away and hidden. And, at any rate, none of it returned to the country of Spain.

This unscrupulous lying she learned by the example of her father, Henry VIII, and of men like Thomas Cromwell, Cranmer, Norfolk and all the leaders, whether Papists or Protestants, who supported Henry of Windsor. And if she had been a man it is conceivable that she would have been as skilful a liar, but I doubt whether she would have been so cool a one.

Philip of Spain being a man and Elizabeth being a woman, this King had nothing to do but to pretend to believe her, as I or any other man would have to do in a drawing-room today. He had to pretend to believe her; he had to answer with courtesy and to thank her for writing the public letters. He probably knew all about the private ones, but he couldn't, being a man and a Spaniard, write to his dear cousin of England that she lied. It is possible that he couldn't have done this even had Elizabeth been a man. For in those days, as today, in the correspondence between States a certain formality, a certain politeness, had to be observed. So that, had Elizabeth been a man according to the desires of my friend, up to this point she might have prospered just as well. But only up to this point and in this special department of the game. For, generally speaking, Philip wasn't a fool; had he had to do with say Edward VI at this stage he would probably not have told Edward in so many words that he lied, but he would have taken the opportunity to declare war about some small point after Edward had been on the throne for about three years. Then there would have been an end of England.

But Elizabeth was a woman, and whilst she could lie as well as any man she had in this particular juncture a power that no man would have had — the power of her sex. With her deceitful correspondence she played a man's game with all the success of a man of that day. She was probably no better at it than Burleigh would have been; she was probably no better at it than Thomas Cromwell or than Gardiner or Reginald Pole had been; she was just like any other man, and she would have had the ups and downs of any other man, and she would have gone under because the odds against her would have been much too great had she been a man. So she availed herself of the accident or of the providence of her sex. She simply remembered that she was a marriageable person, and for years and years she played the game of matrimonial alliances. Philip of Spain had already been King-Consort of England, and for years and years, Elizabeth dangled the bait of marriage in front of his nose. There were Frenchmen also who would have liked to marry her, and she kept the French in a perpetual state of threatening Spain on the flank by perpetually negotiating for a marriage with one French prince or another. Her game was to gain time. Gold in those days was as important as gold is today, and, whilst on the one hand gold during all these years was pouring into England, so on the other hand Spain was being slowly bled to death. And, roughly speaking, the only thing that Elizabeth thought about was gold.

She may have had a heart or she mayn't; she may have had

personal vanity at the beginning of her reign or she may not, but she played the game as if she had had a heart and as if she had had the ordinary susceptibilities of a woman. No man could possibly have effected her economies; no man could possibly have exacted the sacrifices that were hers at the cost of a glance, a pressure of the hand or a sigh. She exacted of men that they should send fleets sailing round the world; that they should go to certain and obscure deaths on the Spanish Main; she exacted of men that they should entertain her with profuse hospitalities which, whilst they saved her purse, had the double advantage of so impoverishing them that they would not be able to resist her royal power supposing that they had been so disposed. With her femininity she dazzled the whole world, whilst with her cool and unscrupulous mind she was for ever attentive to business.

I don't want to over-weight these pages with documents, but if you will take the trouble to go to the Record Office, which is in Chancery Lane, you will see for yourself in the showcases of the Public Museum of that building two documents which exactly exemplify what I have said. Here you will see in one frame a warrant from Queen Elizabeth to Christopher Wray, Chief Justice of the Queen's Bench, for the delivery to Martin Frobisher of twelve specified prisoners condemned or likely to be condemned to death, 'to make a viage of the seas for the discovery of new countryes'. This was written in the year 1577 and is signed Elizabeth R. Thus, whilst Elizabeth sent abroad her felons to plunder and do piracy on the seas, the glory of her virgin fame was spreading abroad beyond the bounds of Christendom. For in another frame you will see a letter from Amurath III, Sultan of Turkey, to the Queen herself. And in this letter he addressed her as 'Refulgent with splendour and glory, most sapient Princess of the magnanimous followers of Jesus, most serene Controller of all the affairs and business of the people and family of the Nazarenes, most grateful rain-cloud, sweetest fount of splendour and honour,' and so on. This was written in the year 1583.

And so Elizabeth paid nobody, cheated everybody, and was mean in a manner in which no man could have been mean. Had she been a fine lady living today she would have been the sort of person who would have underpaid her cabman, docked half the wages of her footman, ridden first-class with a third-class ticket — and at the cabman, at the footman, at the ticket collectors she would have made such eyes that not one of them but would have protested that she was the most charming lady in the world. No man, nowadays, could do such a thing, just as no King in her time could have done it.

I don't mean to say that Elizabeth exhibited femininism in its most creditable form; I daresay a female saint would have left a better taste in the mouth, or a gentleman would have gone to ruin more picturesquely. But we are dealing not with gentlemen nor with saints, but with statesmanship. And statesmanship is always a dirty business. It has to be, because the first business of a statesman is to overreach his opponents for the good of the people who shelter beneath his mantle. He is the man who is sent to lie abroad for the benefit of his country, so that we may say that Elizabeth was a great statesman. The British Empire is alive to this day to testify to it in spite of Charles II and the Georges. But I think it is fairly certain that without the gold that Elizabeth had hoarded up in this country, and without the impetus that she had given to the national spirit, we should never have muddled through as we did to the reign of Queen Victoria. For Elizabeth had her vanities, but, fortunately for England, they were not male vanities. Male vanities are much more expensive things and are things much more ruffling. No King could have cringed as Elizabeth cringed when it was necessary to throw her enemies off the scent of her growing strength, and no King could have economised so in money or could have exacted from the subjects alike their blood and their very honour.

The figure of Queen Victoria is, of course, a very different one. But one has only to consider her with equanimity or with cynicism — one has only to see how difficult this is to know how great was the feeling that the late Queen caused to arise in these islands. And, when one comes to consider how subtle a thing is modern life, with its currents and cross-currents of interests and conflicting tendencies, it is a great thing to be able to get hold of anything so definite as a wide-spread feeling. My friend, the anti-suffragist, said that Victoria was a disagreeable old woman. (I should like, in order to make his point of view more precise, to explain that he wasn't a Socialist, but that he was what you might call a good clubman and an official of the State.) Now it is perfectly possible that Victoria, as a person, was a disagreeable woman. It would, indeed, be odd — it would be almost discreditable if, given her birth and her ancestry, she had been anything else but rather a trying guest at a small dinner. The Chinese proverb says, 'It would be an hypocrisy to search for the person of the Sacred Emperor in a low tea-house', and if the late Queen had been a comfortable person for a small tea-party, she would have been something less than Queen. She would have been inappropriate. And this Queen Victoria never was.

She was without doubt obstinate; she was without doubt not humble; she had without doubt strong preconceptions and strong prejudices. But the real wonder is, considering her descent from George III, from George I — considering the mixed Stuart and Guelph nature of her blood, the real wonder is that these characteristics did not lead her to disasters of tactlessness. This they never did. And this without doubt was due to the fact that she was a woman. It was probably due to the other fact that during the early and impressionable years of her reign she fell under the influences of Lord Melbourne and of her cousin, Leopold I of Belgium — or rather, to be exact in the last particular, under the influence of the extremely skilful gentleman, Baron Stockmar, who influenced all the actions and all the sentiments of Leopold. Under these auspices the Queen learnt what none of her ancestors had ever dreamt of, and that was the value of tact. And I think it may be very much doubted whether, supposing that she had been a prince instead of a princess, and supposing that she had not a feminine desire to venerate distinguished men — I think it is very much open to doubt whether the troublous internal history of England up to the year 1848 would not have been immensely different. For whatever Queen Victoria was or wasn't, she had a very vivid sense of the duties and the responsibilities of kingship as a craft, whereas all the male members of her house had shown nothing but a very strong and obstinate sense of the importance of a King as a King. These two things are immensely different.

And there can be very little doubt that the mere fact that Victoria was a woman did work immensely for peace during her long reign. During the first part of that reign the war menace was nominally from France. It is hardly to be doubted that during the reign of Napoleon III England might several times have come into the most serious difficulties with what at that date it was the custom to call our Gallic neighbours. But, perhaps because the feminine heart of Queen Victoria was won by the figure of that once splendid adventurer and the beautiful bride with whom he made a love match — a thing always appealing to the heart of a woman were she never so much a Queen — or perhaps it was because living perpetually in the consideration of International matters that she was really wiser than her nominal advisers — at any rate, all the great moral and temporal power of Victoria was dedicated to the task of preserving peace with France.

After 1870, the usual menace to England became Prussia. In the case of this latter country, being as it were upon family grounds, the late Queen showed less tactfulness and less patience than she ever showed in any other matter. Without doubt she knew what she was doing. But it is certain that she was the one person in the world who thoroughly worried Bismarck and whom Bismarck thoroughly hated and feared. And here again it is difficult to believe that if she had not been a woman the results of the perpetual intriguing between these two great figures might have been disastrous to the peace of Europe. For it is not in the least fanciful to imagine that in the heart of all the great affairs of State there remain always the facts of personal impatiences and personal jealousies. Bismarck was always a very masculine man, and Victoria was always a very feminine woman. And they were acting against each other always in a sort of family party. Bismarck, of course, was not a member of the family. In a sense he was vastly more important; but in a very real sense he was dependent on his Imperial masters. And he would not want to precipitate unpleasantness between his employers and their close relatives any more than the most domineering of family solicitors would want to precipitate law suits between his own clients and a rather domineering old lady whose estates bordered on his client's estates and who happened to be his client's great aunt. But I think it not in the least unlikely that had this person who troubled Bismarck with her persistence — had this person been a man instead of a woman, Bismarck's anger would have taken much more martial forms. After all, in the Biblical story of the importunate person who troubled a judge that neither feared God nor regarded man — that importunate person was a widow. I imagine that had it been a widower, the judge would have had his head off long before any opportunities for parable had been given.

Diplomatists will, of course, inform you that this personal way of looking at foreign affairs is fallacious, but the business of diplomatists is to surround their craft with a cloud of mysteries. And scientific or democratic historians will again inform you that a personal interpretation of history is fallacious, but that, of course, is a necessary part of their democratic theories. There remain in the end only the results. And in the matter of results the characteristics of these two Reigns and even the characteristics of the Reign of Anne, are all so similar that we may fairly judge that the result of having a woman upon the Throne of these countries has been upon the whole one making for peace, for the extension of the bounds of the Empire, and following upon this peace and this extension come increased wealth, the cultivation of the arts and of the finer and gentler things of life. I am not making any greater claim for these Queens than just the claim of sex. But the claim of sex is good enough when it comes to merely practical matters — it is good enough as long as the results are practically beneficial. How things may be today it is fortunately not my business to say, but, to put the matter with as plain an image as I possibly can — to put it so plainly that no one can fail to understand it, I might compare the home and foreign politics of the last three centuries to a bar in a public-house. It was a cockpit really not more august and really not more high-minded; it was a place in which large numbers of people shouted against each other about their rights and were always ready to back their arguments up with great words and with the shaking of dirty fists. And just as those bar-parlours which are presided over by barmaids are quieter and more decorous places than those which are served by men, so the corner of the European cockpit where England dispensed its ales, did its business better, more quietly, with fewer oaths and with fewer threats, when the person who poured out the ale of preferment and the spirits of promotion was a woman. And I think that upon the whole even in the last war in which we indulged ourselves, our troops went into action or about the business of harrying and counter-marching which war is — they went about it in a slightly nobler, in a slightly more chivalrous spirit because they were fighting in the name of an abstraction that was known as the Widow at Windsor.

I have no sentimental objections to quarrelling as quarrelling, to punching heads or to the large and splendid cutting of throats that is called war. I suppose we all have our moods and emotions in which we should like to see Great Britain once more flinging her battle standards to the breeze. But when it comes to sober reasoning, or when it comes to examination of history in the light of common sense, we can see well enough that war, putting the matter at its lowest, is a great nuisance. Putting the matter again at its very lowest, it is expensive. Any dislocation of cordiality between nations is also expensive — not so expensive as war, but still bad, because it disturbs public confidence and interrupts the regular flow of traffic. And certainly, in the cases of Elizabeth, of Anne, and of Victoria, wars became as seldom as was thinkable, and we did our work of absorbing large spaces of the world peacefully and inexpensively.

I am putting the matter on purpose at its very lowest basis, in order to appeal to your common sense rather than to prove romantic emotions. All that I have tried to prove — and I think I have proved it beyond any controverting — was that in England it has been profitable to have women occupying the highest place of the State. And it seems to me that if it is profitable that a woman should occupy the highest place, it is only reasonable to carry the argument one or two stages further. What those stages are I will leave to the reader. But, just to end this contention upon a slightly higher note, I should like to point out another self-evident fact. The important thing of statesmanship is the State, and that State is best served whose statesmen, being most forgetful of self, most whole-heartedly devote themselves to the ideal of the State such as they see it. And such devotion as was shown, say by Disraeli to the late Queen, is enough in itself to render the State a rather more beautiful place. And such confidence as Queen Victoria was able to repose in Disraeli or in other ministers, such as Melbourne, was also a rather beautiful thing and one fit to dignify the throne. And, upon the whole, that country will have a machinery of state most easily moving whose throne has dignity and moves in harmony with its great officers. And as it was with Victoria so it was with Elizabeth. Here, for instance, are a few sentences of a letter from Robert Dudley, Earl of Leicester. He was lying upon his death-bed, so that we may take it that he was sincere enough.

'I most humbly besech your Majestie to pardon your poore old servant to be thus bold in sending to know how my gratious ladie doth and what ease of her late paine she findes, being the chifest thing in this world I doe pray for, for hir to have good health and longe life. For my none poore case, I contynew styll your medycyn. . . . Thus hoping to finde perfect cure at the Bath. . . . I humbly kyss your foote.'

And it is even pleasant to consider that Elizabeth took the trouble to endorse this writing with the words: 'His last letter.'

from

When Blood Is Their Argument (1915)

Ford wrote this and *Between St Dennis and St George* at the request of C. F. G. Masterman, director of the British Ministry of Information during World War I.

PREFACE

> Resolutely, on the other hand, the Roman surrendered his own personal will for the sake of freedom, and learned to obey his father that he might know how to obey the State. Amidst this subjection individual development might be marred, and the germs of fairest promise in man might be arrested in the bud; the Roman gained in their stead a feeling of Fatherland and of patriotism such as the Greek never knew, and alone among all the civilised nations of antiquity succeeded in working out national unity in connection with a constitution based on self-government — a national unity which at last placed in his hands the mastery not only over the divided Hellenic stock, but over the whole known world. — Mommsen, *Roemische Geschichte*, vol. I, p. 31.

I HAVE been charged with deliberate unfairness to the traditions of German learning and of German scholarship. The following must be my reply as far as the following pages are concerned:

I have approached the form but not the matter of this work with the deepest misgiving. The matter of it has been familiar to me all my life. From my father as from my grandfather, Madox Brown, I imbibed in my very earliest years a deep hatred of Prussianism, of materialism, of academicism, of pedagogism, and of purely economic views of the values of life. At the same time I was, by those same men, inspired with a deep love and veneration for French learning, arts, habits of mind, lucidity, and for that form of imagination which implies a sympathetic comprehension of the hopes, fears, and ideals of one's fellow-men. So that, since this work is, in essence, a reassertion of the claims of, or of the necessity for, altruism, whether

Christian or Hellenic, I may be said to have passed the whole of my life reflecting upon these propagandist lines.

At the same time my father's South German Catholic origin left me in a position, fortunate for the purposes of this work, of being able to regard at any rate South Germans as ordinary human beings. My grandfather, on the other hand, having been born in Calais and being, to the end of his life, more French than English in manners and point of view, I have similarly never had any feeling of foreignness in France. The French in fact have always seemed to me to be 'just people', like the South Germans or the English. For as long as I can remember, therefore, I have been accustomed to think indifferently in French, in German, or in English, and I am indeed conscious that whilst I was framing this sentence in my mind, since I am writing with extreme care, I began to phrase it in French before committing myself to its final form.

I might indeed say that, throughout my life, whenever I have thought with *great* care of a prose paragraph, I have framed it in my mind in French, or more rarely in Latin, and have then translated into English; whereas when it was a matter of such attempts at verse as I have made my thinking has been done exclusively in colloquial English. When, on the other hand, it has been a matter of pleasures of the table, of wines and the like, I have been quite apt to think in German. When I have been in the mood, in short, for exact thinking and a practicable grip upon the arts I have gone to France; when I have desired to lead an ordinary home life with a certain homely poetry about it I have remained in this country; when I have desired still more homely, kindly and material pleasures, cool and delicious wines and the shadows of great mountains falling across a mighty river, I have spent a month or two in South Germany. But I have never, I think, done any of that spying into the habits of these people which is usually connoted under such a heading as Notes and Observations of Foreign Travel. Going into Western Europe has never, for me, seemed to be travelling; it has been merely a change of abode, as it were, from one county to another.

I have had therefore no difficulty about the matter of this work. I have had no difficulty whatever in getting together what in German professorial language are called 'Quellen'. Indeed my special difficulty has been not so much to select matter to lay before the reader, since my whole life as a conscious artist has been a matter of selecting this or that illustration so as to convey to readers this or that impression; and my difficulty has not been so much any lack of that passionate interest in the subject which would underlie any work of art. No, my difficulty has been simply and solely to decide to what extent I can afford to me impersonal and to what extent I must force myself to be personal.

To be impersonal, to acquire an aspect of a certain factitious weight by shrouding oneself in indefinite allegations, generalizings, and apparently sober statements without giving the grounds that one has for arriving at conclusions is so extremely easy — and so extremely unfair. Nothing, for instance, is easier than for Professor Delbrueck to write of the 'somewhat naïve metaphysics' — the 'etwas naive Metaphysik' — of English constitutional theories, and so to attain to an aspect of aloof generalization which would be altogether lost if he were to write: 'I, Professor Hans Delbrueck, am a paid official of the Prussian State who was once fined five hundred marks for criticising the action of the Prussian State. By inclination, by self-interest, by national interest, and by conscientious belief I am forced into thinking that the methods of the Prussian State are beneficent and necessary if I and humanity who are of good will are to prosper. I am therefore ransacking history in order to find incidents and precedents that shall make effective propaganda. I am, in fact, a barrister employed by Prussia and I am doing my best for my client. Therefore, I call all theories of constitutionalism "somewhat naïve metaphysics".'

Such a statement would be neither as effective nor as impressive as the method usually employed by Professor Delbrueck and his colleagues of the Prussian professoriate — but it would be much more fair, and in the end much more convincing. For, as it is, one approaches the works of this illustrious professor with respect, almost with awe. One says to oneself that one will be perusing the products of an extraordinary mind that has concerned itself judicially with the high facts of history and has distilled therefrom subtle empiricisms and high truths. One leaves the perusal with a feeling that one has been in contact with a mind ordinary and commonplace beyond the ordinariness and commonplaceness of the mind of a police-sergeant, who is distorting facts in order to secure a conviction of an innocent female accused of streetwalking. One doubts every historic instance adduced by this special pleader; one suspects him of forging his 'Quellen' and of exaggerating even his own beliefs; and one feels that any Berlin shopkeeper or any prince of a

German reigning house, given the assistance and the resources that have been at the disposal of Herr Delbrueck, could have done his 'job' just as well or better.

Of course that is not fair to Professor Delbrueck; it is the natural reaction which occurs in one's mind when one discovers that a professedly impartial scientist is really a passionate pleader briefed for some special cause or other. Such a reaction will not occur in the case of such a special pleader if he announces that, whilst striving to be fair in his methods of argument and not falsifying his authorities, he has a distinct bias in favour of one party or another. Whilst maintaining that I have certainly not falsified any sources or employed any form of argument that seems to me to be unfair, I do not lay claim to any aspirations after fairness of mind. Let me say frankly that I consider myself to be a special pleader, briefed on behalf of altruism, of constitutionalism, and of such forms of art and learning as promote a sympathetic comprehension of my fellow-men, briefed more particularly on behalf of French learning, French art-methods, habits of mind, and lucidity, and briefed on behalf of Anglo-Saxon opportunist constitutionalism.

I hope the reader will take it for granted that I am bringing forward and putting as incisively as possible everything that I can select to make these things appear lovely and desirable and that I am selecting, bringing forward, and putting with a hatred inspired by a cruel and cold indignation everything that I can think of that can make Prussianism, materialism, militarism, and the mania for organization appear hideous in their products and disastrous for humanity. That a rat has as great a moral right to exist as I myself I am ready to concede. But if I can kill it I will kill it, and its death seems to me to end its rights to existence. And in writing the present book I am attempting to cast such a stone at the rat of Prussianism as posterity will not willingly . . . well, the reader may complete the simile himself.

That being so, I determined to adopt as far as possible the personal tone in this work. I am aware that to adopt a personal tone is to subject oneself to the charge of immodesty — but I am indifferent to the charge of immodesty. Indeed I might say that this book is levelled as much against the professorial hypocrisy of impersonalism as against any other hypocrisy or evil of the world. For impersonalism is a professorial product, the refuge of an empty and non-constructive mind that is afraid of setting down its own conclusions as its own conclusions. Robert of Gloucester wrote a chronicle and it is true that Robert of Gloucester's Chronicle is only made up of Robert of Gloucester's own observations and his records at second-hand. You say: 'Oh, he is only an individual writer.' But when Professor Maetzner, writing impersonally, makes various deductions from the story of King Lear as recorded by Robert of Gloucester, one says: 'This is very learned: this is very erudite.' And when Professor Sievers makes further deductions from Professor Maetzner's deductions from Robert of Gloucester's deductions one says: 'This is still more learned; this is still more erudite.' Yet if you come to consider it, you will see that Robert of Gloucester's deductions must obviously have been made at least at second-hand, Professor Maetzner's at third-hand, and Professor Sievers' at fourth-hand.

Let me briefly illustrate what I mean by the difference between personal and impersonal methods. At the end of the first chapter of this book I am concerned to illustrate the extreme poverty of Germany at the end of the eighteenth century, and I do it by an anecdote concerning a letter written by a schoolmaster to an ancestress of my own. This makes fairly entertaining reading and I have put it as entertainingly as I could. That, then, is the personal method. Had I wished to be impersonal I might have quoted at enormous length from innumerable works by professors and others which would demonstrate at once the wideness of my reading and the weight that must be attached to my pages. Supposing I had wished to show the poverty of school-teachers in the German eighteenth century by this method, I should have quoted from the Report of the Oberkonsistorium of the Kurmark to the Oberschulcollegium to the effect that:

> The condition of the country school-teachers was lamentable. Many posts had a salary of from 5 to 10 thalers per annum (from £2 to £4). The average was from 20 to 30 thalers (£8 to £12); positions worth more than 100 thalers were extremely rare. Teachers who had no supplementary profession were recommended to beg. . . .[1]

And I should have gone on to quote from Frederick Gedicke's *Annalen des preussichen Schul-und Kirchenwesens*, from Thilo, from Harkort, and from Clausnitzer and Rosin's *Geschichte des preussischen Unterrichtsgesetzes*, so as to prove that Prussian elementary school-

[1] Quoted in Heppe's *Deutsches Volksschulwesen*, vol. III, p.78.

teachers were mostly tailors, carpenters, and old soldiers, dependent upon the bounty of the peasants for their bare maintenance. I might, in fact have so overloaded the pages of this work with footnotes that the pages themselves disappeared. But in that case I could expect to find only very few readers. I have attempted therefore to play rather the part of Robert of Gloucester than of Professors Maetzner and Sievers; to write rather a Chronicle than a compilation. I claim in short to be the 'Quellen'. '. . . Quaeque ipse miserrima vidi/Et quorum pars magna fui. . . .' And by 'pars magna' I do not mean to claim that I have played any large part or any part at all in the evolution of the Prussian professorial habit of mind or methods of instruction, but that all my life a large part of my miseries have been caused by these phenomena. The stupidities of the ordinary English reviewer; the extreme difficulty of finding any soul in the Occidental hemisphere who is not *ergoteur* and *ergoteur* and again *ergoteur*; the impossibility of conducting any unconstrained and pleasing conversation about the feast of Trimalchio without being brought up short by some one who will have read Professor Friedlaender's *Cena Trimalchionis mit Uebersetzung und Anmerkungen* or Professor Buecheler's *Satirarum reliquiae* — these things are not merely the humorous disagreeables of life; they are real and actual causes of intellectual death. And they are all the products of Prussianism; they are all the products of a type of mind that desires to see every phenomenon of life encyclopaedised, laid upon the shelf and done for.

The ordinary English reviewer really wishes not to be troubled with the consideration of new metrical forms, and therefore, very gladly, he takes refuge in the fact that Professor Alois Brandl may have said something about the metre of Tennyson in the introduction to the Standard Library of International Literature; the *ergoteur* is a gentleman whose passion is to side-track main arguments by dilating upon infinitely unimportant immaterialisms — the type of gentlemen who maintain that Jesus Christ is unworthy of attention because Professor Kuno Meyer may have discovered five grammatical errors in a Celtic translation of the Sermon on the Mount; and the gentleman who will silence a pleasing conversation about Petronius Arbiter by quotations from Professors Friedlaender and Buecheler is a gentleman who does not really wish the beauty of Hellenic literature or of Roman-Hellenic derivative literature to play about the modern tablecloth.

I have been reproached, as I have said, with unfairness to the really great traditions of German learning — to the great service they have rendered to the classics in the settling of texts and of ascriptions. But I do not think that any one who will read my chapters upon the defects of the Prussian University system will accuse me of having been unfair to German learning. It is of course a splendid, if a secondary, thing to have purer classical texts. But before the desirability of pure texts comes the desirability that any kind of a text should be spread broadcast about the world — should, in fact, be in every household of the Occident. And if the discussion as to whether the word '*at*' should be read into the text of line 21 of Catullus' version of 'The Rape of the Lock of Berenice' — if this and similar discussions are to render the reading of Catallus burdensome to the lover of learning, then these discussions should be made penal offences. If every schoolmaster who has given a boy a distaste for the works of Shakespeare by insisting on the boy's attending to learned annotations rather than to the story of the play — if every such schoolmaster had been imprisoned on the occasion of his first offence of this sort Shakespeare would be better beloved in England and England a more lovable and a better place.

And this is very serious writing; it is in addition sound commonsense and Christian charity. It in no way detracts from its soundness that, to some extent these remarks are platitudes; it no way detracts from the Christianity that these remarks run counter to the accepted conceptions of two Prussianised generations. The first duty of philosophy is to help men to live their lives; the first duty of learning is to teach the children of men that the objects of learned study are beautiful. It is better to induce fifty thousand men to read a defective text of Tibullus than to grant fifty doctorates for emendations of that text. The obverse of these doctrines is to produce what Professor Huber calls 'monomaniacs of their special subject'. But the production of monomaniacs is hardly a proud record for a great civilization. Yet it is nearly all that Prussia has to show in the realms of the humaner occupations.

By speaking of Prussia it should be understood that I imply Prussia since 1848. Before 1848 the German universities produced men of great erudition who were also men of great constructive ability. Mommsen's *Roemische Geschichte*, which I have lately been re-reading, remains for me still one of the immense masterpieces of the world — it ranks, as far as I am concerned, with Maine's *Ancient*

Law, Clarendon's *History of the Great Rebellion*, and Mr Doughty's *Travels in Arabia Deserta*. But Mommsen was a product of pre-1848 Germany.

And of course I am not saying that none of the constructive ability that distinguished the great men of the German universities between 1810 and 1848 remains in Germany of today. I have only tried to point out that Prussia and that the Emperor William II with the aid of his Ministers of Education have done everything that they could to crush out the constructive spirit and to limit academic activities purely to what are known as 'Forschungen'. And 'Forschungen' Prussia conceives primarily as exercises having no necessary relation to learning, to philosophy, or to the arts, but simply as exercises in discipline. As far as Prussianism is concerned a young man might as well receive his doctorate for tabulating the number of times the letter 't' was defectively printed in British Bluebooks between the year 1892 and the year 1897, as for a collection of theories since Sir Thomas Browne's days as to what songs the Sirens sang. Industry, in fact, not gifts, is what the Prussian Government demands of its learned — and industry that shall provide a population tenacious in acts of war, infinitely courageous in the contemplation of death, and utterly and finally at the disposal of the State, whether the actions of the State be good or evil.

And this tendency has coloured even the activities of such professors in Germany as have kept alive some of the flame of constructive classical learning. I have been particularly requested by an erudite Englishman who has been pained by my attacks upon Prussian learning — for there are erudite Englishmen who cherish affection or reverence for the Prussianisation of the sources of knowledge — to pay some attention to the works of Professor Wilamowitz-Moellerndorff. I must confess to having heard very little of this professor, but I have read carefully his *Reden und Vortraege* — which is a collection of his public utterances during nearly forty years. And I will admit at once that Professor Moellerndorff's work contains at least one very charming and almost ideal dissertation — upon the 'Berenice'. It contains articles also on the sources of 'Clitumnus', upon 'Egyptian graves', and upon the 'Zeus of Olympia', which have a very nearly equal charm and a great beauty and distinction of writing.

But it contains also — though these too are charmingly written — patriotic orations on the Emperor's birthday in 1877, on the jubilee of William I in 1885, on the Emperor's birthdays in1897 and 1898, and on the opening of the new century in 1900. And all these orations, though they are delicately expressed, and though they do take into account the existence of France and the United States, are none the less glorifications of German culture. They state that there is a German culture; that it is wonderful that there should be a German culture; that German culture can take its place alongside the culture of the United States and France. One asks oneself, in short, what other professor of what other civilized State would exhibit such a singular national self-consciousness, such astonishment, or such pride. And one says to oneself that it is lamentable that a professor with the lovely and lovable gifts that are exhibited in the classical orations should be forced to waste his time upon innumerable demonstrations of what should either be self-evident or, if it be not self-evident, is unworthy of attention.

My attack, in fact, is not upon German learning, which, when its exponent has a sense of form and a gift of expression, is a thing fine enough; my attack is simply upon the paucity of the products of German learning. Professor Wilamowitz-Moellerndorff writes beautifully, but he does not write enough; Mommsen writes clearly, colloquially, and suggestively, but there are not enough Mommsens, and the present system of German university education at best affords little chance of rising to intellects of the type of Mommsen's, and, at worst, crushes out such intellects. And such intellects as those of Herren Fontane and Liliencron are forced by the exigencies of their careers and by what in the eyes of the Prussian educational authorities appear to be national and imperial necessities into wasting an unreasonable amount of time in patriotic and semi-militarist orations and writings.

It may be argued that Prussia is within her rights in exacting these sacrifices of her loyal sons. And one has nothing to say against that claim. But Prussia cannot, whilst asserting that claim and exacting these sacrifices, assert at the same time a claim to dominate the culture of the entire Occident and of the entire world. What Prussia may do within her own boundaries is the concern of no mortal being outside Prussia; it is only when Prussia emerges from the territories east of the Elbe that Prussia must expect to be judged and will very certainly be found wanting. And the very definite defect of Prussianism is the fact that its chief characteristic is an intellectual laziness and a constructive cowardice. Not gifts but industry is, as it were, the motto of Prussia, just as not individual perfection but organization is another of her mottoes. It is largely to be laid to the account of Prussia that prominent chairs of learning throughout the world are occupied by non-gifted individuals whose claim to occupy those chairs is solely that of an uninspired capacity to aggregate facts.

There is, I am aware, a great deal to be said for the fascination of absolute learning. But the fascination of absolute learning in no way correlated to life or the arts is a fascination purely private. There is no reason in the world why a man should not pass a large portion of his time or his whole time in collecting instances of misprints or any other similar 'Forschungen'; there is no reason why a man should not pass a great part of his time playing patience or in collecting postage-stamps. These are innocent and innocuous occupations, and all of them are mental soporifics and anodynes in a world that is sad enough and tragic enough. But let me repeat for the hundredth time that though these occupations may be absolutely innocent they do not confer upon their followers the right to rule an immense world teeming with passionate and erect sons of men.

Let me labour these points and re-labour these points. The first province of philosophy is to throw a light upon life; the first province of an historian is to throw a light upon how men act in great masses; the first province of learning is to render the study of beautiful things attractive and practicable for proper men. But all these things have secondary and higher provinces. The higher province of philosophy is to lead the individual men to pass better and saner lives; the higher province of an historian is to lead those large bodies of men which are called nations so to learn from the experience of the past that in future they may avoid what in the past were national crimes; and the higher province of learning, which is the highest province of all and the noblest function of humanity, is so to direct the study of the beautiful things of the past and the present that the future may be filled with more and always more beauties. The true and really high function of our professors is to teach us so to read the Sermon on the Mount and the Beatitudes that more such poems may be written by our children for our children even to the furthest generations. And until a civilization shall arise whose professors can do this no civilization has a right to claim world-dominance.

In this direction the civilization of the French has gone farther than any other; the civilization of the English has gone less far, but still has had some glimmerings of this ideal. The civilization of Prussia, on the other hand, has struck constantly and remorselessly at this ideal. And will the world see with equanimity the beautiful and beneficent civilization of France and the more homely, more domestic, but still charming civilization of Anglo-Saxondom disappear before a rudely machined organization, the product of a quarter of a century of desperate and bitter strivings, whose chief characteristic, whose chief province of life is the provision of 'monomaniacs interested in their special subjects'? That question still waits its answer. That enigma, terrible with the possibilities of horror for children and the children's children of all the world, still remains unsolved.

It is at any rate this problem that I have attempted to put in bold outlines before the reader of the present book. That the present book may well be styled sketchy, didactic, and insufficiently impersonal I am well aware. But I have been faced with the problem of producing in a form that may be easily handled and read without too much effort the history of an entire civilization. It is very widely held that a really learned and serious work should not be 'written', using the word in the sense of the creative artist. Why this should be held I do not know: it is, I suppose, merely another product of the Prussian habit of mind. But I desire to be read as widely as possible. I desire that this book should be read by every person in the habitable globe since the subject is a subject of the greatest importance to every inhabitant of the habitable globe at the present moment. Therefore I have limited myself to the utterances of certain representative personalities and I have adopted a form of narration as readable as, to the measure of the light vouchsafed to me, I could contrive.

Put into four or five words the problem that is now before humanity is whether the culture of the future, the very life and heart of the future, shall be materialist or altruist. The form in which this problem is presented to the reader matters very little; but I am anxious, if I can, to avoid the charge of egoism, since, if such a charge can be maintained and substantiated, by behaving discreditably I should bring discredit upon the cause which I have at heart. I have, then, written personally throughout great portions of this book because I wished to make it as readable as possible — because I wished to suggest to as many people as possible lines of attack upon the chief enemy of humanity and the human letters. It is, in short, the merest rough pioneer work that I have attempted. If I knew of any other form that would have been as readable I would thankfully have adopted it. But readability, as far as I have observed it in its effects upon myself, has seemed always to resolve itself into relating anecdotes and drawing morals from those anecdotes.

This is all that I have done and all that I ask is that ten thousand other pens more skilled, using as many other forms more adapted for the purpose, should take up this attack, for, in the end an attack upon a form of civilization can only be made by the many pens and the many tongues of another civilization. Looking at the world as I see it I can only perceive that the Anglo-Saxon and Latin civilizations have for the last forty years been browbeaten into timidity by the formidable productions of an alien barbarism; and all that I have been trying to do is by hook or by crook, employing now colloquialism, now rhetoric, to unmask the face of this barbarism and, in that way, as far as I might, to put some heart into unnecessarily depressed populations.

London
3 February 1915

[New York and London: Hodder and Stoughton, 1915: pp. vii-xx.]

from

Women and Men (1923)

Women and Men was published by the Three Mountains Press in Paris in an edition of 300 copies as a prose booklet in a series chosen by Ezra Pound, which included Hemingway's *In Our Time* (see p. 247). Pound, recognizing 'the real stuff', had already arranged for the publication of the individual essays in the *Little Review* in 1918 in six issues. Some of the pages in this chapter first appeared in *The Heart of the Country*, 1906; Ford rewrote the Meary Walker material for the chapter 'Cabbages and Queens' in *Return to Yesterday*, 1932.

When Ford first thought of writing *Women and Men* in 1911 (the year before he wrote *This Monstrous Regiment of Women*), he intended 'a sort of philosphical discussion on the relations and the differences between the sexes'. The original title was to have been 'Men and Women'.

AVERAGE PEOPLE

I HAVE reflected for a long time; I have reflected for a very long time. I have really done my best to make a discovery which most people would regard as the easiest in the world. It is one of those matters which every one would say at first sight was known to everyone, but which no one ever really knows. If you ask any person in the world how many steps lead up to his front door he will not be able to tell you: or if you ask him whether the figures on his watch are Arabic or Roman. And yet there will be a portion of that man's brain that knows these things, though from his consciousness they are entirely absent. Thus, every man can descend his own steps without paying attention to the number of them, which proves that somewhere in his automatic memory the knowledge is hidden away. And every man, if presented with his own watch and the watch of another precisely similar in every detail save that of the dial plate, will know his own watch by its 'look'. Along somewhat similar lines is the discovery that I am trying to make. For what I want to know is: 'What is an average man?'

What, for the matter of that is an average woman? Who has seen either of these impossible monsters? Assuredly neither I nor you. 'For such a sunflower never bloomed beneath the sun.' We all have very strongly within us the belief that there is such a thing. The belief is as strong as that in the immortality of our souls. And we think, when we are not thinking about it, that we know a large number of quite average men and women. We should laugh loudly if we were told that we could not put our finger immediately upon a perfectly average man or a perfectly average woman. And yet, the moment you come to try to do it you will find that it is absolutely impossible.

By carefully going through the Alphabet, and my calling book, I have found that I know at the present moment 1,642 men and women. I know them, that is to say, all of them to speak to. And, having a fairly tenacious memory, which practically never forgets even very small things connected with the careers of other people, I may say that I know something of the circumstances and the characters of all these people. My own acquaintance divides itself into three main bodies — the distinctly lower classes, the intellectual classes and the distinctly leisured and upper classes. Of the commercial middle classes I know practically very little. These distinctions are of course arbitrary, but they more or less express what I mean. I am aware that the objections will at once be made: 'If you know nothing of the middle classes you cannot of course know anything of the average man, for it is precisely amongst the middle classes that the average man is to be found.' And of course there is something to be said for the objection until one comes to regard it scientifically. Then at once it disappears. For, in the very nature of the case the middle classes are numerically small by comparison with the bulk of the people.

And indeed every aspect of this bewildering subject bristles with difficulties as soon as one approaches it. Thus, let us for the moment accept the dictum that the average man is to be found among the middle classes. Let us carry it even a step further and say that the middle-class man is the average man. For of course the great bulk of readers will be found among the middle classes — or they would have been so found until yesterday when the coming of the cheap press spread some kind of printed matter into the hands even of the very poorest of servant girls. Here then is another difficulty of classification. One cannot really say that the middle classes are the reading classes. One cannot even really say that the middle classes are the classes that most read thoughtful literature.

In a book dealing specifically with the life we live today it is almost impossible to avoid mentioning the names of individuals or of institutions. And, to name individuals or institutions is always open to certain objections. These objections, grave as they are, I must just face as best I can, or rather I must just ignore them. If I could, I would just deal with my own readers, but I haven't the least idea who my own readers may be. No author ever has or ever can have. A certain number of people tell me that they have read my books. They may have or they may not have, but I have no means of classifying them. I don't in fact know my own 'public'. But as soon as it comes to the 'publics' of other authors, or more particularly of various journals, one arrives at much more definite ground. One knows at least what sort of person will not read the *Sporting Times*.

Yet having written the statement down I am at once driven to hesitation. For it occurs to me that I know very well a lady most of whose interests are intellectual or are connected with public movements in one way or another, and she quite frequently mentions this journal, calling it by its orthodox name — 'The Pink Un'. Or again, I was once an inhabitant of a very remote village and became rather closely friendly with the vicar. This gentleman was just a vicar. He was quite unworldly, he preached simple, gentle sermons; he was good to the poor in the ordinary clerical manner. He spent a good deal of time in fishing. But every now and then, he would astonish me by letting drop startling pieces of gossip as to rather 'smart' people with whom he could not possibly have come into contact. One day he said something so odd, concerning a notoriety in the world of sport who was at that time on his trial for an offence against the laws of the country — something so odd that I could not help questioning him. He said:

'I have it on the authority of a journal that I read regularly. I have never heard its statements questioned. But I dare say you do not read it yourself.' He uttered these last words as if the paper was a little over my head for social or for learned reasons. Of course the good man was quite nice about it, but he could not get it out of his head that he was the clergyman of the parish while I was some casual nobody who happened to have taken a house within the limits of his cure of souls. Then he told me the name of his paper. It was the *Pelican*!

So that it is almost impossible to say even who will not read any given paper. I have pursued this argument with such tenacity that I am aware that the matter I have in hand for the moment may have escaped the remembrance of the reader. It is whether or no the middle classes may be said to make up the bulk of the thoughtful reading classes.

I have a friend whom I will call T. T went to Rugby and Oxford. He ate his dinners at the Middle Temple. He was called to the bar and he once had a brief for a mining company of which one of his uncles was the chairman of directors. Just after this — when T was twenty-five — he came in for six thousand a year. From that day to this he has never done anything. Nothing. Nothing at all. I meet him from time to time at my club and for some reason or other I like him very well and he likes me. He tells me a good deal about racing. And this is the mode of his regular life.

He is forty-one — and a bachelor. He has an immense house in Palace Gardens, Kensington. The house contains thirty rooms and T has six servants. The house is an inheritance from his uncle which T has never taken the trouble to get rid of. The six servants are needed in order to keep it tidy. The only one of them that T ever sees is his 'man'. He rises from his bed every morning at 8.30. Over his bath and his dressing he spends exactly an hour — breakfasting at 9.30. Over his breakfast and the *Morning Post* he spends exactly an hour, finishing at 10.30. Half an hour he spends with his 'man', discussing what he will have for dinner, what tie he will put on with what suit; or, if he wants any new clothes, which he does very frequently, he discusses what is being worn by various gentlemen whom his 'man' has seen. At 11 he puts on the suit and the tie that his 'man' has sanctioned and laid out in his dressing room. At 11.30 he walks across Kensington Gardens where he strolls, or sits upon a penny chair. This lasts him until a quarter to one. A quarter of an hour takes him to his club in the neighbourhood of King Street, St. James's. At his club he sits for half an hour in a deep arm chair reposing both his soul and his body. This is for the good of his digestion for he knows that it is unhealthy to eat immediately after having taken exercise. After lunch, which consists of a soup, a meat and cheese or apple tart, washed down with either barley water or very weak whisky and vichy — which is excellent against the gout, — after lunch he sits until 3.30 in the same deep arm chair. At 3.30 he strolls a little farther eastward where he finds an institution which keeps one's health in order by means of various exercises with dumb bells. Here he exercises himself for an hour, wearing practically no clothes and standing before the open window for the benefit of the fresh air. Dressing himself occupies him for half an hour. At five o'clock he takes a cup of tea and one slice of buttered toast. At half past five he walks to the Bath Club. Here he takes a Turkish bath with a plunge afterwards into the swimming bath. This occupies one hour and a half. At seven o'clock he takes a taxi cab and goes home, arriving there at 7.15. Three quarters of an hour he devotes to dressing for dinner. At eight o'clock he dines, always alone because conversation is unhealthy during serious meals. By nine o'clock he has finished dinner. From nine until ten he takes a nap, being awakened as the hour strikes by his 'man'. From ten to eleven he reads the evening papers. At eleven o'clock he goes to bed. And he tells me that he falls asleep the moment his head touches the pillow and that he sleeps the dreamless sleep of infants and of the pure in heart, until eight o'clock when his 'man' wakes him up with a cup of tea and the first post. So the ideal day of this ideal average man runs its appointed course. And it is a positive fact that my friend once uttered these words. He said:

'My dear chap. How could you pass your day better? Tell me how? I once read a hymn and it struck me so much that I copied it out.' And Mr T produced a little note book from which amazingly he read out the words:

> Sweet day so cool, so calm, so bright,
> The bridal of the earth and sky.
> The dews shall weep thy fall tonight,
> For thou, with all thy sweets, must die.

'That,' Mr T said, 'exactly reminds me of my days. Of course I shall die one day and if it isn't wrong to say so I hope to go to Heaven for I have never done any harm in my life. I behave always I hope like an English gentleman and I look carefully after my health which is cherishing the image of Himself that God has given me.' Mr T was speaking in a tone of the deepest seriousness. And indeed he really had cherished in himself the image of his Maker. His gentle walks, his sobriety in both eating and drinking, his careful avoidance of all disturbing emotions, his daily health exercises, his naps and his Turkish baths — all these things really had made him a perfect man of forty-one in the very pink of health. The flesh of his cheeks was vivid and firm, his eyes were clear and blue, his hair crisp, blond and in excellent condition. His walk was springy, his back erect and he was beautifully and unobtrusively dressed. So perhaps this is the average man . . . Let us now turn to the average woman.

About fifteen years ago I wanted some mushroom catsup. It was in a scattered, little-populated village of the South of England. The village stood on what had formerly been common land, running all down the side of a range of hills. But this common had been long since squatted on, so that it was a maze of little hawthorn hedges surrounding little closes. Each close had a few old apple or cherry trees, a patch of potato ground, a cabbage patch, a few rows of scarlet runners, a few plants of monthly roses, a few plants of marjoram, fennel, borage or thyme. And in each little patch there stood a small dwelling. Mostly these were the original squatters' huts built of mud, white washed outside and crowned with old thatched roofs on which there grew grasses, house-leeks or even irises. There were a great many of these little houses beneath the September sunshine and it was all a maze of the small green hedges.

I had been up to the shop in search of my catsup, but though they sold everything from boots and straw hats to darning needles, bacon, haricot beans, oatmeal and British wines they had no catsup. I was wandering desultorily homewards among the small hedges down hill, looking at the distant sea, seven miles away over the marsh. Just beyond a little hedge I saw a woman digging potatoes in the dry hot ground. She looked up as I passed and said:

'Hullo, Measter!'

I answered: 'Hullo, Missus!' and I was passing on when it occurred to me to ask her whether she knew anyone who sold catsup. She answered:

'Naw! Aw doan't knaw no one!'

I walked on a little farther and then sat down on a stile for half an hour or so, enjoying the pleasant weather and taking a read in the country paper which I had bought in the shop. Then I saw the large, stalwart old woman coming along the stony path carrying two great trugs of the potatoes that she had dug up. I had to get down from the stile to let her pass. And then seeing that she was going my way, that she was evidently oldish and was probably tired, I took the potato trugs from her and carried them. She strode along in front of me between the hedges. She wore an immense pair of men's hob-nailed boots that dragged along the stones of the causeway with metallic sounds. She wore an immense shawl of wool that had been beaten by the weather until it was of a dull liver colour, an immense skirt that had once been of lilac cotton print, but was now a rusty brown, and an immense straw hat that had been given to her by some one as being worn out and that had cost two pence when it was new. Her face was as large, as round and much the same colour as a copper warming pan. Her mouth was immense and quite toothless except for one large fang and as she smiled cheerfully all the time, her great gums were always to be seen. Her shoulders were immense and moved with the roll and heave of those of a great bullock. This was the wisest and upon the whole the most estimable human being that I ever knew at all well. Her hands were enormous and stained a deep blackish green over their original copper colour by the hops that it was her profession to tie.

As we walked along she told me that she was exactly the same age as our Queen who was then just seventy. She told me also that she wasn't of those parts but was a Paddock Wood woman by birth, which meant that she came from the true hop country. She told me also that her husband had died fifteen years before of the sting of a viper, that his poor old leg went all like green jelly up to his thigh before he died and that he had been the best basket maker in all Kent. She also told me that we can't all have everything and that the only thing to do is to 'keep all on gooing'.

I delivered up her trugs to her at her garden gate and she said to me with a cheerful nod:

'Well I'll do the same for you, mate, when you come to be my age,' And, with this witticism she shambled over the rough stone of her garden path and into her dark door beneath the low thatch, that was two yards thick. Her cottage was more dilapidated than any that I have ever seen in my life. It stood in a very long narrow triangle of ground, so that the hedge that I walked along must have been at least eighty yards in length, while at its broadest part the potato patch could not have measured twenty spade breadths. But before I was come to the end of the hedge her voice was calling out after me:

'Measter! Dun yo really want ketchup?'

I replied that I really did.

She said:

'Old Meary Spratt up by Hungry Hall wheer ye see me diggin' – she makes ketchup'.

I asked her why she had not told me before and she answered:

'Well, ye see the Quality do be asking foolish questions. I thought ye didn't really want to know.'

But indeed, as I learnt afterwards it wasn't only the dislike of being asked foolish questions. In Meary Walker's long, wise life she had experienced one thing — that no man with a collar and a tie is to be trusted. She had had it vaguely in her mind that, when I asked the question, I might be some sort of excise officer trying to find out where illicit distilling was carried on. She didn't know that the making of catsup was not illegal. She had heard that many of her poor neighbours had been fined heavily for selling bottles of home-made sloe-gin or mead. She had refused to answer, out of a sense of automatic caution for fear she should get poor old Meary Spratt into trouble.

But next morning she turned up at my cottage carrying two bottles of Meary Spratt's catsup in an old basket covered with a cloth. And after that, seeing her rather often at the shop on Saturday nights when all the world came to buy its Sunday provisions and, because she came in to heat the bake oven with faggots once a week, and to do the washing — in that isolated neighbourhood, among the deep woods of the Weald, I got to know her as well as I ever knew anybody. This is her biography:

She was the daughter of a day labourer among the hopfields of Paddock Wood. When she had been born, the youngest of five, her own mother had died. Her father had brought a stepmother into the house. I never discovered that the stepmother was notably cruel to Meary. But those were the Hungry Forties. The children never had enough to eat. Once, Meary cut off one of her big toes. She had jumped down into a ditch after a piece of turnip peel. She had of course had no shoes or stockings and there had been a broken bottle in the ditch.

So her childhood had been a matter of thirst, hunger and frequent chastisements with the end of a leather strap that her father wore round his waist. When she was fourteen she was sent to service in a great house where all the maids slept together under the roof. Here they told each other legends at night — odd legends that exactly resembled the fairy tales of Grimm — legends of princes and princesses, of castles, or of travelling companions on the road. A great many of these stories seemed to hinge upon the price of salt which at one time was extravagantly dear in the popular memory, so that one princess offered to have her heart cut out in order to purchase a pound of salt that should restore her father to health.

From this house Meary Walker ran away with a gipsy — or at least he was what in that part of the world was called a 'pikey' — a user of the turnpike road. So, for many years they led a wandering existence, until at last they settled down in this village. Until the date of that settlement Meary had not troubled to marry her Walker. Then a parson insisted on it, but it did not trouble her much either way.

Walker had always been a man of weak health. To put it shortly, he had what is called the artistic temperament — a small, dark, delicate man whose one enthusiasm was his art of making baskets. In that he certainly excelled. But he was lazy and all the work of their support fell on Meary. She tied hops — and this is rather skilled work, — she picked them in the autumn; she helped the neighbours with baking and brewing. She cleaned up the church once a week. She planted the potatoes and cropped them. She was the first cottager in East Kent to keep poultry for profit. In her biography, which I have related at greater length in another book, you could find traces of great benevolence and of considerable heroism. Thus, one hard winter, she supported not only herself and her husband, but her old friend Meary Spratt, at that time a widow with six children. Meary Spratt was in bed with pneumonia and its after effects from December to March. Meary Walker nursed her, washed and tended the children and made the livings of all of them.

Then there came the time when she broke her leg and had to be taken against her will to the hospital which was seven miles away. She did not want to be in the hospital; she was anxious to be with Walker who was then dying of gangrene of the leg. She was anxious too about a sitting hen; one of her neighbours had promised her half a crown for a clutch of chickens. She used to lie in hospital, patting her broken knee under the bed clothes and exclaiming:

'Get well, get well, oh do get well quickly!' And even twenty years afterwards when she rehearsed these scenes and these words there would remain in the repetition a whole world of passionate wistfulness. But indeed, she translated her passion into words. One night, driven beyond endurance by the want of news of Walker and of her sitting hen she escaped from the hospital window and crawled on her hands and knees the whole seven miles from the hospital to her home. She found when she arrived in the dawn that Walker was in his coffin. The chickens however were a healthy brood. Her admiration for Walker, the weak and lazy artist in basket making, never decreased. She treasured his best baskets to the end of her life as you and I might treasure Rembrandts. Once, ten years after, she sat for a whole day on his grave. The old sexton growing confused with years had made a mistake and was going to inter another man's wife on top of Walker. Meary stopped that.

For the last twenty-six years or so of her life she lived in the mud hut which I had first seen her enter. She went on as before, tying hops, heating ovens, picking up stones, keeping a hen or two. She looked after, fed and nursed — for the love of God — a particularly disagreeable old man called Purdey who had been a London cab driver. He sat all day in a grandfather's chair, grumbling and swearing at Meary whenever she came in. He was eighty-two. He had no claim whatever upon her and he never paid her a penny of money. She could not have told you why she did it, but no doubt it was just the mothering instinct.

So she kept on going all through life. She was always cheerful: she had always on her tongue some fragment of peasant wisdom. Once, coming back from market she sat down outside a public house and a soldier treated her to a pot of beer. Presently there rode up the Duke of Cambridge in his field-marshal's uniform and beside him there was the Shah of Persia. They were watching a sham fight in the neighbourhood. Meary raised her pot of beer towards these Royal personages and wished them health. They nodded in return.

'Well,' Meary called out to the Duke, 'you're only your mother's son like the rest of us.' Once, the Portuguese ambassador amiably telling her that, in his language, bread was 'pom' she expressed surprise but then she added —

'Oh well poor dear, when you're hungry you've got to eat it, like the rest of us, whatever you call it.'

She was sorry for him because he had to call bread by such an outlandish name. She could not think how he remembered the word. Yet she knew that *Brot* was the German for bread and *Apfel* for apples because, during the Napoleonic Wars of her youth, the Hanoverian Legion had garrisoned that part of the country. One of what she called the jarman legions had murdered a friend of her mother's who had been his sweetheart and when he was hung for it at Canterbury he asked for *Brot* and *Apfel* on the scaffold. She saw him hung, a pleasant fair boy, and when she looked down at her hands she said they were as white as lard.

So she worked on until she was seventy-eight. One day she discovered a swelling under her left breast. It gave her no pain but she wanted to know what it was. So she put a hot brick to it. She knew that if it was cancer that was a bad thing to do, but she wanted to get it settled. The swelling became worse. So she walked to the hospital — the same hospital that she had crawled away from. They operated on her next morning — and she was dead by noon. Her last words were:

'Who's going to look after old Purdey?'

She was buried in the workhouse cemetery. The number of her grave is 1642. Mr Purdey was taken to the Union that night. And there he still is, aged ninety-seven, a disagreeable old man.

And so we come back to the question of the average woman. Was Meary Walker this person? I wonder. If so the average among women is fairly high. Yet, in her own village nobody thought very much of Meary. She was popular with many people and hated by a few. Yet, as far as I can say her life, in each of its days, was as perfect as that of my friend Mr T. She never had a penny from me that she had not worked for, or never so much as a pair of old boots from anyone else. Was she then the average woman? I should not like to say that she was not. For, in spite of all our modernity, still the widest of all classes of employment is given by the land. There are more peasants in the world than there are anything else. And Meary was just a peasant woman, attracting no particular notice from her fellows. On the other hand there was Meary Spratt her bosom friend.

Meary Spratt was much more like the average woman of fiction. She was decidedly emotional, she was certainly not truthful: she begged, and when she begged she would scream and howl and yell in the highest of keys, pulling her gnarled, rheumatic fingers into repulsive shapes and screaming like a locomotive to show how much they pained her, or sobbing with the most dramatic emphasis when she related how Meary Walker had saved her six little children from starvation. On the other hand she would relate with a proper female virtue the fact — I fancy it may have been true — that, at some portion of her career Meary Walker had a daughter by somebody who was not Walker and that the daughter was in service in Folkestone. She would also say that Meary Walker was an arrant miser who had saved up a large fortune in bank notes which were quilted into her stays. She said she had heard the stays crackle.

Meary Spratt had never had a child by anyone but a husband. But then she had had four husbands as well as nineteen children, all of whom had lived. She is quite a small woman with an appallingly shrill voice and no doubt she is feminine in that her tongue never stops. In the early morning among the dews you will hear her voice.

She will be picking what she calls musherooms for her catsup. You will hear her all the while like this screaming quite loudly while you listen from your bedroom window, she being in the field beyond the hedge and it being four o'clock of a very dewy morning.

'He! He! He!' she will scream, 'here is a nice little one! A little pinky one! Now I'm going to pick you! Up you come, my little darling! Ah, doesn't it hurt!' And then she will give a shrill yell to show the pain that the musheroom feels when it is being picked. And then she will continue: 'Oh, oh, oh Lord! Oh my poor shoulders! Oh! my poor legs! They do fairly terrify me with rhumatiz! Oh, oh, Lord!'

And you will hear her voice seeming to get shriller as it gets fainter and she goes over the marshy grass, into the mist, until she comes on another little pink one. She is seventy-six and it is cold out on the marshes in that October weather.

Yes, she is decidedly feminine. She has only been married three years to Mr Spratford — so she gets called Meary Spratt. Mr Spratford was eighty-two when they married. Between them they have had thirty-one children. And they lived in a little brick cottage not much larger than a dog kennel. When you ask Mr Spratford why he married — Mr Spratford was a most venerable looking peasant, like a Biblical patriarch, with very white hair curling round a fine bald head and with noble faded blue eyes; and when he spoke he always gesticulated nobly with one hand and uttered the most edifying moral sentiments. He was extremely dishonest and had three times been to prison for robbing poor old women. Indeed, when I first made his acquaintance he did a week's work for me, charged me double prices and begged me not to tell anybody that I had paid him at all because he was on his club — and this is about the meanest crime that any peasant can commit. It was an offence so mean that even Meary Spratford — who you will observe was a woman and who would have had no scruple at all about pilfering from any member of the quality — even Meary Spratford was outraged and made him pay back his club money for that week. She could not bear to think of the members of the club being defrauded, because they were quite poor people. It is true that she came to me afterwards, and, groaning and sobbing, she tried to get the money out of me to make up for her noble act — but when you asked Mr Spratford why he married he answered:

'Well, you see, sir, in a manner of speaking us do be very poor people and us bean't able to afford more than one blanket apiece, and one small fire for each of us, coals do be so dear.' (He got all his coals for nothing from the poor old parson and so did Mrs Spratt.) 'So iff we do marry we do have two blankets atop of us at night and we have one big fire and sit on either side of it.'

So said Mr Spratford. But when it came to his wife she would scream out:

'Why did us marry? Why I like to have a man about the house and a woman looks better like among her neebours if she do have a husband.' So that no doubt Mrs Spratt was feminine enough, just as Mr Spratford was undoubtedly masculine. He died raving on the mud floor of his hut. His wife had not the strength to lift him into bed and the four men who had held him down during the night had had to go to work in the morning. He tore his bald head to ribbons with his nails and Mrs Spratt for years afterwards could make anybody sick with her dramatic rehearsals of how he died. When she was really worked up over this narration she would even scratch her own forehead until it bled. So perhaps she was really a more womanly woman than Mrs Walker. She kept on going just the same: she is still keeping on going. But she made much more noise about it. That, I believe, is what is demanded of man's weaker vessels.

But even in the village, Meary Spratt was regarded as unusually loquacious whereas Meary Walker attracted, as I have said, no attention at all. It was as if Meary Walker was just a woman whereas Meary Spratt was at least a super-woman, or as if she were a woman endowed with the lungs of a locomotive whistle. Indeed, I am certain that anyone there would have told you that Meary Walker was just an average woman.

[pp. 47-61]

from

Provence (1935)

THE secret ambition of Lord Palmerston at sixty was to become a ballet-dancer and I can parallel that ideal of the great and virtuous minister by saying that, years ago when I met Miss Adeline Genée one of the first things I asked her was whether with her lessons she could not turn me into a clog-dancer. I did not ask very seriously but I was expressing a certain longing. For my frivolity she gave it to me; as the saying used to be, in the neck, by answering uncompromisingly: 'You're too old. . . . And too fat!' . . . And that must have been in 1909. . . . *Eheu fugaces!*

But at least I cannot be accused of disliking dancing or of having any contempt for the most lovely as it is the most fugitive of all the Arts. And indeed of all the beautiful and mysterious motives and emotions that go to make up the frame of mind that is Provence the most beautiful, moving and mysterious is that of the Northern Boy of Antibes. They boy danced and gave pleasure, died two thousand years ago and his memorial tablet set into the walls of Antibes which is Antipolis of the Greeks sets forth those salient facts of his life and portrays in the lasting stone the little bag in which he used to make his collections. . . . He indeed along with Herod's daughter who came after and King David who preceded him must be amongst the earliest dancers upon whom Destiny has conferred the immortality of stone, papyrus or wax. . . . The most mysterious and the most beautiful.

And that is the note of the frame of mind that is Provence — that and the sculptured tablets of the cloister of St Trophime at Arles, of the façade of the church at St Gilles, of the Maison Carrée at Nîmes, of the triangular white tower of Beaucaire and the legends of the Good King René, the Good Queen Joan, the ruined city of les Baux and the wine called *Sanh del Trobador*, the blood of Guillem de Cabestanh.

* * *

So my feeling for Provence is a loving equanimity. Provence shall always be there and, if not with the eyes of the flesh, then at least with those of the spirit, I shall always see it as I see it here in spite of the fog and the tumult.

And yet that is not the state of mind of the Teuton who is always filled with *Sehnsucht* and sighing for the land *wo die Citronen bluehen*. That state of mind is probably unhealthy and certainly it is a misfortune for the rest of the world, if most particularly for France which stands between Germany and the lemon trees. But one may attain to a firm and quiet resolution to go to, to finish one's days in that home and cradle of one's kind without either loss of dignity nor yet sword and torch in hand.

To understand what that means it is necessary at least once to have seen the Roman Province. Having once seen it you may, like a lover who is convinced that his young woman still desires him beyond the mountains and across the seas, draw strength from the knowledge that that land exists and is unchanging. There will be no actual need to visit it again.

Obviously the ball we inhabit and whose surface we scratch will, after million-wise gyrations, one day fall back into the sun, and nothing earthly is in the absolute sense immutable. But, for all working purposes, Provence is. In forgotten and prehistoric days, before even the Great Trade Routes had been trodden through her valleys, her grey stone hills may have been scratched and scored by the glaciers and moraines of an unremembered ice age. But, standing on a rock above les Baux and looking inwards, we see astonishingly exactly what was seen in turn by any individual of the cohorts, legions, phalanxes, hordes and chevauchées that, since thousands of years ago have poured in uninterrupted succession through the Rhone valley. You could not say the same for the valleys of the Danube or the Rhine, for Palestine or Greece, for old England or for New or for any lands fashioned of clay or chalk or loam or sand or alluvial soil. They and their contours and surfaces will have been ploughed, or flooded or blown away. Above all, man with his next most dangerous competitors, the goats, will have deforested whole regions and there is no saying how in any given hundred years their aspects and very climates will not have altered. Palestine, like Greece, was once a very garden of Eden, to become a bitter desert and now again to be in process of being made to bloom. The Sahara was once a sea-bottom; and consider the climate of the Mississippi valley today! . . . But the sun-hardened rocks of Provence, fretted by neither rain nor frost, have in the meanwhile changed hardly at all. You may go back to les Baux after forty years and find no changes either in the most distant landscape or the objects nearest you.

Nor do sudden, devastating changes much affect the old cities of Provence. M. Bonhoure may re-face his old shop-front with marble and a café here and there may have some scagliola stuck on to its inner walls but, except on the littoral, the aspects of these ancient places remain almost unchanged. That is partly because the Provençal, being a fatalist, is by nature conservative. But it is still more because there are no remarkable deposits of precious minerals or mineral oils and the Rhone is for the most part hardly navigable. So neither gold-rushes nor sudden crowdings of populations have there taken place. Provence itself has been continually 'rushed' by every known type of barbarian. There can be no part of the earth's surface to have been as consistently taken by the sword. But the tides of men making those incursions have, like other rivers, spread themselves out in places they found attractive or unoccupied and the only pocket into which they have at all crowded has been Marseilles.

* * *

I am giving you my Provence. It is not the country as made up by modern or German scholarship; it is the Roman Province on the Great Trade Route where I have lived for nearly all my spiritual as for a great part of my physical, life.

I drink deep into my lungs wind that I know comes from Provence;
From that country everything that comes gives me pleasure
And listening to the praises of her I smile.
For every word of praise that is said I ask you for a hundred
So much am I pleased by the praises of that land.
From the mouth of the Rhone to Valence, between the sea and the
Durance!
In that noble land did I leave the joy of my heart.
To her I owe the glory that the beauty of my verses and the valour of
my deeds have gained for me,
And, as from her I draw talent and wisdom, so it is she that made me
a lover and, if I am a poet,
To her I owe it.

I am reminded of Henry James saying that he had loved France as he had never loved woman. Like the Author of *Daisy Miller*, Peire

Vidal, who is for me *the* Troubadour as for me Henry James is *the* Expatriate, was when he wrote those lines away from the country he loved, though no further away than in the castle of la Louve, in the Black Mountain, behind Carcassonne, in the Narbonnais. To be sure St James's Park, where the Master of the London novel spoke those words, is no further away from France than is Carcassonne from Tarascon. But, just as poor dear old London is a Paris without effervescence, so the Narbonnais, like a cake that has been baked in a too slow oven, is a heavier Provence. Running water cuts off the power of witches — which is why you must always make a hole in your egg-shells — so the Rhone and the Channel form barriers for lightnesses.

It is queer what powers of insulation those waters have. I sit here in my garret and hammer at phrases; I walk these streets with the dove-coloured paving stones, bemused; if I want to see anything I must make an effort of the will; if I write a sentence it comes out as backboneless as a water-hose; to give it life I must cut it into nine. It is no doubt no more than indigestion; when I get back to Provence the world will be astonishingly visible. I shall write little crisp sentences like silver fish jumping out of streams.

* * *

I came yesterday, also in Fitzroy Street, at a party, upon a young Lady who was the type of young lady I did not think one ever could meet. She was one of those ravishing and, like the syrens of the Mediterranean and Ulysses, fabulous beings who display new creations to the sound of harps, shawms and tea-cups. What made it all the more astounding was that she was introduced to me as being one of the best cooks in London — a real *cordon bleu*, and then some. She was, as you might expect, divinely tall and appeared to appear through such mists as surrounded Venus saving a warrior. But I found that she really could talk, if awfully, and at last she told me something that I did not know — about garlic. . . .

As do — as *must* — all good cooks, she used quantities of that bulb. It occurred to me at once that this was London and her work was social. Garlic is all very well on the bridge between Beaucaire and Tarascon or in the arena at Nîmes amongst sixteen thousand civilized beings . . . But in an *atelier de couture* in the neighbourhood of Hanover Square! . . . The lady answered mysteriously; No: there is no objection if only you take enough and train your organs to the assimilation. The perfume of *allium officinale* attends only on those timorous creatures who have not the courage as it were to wallow in that vegetable. I used to know a London literary lady who had that amount of civilization so that when she ate abroad she carried with her, in a hermetically sealed silver container, a single clove of the principal ingredient of *aioli*. With this she would rub her plate, her knife, her fork and the bread beside her place at the table. This, she claimed, satisfied her yearnings. But it did not enchant her friends or her neighbours at table.

My instructress said that that served her right. She herself, at the outset of her professional career, had had the cowardice to adopt exactly that stratagem that, amongst those in London who have seen the light, is not uncommon. But, when she went to her studio the outcry amongst her comrades, attendants, employers, clients and the very conductor of the bus that took her to Oxford Circus, had been something dreadful to hear. Not St Plothinus nor any martyr of Lyons had been so miscalled by those vulgarians.

So she had determined to resign her post and had gone home and cooked for herself a *poulet Béarnais*, the main garniture of which is a kilo — two lbs — of garlic per chicken, you eating the stewed cloves as if they were *haricots blancs*. It had been a Friday before a Bank holiday so that the mannequins at that fashionable place would not be required for a whole week.

Gloomily, but with what rapture internally, she had for that space of time lived on hardly anything else but the usually eschewed bulb. Then she set out gloomily towards the place that she so beautified but that she must leave for ever. Whilst she had been buttoning her gloves she had kissed an old aunt whose protests had usually been as clamant as those of her studio-mates. The old lady had merely complimented her on her looks. At the studio there had been no outcry and there too she had been congratulated on the improvement, if possible, of her skin, her hair, her carriage. . . .

She had solved the great problem; she had schooled her organs to assimilate, not to protest against, the sacred herb. . . .

* * *

A great man cannot get off the responsibility for the quality and behaviour of his admirers, because his poetry or doctrines will have had a large share in moulding their characters and demonstrations.

* * *

But the authentic note of the great poet is to modify for you the aspect of the world and of your relationship to your world. This [Frédéric] Mistral very astonishingly does. I have said that for a great many years I misestimated this great poet. But of late I have been reading him a great deal — notably since I have been in this city . . . And the curious effect has been to render London infinitely more supportable. It is, I suppose, because Mistral is the poet of little, unassuming people who are near the earth and have no claim to dictate destinies to their fellows . . . Whilst the High Gods thunder above, they find cracks in the earth in which to play their concertinas and carry on the arts, the amenities and the realities of life. London is more stupidly misgoverned than any place on the earth simply because its people are so docile and contented with so little that it should be easy to make of the Thames valley a paradise of harmony. It is instead one vast blunder — an immense muddling through about which its kindly people go with forever, on their lips the shibboleth:

'You can't bloody well have everything.'

I think if the politicians of Westminster and the ediles across the Thames could be removed to a desert and shut up in cells with nothing but *Mireille* to read and the *Trísor Félibrige* to help them out in the interpretation, London might get its deserts. For though it may be an exaggeration for M. Turle to say that Mistral puts the soul of Jesus into the measures of Virgil, it is nothing but the truth when he says: 'Tu ne pourras pas vivre ainsi que de coutume/Si les chants de Mistral t'ont chanté dans l'oreille . . .' . . . You cannot continue in your old, bad courses once the songs of Mistral have sounded in your ears.

* * *

I have spoken with some contempt of scholars and scholarship. Nevertheless during all my life I have been aware — or it might be more true to say that I have had the feeling, since never till this moment have I put it into words — that there are in this world only two earthly paradises. The one is in Provence with what has survived of the civilizations of the Good King, of the conte-fablistes of the Troubadours and of the painters of Avignon of the Popes. The other is the Reading Room of the British Museum.

It is — it has always been — to me delightful, soothing like the thought of a blessed oasis in the insupportable madhouse for apes that is our civilization, to remember that, rage the journalists how they may, there at the other end of the scale sit in an atmosphere of immutable calm, in that vast, silent place, all those half-brothers of the pen intent on the minutiae of the arts, the sciences and of pure thought. I think they must be the next to most happy people in the world, bending above their desks whilst the great clock marks the negligible hours of the next to Best Great Place. It is like the other consoling thought that I have always not very far from the back of my mind — that of innumerable nuns in forgotten convents praying for the redemption of all our miserable souls. . . . Yes, yours as well as mine and that of my patient non-Anglo-Saxon New York friend . . . who would really rather be damned than saved by the intervention of the pale daughters of the Scarlet Woman.

I don't know that the application of scholars is of more service to the arts than the supplications of the Praying Orders are effectual in changing, here in earth, our hearts. Nevertheless, just as praise is due to the poor dear old Church for the invention of those Orders, so the evolution by the poor dear old rag-bag that London is, of the British Museum Library may be accounted the one just act that, according to the Russian liturgy, may just save her soul. And in the long roll of her citizens that on the last day shall be offered to the Recording Angels, I do not believe that any two names could more fittingly head the list than those of Sir Anthony Panizzi[1] who began and of Dr Richard Garnett who completed the task of making the Reading Room fit for scholars. It would be a good precaution for they at least are certain to be acceptable as the two just men that will be necessary to save our poor, ragtime Sodom.

It is of course absurd to decry scholarship. Accuracy of mind and a certain erudition are as necessary to the imaginative writer as is native genius. But I was born in the days of the full desert breath of the terrible commercial scholarship of Victorian times. In those days it was sufficient to have prepared — say in Goettingen — a pamphlet

[1] Anthony Panizzi, the first Librarian of the British Museum to have left any mark and the friend of Prosper Merimée who published a volume called *Lettres à Panizzi*, was born in Brescia three years before the end of the eighteenth century and so carried to his task the classical tradition and the spirit of the last of the great centuries. He began the cataloguing of the Library, a task finished so brilliantly by the never sufficiently to be lamented Dr Garnett and, more important still, they bequeathed to the Reading Room that spirit of urbane serviceability that most gives to London the right to assert that she is a centre of civilization.

about 'Shorthand in the Days of Ben Jonson', 'Shakespeare's Insomnia, Its Cause and Cure' or 'A Tabulation of the Use of Until as Against That of Till in *Piers Plowman*' — and you were at once accorded the right to improve the prose of Daudet, correct the use of similes by Shakespeare and bury to the extent of a page to a line the poems of Chaucer and Arnaut Daniel beneath your intolerable annotations. . . . Those fellows must have done more to contribute to the barbarism of our day than all the brutalities of ten thousand big battalions thundering across a shuddering earth. For how can the English be civilized beings if they do not know the wisdom, the good-humour, the human instances of the *Knight's Tale* which is the supreme monument of the letters of our country? And yet how could any man who was a boy when I was a boy have any idea of what lay buried beneath those absolutely unreadable annotations as to Chaucer's employment of the Mittel-Hoch-Deutsch 'v' for the Greek digamma in dialect passages. . . . No, as Marwood used to say, we could not bear — for sheer boredom — to think of either Shakespeare or Christ because they had the faces, for us, of Fourth Form Masters. . . . You speak of the Lost Generation as having followed the War. Alas, it was us who were lost before ever Gemmenich heard the dawn-sound of guns. . . .

Obviously in the preparation, in the thinking out, of works of the imagination that can alone save humanity we must be fortified by erudition, if not by that of annotated books, then by that of Life. Neither Homer nor Catullus, nor yet Arnaut Daniel, Dante, Chaucer, Shakespeare, Mr Pound's friend, Confucius, or Doctor Johnson or Stendhal or Flaubert could have written their books unless they were masters of all the knowledge of their day or of how to use an encyclopaedia and to discount the newspaper accounts of current events. And the production of a great work, inspired by next-to-all knowledge and rendered beautiful by cadence, just wording, toleration, pity and impatience is the greatest benefit that humanity can confer on the Almighty. The one thing that can save a Sodom from its fate! . . .

★ ★ ★

In Avignon, on the other hand, almost all of life passes and has always passed in the open air. So you had the great school of Art in the time of the popes and the continued practice of the arts by almost the entire peasant population — a practice that has filled the churches of Provence with the thousands of little votive paintings that have had so great an influence on the living art of today. For, just as the writing of *conte-fables* has occupied the small trade- and craftsmen all over Provence ever since the days of the Troubadours, so painting, domestic architecture and sculpture in miniature have continued to be produced by small people in the small towns and hamlets all over Gallia Narbonensis, to this day.

That is a phenomenon very largely climatic; but it has also its social side. A peasantry that has seen its feudal lords engage in poetic contests and many of its sons ennobled because of their poetic gifts and that has seen painting and sculpture and painters and sculptors held in high honour in the courts of the sovereign spiritual director of the world will not look askance at the practitioners of those arts and so in Provence there arose and continued the tradition that occupation with one art or the other is a proper thing for sound men.

My house in Toulon has its rooms frescoed, very primitively, by the retired naval quartermaster who built it — himself and his wife, with their own hands, using a cement, said to be of their own manufacture, made from burning oyster-shells according to the Roman tradition and so hard that it will turn any cold chisel. How that may be — as far as the tradition of cement — I do not know — but there the pictures are: scenes of rural life, dovecotes, ponds, fish-stews, swans, wild-fowl, carp, small fish, men rowing boats, men fishing; all under the shadow of the great mountains that are in the Toulon hinterland and all amidst a profusion of leafage and flowers . . . And all a very charming decoration. . . .

Another room is decorated — I imagine by the wife alone, since the paintings are more traditional and she probably went to an art-school — with bouquets of flowers, only some of which are naïve, alive and charming, and all this having been done about 1890 or so.

But imagine an English retired naval quartermaster, in the suburbs of Portsmouth, building, along with his lady and with their own hands, a house of Roman cement, tiled with Roman S-shaped tiles . . . And then frescoing it! . . . Or, for the matter of that, what would be the emotion of an English or American ex-naval officer of high rank on learning that he had let one of his houses to a 'poet'? Yet, as I have elsewhere related, the first emotion of my landlord here in Provence when he had that news was to get into his car and drive a hundred and fifty miles to fetch me a root of asphodel.

Because all poets must have in their gardens that fabulous herb. . . .

And, if towards Christmas, I go out from my frescoed rooms, down into the town I shall pass near a village where they are performing their *pastorale* and at every street corner there will be booths where peasants will be offering for sale *saintons* such as their ancestors have made in these parts ever since the first Attic-Boeotian colonists came to these parts from the Oropos three thousand years ago and moulded from the red clay their Tanagra figures. Today the little images are there manufactured in honour of the Saviour and represent every condition of man and every craft, so that all humanity may be shewn standing before the *crêches* in the homes of the peasants and townsmen — fishermen with their nets, market-gardeners with their melons, vintners with their casks; white, yellow and black kings with their crowns to remind you of the Magi, and all standing or kneeling before the straw cradle of a little, pink, naked celluloid doll in a plaster of Paris stable. . . . You will not find the like of those *saintons* till you get to Mexico. There Indian peasant families have maintained the art for generations in their families and manufacture still such *saintons* as they learned to make at the points of the swords of the Conquistadores — the early Spaniards having brought the art from Barcelona and Aragon and Barcelonese and Aragonese having learnt the art from Provence at a time when Spain was part of Provence. Or Provence part of Spain, if you prefer it.

And if, on Christmas day, I go down to the harbour I shall see, lying in the sun beneath the exquisite caryatids of Puget on the Mairie and behind his incomparable 'Navigator' an 'oil-paintist'. He will have ranged beside him along the Mairie wall ten or a dozen panel-paintings. Not deathless masterpieces of course for he will be neither a Monticelli nor a Douanier Rousseau. But like those two, and lying contentedly in the sun, he will earn his years' bed and board by those sincere crudenesses and neither you nor the burgesses of the city need feel disgraced at having paid twenty-five francs for one or the other of them.

And up in the town you will find one who will write for you your letters in verse — in classical Alexandrines at thirty lines per half hour for ten sous a line . . . But he will ask more if you want more tricky metres.

The point is that, in Provence, the arts live, if hidden from Missouri then in the hearts of the people. And you cannot call it either a proletariat art or one induced from above, since it is the product of peasant-proprietors — and not of peasant-proprietors only. The sons of not too rich newspaper proprietors paint pictures; those of millionaire tanners write epics; naval officers paint water-colours from Cap Sète to Annam . . . and proud of it! . . . That is the point.

I do not say that the production of masterpieces is enormous; but the presence of the celluloid doll before the three-thousand-year descended *saintons* is a proof of how intimately the native arts enter into the real life of the people even today. They are a part of life as unnoticed as the daily bread, the prayers, the games of boules, the furniture and the Sunday bullfights.

★ ★ ★

And it is to be remembered that the motive of the artist was always sensual and never representational. He desired to give pleasure to the saint to whom his picture was addressed; to win with its prettiness one more smile from Ste Thérèse of the Roses in Heaven. It is unnecessary to record for her how the miraculous preservation looked. She was there. But you can add one more to her heavenly joys . . . and he, the painter, desired to add more beauties to the church in which his offering should be suspended.

It is that that has caused these works to have such a tremendous influence on the art of today.

Obviously the Avignon atelier drew inspiration from the Italian primitives of the fourteenth century so that they could continue and keep fresh a real art long after the gradually sophisticated Italians had abandoned the greatest of their traditions. For it was in the age of Raphael that the 'easel-picture' was invented and the *image* reached it quintessence and evolved its stultifying conventions and the ateliers of Avignon and Nice were at their most flourishing just between 1480 and 1520.

Those earlier painters, whether of Siena or Avignon, painted to adorn spaces. If it was their aim to aid religion it was far more their aim to exalt the mind of the onlooker . . . to create in him a religious frame of mind by letting him see what good inventions of beauty they could see in the world of God. And the idea of making portrait-images of the Virgin and Child or journalistic records of the Crucifixion never entered their minds. They painted to make churches glow and tired eyes be rested by the assured beauty and movements of their designs. That was Art.

It was also an intellectual feat. The intellect of plastic art manifests itself not in portraits of thinkers or in the portrayals of the blessings conferred on humanity by the applied sciences. It expresses itself in design and pattern and in the movement of the eye running from place to place on painted walls.

Aesthetically speaking, movement in a picture has nothing to do with the correct anatomical representation of a javelin thrower in action or of a lion in mid air springing on its prey. It consists in such inspiration of line, colour and mass that the confiding eye, coerced by the art of the painter, can let its glance meet the surface of a painting and be conveyed unerringly from place to place on that surface. That ocular progress is what causes aesthetic pleasure and emotion.

The quattrocentists and their predecessors back to the Byzantines treated the subjects on their wall-spaces exactly as composers treat their themes in abstract music. The — literally and only literally — meaningless contrapuntal passages of Bach are infinitely emotional and the cause of emotion — and they are much more mystically so than the most realistic programme-music founded on the most earnest and ingenious renderings of the snortings of dragons, Valkyrs or serpents. So the Virgins and Children of the primitive Italians or French, like the mosaics of the Byzantines, are no more presentations of sacred individuals than Bach's *Matthew Passion* is a representation of divine searchings of the soul. They are, as I have said, abstract variations on an aesthetic, given theme.

And there is as much movement in a Byzantine mosaic, a design of Cimabue, Giotto, Simone Martini, Quarton, Clouet or Fromentin, or of the Master of St Anne, the Unknown Master of Cologne, Cranach, El Greco, Poussin, Cézanne or Matisse — to name the whole apostolic succession — as in any of Bach's fugal writings. And as much thought as in any of the writings of Einstein.

* * *

Next day we were in a train, going South.

I ask to be regarded, from this moment, not as Moralist; nor as Historian; but simply as prophet. I am going to point out to this world what will happen to it if it does not take Provence of the XIII century for its model. For there seems to be a general — and universal — impression that our Civilization — if that is what you want to call it — is staggering to its end. And for the first time in my life I find myself in agreement with the world from China to Peru.

Do you happen to know Haydn's symphony? . . . It is a piece that begins with a full orchestra, each player having beside him a candle to light his score. They play that delicate cheerful-regretful music of an eighteenth century that was already certain of its doom . . . As they play on the contra-bassist takes his candle and on tiptoe steals out of the orchestra; then the flautist takes his candle and steals away . . . The music goes on — and the drum is gone, and the bassoon . . . and the hautbois, and the second . . . violin . . . Then they are all gone and it is dark. . . .

That is our Age . . . There have stolen away from us, unperceived, Faith and Courage; the belief in a sustaining Redeemer, in a sustaining anything; the Stage is gone, the Cinema is going, the belief in the Arts, in Altruism, in the Law of Supply and Demand, in Science, in the Destiny of our Races . . . In the machine itself . . . In Provence there is every Sunday a *Mise à mort* that is responsible for the death of six bulls. In the world outside it one immense bull that bears our destiny is at every hour of every day slowly and blindly staggering to its end.

★ ★ ★

In Provence the atmosphere has no obstacle to offer to the eye. In the bright sunshine your sight travels as far as it can carry. On my terrace looking over the sea I can see across the bay the windows in the chapel of the miraculous Virgin on top of Cap Cepet which is twenty miles away — and on the slopes of the mountain the shadows of the umbrella pines — The young as a rule do not see so well.

In Sussex the effect is reversed. Between you and the downs in the brightest sunlight there is the curtain of moist particles, bluish, drawn up by the sun. . . . The effect, to the eye used to Provence is to throw the downs back four or five miles — and then the tufts of small firs and the little, paintbrush yews, each throwing its defined shadow, exactly resemble the umbrella pines and tufts of lavender, thyme and rosemary of the Alpines. . . . You might indeed call that part of Sussex the Provence of England — but a Provence so fugitive. For this is a country where you are for ever, mechanically, cocking one eye at the sky and, in spite of yourself, your subconsciousness whispers inside you: 'It can't last!' . . . Always!

★ ★ ★

I don't, you understand, speak as a politician but merely as an observer of life. I don't care a bit whether Fascism or Communism of the Russian type eventually prevail in the Western World. But if Lenin had preferred to establish agricultural rather than industrial communities I should have been wholeheartedly in favour of them. The curses of humanity are not property but the sense of property, not War but the ill-nature and ignorance that lead to Wars. Both these evils would have been swept away by Christianity, that tide that, sweeping from the extreme eastern shores of the Mediterranean, carried along the Great Trade Route the stream of Graeco-Jewish altruism. . . . To the extreme limits of the habitable globe. Even Prussia was temporarily Christianized towards the end of the XVIIIth century. . . .

* * *

Faith, in short, died after the war — every sort of Faith and it is time to get back to life. . . . And Paris, curiously enough, is the one of the great cities — the one tract of land outside Provence and Burgundy which is her appanage — where closeness to life has been most tenaciously maintained. You get there the most and the best manual domesticity; the most tolerable cooking; the fewest canned goods and departmental stores; the most *petites industries* and non-machine craftsmanship. And above all — of course once more outside Provence and Burgundy — the most amazingly efficient market-gardening — which is the only way of innocently getting something for nothing, or for so little as makes no difference. . . . And considering the difficulties of her climate you might well say that that is the proudest feat of no mean city. . . .

* * *

It is, you see, all very confusing. But the principle that each countryside should produce only that for which it is most fitted and that such products should circulate freely through the world — preferably by barter — that principle is so blindingly clear that no human being can miss it . . . And the putting into practice of that principle must of necessity abolish wars since no country could dispense with the products of any other country . . . And then we should be back again to the manner of the Great Trade Route with the sacred and honest merchants travelling with their wares from tabu ground to ground . . . and civilizations flowing backwards and forwards from China to Peru . . . And all of us sitting gasping with admiration for the tales of other races that they brought back and at the films that also they should bring shewing the marvellous accomplishments, virtues, frugality and beauty of all the foreign parts of the great world . . . For I think that civilizations are better things to exchange than bombs containing poison gases and loathsome infections. . . .

After the bull-fight at Nîmes the crowd is so thick throughout the large and beautiful town that for minutes you cannot move. But after the matadors have passed from the arena gate to their *posada*, opposite, slowly and gravely, you are carried along the streets. We went, so pressed, down the broad, and as it were gradiloquent, avenue that leads from the Arena to the Bourse and the Theatre. It was impossible for any of us to converse . . . From time to time we could exchange a shouted word whilst all the time went up the words *mise à mort*; *mise à mort*; now no longer with the shouted gaiety of anticipation of the autobus but with the grave, savouring softness of those criticising and assaying what has passed . . . So we progressed as it were ritually, like Spanish women in black mantillas pigeon-stepping along the Rambla. . . .

The whole crowd at one moment stopped still. And in the silence my New York friend said from behind me into my ear:

'By Jove I should not like to be the woman that Lalanda wanted to put the comether on' . . . and added: 'But perhaps if I was a woman *I should*.' Then we all flowed on again. . . .

We were beneath and between trees and trees and trees and kiosques and shopfronts and sweet-stalls . . . And then slowly a large open space and, on high, in the centre of it . . . You know the tiny crescent of the moon, gleaming through a veil of orange, just born and wavering down to the horizon above the islands in a breathless night . . . It has that tranquillity . . . the *Maison Carrée* . . . That very tranquillity and the ineffable perfection of all the quiet words that were ever written by Sappho and Catullus. And whenever I see it I seem to be reading the words that seem to me the most beautiful in the world

ERAMEN MEN EGO SETHEN ATHI PALAI POTA

Or

TE SPECTEM SUPREMA MIHI QUUM VENERIT HORA

Or

Less than a God they said there could not dwell

Within the hollow of that shell
That spoke so sweetly and so well . . .

This is by way of being a testament and so, though I ask pardon, I take pleasure as it were in laying before the most beautiful building that was ever built what have all my life been for me the most beautiful words that were ever written or said.

And then the singular Destiny of Provence gave one of her enigmatic smiles . . . An automobile coming from behind our backs knocked down — before the very portals of that House — just under our faces and so that he actually touched one of our unfortunate American ladies, a poor old peasant. And there he lay dead . . . And she had never seen either the Maison Carrée or a dead man before . . . It was a queer way of what we used to call coming to the end of a perfect day . . . Queer. There is no other word for the destinies of this country and the manifestations they choose. . . .

I went down just now to see that the irrigation was turned on ready for the water when it comes. It is just after noon . . . Pan's hour . . . One ought not to go into one's garden in Pan's hour. On these absolutely still days you may well get sunstroke . . . And then . . . things are abroad.

And sure enough, descending, I had to step across the body of the great snake that I have not yet seen this year. His head was in one hedge and his tail in another. I suppose he knows my step for he was moving very slowly and did not hurry when I stepped carefully over him . . . I do not know what that omen means. The great snake is the attendant on Aesculapius, so I may soon have to go to a doctor. On the other hand he may be benevolent and his return may mean that I shall not have to call in Demoulin for a long time.

[London: Allen and Unwin, 1934; pp. 50–52, 91–3, 142–3, 149–50, 161, 166, 221–3, 233–7, 238–40, 261–2, 299, 304, 315–16, 362–5.]

from

Great Trade Route (1937)

I HAVE written so much on the ancient Great Trade Route proper that the reader may have come across some of those writings. In case he have not I had better put down what to me it means. To me in the first place it means a frame of mind to which, unless we return, our occidental civilization is doomed.

Less mysteriously, however, it was a broad swathe of territory running from East to West for the most part on the 40th parallel N. For, singular as it may seem, on the planisphere, Pekin and Washington and Samarkand and Constantinople are all exactly in line with one another. The route started then in Pekin, ran level to Constantinople, turned a little North above Greece to reach Venice and Genoa and to skirt the Mediterranean as far as the mouth of the Rhone. It turned north up that stream passing Lyons and then descended the Seine passing Paris. It left Paris still going North and reached the shores of the Channel at Calais. It crossed in dug outs and rafts to somewhere about Rye, West of Dover on the English South Coast, followed the coast, and reached according to legend and worked-out history, the country of King Arthur and the Land's End. As they could go no further the merchants and civilizers of the Great Route there turned back and returned to Pekin.

They had started from the site of that city laden with manufactured products of their looms and craftsmen, with fruits, spices, tools, jewels, treasure chests. The inhabitants of the countries and cities by which they passed laid out tabu grounds on which the Merchants bartered their goods for such indigenous products as they needed, and on their journeys between such bartering places they were protected by the strictest of tabus upheld by the native chiefs, headmen, priests, or elders. The tabu still exists in Polynesia. The word itself is Polynesian but in the days of the ancient Great Route the principle was of world wide observance.

In consequence you had running all across the Old World the age called Golden since all the desirable things of the life of that day were tabu. Thus there was neither occasion nor necessity for theft, murder for possession, chicanery, or any of the legalized crime by which today we possess ourselves of the goods, gear, and specie of our neighbours. The Sacred Merchants were at once civilizers, gift bringers, educators, and the trainers of priesthoods. How this all worked out you will read in the records of my meditations on the disappearance of the Merchants. . . . At odd places like Flemington, N. J., Paoli, Pa., Madeira, Monte Carlo, and elsewhere on the original route and its oval prolongation, we shall suddenly sit down and think. Now and then we shall go outside the Route itself to places like Geneva or New York so as to get it better into perspective.

What is certain is that our civilization — I am not talking of our ability to evolve and make others work machines — our civilization was born on the great Route and, in so far as our civilization has beauties and virtues it derives them from the Merchants and their pupils. You can put it that in so far as we are civilized beings — beings fitted to live the one beside the other without friction — it is because of the workings in our minds of that Chinese-Greek-Latin civilization's Mediterranean leaven. Where we Nordics are predatory, bloodthirsty, blind, reckless, and apt to go berserker, it is because we have in our veins the blood of peoples that, after or towards the end of the Age of the Sacred Merchants, were born, multiplied, and overpeopled the forests, swamps, and heaths to the North of the Great Route.

To get working ideas of things in the mind it is necessary to imagine a sort of pattern or map of things ascertained. From that we may make mental excursions in hypotheses into the realm of the unascertained. If those hypotheses in the course of further investigation are confirmed by data, they take their part in the pattern.

Let us then imagine as the basis of our original Route a sort of Mason and Dixon Line running in a great swathe round the world on or about the fortieth North parallel of latitude — the latitude of Washington, Constantinople, Samarkand, and Pekin. Let it be a fairly broad swathe extending, as far as we are immediately concerned as far south as Madeira in the old world and Florida in the new — and as far north, irregularly, as Turin, Geneva, Paris, and a thin strip along the south coast of England and as far north as New York City in the new one.

It is more than anything a swathe of equable climate rather than a geographical delimitation, a swathe of fertile land rather than a matter of races. It is above all a belt of the world in which men tend to be distinguished by equanimity of mind, frugality, and moderation rather than by huge appetites, crowd massacres, and efficiency. It is in short the tract of land that produced Jesus — or if you prefer it, the Rabbi Hillel — rather than that which produced Calvin.

Or, to drive the matter home, it is the part of the world for whose inhabitants the life motto is: 'Sit comes non dux voluptas.'

LET COMFORT BE YOUR COMPANION NOT YOUR LEADER

* * *

The Great Trade Route began its course, then, in Cathay and for the beginnings of its stretch ran perforce inland. You imagine it starting in the market of Pekin where they made beautiful, intricate and improbable, stuffs, gadgets, perfumes, bales of sweet herbs, painted furnishings, cloth of gold, lacquer chests, teas, silks, porcelains. Swords, even, for protection from the mountain tigers. The Chinese have always despised soldiers and soldiering as being more contemptible than the slaughtering of domestic cattle but they will let you kill wild beasts. The immense caravans set out, whole holy cities at a time, to spread the sweetness of herbs, the softness of silks and ritual and cults and the arts of lacquering and the dance before altars. — Up the course of the Hoang Ho it went, through the plains of Lob Nor and the Ta Rim, through Chinese Turkestan, north of the Pamirs and the roof of the world to Samarkand, and through the gap at Herat and past Ispahan to Moussoul and Aleppo and Damascus. And then to the sea-shore which from then on they skirted.

Dropping ivory, gold, apes, and peacocks for the predecessors of Solomon they went round the shores of Asia Minor to Smyrna and Constantinople; they crossed the Bosphorus on great rafts, went across Greece, skirted the Adriatic to Venice, crosssed Italy to Genoa, went along the coasts of the Italian and French Rivieras up the Rhone to Burgundy and Paris; down the Seine to the Channel. And so, across the Channel at its narrowest; along the South coast of England to Cornwall and the Court of Arthur. They passed lifetimes passing backwards and forwards. Where they went they left civilizations — the ancient civilizations of the resounding and romantic names — Samarkand and Ispahan and Trebizond and Damascus and Venice and Paris and Tintagel. And their traces remain for ever since it is to them that we owe our arts, our cults, our thought and what is left to us of the love of peace and sunshine. . . .

There was once a Golden Age when all humanity combined to stave off barbarism and to shut the lust for lucre up in northern forests. Humanity has been running for millions of years. There is nothing to wonder at that civilizations wiser and richer than ours should have been swallowed up behind the veils of the years, leaving us nothing but the echoes of traditions and a faint hope of once again leaving behind us legends shining with gold and peacocks. That is really our task.

And to set about it we have to jettison most of what we regard as precious. We have to consider that we are humanity at almost its lowest ebb since we are humanity almost without mastery over its fate.

* * *

It is a good legend [the story of the Holy Maries and the gipsies]. Just as impressionist art tells things more truly than photographs, so such a story reveals the true history of the earth far more truly than it can ever be revealed by the scientific historian. For nothing is more invariable in the course of history than that when new faiths seep into and over-run countries the priests of the old faiths fall into poverty and disrepute. But the ancient tenets remain strongly in the memory of the peoples; almost to the end of time, traces of the earlier religion remain inextricably mixed in with the faiths that have become fashionable. And the priests of the older faith are reputed to retain mysterious gifts that have never descended to the clergy who have succeeded them in their cures. In rural England if the country people have occasion to have a ghost laid they will call in thirteen Anglican clergymen to pronounce exorcisms. But if that fails they call in a Roman priest and at the first shower of his holy water, they will tell you, the unhappy spirit is laid at rest for ever. Or in Latin Catholic countries if the holy water of the priest fails to keep the murrain from flocks they will first have the shepherds — who from their continually remaining solitary with their sheep are acquainted with the old dispossessed Gods that still haunt mistletoed oak groves — will first have the shepherds perform incantations that the Church forbids. Then they will have the gipsies do things with twisted twigs of hazel called *patterans*. After that, so they say, the murrain will certainly leave their beasts. . . . And have we not all lately seen how the Germans, first extirpated the Jews because they slew the Saviour of Humanity, and, then, finding that their financial credit was not thus to be established, fell upon the priests and re-established the cult of Wodin and Thor, who they say flourished in and produced, the

Heroic-Bloodsplashed Age from the Lueneberger Heide to the Teutoburger Wald.

It is thus always, in the minds of the people, that Old Gods preside over fortunate and vanished times, the 'our day' of succeeding generations growing steadily more and more hard. King Arthur and his knights sleep in one cave awaiting the call; Charlemagne and his paladins sit in another, their beards growing through the table beneath them; I have heard peasants in Germany say that nothing will be well till der Alte comes again, only der Alte is so fast asleep — the Old One being Bismarck whom I remember to have seen walking along the Poppelsdorfer Allée, after his fall, his head dejected and his great hound dejected also, following him, his immense dewlaps almost touching his master's heel. . . . Thus in one life-time of a man a solar myth of an age of gold has developed itself. . . . In a country that has surely been sorely tried.

* * *

Theft in those days had not been invented, nor yet metals. Gold was so used for ornament that that was known as the golden age. So, the last sleds of the great caravan that had continually been passing, began to approach after a day or rather more. The merchants loaded up their own sleds with such food and perishable articles as they had taken and fell in in the rear. The permanent things — the amber, agates, sharks' teeth, sea-ivory, jars of wine that kept well — they cached in the tabu ground where they would remain until they came again, going, after years, homewards. They would leave behind an instructor in the use of those tools they left and in the making and ornamenting of the stuffs and of how most fittingly to worship the supreme Principle. When they came again, if the villagers had shewn themselves apt craftsmen, they would be pleased and leave them gifts from the lands that King Arthur afterwards ruled over.

Their teachings may today be read in the *Chou-King* which is a compilation of the most ancient examples of moral and political wisdom of ancient East, made by Confucius.

I came this morning in another sort of compilation on an example of moral and political wisdom that has kept me pleased all day.

Sir Walter Raleigh was telling Lord Chancellor Bacon, who was a grafter compared with whom many of our overlords today were mere beginners, how he planned certainly to enrich his sovereign James VI of Scotland and I of England. The country was at peace with Spain, after the days of the sack of Cadiz and the Armada. Nevertheless, said Raleigh who was preparing to set out on his last expedition to the Indies, if he failed to find the famous and fabled gold mine on the Orinoco that he purposed finding, he intended to set about the Spanish treasure ships in returning, and so to lay at the feet of the Scottish Solomon wealth surpassing that of the Golcondas.

Lord Bacon, expressing the utmost horror, exclaimed that that would be the rankest piracy. In those days James was seeking to curry favour with the king of Spain and it was death, as Raleigh afterwards found, to tamper with that king's subjects . . . 'The rankest piracy', said the Lord Chancellor.

But no, Raleigh answered, if you take millions it is not piracy.

§

And with that speech Raleigh withdrew the curtain that concealed the New World from the Old. . . . I don't mean the Western from the Eastern Hemisphere; I mean the millions of years that had preceded from the three centuries that have since lapsed. He had prophesied Mass Production. . . . And, as a corollary, looking at his kettle lid he prophesied . . . say television. Or if there is anything later, say that.

But the second discovery is a very minor affair. The Machine itself is a stupid Moloch; it is the stealing-a-million-isn't-piracy psychology, the gradually evolved mentality of the Technocrat of Mount Kisco at Christmas, that has brought about our ruin. . . . That psychology behind the Machine. We appear, as a civilization, to be about to go down in flames. The immediate cause seems to be that our Italian kinsmen think that, sheltered behind the Machine, they will be able to do what no other race ever accomplished . . . steal millions with impunity from Africa. It can't be done.

§

The partition of Africa which went on between 1882 and 1914 was the occasion of what happened in that latter year . . . and ever since.

§

I am not trying to draw down your reprobation on the descendants of Q. Fabius Maximus. They played in their day their beautiful, massacring, martyred role on the Great Route. You cannot much blame them if naïvely they now think they should have their share in the heritage of Raleigh. They are a little late, that's all. . . . It is true that they it was who began the partition of Africa.[1] That only proves how fully in sympathy they are with our modern spirit.

§

This partition of a continent from whose results we have for so long been suffering is, when it is tabulated, an amazing instance of an afflatus that, arising no one much knows why, spreads with an amazing rapidity half across a world. No one knows why Italy

[1] The salient dates of this partition are as follows:

1883 March 15. Italy occupies part of the sea-shore territory of Aussa on the Red Sea . . . by 'agreement' with petty sultan.

1883 A fortnight later, a Bremen merchant called Luederitz obtained a similar cession of territory on the Orange River from a South African native.

1883 June 13. French occupied Tamatane in Madagascar.

Feb. 1884 Great Britain assumes control of foreign affairs of Transvaal.

May 1884 Great Britain establishes protectorate over territory N. of Transvaal to 20°S.

June 1884 London conference between Gt. Britain and France ref. partition of Egypt. Abortive.

July 1884 Germany establishes protectorate over Togoland.

July 1884 Germany establishes protectorate over Cameroons.

Nov. 1884 Germany establishes protectorate ultimating in German E. Africa.

Dec. 1884 Great Britain annexes St Lucia Bay.

Jan. 1885 Spain announces protectorate over part of W. coast of Africa.

Feb. 1885 Berlin Conference recognizes possession of Congo region by trading association of Leopold II of Belgium.

Feb. 1885 Portugal receives compensation on the Congo for recognizing rights of Leopold II.

Feb. 1885 Khartoum taken by Mahdi. Gordon killed.

Mar. 1885 London lends £9,000,000 sterling to Egypt.

Apr. 1885 German S. W. Africa Co. given rights of sovereignty.

Oct. 1885 Turko-British convention ref. Partition of Egypt.

Dec. 1885 Foreign relations of Madagascar placed under control of France.

These are the happenings of only the first three years of the Partition. But these million-stealings went on as thickly with the usual fallings out of the thieves right up to the Turkish War of 1913 and into the shadow of Armageddon. In March 1896 France annexed Madagascar; and the Italians were wiped out of existence by Menelik in Abyssinia. In June '98 the Fashoda Incident set Great Britain and France within an inch of War. In October '99 the Transvaal invaded the British South African possessions. The war lasted three years and a half. In 1911 for several months France and Germany, at Agadir, were within an inch of War over Morocco. Under cover of that tension Italy declared war on Turkey with the intention of annexing Turkish N. Africa. This led directly to the first and second Balkan Wars of 1912 & 13 . . . And those wars, by bottling up Germany from the Near East, led directly to her invasion of Belgium in 1914.

should in 1883 have suddenly taken it into her head to imitate her ancestors of the Punic War. But once the country of St Francis of the Birds had shewn the way, every inhabitant of every country anywhere within reach of the poor Dark Continent seemed suddenly to be visited by a new and blinding revelation. It became obvious to each such man that he could only fulfil his Imperial destiny, properly worship his God, sleep sound at night, and wallow in prosperity, if his government went on one or other billion-stealing expedition amongst dark-skinned peoples. Nor indeed was the mania restricted to the Old World. Imperial adventures are opposed to the American tradition and suspect to the better sort of inhabitants of the republic. But by 1893 America was already in the game. A U.S. 'reform party' in Hawaii, called in U.S. marines, deposed the queen and succeeded in getting an annexation treaty signed at Washington. . . . And several times during the decade the United States was within an inch of war with Germany . . . over Samoa. It is difficult to imagine anything more fantastic.

§

Afflati of that sort run across the world, the world for no ascertainable reason being suddenly ripe for them as it gets at other times ready to be decimated by plagues. You will have suddenly Buddhism, Christianity, Mahometanism, Platonism, Aristotelianism, Renaissances of Helleno-Latinity, spirits of the Crusades, of chivalry . . . *I pray thee Sir Lancelot that thou come again to this Land* . . . of anti-chivalry. For a couple of centuries or more you had the whole Old World in a state of unease at the idea of passage to the West towards an India that should be billion-robbed. It was succeeded by Cortez-Pisarrism. A hundred years after Columbus even Anglo-Saxondom took courage and you had Raleighism which was the meanest kind of million-stealing, tacked oddly enough onto a kind of murderous Small Producerism. It exported unfortunate people who were to take from the natives not only their gold ornaments but their very food. It is at any rate a comment on the relative mental activity of the Mediterranean peoples and us Nordics that the first colony of Spain should have been founded on the Island of Hayti and called Novidad in 1493, whereas the abortive Roanoke Island attempt of Raleigh should not have been made till 1585. Virginia Dare founded the F.F.V. two years later. Her fate is not known.

§

Let us agree to set down as part of our pattern that the wheelless New World of pre-Cortez and Raleigh days was a near-earthly paradise. It remained over after the Old World's Golden Age had succumbed to one inventor or another. . . . There is this note to be made: on the island of the Madeiran archipelago that is nearest to Africa a primitive form of wheel is used in carts and ploughs. The island is Porto Santo. It is there that Columbus is said to have married and got his Atlantic lore. The geological formation of Porto Santo is African; that of Madeira proper is American. (Geologically considered America is older than Europe.) And in between the two islands the sea runs two miles deep. So let us consider that there is the parting of the ways and that it was Europeans rather than Amerindians or other Westerns who first used wheels.

And let us consider also that the Wheel is the fruit of the tree of evil. . . . Just consider how satisfactory the world would become if, for a year wheels lost the property of turning. . . . Think how the atmosphere of Pittsburgh would be improved. . . . And of the satisfaction in Ethiopia. Well, you can think all that out for yourself. . . . We shall be in Pennsylvania soon enough. . . . Before then we must think out some means of restoring the World to the Golden Age. . . . Or of restoring the Age to the World.

§

We are perhaps nearer to that than you think. . . .

We are all sick of today. There is none of us that is not. We are all waiting for a new revelation. We are all certain that our Age — that of the Wheel — is wrong. We are all dreaming, whether at Geneva or at Baton Rouge, of a New Order when Lancelot may come again to this oval realm. The soil is ready, and History is waiting to repeat itself.

§

There is nothing History likes better.

We are today in the exact situation of the inhabitants of the world before the Deluge. That cataclysm is a few hours off. It will submerge us like a wave. When it has passed there will be very few of us left. It does not matter whether God shall assail us with water, for our sins, or whether we shall, to the greater glory of Science, murder with wheel-byproducts . . . nearly everyone of us murdering nearly everyone else. There will be almost none of us left. . . . Half a dozen in Schenectady; a hundred in the delightful little Delaware-Maryland-Virginia peninsula that I hope we may get to before we are done. A few thousand will be in the Azores, the Madeiras, in Ceuta, Algeciras, the Saintes Maries, Diana Marino, Asia Minor, Herat . . . on the Hoang Ho. . . . Then round the world, re-emerging from the clouds of poison gas, will go an afflatus. Suddenly it shall be manifest to us what we must do to be saved. History will have repeated itself.

§

Just so, after the last Deluge — the one that destroyed the unfinished Palace of the Nations, not at Geneva, but at Babel — an afflatus — an immense Will went round the fortieth parallel of latitude. The former Mason and Dixon Line re-established itself. (We Nordics had naturally, with our efficiency, completely eradicated ourselves . . . then, as tomorrow we shall.)

That immense Will kept humanity to the decencies, not by Laws but by custumals. If you like it was the product of thousands of years of pre-deluvian experience. If you prefer, it was the manifestation of innocence. No one desired to harm anyone else because the world needed all its man-power; no one desired to dispossess anyone else because there were too many possessions. . . . As if four people had been turned loose in an empty Macy's and told to help themselves.

In other words, there is no imaginable reason why in a world of softly equable climate and fertile soil with no excess of population, the idea of murder as the chief, if not the sole means to wealth should ever have been born.

§

What we need is before all to realize that there are *no* short cuts in the world.

§

The brand of Cain was set on a brow tortured by jealousy, not by covetousness, and the sons of Noah had all their possessions in common. Yet today, it is not merely in New York that the only road to Utopia seems to be attainable by setting millions of people up against a wall.

'. . . There are sixteen million Jews in the United States, said the Technocrat.

. . . *That's* a problem said Dreiser.

. . . Set 'em up against a wall, said the Technocrat.'

You will hear that conversation going on on Mont Blanc as on Mount Kisco; in Tokio as in Buenos Aires. Therefore I beseech thee, Sir Lancelot, that thou return again into this realm. . . . . .

For unless something of the sort happens, unless some Arthur and his Paladins return, I do not see how this universal wave — this Deluge — of bloodthirstiness can do anything but return us to the Dark Ages.

★ ★ ★

We are told by one set of authorities that the movements of the priest in the Holy Ceremony of the Mass represent the journeys made by the Redeemer in His passage through the world; when the officiant prays to the right he is expressing Christ's submission to the elders in the Temple, when he moves to the left to read the Gospels that represents the journey into Galilee; other authorities assert that the mass is the dance that David danced before the ark of the tabernacle. No doubt both are right. What matters to me is that you should observe that, whether these rituals originated on the one hand in the Pamirs, or, in the other, on the plains of the Hoang-ho, one cult must at one time have embraced all the peoples of that swathe that went from Cathay to the Cassiterides and that Augustine was right enough when he said that the Christian religion had existed and come down from times infinitely beyond the memory of man.

★ ★ ★

In this second part of this book I am, as I threatened to be, more interested in agriculture and handicrafts than in anything else, but a few words as to the relationships of the early colonists with the lawful owners of the soil may not be amiss.

The odd thing was that the colonists regarded the Indians as actually the owners of the forests, plains, and rivers that they coveted. The Indians themselves had apparently no such pretensions. They seem to have considered themselves much as do the inhabitants of common land in England to this day. They claimed to roam the country at will and unhindered, to take game, pelts, fish, and firewood unimpeded and to squat temporarily where and for as long as they liked. It seems never to have occurred to them that they or anyone else could contemplate owning the soil from the peak of the heavens to the centre of the earth, as the saying is. So that what they regarded themselves as selling when they received an all-wool overcoat — which for the colonist was taken to be a respectable price for the fee simple of 600 acres of ploughland — what the Indians regarded themselves as selling was the right to roam like themselves and get what good could be gotten of their hunting grounds. The colonists were grotesquely incompetent at woodlore, fishing, or fur-taking so the Indians may well have believed that what they sold had been overpaid.

§

It would be as well to consider that, in the seventeenth century, even the Indians of the Southern States were much more satisfactorily civilized than the settlers. They were men leading a life that satisfied them and one that was adapted to the country in which they lived. They were obedient to laws evolved by custom; they were hardy, frugal, had arts and crafts suited to the manner of their lives and, what was very important, they were not overcrowded. Above all the sense of impersonal property was almost undeveloped among them. Very few of their languages had any word at all for real estate; and the idea of controlling goods, gear, or land in their absence, on the other side of the continent, would have seemed as humorously grotesque to them as to us would be the idea of claiming to dispose of property in the planet Mars. At most, certain very prescriptive rights to territories in which they were accustomed to fish, hunt and trap were vaguely claimed and more vaguely accorded by one sept and its relatives or another. Property that was under their eyes or fingers, in their individual wigwams or on their or their wives' backs was as far as they went.

They were in fact a relatively little degenerated populace of descendants from the people of our Golden Age. They came, as did the peoples of the four great empires of the Southern portion of the Continent, originally from Cathay.

§

In addition their skill in warfare was infinitely superior to that of the colonists. If that branch of human activities is to be taken as a department of civilization it was a case of the redskins first and the rest nowhere. So, had they not been essentially a humane and hospitable people, the unfortunate settlers could never have effected any lodgment at all on the eastern shore of North America. Their arms of the latter were totally unsuited to the country, their eyesight dull, their mobility as grotesque as that of the tortoise. If someone held an Indian still they could stick — a certainly sharp — knife into him or, if he consented to stand motionless for long enough, at the third or fourth discharge they might hit him with a ball from a grotesque musquetoon, swivelled on to the top of a post.

Occasionally the settlers could massacre women and children by penalties; you hung children for stealing rolls of bread and burned in untellable numbers those who took views opposite from your own as to the manner of the conception of the mother of your Saviour. If you retain any moral doubt as to the respective cruelties of the Indian and European nations of those days, read the letters of the tender poet Spenser as to the treatment of Irish captives in the days of the Governorship of the first man to send settlers to Virginia . . . Nay, so strong in Anglo-Saxondom is the hold of the idea that property is more valuable than human beings, that as late as 1886, in the first official biography of Lincoln, the respectable authors — one of whom was John Hay, who in other ways deserved well enough of the world — the authors, then, find it not unnatural that the first settlers in Kentucky executed men for stealing horses or cattle whilst murders as a rule went unpunished. A horse or an ox was a rare necessity; men were all too common.

It is a noteworthy pendant that after the massacre at Bad Axe in the war of 1831 the aged fallen chief Black Hawk when carried in triumph to Washington said to President Jackson, true to the spirit of his ancestors: 'You cannot sell land'. . . . Because they forbade him to visit the tomb of his daughter which lay in ground that they professed to have bought and that he denied having sold.

Lincoln himself served as a volunteer in that war and it is suggestive to remember that in his proclamation at the opening of the Civil War he uses identically the same argument as did the old chief he helped to subdue.[1]

§

The successive encroachments of the whites on the Indians may be typified by the legends of the Smith-Pocahontas-Rolfe type in the earlier seventeenth century and by the gradual evolution of the settlers' methods of warfare until, abandoning the false security that armour gave them, they developed methods of scouting that, as had been the case with their agriculture, they had learned from the Indians. So was evolved the type of Virginia mountaineer whose

[1] *Black Hawk to President Jackson*: 'I am a man; you are another. I did not expect to conquer the white people. I took up the hatchet *to avenge injuries no longer to be endured* . . . I say no more; all is known to you.'
Lincoln to Troops: 'I call to you to redress wrongs already long enough endured.'
It is singular how few arguments are to be found when you are about to take a sword and dror it.

methods of warfare were to prove so fatal to regular soldiers for many centuries. Finally, in the war of 1914–1918 it became the orthodox 'tactics in advance' for all the armies in the field — one more instance of education of a sort travelling backwards along the fortieth parallel.[1]

* * *

Like the Giant Antaeus, who preceded Mithras by a hundred thousand years, our civilization needs contact with the earth for its renewal if it is to be renewed. This has been said so often that no one believes it much. . . . But that we shall either return or be returned to the earth is for all us nations inevitable. Our civilization cannot escape the lot of all the proud civilizations that have preceded us. It is for us to decide whether our return shall be merely an Antaean retouching of the earth to regain strength or whether it shall be cataclysmic — a be-panicked *sauve qui peut* after world-disaster.

In either case it shall be the hut nestling beside the manor that shall be the last to go and the first to return. If we have already chosen the better portion we shall long have had our huts. Returned to our beanrows we shall begin once more building up our proud civilizations. Our predecessors did that after the Fall of Rome: that is why we are here.

The marvellous human brain has discovered how we may fly in the face of God and from the empyrean destroy our fellows by the million. But, fagged out, that brain has flinched before the task of finding out how a machine that can do the work of ten thousand men under the inspection of one man alone can be got to find employment for the nine thousand, nine hundred and ninety-nine that it has dispossessed. Still less has that poor tired thing been able to devise how to prevent us or our neighbours from razing off the earth all our

[1] I had the interesting experience during the late war of commanding in France, though not actually in the trenches, a couple of battalions of French Canadians. These included rather more than two hundred American Indians, mostly, as far as I can remember, Algonquins. They differed from the white troops in being rather remarkably good in discipline, in being noticeably poor shots, but in having a faculty for disappearance when scouting in No Man's Land that appeared almost miraculous. As far as I could check, only two of them were killed whilst actually scouting — except of course by barrages. It is interesting to note that the Japanese serving in the same regiments had almost exactly the same characteristics, except that they were noticeably better shots.

cities with their populations. So that the tired brain of the architect of today has still more to tire itself over devising cellars — into which populations skilled in the use of gas masks — and of nothing else — may at any moment retire.

When they re-emerge there will be nothing for them but to set unskilfully to scratching a subsistence from a soil of rubble from the fallen buildings. But if they have a little kitchen-garden skill and the earth round their cities is in good shape for intensive culture they will have a chance of survival. They can have no other. . . . Or the ruin of our empires will come from civil strife. The end will be the same.

It would be better to achieve that end without the orgies of destruction and the settings up against walls that are so dear to our Technocrats. Our mechanical civilization seems to be crumbling beneath its own weight. It is impossible to escape the conviction that we are in a world of weakening pulses; our intelligences are enfeebled by the blood supplied to our brains by artificially grown, chemically fertilized and preserved foods. And even if our civilization could continue in spite of our degeneration, the problem of the machine dispossessing the worker must grow more and more acute between — and then within — nation and nation.

⋆ ⋆ ⋆

I think I can say — but I *can* say — that never since I was a child have I had a sense even of property of my own. Certainly I never had any sense of impersonal property. I was once left some brewery shares; but the brewery one day by accident mixed arsenic instead of sugar with its malt. So those shares disappeared and I was left with a sense of having some responsibility for quite a number of deaths. . . . Years ago, going into my own — my very own — kitchen in London at night after the cook had gone to bed, suddenly I was like someone struck dumb with amazement. It had occurred to me that I — and no one else — owned that prodigious array of copper stew-pans, basters, flour dredgers, pastry boards . . . a perfect wilderness of things. Like an armoury!

They were my own. I could do what I liked with them. . . . Hug them to my breast; throw them out of the window; decree that they should be melted down; have them all tied on a rope and drag them behind my Studebaker. And I burst into roars of laughter.

I had never thought about them before; or, if my subconscious had, it had imagined them belonging to the cook or anybody else.

Just a sort of public property that happened to have floated into my kitchen. That was nice of it. Because, if you will permit me to say so, my cook was a damn good cook, and she probably would not have been able to do without her apparatus.

And, when I came to think of it, that was my attitude towards every other room in the house — except the book room and the drawer in which I kept my ties, collar studs, and socks. If you had come in and asked me for the wash hand stand, or the dining table I should have said: Take them. Or I should certainly have been ashamed of myself if I hadn't. Even with regard to the books it was not a sense of property. If you had wanted my books you could have had them on condition that you took whole rows, not a volume here or there so that there would be gaps making the remaining books lean up the one against the other . . . for in that case I should go on hitching and fitching for days until I had got other books to fill in the gaps. . . . And then I should go to some friendly carpenter and ask for some wood and knock a washing stand or a table together somehow. I have indeed so often done that, one person and another having gone off with all I possessed, that I cannot any longer remember possessing anything.

I usually write in my home in Provence at an extraordinarily knocked together table with flanking shelves of walnut bed-panels, supported by sawn off chair legs and above me an immense deal shelf supported in turn by sawn off broom handles and nobody is more contented than I or prouder of his atelier. And when neighbours come in and I shew them my contrivance they say: *Tiens, mais vous avez du goût!* as if it surprised them. . . . And sometimes when I shut my eyes and think of my own personal Utopia I imagine myself in a whitewood hut on one of the harsh, bare, sunbaked hillsides of Provence . . . with of course a great black cypress for shade. And nothing in it but a camp bed and a table made out of a bully beef case and a chair made out of two — and an earthenware casserole for boiling or frying and a camp oven which I should build myself outside, for baking or roasting. That I think would be civilization.

* * *

The millionaire cannot exist without mass-production; men cannot exist with mass-production — and remain men. But what is necessary is not the extinction of the millionaire by sociological expedients. What is necessary is such a change of the public heart that the accumulation of immense wealth shall be universally regarded as being as shameful as any other unmentionable sin. Men will then cease to wish for great, sudden wealth and the motive for mass production will be gone. Then we can begin to think of civilization.

§

Do you happen to know Wood River, Ohio? I don't suppose anyone does. It is a junction of oil pipe lines. Under a perpetual stink of mephitic, bluish vapours men there live in a landscape completely of metal, pipes, tubes, containers, poles for wires in an endless complexity, rusted and abandoned boilers, rusted and abandoned tin lizzies, vast piles of cans. There is not a tree for miles, not a blade of grass. The caption for the publicity poster of this world centre runs: 'Here Indians roamed, birds nested, flowers grew before civilization came.'

Near Wood River they are enclosing a tract of thirty square miles to make a State reservation. Because it contains the only stand of white pine left in the State.

⋆ ⋆ ⋆

It is not that honest men are lacking in our ranks; it is that, outside perhaps England, which has a peculiar political genius all its own, honest men have absolutely no chance of making their voices heard or their influences felt. There is in no country — not even in France — a press of any importance that will voice the honest man, since the presses of all countries, for reasons of mere economy, speak in the interests of the interests that capitalize them. And inevitably, 'interests' cannot be honest. The vastness of the sums of money that are today involved; the tendency of humanity to say, that, if you rob in millions it is not robbery; the temptation to tell yourself that if you obtain power over millions of your compatriots you will exert your power for good . . . all these things weigh too heavy in the balance. And most fatal of all, all our electorates without exception, are forced to vote not for measures but for men. And to appeal to electorates so vast, politicians, to be successful, must employ methods that are fatal to their own self-respect and to their own senses of honesty. The gentleman who supplied rotten pipes and chains to the public buildings of his state was, in his own eyes an honest, easy-going citizen who expected if anything your applause; the lawyer who went in public to extremes of taste in defense of his client was at home a cultured and severe citizen; the Reformers were undoubtedly sincere in desiring reforms of abuses in their city, yet to ensure the return of their spokesman they must needs buy the suffrages of the most unpleasant and corrupt inhabitants of their city. To indulge in a political career is in short to have your sensibility deflowered and your morality blunted by continual compromise. Yet it is in such a condition that you take on the very awful responsibility of ruling for a time over vast numbers of your fellow citizens, your compatriots or mankind. I have consorted with politicians a good deal more or less accidentally in the course of my life and I have yet to hear one of them utter in private life concerning their public functions a single sentence shewing the least elevation of views or the least altruistic concern for the welfare or happiness of their constituents. . . . On the hustings of course it was different.

★ ★ ★

Let us begin at once by saying that it is abhorrent that one human being should be the property of another. Let us even premise that it is a natural abhorrence such as all created beings feel for the excrement of their species or all human beings for the reptiles that crawl upon their bellies. That is perhaps going too far since by all the great civilizations of the past slavery was regarded with equanimity. But let us concede it, for our space grows short. Or let us say that Humanity since then has developed a different moral sense. Or let us say merely that Humanity shudders — as I really do — at the thought of the incurable wound to the body politic that is caused whenever one race enslaves another.

There is a point on one of the inextricable tangle of country roads in Tennessee where, whenever I have passed it a voice seems to say:

'Here speaks the Nemesis of Africa.'

For, whatever you believe or disbelieve in the Hebraic compilation that we call Holy Writ, guard yourself from shaking off the belief that God visits the sins of the children unto the third and fourth generation; and if there were no God the effects would be the same. . . .

★ ★ ★

For do not believe that the murders called wars are ever 'gotten over'. They remain curses for ever both for him that murders and to eternal generations of the children of the murdered. The one is accursed by prosperity in sin that time shall fully avenge; the other is accursed by a bitterness that will prove an unending drag on his civilization. And round them all the world is cursed.

⋆ ⋆ ⋆

The last time I came through the Straits of Gibraltar — in the enjoyable, vanished, white *Providence* of the Fabre line, the ship hove to off the Rock. And I got infinite joy watching for hours, in the completely lucid water that was lit up by the reflection of the sunshine from the white sand of the bottom . . . watching the innumerable dolphins that drifted in shoals round and round the ship, hanging in space, and then dived clean under the keel and round and round again.

It was, because the rays darted upwards and gilded the forms of those graceful, fishlike beasts, a spectacle so engrossing that I completely forgot Rock, Peninsula, and Continent and spent the greater part of my stay hanging over the side of the vessel — forgetting not only my own troubles of which I had a peck but also those of a world that had more than sufficient.

The dolphin is a slim elegant creature. Seen from the side its profile resembles that of the saw-fish but with the snout much less developed. Like the puma it is the friend of man and is said to be obedient to him when soothed by music. But it in no way resembles the creature that, in the paintings of the ancients and the Italian Renaissance, carried Arion over the waves on mural decorations, heraldic devices, and fountains. That stylised beast has an enormous and protuberant forehead that swells until it embraces the whole of the body from the blubber lips that resemble a *retroussé* nose to the forked tail. If that is like anything it resembles the porpoise — the despised beast that is called by the French *marsouin* after the Germans' *meeres-Schwein* — sea hog. . . . And whereas the dolphin glides elegantly through the water the porpoise rolls on the waves with the motions of an intoxicated sailor. It pays no attention to music and is in no sense the friend of man except that its hide provides completely water-tight boots. I had a pair made by the village cobbler at Bonnington in 1903 and wore them on every wet day after that, right through the war, in landscapes swimming with mud and they were still going and completely water-tight on the feet of my batman long after the World had been made unfit for War. . . . Alas. . . .

⋆ ⋆ ⋆

I believe that the infinite multiplication of small units of populations alone can save the world. . . . The whole united in such an immense Zollverein or Customs Union that there won't be any more customs duties anywhere . . . and only custumals instead of laws and only world conscience to influence the trend of custumals.

* * *

It wasn't a new thought to me — that the medieval serf was better off than the industrial worker of that day. I was pretty convinced of it. Or that even the negro slave was. You were valuable cattle. It is abhorrent that one man should be the property of another — spiritually degrading. . . . But if you have to waste your whole mind on agonies at being out of work or on agonies at the thought that tomorrow you may be out of work — with all the concomitant agonies for your dependants — it does not seem to me that you are spiritually better off than serf or slave. . . . And it could not be very good for the world if it succeeded in breeding men who were indifferent to those conditions.

§

I don't write as a communist — or that may possibly be reactionary. . . . I don't care. I write rather as a man who should go along a road and see some sheep over the hedge who were not doing well. . . . And I should go to the farmer and suggest his throwing a little sorghum cake on the meadow morning and evening. The cake would increase the nitrates in the dung; and the improved dung would help the grass in the meadow . . . And so on. . . . Talking like that.

[London: Allen and Unwin, 1937: pp. 28–30, 87–9, 98–9, 102–08, 119–20, 137–41, 172–3, 206–07, 214, 220–21, 318–19, 339, 366–7, 385, 395.]

V

Art Criticism

from

Hans Holbein the Younger (1905)

Ford wrote three critical monographs on painters and painting for the Duckworth 'Popular Library of Art' series — *Rossetti* (1902), *Hans Holbein the Younger* and *The Pre-Raphaelite Brotherhood* (1907).

HOLBEIN'S lords no longer ride hunting. They are inmates of palaces, their flesh is rounded, their limbs at rest, their eyes sceptical or contemplative. They are indoor statesmen; they deal in intrigues; they have already learnt the meaning of the words 'The balance of the Powers', and in consequence they wield the sword no longer; they have become sedentary rulers. Apart from minute differences of costume, of badges round their necks, or implements which lie beside them on tables — differences which for us have already lost their significance — Holbein's great lords are no longer distinguishable from Holbein's great merchants. Indeed the portrait of the *Sieur de Morette* has until quite lately been universally regarded as that of *Gilbert Morett*, Henry VIII's master-jeweller.

Holbein obviously was not responsible for this change in the spirit of the age: but it was just because these changed circumstances were sympathetic to him, just because he could so perfectly render them, that he became the great painter of his time. Dürer was a mystic, the last fruit of a twilight of the gods. In his portraits the eyes dream, accept, or believe in the things they see. Thus his *Ulrich Varnbuler, Chancellor of the Empire*, a magnificent, fleshy man, gazes into the distance unseeingly, for all the world like a poet in the outward form of a brewer's drayman. The eyes in Holbein's portraits of queens are half closed, sceptical, challenging, and disbelieving. They look at you as if to say: 'I do not know exactly what manner of man you are, but I am very sure that being a man you are no hero.' This, however, is not a condemnation, but a mere acceptance of the fact that, from pope to peasant, poor humanity can never be more than poor humanity.

It is a common belief, and very possibly a very true belief, that painters in painting figures exaggerate physical and mental traits so that the sitters assume some of their own physical peculiarities.

(Thus Borrow accuses Benjamin Robert Haydon of painting all his figures too short in the legs,[1] because Haydon's own legs were themselves disproportionately small.) One might therefore argue from the eyes of Holbein's pictures that the man himself was a good-humoured sceptic who had seen a great deal of life and took things very much as they came. On the other hand, Dürer, according to the same theory, must have been a man who saw beside all visible objects their poetic significance, their mystical doubles. But perhaps it is safer to say that the dominant men of Dürer's day were really dreamers, whilst those who employed Holbein were essentially sceptics, knowing too much about mankind to have many ideals left.

⋆ ⋆ ⋆

We know . . . that what delighted him was Renaissance decoration, and this was a plastic delight, a personal taste, rather than an influence from without. And, deeper down in the boy, at the very heart of the rose as it were, there was slumbering the deep, human, untroubled, and tranquil delight in the outward aspect of humanity, in eyes, in lips, in the form of hair, in the outlines of the face from ear to chin. This delight in rendering produced the matchless series of portraits of his later years which for us today are 'Holbein'.

⋆ ⋆ ⋆

In his portraits his method was the same throughout his life. He made a silverpoint outline of his sitter — put in light washes of colour on the face; just indicated the nature of ornaments; made pencil notes of furs, orders, or the colour of eyebrows; and then took his delicate sketch home with him to work out the oil picture probably from memory.

⋆ ⋆ ⋆

The likeness [a chalk drawing of himself at twenty-three], which is a masterly piece of pastel work, is so like the mental image of the man that one forms from his works, that one may accept it as a portrait

[1] It will appear later that this very defect characterized for several years the figures of Holbein's own design, though I have never, even in the works of German theorists, seen it imagined that Holbein was short-legged, or in love with a short-legged woman. I offer the theory to commentators.

and retain it privately in one's mind as an image. It is the head of a reliable and good-humoured youth, heavy-shouldered, with a massive neck and an erected round head — the head of a man ready to do any work that might come in his way with a calm self-reliance. The expression is entirely different from that in, say, Dürer's portrait of himself; from the nervous, intent glare and the somewhat self-conscious strained gaze. Holbein neither wrote about his art nor about his religion — nor alas! did he sign and date every piece of paper that left his hand. He was not a man with a mission, but a man ready to do a day's work. And the intent expression of his eyes, which calmly survey the world, suggests nothing so much as that of a thoroughly efficient fieldsman in a game of cricket who misses no motion of the game that passes beneath his eyes, because at any moment the ball may come in his direction.

Dürer signed each of his works, because a friend in early life suggested that in that way he should follow the example of Apelles. He added to his drawings inscriptions such as: 'This is the way knights were armed at this time', or 'This is the dress ladies wore in Nuremberg in going to a ball in 1510', as if he were anxious to add another personal note to that which the drawings themselves should carry down to posterity; as if he were anxious to make his voice heard as well as the work of his hands seen. Holbein once in painting a portrait of one of his supposed mistresses implies that he himself was Apelles. He calls her *Laïs Corinthiaca*, and Laïs of Corinth was the mistress of the great Greek painter. But he scarcely ever added notes to his designs, and he never seems to have troubled about his personality at all.

The eyes of his own portrait are those of a good-humoured sceptic, the eyes of Dürer those of a fanatic. Dürer attempted to amend by his drawings the life of his day; Holbein was contented with rendering life as he saw it. Dürer, after having plunged into the waters of the Renaissance, abandoned them self-consciously — because it was not right for a Christian man to portray heathen gods and goddesses. Holbein, if he gradually dropped Renaissance decorations out of his portraits, did it on purely aesthetic grounds. He continued to the end of his life to make Renaissance designs for goldsmiths, for printers, for architects, or for furniture makers. Dürer identified himself passionately with Luther, in whom he found an emotional teacher after his own heart. Holbein, in one and the same year, painted the *Meier Madonna* and designed head-pieces for Lutheran pamphlets so violent and scurrilous that the Basle Town Council, itself more than half-Lutheran, forbade their sale.

* * *

As a rule, Holbein cannot be called one of these painters who can claim to have painted the 'soul' of his sitters. For there are some painters who make that claim: there are many who have it made for them. The claim is on the face of it rendered absurd by the use of the word 'soul'. One may replace it by the phrase 'dramatic generalization', when it becomes more comprehensible. What it means — to use a literary generalization of some looseness — is that the painter is one accustomed to live with his subject for a time long enough to let him select a characteristic expression; one which, as far as his selection can be justified, shall be *the* characteristic, *the* dominant note, *the* 'moral' of his sitter. The portrait thus becomes, in terms of the painter's abilities, an emblem of sweetness, of regret, of ambition, of what you will. The sitter is caught, as it were, in a moment of action.

Holbein hardly seems to have belonged to this class. He appears to have said to his sitter as a rule: 'Sit still for a moment: think of something that interests you.' He marked the lines of the face, the colour of the hair, a detail of the ornament — and the thing was done. It was done, that is to say, as far as the observation went.

If he wished to 'generalize' about his subject, he did it with some material attribute, giving to *Laïs Corinthiaca* coins and an open palm, to *George Gisze* the attributes of a merchant of the Steelyard. I am not prepared to say whether the method of Holbein or that of the painters of souls is the more to be commended, but I am ready to lay it down that, in the great range of his portraits, Holbein, as a painter of what he could see with the eye of the flesh, was without any superior. Occasionally, as in the portraits of Erasmus in the Louvre, he passed over into the other camp and, without sacrificing any of his marvellous power of rendering what he saw, added a touch of dramatic generalization, or of action. This was generally a product of some intimacy with the sitter.

And it is perhaps this that makes the portrait of Amerbach so charming. It is as if Holbein had had, not the one sitting that was all so many of his later subjects afforded him, but many days of observation when his friend was unaware that he was under the professional eye.

In the course of a summer walk along the flowery meadows of the Rhine near Klein Basel — as the German-hypothetic biographers are so fond of writing — perhaps Holbein glanced aside at his companion. Amerbach's eye had, maybe, caught the up-springing of some lark, and the sight suspended for a moment some wise, witty, slightly sardonic and pleasantly erudite remark. Between the pause and the speech Holbein looked— and the thing was done.

⋆ ⋆ ⋆

The subject of Death was one that very much preoccupied Holbein and his world. There were then, as it were, so many fewer half-way houses to the grave: prolonged illnesses, states of suspended animation, precarious existences in draught-proof environment, or what one will, were then unknown. You were alive: or you were dead; you were very instinct with life: the arrow struck you, the scythe mowed you down. Thus Death and Life became abstractions that were omnipresent, and, the attributes of Death being the more palpable, Death rather than Life was the preoccupation of the living.

In his most widely known designs Holbein, choosing the line of least resistance, shows us this abstraction with its attributes. Employing little imagination of his own, he has lavished a felicitous and facile invention along with a splendid power of draughtsmanship upon an idea that could be picked up from the walls of almost every ale-house of his time. In the *Dead Man*, however, he takes a higher flight, showing us, not a comparatively commonplace abstraction, but nothing less than man, dead. It is the picture of the human entity at its last stage as an individual: the next step must inevitably be its resolution into those elements which can only again be brought together at the beginning of the next stage. It is the one step further — the painting of the inscription upon the rock and of the wound in the side — that identifies this man, dead, and trembling on the verge of dissolution, with that Man, dead, who died that mankind might go its one stage further towards an eternity of joy and praise. And, by thus turning a dead man into *the* Dead Man, Holbein performs, in the realm of literary ideas, a very tremendous fact with a very small exertion — for it is impossible to imagine a human being who will not be brought to a standstill and made to think *some* sort of thoughts before what is, after all, a masterpiece of pure art. It was that, perhaps, that Holbein had in his mind.

It may well be that he had nothing of the sort, and that having, as it were, exhausted, in the search for dramatic and melodramatic renderings of episodes in the life of Christ, every kind of violence that he could conceive of, he here comes out at the other end of the wood and — just as the Greeks ended their tragedies not in a catastrophe but upon a calm tone of one kind or another — so Holbein crowns his version of the earthly career of the Saviour with an unelaborated keystone. Or it may have been merely a product of his spirit of revolt. He may have been tired of supplying series after series of Passion pictures meant to satisfy the hunger of his time for strong meat in religious portrayals.

It was this appetite that caused the existence of the number of works in the Basle Museum — works which must make one a little regret that the Holbein who painted the portrait of Amerbach and the Dead Man had not a greater leisure, since, vigorous and splendid as so many of these conceptions are, they are yet upon a plane appreciably lower, whether we regard them as products of art or as 'readings of Life', to use a cant phrase. In its present, disastrously restored state it is difficult to regard, say, the early *Last Supper* as other than a rather uninspired piece of journey-work. Without the early Passion series on linen one would feel inclined to say that it was of doubtful ascription. It is interesting because it is one more of Holbein's designs that has been 'lifted' from an Italian master, and because it shows Holbein pursuing a sort of pictorial realism to supply the craving for strong meat that I have mentioned. But in the demand for designs for coloured glass he found a refuge which tided him over dangerous years. It called forth, too, qualities, which if they were not amongst his very greatest, were yet sufficient to place him among the rare band of very great decorative artists.

* * *

A busy man, Holbein was under the necessity of working quickly, and being neither a mystic nor a sentimentalist, he struck swift and sure notes. There was in him very little of what Schopenhauer calls *Christo-Germanische Dummheit*; he came before it and before the date of angels who are conceived as long-haired, winged creatures in immaculate gowns — before the date of prettification, in fact. But, being a busy man, he was naturally unequal in his work.

* * *

During these years — to be precise, from June 1521 until October

1522 — Holbein was engaged upon one of those tasks which, along with the Hertenstein frescoes, the Bär table, and the *Dance of Death* remained for some subsequent centuries wonders of the world. This was the decoration of the council chamber in the Basle Rathhaus. The frescoes themselves have vanished so that no man living has seen more than patches of colour upon the walls: the pictures are in that heaven of lost masterpieces where, perhaps, we may one day see the campanile of Venice, the arms of the Venus of Milo, or the seven-branched candlestick of the Temple of Solomon. Vigorous and splendid sketches remain, some copies and many descriptions — but these afford us very little idea of what may have been the actual effect of the decorations, as decorations.

Regarded theoretically they cannot have been perfect or even desirable: here again plain walls were made to look like anything else but walls. But no doubt they were very wonderful things whilst they still existed.

Nevertheless I cannot resist a feeling of private but intimate relief that these tremendous *tours de force* are left to our imaginings. We lose them — but we gain a Holbein whom we can more fearlessly enjoy. For, supposing these things with their nine days' wonder of invention that Holbein shared with many commoner men and set working for the gratification of every commoner man — supposing these extremely wonderful designs still existed, the far greater Holbein — the Holbein of the one or two Madonnas and of the innumerable portraits in oil or in silver-point — the Holbein whose works place him side by side with the highest artists, in that highest of all arts, the art of portraiture — that tranquil and assured master must have been obscured. Those of us who loved his greater works must, in the nature of things, have been accused of paradox flinging: the great Public must have called out: 'Look at that wonderful invention: that compassionate executioner with the magnifying glass, seeking to take out his victim's eye with as little brutality as might be!' And beside that attraction the charms of Christina of Milan or all the sketches at Windsor would be praised in vain. We should have gained another Shakespeare rich in the production of anecdote, we might have lost some of our love for an artist incomparable for his holding the mirror up to the men and women of his wonderful age.

* * *

In 1523 the great troubles and upheavals that saw Rome herself sacked by Lutheran mercenaries were still comparatively at a distance. Writing of that year, one of the greatest of all the rather unsavoury politicians of that wonderful century sums up the topics that were then in men's minds[1]: . . . 'By the space of xvii hole wekes . . . we communyd of warre, pease Stryfe contencyon debatte murmure grudge Riches pouerte penury trowth falsehode Justyce equyte discayte oppreseyon Magnanymyte actyuyte force attempraunce Treason murder Felonye consyliacyon and also how a commune welth myght be edifyed and continuyid within our Realme. Howbeyt in conclusyon wee haue done as our predecessors haue been wont to doo that ys to say, as well as wee myght and lefte where we begann. . . . Whe haue in our parlyament grauntyd vnto the Kynges highnes a ryght large subsydye the lyke whereof was newer graunted in this realme. . . .'

The point about this letter, which is addressed to Cromwell's 'especial and entyrelye belouyd Frende Jno. Creke in Bilbowe in Biscaye', is precisely that at that date there was no burning question in England. Every possible subject was discussed with academic calmness, and the country appeared to be outside the European storm-centre. And such letters went all over Europe in these years, holding out the promise of a halcyon state to such workers as Holbein whose means of subsistence vanished in storms like that of the Peasants' War, and whose very works were destroyed out of all the churches of Protestantism. And not only in Protestant lands, since even such a Pontiff of the plastic arts as Michelangelo was soon to find out that the Pontiff of the Church deemed it expedient to attend almost more to the affairs of his cure than to marbles, however deathless.

Of these bad times for artists we can find, as I have said, little or no trace in the career of Holbein — there are no pictures of his bearing the actual dates 1524 or 1525. It may be convenient therefore to speak here of the *Dance of Death* series and the *Death Alphabet*, although the Trechsels did not actually publish the former until many years had elapsed. This is another of Holbein's wonder-works. It achieved and maintained an European celebrity such as perhaps no other work of art ever did. The only parallels to it that occur at all immediately to one are Bunyan's *Pilgrim's Progress* in Western, and the *Labyrinth* of

[1] 'T. Cromwell to Jno. Creke,' 17 August 1523.

Comenius in Eastern Europe; and these two appeal to a comparatively limited class of races, however widespread. It has struck straight at the hearts of innumerable races, at the hearts of the lowest of peasants as at those of the greatest of artists. It was carried by chap-book pedlars to the remotest hovels of the earth, and Rubens declared that from it he had his earliest lessons in drawing—just as the first master of Michelangelo was, vicariously, Martin Schongauer.

It is easy to say that the appeal of the series came from its subject, and that its subject had been the common property of the mediaeval centuries. Yet the mere fact that of so many *Gesta Mortis* only this of Holbein's held the popular imagination with any lasting firmness, the fact that it was the selected version of all the versions, would go to prove that it was some sort of technical excellence, some sort of technical appeal that caused its apotheosis. And excellent indeed is almost every one of these woodcuts — excellent in the simplicity of design which recognizes so truly what the thick, unctuous line of the wood-engraver can do; excellent in the placing of each little subject on the block; excellent in the way in which each figure stands upon its legs; and above all, excellent in the appeal to the eye, in the 'composition' of each subject.

It is, of course, open to one to say that story-telling is the least of all the departments of designing. But when once such an artist as Holbein sets himself to tell a story, the matter becomes comparatively unimportant. He was so true to himself that his designs had the proper, the individual 'look', whether he were putting on paper something so purely abitrary as the design for a coat-of-arms, or the figure of Death driving a weapon through a soldier. The subject simply did not hinder him: he could employ any object so as to form an integral part of his decorative purpose. And, what is still more to the point, having set himself to tell a story, he did tell it with a quite amazing lucidity. The detail essential to his idea is always what strikes the eye first — or rather it is 'led up to' as skilfully as in the denouement of a good French *caste*. That is, of course, one of the lower merits: but that he took so much trouble over it is proof of how conscientious a worker he was — of how amply he deserved the enormous popularity that became his.

I have hardly space here to trace the evolution of the idea of the *Todtentanz*. It originated, how far back we cannot tell, in a universal, and no doubt praiseworthy, religious desire of 'rubbing in', to each mortal creature, the fact that he or she must die. It was a matter not merely of chalking upon, or carving out of, a wall: 'Remember, oh man, that thou art mortal' — a lesson that each reader, like each hearer of a sermon, was apt to apply rather to his neighbour than to himself. The framer, or inventor of a *Todtentanz* wished to bring the moral home to each beholder, and in order to do this he exhausted his knowledge of the human avocations or estates. Thus a butcher who received a grim joy at seeing his friend the horse-merchant, the lacemaker, or the coney-catcher in the arms of a corpse, was expected to receive a shock and ensue no doubt a moral purging at the spectacle of the representation of all Butcherdom dancing in the embrace of a phantom ox-slaughterer. For, in the original conception of a *Todtentanz*, each man or woman danced, not with Death the Abstraction, but with a dead mortal of his own kidney. Of such 'dances' there were many on the walls of cloisters all over Europe: at Basle itself there is still one to be seen — and no doubt such perpetrations and the fact that they were continually beneath the eyes of men during successive generations did have a considerable influence on the trend of thought. They must, I mean, have smitten very hard the poetic and imaginative few during their childhoods. Perhaps to them may be ascribed the continual preoccupation of the mind of Montaigne with one idea — that of dodging the fear of death when it came by living all his days in a state of mitigated terror.

In Holbein the preoccupation was perhaps natural, since his name means 'Skull', and at times, as in the picture of *The Ambassadors*, he proved that he was not oblivious of the fact. The 'vein' cropped up from time to time in his later works: thus in the rather inferior and very much damaged portrait of Sir Brian Tuke, now at Munich, the hour-glass is in the front of the picture, whilst the background is filled by a skeleton presentation of Death with his lethal instrument. We might almost regard the great *Meier Madonna* as containing one more of these warnings, since, with her shroud half concealing her face, behind the living wife kneels the dead Dorothea Kannegiesser whom Holbein had so beautifully painted a decade before.

* * *

What is interesting is that by this time [1526] Holbein, in his dated paintings, seems to have got rid of the trick of loading his backgrounds with renaissance architecture and what not. The background of the Darmstadt *Madonna* is nearly simplicity itself; behind the head of Erasmus is nothing but a green surface with some decorative stars:

behind the Dorotheas is merely a curtain. He seems to have realized that, by this time, his marvellous painting was a tower in itself and, from this date onward, it is only in 'display' portraits that he troubles himself to be very elaborate.

These, it is significant to observe, are, first, *The Household of Sir Thomas More*, with which he 'introduced' himself to the English on his first visit; secondly, the portrait of Gisze, with which he 'introduced' himself, equally, to the German merchants of the Steelyard on his second coming here. The *Henries VII and VIII and Their Consorts* was also by way of being an introduction, and possibly also the *Ambassadors*, since the two sitters might serve to spread his fame into whatever mysterious court they were accredited from. At any rate, from this time onward, except in such special cases, the master seems to have thrown his glove down to posterity: the human face, the human shape, these were the 'subjects' with which he was to make his appeal. And this 'subject' being the simplest and the most difficult with which a painter can deal, it seems to follow that the achievement is the highest possible. It takes to itself no adventitious aids: it relies upon painting pure and simple.

§

In the late summer of 1526, Holbein left Basle for England. His motives for so doing are not of the first importance and they have been fully discussed by many people. Some will have it that he was unhappy at home; some that his imbroglio with Dorothea Offenburg drove him away. One authority credits him with an invitation to England from a great English lord: it seems more probable that More called to him. No doubt, too, times in Basle were very evil for him, since to all other painters they were very evil. Already painting was an art in disrepute in a Basle coming more and more rapidly under the sway of Lutheranism. Holbein, as I have said, served both masters impartially — for the one side he painted the Madonna, for the other he illustrated pamphlets so violent that they must needs be burned. But for the moment Lutheranism offered only pamphlets. To find room for paintings, Holbein must find a land where there were convents still and churches not whitewashed. It is an interesting little incident, as showing Holbein actually in contact with the troubles of his time, that, when he claimed the painting materials — and more particularly the gold — that his father had left in a monastery he was painting in before his death, the answer he received was that the monastery had been burned by the peasants and that if Holbein desired the gold he must go seek it amid the ashes.

Practically the only other Basle evidences of his life — save for the letter from Erasmus — are the *Dorothea* pictures. One may read into them what one likes. It is usual to consider that, since Holbein painted her first as *Venus* and then as *Laïs*, he must first have been guilelessly in love with her, and then have turned upon his mistress. The amiable apologists for Holbein write eloquently upon the wrongs that he must have suffered at her pretty, but itching palms. But it has always seemed to me, that if a man has enjoyed a woman's favours, it is discreditable of him afterwards to call her even well-deserved names, however excellent an organ his voice may be, and, if I were anxious to apologise for the painter, I should simply adopt another line. I mean that there is no documentary evidence to connect Holbein with Dorothea: thus the portraits may have been commissioned by some other of the very many ill-used lovers of the thus immortalised and beautiful Laïs.

I do not know that it is a matter of much importance. Holbein cannot very easily be whitewashed, since his will gives indisputable evidence of his having led a not strictly regular life in this country. Such things, of course, were not uncommon in those distant days, and Holbein might plead the 'artistic temperament' today. And gossip says too that he was 'unhappy at home' — so that, apparently, for once the desire of the critic to limit his remarks to the man's work, and the desire of the world and his wife to know about everything else, may be brought to coincide. For it would appear that the less we say about Holbein the man — the better.

It is, of course, true that the important thing about a picture is how it is painted, and that the subject matters, by comparison, very little. Nevertheless it is an added, extraneous pleasure — a pleasure added rather to what is called *belles lettres* than to the fine arts — when such a painter as Holbein comes upon 'interesting sitters'. I mean that the charm of Roper's *Life of Sir Thomas More* is infinitely enhanced by looking at Holbein's *Household* — just as the interest of the whole history of the period is made alive for us by Holbein's portraits of Henry VIII's court. Without the court to draw, painting only peasants or fishwives, Holbein would have been a painter just as great. Henry VIII and his men would be lifeless without Holbein. You have only to think how comparatively cold we are left by the name, say, of Edward III, a great king surrounded by great men in a stirring period. No visual image comes to the mind's eye; at most we see, imaginatively, coins and the seals that depend from charters. Thus, if oblivion be not a boon, an age may be thankful for such artists as Holbein. That most wonderful age in which he lived seemed, too, to be well aware of it — since so many of the great sought the immortality that his hand was to confer.

We who come after may well be thankful that Holbein paid when he did his first short visit to this country. Along with the portraits of the splendid opportunists who flourished or fell when the end of the old world came at the fall of More, he has left us some at least of the earlier and more attractive men of doomed principles. Along with More's there decorated then the page of English history the name of Warham, who, for mellow humanitarianism, exceeded Cranmer, his successor, as far as More exceeded Thomas Cromwell in the familiar virtues — and Fisher, Bishop of Rochester, who as far exceeded the later Gardiner. Being men of principle, set in high places, these were doomed to tragedy; and, if Warham died actually in his bed, it needs only Holbein's portrait to assure us that, if the shadows of the future can still affect us on our last pillows, this great man saw, on his deathbed, things enough to make him haggard. Fisher's head has about its eyes a greater intrepidity — but the expression on both is the same; and in these two heads we may see very well how two great men envisaged their stormy times.

Of the portrait of Warham there are two copies in oil extant — both apparently by Holbein, the one in the Louvre, the other at Lambeth: the latter is, I think, the finer example. The oil picture of the *Household of More* has, of course, vanished; but the drawing, a mere sketch with annotations by More, is in Basle, and there are studies for the heads at Windsor. Perhaps, however, the best portrait-picture of this visit to England is the Dresden *Thomas and John Godsalve*, in which the head of the elder man has always appeared to me to be one of the finest pieces of Holbein's painting. The Windsor portrait of *Sir Henry Guildford* is more generally preferred; to my taste it is too much overloaded with decoration — though this was probably to the taste of Sir Henry, a commonplace gentleman, whose successful career was much aided by the king's friendship, and whose position at court made him to a large extent *arbiter elegantiarum*. Thus the portrait has some of the nature of a 'display' picture.

But upon the whole, and if no question of pecuniary value or labour expended need influence, I should be inclined to prefer to either, the wonderful, alert *Portrait of an Englishwoman*, in two chalks, in Basle, or the almost more wonderful body-colour *Portrait of an Englishman* in the Berlin Royal Cabinet. These little drawings of an hour or so are so inexpressibly alive in every touch that the more minutely you examine them, the more excited you will become. In the finished paintings one is presented with a mystery: in these drawings one has the very heart of the secret. Each stroke that one looks at seems to unfold an envelope of the bud — at each unfolding one discovers that the secret lies a little deeper. I suppose Holbein himself could not have told how it was done.

But, of course, these drawings and all the earlier paintings take, as it were, their hats off to the portrait of Holbein's wife and children. . . . As in the case of most of the really impressive portraits of the world, there is here no background, no detailed accessory to worry the beholder's eye. The figures in the picture exist just as at the first sight a great human individuality exists. One has no eyes for the chair he sits in nor much for the kind of clothes he may wear. He overcomes these things and makes them so part of his individuality that they are as much taken for granted as are the number of his fingers. And it is precisely the property of the great portrait that it makes its subject always a great man. It brings out the fact that *every* man is great if viewed from the sympathetic point of view — great, that is, not in the amount of actions done, but in the power of waking interest. It brings out, in fact, in what way its subject is 'typical', since great art is above all things generous, like the strong and merciful light of the sun that will render lovable the meanest fields, the barest walls.

And such a great portrait as this is notable as explaining what must be, always, the artist's ambition — that his work shall look 'not like a picture'. When one stands before it one is not conscious of a break in atmospheric space: one does not subconsciously say: 'Here the air of the room ends: here is the commencement of the picture's atmosphere.' The figures in the picture are figures in the room. It is not, of course, a matter of a Pre-Raphaelite attempt to 'deceive the eye' by a kind of stippling as if the painter had attempted with cuttle-fish to smooth out the traces of his tool, for the tool is frankly accepted and the brush marks visible enough.

The large, plain woman, with the unattractive children, lives before us, luminous, throwing back the light with that subdued quality of reflection that all human flesh possesses. . . .

One so exhausts superlatives in these days that there seem to be none left in which to speak of the almost perfect drawing of the woman's shoulders and head, of the harmony of the whole design, on whose surface, or rather, in whose depths, the eye travels so pleasantly from place to place. The woman's hands are particularly worth looking at — the masterly way in which the one on the boy's shoulder shows in its lines that it rests heavily, and the way in which the pressure on the baby's waist is indicated.

* * *

The magnificent *Samuel and Saul* . . . is to my mind the finest of all Holbein's quasi-decorative subject pictures. The way in which, in this drawing, the figures of the marching troops, of the king, and of the arresting prophet are rendered actual, and at the same time blended into one composition with the strictly decorative scroll-work of smoke from the blazing background, proves that Holbein had at this time reached the very high water mark of genius — of genius which is the comprehension of the scope possible to a certain class of design. It is decoration achieved not by the multiplication of arbitrary details and not by the arbitrary treatment of actual forms — but by the selection of natural objects fitted to fill and to make beautiful a certain space. It is the sort of selection that is given to most of us at rare moments. Thus I remember seeing, whilst I was making a final tour for the purposes of this book, a number of workmen taking a siesta along the bottom of a sunlit wall. There may have been thirty of them in various, but similar attitudes, on the ground, and nearly all of them wore blue blouses. The similarity of their attitudes and costumes and the straight line that they made brought to my lips at once the words: 'If only Holbein had seen that!' I suppose that I had my mind full of the little frieze of *Dancing Peasants* that there is in the Basle Museum.

* * *

I opened this little monograph with a pseudo-comparison of Dürer with Holbein: of course the two are not comparable. For if, to continue the use of a simile of my first page, Holbein be a mountain peak in a chain of hills, we must write Dürer down as a Titanic cloud form, one of a range that on a clear day we may see towering up behind the mountain. The two men differ in kind and in species. Holbein could no more have conceived the *Great Fortune* than Dürer could have painted the *Christina of Milan:* Dürer could not refrain from commenting upon life, Holbein's comments were of little importance.

That essentially was the ultimate difference between the two: it is a serviceable thing to state, since in trying to ascertain the characteristics of a man it is as useful to state what he is not as what he is. Dürer, then, had imagination where Holbein had only vision and invention — an invention of a rough-shod and everyday kind. But, perhaps for that very reason, the subjects of Holbein's brush — in his portraits — are seen as it were through a glass more limpid. To put it with exaggerated clearness: we may *believe* in what Holbein painted, but in looking at Dürer's work we can never be quite assured that he is an unprejudiced transcriber. You will get the comparison emphasised if you will compare Holbein's drawing of Henry VIII with the etching by Cornelis Matsys of the year 1543. The drawing is an unconcerned rendering of an appallingly gross and miserable man; the etching seems as if, with every touch of his tool, the artist had been stabbing in little exclamation notes of horror. The drawing leaves one thinking that no man could be more ugly than Henry: the etching forces one to think that no artist could imagine any man more obscene.

Holbein, in fact, was a great Renderer. If I wanted to find a figure really akin to his I think I should go to music and speak of Bach. For in Bach you have just that peculiar Teutonic type of which Holbein is so great an example: in the musician too you have that marvellous mastery of the instrument, that composure, that want of striving. And both move one by what musicians call 'absolute' means. Just as the fourth fugue of the *Wohltemperierte Klavier* is profoundly moving — for no earthly reason that one knows — so is the portrait of Holbein's family. The fugue is beautiful in spite of a relatively ugly 'subject', the portrait is beyond praise in spite of positively ugly sitters. And there is in neither anything extraneous: the figure, unaided by 'programme', is pure music: the portrait, unaided by literary ideas, is simply painting.

The quality of the enjoyment that we can get from the works of these two is also very precisely identical. I do not know how long the Duke of Norfolk's portrait of Christina of Milan has hung in the Naitonal Gallery: it must have been there many years, since I can hardly remember a 'myself' in which the idea of that 'symphony' in blues and blacks did not play an integral part of my pleasures. I would rather possess that painting than any other object in the world, I think and I have visited the National Gallery, I do not know how many times, simply to stand in front of it — simply to stand and to think nothing. It is not for me a picture; it is not even a personage with whom I am in love. But simply a mood — a mood of profound lack of thought, of profound self-forgetfulness — which assuredly is the most blessed thing which Art, in this rather weary world, can vouchsafe to a man — descends upon me in front of that combination of paints upon that canvas.

It is not merely this portrait that can evoke this mood in us — it is the very quality of Holbein. I happen to possess a very excellent set of reproductions — made for a private person — of the series of Windsor sketches for portraits. One can pass hours with such things as these on the floor before one's chair. Here is the court of Henry VIII from the Groom Falconer to the Earl Marshal. But it is not the former careers of the dead queens, the tiny features of the little prince, or the heavy jowl and weary eyes of the most unhappy king — it is not the history, the intrigue, the gossip of a small kingdom then barbaric and insignificant enough. Here is Regina Anna Bulleyn: but this is not the queen who was done to death by false witnesses. A comely, large featured, slightly sardonic face looks down not very intently upon a book. But it is neither queen nor face that hold those of us who are attuned to the quality that we call 'Holbein': it is a certain collocation of lines, of masses.

We are, literally, in love with this arrangement of lines, of lights and of shadows. The eye is held by no object, but solely by the music of the pattern — the quality that we call 'Holbein'. It is a quality; it is a feeling; it is a method of projection that one admires — and that one might well speak of — in the peculiar phraseology that is reserved for one's admiration of musicians. Thus when one asks another, 'Do you like Beethoven?' he implies, not 'Do you like an old, sardonic, deaf man?' or 'Do you like the Ninth Symphony or any other individual work?' — but 'Are you pleasurably affected when the name Beethoven calls up in you certain emotions — emotions that you have felt when certain notes followed certain others in an intangible sequence; a sequence that cannot be analysed but which is "Beethoven"?'

The quality, the power of Holbein is similar. When we recall him to mind, no particular work of his 'sticks out' in the mind's eye. He is a mass, or a force; he calls up a mood.

This characteristic is most marked when one considers the work that he did after his final establishment in England. One may use a cliché phrase so that it becomes, in this case, vivid and actual: he poured out a stream of pictures. They are better or worse than each other only in accordance with the beholder's private preferences; just as, in a stream, different men standing at different points on the bank and seeing different facets of the ripples see differing lights and shadows differing. You may above all things care for the *Ambassadors*, which moves me very little; I shall never be contented with praise of the *Duke of Norfolk* of Windsor, or the *Unbekannte Dame* of Vienna. Yet, in the mass, and after the review, you and I may both set the abstraction we call 'Holbein' at the same very high level.

He has always seemed to me to be the earliest of 'modern' painters — to have looked at men and women, first of all, with the 'modern' eye. If you glance rapidly along the series of sketches at Windsor you will be astounded to see how exactly they resemble the faces you will pass in the Windsor streets. If you compare them with, say, Lely's portraits of a later court, the characteristic becomes even more marked, since Lely's men and women died a century or so later than Holbein's — and have yet been dead so much longer. He got out of his time — as he got *into* our time — with a completeness that few painters have achieved — hardly even Velázquez or Rembrandt.

The claim is not, really, a very high one: the modern eye looking at things in a rather humdrum and uninspired way. But, of course, the praise appears more high if we put it that Holbein's works may be said to have compelled us to look at things as we do, just as, after Palestrina, the ears of men grew gradually accustomed to hear music only in the modern modes. Artistically speaking it means that Holbein, penetrating, as it were, through the disguise of costume, of hair-dressing, and of the very postures of the body and droop of the eyelids, siezed on the rounded personalities — the underlying truths — of the individuals before him; so that when one looks at the portrait of de Morette, or the wonderful sketch of a dark girl with a figure that rakes back, one neither notices the clothes of the one nor the absence of clothes of the other. Aesthetically, of course, the painting of the clothes and ornaments has a value of its own — in the portrait of de Morette it leads up to and supports the heavy and sagacious face — but, until we consciously examine it for our own aesthetic ends, we are not really aware of the clothes at all, and the figure before us might be that of any prime minister, plumber, or book publisher of today.

★ ★ ★

Nothing was further from Holbein's spirit — and nothing indeed is further from the spirit of his nation and age — than any idea that great results can be obtained with small means. He belonged to a nation to whom display was and remains the readiest means of indicating value of whatever sort. Simplicity and severity were probably distasteful enough to him. Thus nothing could have been further from his sympathy than what is best in modern decorative art, and he had little or no idea, beyond that enforced by the exigencies of space, of adapting his design to the form of the object to be decorated or of reducing the amount of ornament further and further until the best decorated space be that which contains the least ornament. *His* dukes would never have been the worst dressed men of a house of peers.

His is the other end of our line, in this as in so many other things, and to appreciate him thoroughly we have to make mental efforts of one kind and another. As we might put it, he was vulgar, which we are not, but he had more blood and more hope, so that he achieved the impossible so many times, and climbing in places where we are accustomed to say that climbing is wrong or hopeless, he appears on peaks more high than any of ours. That, of course, is what the master does in the realm of the arts.

I have employed freely the words 'actual' and 'realist' in speaking of Holbein's work, and in that I have followed the example of many who use the terms either panegyrically or in contempt. But in the modern sense he was little of a realist, dealing rather in the typical. One can exemplify this best in such drawings as the very beautiful and celebrated 'ship' design. Our present-day 'realist' would give us some moment from the career of some actual ship. But Holbein's is hardly an actual ship at all. It can hardly have been drawn from the life, since, even in that day when ships absurdly unmanageable, top-heavy, and unsteerable made voyages the mere idea of which turns the hair of the modern sailor grey — even in that day no ship so absolutely unballasted would have set sail from any port. But Holbein had got into his head, had made part of his ideas, a representative ship. He had seen ships perhaps at Lyons, perhaps in the channel, and he evolved from his mind a typical form. Equally, too, he had seen ships set sail, had seen men being sea-sick, had seen fat warrior-sailors on board embracing fat women, had seen bumboats casting off, had seen pots of beer handed up to a masthead and gigantic standard-bearers casting loose their flags to the breeze. But in bringing all these things together into his design he overwhelms one with the idea that he could never, upon any one setting sail of a ship, have seen so much at one moment. Thus, admirable and actual as each detail of the drawing is, it impresses one not as a realistic shadowing of any incident, but as an almost didactic portrayal of what it might be possible to see. It is as if he wished to show men of the inlands who had never seen a ship as much as possible in one drawing.

Of course his real purpose may have been no more than a note to remind himself, as in the case of the *Bat* and *Lamb* drawings. But that semi-didactic spirit is visible in much else of his work. It seems to fill the *Dance of Death* series, which, as it were, exclaims continually, 'See what Death can do!' And it is the real 'note' of all his portraits. Whilst going to the bottom of each individual, whilst absolutely searching out his most usable qualities, he seems to be selecting those saliences which will make the individual really noticeable. Dürer wrote upon his drawings: 'This is how the Knights rode in armour in 1515.' Holbein tries to force us to see in his portrait of the Lady Parker: 'This is how women of the narrow-eyed, small-nosed, wide-mouthed, tiny-waisted type looked in the year 1537.' Or, in an exaggerated form the *George Gisze* shows us the merchant with all his arms around him.

This last is, of course, merely material — but it is a material indication of the artist's psychological approach to his sitters. He does not, as I have said, take them in their 'moments', he does not show them under violent lights or in the grasp of strong passions. He rounds them off, catching them always at moments when the illumination, both of the actual atmosphere and of their souls, was transfused and shone all round them. Thus he has left us a picture of his world, as it were, upon a grey day.

Other artists are giving us more light, others again have given us both more light and more shadow or more shadow alone. But no other artist has left a more sincere rendering of his particular world, and no other artist's particular world is compact of simulacra more convincing, more illusory, or more calculated to hold our attentions. He has redeemed a whole era for us from oblivion, and he has forced us to believe that his vision of it was the only feasible one. This is all that the greatest of Art can do, whether it takes us into a world of the artist's fancy or into one of his fellowmen. And, by rescuing from oblivion these past eras it confers upon us, to the extent of its hold, a portion of that herb oblivion, a portion of that forgetfulness of our own selves, which is the best gift that Art has to bestow.

[London: Duckworth, 1905, pp. 6–8, 28, 32, 44–8, 57–9, 62–8, 82, 90–92, 96–106, 112–14, 115–28, 130–32, 146–60, 166–73.]

VI

Poetry

Ford published twelve volumes of poetry in the course of his literary career, beginning with *The Questions at the Well* in 1893 under the pseudonym Fenil Haig. His poems appeared in two collected editions — in 1913, with an important preface, and in 1936, published by Oxford University Press. (The long poem *Mister Bosphorus and the Muses*, 1923, was not included in the second *Collected Poems*.)

Although Ford did not think of himself primarily as a poet, Pound insisted on Ford's importance both as a poet and an influence on the poetic language of his time, his 'long prose training' bringing the quality of naturalness of speech to younger poets. In his obituary of Ford, Pound wrote:

> Apart from narrative sense and the main constructive, there is this to be said of Homer, that never can you read half a page without finding melodic invention, still fresh, and that you can hear the actual voices, as of the old men speaking in the course of the phrases.
>
> It is for this latter quality that Ford's poetry is of high importance, both in itself and for its effect on all the best subsequent work of his time. Let no young snob forget this.
>
> I propose to bury him in the order of merits as I think he himself understood them, first for an actual example in the writing of poetry; secondly, for those same merits more fully shown in his prose, and thirdly, for the critical acumen which was implicit in his finding these merits.

from

Poems for Pictures (1900)

THE SONG OF THE WOMEN
A WEALDEN TRIO

1st Voice

When ye've got a child 'ats whist for want of food,
And a grate as grey's y'r 'air for want of wood,
And y'r man and you ain't nowise not much good;

Together

Oh —
It's hard work a-Christmassing,
Carolling,
Singin' songs about the 'Babe what's born.'

2nd Voice

When ye've 'eered the bailiff's 'and upon the latch,
And ye've feeled the rain a-trickling through the thatch,
An' y'r man can't git no stones to break ner yit no sheep
to watch —

Together

Oh —
We've got to come a-Christmassing,
Carolling,
Singin' of the 'Shepherds on that morn.'

3rd Voice, more cheerfully

'E was a man's poor as us, very near,
An' 'E 'ad 'is trials and danger,
An' I think 'E'll think of us when 'E sees us singing' 'ere;
For 'is mother was poor, like us, poor dear,
An' she bore Him in a manger.

Together

Oh —
It's warm in the heavens, but it's cold upon the earth;
An' we ain't no food at table nor no fire upon the hearth;
And it's bitter hard a-Christmassing,
Carolling,
Singin' songs about our Saviour's birth;
Singin' songs about the Babe what's born;
Singin' of the shepherds on that morn.

[Set to music by Benjamin Britten]

from

Songs from London (1910)

FINCHLEY ROAD

As we come up at Baker Street
Where tubes and trains and 'buses meet
There's a touch of fog and a touch of sleet;
And we go on up Hampstead way
Towards the closing in of day . . .

You should be a queen or a duchess rather,
Reigning in place of a warlike father
In peaceful times o'er a tiny town
Where all the roads wind up and down
From your little palace — a small, old place
Where every soul should know your face
And bless your coming. That's what I mean,
A small grand-duchess, no distant queen,
Lost in a great land, sitting alone
In a marble palace upon a throne.

And you'd say to your shipmen: 'Now take your ease,
Tomorrow is time enough for the seas.'
And you'd set your bondmen a milder rule
And let the children loose from the school.
No wrongs to right and no sores to fester,
In your small, great hall 'neath a firelit dais,
You'd sit, with me at your feet, your jester,
Stroking your shoes where the seed pearls glisten
And talking my fancies. And you as your way is,
Would sometimes heed and at times not listen,
But sit at your sewing and look at the brands
And sometimes reach me one of your hands,
Or bid me write you a little ode,
Part quaint, part sad, part serious . . .

But here we are in the Finchley Road
With a drizzling rain and a skidding 'bus
And the twilight settling down on us.

THE THREE-TEN

When in the prime and May Day time dead lovers went a-walking,
How bright the grass in lads' eyes was, how easy poet's talking!
Here were green hills and daffodils, and copses to contain them:
Daisies for floors did front their doors agog for maids to chain them.
So when the ray of rising day did pierce the eastern heaven
Maids did arise to make the skies seem brighter far by seven.
Now here's a street where 'bus routes meet, and 'twixt the wheels and paving
Standeth a lout that doth hold out flowers not worth the having.
But see, but see! The clock marks three above the Kilburn Station,
Those maids, thank God! are 'neath the sod and all their generation.

What she shall wear who'll soon appear, it is not hood nor wimple,
But by the powers there are no flowers so stately or so simple,
And paper shops and full 'bus tops confront the sun so brightly,
That, come three-ten, no lovers then had hearts that beat so lightly
As ours, or loved more truly,
Or found green shades or flowered glades to fit their loves more duly.
And see, and see! 'Tis ten past three above the Kilburn Station,
Those maids, thank God! are 'neath the sod and all their generation.

from

On Heaven and Poems Written on Active Service (1918)

ON HEAVEN

To V. H., who asked for a working Heaven

I

That day the sunlight lay on the farms;
On the morrow the bitter frost that there was!
That night my young love lay in my arms,
   The morrow how bitter it was!

And because she is very tall and quaint
And golden, like a *quattrocento* saint,
I desire to write about Heaven;
To tell you the shape and the ways of it,
And the joys and the toil in the maze of it,
For these there must be in Heaven,
Even in Heaven!

For God is a good man, God is a kind man,
And God's a good brother, and God is no blind man,
And God is our father.

            I will tell you how this thing began:
How I waited in a little town near Lyons many years,
And yet knew nothing of passing time, or of her tears,
But, for nine slow years, lounged away at my table in the shadowy
   sunlit square
Where the small cafés are.

The *Place* is small and shaded by great planes,
Over a rather human monument
Set up to *Louis Dixhuit* in the year

Eighteen fourteen; a funny thing with dolphins
About a pyramid of green-dripped, sordid stone.
But the enormous, monumental planes
Shade it all in, and in the flecks of sun
Sit market women. There's a paper shop
Painted all blue, a shipping agency,
Three or four cafés; dank, dark colonnades
Of an eighteen-forty *Maîrie*. I'd no wish
To wait for her where it was picturesque,
Or ancient or historic, or to love
Over well any place in the land before she came
And loved it too. I didn't even go
To Lyons for the opera; Arles for the bulls,
Or Avignon for glimpses of the Rhone.
Not even to Beaucaire! I sat about
And played long games of dominoes with the *maîre*,
Or passing *commis-voyageurs*. And so
I sat and watched the trams come in, and read
The *Libre Parole* and sipped the thin, fresh wine
They call Piquette, and got to know the people,
The kindly, southern people . . .

Until, when the years were over, she came in her swift red car,
Shooting out past a tram; and she slowed and stopped and lighted
absently down,
A little dazed, in the heart of the town;
And nodded imperceptibly.
With a sideways look at me.

So our days here began.

And the wrinkled old woman who keeps the café,
And the man
Who sells the *Libre Parole*,
And the sleepy gendarme,
And the fat *facteur* who delivers letters only in the shady,
Pleasanter kind of streets;
And the boy I often gave a penny,
And the *maîre* himself, and the little girl who loves toffee
And me because I have given her many sweets;

And the one-eyed, droll
Bookseller of the *rue Grand de Provence*, —
Chancing to be going home to bed,
Smiled with their kindly, fresh benevolence,
Because they knew I had waited for a lady
Who should come in a swift, red, English car,
To the square where the little cafés are.
And the old, old woman touched me on the wrist
With a wrinkled finger,
And said: 'Why do you linger? —
Too many kisses can never be kissed!
And comfort her — nobody here will think harm —
Take her instantly to your arm!
It is a little strange, you know, to your dear,
To be dead!'

But one is English,
Though one be never so much of a ghost;
And if most of your life has been spent in the craze to relinquish
What you want most,
You will go on relinquishing,
You will go on vanquishing
Human longings, even
In Heaven.

God! You will have forgotten what the rest of the world
  is on fire for —
The madness of desire for the long and quiet embrace,
The coming nearer of a tear-wet face;
Forgotten the desire to slake
The thirst, and the long, slow ache,
And to interlace
Lash with lash, lip with lip, limb with limb, and the fingers of the
  hand with the hand
And . . .

You will have forgotten . . .
                    But they will all awake;
Aye, all of them shall awaken
In this dear place.

And all that then we took
Of all that we might have taken,
Was that one embracing look,
Coursing over features, over limbs, between eyes, a making sure,
    and a long sigh,
Having the tranquillity
Of trees unshaken,
And the softness of sweet tears,
And the clearness of the clear brook
To wash away past years.
(For that too is the quality of Heaven,
That you are conscious always of great pain
Only when it is over
And shall not come again.
Thank God, thank God, it shall not come again,
Though your eyes be never so wet with the tears
Of many years!)

II

And so she stood a moment by the door
Of the long, red car. Royally she stepped down,
Settling on one long foot and leaning back
Amongst her russet furs. And she looked round . . .
Of course it must be strange to come from England
Straight into Heaven. You must take it in,
Slowly, for a long instant, with some fear . . .
Now that *affiche*, in orange, on the kiosque:
'*Six Spanish bulls will fight on Sunday next*
At Arles, in the arena' . . . Well, it's strange
Till you get used to our ways. And, on the *Maîrie*,
The untidy poster telling of the *concours*
De vers de soie, of silkworms. The cocoons
Pile, yellow, all across the little Places
Of ninety townships in the environs
Of Lyons, the city famous for her silks.
What if she's pale? It must be more than strange,
After these years, to come out here from England
To a strange place, to the stretched-out arms of me,
A man never fully known, only divined,

Loved, guessed at, pledged to, in your Sussex mud,
Amongst the frost-bound farms by the yeasty sea.
Oh, the long look; the long, long searching look!
And how my heart beat!
                                        Well, you see, in England
She had a husband. And four families —
His, hers, mine, and another woman's too —
Would have gone crazy. And, with all the rest,
Eight parents, and the children, seven aunts
And sixteen uncles and a grandmother.
There were, besides, our names, a few real friends,
And the decencies of life. A monstrous heap!
They made a monstrous heap. I've lain awake
Whole aching nights to tot the figures up!
Heap after heaps, of complications, griefs,
Worries, tongue-clackings, nonsenses and shame
For not making good. You see the coil there was!
And the poor strained fibres of our tortured brains,
And the voice that called from depth in her to depth
In me . . . my God, in the dreadful nights,
Through the roar of the great black winds, through the sound
  of the sea!
Oh agony! Agony! From out my breast
It called whilst the dark house slept, and stairheads creaked;
From within my breast it screamed and made no sound;
And wailed . . . And made no sound.
And howled like the damned . . . No sound! No sound!
Only the roar of the wind, the sound of the sea,
The tick of the clock . . .
And our two voices, noiseless through the dark.
O God! O God!

(That night my young love lay in my arms . . .

There was a bitter frost lay on the farms
In England, by the shiver
And the crawling of the tide;
By the broken silver of the English Channel,
Beneath the aged moon that watched alone —
Poor, dreary, lonely old moon to have to watch alone,

Over the dreary beaches mantled with ancient foam
Like shrunken flannel;
The moon, an intent, pale face, looking down
Over the English Channel.

But soft and warm She lay in the crook of my arm,
And came to no harm since we had come quietly home
Even to Heaven;
Which is situate in a little old town
Not very far from the side of the Rhone,
That mighty river
That is, just there by the Crau, in the lower reaches,
Far wider than the Channel.)

But, in the market place of the other little town,
Where the Rhone is a narrower, greener affair,
When she had looked at me, she beckoned with her long white hand,
A little languidly, since it is a strain, if a blessed strain, to have just died.
And going back again,
Into the long, red, English racing car,
Made room for me amongst the furs at her side.
And we moved away from the kind looks of the kindly people
Into the wine of the hurrying air.
And very soon even the tall grey steeple
Of Lyons cathedral behind us grew little and far
And then was no more there . . .
And, thank God, we had nothing any more to think of,
And, thank God, we had nothing any more to talk of;
Unless, as it chanced, the flashing silver stalk of the pampas
Growing down to the brink of the Rhone,
On the lawn of a little château, giving onto the river.
And we were alone, alone, alone . . .
At last alone . . .

The poplars on the hill-crests go marching rank on rank,
And far away to the left, like a pyramid, marches the ghost of Mont Blanc.
There are vines and vines and vines, all down to the river bank.
There will be a castle here,

And an abbey there;
And huge quarries and a long white farm,
With long thatched barns and a long wine shed,
As we ran alone, all down the Rhone.

And that day there was no puncturing of the tyres to fear;
And no trouble at all with the engine and gear;
Smoothly and softly we ran between the great poplar alley
All down the valley of the Rhone.
For the dear, good God knew how we needed rest and to be alone.
But, on other days, just as you must have perfect shadows to make
perfect Rembrandts,
He shall afflict us with little lets and hindrances of His own
Devising – just to let us be glad that we are dead . . .
Just for remembrance.

III

Hard by the castle of God in the Alpilles,
In the eternal stone of Alpilles,
There's this little old town, walled round by the old, grey gardens . . .
There were never such olives as grow in the gardens of God,
The green-grey trees, the wardens of agony
And failure of gods.
Of hatred and faith, of truth, of treachery
They whisper; they whisper that none of the living prevail;
They whirl in the great mistral over the white, dry sods,
Like hair blown back from white foreheads in the enormous gale
Up to the castle walls of God . . .

But, in the town that's our home,
Once you are past the wall,
Amongst the trunks of the planes,
Though they roar never so mightily overhead in the day,
All this tumult is quieted down, and all
The windows stand open because of the heat of the night
That shall come.
And, from each little window, shines in the twilight a light,
And, beneath the eternal planes
With the huge, gnarled trunks that were aged and grey

At the creation of Time,
The Chinese lanthorns, hung out at the doors of hotels,
Shimmering in the dusk, here on an orange tree, there on a sweet-scented lime,
There on a golden inscription: 'Hotel of the Three Holy Bells.'
Or 'Hotel Sublime,' or 'Inn of the Real Good Will'.
And, yes, it is very warm and still,
And all the world is afoot after the heat of the day,
In the cool of the even in Heaven . . .
And it is here that I have brought my dear to pay her all that I owed her,
Amidst this crowd, with the soft voices, the soft footfalls, the rejoicing laughter.
And after the twilight there falls such a warm, soft darkness,
And there will come stealing under the planes a drowsy odour,
Compounded all of cyclamen, of oranges, or rosemary and bay,
To take the remembrance of the toil of the day away.

So we sat at a little table, under an immense plane,
And we remembered again
The blisters and foments
And terrible harassments of the tired brain,
The cold and the frost and the pain,
As if we were looking at a picture and saying: 'This is true!
Why this is a truly painted
Rendering of that street where — you remember? — I fainted.'
And we remembered again
Tranquilly, our poor few tranquil moments,
The falling of the sunlight through the panes,
The flutter for ever in the chimney of the quiet flame,
The mutter of our two poor tortured voices, always a-whisper
And the endless nights when I would cry out, running through all the gamut of misery, even to a lisp, her name;
And we remembered our kisses, nine, maybe, or eleven —
If you count two that I gave and she did not give again.

And always the crowd drifted by in the cool of the even,
And we saw the faces of friends,
And the faces of those to whom one day we must make amends,
Smiling in welcome.

And I said: 'On another day —
And such a day may well come soon —
We will play dominoes with Dick and Evelyn and Frances
For a whole afternoon.
And, in the time to come, Genée
Shall dance for us, fluttering over the ground as the sunlight dances.'
And *Arlésiennes* with the beautiful faces went by us,
And gipsies and Spanish shepherds, noiseless in sandals of straw, sauntered nigh us,
Wearing slouch hats and old sheep-skins, and casting admiring glances
From dark, foreign eyes at my dear . . .
(And ah, it is Heaven alone, to have her alone and so near!)
So all this world rejoices
In the cool of the even
In Heaven . . .
And, when the cool of the even was fully there,
Came a great ha-ha of voices.
Many children run together, and all laugh and rejoice and call,
Hurrying with little arms flying, and little feet flying, and little hurrying haunches,
From the door of a stable,
Where, in an *olla podrida*, they had been playing at the *corrida*
With the black Spanish bull, whose nature
Is patience with children. And so, through the gaps of the branches
Of jasmine on our screen beneath the planes,
We saw, coming down from the road that leads to the olives and Alpilles,
A man of great stature,
In a great cloak,
With a great stride,
And a little joke
For all and sundry, coming down with a hound at his side.
And he stood at the cross-roads, passing the time of day
In a great, kind voice, the voice of a man-and-a-half! —
With a great laugh, and a great clap on the back,
For a fellow in black — a priest I should say,
Or may be a lover,
Wearing black for his mistress's mood.
'A little toothache,' we could hear him say; 'but that's so good

When it gives over.' So he passed from sight
In the soft twilight, into the soft night,
In the soft riot and tumult of the crowd.

And a magpie flew down, laughing, holding up his beak to us.
And I said: 'That was God! Presently, when he has walked through
the town
And the night has settled down,
So that you may not be afraid,
In the darkness, he will come to our table and speak to us.'
And past us many saints went walking in a company —
The kindly, thoughtful saints, devising and laughing and talking,
And smiling at us with their pleasant solicitude.
And because the thick of the crowd followed to the one side God,
Or to the other the saints, we sat in solitude.
In the distance the saints went singing all in chorus,
And our Lord went on the other side of the street,
Holding a little boy.
Taking him to pick the musk-roses that open at dusk,
For wreathing the statue of Jove,
Left on the Alpilles above
By the Romans; since Jove,
Even Jove,
Must not want for his quota of honour and love;
But round about him there must be,
With all its tender jollity,
The laughter of children in Heaven,
Making merry with roses in Heaven.

Yet never he looked at us, knowing that that would be such joy
As must be over-great for hearts that needed quiet;
Such a riot and tumult of joy as quiet hearts are not able
To taste to the full . . .

. . . And my dear one sat in the shadows; very softly she wept: —
Such joy is in Heaven,
In the cool of the even,
After the burden and toil of the days,
After the heat and haze
In the vine-hills; or in the shady

Whispering groves in high passes up in the Alpilles,
Guarding the castle of God.

And I went on talking towards her unseen face:
'So it is, so it goes, in this beloved place,
There shall be never a grief but passes; no, not any;
There shall be such bright light and no blindness;
There shall be so little awe and so much loving-kindness;
There shall be a little longing and enough care,
There shall be a little labour and enough of toil
To bring back the lost flavour of our human coil;
Not enough to taint it;
And all that we desire shall prove as fair as we can paint it.'
For, though that may be the very hardest trick of all
God set Himself, who fashioned this goodly hall.
Thus He has made Heaven;
Even Heaven.

For God is a very clever mechanician;
And if He made this proud and goodly ship of the world,
From the maintop to the hull,
Do you think He could not finish it to the full,
With a flag and all,
And make it sail, tall and brave,
On the waters, beyond the grave?
It should cost but very little rhetoric
To explain for you that last, fine, conjuring trick;
Nor does God need to be a very great magician
To give to each man after his heart,
Who knows very well what each man has in his heart:
To let you pass your life in a night-club where they dance,
If that is your idea of heaven; if you will, in the South of France;
If you will, on the turbulent sea; if you will, in the peace of the night;
Where you will; how you will;
Or in the long death of a kiss, that may never pall:
He would be a very little God if He could not do all this,
And He is still
The great God of all.

For God is a good man; God is a kind man;

In the darkness He came walking to our table beneath the planes,
And spoke
So kindly to my dear,
With a little joke,
Giving Himself some pains
To take away her fear
Of His stature,
So as not to abash her,
In no way at all to dash her new pleasure beneath the planes,
In the cool of the even
In Heaven.

That, that is God's nature.
For God's a good brother, and God is no blind man,
And God's a good mother and loves sons who're rovers,
And God is our father and loves all good lovers.
He has a kindly smile for many a poor sinner;
He takes note to make it up to poor wayfarers on sodden roads;
Such as bear heavy loads
He takes note of, and of all that toil on bitter seas and frosty lands,
He takes care that they shall have good at His hands;
Well He takes note of a poor old cook,
Cooking your dinner;
And much He loves sweet joys in such as ever took
Sweet joy on earth. He has a kindly smile for a kiss
Given in a shady nook.
And in the golden book
Where the accounts of His estate are kept,
All the round, golden sovereigns of bliss,
Known by poor lovers, married or never yet married,
Whilst the green world waked, or the black world quietly slept;
All joy, all sweetness, each sweet sigh that's sighed —
Their accounts are kept,
And carried
By the love of God to His own credit's side.
So that is why He came to our table to welcome my dear, dear bride,
In the cool of the even
In front of a café in Heaven.

ANTWERP

I

Gloom!
An October like November;
August a hundred thousand hours,
And all September,
A hundred thousand, dragging sunlit days,
And half October like a thousand years . . .
And doom!
That then was Antwerp . . .
                                        In the name of God,
How could they do it?
Those souls that usually dived
Into the dirty caverns of mines;
Who usually hived
In whitened hovels; under ragged poplars;
Who dragged muddy shovels, over the grassy mud,
Lumbering to work over the greasy sods . . .
Those men there, with the appearances of clods
Were the bravest men that a usually listless priest of God
Ever shrived . . .
And it is not for us to make them an anthem.
If we found words there would come no wind that would fan them
To a tune that the trumpets might blow it,
Shrill through the heaven that's ours or yet Allah's
Or the wide halls of any Valhallas.
We can make no such anthem. So that all that is ours
For inditing in sonnets, pantoums, elegiacs, or lays
Is this:
'In the name of God, how could they do it?'

II

For there is no new thing under the sun,
Only this uncomely man with a smoking gun
In the gloom . . .
What the devil will he gain by it?
Digging a hole in the mud and standing all day in the rain by it

Waiting his doom,
The sharp blow, the swift outpouring of the blood,
Till the trench of grey mud
Is turned to a brown purple drain by it.
Well, there have been scars
Won in many wars . . .
Punic,
Lacedaemonian, wars of Napoleon, wars for faith, wars for honour, for love, for possession,
But this Belgian man in his ugly tunic,
His ugly round cap, shooting on, in a sort of obsession,
Overspreading his miserable land,
Standing with his wet gun in his hand . . .
Doom!
He finds that in a sudden scrimmage,
And lies, an unsightly lump on the sodden grass . . .
An image that shall take long to pass!

III

For the white-limbed heroes of Hellas ride by upon their horses
For ever through our brains.
The heroes of Cressy ride by upon their stallions;
And battalions and battalions and battalions —
The Old Guard, the Young Guard, the men of Minden and of Waterloo,
Pass, for ever staunch,
Stand for ever true;
And the small man with the large paunch,
And the grey coat, and the large hat, and the hands behind the back,
Watches them pass
In our minds for ever . . .
But that clutter of sodden corses
On the sodden Belgian grass —
That is a strange new beauty.

IV

With no especial legends of marchings or triumphs or duty,
Assuredly that is the way of it,

The way of beauty . . .
And that is the highest word you can find to say of it.
For you cannot praise it with words
Compounded of lyres and swords,
But the thought of the gloom and the rain
And the ugly coated figure, standing beside a drain,
Shall eat itself into your brain.
And that shall be an honourable word;
'Belgian' shall be an honourable word,
As honourable as the fame of the sword,
As honourable as the mention of the many-chorded lyre,
And his old coat shall seem as beautiful as the fabrics woven in Tyre.

V

And what in the world did they bear it for?
I don't know.
And what in the world did they dare it for?
Perhaps that is not for the likes of me to understand.
They could very well have watched a hundred legions go
Over their fields and between their cities
Down into more southerly regions.
They could very well have let the legions pass through their woods,
And have kept their lives and their wives and their children and cattle
and goods.
I don't understand.
Was it just love of their land?
Oh poor dears!
Can any man so love his land?
Give them a thousand thousand pities
And rivers and rivers of tears
To wash off the blood from the cities of Flanders.

VI

This is Charing Cross;
It is midnight;
There is a great crowd
And no light.
A great crowd, all black that hardly whispers aloud.

Surely, that is a dead woman — a dead mother!
She has a dead face;
She is dressed all in black;
She wanders to the bookstall and back,
At the back of the crowd;
And back again and again back,
She sways and wanders.

This is Charing Cross;
It is one o'clock.
There is still a great cloud, and very little light;
Immense shafts of shadows over the black crowd
That hardly whispers aloud . . .
And now! . . . That is another dead mother,
And there is another and another and another . . .
And little children, all in black,
All with dead faces, waiting in all the waiting-places,
Wandering from the doors of the waiting-room
In the dim gloom.
These are the women of Flanders.
They await the lost.
They await the lost that shall never leave the dock;
They await the lost that shall never again come by the train
To the embraces of all these women with dead faces;
They await the lost who lie dead in trench and barrier and foss,
In the dark of the night.
This is Charing Cross; it is past one of the clock;
There is very little light.

There is so much pain.

L'Envoi.

And it was for this that they endured this gloom;
This October like November,
That August like a hundred thousand hours,
And that September,
A hundred thousand dragging sunlit days,
And half October like a thousand years . . .
Oh poor dears!

from

Buckshee: Last Poems (1936)

Buckshee, derived from the universal Oriental *backschisch*, has no English equivalent. It is a British Army word — signifies something unexpected, unearned — gratifying. If the cook, at dinner time, slips three extra potatoes into your meat can, these are buckshee potatoes; if, for something you are paid in guineas instead of pounds, the odd shillings are buckshee; if you are a little boy alongside a liner at Port Said and a white passenger throws half a crown instead of a florin into the shark-infested water for you to dive for, the odd sixpence is buckshee, backschisch. Or if you have long given up the practice of verse and suddenly find yourself writing it — those lines will be *buckshee*. — *F.M.F.*

BUCKSHEE

I

I think God must have been a stupid man,
To have sent a spirit, chivalrous and loyal,
Cruel and tender, arrogant and so meek,
Gallant and timorous, halting and as swift
As hawk descending — to have sent such a spirit,
Certain in all its attributes, into this Age
Of our banal world.
            He had Infinity
Which must embrace infinities of worlds.
            And had Eternity
And could have chosen any other Age.
            He had Omnipotence
And could have found a fitting hour and time.
But, bruised and bruising, wounded, contumacious,
An eagle pinioned, an eagle on the wing;
A leopard maimed, a leopard in its spring;
A swallow caged, a swallow in the spacious
And amethystine, palpitating blue;
A night-bird of the heath, shut off from the heath,

A deathless being, daubed with the mud of death,
Haïtchka, the undaunted, loyal spirit of you!
Came to our world of cozening and pimping,
Our globe compact of virtues all half virtue,
Of vices scarce half-vices, made up of truth
Blurred in the edges and of lies so limping
They will not spur the pulse in the utterance;
From a New World that's old and knows not youth
Unto our France that's France and knows not France,
Where charity and every virtue hurt you . . .
A coin of gold dropped in a leaden palm,
Manna and frankincense and myrrh and balm
And bitter herbs and spices of the South
Are you and honey for the parching mouth . . .
  Because God was a stupid man and threw
  Into our outstretched palms, Haïtchka, you!

VII
Miscellaneous

Ford's notes on reading the *Talmud* (1893)

An autograph manuscript, published here for the first time with the permission of the Department of Rare Books, Ford Madox Ford Collection, Cornell University.

THE philosophy of the Jews seems to have been quite as Catholic as that of the Church of Rome. For the credulous there is a perfect infinity of ridiculous miracles taking in all sorts and conditions of people from God Almighty to sea serpents. In the Bible[1] this is not so marked as regards the Deity — but fabulous monsters of course abound and are explained away to this day as allegories by Christians. In the Talmud there are miraculous minutiae of quite as ridiculous calibre as in R. C. legends — but for the more philosophic in both churches there is a great deal of scope. — In the T. moreover are many injunctions to a spirit of forgiveness that is almost Christian.

The symbol of a Rock is not by any means inapplicable to either church — for there are many crannies in which a man may hide and shut his eyes from the light. — The Church of R. being of course more sympathetic and eminently *more* Catholic than any other Western Church Protestant. — I am almost inclined to place the Jewish Philosophy on the whole next to it as regards those qualities — such sympathy for old cock and bull stories being an eminently attractive and aesthetic quality — calculated to seize on one when tired of reason for the time being. — The P.s are far more cold and reasoning and therefore less attractive.

[1] e.g. Jacob wrestling with the Almighty, Genesis. (Ford's note)

'The Mantle of Elijah'

This deft little story was probably written in 1898, the year Ford wrote *Seraphina*, the unpublished novel that was to be the basis for his first collaboration with Conrad, *Romance*. Ford and his wife Elsie had moved to Grace's Cottage in Limpsfield, Surrey, next door to Edward and Constance Garnett. It was a very literary place to live: Ford met Conrad, Galsworthy, W.H. Hudson and Stephen Crane; Henry James lived within walking distance, at Rye. It is no surprise that Ford should have written a story about literary influence, a subject he treated in a much broader vein thirteen years later, when, under the pseudonym Daniel Chaucer, he wrote *The Simple Life Limited* (see excerpt, pp. 40–51), a satirical novel drawing largely on the community in Limpsfield. The manuscript of 'The Mantle of Elijah' is published here for the first time, by permission of the Harry Ransom Humanities Research Center, The University of Texas at Austin.

'MY dear fellow,' Lingen said, 'I can tell you why I took him — with the utmost precision. He was Tomalyn's man and when Tomalyn died I said: — "I must have something of his that actually exhales the air he breathes." I went to his house — but it was really too painful I found to enter and select. This man opened the door to me. I told him to beg his mistress to send me something that my dear friend had used every day — something that she might have chosen for herself. Go in I could not — there seemed to be such a real presence of death in the house. — Well — this grotesque person stood on the door-step, making his remarkable congees to me and the thought came to me that he must know more of Tomalyn, than even — even the pen he wrote with could tell me. I said:

"And you — what are you going to do — Is Mrs Tomalyn going to keep you?"

It appeared not. He did not fit into any place in the changed household. It seemed to me that he might in mine. I had never wanted a man servant before. I suppose I did not actually need him then, but I made him the offer. It seems he had at first thought of reverting from the service of Literature to his appropriate sphere as a retainer of Society — He's very useful, you know. — I don't know that he has any duties to perform — but he is at hand if ever anything chances to want doing. Of course he's grotesquely out of place. — I feel that he ought to be adorning some sideboard covered with ancestral plate. But it amuses me to contemplate him as the servant of a literary bachelor. It puts me into a sort of chuckling good humour. — I don't know why, I'm sure — but somehow he suggests a very dignified cock that's lost its tail feathers. And mind you,' Lingen went on, 'he does seem to keep me remarkably in touch with Tomalyn. He has the outward reserve of the upper servant — but he grows confidential as he moves about the room putting things in order and his way of managing his phrases is very remarkable — very. And what's more it does suggest Tomalyn,' he repeated.

I sat in silence and looked at Lingen. I didn't doubt that that odd fowl his butler did suggest Tomalyn to him. I never knew that noble man and great writer myself — but I knew enough of Lingen himself to realize the arbitrary manner in which his mind established connections between things apparently of the remotest nature. 'Arbitrary' characterizes Lingen. He was born to dictate. Someone once said that he looked like a police magistrate. Consider this abominable conversation.

What did I care about his butler — I, a person who perhaps twice a year pass four nights in London, and then thirst for commune upon topics quite other? I admit that it served me right. I sat there feeling like a baffled — and to wit very mean — detective. I had imposed myself on Lingen's hospitable hearth with a discreditable end in view — you guess it to be the solution of the Lingen-Tomalyn question. I was consequently longing to hear Tomalyn discussed by Lingen. Instead: Lingen analysed his accursed butler.

I found myself listening abstractedly, and saying to myself over and over again:

'All very well — all very well — but why do you write like Tomalyn now — why after writing pure Lingen for all these years and years do you suddenly become — not exactly a copyist of Tomalyn — but just Tomalyn?'

Before Tomalyn's death one had naturally linked the two. They were the two most polishing writers of the day. Every sentence that each of them wrote was a lesson in perfection. But each in its kind. There was no more similarity between that nervous, exhilarated, buoyant style of Tomalyn and the utterly refined ungraspable nebulousness of Lingen than there is between etching and silver-point. If Tomalyn had evolved his methods through years of starvation and neglect Lingen had given years to the perfection of his vehicle of expression. In all human probability it had seemed that Lingen had attained his definite level.

Yet when I came to read the first volume that he produced after Tomalyn's death I found myself exclaiming with absolute amazement:

'But this is pure Tomalyn.'

And as time went on his work became more pronouncedly Tomalyn and the fact became patent to the world — the world, that is, that troubled itself about such matters.

I frankly confess that it grieved me to the soul. It meant that Tomalyn still lived — but that Lingen was dead, and though I am free to concede that Tomalyn was as great a man — I craved mere Lingen. It puzzled as well as saddened me.

Lingen I have said was arbitrary. It seemed to me incredible that so strongly individualized a man could, with what seemed like meekness, indue the mantle of any other prophet however well beloved.

The only answer that came to me was that Lingen so lamented his friend that he had bent his indomitable will to snatching him from death at the cost of his own life. — But there was no absolute conviction — no rest for me — in this. Lingen himself gave me no further clue.

I stayed my four days under Lingen's roof and then found that I must needs extend my stay to double that period. I came a good deal into contact with the preposterous domestic that Lingen dwelt upon. I have no doubt that Lingen was right as to his adorning an aristocratic sideboard — though I never remember to have sat before one. The quaintness of his remarks was incontestable: their flavour seemed to hang in the mouth, and the turns of his phrase to crop up in one's subsequent intercourse with quite incongruous mortals. When one left Lingen's chambers it was as if one went out from a strongly-hued light, or a room filled with a powerful clinging odour into a normal-coloured, odourless world. The days that a countryman spends in Town are so crowded with sensations as to seem years of tranquil greensward life. I seemed to have been for a season rather than a mere sennight subject to Lingen's own 'home influences' on the day when I found myself still in Lingen's room taking up a forgotten pen and framing a too belated piece of copy.

The words came trippingly to my tongue and transferred themselves with unaccustomed effortlessness to the paper. I had a vague sense that something was amiss — as though I were working with the aid of a strong stimulant.

I faltered a moment — a word didn't come. Lingen was polishing a pile of type-written matter on the other side of the table. He was digging his pen impatiently into his blotting paper. I know that like myself he was word hunting.

The butler opened the door to ask some trivial question. Midway in his phrase came the word I sought. I captured it and glanced at my last sentence. I found myself exclaiming:

'But good God — this is pure Tomalyn.'

I cast back — there were the butler's quaint pregnant phrases — all the strong savour of his antiquated speech — all its forgotten, preposterous courtly convolutions.

I tore my copy in half and then placed it carefully in a notebook. 'A few days of country life will blow away these cobwebs — a few good gusts of our south west wind. My style will resume its familiar baldness.'

I looked across at Lingen. He too had found his word and was buried in his work, but I interrupted him.

'I must be catching my train,' I said. — 'Do you think you will ever get rid of your butler?' I continued tentatively.

He disentangled his mind for a moment to bid me farewell.

'No — I don't suppose I shall surrender him unless I outlive him.'

Till then we shall have no more Lingen.

from

The Cinque Ports: A Historical and Descriptive Record (1900)

This account of the five towns of Kent and Sussex that once formed an autonomous kingdom was a work of both history and personal commentary, an early example of the 'sociological impressionism' that Ford made into a characteristic genre and developed throughout his career. (See particularly the three books on England published together as *England and the English*: *The Soul of London*, 1905, The *Heart of the Country*, 1906, and *The Spirit of the People*, 1907; the two books of propaganda for the Allies, *When Blood Is Their Argument*, 1915, and *Between St Dennis and St George*, 1915; and the better known *Provence*, 1935 and *Great Trade Route*, 1937.) In this excerpt, readers will recognize the germ of the story of Conrad's 'Amy Foster', which Ford, having heard in Winchelsea as a local anecdote, told to Conrad.

BESIDES the lighthouse there is at Dungeness Point a Lloyd's station which, on a busy day, adds a touch of colour to the place with its strings of flags. Walking along the shingle one comes upon a solitary telegraph-station, almost within reach of the waves. It is used, I believe, by shipmasters, who send messages ashore by boat. Farther along one will find a cluster of fishermen's cottages grouped round a dismantled fort. The little village — Lambarde calls it Nesh — is perhaps as difficult of attainment as any in the kingdom. The fulls of shingle make walking an absolute torture, make one envy the pilgrims who had nothing worse than parched peas underfoot. The inhabitants, however, make use of what they call backstays, an instrument after the manner of a snow-shoe, and on these they glide in an enviable manner. The village, when one has reached it, is picturesque, though, perhaps, 'suggestive' is the better word. Its black, weather-boarded houses have no better foundation than the shingle; not a herb is to be seen. According to Mr Lucy, however, there was once a garden in the place. Its owner had carried the soil for it from Lydd sack by sack over the terrible road. It has now, I think, disappeared; I, at least, have never seen it. A few hens peck the ground round the shanties, though what they find to nourish them it is difficult to say. There is not even soil enough for the sea-poppy, though a little nearer the railway a miniature wood makes a shift to cover a plot of ground not much larger than a suit of clothes. The firewood of the village is composed of stacks of wreckwood; indeed the whole neighbourhood has an air of having been washed from the depths of the sea. If one is in luck — still more, if one has the gift of making those of few words talk — one may hear stirring stories of the ships that come ashore on stormy nights; for Dungeness is very terrible to those that fail to give it a wide enough berth. Moreover, it is no unusual thing to see a sad piece of human jetsam, done to death miles and miles away, come bobbing along the currents that sweep the bay near the point. One of the most tragic stories that I remember to have heard was connected with a man who escaped the tender mercies of the ocean to undergo an almost more merciless buffeting ashore. He was one of the crew of a German merchant that was wrecked almost at the foot of the lighthouse. A moderate swimmer, he was carried by the current to some distance from the scene of the catastrophe. Here he touched the ground. He had nothing, no clothes, no food; he came ashore on a winter's night. In the morning he found himself in the Marsh near Romney. He knocked at doors, tried to make himself understood. The Marsh people thought him either a lunatic or a supernatural visitor. To lonely women in the Marsh cottages he seemed a fearful object. No doubt he was, poor wretch. They warned their menfolk of him, and whenever he was seen he was hounded away and ill-used. He got the name of Mad Jack. Knowing nothing of the country, nothing of the language, he could neither ask his way nor read the names on the signposts, and even if he read them, they meant nothing to him. How long this lasted, I do not know: I remember hearing from the village people at the time that a dangerous person was in the neighbourhood. The fear of the cottage folk was real enough. For a fortnight or so hardly one of them would open their doors after nightfall. The police at last got to hear of him, and, after a search of some days, he was found asleep in a pigsty. He had the remains of an old shirt hanging round his neck; and under one arm, an old shoe that he seemed to use as a larder; it contained two old crusts and the raw wing of a chicken. In all the time of his wandering he had not come more than nine miles from the place where he had come ashore.

I had the story rather curiously confirmed — paralleled — the other day. A man knocked at my door and asked me in German if I were a Jew. I told him that I was not, without much affecting his belief that the only German-speakers in the kingdom were members of the chosen people. He was one of the many Germans who leave their country to escape the military service; had taken a ticket for London from Cologne, and had persuaded his aged mother to accompany him to the town whose streets are paved with gold. They had reached Dover in safety, and were in the train bound for London when a German in the same compartment advised them not to go to London; there were too many Germans there already, too many thieves. Jakob Schmitz decided to alight at the next station. At Folkestone, therefore, he attempted to explain his wishes to the porter at the gate. The porter called the guard of the train, who, seeing that Schmitz had a London ticket, caught him by the arm and bundled him and his mother into the train again, locking the door upon them. Schmitz, however, determined not to go to London, descended on to the six-footway at the next station — Sandling Junction. When the train moved off Schmitz and his mother were discovered and conducted to a waiting-room for consignment to the care of the guard of the next train. This Schmitz and his mother did not await. They seized a moment when the coast was clear and departed into the wide world. They had to undergo an agony as acute, though fortunately not so protracted, as that of their predecessor in misfortune. The mother was in want of a cup of coffee, but whenever Schmitz knocked at a cottage door he was roughly repelled. The folks told him afterwards that they had taken him for a ghost or a murderer or a pikey — as we call the gipsies.

After nine hours' wandering, the Schmitzes reached Hythe. It was then eight o'clock of a January night. Here Frau Schmitz fainted in the open street — a small crowd collected, and amongst the number a man who had passed some time with German workmen in New York. He conducted them to a hotel where there was a German waiter, and their troubles were at an end. But for the fainting of the mother, however, they might have fared nearly as badly as the other did.

Stories as cheerless as these may be heard in plenty among the dwellers at Dungeness.

[London: Heinemann, 1900: pp. 162–4.]

from

Conrad's *Nostromo*

Nostromo was originally serialized in *T.P.'s Weekly* in consecutive issues from 29 January to 7 October, 1904. When the instalment for the 8 April issue was due, Conrad 'was taken with so violent an attack of gout and nervous depression that he was quite unable to continue his instalments.' (Letter from Ford to George T. Keating, cited by John Hope Morey, 'Joseph Conrad and Ford Madox Ford,' Diss. Cornell University, 1960, pp. 120–21.) Ford wrote the section, which constitutes roughly the first half of Chapter V of Part II, 'The Isabels'.

The text published here is the editor's transcription of the autograph manuscript in the Beinecke Rare Book and Manuscript Library, Yale University. Editorial brackets indicate gaps in the manuscript due to missing pages, filled by using the text from *T.P.'s Weekly*, which is closer throughout to Ford's pages than is the first English edition of the novel.

[THE Gould carriage was the first to return from the harbour to the empty town, for all the populace, high and low, had poured out to the military spectacle. On the ancient pavement laid out in patterns, sunk into ruts and holes, the portly Ignacio, mindful of the springs of the Parisian-built landau, had pulled up to a walk, and Decoud in his corner contemplated moodily the inner aspect of the gate. The squat turreted sides held up between them a mass of masonry with bunches of grass growing at the top, and a grey, heavily-scrolled, armorial shield of stone above the apex of the arch with the arms of Spain nearly smoothed out as if in readiness for some new device typical of the impending progress.

The explosive noise of the railway trucks seemed to augment Decoud's irritation. He muttered something to himself, then began to talk aloud in curt, angry phrases thrown at the silence of the two women. They did not look at him at all; while Don José, with his semi-translucent, waxy complexion, overshadowed by the soft grey hat, swayed a little to the jolts of the carriage by the side of Mrs Gould. Neither did he look at the young man; one could almost detect under the clothes the emaciated condition of that body held up in an unyielding rigidity by the force of will, inspired by imperishable convictions.

'This sound puts a new edge on a very old truth.'

Decoud spoke in French, perhaps because of Ignacio on the box above him; the old coachman, with his broad back in short silver-braided jacket, had a big pair of ears, whose thick rims stood well away from his cropped head.

'Yes, the noise outside the city wall is new, but the principle is old.'

He ruminated his discontent for a while, then began afresh with a sidelong glance at Antonia:

'No, but just imagine our forefathers in morions and corselets drawn up outside this gate, and a band of adventurers just landed from their ships in the harbour there. Thieves, of course. Speculators, too. Their expeditions, each one, were the speculations of grave and reverend persons in England. That is history, as that absurd sailor Mitchell is always saying.'

'Mitchell's arrangements for the embarkation of the troops were excellent!' exclaimed Don José.

'That! — that! oh, that's really the work of that Genoese seaman! But to return to my noises; there used to be in the old days the sound of trumpets outside that gate. War trumpets! I'm sure they were trumpets instead of those noises! But it's the same thing. Drake, who was the greatest of these men, used to dine alone in his cabin on board ship to the sound of trumpets. In those days this town was full of wealth, those men came to take it. Now the whole land is like a treasure house, and all these people are breaking into it, whilst we are cutting each other's throats. The only thing that keeps them out is mutual jealousy. But they'll come to agreements — and by the time we've settled our quarrels and become decent and honourable, there'll be nothing left for us. It has always been the same. We Spaniards are a wonderful people, but it has always been our fate to be' — he did not say 'robbed', but added, after a pause – 'exploited!'

Mrs Gould said: 'Oh, this is unjust!' And Antonia interjected: 'Don't answer him, Emilia. He is attacking me.'

'You surely don't think I was attacking Don Carlos!' Decoud answered.

And then the carriage stopped before the door of the Casa Gould. The young man offered his hand to the ladies. They went in first together; Don José walked by the side of Decoud, and the old porter trotted after them with some light wraps on his arm.

Don José slipped his hand under the arm of the journalist of Sulaco.]

'The *Porvenir* must have a long and confident article upon Barrios' [sic] and the irresistibleness of his army of Cayta! The moral effect should be kept up in the country. — We will cable extracts to Europe and the United States. After all we must maintain the favourable impression abroad.'

Decoud muttered:

'Oh yes, we must comfort our friends the speculators.'

This side of the open gallery was in the shadow, with its screen of plants in vases along the balustrade holding out motionless blossoms and all the glass doors of the reception rooms thrown open. A jingle of spurs died out at the further end.

Benito, standing aside against the wall said in a soft tone to the passing ladies:

'The Señor Administrador is just back from the mountains.'

In the great Sala with its groups of ancient Spanish and modern European furniture making as if different centres under the high white spread of the ceiling, the silver and porcelain of the tea service gleamed among a cluster of dwarf chairs like a bit of a lady's boudoir putting in a note of feminine and intimate delicacy.

Don José in his rocking chair placed his hat on his lap and Decoud walked up and down the whole length of the room, passing between tables loaded with knick-knacks and almost disappearing behind the high backs of leathern sofas. — He was thinking of the angry face of Antonia; he was confident that he would make his peace with her. . . . He did not stay in Sulaco to quarrel with Antonia . . .

Martin Decoud was angry with himself. All he saw and heard going on around him exasperated the preconceived views of his European civilization. To contemplate revolutions from the distance of the Parisian Boulevards was quite another matter. There on the spot it was impossible to dismiss their tragic comedy with the expression: '*Quelle farce*!'

The reality of the political action, such as it was, seemed close, and acquired poignancy by Antonia's belief in the cause. Its crudeness hurt his vanity. He was surprised at his own sensitiveness.

'I suppose I am more of a ["Costaguanero" than I would have believed possible,' he thought to himself.

His disdain for it grew like a reaction of his scepticism against the action into which he was forced by his infatuation for Antonia. He soothed himself by saying he was not a patriot, but a lover.

He continued to walk after the ladies came in bare-headed, and Mrs Gould sank low before the little tea-table. Antonia took up her usual place at the reception hour — the corner of a leathern couch, with a rigid grace of her pose and a fan in her hand; then Decoud, swerving from the straight line of his march, came to lean over the high back of her seat.

For a long time he spoke into her ear, softly, with a half-smile and an air of apologetic familiarity, watching the while the fold of the frown on her forehead smooth out gradually. Her fan lay half-grasped on her knee. She never looked at him. His rapid utterance grew more and more insistent] and caressing. At last he ventured a slight laugh:

— 'No. Really. You must forgive me. One must be serious sometimes.' He paused. Her blue eyes glided slowly towards him, slightly upwards, as if mollified and questioning.

'You can't think I am serious, when I call Montero a *gran bestia* every second day in the *Porvenir*? — That isn't a serious occupation. No occupation is serious, not even when a bullet in the heart is the penalty of failure.'

Her hand closed firmly on the fan.

'Some reason, — you understand I mean some sense, — may creep into thinking, some glimpse of truth, I mean some effective truth for which there is no room in politics or journalism. I happen to have said what I thought. And you are angry! If you do me the kindness to think a little you will see that I spoke like a patriot.'

— She opened her red lips for the first time, not unkindly:

'Yes! But you never see the aims. Men must be used as they are. I suppose nobody is really disinterested, unless perhaps you, Don Martin!'

— 'God forbid! It's the last thing I should like you to believe of me.' He spoke lightly and paused. She began to fan herself with a slow movement without raising her hand. After a time he whispered passionately:

'Antonia!'

She smiled and extended her hand after the English manner towards Charles Gould who was bowing before her; while Decoud with his arms spread on the back of the sofa dropped his eyes and murmured: 'Bonjour.'

The Señor Administrador of the San Tomé mine bent over his wife for a moment. They exchanged a few words of which only the phrase: 'The greatest enthusiasm,' pronounced by Mrs Gould, could be heard.

— 'Yes,' Decoud began in a murmur. 'Even he!'

— 'This is sheer calumny,' she said not very severely.

— 'You just ask him to throw his mine into the melting pot for the great cause,' Decoud whispered furiously.

Don José had raised his voice. He emitted slight laughs and rubbed his hands. The excellent aspect of the troops and the great quantity of the new, deadly rifles on the shoulders of those brave men seemed to fill him with a sort of ecstatic confidence.

Charles Gould, very tall and thin before his chair, listened but nothing could be discovered in his face except an expression of kind and deferential attention. Meantime Antonia had risen and crossing the room stood looking out of one of the three long windows giving on the street. Decoud followed her. — The window was thrown open and he leaned against the thickness of the wall. The long folds of the damask curtain falling straight from the broad bronze cornice hid him partly from the room. He crossed his arms on his breast and looked steadily at Antonia's profile.

The people returning from the harbour filled both pavements; the shuffle of sandals and a low murmur of voices ascended to the window. Now and then a great family coach rolled slowly along the disjointed roadway of the Calle de la Constitucion. There were not many private carriages in Sulaco; at the most crowded hour on the Alameda they could be counted with one glance of the eye. The great family arks, swaying on high leathern springs, full of pretty, powdered faces in which the eyes looked intensely alive and black. And first, Don Juste Lopes the president of the Provincial Assembly, passed, portly in a black coat and cravat as when presiding over a *séance* with his three lovely daughters, and though they all raised their eyes Antonia did not make the usual greeting gesture of a fluttered hand, and they affected not to see the two young people, Costaguañeros with European manners whose doings were discussed beyond the barred windows of the first families in Sulaco. — And then Señora Gavilaso de Valdes rolled by, handsome and dignified, in a great, cumbrous machine in which she used to travel to and fro to her country house, surrounded by an armed retinue in leather suits and big sombreros with carbines at the bows of their saddles. She was a widow of most distinguished family, proud, rich and kindhearted. Her second son Jaime had just gone off on the staff of Barios [sic]. The eldest, a worthless fellow of a moody disposition, filled Sulaco with the noise of his dissipations and gambled heavily at the club. The two youngest boys with yellow Ribierist cockades in their caps sat on the front seat. She too affected not to see the señor Decoud talking publicly with Antonia in defiance of every convention and he not even her *novio* as far as the world knew, though even in that case it would have been scandal enough. But the dignified old lady, respected and admired by the first families, would have been still more shocked if she could have heard the words they were exchanging:

— 'Did you say I lost sight of the aim? I have only one aim in the world.'

She had an almost imperceptible negative movement of her head, still staring across the street at the Avellanos' house, grey, marked with decay and with iron bars like a prison.

— 'And it would be so easy of attainment,' he continued, 'this aim which, whether knowingly or not, I have always had in my heart — ever since the day when you scolded me so horribly once, in Paris you remember.'

A slight smile seemed to move the corner of the lip that was on his side.

— 'You know you were a very terrible person, a sort of Charlotte Corday in a school girl's dress. — A ferocious patriot: I suppose you would have struck a knife into Guzman Bento.'

She interrupted him:

— 'You do me too much honour.'

— 'At any rate,' he said, changing suddenly to a tone of bitter levity, 'you would have sent me to stab him without compunction.'

— 'Ah, *par exemple*!' she murmured.

— 'Well,' he argued mockingly, 'don't you keep me here writing deadly nonsense? — Deadly to me! It has already killed my self-respect. And you may imagine,' he went on, his tone passing into light banter, 'that Montero, should he be successful, would get even with me in the only way such a brute can get even with a man of intelligence who condescends to call him a *gran bestia* three times a week. It's a sort of intellectual death but there is the other one in the background for a journalist of my ability.'

— 'If he is successful,' said Antonia thoughtfully.

— 'You seem satisfied to see my life hang on a thread,' Decoud replied, with a broad smile. 'And the other one, the "dear brother" of the Proclamations, the guerrillero, — haven't I written that he was taking the guest's [sic] overcoats and changing plates in Paris at our Legation in the intervals of spying on some of our refugees there in the time of Rojes [sic]. He will wash out that sacred truth with blood. With my blood! — Why do you look annoyed? This is simply a bit of the biography of one of our great men. What do you think he will do to me? There is a certain convent wall round the corner of the Plaza opposite the door of the Bull Ring. You know? Opposite the door with the inscription: *Intrada de la Sombra*. — Appropriate perhaps! That's where the uncle of our host gave up his Anglo-South American soul. *Quel héroisme!* For, note, he might have run away. A man who has fought with weapons may run away. You might have let me go with Barrios if you had cared for me. I would have carried one of those rifles in which Don José believes, with the greatest satisfaction in the ranks of poor peons and Indios that know nothing either of reason or of politics. The most forlorn hope in the most forlorn army on earth would have been safer than that for which you made me stay here. When you make war you may retreat but not when you spend your time in inciting poor ignorant fools to kill and to die.'

His tone remained light, and as if unaware of his presence she stood motionless, her hands clasped lightly with the fan hanging down from her entwined fingers. — He waited for a while and then said:

'I shall go to the wall,' he said with a sort of jocular desperation. Even that declaration did not make her look at him. Her head remained still, her eyes fixed upon the house of the Avellanos, whose chipped pilasters, broken cornices, the whole degradation of dignity was hidden now by the gathering dusk of the street. In her whole figure her lips alone moved forming the words:

'Martin, you will make me cry.'

He remained silent for a minute, startled as if overwhelmed by a sort of awed happiness, with the lines of the mocking smile still stiffened about his mouth and incredulous surprise in his eyes. The value of a sentence is in the personality which utters it, for nothing new can be said by man or woman — and those were the last words, it seemed to him, that could ever have been spoken by Antonia. He had never made it up with her so completely in all their intercourse of small and sharp encounters. — But even before she had time to turn towards him, which she did slowly with a rigid grace, he had recovered his voice.

'My sister is only waiting to embrace you. My father is transported. I won't say anything of my mother: our mothers were like sisters. There is a packet south next week . . . That Fernandez is a fool. Why, a man like Montero is bribed. It's the practice of the country. It's tradition: it's politics. Read: *Fifty Years of Misrule*.'

— ' Leave poor papa alone, Don Martin. He believes. . . .'

— 'I have the greatest tenderness,' he began hurriedly. 'But I love. I love, Antonia! And Fernandez has miserably mismanaged that business. Perhaps your father did too. I don't know. Montero *was* bribeable. Why, I suppose he only wanted his share of this famous loan for National Development. Why didn't the stupid Sta. Martha people give it him, or an Embassy or something. He would have taken five years' salary in advance and gone boosing [?] in Paris, this stupid, ferocious Indio!'

'The man,' she said thoughtfully and very calm before this outburst, 'was intoxicated with vanity. We had all the information, not Fernandez' only, and then there was his brother intriguing too.'

'Oh yes,' he said. 'Of course, you know. You know everything. You read all the correspondence, you write all the papers — all those State Papers that are inspired here, in this room. — In blind devotion to a theory of political purity. Hadn't you Carlos Gould before your eyes? Rey de Sulaco! He and his mine are the practical demonstration of what could have been done. Do you think he succeeded by his fidelity to a theory of virtue? And all those railway people with their honest work? Of course their work is honest! But what if you can't work honestly till the thieves are satisfied? Couldn't he, a great man, have told that Sir John What's his name that Montero had to be bought off — he and his Negro liberals hanging onto his gold-laced sleeves? He ought to have been bought off with his own stupid weight of gold, his weight of gold, I tell you, boots, sabre, spurs, cocked hat and all.'

She shook her head slightly:

'It was impossible,' she murmured.

— 'He wanted the whole lot? What?'

She was facing him now in the deep recess of the window, very close and motionless while her lips moved rapidly; and an effect of passionate interest in her eyes. She defended Fernandez, the President-Dictator Ribiera; they had aspirations, those men. Other names fell fluently from her red lips with justificative comments and a deep knowledge of the secret counsels of the party. She was, with a sort of reasonable ardour, justifying her father, really. Decoud, leaning his head back against the wall, listened with crossed arms and lowered eyelids. He drank in the tones of her low voice and watched the agitated life of her throat as if waves of emotion had run a pulse from the heart to pass out into the air in her reasonable words. He also had his aspirations; he aspired to carry her away out of these deadly futilities of pronunciamentos and reforms. All this was wrong — utterly wrong, but she fascinated him and sometimes the sheer sagacity of a phrase would break the charm, replace the fascination by a sudden, unwilling thrill of interest. Some women hovered, as it were, on the threshold of genius, he reflected; they did not want to know or think or understand. Passion stood for all that and he was ready to believe that some startlingly profound remark, some appreciation of character, or a judgement upon an event, bordered on the miraculous. In the mature Antonia he could see with an extraordinary vividness the austere schoolgirl of the earlier days. She seduced him against his judgement; sometimes he smiled, now and then he threw in a word. He began to argue; the curtains half hid them. They talked.

Outside it had grown dark, and from the deep trench of shadow between the houses the glimmer of rare street lamps ascended the evening silence of Sulaco — the silence of a town with few carriages and no wheeled traffic, of no shod horses and soft-sandalled populace; the lights of the Casa Gould flung their shining parallelograms upon the house of the Avellanos. Now and then a shuffle of feet, subdued like a whisper, passed by with the gliding, red glow of a cigarette under the darkness of the walls, and the night air, as if cooled by the snows of Higuerota, refreshed their faces.

'We Occidentales,' said Martin Decoud, using the usual term the Provincials of Sulaco applied to themselves, 'have been always so separated. As long as we hold Cayta nothing can reach us. In all our troubles no army has been marched over those mountains. A revolution in the central provinces isolates us at once. Look how complete it is now! — The news of Barrios' movement will be cabled to the U.S. and only in that way it will reach Sta. Martha by the cables of our other seaboard. They will know it tomorrow. It's astounding to think of! We have the greatest riches, the greatest fertility, the purest blood in our great families, the most laborious population. The Occidental Province should stand alone. The early Federalism was bad enough for us; then came worse, union. The rest of Costaguana hangs like a stone round our necks. The territory is large enough to make any man's country. Look at those mountains! Nature itself seems to cry to us: "Separation!" '

She made an energetic gesture of denegation. A silence fell.

— 'Oh yes, I know it's contrary to the speculations laid down in the *History of Fifty Years' Misrule*. I am only trying to be sensible. But my sense seems always to give you cause for offence. Have I startled you very much with this perfectly reasonable aspiration?'

She shook her head. No she was not startled, but the idea was contrary to all her convictions. Her patriotism was larger. She had never considered that possibility.

'It may yet be the means of saving some of your convictions,' he said prophetically.

She did not answer. She seemed tired and they [leaned side by side on the rail of the little balcony, very friendly, having exhausted politics, giving themselves up to the silent feeling of their nearness, in one of those profound pauses that fall upon the rhythm of passion. Towards the plaza end of the street the glowing coals in the brazeros of the market women cooking their evening meal gleamed red along the edge of the pavement. A man walked without a sound past a street lamp, showing the coloured inverted triangle of his bordered poncho, square on his shoulders, hanging in a point below his knees. From the harbour end of the Calle a horseman walked his soft-stepping mount, gleaming silver-grey abreast each lamp under the dark shadow of the rider.

'Behold the illustrious Capataz de Cargadores,' said Decoud gently, 'coming in all his splendour after his work is done. The next great man after Don Carlos Gould. But he is good-natured, and let me make friends with him.'

'Ah, indeed!' said Antonia. 'How did you make friends?'

'A journalist ought to have his finger on the popular pulse, and this man is the king of the populace. A journalist ought to know remarkable men — and this man is remarkable in his way.'

'Ah, yes!' said Antonia thoughtfully. 'It is known that this Italian has a great influence with the people.'

The horseman had passed below them, with a gleam of dim light on the shining broad quarters of the grey mare, on a bright heavy stirrup, on a long silver spur; but the short flick of yellowish flame in the dusk was powerless against the muffled-up mysteriousness of the dark figure with an invisible face concealed by a great sombrero.

Decoud and Antonia remained leaning over the balcony, side by side, so close that their elbows touched. They had barely standing room on the rounded projection, half in, half out of the window, with their heads overhanging the darkness of the street, and the brilliantly lighted Sala at their backs. This was a tête-à-tête of extreme impropriety; something of which in the whole extent of the Republic only the extraordinary Antonia could be capable — the poor, motherless girl never accompanied, with a careless father, who had cared for nothing but to make her learned. And even Decoud himself seemed to feel that this was as much as he could expect of having her to himself till — till the revolution was over and he could carry her off to Europe, away from the endlessness of civil strife whose folly seemed even harder to bear than its ignominy. After one Montero there would be another, the lawlessness of a populace of all colours and races, barbarism, irremediable tyranny. As the great Liberator Bolivar had said in the bitterness of his spirit, 'America is ungovernable. Those who worked for her independence have ploughed the sea.' He did not care, he declared boldly; he seized every opportunity to tell her that though she had managed to make a Blanco journalist of him, he was no patriot.]

from

Zeppelin Nights: A London Entertainment (1915)

The book is a collection of twenty-four historical vignettes, all of them republished from the *Daily News* and *Outlook*. They are tales told in war-time London, each about an historical moment that could give courage and perspective to an audience having to face the German Zeppelins overhead. Violet Hunt, Ford's collaborator in this book (and in *The Desirable Alien*), provided a loose sort of framework to contain the stories, in the manner of *The Decameron*.

On the whole, Ford did not feel comfortable with the short story form: he could not, he complained, write 'short'. But these stories — miniature historical novels — are among the best he wrote, and as late as 1938, he hoped to find a publisher 'to reprint one or two of the little historical sketches which I think are some of my best writing'.

NO POPERY

June 7, 1780

THE very long, very high, dimly lit and panelled room of the great mansion in Red Lion Square contained no furniture upon its polished floors save a few bow-legged gilt chairs with white silk seats and backs. The light from two wax candles shone tremulously, reflected down the boards as if upon water. A burly man in a black satin coat with heavy flounces, black satin knee-breeches, black silk stockings, with a touch of a white ruffle at his neck and large white ruffles at his wrists, was leaning over a music-book that lay upon the harpsichord. The lid of the harpsichord stood high and sent an immense shadow over the tall panels of the walls. Its inner leaf was painted with a reddish lacquer, and, with the illumination from the candles in the great dim room, it resembled one of those large black moths whose inner wings are orange and vermilion. The man in black, leaning on the harpsichord, exclaimed, in imperious tones that were marked by a strong Italian accent: 'My good friend, I can sing anything in this partition with anyone you like at any time and upside down and how you will.'

The man at the harpsichord, who was dressed in a blue silk coat with white China-silk breeches, answered nothing. His very white wig had many little curls over the ears and, whilst his face was nearly as white as his wig, he appeared to listen not at all to the Italian, and his face had the expression of those who hearken in terror for sounds in the distance. The Italian threw the book on to the music-stand in front of this gentleman and exclaimed: 'I will sing this tonight if anybody comes.'

'Nobody will come,' Sir Charles Eastman answered. He was the Secretary of the Royal Cecilian Society of Consorts, which met in those rooms by permission of the Lord Sincere, and he considered that he had exhibited heroism enough in merely coming to that house at all through the dangerous streets. Now he was trembling at the thought that he must go back home. It was all very well for Signor Privaldi, whom my lord permitted to lodge in that house, though all the servants save a very old woman had fled. And Sir Charles Eastman's hat, which lay upon one of the chairs, was decorated with a blue cockade as large as a cabbage to show his attachment to the Protestant religion. . . .

'Play that now,' Signor Privaldi exclaimed imperiously. The top of the page in the thin warm candlelight showed, written with a flourish, the words *Orfeo ed Euridice*. Sir Charles glanced miserably at the page, laid his hands on the black keyboard, and a thin tinkle came from the instrument — a little reedy, metallic, and tremulous sound.

'Good God,' Privaldi exclaimed; 'do you think I am going to sing to that noise? Put down the third pedal from the right — the simpatico — what do you call it? — and lock it. Then put down the one all alone to the left and keep your foot upon it — the sostenuto — until I make a sign with my hand. . . . So!'

Sir Charles having manipulated the pedals as Signor Privaldi desired, placed his hands once again on the black expanse of the notes and the air came out sustained, rounded, and swelling. Leaning upon the corner of the instrument, the Italian, with his masculine and fierce features, opened in his fat face a little mouth from which then issued the wonderful full tones, the wonderful rounded air, the wonderful volume of sweet sound that a week later ravished and exhausted with ecstasy two thousand exquisites in the new Assembly Rooms at Bath. Even Sir Charles at that moment, or at least when Signor Privaldi came for the third time to 'Dove Andrò', with the little shake — even Sir Charles for three whole bars forgot his fears, and later he was accustomed to declare that the Signor's voice had entirely rapt and ravished him away from that grim and portentous moment. 'Ah, what passion indeed,' he would say, 'cannot musick raise and quell! I forgot entirely such small apprehension as I had, and truly

> Less than a god, I said, there could not dwell
> Within the hollow of that shell
> That spoke so sweetly and so well.

But then Sir Charles, as Secretary to the Cecilian Society, was naturally anxious as much as possible to enhance the marvels of Signor Privaldi's voice, since that Society was responsible for the musician's introduction not only to London but to Bath, which was a very much greater matter.

Several members of the Dilettanti Society, who happened to be also members of the Cecilian, had heard this fiery, irascible, masculine tenor during the grand tour, and they had combined to beseech him to visit this town of London. There should have been a meeting of the Society that evening to hear him sing, but not a soul had come — since the mob had burnt the Sardinian Embassy's Chapel the night before and many other chapels, had invaded the Houses of Parliament and crushed-in the heads of every soul they met in the streets not wearing a blue cockade — not a single member of the Society, not a fiddler, not so much as the harpsichord player, had ventured through the streets. The Lord Sincere himself, suspected by the mob of being no true Protestant, had gone with all his household to his seat at Pinner, where he considered himself far enough off, and they were all alone in that great mansion with only the old woman down somewhere in the basement.

But what really happened on that occasion in the matter of Sir Charles' enraptured and ravished soul was this: Signor Privaldi's voice blending with the perfect tones of the beautiful instrument sang on and on, whilst Sir Charles' fingers shivered upon the keys. And they had got as far as the resolution of the last half-close, and four bars would have finished it, when Sir Charles screamed out, 'My God, look!'

He had glanced aside at the dark windows which faced towards the west, and those two of the tall six that were mostly to the right and consequently most to the northward, appeared to be painted-in, tremulously and ghastily, with diluted blood that faded out and glazed them in again. Sir Charles sprang up from the music-stool and stood, visibly shaking. Privaldi exclaimed roughly, 'Good

Lord, what's this?' And Sir Charles bleated out, 'Lord Mansfield's house! They are burning out Lord Mansfield's house.' He ran to the window. Just to the north the sky had become and was becoming more and more blood-red — the colour of your fingers when you hold them out and let a flame shine through them. Against this redness the crooked chimneys and roofs of the houses of Red Lion Square stood out black, distorted, and grotesque, in a long line.

'Well, that will be amusing,' Signor Privaldi said. 'When it is well alight we will go and see it.'

Sir Charles was glued against the window-pane, drumming upon it with his panic-stricken fingers. 'My God, no,' he said, 'we must fly. They will be coming here. In a minute they will be coming here.'

Signor Privaldi, judging that the conflagration was not yet at its height, and considering that it was not two minutes' walk to Lord Mansfield's house, which was in Bloomsbury Square, sat himself down at the harpsichord and began to puzzle out a tune called 'Brighton Camp', which he had heard the mob singing that day whilst his chaise had been held up during his entry into London. Because this had struck him as a jolly, strong, heartful, and masculine tune it had given him a good impression of this city, which he was visiting for the first time. And once he had got a good impression of the city it was difficult for his tenacious nature to modify his views. He began to play the melody of 'Brighton Camp' with two of the five pedals down and both of the keyboards going, so that it had a fine lilt and a martial suggestion of flutes. This tune is that to which we now sing the words of 'The girl I left behind me', but the rioters of that day had set it to words implying that his Holiness of Rome would have an unpleasant end; whilst they assured their bemused leader, Lord George Gordon, that it was really a Protestant psalm. So Signor Privaldi played on.

Suddenly Sir Charles sprang for his hat with the blue cockade, which was on a chair, and his clouded cane which was beside it. 'To think,' he exclaimed, 'that I should be found here with you, a Papist! For you are a Papist, aren't you?'

'Of course I am,' Signor Privaldi answered; 'there is nothing unnatural in that. In Monza, where I come from, we are all Papists.'

Sir Charles pulled open his coat; inside it there was pinned another huge blue cockade. He unpinned it and thrust it tremulously into the singer's hands. 'For God's sake,' he said hoarsely, 'wear this upon your person when you are in the house and upon your hat when you are out-a-doors.'

The singer regarded the blue object curiously. 'If I hold this upside down,' he said, 'it resembles a comet. Now the sign for the feast day of St Gabriel of Monza is a blue comet, since St Gabriel, who is my patron saint, once stayed the devastations caused by one of these flails of heaven. I see no reason why I should not wear the badge of my patron saint.' He approached his huge black hat, pinned the blue cockade on to it upside down, so that when he set the hat on, the tail of the comet drooped over his left eye.

'We must fly! We must fly!' Sir Charles cried out, and he ran out of the great room and down the echoing stone stairs. It was very dark in the hall, save that the conflagration at Lord Mansfield's shed some illumination through the pale fanlight above the door. Nevertheless Sir Charles managed to throw back the bolts and to turn the immense key. When he opened the door a joyful and ruddy light illumined all the pillars of the great stone hall. He fled.

Signor Privaldi followed him so much more composedly that, after he had taken the great key out of the door, closed it, and gone down the front steps, Sir Charles had vanished round the corner of the Square. He walked towards the conflagration, swinging the great key round his fingers. He thought that that would be all the arms that he needed, for it seemed to him to be so natural a thing to be a true Christian — so he regarded it! — that he could not imagine this jolly English mob could harm him for it. All the shutters of the Square were back and all the windows of the houses boasted rows of candles, the inhabitants deeming it prudent thus to illuminate, so as to indicate their joy that the populace were demanding the repeal of the Emancipation Bill. Thus there was a good glittering light. Signor Privaldi passed a man bearing a gilt settee upon his head, and he laughed, for that appeared to be humorous and jolly. He passed a man rolling a barrel along; and then, just as he was passing a woman, she fell clean through a great mirror that she was carrying. It is a very difficult thing to carry a mirror with the glass towards you. Signor Privaldi roared with laughter. This was loot from Lord Mansfield's house. He perceived that most of the fronts of the houses or most of the doors were inscribed with huge whitewashed letters, *No Popery*. Then he came upon the thick of the crowd. Swirling round Bloomsbury Square, in Southampton Row, in Theobald's Road, there was a crowd of forty thousand people. They screamed, they swore, they shouted, some pushing their way in to get loot from Lord Mansfield's house, some pushing their way out with loot that they had already obtained. All their distorted faces were lit up with the flames that climbed to heaven or with the reflection of them. Since Signor Privaldi did not desire any loot and did desire to keep his black satin coat undamaged, he pushed no farther into the crowd, but turned eastward. He walked slowly, without being incommoded, until he came to the top of Holborn Hill. Here he must spring across several runlets of blazing alcohol, coming from the vaults of Mr Langdale, the Catholic distiller, and across the bodies of several men and a great many women, who had drunk themselves dead with these fiery fluids. The night was one blaze of black and scarlet. Flames danced everywhere. The house of Mr Ackerman, the Governor of Newgate, blazed to heaven; a pyre of furniture was lit before the great gate of the gaol to burn it down, so that the rioters might go in and rescue those of them that had been taken prisoners, as well as all the murderers, thieves, felons, and other true Protestants that lay there under sentence of death. Signor Privaldi turned down Hatton Garden to get a little quiet. His eyes were tired with beholding these spectacles, and he felt that he had enough to reflect upon for a month of Sundays. Right across the front of a shop, kept by a man called Gutenberger, a good Jew, he perceived in white letters the words, 'This house is a true Protestant'. And this brought into his mind that he owed some return for hospitality received. He did not remember to have seen any inscription upon the mansion of Lord Sincere, who had hospitably afforded him a roof, and he considered it his duty to hurry back and repair this omission. At the same time he had no strong idea as to what he should inscribe upon the house when he got there. Lord Sincere, he knew, was suspected of being a concealed Catholic, but on the other hand he had never heard his lordship utter any less blasphemies, obscenities, and filth than would have done credit to the most Protestant of Lord George Gordon's cheerful followers. Moreover, Lord Sincere, in his cups, was in the habit of proclaiming himself an atheist. It was therefore a very nice problem for Signor Privaldi's conscience, and his quite considerable obstinacy would not permit him to relish ever writing up the words, *No Popery*. He was a Papist, if not a very good one.

He reached Lord Sincere's house, and, having penetrated to the basement, he found, after searching for long in the basement, a leathern pail containing some whitewash and an old brush. With this he once more ascended to the front door and, having closed it upon himself, he began with the brush to stir up the whitewash. The Square was no longer so deserted, and, although the illumination of candles still burned in all the house windows, the glow in the sky from Lord Mansfield's house was much diminished, and the sparse forerunners of a crowd were drifting slowly, and in a sinister manner, into Red Lion Square. They were indeed halting and mumbling before the house of Lord Sincere. With a fine sweep of his brush — for after all Signor Privaldi was a public performer — he inscribed high up on the door the letters N O. Behind his back there seemed to arise from the shadows a sound that was at once a token of sinister congratulation and sinister disappointment. Brushing footsteps hastened up and fierce whispers seemed to come from all the shadows. There were some torches too. Because he was writing so large he found room beneath the word NO only for the three letters R E L, beneath that for I G I, and at the bottom for O N. It seemed to him that that adequately met the case of Lord Sincere.

He turned round, and, describing a fine sweep with his brush, he bowed low before an audience that was already over a thousand strong, so quickly did it appear to have sprung out of the cobbles.

Such applause greeted him as he had never had upon any stage. It grew and grew as more thousands and more came pouring in from Bloomsbury Square. He put the great key in the lock, let himself quickly in, and ran up the echoing stairs to the great room. The candles upon the harpsichord had guttered nearly away, but he took from the sconces all that there were upon the walls, and, lighting them, set them in rows along the windows. He threw up all the sashes and then, plainly visible to the packed mass in the Square, he sat down at the harpsichord. Three of the pedals he set down and locked, upon the third he kept his left foot warily, so that when he began to play upon the keys there pealed out from that magnificent instrument a deathless rendering of 'Brighton Camp'. It had the quality of organ notes, of fifes, of drums, of the cry of crowds, and of sergeants' commands. It was the marching-away tune for a regiment, for a division, for an army, and for this mob that was forty thousand strong. And this mob began to march; it sent them marching with the cheers, with the cries, with the casting up of hats, with the bold waving of torches. And, as they went away, there pealed after them the triumphant and mournful strains of the tune that now goes with the words, 'It's lonesome since I left the town' —

the tune of 'The girl I left behind me'.

My lord left the inscription upon his street door for a full six months — it tickled his sense of the ridiculous immensely.

[London: John Lane, The Bodley Head, 1915: pp. 200–14.]

'A Day of Battle'

by Miles Ignotus [the Unknown Soldier]
(Written on the Ypres Salient: 15th Sep. 1916)

I ARMS AND THE MIND

I HAVE asked myself continuously why I can write nothing — why I cannot even think anything that to myself seems worth thinking! — about the psychology of that Active Service of which I have seen my share. And why cannot I even evoke pictures of the Somme or the flat lands round Ploegsteert? With the pen, I used to be able to 'visualize things' — as it used to be called. It is no very valuable claim to make for oneself — since 'visualizing' is the smallest, the least moving, of the facets of the *table diamant* that art is.

Still, it used to be my métier — my little department to myself. I could make you see the court of Henry VIII; the underground at Gower Street; palaces in Cuba; the coronation — anything I had seen, and still better, anything I hadn't seen. Now I could not make you see Messines, Wijtschate, St Eloi; or La Boiselle, the Bois de Bécourt or de Mametz — although I have sat looking at them for hours, for days, for weeks on end. Today, when I look at a mere coarse map of the Line, simply to read 'Ploegsteert' or 'Armentières' seems to bring up extraordinarily coloured and exact pictures behind my eyeballs — little pictures having all the brilliant minuteness that medieval illuminations had — of towers, and roofs, and belts of trees and sunlight; or, for the matter of these, of men, burst into mere showers of blood and dissolving into muddy ooze; or of aeroplanes and shells against the translucent blue. — But, as for putting them — into words! No: the mind stops dead, and something in the brain stops and shuts down: precisely as the left foot stops dead and the right foot comes up to it with a stamp upon the hard asphalt — upon the 'square', after the word of command 'Halt', at Chelsea!

As far as I am concerned an invisible barrier in my brain seems to lie between the profession of Arms and the mind that put things into words. And I ask myself: why? And I ask myself: why?

I was reading, the other day, a thoughtful article in one of the more serious weeklies, as to a somewhat similar point — as to why the great books about the psychology of war (such as Stephen Crane's *Red Badge of Courage* or even the *Débâcle* of Zola) should have been written by civilians who had never heard a shot fired or drilled a squad. But the reason for that is obvious: it was not Hector of Troy — it wasn't even Helen! — who wrote the *Iliad*: it wasn't Lear who wrote *Lear*; and it was Turgenev, not Bazaroff, who wrote *Fathers and Children*. Lookers-on see most of the Game: but it is carrying the reverse to a queer extreme to say that one of the players should carry away, mentally, nothing of the Game at all.

I am talking of course of the psychological side of war like operations. I remember standing at an O.P. during the July 'push' on the Somme. It was the O.P. called Max Redoubt on the highest point of the road between Albert and Bécourt Wood. One looked up to the tufted fastness of Martinpuich that the Huns still held: one looked down upon Mametz, upon Tricourt, upon the Ancre, upon Bécourt-Bécordel, upon La Boisselle, upon Pozières. We held all those: or perhaps we did not already hold Pozières. Over High Wood an immense cloud of smoke hung: black and as if earthy. The push was on.

And it came into my head to think that here was the most amazing fact of history. For in the territory beneath the eye, or not hidden by folds in the ground, there must have been — on the two sides — a million men, moving one against the other and impelled by an invisible moral force into a Hell of fear that surely cannot have had a parallel in this world. It was an extraordinary feeling to have in a wide landscape.

But there it stopped. As for explanation I hadn't any: as for significant or valuable pronouncement of a psychological kind I could not make any — nor any generalization. There we were: those million men, forlorn, upon a raft in space. But as to what had assembled us upon that landscape: I had just to fall back upon the formula: it is the Will of God. Nothing else would take it all in. I myself seemed to have drifted there at the bidding of indifferently written characters on small scraps of paper: W.O. telegram A/R 2572/26: a yellow railway warrant; a white embarkation order; a pink movement order; a check like a cloakroom ticket ordering the C.O. of one's Battalion to receive one. But the Will that had brought me there did not seem to be, much, one's own Will. No doubt what had put in action the rather weary, stiff limbs beneath one's heavy pack had its actual origin in one's own brain. But it didn't feel like it. There is so much — such an eternity of — waiting about in the life of any army on the move or up against the enemy trenches, that one's predominant impression is one of listlessness. The moments when one can feel one's individual will at work limit themselves almost to two types of event — the determination not to fall out upon the march and the determination not to be left behind in 'going over'.

Even work that, on the face of it is individualistic, is too controlled to be anything other than delineated. If you are patrol officer your limits are laid down: if you are Battalion Intelligence Officer upon an Observation Point the class of object that is laid down for your observation is strictly limited in range. And, within the prescribed limits there is so much to which one must pay attention that other sights, sounds, and speculations are very much dismissed. And of course, if you are actually firing a rifle your range of observation is still more limited. Dimly, but very tyrannically, there lurking in your mind the precepts of the musketry instructors at Splott or at Veryd ranges. The precepts that the sights must be upright, the tip of the foresight in line with the shutters of the V of the backsight are always there, even when the V of the backsight has assumed its air of being a loophole between yourself and the sun and wind and when the blade of the foresight is like a bar across that loophole. And the dark, smallish, potlike object upon whose 'six o'clock' you must align both bar and loophole has none of the aspects of a man's head. It is just a pot . . .

In battle — and in the battle zone — the whole world, humanity included, seems to assume the aspect of matter dominated eventually by gravity. Large bits of pot fly about, smash large pieces of flesh: then one and the other fall, to lie in the dust among the immense thistles. That seems to be absolutely all. Hopes, passions, fears do not seem much to exist outside oneself — and only in varying degrees within oneself. On the day on which I was sent to Max Redoubt O.P. to observe something, I was ordered further to proceed to the dump of another Battalion in Bécourt Wood and to make certain preliminary arrangements for taking over the dump.

The preoccupations of my mission absolutely numbed my powers of observation. Of that I am certain. It is, in fact, the sense of responsibility that is really numbing: your 'job' is so infinitely more important than any other human necessity, or the considerations of humanity, pity, or compassion. With your backsight and foresight aligned on that dark object like a pot you are incapable of remembering that pot shelters hopes, fears, aspirations, or has significance for wives, children, fathers and mothers . . . It is just the 'falling plate' that you bring down on the range. You feel the satisfaction that you feel in making a good shot at golf.

It is all just matter — all humanity, just matter; one with the trees, the shells by the roadside, the limbered wagons, the howitzers and the few upstanding housewalls. On the face of it I am a man who has taken a keen interest in the aspects of humanity — in the turn of an eyelash, an expression of joy, a gesture of despair. In the old days when I saw a man injured in a street accident or in an epileptic fit by the roadside, I felt certain emotions: I should wonder what would become of him or what I could do for him. Or to put it even nearer home, when by Turnham Green in the Swiss Cottage, in peace time, I have seen dusty 18 pounders, khaki coloured and [illegible], jingling along behind the brave horses, I can remember to have felt emotions — to have felt that the guns looked venomous, dangerous, or as if they had been peering, like blind snakes.

But, stepping out of Max Redoubt into the Bécourt Road, that day, I came right into the middle of ten or a dozen lamentably wounded men, waiting by a loop of the tramline, I suppose for a trolley to take them to a C.C.S. I remember the fact: but of the aspects of these men — nothing! Or so very little. They were in khaki: some of them had white bandages round their heads: they grouped themselves on a bit of a bank: they were just like low, jagged fragments of a brown and white wall ruined by shell fire. And they are as dim in my memory as forgotten trees.

And so with the guns that in peace time I had found interesting or picturesque: they rattled past me there in an endless procession: they crushed slowly into the sandy road behind immense tractor monsters like incredible kitchen stoves. Further down in the wood they were actually at it: a dozen converted naval howitzers like enormous black toads that wheezed, panted out flame, shook the earth, and ran back into shelters of green boughs. The shells went away with long, slow whines . . .

But it all seemed to signify nothing. One did not think of where the immense shells struck the ground, blowing whole battalions to nothing. One did not think that the R.F.A. guns, hurrying forward, meant that the Push was progressing. Even the enemy shells that whined overhead were not very significant — and the visible signs that, shortly before, these shells had pitched into the new British graveyard, seemed to mean nothing very personal. One *reasoned* that the shells might pitch there again any minute: but one *felt* that they would not. I don't know why. And of course it meant nothing. In moments of great danger I have felt convinced that I was immune: five miles behind the lines I have been appallingly certain of immediate death because an aeroplane was being shelled a mile away. Mainly the reason for these moods is very commonplace. If one has plenty to do one is not afraid: in one's moments of leisure one may be very frightened indeed. The mere commonplaceness of one's occupation, and of the earth and the grass and the trees and the sky, makes the idea of death or even of wounds, seem exaggerated and out of proportion. One is in a field, writing a message on an ordinary piece of paper with an ordinary pencil — 'from O.C. no. 1 platoon, B. Co. to O.C. anything. . . .' Nothing could be more commonplace . . .

So the idea of tragedy is just incongruous and death quite inappropriate. No! Reason has very little to do with it. For you may be in a large field — a 40-acre field — and the Huns may be dropping their usual triplet of 4.2's into it. Your reason — if you are not employed for the moment — will tell you that your chances of being hit are 400 to 1 against. But it does not in the least comfort you. On the other hand I have been lifted off my feet and dropped two yards away by the explosion of a shell and felt complete assurance of immunity.

The force of one's sense of responsibility is in fact wonderfully hypnotic and drives one wonderfully in on oneself. I used to think that being out in France would be like being in a magic ring that would cut me off from all private troubles: but nothing is further from the truth. I have gone down to the front line at night, worried, worried, worried beyond belief about happenings at home in a Blighty that I did not much expect to see again — so worried that all sense of personal danger disappeared and I forgot to duck when shells went close overhead. At the same time I have carefully observed angles, compass bearings, landmarks and the loom of duckboards: and I have worried — simultaneously with the other worries — to think that I might have neglected some precaution as to the safety of the men, or that I might not be on time, or that I might get some message wrong — till gradually the feeling of the responsibility eclipsed all other feelings . . .

Still, as I have said, one's personal feelings do not get blotted out, or one's personal affections. If, for instance, those wounded that I had seen by Max Redoubt had been men of my own Bn. or another Bn. of the Welch Regiment that was side by side with us, I should have tried to do what I could for them — and I should certainly remember them now. For I do remember all the wounded of my own Bn. that I have seen. The poor men, they come from Pontypridd and Nantgarw and Penarth and Dowlais Works and they have queer, odd, guttural accents like the croaking of ravens, and they call every hill a moun*tain* . . . and there is no emotion so terrific and so overwhelming as the feeling that comes over you when your own men are dead. It is a feeling of an anger . . . an anger . . . a deep anger! It shakes you like a force that is beyond all other forces in the world: unimaginable, irresistible . . .

Yes, I have just one War Picture in my mind: it is a hurrying black cloud, like the dark cloud of the Hun shrapnel. It sweeps down at any moment. Over Mametz Wood: over the Veryd Range, over the grey level of the North Sea; over the parade ground in the sunlight, with the band, and the goat shining like silver and the R.S.M. shouting: 'Right Markers! Stead a......ye!' A darkness out of which shine — like swiftly obscured fragments of pallid moons — white faces of the little, dark, raven-voiced, Evanses, and Lewises, and Joneses and Thomases . . . Our dead!

That is the most real picture of war that I carry about with me. And that, too, is personal, and borne along with, not observed in spite of, responsibilities . . .

[Autograph manuscript, edited by Sondra J. Stang, published with the permission of the Department of Rare Books, Ford Madox Ford Collection, Cornell University. Another version of this ms. was previously published in *Esquire*, December, 1980.]

VIII

Sixty Unpublished Letters

To Olive Garnett

1 [November] *Hythe*

Dear Olive, Mille pardons; what I wrote about Sylvester was meant to be 'chip at', not chop out. I don't for a moment say that you ought not to have tried to realize Miss Emmie & Sylvester; what I desire to drive home is that you have not realized them sufficiently, I mean as far as my perception goes. These things are matter of convention. In the Secret, Barry & Mrs B. are seen — the one in a grey suit, the other with her back hair like a tea-pot-handle; but neither Miss E. nor S. are more than ideas. Now the value of the work of art is not the idea, but the selection of the facts with wh. the idea is presented or at least, the idea should not be continually in contrast with the individuals. This is why I find fault. The Secret is neither one thing nor the other; it wavers, is in two pitches. Either Miss E & Sylvester should be tuned up or Barry & Mrs B. tuned down. You either see or feel this well enough. In the Voice the man is called a lunatic by an unfriendly person, & lives on that account. If someone unfriendly had handled, for the merest moment, Miss Emmie & S. they too would be more get-at-able &, what is more, the world in which they lived — which was inside them — would have jumped into life. But don't take me too seriously: these remarks are not criticism but the observations on technique of a confused creature.

When I have had time to think about it I will say what I think of the Voice. Of course it is not a bore but a delicate attention in you to have sent it.

Yrs in haste *F.M.H.*

Olive Garnett was the daughter of Richard Garnett, Keeper of Printed Books in the Library of the British Museum. As a 'very young lady' she published Ford's first poems on her 'anarchist printing press'. She wrote stories and novels, and in this and the following letter Ford responds to some of her work in manuscript. He later published her in *The English Review*.

2 [1900–1901] *Stock's Hall, Aldington nr Hythe, Kent*

Dear Olive: Forgive my protracted silence re 'The Voice'. I have been bothered in all sorts of ways lately.

As far as I am concerned, the story, its convention once accepted, stands on its own legs. The convention is, of course, outside my more material line, but I am perfectly willing to accept it. I mean that personally I want to feel more satisfied as to the externals of the characters, how they got their bread, what they looked like. I always want to begin: 'He was six feet high; dark & with a pronounced stoop. His father had been a minor poet who made a living by writing fashion articles for the Morning Post. I was &c &c'. You know, of course why one does that & you don't do it & I don't cavil. Only, when I approach 'The Voice' I am definitely out of it as far as the craftsmanship goes. What you have is an atmosphere, very excellently done; two psychologies well brought into that atmosphere & a problem of ethics well in tone. The whole makes a work of art & that is what one asks for. When one descends to details I can make a few suggestions as to writing & the Machinery. I don't think I would begin 'It was a still autumn evening', but would move the sentence one or two places down — to before the one beginning 'Our wills & our nerves happily at rest . . .' And I think I would cut out '& then' & divide the long sentence 'I was . . . coatsleeve' into three. But these are mere proof-sheet details. When it comes to the Machinery I think the inception of the Voice idea comes near danger. It brings the man too near either actual lunacy or posing [?] for him to run out into the street. He ought, in listening to a song to say something subtle about what musicians call the overtone, not to ram the idea of 'the Voice' home by running out & returning covered with mud. The Voice separates them by a cumulative effect later on, yet finds its actual manifestation at the outset. If the she of the story is not moved to give him his congé at the beginning she would hardly be so moved by merely indefinite, altho' just as real, disappointments at the last.

I put this in as Philistine a way as I can; because one has to meet the Philistine whenever one can, half-way; the Philistine being always half right. Why I really mention it is in the interests of the progression d'effets. Let the Voice begin as a vague doubt alone & let that vague doubt gradually grow until you reach the parting, which in musical parlance one would call the end of the first movement; then your working out & your re-statement of first & second subjects, coda & close would move naturally enough. (The working out is III, the restatement, IV, the peaceful coda pp. ~~44–6~~.)

I think that, for much the same reason, you should go cold-bloodedly thro' the m. s. & erase the definitely erotic expressions. They jar a little; because, altho' expressions like 'the Beloved' and 'folded me in his arms' are not per se culpable they do not seem to belong to your vernacular; &, at the other end of the scale, the 'throat' jars a little, too. A sympathetic reader will justify it & it is necessary to the 'story', but I would introduce the actual word in the course of the text not in the speech of the woman. Because the words in speeches have a way of getting themselves embossed, so to say. Conversations, I always think, need vastly more attention than anything else. I don't mean to say that you should alter the motive but merely the wording of the speech in question.

Katharine Mary is uttering doleful wails in a distant room & as I am, officially Nurse-tender for the afternoon, I must cease & pay attention to her wants. I have just finished an Article on the Making of Modern Verse and the Choice of the Just Word in Poetry & so feel limp at the best, moreover I swallowed yesterday the Chronicle on Cinque Ports which was like eating a pound of breadless honey & a paragraph in the Morning Post, a spoonful of brimstone & treacle without much treacle.

Yours

Elsie has gone to a Sale with Mrs Walker.

3 [c. 1901]

Dearest O: I called with my bosom friend Marwood as chaperone, but, tho' the bell pealed this time, the wrong lady came forth. So there we are, as H. J. [Henry James] wd. say.

E. [Elsie] is a good deal better (Unberufen!) & turning her thoughts to gardening. She asked me to find out what was the best manual of gardening for a beginner. Wd. you ask Arthur to drop her a p. c. with that information as I'm sure he *ought* to know. But if I were asked — or you — what was the best manual of the art we cultivate on a little thin oatmeal — what cd. *we* reply.

We had such a miry tramp from Hampton Ct. I wanted you to know Marwood whom I consider to have the greatest intellect of any man living. (That is the Huefferism for 'any man that I know!')

Good night: sleep well

Yrs. *Ford M. H.*

4 [11 July 1902] *The Bungalow, Winchelsea nr Rye, Sussex*

Dear Olive — All right; have it — with yr. *a priori* criticism — your own way.

I haven't the spirit to bother, gallant soul tho' I be. Xtina has the measles; there's — (as there must be) a crisis of a domestic's raising & all our plans for the summer have melted like an ice pudding. It's been for us too miserable a year for anything in the nature of the criticism of a criticism to matter more than a thin ghost.

I'll send you a copy of the poems when I can muster energy to drag away the sofa from before the cupboard in which they are. Elsie sends her love & I'm

Yrs *Ford M. H.*

We've just seen the new moon — that *always* means ill luck. My only, firmly rooted superstition! But it's inevitable and deadly.

To Edward Garnett

5 [1902]

Dear E. Herewith the m.s. — I have as you will observe accepted all your emendations except the following for wh. I crave yr. earnest consideration.

P.2. I have inserted your words in inverted commas because personally I don't agree with the matter. — The very first thing that strikes *me*, as beholder, of Lilith is strong dislike for the lady.

P.4. This is a matter entirely for you to decide. — I use 'sensual' always as a technical term, as explained on the back of the leaf.

P.5. I have said all that I can conscientiously or temperamentally say in praise of R's [Rossetti's] work. — It's part of technique and treatment — and humility. When I praise a thing I always feel unconvincing and *brassy* in tone; I want always to keep myself in hand. I say, below yr. note, what I think to be true and convincing — that R's true significance is indicated in his sketches and projections. I feel sure that flowery periods wd. defeat the whole purpose of my tone. — But please insert what you like; I wd. myself but I simply don't know what to say — after having considered the point for some time.

P.18. *Please*, I cannot enter into these pathological details; I should have to consider the matter for a long time, consult toxicologists for symptoms and ponder for ever or long on a matter to me very repellent. Because how *can* I distinguish between the symptoms, on canvas, of chloral, uraemia, gout in the wrist and incipient blindness, all of wh. (not to mention chronic delusions) had a share?

With regard to p. 20: Please carefully consider these points: 'must be lost' is true; a good phrase and is worth saying. 'Few can win' is not true; is a half statement and, in any case, *ne vaut pas la peine de dire*.

Certainly all Artists do confess to failure in the face of the immensities etc. — i.e. when they measure their achievements by their ideals. — The greater the artist the more certain this is; it is so very obvious. — With regard to the 'Immortals' you [illegible] — Homer I don't know about but Dante in the *Paradiso* xxxiii ll.72 et seq. says exactly that; so does Michelangelo in the sonnets to Victoria Colonna commencing: 'Poscia ch'appreso', and 'Per esser manco'; in several conversations with Jul. II and in half a dozen other places. Shakespeare says the same again and again in his sonnets, and all the Elizabethans said nothing else. Acknowledgment of failure — and often of the necessity of failure — is always the essential note of the Artist.

You and I may say that 'some score in some score ages' have

not failed or rather have comparatively succeeded — but not one of these twenty would say so, simply because if he ever reached the point when his abilities compassed and equalled his *ambitions* he would drop dead. That is, after all, the essential characteristic of humanity — and the great artist is the sane man, the man who sees all problems — and that among them — in the right light. The passage itself doesn't matter. Cut it out if it offends, but to modify it would be to render it purely nugatory — a *longueur*.

P.25. Rossetti undoubtedly did *fail* — the point is whether his failure was or was not *ignoble*. I personally, therefore, disagree with your insertion. But if you want it put round your way, [illegible]. Here again the whole point is one of technique and temperament: if you advance the statement that R. did *not* fail the onus of proof is on you. If on the other hand you say that he did not fail *ignobly* (failure being the lot of man) you advance as considerable a claim — but do it in an inoffensive way. — In these matters *reticence* and a low key are of immense value. But it is obvious enough that you cannot be I and, the matter being yrs. rather than mine, please change it or leave it, as you like.

A small matter —: Wd. you mind my stipulating for a small royalty (I don't care how small) after a sale of 10,000 copies? It isn't a matter of money but I don't wish to sell the copyright and let it get quite beyond my control. Duckworth, I mean, might in years to come sell it to God knows whom and I might reach a frame of mind when it wd. be excessively distasteful to me to have it republished suddenly. — I wrote once an introduction to a catalogue and it got reprinted in an extraordinarily distastefully garbled version last year — in spite of my remonstrances. I wd. like to guard against this if you don't much object.

Yrs. *Ford M. H.*

Edward, Richard Garnett's second son, was the husband of Constance Garnett. As the reader for T. Fisher Unwin, he arranged for the publication of Ford's first books — the fairy tales *The Brown Owl* (1891) and *The Feather* (1892) and the novel *The Shifting of the Fire* (1892). In this letter Ford refers to the manuscript of his book on Rossetti, the first of his three critical monographs on painters and painting for the Duckworth 'Popular Library of Art' series.

To Richard Garnett

6 [May or June 1904] *Winterbourne Stoke*
nr Salisbury

Dear Dr. Garnett: I am really extremely obliged to you — & extremely sorry to have given you so much trouble, under a species of false pretences. Heaven forbid that I shd want to write about these matters — I only wanted to read: to enlighten my own mind rather than to illumine those of others.

I'm engaged upon the amiable task of 'whitewashing' Katharine Howard — & it occurred to me — quite as a side issue — to speculate upon how the varying strains of Latinism (from Seneca's to the writer's of Il Principe whose maxims were upon so many English lips H. VIII rege) operated upon the human animal in those days. . . . Writing of course is quite another matter.

As for the earnings of literature: alas, if I don't neglect them, they neglect me — & editors look as askance at my papers, sketches and tales as critics do upon my poems — Only three London papers have as far as I know acknowledged the existence of the latter. — Subjects I fancy — or indeed as you so very kindly point out — don't lack here: but I seem to be out of the way of books & I'm still in such a physical condition that I can't walk three steps in a town — whilst the only comprehensive history of this district that I've come across — Hoare's — costs £45 in Salisbury, & the only bookseller I've come across there appeared to be a miracle of unintelligence.

. . . I was going to ask more questions, but that would force yr. kindness, probably, to write more letters, so I *refrain*. But I'm most grateful all the same. I really rejoice to know that you are writing about the Borgias. Elsie sends you her love — she heard lately from Lucy who appears to be flourishing — tho' in want of servants.

Yrs. very truly *Ford Madox Hueffer*

Is there a convenient life of Thicknesse?

[Ann Ford Thicknesse (1737–1824), novelist and musician, who gave concerts in which she sang and accompanied herself on the musical glasses.]

To James B. Pinker

7 [c. December 1904] *3 St Edmunds Terrace, N.W.*

Dear Mr Pinker: Thanks: the terms suit me well enough.

As to the title [*The Soul of London*]: if the Alston people can suggest a happier one I shall be delighted. I find titles difficult things to evolve.

Yrs. truly *Ford M. Hueffer*

Pinker set up as a literary agent — then rather a novelty — in 1896; one of his first clients was H.G. Wells, who was quickly followed by Henry James and Arnold Bennett. Conrad was another of his clients, and through Conrad, Pinker became Ford's agent as well — from the turn of the century until his sudden death in 1922. Ford seems not to have liked Pinker's son Eric, who inherited the agency (see letter 29).

To George Bernard Shaw

8 25 November 1908 *84, Holland Park Avenue, W.*
THE ENGLISH REVIEW

Dear Mr Shaw, My charges for receiving post-cards containing defamatory words are £2,700 per post-card. You will thus see that when I have printed 'Getting Married' you will owe me £12,000, cheque for which will oblige. You say 'it would mean if I accepted it, license to print in one issue of the English Review for one month or for a definite maximum number of copies.' Supposing I pay you £1,500. for the American and English rights and get back £700 from the United States this would mean that in order to pay myself right out, taking the copy of the Review as 2/-, that I should have to increase my circulation on your account by 8,000 copies, to make it just barely pay yr. fee alone. You would have therefore to give me license to sell at least 20,000 copies (to pay for printing etc.). I, on the other hand would guarantee that it was not sold as a remainder. Or how would it suit you as a more distinctly equitable idea, that I should pay you a royalty as big as you like on the number sold above the average circulation? (These proposals are merely tentative). In that case I would copy-right it for you in the United States but leave the American rights in your hands. Let me have a reply to this as soon as you conveniently can will you?

With regard to the National Theatre, I offered at the first meeting of the Committee which I attended to guarantee a sum not exceeding £40,000 from various papers in France and Germany on condition that the National Theatre set aside a week each for the classical Theatres of each of these countries to perform pieces from their repertoire in the National Theatre. This offer was refused in two contemptuous words by Mr T. P. O'Conner and one contemptuous phrase of Mr George Bernard Shaw. I thereupon informed the papers who had made the offer that it would be unacceptable as Britons (Celtic variety) never would be Slaves. I don't think I could make the offer again but I am prepared to try if I could be certain of being treated with any courtesy — not that I care about courtesy myself but because I should have to report the answer to various foreign friends who consider forms and ceremonies. Why don't you let me have an article or an appeal for funds to print? I will give it plenty of publicity.

Yours sincerely, *Ford Madox Hueffer*

To James B. Pinker

9 [1908 or 09] *84, Holland Park Avenue, W.*

Dear Pinker: I do wish you wd. hurry up Nelson's and let me have the money, for really it is no exaggeration to say that I am practically at starvation point.

Yrs. *Ford M. H.*

0 [1909] *84, Holland Park Avenue, W.*

Dear Pinker: I am rather in need of money to meet my month's bills. I think that with the 'Half Moon' cheque (Nash ought to pay royalty in advance as par suite of the *Fifth Queen* up to date of publication) and the Methuen novel there ought to be a balance in my favour after yr. commission and interest are paid: wd. it will be troubling you too much to ask you what this amount will be and either letting me have it, deducting of course yr. interest, or giving me such particulars as will let me raise it commercially. I want about £150 and imagine it ought to run to that or thereabouts. I am sorry to trouble you but the English Review so eats up my resources that I have nothing to pay my household bills with.

Yrs. *Ford Madox Hueffer*

11 26 March 1909

84, Holland Park Avenue, W.
THE ENGLISH REVIEW

Dear Pinker, Certainly the articles will be fitted for the most family magazine which you could imagine, and will not bring the blush to any cheek. It is really a matter of pointing out that now that the press really seems no longer to voice — if it ever did — the normal public opinion that music-halls are almost the only place for keeping one's finger on the national pulse. This solemn lesson will, however, be very gently rubbed in, not forced down the unwilling reader's throat. I should like to make it a matter of six articles of say 1500 words each.

Yours sincerely, *Ford Madox Hueffer*

12 3 June 1912

South Lodge
Campden Hill Road
Kensington, W.

Dear Pinker, I really think it is time that you let me hear something about Constable's intentions in publishing the Panel.[1] You worried me in their interests until I wrote the novel in about a month and induced a very severe nervous breakdown from which I am still suffering.

Now they not only do not publish it or pay for it but you do not even let me know what are their intentions. I really do think that you ought at times to remember that you are supposed to be acting in my interests at least to the extent of keeping me informed. I am now tied up to these people and cannot write novels for any other publisher till they choose to publish me — and they simply sit on my mss. which may be ingenious and pleasant for them but is quite the reverse for me.

[1] Ford's novel *The Panel*, published by Constable in 1912, with some changes was published as *Ring for Nancy* in America.

I think I must therefore ask you to warn them that unless they publish and pay for the Panel within the next fortnight I shall disregard that portion of my contract with them that gives them my next novel and shall accept the commission of another publisher to give him my next book, leaving the last for Constable's until it suits me to write it.

Yours faithfully *Ford Madox Hueffer*

3 [February 1913] *South Lodge*
Kensington, W.

Dear Pinker, I am upon the whole in agreement with the sentiments of your letter, but with regard to saddling Byles[1] with the historical novel as well as the modern one I am not so sure. You see, other things being equal, there will be three instalments of the novel Byles is to have and that ought to be enough for any one publishing house.

What I should have preferred would have been that you should have got me a commission for the historical novel that I am just completing from some other firm. I suppose that ought not to be very difficult. I have, by the way, written Constable's as polite a letter as I know how, which I thought I owed them and, in the course of it, I suggested that they should publish all the historical novels that I write, leaving the modern ones to Byles who is enthusiastic and will spend a great deal of money on advertising them. Subject to your approval I think this would be a good and also an equitable plan.

But of course there are other publishers — for instance Hodders ought to be favourably inclined to me. At any rate, Robertson Nichols always writes about me as if I were Shakespeare, Robert Lewis [sic] Stevenson and God almighty rolled into one; just think about it will you?

Yours *Ford Madox Hueffer*

[1] René Byles managed the publishing firm of Alston Rivers, which published seven of Ford's books. Byles became, as Ford writes in *Return to Yesterday*, 'one of my most intimate friends' — such a believer in Ford's gifts that 'he almost made me believe in myself'. He credits Byles moreover with being 'almost' the first English man of business to use a card index.

14 4 March 1913 *Gd Hotel de Provence*
Saint-Remy-de-Provence

Dear Pinker, Certainly I will lengthen 'The Panel' a little and alter it here and there for Bobbs-Merill & Co. I have sent for a copy of it and will do it as soon as I get it.

I am glad you are going to let Byles have his way; as it is really rather more in the nature of a present to him than anything else. Let me whisper into your secretive ear that the novel I am now writing [*The Young Lovell*] is going to be one of the great historical novels of the world; no doubt you will let that fact be reflected in the contract that I understand you to be making for me.

Yours *Ford Madox Hueffer* p. V.H. [Violet Hunt]

I am getting the German book [*The Desirable Alien*] finished [and] ready for you. I want you to begin on it as soon as I get home. *V.M.H.*

To F. S. Flint

15 [2 June 1914] *South Lodge*
Campden Hill Road
Kensington, W.

My dear Flint, It is an honour to have a poem addressed to one by you; but I hope, if you publish it, that you will leave out the superscription because — though I don't know why one should — one dislikes having one's psychology presented to the world. Come up and sit in the garden again during another hot evening.

Yours, *F.M.H*

F. S. Flint (1885–1960), poet, translator, and prime mover in the Imagist movement, with which Ford was associated.

To John Lane

6 17 December 1914

South Lodge
Campden Hill Road
Kensington, W.

My dear Lane/ I should have thought that you publishers had had eye-openers enough about monkeying with authors' titles, at the request of travellers. 'The Saddest Story' — I say it in all humility — is about the best book you ever published and the title is about the best title. Still, I make it a principle never to interfere with my publisher, but to take it out in calling him names. Why not call the book 'The Roaring Joke'? Or call it anything you like, or perhaps it would be better to call it 'A Good Soldier' — that might do. At any rate it is all I can think of.

Yrs *Ford Madox Hueffer* [per Violet Hunt]

Lane (1854–1925) founded The Bodley Head publishing firm in 1887; he published *The Good Soldier*, pressing Ford for a new title, the original — *The Saddest Story* — having struck him as too gloomy to be saleable during wartime. In the second of these two letters to Lane, Ford adopts an ironic position toward readers like the gentleman from Liverpool who attacked the novel for its sexual content. Within the following week, Rebecca West reviewed *The Good Soldier*: '. . . It is as impossible to miss the light of its extreme beauty and wisdom as it would be to miss the full moon on a clear night.'

7 28 March 1915

The Knap Cottage, Selsey
Sussex

My dear Lane, Alas, it does indeed seem a monstrous thing, but after all, what is chaste in Constantinople may have the aspect of lewdness in Liverpool, and what in Liverpool may pass for virtue in Constantinople is frequently regarded as vice. Let us hope that when the Allies have entered the Dardanelles 'The Good Soldier' may come into his own, in several senses. You see, that work is as serious an analysis of the polygamous desires that underlie all men — except perhaps the members of the Publishers' Association — as 'When Blood is Their Argument' is an analysis of Prussian Culture.

I have however heard that really iniquitous publishers have got quite good 'ads.' out of similar positions. I remember that when the

Public Librarian of Southend publicly announced that one of my books about Henry VIII would not be lent out by the Southend Municipal Library the good citizens of that illustrious place bought next day four hundred copies of the said work. Why not send the correspondence to the Liverpool papers and add that in your opinion the book would be proper reading for Birkenhead Police recruits who, by recommendation of the Home Office, must all be men of mature years. I cannot think of anything else to do about it.

Yours, With kind regards, *Ford Madox Hueffer*

P. S. It has just occurred to me that if that gentleman is circulating the labelled copy of that book we might have rather fun because it would show that he has resigned himself to corrupting Liverpudlians rather than lose the benefit of what he has paid 4/2 for. Could you find out?

To The Adjutant, 9/Welch B. E. F.

18 7 September 1916

Sir, I have the honour to request that leave of absence may be granted to me from 9/9/16 to 11/9/16 for the purpose of proceeding to Paris on urgent financial affairs — these being the publication in Paris of a work by myself entitled *Entre St Denis et St Georges*, the said work having been written at the request of H. M. Government for the Government of the French Republic. My financial affairs having become exceedingly embarrassed owing to my having done this & other work without pay, for H. M. Government, it would be of the greatest advantage to me if this short leave could be granted to me. In the case of its being so granted my address would be c/o Mess. Payot, 106 Boulevard St. Germain, Paris.

I have the honour to be, Sir, Your obedient servant, *Ford Madox Hueffer*

2/Lt attd 9/Welch

To James B. Pinker

19 22 January 1920 *Red Ford*

Dear Pinker: I am returning *English Country* [*No Enemy*] herewith.

You speak of it as a 'novel' & that rather troubles me. If it is a novel it simply has to go to Lane. I regard it as what is called a 'serious book' — I suppose it is really betwixt & between.

Can you approach Lane about it? Or should I? I do so dislike being in false positions about books — yet I always seem to get into them, with the best intentions in the world. I wish you could get over your antipathy to J. L. [John Lane] — at any rate for the occasion — & put the matter to him. I would — but then I might seem to be going behind *your* back & there we should be again!

I meant *English Country* to be a 'piece of writing', like the *Soul of London* and to go, eventually, to Duckworth.

I wish you wd. send me that Northern Newspapers money. My pigs have been sick — and that is ruinous as well as distracting.

I suppose you wd. not care to buy a pig — not a sick one — about 20 st. [stone].

Yrs. *F.M.Ford*

8 July 1920 *Red Ford, Hurston*
Pulborough

Dear Pinker; I think the psychological moment is approaching when you might suggest to Lane that he produce the contract for my Collected Edition. I have got a long novel nearly completed and Lane is bound to have that. But I do not care to let it go without some sort of business arrangements being made.

As far as I know the matter stands thus: during, or just before the war some sort of arrangement was made between Lane and a third party that he was to take all my future novels on a basis that I do not remember. I don't know that I even saw the agreement. At any rate except that, vaguely, advances were to be made on succeeding novels on a basis of some kind calculated on the sales of the previous novel — which in this case would be the *Good Soldier* — I either never knew or have quite forgotten what the arrangement was. I do not possess a copy of the agreement and see no chance of getting hold of it . . . During the war I suggested myself to Lane that, as he had this agreement he had better undertake to collect all my previous novels and re-publish them. To this he cordially agreed. I asked you then to take steps for getting the copyrights back and you said you would. After the Armistice I again saw Lane and asked him when he was going to begin. He said that paper was at that date so dear that he could not fix a date but he gave me his word that he would begin quite soon or as soon as things settled down. This is as far as I have got.

Could you now, please, ascertain for me what were the terms arranged for the novels succeeding the *Good Soldier*? And would you, at the same time, take steps to get the agreement for the Collected Edition drawn up? I am getting back into work again and dislike going on on vaguenesses.

Ref. your last letter and the cinema rights of the *Panel*. I was quite aware that the arrangement with the American people had fallen through. But you will remember that, when you advised me to refuse the offer, you said you could get much better terms, I supposed elsewhere. It was to this that I was referring when I last wrote. I should be glad if you could now put this through. The book is a bad book but it would make a good film.

Yours *F. M. Ford*

P.S. Would you please have cheques made out to me as 'Ford'?

21 13 July 1920 *Red Ford Cottage, Hurston*
Pulborough

Dear Pinker; Yes, I daresay there may be difficulties about paper and the rest for Lane — but they apply equally to me. I do not want to press for an entire re-publication in six months, or anything of that sort, but I do want a definite agreement. As things stand I have Lane's word and for today that is quite good enough — but Lane might die, or become permanently ill or sell his business and I should have nothing to shew. Also I want to know the terms. For a long time — I daresay for ten years or so — I never really knew anything about my business affairs; but the years go on and that seems an unsatisfactory sort of position. As I understand things Lane got the Good Soldier at a very easy rate — but I don't even know what the rate was — on condition that he did publish the collected edition. I am quite content that that should be so but I think it ought to be in black and white. That's all.

Yrs. *F.M. Ford*

To Harriet Monroe

2 10 February 1921

Coopers, Bedham
Fittleworth, Sussex

Dear Miss Munroe [sic]; Thank you for your cheque and still more for your appreciative letter — and still, still more for the good work that you do with POETRY. I am sure that there will be a special niche for you on Parnassus, or the Heaven of Good Poets, wherever it be. I don't know the United States well enough to lecture you about yourself — but as far as I *do* know the United States I think — as you will find me shortly saying in the N. Y. Evening Post — at least for its periodicals, that nation is infinitely ahead of all its Anglo-Saxon brethren. And, if that periodical literature has a little peak, a little crown, raising it to the best of European cosmopolitanism, or at any rate in that direction, it is because you and your small paper shewed how it could be done. It is a fine achievement!

Perhaps you would be good enough to note that, since Ezra sent that poem to you, I have changed my surname, so as to fulfil the terms of a small legacy and that I have bought a small farm, the address being as above, the name being FORD. I shall continue to write — if I *do* continue to write! — as Hueffer but if you have occasion to address me perhaps you would write as to F. M. Ford, Coopers etc. I pass my time mostly in the raising of pedigree pigs, as the war has left me under the necessity of living in the open air; but sometimes I go indoors and write fabulous attacks on Academic poets and ferocious applause of Vers Libristes and the like. Of that sort, I have a book coming out in the Spring [Thus to Revisit]. It is going to get me ostracised here — but on looking it through it is astonishing to me to observe how, from Stephen Crane to James and from him to Ezra and T. S. Eliot, your country right or wrong figures in one's reminiscences!

Anyhow, more power to your elbow.

Yours cordially *Ford Madox Ford*

I enclose one or two little verses that you might print. If they are too domestic, pass them on to HARPERS or the LADY'S HOME JOURNAL [sic] or something, or drop them into the W. P. B. Price to you fourpence, or what you will.

Harriet Monroe was editor of *Poetry: A Magazine of Verse*, which she founded in Chicago in 1912.

23 10 August 1921 *Coopers, Bedham*
Fittleworth, Sussex

Dear Miss Monroe; I think the quotation would read better if it ran:

> If American periodical literature has today a peak, a little group of journals, raising it to the level of the best of European cosmopolitanism, or at any rate in that direction, it is because you and your small paper showed how, editorially and economically, it could be done.

I think that reads more comprehensibly, and makes a better cadence. But if you prefer the first version by all means stick to it. I shall naturally be much pleased if you print either version — as I should be if there were anything else I could do to be of service to you.

You never sent me, as you promised, that Western poet's poem — I cannot remember his name: was it Sarett. He wrote me a nice letter and I should like to write him something nice in return. So send it me, will you?

Yours in haste *F.M.Ford*

To H. S. Latham

24 14 August 1921 *Coopers, Bedham*
Fittleworth

Dear Mr Latham; I wrote you the following immense long letter on the 4th inst; but it seemed to me so preposterous that, intending to shorten it a great deal, I did not post it. Emboldened however by your very kind letter of the 2nd inst, I am copying it out and sending it after all:

'As I am afraid I shall have to trouble you with a long letter, I am forwarding you herewith in a separate fascicle, synopses of, or notes on, several books that I have in various stages of in-hand-ness. They will thus I hope appear less appalling than they would in the body of a letter.

As you will see I have been thinking of most of them for some years — one or two of them for several years, or indeed a great many. This does not mean that I have any doubts of them as subjects;

I always do think of my books for very long periods before setting pen to paper, when I write them, usually, very rapidly. Moreover, I have not been well enough since being invalided out of the Army, to risk the strain of such prolonged indoor work as has been entailed by anything other than very desultory writing. But I think I could now begin on any one of the books foreshadowed in that fascicle and carry it to a fairly speedy conclusion. If therefore one of these subjects appealed to you and we came to terms — as I hope we may, for I do not think I am exacting — I could begin at once on hearing from you.

I should like to say, however, as a preliminary, that I want to get into relations with a publisher with whom I could reasonably hope to remain for the rest of my life. In the course of what is beginning to be rather a protracted literary career I have been — as is not unusual — published by several firms, so that, at present, although my kindlier critics assure me that I have written several books of permanent interest, the public finds it very difficult to know where to go to obtain my works. Five or six of them, such as my 'Soul of London' series [published by Alston Rivers] and some monographs on artists [*Rossetti*, *Hans Holbein* and *The Pre-Raphaelite Brotherhood* published by Duckworth] and other critical works — all what are called "serious books" — are in the hands of one publisher and have a steady — one or two even a large — sale. But all my historical and modern novels as well as my volumes of poems are divided up amongst four or five publishers, whilst several have gone out of print owing to the disappearance of the firms that published them. This is naturally very disadvantageous to a writer like myself who have always written with a view to a steady and continuing, rather than an immediate and sensational, sale.

What I want now to find is a publisher — and I should be extremely pleased if it could be your house — who would whilst commissioning some of my future work, publish two or three of my historical and modern novels and a fairly large representative selection of my poems as coups d'essai and who would then go on to publish more if the experiment proved successful. Of course if it did not, after a fair trial, the experiment would be dropped: but if it proceeded we might proceed to a fairly complete and definitive edition.

I may mention that since I acknowledged your letter I have received, amongst several proposals from American publishers and editors one in particular to re-publish a number of my earlier works.

I do not of course say this in order to force your hand in one way or the other. I mean that I should be very glad to publish new work with you and old with the other firm: but I imagine it would be advantageous to both myself and whoever my publisher was if all my books could be under one roof — whilst the fact that, since the beginning of this year, I have received in one way and another a great deal of attention in and offers of commissions from the United States encourages me to think that my day, as the saying is, has dawned in your country — at any rate sufficiently to make such a proposal from me not seem altogether absurd.

The question of terms I should prefer to leave to you.'

That was the contents of my original letter to which I do not see that there is anything to add except that yours of the 2nd of August gratifies me very much and that I really hope that we may, as the saying goes, do business together.

Yours very sincerely

P.S. The accompanying synopses are I think fairly plain. I was, when I wrote them, taking stock of my own position as much for my own benefit as for yours — and, after all, if they are too much of a bore there is no particular reason why you should read them!

H. S. Latham was Editor at the Macmillan Company in New York.

To T.S. Eliot

25 8 October 1923

THE PARIS REVIEW
65 Boulevard Arago
Paris[1]

My dear Eliot, Thanks very much for your friendly letter. I enclose herewith a rough draft of the circular that I shall be sending out in vast numbers next week. It will give you an idea of the aims of this infernal enterprise which, since it appears three times as often as The Criterion will kill me three times as fast as The Criterion kills you. (The draft is *very* rough). The history of British literature has not, by the by, yet reached me. If you could see that it is sent off at

[1] The letterhead shows that *The Transatlantic Review* was originally to be called *The Paris Review*.

once or do anything to get it here as quickly as possible I should be much obliged but I am much more concerned to have your note than anything else.

Yours always in haste, *F.M. Ford*

To F. S. Flint

6 15 October 1923

THE TRANSATLANTIC REVIEW
65 Boulevard Arago
Paris XIII

My dear Flint:— I am starting a Review here with the above title which will be published also in London and New York and, as you were a contributor to the old English Review of which this will be a replica I should very much like to inscribe your name on the list of those who are going to write for me now.

I hope you are well.

Yours very truly *F.M. Ford*

P.S. We have had as is always the case to change our name at the last moment. Hence the heading.

To William Aspenwall Bradley

27 Friday [1924]

Dear Bradley: I've finished the novel [*Some Do Not*] as far as I am concerned: I say as far as I am concerned because, for the English market it is shortish — not longer than 70,000 or at most 75,000 words. I'd much rather leave it at that artistically — & this book is so closely written that, if it were longer I believe it wd. be intolerable to a reader.

But I am afraid I shall have to add 6 or 7,000 words for England because the Libraries insist on so much avoir du pois — so I shall add matter that artistically ought to go into the next book.

What do you think? I fancy the U.S.A. does not object to short books & I'd much rather leave this short; but I don't want Boni's to think I've stinted them.

Let me know by return, will you?

Yrs. *F.*

If you've nothing better to do, come around about 7 and look at the end [of the book] and we'll eat together after.

William Aspenwall Bradley was Ford's literary agent in the 1920s. Bradley was an American who lived in Paris; his wife, Jenny Serruys Bradley, a Frenchwoman, carried on the agency after his death. Both were close friends of Ford's. See Jenny Bradley's tribute in *The Presence of Ford Madox Ford*, ed. S. J. Stang (Philadelphia: University of Pennsylvania Press, 1981), p. 199.

To M. Roché

28 5 March 1924 *29, Quai d'anjou, Paris-4°*

Dear M. Roché: I am forwarding you under another cover a copy of No iii of the Review containing the Art Supplement towards the preparation of which you gave such much-valued assistance.

Mr Quinn[1] is anxious that our No vi (June) Number should 'feature' as the cinemas say, *Derain* — and I see nothing against this, except that Derain is almost *too* well known already and I have leanings myself toward *Segonzac*, who would help our English circulation, his exhibition there having been a great success. I should like also to put in one or two *Bissières* as he has been very obliging about the Braques. Perhaps you would let me know what you think about this. We might do say *6 Derains*, *4 Segonzacs* and *4 Bissières*, with a couple each of English and American artists to keep the *international note* which I have to consider. You will perhaps by then have something for me to publish — say by the 1st of May when I should need your m.s.

Thanking you again

I'm yours very sincerely *Ford Madox Ford*

[1] John Quinn was the American lawyer who defended Joyce's *Ulysses* in court. He owned a large and significant collection of modern European art, dispersed after his death. Quinn was a principal backer of the *Transatlantic*.

To William Aspenwall Bradley

29 25 January 1925 *Guermantes Près Lagny*

My dear Bradley, Yours of yesterday. Miss Rhys is here but has been too ill to do anything about that ms. She is of course quite agreeable that you should handle it in Germany. I will send it along as soon as she has gone through it again, which should be about Thursday next.

Ref my own work for Germany and elsewhere:

Some Do Not and the Conrad book are free for you to handle in Germany. With regard to both of them for France *Some Do Not* is to go to Kra and someone (I am not certain whether it was Llona or Chadourne)[1] asked me whether I had any arrangements about the French translation and I answered that I was open to receive an offer. I have not however heard anything further.

Future work.

The book I am writing now is a novel called *No More Parades*. The English book rights of this as of all my books go to Duckworth, but the American book rights and all serial rights are not disposed of. Seltzer, through Brandt, made an offer for it: what it was I have forgotten and I am not sure that I even read it as I cannot and will not have anything more to do with Seltzer.[2]

If you would care to handle it for American book and serial rights (British serial rights as well) I would send you the mss along in chunks and you could get it typed if that would suit you, but I usually get Duckworth to print a set or two of proofs off right away and thus save myself the expense and bother of typing.

I rather think, don't you?, that we ought to have a written agreement about these things. So many people come to me and ask me for this and that and I always forget what they want or what I

1 Victor Llona, Peruvian-French novelist. Paul Chadourne, French translator of Ford and Conrad's *Romance*, published by Kra in 1926. Ford thought the translation 'very admirable'. He wrote the preface in 1927 to *Vasco*, a novel by Paul's brother, Marc Chadourne.

2 Thomas Seltzer, uncle of Albert Boni, the publisher, published the first American edition of *Some Do Not* in 1924; he was also Ford's agent for *The Transatlantic Review* in New York. Ford held Seltzer at least partly responsible for the financial failure of the magazine. In addition, for three years Seltzer paid Ford no royalties on *Some Do Not*.

answer and enormous muddles might result, but if we had a definite written agreement I should remember it, or even if I didn't, I could refer them to you and you could make arrangements with them. I used to have an arrangement like that with Pinker till his death and it worked satisfactorily for both parties I think, but I do not get on with Eric Pinker. It did not apply to articles commissioned by periodicals writing direct to me, but did to everything else. Think about it, will you? I have not at the moment either time or brains to draft anything.

I enclose a small cheque. I would be infinitely obliged to you if you would send me the equivalent in notes, even if against the law, because a mandat is almost unnegotiable in these rustic solitudes and if I write to my bank for money they take intolerable ages to send it. I would not bother you, but Stella is in bed with the flu, rather seriously, and I do not know when we shall get up to Paris or a bank and in the meantime the house is full of people, Miss Rhys being also sick and I have to do all the cooking and most of the house work, so I am too moider [American slang: murdered] to think of anything else but bothering you. If you could wire the money it might be almost better for heaven only knows when this letter will go. We really might here be in the centre of the bogs of Ireland or any other remote place. I am dreadfully sorry to be such a bother.

All sorts of good wishes to Madame: Stella would send the same but she is asleep.

Yours always *F.M. Ford*

30 Sunday 21 June 1925 *16 Rue Denfert-Rochereau*

Dear Bradley, I left the page proofs of No More Parades on [sic] you yesterday evening.

I have added to the reverse of title page the words Copyright in the U.S.A. by Madeleine Boyd 1925, as I think we agreed that she would copyright the book as soon as she has copies which I will have sent to her straight by Duckworth. Perhaps you would let me have her address for that purpose. She does not have to apply for provisional copyright until two months after date of English publication and it remains valid for six months after that so there is really plenty of time but the American publisher would be well-advised to publish as early as possible, for, much to Seltzer's disgust the English edition was selling — of Some do Not — in New York before he got his edition out. In that case I did not mind because I got the royalty on those copies which I should not have if Seltzer had got in first.

I think it is really quite a good book which is a relief to me, for it seemed to me to be appalling in slip proofs and I have been going about in a state of deep depression. But in page proof it really seems to be something heavy and gloomy and big. So I may yet knock spots off Mr Dostoevski, though that secret ambition of mine should be kept between ourselves.

I have been reflecting upon the Conrad controversy. It seems to me that the obvious thing to do is for Little Brown to issue a new edition in which, *without any comment at all* I will add an appendix giving quotations and documents which will knock that nonsense on the head. It is a pity that Little Brown did not publish the facsimile letter which appears in the English edition of the book. Mrs Conrad is really already answered by that and quotations in the book itself which she has never seen, she having written her letter on the strength of the first three instalments that appeared in the Transatlantic Review. I think it would be a mistake to do even this, but if Little Brown wanted to do it I am ready to give them the material.

I hear famous things of Mrs Bradley: I suppose she will soon be restored to you.

We are stopping in Town for this week.

Yours *F.M.F*

31 [1926]

Dear Bradley, Would you just put this copy in your safe? It is incomplete but nearly complete. When I get towards the end of a book I always hate to have all the copies of a ms in one place for fear of fire.

I am very nearly finished: in both senses of the word.

I will undertake never to mention Selzer's [sic] name again — except in connection with brandy. I never even want to think of him again.

The title then is:

3 A Man Could Stand Up? Or had you some other form?

In haste and complete exhaustion *F*

You have already had duplicates of the earlier chapters — to Part II. 1.

32 8 March 1926 *Hotel Victoria, Toulon*

Dear Bradley: This here correspondence business is becoming portentous!

A. Yours enclosing Boni's of 20th ult.

I have got a practising journalist of the N.Y. Times Sunday Edn, to interview me here, said interview to be sent to Boni to use as they like. Suppose they will pay him some sort of space rates. This is the best I could do.

Juan Gris is making a portrait of me which B's [Boni's] can use if they like. If they do Gris must be paid a little. I am also getting photographed at work here.

I don't like this publicity business and don't really believe it does good: but B's perhaps know better.

B. Yours enclosing Boni's letter and Pond Contract.[1]

You can regard it as quite certain that I shall accept Pond, but I want a day or two to think about dates etc. before signing the contract. When I do I will post it to you.

Emmerich we may consider as W.O. — equals a wash out!

C. Letter of Duckworth enclosed.

Perhaps you will deal with this. On principle I do not want N.M.P. [*No More Parades*] translated for the Huns' delectation as it rather wallops my own country, but I would do it if they would undertake to publish also translation of my next book which redresses the balance as against *them* and gives a fairly impartial picture of the Late Great.

We are going to become very hard up in a fortnight. Do you suppose that Boni's have sent cheque for their acct. up to March 1st as per their contract as I had calculated they would? If not I shall have to stick Duckworth for some more which I do not like doing as the poor dear is hard up owing to the late great Strike. Of course if Boni's cheque is on the high seas now it would be all right. Or could you do anything magic with cables?

[1] James Pond, an American agent, arranged a ten-week lecture tour in America for Ford.

To Harriet Monroe

33 20 November 1926 *51 W. 16*

My dear Miss Monroe: Thank you for your very kind letter. I hope I shall get to Chicago — if only to see you and have a good talk.

I have sent on your message about the two clubs to Pond who will attend to that.

If I come I'd like to read *On Heaven* and the *House* to some of your people — if you'd like it. I don't of course want to be paid for that. I mean that I daresay you'd like it and I'd like to do it. . . . But I've a clumsy way of expressing it. I only mean that I'm grateful to you and if anything of the sort would be useful to *Poetry* I'd be glad to do it.

I don't wonder the lecturing field is crowded: there seem to be mornamillion English — not to mention native — novelists in the field. But I don't much care about lecturing and would just as soon work quietly here — as I propose to do for the next three months or so.

Anyhow I'll try to see you before I go and in the meantime I'm yours very truly *Ford Madox Ford*

I see your letter is dated the 13th. It only reached me yesterday as I've been moving about.

34 7 February 1927 *51 West 16th Street*
New York

Dear Miss Monroe: I return herewith the proofs, corrected.

You could render me a very great service. Miss Durkee tells me that there is in her library a copy of an early work of mine called *The Cinque Ports* [see pp. 00–00 of this volume] which does not appear to be discoverable anywhere else in this country. On or about page 162 of this work is a passage telling the story of a foreigner cast ashore in the Romney marsh and starving because he can't make himself understood whilst the country people think him a dangerous lunatic. I very much need this passage copied out. Could you get somebody to do it for me? It is only a matter of perhaps ten minutes' work and I would willingly pay for it handsomely, whilst you would earn my great great gratitude by getting it done for me. I really had not time to do it myself in Chicago.

Yes, I wish I could have stopped longer in the neighbourhood of the Loop but you made things so nice for me that, had I done so, I should have been spoiled, so perhaps it is better thus. In any case I am very grateful to you. I hope we shall meet again in the not distant future.

Yours always, sincerely, *Ford Madox Ford*

So glad you left Tate in!

To Ferris Greenslet

35 20 February 1927 *51 West 16th Street*
New York

My dear Greenslet: Alas, I have decided that I cannot afford to cross the ocean with any jovial crew because I am so dreadfully behind hand with my work that I must positively write all the time I am on board ship. So I am going by the American Banker on Thursday. There are on it practically no passengers and I shall have a cabin all to myself to write in besides the one in which I sleep. If I went with you who knows how many master pieces might not get written. But maybe we shall meet in London.

In any case I hope we shall meet before that because as Mrs Foster[1] will have told you I am coming to Boston on Tuesday. If you would once more put me up at the St Botolph's Club I should esteem it a great favour. I shall arrive in Boston at ten o'clock on Tuesday night. *A tantot* then,

Yr. *F.M. Ford*

Greenslet was Editor at Houghton Mifflin — 'a pillar of the august and ancient House of Houghton Mifflin' (*Return to Yesterday*, p. 318).

[1] Jeanne Robert Foster, whom Ford described as a 'ravishingly beautiful lady', was a close friend of John Quinn and of John Butler Yeats. She was the American editor of *The Transatlantic Review*.

To James F. Drake

36 24 October 1927 *15 Gramercy Park Manhattan*

Dear Colonel Drake: You asked me the other day if I wanted to sell my Conrad letters. I don't — but I wd sell — as of interest to Conrad collectors — the ms. of my Conrad book — mostly in ms. but a portion typed. I wd add to it the letter of Conrad's which forms the frontispiece of the English edition & the letters I wrote to the *Herald-Tribune* and the *Times* last year on the subject of the plot of C's *Amy Foster*. The ms. is interesting because it contains a number of passages I excised for fear of hurting various susceptibilities.

If this wd. fetch a good price I wd. not mind selling it; perhaps you wd. drop me a line?

Yrs. vy sincerely *Ford Madox Ford*

To J. B. Manson

37 11 January 1929 *32 Rue de Vaugirard, Paris VI*

My dear Sir: I am much touched by what you have said about the Tietjens books; where the result upon the public of one's work is so infinitesmal or so completely non-existent as is the case with mine a little private praise is much to be appreciated. However I don't really complain of the reviewers in England for they write about me often enough in terms suited only for, say, Shakespeare and Emerson rolled into one. The curious thing is that their voices seem to make no impression whatever upon the public and my sales in England are so small that I have nearly come to the conclusion not to publish there at all — not so much because of the lack of sales but as a protest against the miserable policy of the government in imposing an enormous super-tax on such unfortunate writers and artists as are doomed to live abroad because they can't afford to live at home. It is a curious thing, if you come to think of it, that writers who ought to be the most vocal of creatures have to submit to the worst sort of pillaging at the hands of our fiscal authorities — the worst sort of pillaging that is suffered by any class of the body politic. It is a joint product, I suppose, of the real hatred for the arts that exists in the

British administrative classes and of the sort of shyness to write about their private matters that distinguishes authors and artists and the like. I suppose it ought to be my duty to write to the Times, to state that my income from books in the United Kingdom is seventy-five shillings per annum less than nothing solely owing to taxation and to head a clamorous movement for the liberation of the poor old Andromeda of British Literature from her chains, but I shan't do it, nor yet will any one else. Anyhow thank you very much. I will certainly ask for you if I ever come to Millbank [where Manson worked at the then National Gallery], but I think the chances are that you are more likely to come to Paris before I come to London. In that case pray give me a ring at the telephone number that you see above. There are so many things I should like to ask you,

Yours very sincerely, *Ford Madox Ford*

To William Carlos Williams

38 5 July 1929 *30 West Ninth Street*
New York City

My dear Williams, I am so sorry. I knew that would happen, though I did my best to prevent it. A man insisted on motoring me to White Plains on the plea that there were many trains there and none at Paterson. It turned out however that there were no trains at White Plains whereas if I had taken the train from Paterson I should have been in good time for you.

Do choose another day for lunch next week and pardon me this one? Almost any day — or indeed absolutely any one!

Yours apologetically *Ford Madox Ford*

To Harriet Monroe

39 2 November 1931 *32 R. de Vaugirard, Paris VI*

Dear Miss Monroe, Alas, after prayer and fasting and the greatest desire in the world to meet your wishes I can't let you truncate that series.[1] You see, it is a single work with a design of its own and if you cut out two of its main notes you will completely change the effect. I am very sorry. I know how limited your space is. If you would like to publish the whole in two instalments I should not so much object — say to the end of FLEUVE PROFOND and from there to the end of the poem [sic]. But I daresay you will not care to do that.

It is good to hear that you are flourishing. We have just returned for the winter to my old apartment which, alas, they are going to pull down very shortly in the attempt to make the quarter more resemble Michigan Avenue. In the meanwhile the sun shines and Paris is very much Paris.

Always more power to your elbow.

Yours always, *Ford Madox Ford*

To Victor Gollancz

40 3 January 1932

Dear Sir, It is annoying that you are not going to be able to be in Paris. I hope the lawsuit went favourably for you.

Briefly, I am in search of an English publisher with whom I can end my days. I have a long programme of work that I hope to do before then. It is all settled for in New York, the only question remaining is whether I shall publish in England and, if so, how to synchronise the publications.

If you think, from your experience with RETURN TO YESTERDAY; that you would care to handle my work I will send you a sort of synopsis of my plans, but I should dislike doing so without a prima facie likelihood of your contemplating a prolonged relationship.

I hope RETURN TO YESTERDAY has done well, but as I see neither cuttings nor English papers I have no means of knowing.

Perhaps you would let me have an answer at your convenience.

1 *Buckshee*, the series of nine poems Ford wrote for Janice Biala. Subtitled *Last Poems (for Haitchka in France)*, they are in fact the last poems he wrote.

Reciprocating your wishes for the three day old year I'm
Yours sincerely

Victor Gollancz published only one of Ford's books, *Return to Yesterday*.

To Jonathan Cape

41 6 March 1932

Dear Sirs, WHEN THE WICKED MAN

I am forwarding you by this mail under another cover one copy of the American edition of the above with Mr Ford's emendations and a prefatory note [see p. 00 of this volume]. Mr Ford would be glad to have your proofs as soon as possible as he will shortly be travelling.

He asks me to say that you may if you wish transpose Chapters II and III with the idea of making the book more of a straightforward narrative. At the same time he thinks your advisers underrate the intelligence of the British reader. English novels have not of course caught up with the general run of European and American fiction in matters of form but that is largely because of timidity or old-fashionedness in the producers rather than because the English reader is markedly less intelligent than his foreign contemporaries. English books would probably sell better if they were better constructed.

Yours faithfully *Secretary*

P.S. Will you please ask your printer to treat the copy as tenderly as possible? It is a copy of the first edition which is rare and will have a certain added value from Mr Ford's emendations.

To Victor Gollancz

42 6 August 1932

Dear Sir, I have been away and have only just received your letter of the twenty-fifth of July. I suspect that you must be as bad at reading and answering letters as I am myself for I wrote you three times on the subject at the beginning of the year. But the matter was not particularly urgent so I left it alone. I am glad you want the book. As to terms I must ask you to make several modifications in the form of the contract. I will outline these in a day or two when I have made my final arrangements for the American contract.

In the meantime, on another subject, Ezra Pound is publishing his XXX CANTOS with Farrar and Rinehart in New York next autumn. He has not got an English publisher and this is a defect which it seems to me ought to be remedied. Could you not take some sheets from Farrar's? I don't guarantee that you will make money by the transaction but I do guarantee that it will redound to the honour of your house long after most of your other enterprises are buried in the oblivion which is destined for most of us. If you decide to do it the negotiations should be entered upon telegraphically for I think it important that the book should appear in England before American publication. I have spoken to Mr Pound about it and he is quite content to leave the matter in my hands. As the matter is rather urgent I should be obliged if you would depart from your usual custom and let me have a reply by return.

With kind regards, Yours faithfully,

To James Joyce

43 29 August 1932

Villa Paul
Chemin de la Calade
Cap Brun. Toulon. Var

My dear Joyce, Ezra Pound is publishing his Cantos in New York next January and I am trying to get him what is called a good press in that country. To that end I am getting together a pamphlet containing testimonials to Ezra as a literary figure in general and to the Cantos in particular, if the writers of said testimonials chance to have read them. We all I think — if you will excuse my saying so — have owed at one time or another at least something to Ezra and some of us a good deal. And this is his first real public appearance in the United States for what is called donkey's years. Moreover he is as completely unknown to the American press and public as he is to the English. I know with what difficulty your writing is beset but if you would add just a word or two to the collection it would be very delightful. If you would just dictate a letter with a cordial word or two in answer to this it would be quite sufficient but of course if you would write something studied it would be of much more service.

I hope you are well. I wish we met more often but I am nearly permanently anchored and no good breezes seem likely to blow you this way. Our very kind regards to Mrs Joyce.

Yours as always, *Ford Madox Ford*

To Hugh Walpole

44 25 October 1932

Villa Paul
Chemin de la Calade
Cap Brun. Toulon. Var

Dear Walpole, Be an angel or at least a sport and write me one or two words of enthusiasm or amiability for the pamphlet about Ezra and his CANTOS that I am getting up to accompany the American edition of that work. Joyce and Paul Morand and Gerhart Hauptmann and Hemingway and Eliot and all sorts of non-English people have written long or short but at anyrate enthusiastic screeds about them whereas, try as I will, I cannot get an English publisher for them so do do something to redress this monstrous balance of the Old World. I will send you the proofs of the CANTOS if you like but any amiable personal remarks would do if you don't want to be bothered to read them.

We were in Germany for some time just now but the weather was cold and the state of things depressing so we did not get much out of it. If you are coming south do not neglect us.

Yours always *Ford Madox Ford*

Sir Hugh Walpole (1887–1914), a prolific writer whose novels — notably *The Herries Chronicle* (1930–33) — were enormously popular in his lifetime.

To Theodore Dreiser

45 12 September 1933

Villa Paul
Chemin de la Calade
Cap Brun. Toulon. Var

My dear Dreiser, In answer to yours of the 26th January I wrote you a letter of which the enclosed is a copy. I have just got it back in the envelope also enclosed. I suppose it is my fault for not having put the name of THE AMERICAN SPECTATOR after yours on the address. And now I am completely at sea. I hear you have left W.57. Liveright's I see today in POETRY have gone bankrupt. Ray Long and Smith[1] as I know to my cost have also failed and, since the AMERICAN SPECTATOR belonged to them it may have stopped. So where am I to address you? If you get this wouldn't you let me know an address to which I can write? I like to drop you a line from time to time and like to have your news. But the present situation is discouraging. As for me I am generally here but c/o the Guaranty Trust, 4 Place Vendome, Paris is good at all times.

I hope the collapse of Liveright's has not seriously hit you. Who are your present publishers? I hope you have found somebody stable — if there is anybody. For myself I have gone to Lippincott's. I suppose they will last as long as anyone and they are pleasant people to have to do with. Moreover they read one's letters which I never knew any other American publisher do, but of course the collapse of the dollar has hit us pretty hard here.

Do you never come to Europe? We'd be extremely glad to put you up here and it is a lovely place. I wish I could come to New York but the financial hurdles are too high to take. I never come to that city without spending about twice as much as I make there and in these days that is no good.

Drop me a note when you have time, won't you?

Yours always, *Ford Madox Ford*

If the AMERICAN SPECTATOR is still alive I would not mind putting the French case for it, but I suppose that is the last thing it would want.

To Graham Greene

46 24 September 1934

Villa Paul
Chemin de la Calade
Cap Brun. Toulon. Var

My dear Sir: Thank you very much: yr. letter being undated I can't tell how long I have left it unanswered — but at any rate during the

[1] This firm had contracted to publish Ford's *A History of Our Own Times*. He never succeeded in finding another publisher for it.

interval, the occasional remembering of it has given me little touches of pleasure and the feeling that all is not lost!

My only complaint is that you shd. say: 'I am a novelist' & then not send me one of yr. novels! It makes correspondence rather like duelling in the mist with an opponent armed with one doesn't know what weapon!

Send me something — & then we can go on!

Yrs. vry. sincerely *Ford Madox Ford*

47 4 December 1934

61 Fifth Avenue
New York City

Dear Mr Graham Greene: Thank you very much for It's a Battlefield; it's a truly admirable work: I can hardly express how highly I think of it — construction impeccable; writing very good indeed & atmosphere extraordinarily impressive. . . . I can't write sense in this city: I wish I cd. meet you & talk about it. At any rate, believe that it seems for me to make a shaft of sunlight through the gloom that seems to hang over our distant land! I wd. not have believed that such writing cd. come out of England.

Write and let me know what you are doing now — and more about yourself. I expect to be here till about March and hope then to get back to Toulon.

All good things in the meantime!

Yrs. very sincerely, *Ford Madox Ford*

To Lewis Gannett

48 27 June 1935

c/o Dr Lake
50 West 12th Street, N.Y.C.

Dear Mr Gannett: I have lately re-read here the complete works of Conrad and Henry James and am engaged on reading all the books of

Stephen Crane that I can lay my hands on — for the to me astounding fact is that the works of those three writers are here out of print and practically unobtainable, such being glory! I had to borrow the Conrad and James from Doubleday and Scribner's respectively and Knopf has only been able to lend me Crane's *George's Mother* . . . after ringing up more than twenty new and second hand booksellers.

Of Conrad I was most re-impressed by *Under Western Eyes*, *Nostromo* and the *Secret Agent*; of James the *Spoils of Poynton*, the *Wings of the Dove*, the *Turn of the Screw* and a dozen short stories.

I have also been reading during a fortnight in Tennessee from which I have just returned, the *Agricultural Census* of the United States, several lives of Lee, Stonewall Jackson, Boone, Crockett and minor Southern Notabilities, the new (as yet unpublished) volume of poems by Allen Tate; the new (as yet unpublished) novel of Robert Penn Warren — both these admirable; and a number of other works in ms.

Of lately published work I have vivid recollections of and admiration for *Aleck Maury, Sportsman*, by Caroline Gordon, *Act of Darkness* by John Peale Bishop, *Walls Against the Wind* by Frances Park, *Little Candle's Beam* by Isa Glenn and Graham Greene's *It's a Battlefield* and Arnold Gingrich's *Cast Down the Laurel*.

In the immediate future — on the S.S. Roma I shall read all of Crane and Hudson I can get hold of and the proof sheets of my own *Collected Poems* which the Oxford University Press are publishing here in the Fall.

We shall leave on Saturday for Naples, working back from there to Toulon where I shall set to work on another book about the Great Trade Route, taking in this time, the North and Mid Atlantic which also the Oxford University Press is publishing here and for which Biala is again making the illustrations — from Naples to New Orleans!

That is all I can think of for the moment — and more than enough, says you.

Our kind regards to Mrs Gannett

Yours very sincerely *Ford Madox Ford*

We shall be back next January and shall hope to see you again.

Gannett was a book columnist for the *New York Herald-Tribune*.

To R. A. Scott-James

49 5 September 1936

4 Place de la Concorde
Paris

Dear Scott-James, If my friends the Porter-Pressly's (Katherine Anne Porter, author of FLOWERING JUDAS and generally regarded, I should say with justice, as the finest prose writer bar none in U.S.A. and one of the most amusing women; plus Eugene Pressly, Embassy attaché at Paris and great — but incredibly silent and discreet — authority on international finance, husband of said K.A.P.) ring you up in the next few days you might be a little nice to them . . . socially I mean. Pressly is probably going to be attached to the Embassy in London. Let 'em if you can without trouble meet a few amusing people. They are very intimate friends of ours.

The weather has been gorgeous, but my foot has troubled me a good deal ever since we got here; however, now I'm beginning to hobble around. Do you get away, or do they keep your poor nose to the grindstone all the time?

All good luck, anyhow
Yours *F.M.F.*

If you're sending the proofs of that article for next month, send them a little earlier, will you? The poem only reached me about the 25th ult and, as I didn't see it needed correction, I thought it hardly worthwhile to return it . . . Thanks for giving me pride of place.

I hope you are reducing the L.M. [*London Mercury*] to an ordinary octavo. Those long lines are very tiring to the eye used to 8° and I always think that dulls the sense of everything one writes. I'm glad you have got Kay Boyle. See if you can't get hold of Djuna Barnes who is another of my babies. Fabers would give you her address: they and Eliot are crazy about her — printing her next book in spite of danger of gaol and all.

Former Editor of the *Daily News*, for which Ford had written weekly pieces, and contributor to Ford's *English Review*. He wrote the Preface to the Penguin edition of *Some Do Not*.

To the Director of Libraries, University of Buffalo, N.Y.

50 13 December 1936 *Ten Fifth Avenue*

Dear Sir: I'm very sorry: I don't keep my mss. so I can't send you one, much as I am flattered by the request. But I transcribe a little verse below — if it's of any use to you.

Yrs. faithfully *Ford Madox Ford*

Thank Goodness, the moving is over,
They've swept up the straw in the passage
And life will begin. . . .
This tiny, white, tiled cottage by the bridge! . . .
When we've had tea I will punt you
To Paradise for the sugar and onions . . .
We will drift home in the twilight,
The trout will be rising.

— *When the World Was in Building*

I wrote this, I should think in late '13 or early 1914. It pleases me still more than most of my things. I don't think I made any corrections in the original m.s. wh. must have looked much as above. *F.M.F*

To William Carlos Williams

51 28 January 1937 *Ten Fifth Avenue*

My dear William Carlos Williams, I wish you would lend me some — or for that matter — all of your books. I want to write something about you for VOGUE.[1]. It's a pretty silly sort of paper, but it might make some publisher do his duty.

When and how are we going to see you? Couldn't you and Mrs Williams come and have a meal with us on Friday? I think that is your day in town.

[1] In an article 'The Fate of the Semi-Classic' in *Forum*, September 1937, Ford wrote in praise of Williams, Edward Dahlberg, and e.e. cummings.

Janice is having her exhibition at the Passedoit Gallery on the 23rd of February. I do hope you'll manage to get and see it. I send you also a catalogue of Zadkine's show. You certainly ought to see that.

I hope you and yours all flourish. We manage to get along somehow.

Yrs always. *Ford Madox Ford*

52 10 February 1937 *Ten Fifth Avenue*

Dear William Carlos, Thanks for your letter. I will minutely observe all its directions and I think I shall try and make a more extended piece about you than I had contemplated though that will take longer.

Curtis Bok says 'I will be glad to see Doctor Williams for I am very much interested in music, and if he will get in touch with me when he wants to come I shall be glad to make an appointment.' His address is: Judge Curtis Bok, Orphans' Court, Philadelphia.

It is nice to think of you and Mrs Williams coming to see us and we shall be delighted to come and see you, too, in turn.

With kind regards, *F.M.F*

To George T. Bye

53 8 March 1937 *Ten Fifth Avenue*

My dear Bye, *Ref Publisher.*

With regard to Doubledays or any other publisher I want all my books, past and to come, taken over; publisher to pay me $150 monthly as against what is called in England a hotchpotch of my work — that is to say payment in advance of royalties of each work of a sum earned in royalties by preceding work of same type; those advances to be credited to general account; each book to be accounted for separately . . . and in addition a sum of from $1,000 to $1,500 on signature of contract for purchase of books, travelling and other expenses.

As against that I undertake to furnish the publisher with two books yearly, one fiction and one non-fiction or, say, a minimum of 150,000 words a year.

The books I plan writing are — in addition to the history of literature which you may or may not transfer as you like — 1. A continuation of GREAT TRADE ROUTE, then a novel; then A HISTORY OF OUR OWN TIMES — say 1880 to 1930 —; then another novel. I haven't planned anything beyond this.

All these books are contracted for with Allen and Unwin in England they being ready to collaborate in the production with any American firm of standing.

Further, they are planning a collected — or rather a subscription edition — of twelve of my former books: about eight novels and four non-fiction and I should wish my American publisher to take these up too — indeed that is indispensable for me. In addition to these twelve there will be a thirteenth — a new edition of ROMANCE by Conrad and myself with new biographical introductory matter and illustrations. My agreement with Conrad was to the effect that either or both of us could include collaborated matter in our collected editions.

I should propose to begin the collected edition with the three Tietjens books in one volume. I understand that Duckworth's of London, the original publishers, are proposing to bring out a one volume edition next spring. In that case the American publisher could make a photographic edition so as to avoid my losing copyright in this country. In case said publisher agreed to above terms — i.e. $150 per mensem and lump sum on signature — I should not, at any [rate] provisionally propose to ask for any advance on re-printed books.

Above details are of course all provisional, the general principle being that I want a publisher with whom I can remain for good, who will assure me of a modest income and who will arrange for a collected edition.

Yours faithfully *Ford Madox Ford*

P.S. All serial rights to remain mine; other rights by arrangement.

Bye was Ford's literary agent, who worked for the firm of Curtis Brown.

To Morton D. Zabel

54 18 May 1937

c/o Mrs Allen Tate
Benfolly, Clarksville
Tennessee

Dear Mr Zabel: As I telegraphed to you today, I have decided to accept your kind invitation and will come to Chicago in time for the date which you have indicated. I shall be glad if you have arranged that the lecture to Chicago University [sic] will follow as soon as possible upon the dinner because I want to get back here as soon as may be. What I want to do, if possible, is to get a day train to Chicago on the 26th, arriving in time for your dinner and to speak at the University the next day in time to catch a night train back here. I have not been able yet to ascertain the time of trains but I shall stick to that programme as nearly as possible. In the circumstances will you please excuse my not writing the article on Whitman? I have tried very hard to do this but I can't think of anything profitable to say about that good, grey poet and I find I can't say anything at all sincere that wouldn't hurt the feelings of my great friend, Mr Masters. And besides I am dreadfully behind hand with my book and this Chicago trip will put me two days more back. A little later I will try to write about something more congenial for you. Or you might possibly get someone to shorthand some passages from my speech at the dinner which might be useful to you. By the bye, my voice is not enormous and if your audience or that of the university is likely to be above 200 or 250, or if the acoustics of either place are at all bad, I would take it as a favour if you could provide a mike.

Yours very sincerely, *Ford Madox Ford*

By the bye: Tate says that, as the Whitman book is here he would, if you liked, write something about it for you.

Literary critic, Professor of English at the University of Chicago, and editor of *Poetry*.

To George T. Bye

55 29 November 1938

Ten Fifth Avenue

Dear Bye: The three books I discussed with [Quincy] Howe are as follows:

1 — The quite provisional title, *Forty* (?) *Years of Travel in America*. This will be a book similar in plan to my *Provence* and the other books of the same type. It will show the writer moving from Boston via New York to Washington, D.C.; Nashville, Tennessee; Denver, Colorado; St. Louis, Chicago, Detroit, and not so much commenting on those places as sitting down in those places and thinking about anything under the sun. Thus, in Boston, he would probably think a great deal about American education; in Washington about world politics; in Nashville about the WPA [Works Progress Administration], and, as far as is permitted to a foreigner, about the American social, industrial and political scene: in Denver about the American tendency to regionalism in the Arts; in Chicago about American food and food-products and in Detroit about agriculture in general and self-sufficiency farming in particular against the problem of machinery as displacing labour. And in various places on the road, as in Lexington, Virginia or Grand Rapids, Michigan, he might think about various allied topics such as American roots — i.e. colonial as against pioneering traditions, and American colonial versus modern architecture and furnishings.

Note: This book is to take the place of the proposed book on the international situation which will be treated of in the section treating with Washington, D.C.

2 — A novel. This will be a treatment in fictional form of world and particularly United States conditions today, the central figure having to accommodate himself in life, finance, love and the rest of his personal and social affairs — to the changing conditions around him.

3 — *A History Of Our Own Time* from 1895 to the present day. This is a book which has been commissioned for many years now by my English publishers and I shall have finished collecting the material for it and be ready to write it in about eighteen months' time — i.e. after the other two books are finished.

4 — The Anthology. We have talked sufficiently about this. I should propose to carry it on simultaneously with the other books as a spare time occupation, as I have got a very good assistant who will do most of the work. The publishers might expect to have the book within eighteen months after signing of contract.

Terms:

Mr Howe badgered me a good deal about these but I said that you must negotiate these but that as a general principle, I wanted in this country a permanent agreement for all my future work similar to that which I have had for many years with my English publishers, Allen & Unwin. The principle of this is that Allen & Unwin pay me as advance of royalties whatever has been actually earned by the previous book of the same character. Thus, they paid as advance on the *Great Trade Route* what had been earned by *It Was The Nightingale* and for *Provence*, which has just appeared there, what was earned by *Great Trade Route*. And similarly with novels, the two categories being regarded as separate. I said that, roughly speaking, I should be prepared to take in advance for the American travel book what has been earned to date of signing the contract by *The March of Literature* plus a certain sum not exceeding $250 for Mrs Ford's illustrations. But you might ring me up and talk about these last before talking to S and S [Simon and Schuster]. These payments should be made as to one half on the signature of contract and the other upon the receipt of the manuscript by the publishers.

I think that that is all I have got to say for the moment. If there is anything in the above that does not explain itself, please ring me up at your convenience.

Yrs *F.M.F.*

To Stanley Unwin

56 16 February 1939

Dear Mr Unwin; I was much flattered to find myself on the front page of your catalogue with such an extremely charming blurb. It has really warmed the cockles of my heart because things are extremely gloomy here.

I owe you an apology for having left so many things in a muddle but I really could not help myself. To begin with: about the international book. I have not been able to find a publisher to take it here. And as I depend entirely on my makings here I have almost had to give up the idea. On the other hand quite a number of publishers here have asked me for a novel so I have decided that I shall have to write a novel and indeed, I have begun one. But practically all the publishers here refuse to give any advances to writers who are not amongst the best sellers so that being far indeed from amongst the best sellers I shan't be able probably even to continue the writing of the novel because I shall have to by hook or by crook make a living by writing for the really atrocious journals of this city. And I've been so ill for so long that my brain is not up to that sort of slickness. It is very curious: I have really an enormous reputation here. I am generally regarded as the Dean of American Letters and I am told that if I were American I should be a certainty for the Nobel prize. In witness of that the local branch of the PEN club gave me a dinner in company with the two American Nobel Prize winners, Sinclair Lewis and Miss Pearl Buck and in the course of it Mr Lewis made a speech in which if you please he styled me not only the Dean of American Letters but the most eminent man of letters not only in English but in the world and the sentiment was received with unanimous applause. In spite of that my books sell very little and, as I have been able to do no occasional work since July when I finished the *March of Literature* I am at the moment almost without funds and with nowhere really to turn to, for the people I live with here are all writers or painters and extremely poverty stricken.

I am therefore going to ask you for some temporary assistance. If you could possibly see your way to lending me say £250 it would be of most immense service to me and in the end would be of some benefit to yourself because it would mean that I could return to France and finish my novel in some peace of mind which of course would mean that the novel would greatly benefit. And of course I would repay the money by degrees as the American publisher pays me for the book. In addition I have a complete novel which I wrote some time ago but for personal reasons do not wish to have it published until after my death — or rather until after the deaths of several people who might possibly recognize themselves in one or other of the characters. I shall be very glad to let you have this to hold in what they call escrow here until either I repay the money or feel that the time has come to publish the book. As this book was written some time ago — just, indeed, after the Tietjens books when my writing was at its most popular, it does not fall under my agreement with Mrs Bowen so that you could have both the English and the American rights as security. I know that it is very indecent of me to make this request but my necessities at the moment are very urgent and I see nothing else whatever to do.

I might say that if you are not otherwise provided I'd be quite glad to act as what is called here and in Paris your scout as some return for your kindness — I mean for books of more commercial value than those of the young things I've been sending you. I have so many contacts here and indeed in Paris that I think I could keep you advised quite easily as to what the better publishers have in hand. I do hope you will see your way to do me this very considerable favour. If you can, would you pay £250 to my account at the Guaranty Trust, 4 Place de la Concorde, Paris and if you do see your way to it if you would send me a cable to the effect that you are doing so, you would add immensely to the benefit conferred.

Please forgive me for giving you what I know will be the pain of having to read this letter.

Yours very sincerely,

P.S. I omitted to say that I had to break with the new proprietors of the Dial Press rather more because I found them insupportable as individuals than because they were also rather too skilful in making up their accounts.

To Eudora Welty

57 3 November 1938 *Ten Fifth Avenue*

Dear Miss Welty: I am not proposing at present to deal with short stories in my own undertaking but Miss Porter speaks so highly of your stories that if you will send them to me and if I like them, of which I have not much doubt, I will do my best to find a publisher for them here and you can feel fairly confident of my placing them in England to which, I suppose, you would have no objections. But will you please send with them an envelope or other container for their return or their forwarding to a publisher?

Yours faithfully, *Ford Madox Ford*

58 7 January 1939 *Ten Fifth Avenue*

Dear Madam: I have now read your short stories with a great deal of real pleasure and interest. I think you have a very remarkable gift and if you continue in the way you are going, you should arrive at great things.

For the moment would you tell me what you want me to do with these stories? Have you submitted them in book form to any publishers hitherto? In any case, I would be very pleased to recommend them.

And would you care for them to be published in England? If so, I will recommend them to my English publisher who quite usually pays attention to my recommendations.

Let me have your answer to these questions at your convenience, please, and we can then proceed.

Yours very sincerely, *Ford Madox Ford*

9 19 January 1939 *Ten Fifth Avenue*

Dear Miss Welty: Thank you very much for the information in your letter of the 10th inst. If you have a second copy of your short stories, would you now mail this to Stanley Unwin, Esq., c/o Allen & Unwin, Ltd., 40, Museum Street, London, W.C.1, England, marking the parcel as coming from me and being personal to Mr Stanley Unwin. The copy I have, I will do my best with in New York. Let me know, when you have mailed the other to London, please.

Yours very sincerely, *Ford Madox Ford*

0 25 May 1939 *Ten Fifth Avenue*

Dear Miss Welty: Stokes finally came to the conclusion that they couldn't publish your stories — for the usual reason of alleged public distaste for short stories. In the meanwhile, Mr Strauss of Knopf wrote to me for the manuscript and I have sent it to him with very strong recommendations that he publish it. So let us go on hoping.

Is there, by the bye, any reason why you shouldn't write a novel? I should think you could do a very good one — or have you any reason for not making the attempt?

I shall be leaving for Europe on the 30th and don't expect to be back here before October. In the meantime my European address will be 4 Place de la Concorde, Paris, France, should you wish to write to me.

Hoping so much that you will have good luck with Knopf, I am

Yours very sincerely, *Ford Madox Ford*

Chronological List of Ford's Books

(Including Collaborations and Ford's own Translations)

Date given is actual year of publication, not necessarily year on title-page.

1891 *The Brown Owl*. Children's fairy tale.
1892 *The Feather*. Children's fairy tale.
1892 *The Shifting of the Fire*. Novel.
1893 *The Questions at the Well* [pseud. 'Fenil Haig']. Poems.
1894 *The Queen Who Flew*. Children's fairy tale.
1896 *Ford Madox Brown*. Biography.
1900 *Poems for Pictures*. Poems.
1900 *The Cinque Ports*. 'A Historical and Descriptive Record' (half-title) of Kent and Sussex port towns.
1901 *The Inheritors*. Novel, written in collaboration with Joseph Conrad.
1902 *Rossetti*. Art criticism and biography.
1903 *Romance*. Novel (historical adventure story), written in collaboration with Joseph Conrad.
1904 *The Face of the Night*. Poems.
1905 *The Soul of London*. Sociological impressionism.
1905 *The Benefactor*. Novel.
1905 *Hans Holbein*. Art criticism.
1906 *The Fifth Queen*. Novel (historical romance; first of the 'Katharine Howard' trilogy).
1906 *The Heart of the Country*. Sociological impressionism.
1906 *Christina's Fairy Book*. Children's fairy tales.
1907 *Privy Seal*. Novel (historical romance; second of the 'Katharine Howard' trilogy).
1907 *England and the English*. Sociological impressionism; published only in America; composed of the previously published *The Soul of London* and *The Heart of the Country* plus *The Spirit of the People*.
1907 *From Inland*. Poems.
1907 *An English Girl*. Novel.
1907 *The Pre-Raphaelite Brotherhood*. Art criticism.
1907 *The Spirit of the People*. Sociological impressionism; previously published, only in America, in *England and the English*.

1908 *The Fifth Queen Crowned*. Novel (historical romance; third of the 'Katharine Howard' trilogy).
1908 *Mr. Apollo*. Novel.
1909 *The 'Half Moon'*. Novel (historical romance).
1910 *A Call*. Novel.
1910 *Songs from London*. Poems.
1910 *The Portrait*. Novel (historical romance).
1911 *The Simple Life Limited* [pseud. 'Daniel Chaucer']. Novel (satire).
1911 *Ancient Lights*. Reminiscences; published in America in 1911 as *Memories and Impressions*.
1911 *Ladies Whose Bright Eyes*. Novel (historical fantasy).
1911 *The Critical Attitude*. Essays in literary criticism.
1912 *High Germany*. Poems.
1912 *The Panel*. Novel (farce).
1912 *The New Humpty-Dumpty* [pseud. 'Daniel Chaucer']. Novel (satire).
[1912] *This Monstrous Regiment of Women*. Suffragette pamphlet.
1913 *Mr. Fleight*. Novel (satire).
1913 *The Desirable Alien*. Impressions of Germany, written in collaboration with Violet Hunt.
1913 *The Young Lovell*. Novel (historical romance).
1913 *Ring for Nancy*. Novel (farce; adaptation of *The Panel;* published only in America).
1913 *Collected Poems*.
1914 *Henry James*. Critical essay.
1915 *Antwerp*. Long poem (pamphlet).
1915 *The Good Soldier*. Novel.
1915 *When Blood is Their Argument*. War propaganda (anti-Prussian essays).
1915 *Between St. Dennis and St. George*. War propaganda (pro-French and anti-Prussian essays).
1915 *Zeppelin Nights*. Historical sketches (told Decameron-fashion against the background of the war), written in collaboration with Violet Hunt.
1917 *The Trail of the Barbarians*. Translation of the war pamphlet, *L'Outrage des barbares* by Pierre Loti.
1918 *On Heaven*. Poems.
1921 *A House*. Long poem (pamphlet).
1921 *Thus to Revisit*. Literary criticism and reminiscence.
1923 *The Marsden Case*. Novel.
1923 *Women & Men*. Essays.
1923 *Mister Bosphorus and the Muses*. Long narrative and dramatic poem.
1924 *Some Do Not. . . .* Novel (first of the 'Tietjens' tetralogy).
1924 *The Nature of a Crime*. Novella, written in collaboration with Joseph Conrad; previously published in 1909 in *English Review*.
1924 *Joseph Conrad: A Personal Remembrance*. Biography, reminiscence, and criticism.
1925 *No More Parades*. Novel (second of the 'Tietjens' tetralogy).
1926 *A Mirror to France*. Sociological impressionism.
1926 *A Man Could Stand Up —*. Novel (third of the 'Tietjens' tetralogy).
1927 *New Poems*.
1927 *New York Is Not America*. Essays in sociological atmospheres.

1927 *New York Essays*.
1928 *The Last Post*. Novel (last novel of the 'Tietjens' tetralogy; titled *Last Post* in England).
1928 *A Little Less than Gods*. Novel (historical romance).
1929 *The English Novel*. Essay in literary criticism and history.
1929 *No Enemy*. Disguised autobiography (concerning the war years; written shortly after the war).
1931 *Return to Yesterday*. Reminiscences (up to 1914).
1931 *When the Wicked Man*. Novel.
1933 *The Rash Act*. Novel.
1933 *It Was the Nightingale*. Autobiography and reminiscences (from 1918).
1934 *Henry for Hugh*. Novel.
1935 *Provence*. Impressions of France and England.
1936 *Vive le Roy*. 'Mystery' novel.
1936 *Collected Poems*.
1937 *Great Trade Route*. Impressions of France, the United States, and England.
1937 *Portraits from Life*. Essays in personal reminiscence and literary criticism about ten *prosateurs* and one poet; published in England in 1938 as *Mightier than the Sword*.
1938 *The March of Literature*. Survey of literature 'From Confucius' Day to Our Own'.
1965 *Letters of Ford Madox Ford*, ed. Richard Ludwig. Princeton: Princeton University Press.
1982 *Pound/Ford. The Story of a Literary Friendship*, ed. Brita Lindberg-Seyersted. New York: New Directions; London: Faber and Faber.

Adapted from David Dow Harvey, *Ford Madox Ford 1873–1939: A Bibliography of Works and Criticism* (Princeton: Princeton University Press, 1962).